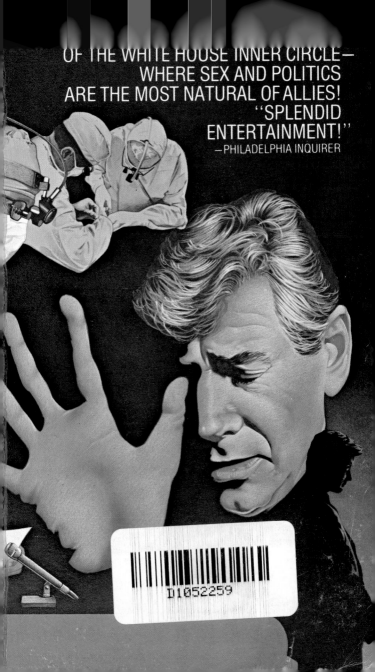

OF THE WHITE HOUSE INNER CIRCLE—
WHERE SEX AND POLITICS
ARE THE MOST NATURAL OF ALLIES!
"SPLENDID
ENTERTAINMENT!"
—PHILADELPHIA INQUIRER

FULL DISCLOSURE

William Safire

BALLANTINE BOOKS · NEW YORK

For Helene

Library of Congress Catalog Card Number: 76-18365

ISBN 0-345-27195-5

This edition published by arrangement with Doubleday & Company, Inc.

Manufactured in the United States of America

First Ballantine Books Edition: July 1978

Prologue

"What is the extent of the term 'disability' and who is to be the judge of it?"—John Dickinson of Delaware, August 27, 1787, at the Constitutional Convention, in the only recorded reference to the clause on presidential succession. The Dickinson question did not receive an answer.

The Twenty-fifth Amendment to the Constitution of the United States, approved by the Congress July 6, 1965, and ratified by the necessary three fourths of the states on February 10, 1967:

"Section 1. In case of the removal of the President from office or of his death or resignation, the Vice President shall become President."

"Sec. 2. Whenever there is a vacancy in the office of the Vice President, the President shall nominate a Vice President who shall take office upon confirmation by a majority vote of both Houses of Congress.

"Sec. 3. Whenever the President transmits to the President pro tempore of the Senate and the Speaker of the House of Representatives his written declaration that he is unable to discharge the powers and duties of his office, and until he transmits to them a written declaration to the contrary, such powers and duties shall be discharged by the Vice President as Acting President.

"Sec. 4. Whenever the Vice President and a majority of either the principal officers of the executive departments or of such other body as Congress may by law provide, transmit to the President pro tempore of the Senate and the Speaker of the House of Representatives their written declaration that the President is unable to discharge the powers and duties of his office, the Vice President shall immediately assume the powers and duties of the office as Acting President.

"Thereafter, when the President transmits to the President pro tempore of the Senate and the Speaker of the House of Representatives his written declaration that no inability exists, he shall resume the powers and duties of his office unless the Vice President and a majority of either the principal officers of the executive department or of such other body as Congress may by law provide, transmit within four days to the President pro tempore of the Senate and the Speaker of the House of Representatives their written declaration that the President is unable to discharge the powers and duties of his office. Thereupon Congress shall decide the issue, assembling within forty-eight hours for that purpose if not in session. If the Congress, within twenty-one days after receipt of the latter written declaration, or if Congress is not in session, within twenty-one days after Congress is required to assemble, determines by two-thirds vote of both Houses that the President is unable to discharge the powers and duties of his office, the Vice President shall continue to discharge the same as Acting President; otherwise, the President shall resume the powers and duties of his office."

Contents

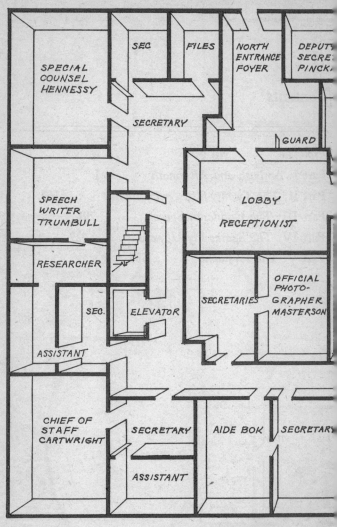

FIRST FLOOR PLAN
WEST WING, THE WHITE HOUSE

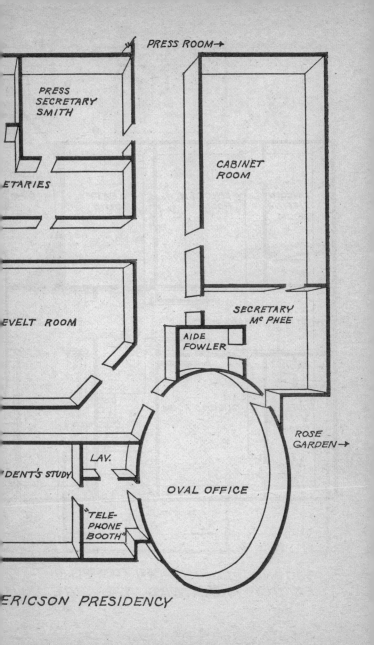

PRESS ROOM→

PRESS
SECRETARY
SMITH

CABINET
ROOM

ETARIES

EVELT ROOM

SECRETARY
McPHEE

AIDE
FOWLER

ROSE
GARDEN→

LAV.

"DENT'S STUDY

OVAL OFFICE

"TELE-
PHONE
BOOTH"

ERICSON PRESIDENCY

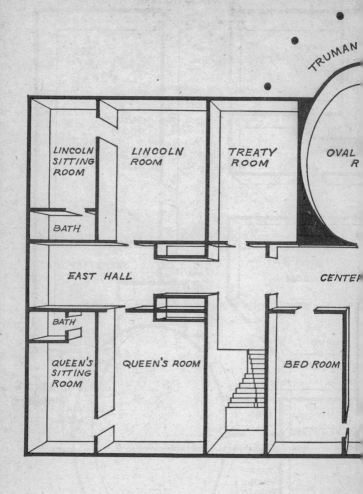

TRUMAN

LINCOLN SITTING ROOM

LINCOLN ROOM

TREATY ROOM

OVAL R

BATH

EAST HALL

CENTER

BATH

QUEEN'S SITTING ROOM

QUEEN'S ROOM

BED ROOM

SECOND FLOOR PLAN
FAMILY QUARTERS

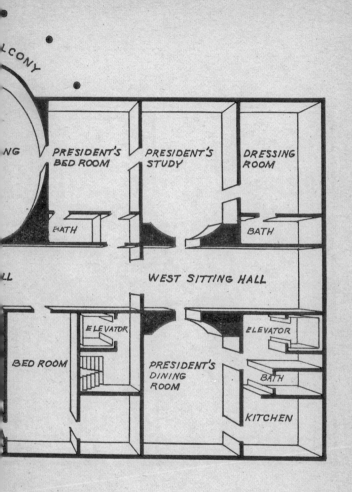

THE WHITE HOUSE ···
THE ERICSON PRESIDENCY

I

Ambush
and Aftermath

The Secret Service Agent / 1

Counterfeiting, that was for him. Meticulous work, satisfying results. Harry Bok took a phony hundred-dollar bill out of his wallet and studied a well-engraved picture of Benjamin Franklin. He crinkled the bill in his hand; the paper was not quite right. A touch too heavy. He felt sorry for the engraver, to work so painstakingly and then to lose out on the failure of his paper supplier.

Harry looked out the window of *Air Force One* and concluded that he had been in the wrong end of the Secret Service for too long. All these years—a twenty-five-year veteran, he had joined the Service when he turned twenty-one—he had been stuck in protection, mainly presidential protection. A bodyguard.

The brown Russian countryside gained contour as the aircraft slowly descended toward the Black Sea resort. He wondered about counterfeiting in the Soviet Union. The man in the seat next to him was a Russian guard, protecting the Soviet Foreign Minister, who was up in the President's cabin meeting with President Ericson and the Secretary of State.

"You get much counterfeiting in Russia?" Harry asked. He had to explain what counterfeiting was. The Russian shook his head, no; lot of prostitution and drunken brawling, some holdups and street crime, no counterfeiting. Harry nodded and went back to his reverie. The U. S. Secret Service began because of counterfeiting. In the 1860s, with all the different banks issuing specie, one out of every three dollars had been counterfeit. Big national problem. Lincoln ordered the creation of an anticounterfeit crew, called

FULL DISCLOSURE

the Secret Service, the morning of the day he was shot.
After Lincoln's assassination, there was still no protection assignment, and the Service launched its war on
bogus bills. Harry remembered the irony pointed out
to him by the teachers at the training center in Belts-
ville, Maryland, so long ago: A gang of counterfeiters,
trying to get their leader out of jail, cooked up a plan
to steal Lincoln's body from his grave in Springfield.
They intended to trade the dead body for their live
confederate, but the Service got wind of it and there
was a shoot-out at the cemetery. So the first President
the Secret Service protected was a dead body; after
that, since it was the only federal law enforcement
agency, the Service was given the protection function,
and in a century the protection tail had outgrown the
anticounterfeiting dog.

"I never met an agent as old as you," said the Russian, whom Harry decided spoke too much English.

"I'm only twenty-six, but I drink a lot," Harry replied. His seat-mate fell silent. The Russian was right,
of course: Harry was in a job that ought to have been
filled by a younger man. Harry Bok, forty-six, was an
anachronism, perhaps a danger. He did not have the
reflexes he used to have, nor could he be sure any
more that he was ready to put his body between a
President and a bullet. That was why he wanted to get
a counterfeiting assignment where he could compete
with artists and not with nuts. The sound of a balloon
popping was like a clutchfist in his heart. In protection,
he had to live on the balls of his feet, but in counterfeiting, he would not have to be a jock to be a cop.

Harry was ready to face the fact that he was an aging agent, but nobody else was. He was a presidential
favorite and always had been, the choice of four Presidents to be the agent in close, at the right hand and
slightly to the rear, available to handle diapers and
dames, cronies and crazies. And to talk to. Harry wondered why Presidents thought he was so easy to talk
to. Probably it was the sympathetic expression his face
fell naturally into, even when he was not feeling especially sympathetic. All the furrows and the jowls

4

and the soft brown eyes seemed to reach out to assure the speaker of top secrets that Harry was a safe and understanding repository.

Presidents kept passing him along to their successors, over the mild objections of the Service director and his own stated preference for less athletic and more creative police work. He knew why. Herb Abelson, President Ericson's physician, put it to him straight only six months ago, when the forty-first President of the United States took office: "He has plenty of gung-ho types, Harry, all wound up and on a hair trigger ready to throw themselves in the line of fire. What Sven Ericson needs is a paunchy, middle-aged agent afflicted with self-doubt. Not a robot, and I'm not knocking your colleagues, Harry, but a *mensch*."

The ground was getting closer. Harry grunted out of his seat, stepped around the Soviet guard, and inserted himself into the washroom. He hung up his jacket and opened the tiny cake of soap with the presidential seal on the wrapper. A sliver of soap, not a cake; a cake of soap was what you had at home, in your own soap dish, which you could complain about being soggy on the bottom to your wife, who would complain back that you were not home often enough to turn the soap over regularly. He splashed himself liberally with the aftershave, one of the fringe benefits of *Air Force One*. He attached a battery to his belt, ran the wire around his collar, making sure not to entangle it in his shoulder holster, inserted the flesh-colored receiver in his ear, and put his jacket on over all the paraphernalia, checking the green and white pin in his lapel, which would be changed in a couple of days to a different color and shape. He looked in the mirror at the image all wired for sound and wondered what it would be like if a Secret Service agent were hard of hearing. Would he be the only one on the detail to walk around without an earpiece in his ear, standing out unnaturally, like a male harpist in an all-girl orchestra?

Buffie Masterson was waiting for him outside the washroom. Strawberry-blond hair, no make-up, athletic young body in a green jumpsuit, and as usual, insistent: "I want to ride in the chopper, Harry. Can you get me on?"

He automatically said no, knowing Buffie would soon go over his head. She was the President's official photographer, and the best picture taker to hold that job in years—won all kinds of prizes—and part of her talent was a likable pushiness. The President's lawyer, Hennessy, called her "insouciant," and he should know, he was a specialist in the calibration of abrasiveness.

"Would you make the pitch for me in return for a bribe?" She held up a sketch of Harry in profile against the aircraft porthole, charcoal on grainy artist's paper, which the White House carpenter would be able to frame impressively and Harry could hang in his den. When Buffie could not take a camera into a situation, as in a courtroom, or in some meetings, she could take her sketch pad, and come out with a recorded impression. That made her doubly valuable.

"Spritz the fixative on it," he told her. "The last bribe you gave me got all smudged. You come up to the Boss's cabin about five minutes after I do, and you ask him yourself. It's a Russian chopper, all the seats are assigned, and you're a very big woman. I dunno."

She was not a big woman. Her body was well crafted to squeeze into tight situations, but Harry did not know if President Ericson wanted her to go with him on the chopper or to ride with the press corps and keep her ears open. The plan called for the President, accompanied by the Secretary of State and the Soviet Foreign Minister, to arrive in Simferopol Airport in a few minutes to be greeted by General Secretary Kolkov. Ericson and Kolkov had been meeting in Moscow for four days; while Ericson was touring Leningrad, Kiev, and Minsk, Kolkov had gone down to his dacha on the Black Sea to await the American President for the final weekend of the visit. The Crimean airport was almost two hours by car from the Yalta dacha. At the Soviets' suggestion, the two leaders—accompanied only by guards and an interpreter—were to be helicoptered to the dacha, followed by a guard chopper. The rest of the party—about two hundred correspondents and another hundred staffers and hangers-on—would meet and be briefed at the airport hangar, then driven to Yalta's Oreanda Hotel in a motorcade. That would give Ericson and Kolkov a couple of unofficial hours alone together, with no press pool to complain about not being near enough to see them.

Harry stood in the wide aisle, not as worried as usual about security. In Russia, as in China, the danger of a loose nut was minimal; the police were stationed every fifty yards along the highways, the electronic security around the dachas was intense. More important, there was no recent tradition of assassination in those societies, as there was in the Middle East and in the United States. When the Americans asked that their President be permitted to fly around the Soviet Union in *Air Force One,* contrary to protocol, it was not for safety's sake, but rather a reluctance to serve Soviet propaganda by appearing on their supersonic jet. Also, Harry added to himself, to stay in touch. Overseas, when away from *Air Force One,* the only secure communications area was the President's limousine, and it was awkward having all those staff meetings in the car.

Harry was not all that happy about the forthcoming chopper ride, but security was not the reason: Choppers made his stomach queasy. He would have preferred that they all take the motorcade, but the Foreign Minister, Vasily Nikolayev, was anxious to show off the new Soviet equipment, so the White House advance men had agreed. Just as well, Harry conceded, the chopper ride would only be twenty minutes, and those noisy egg beaters were safer than motorcades. Even if engine trouble were to develop, choppers have a way of sinking to the ground safely. With another helicopter following along, security was no problem.

Frankly, Harry told himself, he was more concerned about the trip home. First to Lajes Field in the Azores, which had just become American territory—

the President felt he had to touch down on it—and then Andrews Air Force Base in Washington, D.C. Big crowds, always a problem. His stomach juices started to bubble angrily at the prospect, and he calmed them by thinking of the security inside a dictatorship, especially a country run as tightly as Kolkov's Russia.

That thought of Kolkov reminded him of a question he wanted to ask out of curiosity, unrelated to his job. Harry took an empty seat next to Lucas Cartwright, the President's chief of staff. Ordinarily, the chief of staff would be seated up in the President's cabin during any meeting, but Ericson had asked Secretary Curtice to join him up there and Cartwright was not the sort to insinuate himself. Harry figured Cartwright thought that the President was shoring up George Curtice's morale, by being alone with him and the Soviet Foreign Minister. Curtice needed the reassurance, and the veteran Cartwright surely did not.

Cartwright was reading a novel. Nobody else on *Air Force One* would be caught dead reading a novel, for it was assumed that if the passenger was on the world's most important aircraft, the passenger occupied himself importantly, reading what nobody else could read or would be inclined to read: top secret briefing materials, detailed presidential schedules, code books, position papers in draft form, high-domed magazine articles on foreign policy, or the President's News Summary. But Harry Bok and Lucas Cartwright were old-timers; off duty, Harry was expert in the quick cat nap, and the staff chief would usually immerse himself in some imitation of *Gone With the Wind*.

"Are you having a pleasant voyage, Mr. Bok?" The white-haired adviser was the last courtly gentleman left around the White House. Harry and Cartwright had worked together back in the Johnson days, and Cartwright dated back to White House service under Truman—"as a lad, a mere stripling," he liked to add. Presidents liked Cartwright, but not the way they liked Harry Bok: The Tennessee gentleman farmer was the consummate presidential adviser, the unflappable man

8

who never needed supervision or handholding, selfless and self-assured, happy to serve and willing to leave. Cartwright was the only man around to hold Cordell Hull to be his hero. Harry had seen him in crisis situations, always dependable and cool, usually sage, sometimes wrong but never far off the mark, providing that continuity to previous presidencies that—without him—would be left to butlers, gardeners, and guards. Cartwright's was a familiar face that rarely invited familiarity, and Harry liked him because he added a note of mock formality to an administration that tended to be too lazily with-it, the appointees straining to match the loose and easy Ericson style. The President liked Cartwright, too—not in a personal way, the two men were only professional associates—because he felt a President approaching fifty should have a chief of staff approaching seventy, who had useful memories, Washington connective tissue, and a low personal center of gravity.

"It's none of my business," Harry said, "and I don't hear this from anybody, but I get the feeling that this summit is a big, fat flop."

"Not so," Cartwright said deliberately. "A President's first trip abroad is never a flop. Either it is an astounding personal triumph, or—if things don't quite work out as well as he had hoped—the trip is the beginning of an invaluable process of exploration and a fruitful exchange of views."

"Why did it fizzle?" Harry asked. "Ericson's supposed to be smart as hell on the foreign economic stuff. He was a professor and all."

Cartwright carefully turned down a corner of a page and closed his novel. "The party line," he answered, "as the Secretary of State gave it to the press secretary this morning, is this: The purpose of President Ericson's visit was, first, to get acquainted with Comrade Kolkov, which he has done brilliantly."

"They drank a lot of toasts," Harry allowed.

"Second, the President was determined to find out if the rumors of a rift in the U.S.-U.S.S.R. alliance was true, and if the Soviets were putting out feelers to

9

the Far Eastern powers. This limited purpose was accomplished."

"That's good," said Harry.

"Actually, that's bad," Cartwright continued. "This is in confidence, but what little the President found out is troubling. General Secretary Kolkov is a wily old fox"—the staff chief checked himself—"I'm beginning to sound like a news magazine. Kolkov keeps his own counsel, and as far as we know, not even Nikolayev, who is supposed to be his protégé, can assure us of the old boy's tendencies."

"So the trip was a flop," Harry summarized.

"The beginning of an invaluable process," Cartwright agreed.

"Our boy Curtice is pretty chummy with Nikolayev, though. Could be useful."

"Harry, the nation's first black Secretary of State is never referred to as 'boy.' "

"I'm Polish," Harry protested. "I'm allowed ethnic slurs."

"A chink in your armor." Cartwright smiled, then became serious. "I never know if that's a good idea, pretending to get along as individuals. Friendship really has nothing to do with these dealings, interests always come first."

Harry Bok, who had been on some thirty summits —more than any man alive—agreed. From listening at doorways, or chewing things over with Presidents at night in the limousine in his sounding-board role, he knew that personal relationships were useful to brag about at home, but rarely helpful in dealings between nations.

"Ericson good at this?" he asked Cartwright. Harry had been observing Ericson for about a year—six months of the campaign, then the interregnum, and less than six months since Inauguration—and was not as confident about Ericson as the President was confident of himself.

"Too early to tell. You know him, better than I. You, and Dr. Abelson, and Hennessy, and Melinda McPhee—what does the inner circle think?" Cartwright's realistic exclusion of himself from the inner circle was said without resentment.

"Herb Abelson never gets his nose out of his black bag, he's too worried he forgot to bring along some pill. Hennessy's back home, sore because he didn't get to go on the trip. Melinda thinks the President is a little cocky," Harry reported.

"Melinda has good instincts," Cartwright said obliquely. "The President is fortunate to have a secretary like her."

So Cartwright thought the President was flying too high, as well—Harry's own suspicions must be valid, he decided. The world stage stuff really gets to a man: a President begins to think his own personality makes a big difference.

The page-boy alarm on his hip went off, sending vibrations through his body and making him want to pee down his leg. Harry left the seat next to Cartwright and checked in at the command post ahead of the President's cabin. The deputy chief of detail spread out a map and went over the assignments for each of the twelve men on the plane. Harry was to be the only agent with The Man on the chopper. He reminded himself to get some Dramamine from Herb Abelson, he would hate to be sick in the President's lap. He always thought about that but the horrible moment had never happened. If it ever did, he thought, that would be a short cut to the counterfeiting division.

The Soviet Leader / 1

"Go ahead, push the button," the President said, smiling. "It doesn't blow up the world."

Vasily Nikolayev pushed the button. The desk in the working cabin of *Air Force One* lowered until it had transformed itself into a coffee table. A modular unit containing pens, paper clips, and writing paper recessed into the top and was covered over by a sliding Formica panel, as another unit uncovered itself to reveal nuts and dried fruit. The Soviet Foreign Minister leaned forward and helped himself to a nut. It was fresh, and he permitted himself to look impressed.

"Your plane may be slow, but it is well appointed," he said to the American leader. Nikolayev felt himself to be on informal enough terms with President Ericson to twit him about the relative slowness of the Boeing 747 jumbo jet. The United States was still a year away from the introduction of its supersonic airliner, and this President had chosen not to keep up with the Concordes and Tupolevs of other world leaders by using a military jet. Nikolayev thought Ericson's decision had been wise; the Americans could afford to shrug off the temporary lead that other nations had in commercial aviation. They would leapfrog the rest of the world in a few years. The huge, lumbering 747 as the presidential aircraft was an expression of confidence. Only the United States could say, "What's the hurry?"

"We appreciate your understanding," said the third man in the cabin, the U. S. Secretary of State, "about our using this plane in traveling inside the Soviet Union." Nikolayev gave a polite nod. His counterpart was formal, inexperienced, and black, without the *sang-froid* of President Ericson. There was no need to refer again to the Soviet acquiescence to the American request.

"It must be nice to be surrounded by all these amenities," Nikolayev answered. "Our planes are strictly functional." Diplomatically, he ignored the real reason why the Americans had been anxious to use their own plane on these internal flights: On President Ericson's first visit to the Soviet Union, he undoubtedly felt safer in close and secure contact with command center in Washington.

This was the seventh day of the nine-day visit. The four days of negotiations in Moscow had been curiously inconclusive; some prepackaged sea-bed agreements had been signed, but old Kolkov had been unusually evasive on a broad range of issues to the Americans and to his own colleagues. Nikolayev visualized Kolkov at that moment, pacing up and down the tarmac at Simferopol, much too early as always, hands clasped behind his back, his belly pulling him forward, gray, distant, his lips moving silently, rehearsing what he would shout into the cameras with the lanky figure of the American President towering next to him.

The plan called for a handshake and brief speech at the airport in front of the photographers. Then the two leaders, accompanied only by an interpreter and a couple of guards, were to fly by Soviet military helicopter to the dacha selected for the President's use, a large guest house near the General Secretary's dacha. The American advance men had not liked the chopper idea, but the trip from the airport to the dachas was over an hour by automobile, and it would have been insulting to turn down an invitation on the Soviet Union's most advanced helicopter.

"I think the summit meetings have gone well so far," Secretary of State George Curtice offered. Nikolayev nodded as if he agreed. In fact, the talks had gone badly, almost disastrously. Not just for the Americans, but from Nikolayev's point of view, for the Soviet

Union as well. Kolkov, now in his late seventies and getting meaner and more paranoid every day, had tried to lull the Americans with promises of further strategic arms limitations and mutual force reductions in Europe. Ordinarily, that would have pleased Nikolayev, but not in this case. Vasily Nikolayev was certain that old Kolkov, in his waning days, was secretly and singly taking the Soviet Union into a policy that would be ruinous.

Nikolayev began on the dried fruit, selecting one apricot, one pear, and one peach, rejecting the prune. Making his selection as if with deliberation, he thought of Kolkov taking him into his confidence only two weeks before: "Vasily, I am forced to trust you," the old man had told him. "For fifteen years, the Americans have been exploiting the split in the communist world. In the seventies, that was an annoyance. But since the Far Eastern powers have joined together, American influence there has become intolerable. We cannot afford to have a billion Chinese, with Japanese technology, in opposition to us. We must work with them, lead them, not fight them. I have begun the *rapprochement*."

Vasily Nikolayev guessed then that the old man had lost touch with reality. The only way a balance of power could be maintained, in Nikolayev's judgment, was for the Soviet Union and the United States to work together; if Moscow tried to ally itself with Peking-Tokyo, it would find itself the junior partner in a communist world, not the leader but the led. Defeating capitalism and all that was fine talk, Nikolayev thought, but not if it meant the subjugation of Mother Russia to the hordes of Orientals.

As if reading his mind, the American President said to him, "We hear the Soviet trade mission in Canton is about to make a deal to exchange your computers for their oil. You think that's wise?"

Nikolayev smoothly assured the President that the deal was insignificant, only a counter to the trade openings of the Western consortium.

"Tell that to the marines," President Ericson said

in his easy way. "You're trying to get something going over there."

To change the subject, Nikolayev asked what the President's reference to the marines meant, and learned some unnecessary information about American slang. President Ericson, who evidently liked language, recrossed his long legs and went into a long explanation about seamen's opinion of gullible marines who helped man ships in the early days of the American Navy. Nikolayev even began to enjoy it; he liked the new American President, if a realistic politician could be said to "like" the head of a foreign power. Ericson was tall—6′3″—and angular, sitting far back in his chair and talking over his jutting knees. "Lincoln-esque" was the word admirers liked to use frequently about him, and he had obviously adopted the great man's stoop and mannerisms to his political profit. Interesting and uncommon face, too, Nikolayev thought, with the craggy features and stark lines that women find so attractive. The Russian could hardly fault the American for tacitly likening himself to Lincoln. If he, Nikolayev, resembled Lenin, he would sport a Vandyke, but he was cursed with a Slavic look. The broad planes of his face and low forehead concealed what he knew to be the intellectual beneath.

A genuine tragedy, in many ways, that President Ericson would be killed in a helicopter ambush in approximately one hour. The Russian recrossed his legs in the roomy cabin and looked interested in what the American was saying. Nikolayev felt he had much in common with Ericson: Both were nearing fifty, coming into the prime of life and peak of power. They shared an understanding of the need for power, and both displayed confidence in the ability to wield it. Like Ericson, Nikolayev felt at home at the center of action, stimulated rather than intimidated by the possibility of great failure; unlike Ericson, Nikolayev had not yet taken command, but that was only a matter of a few hours or days after today's assassination.

Nikolayev decided yes, he was definitely saddened by the requirements of the assassination plot he had conceived—not about old Kolkov, who had lived too long and had richly earned his execution, but about Ericson, with whom he would like to have dealt on the world scene.

"Tell me about Kolkov," the President was saying. "You know him better than anybody, Vasily—has he changed much in the past ten years? Hardened? Sharpened?"

Nikolayev knew that Ericson wanted to know if the General Secretary was getting senile. That was not the problem with Kolkov, not the reason he had to be removed. Senility would have called for a gentle easing-out, not these drastic measures.

"Sharpened is a good description," Nikolayev replied, not wanting to lie. "The General Secretary is less patient than he used to be. He wants to get to the heart of the matter quickly." The full truth was that the old man had become paranoid, shifting his suspicions and loyalties almost daily, clinging to two posts —General Secretary of the party and Premier of the government—for fear of a rival. Kolkov's latest impulse—and it was surely only impulse, with no basis in *Realpolitik* or rational grasp of the greatest danger —would destabilize the world order. To sacrifice the U.S.-U.S.S.R. co-operation, built so painstakingly over recent years, for a realignment with the Oriental powers on a communist ideological base was, in Nikolayev's opinion, so wrongheaded as to cross the line into madness. The trouble was that Kolkov had the power and the cunning to bring the realignment off. Then the old man would die happy, leaving it to Nikolayev and others to face domination by a billion Chinese. For that is what was surely in store: Without the American alliance, the Soviet Union would be Oriental communism's junior partner.

The only way to prevent Kolkov's secret move was to kill Kolkov today. Nikolayev had never before been involved in a murder conspiracy. His steady rise to Foreign Minister had always been smoothed by Kolkov, his sponsor, who had sheltered his protégé from the harsher side of Kremlin maneuvering. Nikolayev was interested in his own reaction to his first violent power play: neither elation nor guilt, just some nervousness. He owed Kolkov his position, but nothing else; what the world perceived as the old man's affection for a protégé was nothing but Kolkov's less intense dislike of him than for most of the other steering committee members.

The inclusion of the American leader in the ambush was unfortunate. Regrettable but necessary. Nikolayev felt Ericson's eyes on him—cool, intelligent eyes, Nordic blue, which inspired trust without inviting intimacy—and he wished now that he had not let himself be affected by what the American press liked to call Ericson's "brooding magnetism." As the Russian talked around the subject of Kolkov's changing character, he sought to reinforce his decision that the two world leaders had to die together.

The assassination of Kolkov alone would split the Politburo into its pro- and anti-Oriental camps; Nikolayev could not be certain of getting the upper hand. But the deaths of the two leaders together—blamed on the Far Eastern powers—would anneal the alliance of the Soviet Union and the United States. In Moscow the pro-Chinese faction would have to be concerned with the reaction of the American people to the death of their leader on Soviet soil. The death of Kolkov would help expiate that Russian guilt. In Washington the death of the two leaders would be a blood tie that would bind, with the death of Kolkov a kind of apology for the death of Ericson. The natural tendency for the Americans to seek a villain would alienate the Americans from the Chinese and Japanese for decades.

The plan made sense to Nikolayev, a realist. The opportunity of sealing the U.S.-U.S.S.R. alliance, of isolating the Far Eastern powers, and—most urgently —of preventing Kolkov from upsetting the world order came together here in Yalta. The opportunity would take the form of an ambush, presumably by the Chinese, on both the Soviet and American leaders. The helicopter conveying the two men from the airport to the Kolkov dacha would be shot down by the escort chopper.

The Russian, examining a dried peach, wished the American President could know in what noble cause he was to die. The reaction to the Kolkov-Ericson assassination would prevent a shift in world power that would surely have isolated, and might ultimately have destroyed, the United States. Although Nikolayev's primary reason for the joint assassination was to prevent the subjugation of the Soviet Union to the Peking-Tokyo axis, the sacrifice of the American President's life would directly contribute to the protection of the American continent. Ericson was scheduled to die in his country's best interest, and there was no better way for a leader to lose his life. Nikolayev suppressed a sigh.

A burly man in a cheap-looking gray suit with holster bulges put his head in the doorway and asked, "Mind if I join you for the landing?" That was Harry Bok, Nikolayev knew, from a study of the records and a few meetings in Moscow. The Secret Service agent's job required him to be seated next to the President on landings.

"You've met Harry," Ericson said, waving him in.

"We know all about him," Nikolayev said pleasantly. The report on Bok identified the agent not only as presidential bodyguard but as friend, sounding board, and occasional procurer. "The Mona Lisa's friend," Nikolayev added, to inject a note of mock intrigue.

"You must have some file on me at Dzerzhinski Square," Harry Bok said, buckling his seat belt ostentatiously, so that the President would do the same, which Ericson did not do.

"Dzerzhinski Square," said Secretary Curtice slowly, working out the puzzle, "is where the headquarters of the KGB is. Lubyanka Prison. That's where they would keep a file on a Secret Service man, especially one like you, Harry, with your picture next to three or four Presidents about a thousand times. But I don't get the Mona Lisa reference, Vasily."

"It's Harry's smile," the President said. "Some people think it's enigmatic, but I think he looks that way when he has cramps."

"My first job in the Secret Service," the agent explained to Curtice, "was in 1963, when the Mona Lisa was sent over from France to be shown at the National Gallery. I guarded that painting for three months. After a while, that smile of hers began to bug me. So I asked for a transfer, and they sent me to the White House. It was in a profile in the paper about me, the sort of thing Soviet intelligence would keep in a file."

Nikolayev knew that Bok was scheduled to die in the ambush. Not Secretary Curtice; he and Nikolayev, along with the press buses and White House staff, would motorcade to the Oreanda Hotel. Only Ericson, the Soviet interpreter, Kolkov, one Soviet guard, one American guard—this Harry Bok—and two pilots and a woman steward would be on the helicopter leaving for the Kolkov dachas. After five minutes in the air, at a scenic spot near the Black Sea shore etched with the yellow flower Spanish broom, the backup helicopter supposedly accompanying the General Secretary's party as a safety precaution would shoot down the craft with the two leaders aboard. A single rocket exploding amidships would carry out the execution. Traveling at the same speed, closing to twenty-five yards from his target, the gunner's accuracy was assured.

The assassins—four trusted airmen, all Mongolians, acting on orders from the chief of the Soviet Air Force, who was Nikolayev's closest ally in this enterprise—would then land near the shore, embark in a small speedboat for what they thought would be a waiting submarine. There would be no submarine, of course; the speedboat would be destroyed by Soviet pursuit aircraft to avenge the deaths of the U.S.S.R.'s martyred leader and his guest. Evidence would quickly be produced to prove that the assassinations were the work of the Chinese.

"Who was Dzerzhinski?" the President wanted to know.

"The first head of the Soviet secret police," Nikolayev replied. " 'Iron Felix,' he was called. Hateful man, a pioneer of torture and murder. In our histories, he is almost a nonperson."

"Still," Curtice reminded him, "you haven't renamed the square."

"An oversight." Nikolayev could not relax with Curtice, as he could with Ericson and Bok. It was unfortunate he could not replace Bok with Curtice on the helicopter. The black man appeared to be always under strain, always wary. Nikolayev was accustomed to dealing with African leaders, with their posturing and sensitivies, but had never dealt with an American black. Curtice was not flatterable, possibly not even bluffable; Nikolayev would have to look for a different lever to use on him.

A white light flashed on at the telephone near the President, who picked it up, listened, said, "Sure, send her in," and put it down. In a moment, a striking young woman appeared in the doorway, draped in three cameras. "Don't get up, Vasily," Ericson said. "This is our Official Photographer." He pronounced the words with capital letters. "She's going to record this moment in history." Nikolayev watched Ericson watch the eyes of the other men in the room as the photographer leaned against the doorjamb, in a pose of her own, to snap off a few frames. Ericson's deepset pale blue eyes registered amused pleasure at that moment; Nikolayev had seen those eyes, over the past week, flash in anger, become intimidatingly cold, drill into negotiators across a table, and adopt a unique detached-observer cast, as if the President were not a participant in these meetings at all. When Ericson's gaze came around to Nikolayev, the Russian looked appraisingly at the young woman, to flatter the President's taste.

As was well known in intelligence circles, but was discreetly held to a small group in the White House, the official photographer was President Ericson's most frequent bed partner. He was obviously proud of her, Nikolayev noted, and had much to be proud of: Even with her figure concealed in a strange green one-piece suit, the young woman radiated excitement, and her smile was difficult not to return. She obtained good pictures, too. One reason the gossip was held to a minimum was that her talents as photographer and artist were recognized, and she fiercely attacked as "chauvinist" the suggestion that she held her job for any reason other than her professional standing. The most significant gossip-suppressor was the fact that the President was a divorced man; a discreet affair, with no adultery involved, was no scandal.

After she poked about the cabin, taking shots at different angles, she said to the President, "Any chance of me coming along for the chopper ride? Big historic moment."

Ericson's eyes turned that question to Nikolayev. The Russian tried to put himself in the President's shoes: If he were about to die, would he want his mistress to die with him? Something romantic about that —like Mayerling—dying together, denying to any other man the woman who was yours. On the other hand, Ericson seemed to have a streak of humanity in him and Nikolayev judged he would probably prefer to have the girl live on after his own death.

"What do you say, Vasily," the President put it to him, "is there a jump seat on that chopper?"

"I can scrunch together very small," added the girl, squatting down in a corner, illustrating the meaning of the unfamiliar word, "scrunch."

Nikolayev shook his head sadly, as if the decision was not his to make. "The security people never like last-minute changes."

He pretended not to hear the girl mutter "Balls," at her reprieve, and watched her bounce up and slip out the door. She would look back on this moment with terror and relief. Nikolayev found no pleasure in playing God, and would be glad when his tragic duty was done. He told himself that he was sacrificing a few lives to save millions; in a sense, it was what the

21

French called *triage:* On a battlefield, some wounded would recover without help; others were beyond help; the decision maker had to expend his medicine and time on the middle third, those who could be saved. The assassination of Kolkov and Ericson, along with a dozen or so other deaths, was necessary to save thousands, perhaps millions, who would be casualties of a sudden imbalance and instability in the world power. He sadly saluted this good man, Ericson, and the man of Polish descent who was his bodyguard. But Nikolayev felt no shame at what he had set in motion.

The Official Photographer / 1

"Not even you got to go along on the chopper, Buffie?"

The President's official photographer, who had indulged in ten minutes of grumpiness until she felt better, grinned and shook her head. She didn't mind being one of the guys for a while. As a member of the advance party two weeks before, Buffie had flown and driven over most of Greater Yalta from Simferopol Airport where today's press briefing was about to get under way. She had shot the route across the Crimean Game Preserve, which the General Secretary's helicopter was probably crossing at that moment, over the coastal ridge of mountains to the Black Sea, then down past Yalta where the press and staff were staying, to the President's guest quarters at Vorontsov Palace in Alupka.

"I shot most of the area stuff already, Charley." Buffie called every member of the press corps Charley except other photographers, whom she treated with more respect. She had had some difficulty figuring out what to call Sven Ericson in private. First-naming a President struck her as awkward and their intimacy made "Mr. President" ludicrous, so she had settled on the acronym on his telephone call director: "Potus," for President of the United States. The President had given some thought to the title of Buffie's job, too, changing "personal photographer to the President" to "official photographer" as if people would think their relationship was official and not personal. Potus had given her every break on this first foreign trip, letting her travel ahead with the advance crew and telling her to forget the budget, to shoot everything and print up as much as she liked. Her first batch of negatives had already crisscrossed the Atlantic and now she was able to show prints of the points of interest and likely setups to the news photographers.

James Smith, the President's press secretary, was at the microphone, blowing into it for a sound check, and called to her, "How do you spell Vorontsov Palace, Buffie?"

"P-A-L-A-C-E," she called back helpfully, and when no laugh was forthcoming, added the spelling of the Russian name. Another voice asked her how the Oreanda Hotel was, and she flipped back, "Real fleabag. Fifty years old, more maybe. We sleep four in a room, everybody gets to know everybody."

"Who you rooming with, Buffie?"

"Three Secret Service guys and they're terrified, Charley." She had been assigned to a room with Marilee Pinckney, Smitty's deputy press secretary, which was a good break. Marilee was an aristocrat, not only well educated but smart, a willowy beauty who knew all about Buffie and the President. The two women admired each other and did not compete; coming from different worlds, they knew they would return to different worlds when the eight-year fairyland existence was over. Unlike Buffie, Marilee was a feminist, but because of her good brain and good looks she had trouble finding people who would discriminate against her. Buffie thought she was a regular guy, and appreciated the way Marilee demolished anyone who suggested the President's official photographer had gained her position by anything but professional talent. That perversely brought to mind Melinda McPhee, the President's secretary, whom Buffie classified as a tight-assed bitch on the far side of her mid-thirties because she treated the President's photographer like a slut. Possessive, protective, thinking—in Buffie's eyes—that her loyalty was so fierce and her memory of political favors and slights so good that she could afford to mother-hen Ericson. Didn't approve of the President dallying with his photographer, Buffie knew, and since Melinda couldn't have the President for herself, probably wished he would take up with Marilee or someone else of his social class. Someone with a manicure and feet with no calluses and no sense of fun. Buffie wondered quickly if Melinda McPhee had ever made it with Ericson ten years ago, when they started working together at the university. Could be; she was attractive enough for a woman her age, jet-black hair, fine bosom. Nothing going on now, though, Buffie was sure of that. She looked around for the White House staffer she liked least, spotted Melinda against the wall, arms crossed, intense, waiting for Smitty to start the briefing. Buffie took a quick shot of her with a sour-pussed look on her face. She would make Melinda a present of it later. Another Charley asked Buffie about the food at Yalta.

"There's a place called the Pectopah," she said innocently. "Actually, it must be a chain, there's a lot of them. Very good. Order chicken." She knew that "pectopah" was the way the sign for "restaurant" looked in the Cyrillic alphabet, but she liked to play dumb broad as long as everybody knew she was kidding. "You'll see," she added seriously, "it's easier working here than in Moscow or the other cities. You can wander all over the place, nobody stops you. And at a resort, Russians are willing to talk. Real people, and some of them speak English. Nothing like Moscow." She would pass the word later to a few of the nicer Charleys about the "horosho girls," amateur whores on the make along the promenade, who probably were not much in the sack but who spoke good enough English and could tell the reporters plenty about the seamy side of Soviet life. Buffie piped down because Smitty was beginning the briefing from a long podium with two lecterns, like a debate setup, with his Russian press counterpart.

"I will brief," Smitty said, "and my colleague here, Mr. Mishnikov, will interrupt me if I go astray." The people in the corner of the hangar settled down quickly. Reporters and White House staffers, laden with typewriters, recording machines, cameras, souvenir fur hats, and balalaikas from Kiev that were too fragile to send along with the regular luggage, wanted to get the briefing over with and start the motorcade to the fleabag. An undercurrent of resentment ran through the press, Buffie had heard, because the President and General Secretary were off by themselves with no press pool trailing along, and were therefore likely to be unobserved for most of the day. "The President and the General Secretary," Smitty went on, "will be arriving at their quarters momentarily. The chopper ride is about nineteen minutes. They land on the lawn at Alupka Park and the President checks in at Vorontsov Palace."

"That the place FDR stayed?"

Smitty looked over to the Soviet spokesman, who replied, "No, President Roosevelt stayed at Livadia Palace, which is now a sanatorium providing free medical care for Soviet citizens."

"To go on," Smitty picked up, "the two leaders have nothing on their schedules for the rest of the morning. I expect they will get together for an informal lunch and a swim or something." Smitty listened to someone whisper in his ear—the press secretary was not too well organized, Buffie knew, and relied heavily on Marilee—"I'm informed they will be joined at luncheon by Secretary of State Curtice, Foreign Minister Nikolayev, and two interpreters." And Lucas Cartwright and Melinda McPhee, Buffie assumed, but they were staff and didn't get their names mentioned.

FULL DISCLOSURE

Why not the official photographer? If Potus didn't need photographs, she could make pen and ink sketches. The photos she shot belonged to the public, and were distributed to the press fairly, but the sketches belonged to her and someday she would make a killing on a book or a show or whatever. It would help if Potus would let her come along. She was getting grumpy again, and told herself to cut it out, she had the best deal she ever had in her twenty-six years, dating a fascinating man who was affording her a big leg-up on a career.

"You heard the airport remarks," said Smitty. "Texts will be available at the hotel when you arrive. There's a press room as usual. No statements today. You're free until four-thirty this afternoon, at which time there will be a 'photo opportunity,' or as we used to call it, a chance to grab a picture. The buses will leave from in front of the Oreanda Hotel at four."

"That's a lousy time for photographs," shouted a magazine photographer. Buffie looked up from the contact prints in her hand to see Smitty looking her way. He asked her if that was a lousy time for photographs.

"Cuts it a little close for color, Smitty. Sun going down, you get a lot of red."

The press secretary shrugged his regrets, but was not about to change the schedule that had been worked out with Soviet security. "This is a black-and-white photo opportunity."

"Why no pool, Smitty?"

Buffie hoped, for the President's sake, that Smitty had a good excuse for letting the leaders go off incommunicado. It wouldn't have killed them to bring a few reporters along to the palace in the choppers, just to get the feel of the situation and to file a color pool report. "With no pool," the voice added angrily, "we're out of touch for eight hours, for Chrissake. We didn't drag our asses halfway around the work to look at each other."

"There's no pool because the General Secretary and the President wanted to be alone together, that's why," Smitty told him. An honest answer, Buffie had to admit. "And I'm in touch with Harry Bok at all times," Smitty added, slapping the radio on his hip, "and when I'm in touch, you're in touch. If anything develops, I'll get word around the hotel, but meantime, there's a lid till four-thirty." That was welcome to many of the reporters; the "lid" meant they could go wandering about Yalta all day without worrying about missing any sudden press conference.

Her grumpiness vanished when it occurred to Buffie that the all-day lid freed her for stretching out on the black sand beach in front of the hotel. She would wear her next-to-nothing bikini, and the guys, with nothing to do, would probably put a picture of her on the wires. That would irritate Melinda, but Potus wouldn't mind and the personal publicity would be useful when the White House stint was over. Make the most of every chance, was Buffie's philosophy. She hoped she could find a spot on the beach to stretch out: The Russian tourists were there like lemmings, up at dawn to get their places on the beach, where they sat all day, wringing every second of sunshine out of their vacations.

"Do we have to spend all this time on housekeeping details?" boomed a voice from the rear, a few steps from Buffie's position. "When can we expect a substantive briefing?" That was Samuel Zophar, the columnist, a certified media big shot, and not somebody that Smitty would brush off with a snarl or a joke.

"I'm aware of your concern, Sam," said Smitty in a different tone. "We hope to set something up as soon as the President and the General Secretary have something to pass along." He'd better, Buffie thought, or Zophar and the big guns like him would file thumbsuckers—she liked that word for think pieces—about how the two leaders had developed a rift. "Rift" was one of those words, when it got out and around, everybody had to use. Buffie was glad she didn't have to use clichés in her pictures; even a couple of pols shaking hands could be done differently every time.

At that thought, she made a note on her shot sheet to get a close-up of Ericson and Kolkov with hands clasped. Kolkov had small, wiry, old man's hands, and Ericson had the huge hands of a very tall man, with the powerful fingers of a pianist or a basketball player. She could feel those big hands on her shoulders; the fingers sometimes left marks, which did not bother her at all. She noticed how Kolkov used both hands in his handshakes with Ericson, covering the handclasp with his other hand as if to conceal the difference in size. Be a good tight shot, the big Ericson hand enveloping the Russian's; if not, she could always sketch it.

Buffie sighed happily. A cameraman on the platform above heard her tut-tutted and reached down to pat her red-blond head. She smiled up at him thankfully, and when he turned back to his job, she reached up and goosed him savagely, then turned and raced for the press bus.

The first aboard, she punched the driver's arm and spun his hat around, taking the seat nearest the door for first exit. With her contact prints in hand, puffing a little, she looked over the shots she had taken two weeks before of the Crimean Game Preserve, over which the President and his host must have just flown. Trees, foliage, heavy undergrowth, but not one shot of an animal. Buffie had been told that bears, boars, ostriches, and even llamas abounded, along with colorful birds, but she hadn't spotted anything from the scouting helicopter. She was slightly afraid of animals and had not been about to ask the pilot to put her down in that jungle. Good shots of foliage: too many treetops, but masses of a beautiful yellow flower called Spanish broom.

The Secret Service Agent / 2

Conversation was impossible in the noisy chopper, so the two leaders faked communication by pointing out the window at some object on the ground, nodding sagely, raising impressed eyebrows, and mouthing meaningless questions and answers which the interpreter dutifully shouted back and forth. Ericson and Kolkov faced each other in swivel seats: Harry Bok and the Soviet interpreter faced each other alongside. A couple of Kolkov's guards were seated in back.

Harry focused his mind on forgetting about his stomach. As the helicopter lifted off for its twenty-minute journey, he fixed on his wife and children back in Washington. Then he mentally contemplated Buffie in a bathing suit, stretching on the high board at the swimming pool behind the White House, and compared her body, point for point, with Nurse Kellgren, the tall, buxom Swede who worked for the President's physician. That took his mind partially off the lurch forward, as the chopper gathered speed. Settling in to flight, the agent went into his usual mental litany of Presidents he had protected, and the reasons they gave him for not placing him in counterfeiting yet. He thought of his first President, who had a fatherly nonreaction when Harry first began to flunk the target-shooting test: "Harry, I trust your judgment and your instincts, which is a hell of a lot more important than your being able to shoot down somebody after he's shot me. . . ." He moved along to his second President, who had an exaggerated respect for Harry's war record, and thought that a gung-ho kid who would walk through a hail of machine-gun bullets and win a medal in the earliest days of Vietnam would automatically lay down his life for the man he was hired to protect.

As the years went by, the Presidents kept finding other reasons: Bok was totally discreet, he could ski, the first ladies and their daughters swore by him, he remembered sports statistics and trivia about old movies. Meanwhile, he was slowing down, avoiding target practice when he could, and worrying more about disgracing himself and the Service if and when the moment came. His latest President, Ericson, gave him this ray of hope: "You're good luck. Since you've been around, no President's been killed. Harry, I feel safer with a lucky old retread than an unlucky decathlon champ."

He looked out the window and saw they were getting away from the housing around the airport complex and coming up on the forest, a national park and game preserve. Looking down did nothing good for his stomach. He looked up and back, at the trailing helicopter, with two of the agents of the White House detail aboard, plus one of the medical technicians, along with a group of Russian guards. The second chopper was about a thousand feet back and a hundred feet higher, as called for in the flight plan.

The stocky Russian stewardess came back with a vodka bottle embedded in ice. Kolkov and Ericson each took up a shot glass, toasted the other silently, and knocked it back in fine style. Harry and the interpreter declined the drink. Harry started to accept the caviar hors d'oeuvre, then thought better of it. He noted that the President's long legs caused a problem, as Ericson obviously didn't want to play kneesies with the General Secretary and the aircraft was not built for knees that jutted out so far. The President swiveled and kept his knobby knees in the aisle.

Harry took a couple of deep breaths, checked to see where the air-sick bag was but did not touch it, and decided he would fix his eyes on the following chopper, which was out there in the clear fresh air and offered something to concentrate on.

He frowned. The guard chopper was only a few hundred feet off and maybe fifty feet higher, which was not in the plan. If the Russian pilot didn't know what the flight plan was, why hadn't one of Harry's agents of the White House detail on board reminded him? Those guys were not sight-seers, or amateur photographers who needed a close-up—they were supposed to be flying in formation.

Worse, they were opening the side door in flight, which was stupid. Harry would have to write a report on that and it would be somebody's ass. He could understand the desire for fresh air, and wished some window on his own chopper had been left ajar, but the rules were the rules. He started to reach for his pen but what he saw next made him bring out his gun.

A man's body was being pushed out the side door of the guard chopper. It was not a man jumping, but a body being rolled out and drifting downward in the air until it was past Harry's line of sight. A second body followed. Harry motioned to the Soviet guards in the back of his chopper to look out the back window; they were startled by his drawn gun and pulled their own, one looking out, the other watching Harry in case he were pulling a fast one.

A third body, clothed in white, rolled out. The American medical technician, Harry thought, which meant the other two bodies had been his agents. A long metal tube, which could be a gun barrel, or rocket launcher, appeared in the doorway of the following chopper, with a couple of men behind it.

Harry stuck his gun in his belt, turned and grabbed the President by the shoulders, and forced him to the floor. Then he lurched to the front of the helicopter, pulled open the pilot's door, reached over his shoulder, and jammed the control stick forward, plunging the aircraft downward just before the explosion.

The chopper shuddered and careened. The Russian pilot, who must have thought Harry was the danger, began wrestling with him, and Harry savagely silenced him with a chop of his pistol. He grabbed the headset as he felt a rush of cold air; behind him, the copilot was hanging out of the aircraft through the shattered bubble of glass that housed the flight deck. A body of a stewardess was underfoot.

The stick was loose, there was no control. Harry assumed the rocket had hit the high rear tail and not amidships as intended. His lunge to change the chopper's direction had staved off disaster for a few seconds. He grabbed the pilot's headset and yelled "Mayday! Mayday!" into the speaker and pulled his way back into the main cabin where the President and Kolkov were on the floor. The engine was out and the chopper was sinking, but not crashing like an airplane —the rotor blade was still spinning, probably—dropping down toward the treetops.

One of the Russian agents was firing his pistol through a shot-out window while the other was bringing a submachine gun that had been stowed under his seat into position. Harry knew he was not much of a marksman so he let the Russians return fire while he squatted down, jamming seat cushions under and next to the President's head—Kolkov could shift for himself—and prepared for a crash. The attacking chopper suddenly loomed out the window, not twenty yards away, dropping with them, and Harry could see the rocket barrel in the open doorway come into view again. So could the Russian guard with the submachine gun, and three long bursts poured bullets into the attacker's emplacement and then sprayed along toward the pilot's cabin suppressing fire until the second craft veered up, away from the trees, and Harry heard tearing sounds and the blade thrashing and the crash.

Harry was conscious. His elbows braced on both sides of the President's head, which was bleeding— one of the cushions had jarred loose. He smelled gas and felt the heat of flames. He grabbed Ericson under the armpits and dragged him out of the wreckage, into the forest shadows, as far as he could from the chopper, before collapsing. He felt for the President's chest and could feel the heartbeat. He looked up to see one of the Russian guards with Kolkov on his back in a fireman's carry, and the more welcome sight of the man with the submachine gun following behind.

The Russian with the gun motioned upward, and it was then that Harry realized the roar he could still hear was not in his head, but from the second chopper, which was overhead and coming down, probably looking for a clearing to unload for a final assault. Harry shook his head, no; he had already saved the President's life; he did not want another firefight. And they could not run, with the two unconscious men. He remembered that he had radioed for help.

The burning chopper nearby disintegrated in a fierce blast; now there must be some kind of clearing. The pilots, stewardess, and interpreter were gone, and Harry staggered to his feet, following the directions of the Russian with the submachine gun, who seemed to be picking out a small ravine to set up a defense perimeter. Harry hated to move the President, whose scalp wound was running blood down his face and who had God knows how many other internal injuries, but there was no choice. He got under him and followed the others down into a little crater.

The other chopper had landed and cut its engine. Harry could hear men's voices and crashing-about in the bushes, coming their way. Five or six, he figured. Harry and the two Russian guards made no sound, waiting for a clear shot, Harry cursing the days he'd cut target practice. There was hardly any field of fire, bad for the defenders.

A Chinese face was the first surprise to Harry. He shot at it and his next surprise was to see the face come apart. But now their position was known and carbine gunfire began to chatter in from three sides. The Russian guard took a chance and rose to his knees over the rim of the gully to spray the area in front of them and was immediately cut down.

The other Russian guard handed Harry his revolver and took up his mate's weapon, lying on the edge of their hole, shooting bursts at sounds. Then the sounds stopped. In a moment, hand grenades began exploding around them, killing the other guard, raking

Harry's back and side with shrapnel. He looked to see if President Ericson was alive, which he was, but Kolkov had taken the blast of a grenade and was dead or dying. Harry dragged Kolkov's body over Ericson's, making a shield for the President's head and back, letting his legs stick out, and picked up the submachine gun to await the last assault.

Off to his left, a great crashing and snorting began which sounded weird. Harry held his fire. A human scream ripped the forest and three men rose, exposed, to run from the source of the noise. Harry killed the group with one burst. The crashing and snorting crossed to the center in front of him and another body rose to run and before Harry could squeeze the trigger, he froze at the sight of a man being gored by the horns of a wild boar, the most ferocious-looking beast Harry had ever seen, like ugly bull-hog lusting for blood. He shot at the dying man and the wild animal until the screams and the thrashing ceased.

Harry waited, conscious now of his own bleeding back and inability to move his legs, out of ammunition and out of fight. Nobody else in the area moved. He looked back behind him at Kolkov's body draped over the President's, who might be alive and might not. What the hell had happened? Why did the attackers show themselves in terror so he could easily cut them down? Where did wild animals come from in a goddamn summer resort?

The Crimean Game Preserve. The realization that he was surrounded by animals and more unknown dangers was too much for Harry to cope with and he passed out on his gun, a couple of feet from the dead body of the General Secretary of the Soviet Communist party lying on top of what Harry hoped was not the dead body of his President.

The Ophthalmologist

"But why me?"

Dr. Perry Lilith had never been routed out of bed on an emergency call in his entire, brief medical career. He was an ophthalmologist, a specialist in diseases of the eye, and one of the reasons he had chosen that field was that he did not like the frenetic business of night calls that afflicted most medical men. Of course, all eye doctors at Bethesda Naval Hospital on the outskirts of Washington, D.C., had their fair share of night duty, but it had always been scheduled well in advance and accompanied by compensatory time off.

The commandant of the hospital waking him by telephone used Lilith's naval rank, to remind him he was not a civilian doctor, which the eye doctor immediately resented. "To be truthful with you, Commander, the two ophthalmologists senior to you are unavailable. One's sick and the other's off on vacation. That leaves you."

"But what's it all about? I don't know what to bring or anything."

The admiral had been unnecessarily acerbic at that point, Lilith felt. "Doctor, you are an officer in the United States Navy. I am ordering you to pack a bag containing whatever you need for emergency eye treatment and to be ready to be picked up in front of your home in exactly twenty minutes by a White House vehicle. The car will be there at 0400 hours. You will be transported to Andrews Air Force Base where you will be met by some other doctors and some additional ophthalmological supplies. Do you read me so far?"

FULL DISCLOSURE

"Aye-aye, sir," Lilith said sarcastically. He only had a year to go on this hitch. "May I be permitted to know where we go from there, and who is to cover all my appointments for tomorrow?"

"You will learn the destination in due course," the admiral snapped, "and I'll get somebody to cover for you from NIH or someplace. Tell nobody of your assignment including your wife. Make no calls. This is a top-secret operation and security will not be broken by anyone in my command."

"Admiral—I am not a security risk."

The admiral had seemed to soften at that, and Lilith was pleased that he had held his ground. "Perry, we've been asked to assemble a team of doctors immediately, and the request included an ophthalmologist. The hospital and the Navy are counting on you."

He had put down the receiver, fumbled into his clothes—he fretted because he didn't know where he was going or what to wear—and pushed all he could think of into his black bag. Now he was hurrying out the path in front of his suburban home to the black Mercury that had arrived before 0400, or as he told himself a normal human being would call it, four o'clock in the morning. There was another passenger in the back seat, a civilian.

"I've got both of them now," he heard the driver say into a hand microphone attached to the dashboard, "proceeding to Andrews."

"Are you a doctor?" Lilith asked the man next to him.

"No, I'm a lawyer. I chase ambulances, make big money on lawsuits."

A wise guy. Just what Lilith did not need at this hour of the morning. The car swung out to the capital Beltway and headed for the airfield at a lawbreaking speed. The man slumped in the other corner of the back seat was a small, pugnacious-looking fellow smoking incessantly. When he lit his flame-throwing lighter, he showed curly red hair and a freckled, mottled skin.

"I wish you wouldn't smoke," said Lilith.

"Get used to it," the man said, "this is the smoking car. And the plane doesn't have a no-smoking section."

Lilith said "Hmf" in as caustic a way he could muster and rolled down his window. At eighty miles per hour, the wind blew hot sparks from the cigarette tip all around the back seat and the smoker hurriedly stubbed out his smoke. Surprisingly, the man stuck out his hand and said, "I'm Mark Hennessy, the special counsel to the President. I like people who push back. I take it you're the best damn eye doctor in the D.C. area."

"Thank you," said the startled Lilith, neither denying nor confirming the opinion. "Do you know what this is all about?"

"No," Hennessy stated firmly, and Lilith could tell he was lying. The eye doctor had an idea. He leaned forward to ask the driver to turn on the all-night, all-news radio station. He had a hunch this had to involve the President, who was thousands of miles away meeting the Russians at Yalta; if there had been an accident, it would be on the news.

No luck. The newscaster, when he came to a presidential story in his wrap-up, said only that President Ericson and General Secretary Kolkov had greeted each other at some Crimean airport a couple of hours ago, and had helicoptered to an old palace where they would be meeting for the next few hours. It was lunchtime in Yalta. The President was fine. Lilith was miffed. "I didn't bring an extra set of contact lenses," he complained, "in case that's what this is all about."

"Relax," said Hennessy, "enjoy the high drama of Washington life. You going to leave that window open all the way?"

Lilith rolled up the window and sat fingering the handle on his black bag. The man next to him might have been only kidding about high drama, but in a sense it was. Maybe events lay ahead that would have an effect on his career. "You think the President would tell his own lawyer," he needled the White House aide, "if it was something important."

That needle got to Hennessy. "Ain't you the prissy one!" Lilith stiffened at the lawyer's snide reference to effeminacy, but smiled at having touched a sensitive nerve. "All I know is," Hennessy fulminated, "I was told to get my ass on a plane to Lajes in the Azores and make sure I was with the eye doctor. And then I was told something not to do, which is none of your business, and I wasn't given a goddamn word of explanation either. If I'd have been on that Russian trip, which I should have been, Cartwright wouldn't have had to send out this hurry-up shit."

In those remarks was a tidbit of information: Lilith thought about the Azores. He had read something about the President's visiting there on the way back from the Crimea, since the islands had recently become United States territory. The people there had gotten angry at Portugal, or something. "There must be a hospital and doctors in the Azores," he said.

His companion went off on a tangent. "Do you pronounce the 'ph' in ophthalmologist like the 'ph' in diphtheria?"

"I guess so," he replied tightly, a delayed irritation building over that prissiness comment. Lilith saw himself not as prissy, but as well organized. "Most of the time, I say 'dip-theria' because laymen call me an optometrist. It's from the Greek—*oph* is 'eye,' and *thalmus* is 'chamber,' which is where I work." How did he get into an explanation of this? Hennessy wanted to steer him away from asking more questions. Lilith began to remember what he had read about Hennessy in some newspaper profile—a New York divorce lawyer, who had met Ericson five or six years ago, when he was governor, handled his divorce, and then became his confidant and hatchetman. Supposed to have been the White House chief of staff, but was passed over because he made too many enemies in the presidential campaign, and also—now it registered with Lilith—because he was mercurial, hot-tempered, disorganized. So he was relegated to special counsel. The eye doctor smiled to himself. He would have a few inside things to tell at the next cocktail party about the people he met on this assignment. Cautiously, he began to look forward to whatever lay ahead. If only he could be sure he brought the right equipment and medicines.

The White House car pulled to a stop in front of the VIP lounge at Andrews. Inside, Lilith was introduced to six other physicians, an X-ray technician, anesthetist, and several nurses, all unrumpled and alert, making him feel slightly unpatriotic at not having been thrilled originally at the chance to go riding off into the middle of the Atlantic. Outside, a medium-sized jet was warming up, floodlighted, blue and silver, with black lettering that said, "The United States of America." He saw Hennessy take a large envelope out of his breast pocket, look at it to make sure he had it, and put it back with a pat for security. Lilith was pleased by the distinguished medical company he was in: The other doctors included the leading heart specialist and best-known brain surgeon in the area. He was glad the ophthalmologists senior to him had not been available. The medical team he was a part of was tense but not upset; the young eye doctor told himself to relax, as Hennessy had advised, and to go with the flow of events. But he would get back at the President's lawyer someday for that prissiness crack.

The Nurse

Nurse Inge Kellgren, First Lieutenant, U. S. Air Force, attached to the office of the personal physician to the President, knew enough not to try to plump up the pillow of the injured agent, Harry Bok. Grenade shrapnel was embedded all along his spinal column, his legs were paralyzed, and despite sedation, his slightest movement caused every unparalyzed muscle in his body to spasm.

She did not like the idea of the three visitors coming to talk to him in that condition, but since one of them was her superior, Dr. Herbert Abelson, she could not object. Dr. Abelson, who was the President's long-time friend, made no claim to being much of a doctor, as everyone knew. That was why the M.D. nearest the President had usually been Abelson's assistant, a doctor listed as a medical technician, who was trained in emergency procedures. Unfortunately the assistant had been killed in the ambush.

Dr. Abelson was accompanied by Secretary of State Curtice and Chief of Staff Cartwright. The two senior men stood at opposite sides of Harry Bok's hospital bed and the doctor positioned himself at the foot. The doctor dismissed her with a nod, and Nurse Kellgren walked to the other end of the long ward that had been cleared to make a private room for the American. This was no modern hospital, but an old Czar's palace that had been converted to a sanatorium, and the sixty-foot room chosen for isolation was under a domed ceiling.

She sat at the far end of the room, and to her surprise could hear what was being whispered around the patient's bed. Some trick of sound under the dome, she guessed, and did not quite know whether to get up again and walk out the only door, which was near the patient's bed. She decided to stay put.

"You're going to live, Harry," she heard Dr. Abelson say in a formal voice. "You have some metal chunks in your spinal column that will have to come out, and you won't be able to move for a couple of weeks, but you'll be all right."

She could not see Harry's face, but she could hear his croaked question: "President?"

"The President is alive," Lucas Cartwright said. "He regained consciousness about a half hour ago,

about two hours after the ambush. He has his problems, but he's all right. The General Secretary was
killed."

Harry started to move and his body arched in a
painful grip of angry muscles. When he could, he
asked, "Bug?"

"Your fellow agents thought of that," said Cartwright. "They assure us that the bed and the area
nearby have been swept and contain no transmitters
or microphones." Nurse Kellgren wondered if she
should get up and tell them that the acoustics of this
old room were strange, and she could hear them
across the room when she could not hear them a few
feet away. But that would make everybody look foolish, and perhaps she was wrong. She continued to sit
and could not help but hear.

"Mr. Bok," the Secretary of State said in his deep
voice, "it is now eleven-thirty in the morning. The
helicopter was shot down a little over two hours ago.
In Washington it is four-thirty A.M. Are you oriented
in terms of time?"

"Yes."

"Nobody knows anything yet," said the Secretary.
"Not the traveling press corps, not the Russian people.
Only a small number of Soviet security people under
the direct command of Foreign Minister Nikolayev.
He has placed an absolute blanket of secrecy on this,
on the grounds of protecting the President, but
actually to inform the members of the Politburo first."

"We've objected strenuously," said Cartwright.

"But we can use the time ourselves, with you," said
the Secretary. "That's why we asked Dr. Abelson not
to give you too much painkiller. We need to know,
from you, exactly what happened. There are no other
witnesses."

Harry began to tell the story of the ambush. The
three men leaned forward to hear his whispering, and
Nurse Kellgren could only make out snatches of his
recounting of the tragedy. ". . . then I dragged him out
of the wreck . . . set up a perimeter . . . Chinese face,
right between the eyes . . . guy with the burp gun

caught it . . . grenades got me, killed Kolkov, and I dragged his body over the President's . . . goddamn wild animal and they were all sitting ducks . . . musta passed out."

Nurse Kellgren used a Kleenex on her eyes. Harry Bok was a kind man, who often kidded her in a fatherly way about her statuesque figure with its oversized bosom, and who made sure she was treated with respect by all the other agents. He called her "Silent Sam," because she did not say much, and he sometimes confided in her. She had told him about Dr. Abelson's order not to sedate him completely until he could be debriefed and he had accepted the pain as part of his duty. She had not told her patient, of course, that she had heard from one of the Russian nurses who spoke some English that the Soviet doctors did not think Harry Bok would ever walk again.

"The Russians who answered your Mayday call found the President with Kolkov lying over him," said the Secretary. "Now this is important: Might it have been possible that Kolkov, while still alive, tried to protect the President with his own body?"

"Dead, I think. Dragged him over."

"But might it not have been possible that Kolkov was not dead, and he tried to crawl over to protect the President?"

Lucas Cartwright interrupted Harry Bok's second denial to say, "The Secretary isn't asking you to be sure about anything, Harry. It's just that everybody is terribly nervous after the assassination of Kolkov. Nobody can say for sure who was behind it. The Russians are not letting us get out of here as quick as we want, and not telling the press right away is going to cause trouble."

"They'll go through the roof," Dr. Abelson put in.

"So the Secretary is looking for something that might help ameliorate the situation. Like some heroism on the part of Kolkov," Cartwright explained.

"Something that the Russians can be proud of and the Americans can be thankful for," said Secretary

Curtice. "But we're not asking that you not tell the truth."

"Lucas, this okay?" Harry Bok asked.

Cartwright said, "The Secretary thinks it is very important. It was a hectic moment, Harry—nobody expects total recall. Just sketch out some of the possibilities, that's all. Nothing definite. Might buy us a quicker exit."

"Okay," Nurse Kellgren heard Harry say. "Coulda been that Kolkov crawled over, I dunno, everything was happening."

"Then it is possible," said Curtice, "that Kolkov saved the President's life?"

"Possible, yeah."

"It would surely lessen the anti-Soviet reaction at home," Curtice said, and the nurse wished he would leave Harry alone.

"Wouldn't swear to it. Coulda been."

Nurse Kellgren rose and began walking across the room. Dr. Abelson saw her and said something to the others about not overstraining his patient. Halfway there, Nurse Kellgren could hear nothing of what was being said near Harry's bed. As she approached, Cartwright was saying: "—priority is to get the President the best American medical attention. On American soil. Herb, is the President fit to travel?"

"It's always a risk . . ."

"We need to decide, Herb."

"The ride to the airport worries me," the doctor hesitated. "A chopper would be better than a car, if it doesn't get shot down. We're okay once we get to *Air Force One*. The thing is we need a specialist . . ."

"Is Harry here fit to go along?" At Cartwright's question, the nurse gave the doctor a look of alarm.

"No," said the doctor, and Nurse Kellgren nodded. "Harry can't be moved until he's had an operation."

"Lieutenant," Cartwright said to her, reminding her gently of her position in the armed forces, "would you volunteer to remain with Agent Bok and bring him back with you as soon as he's better?"

"Yes, sir."

"Mr. Secretary," Cartwright said formally, "you are the ranking American on the scene. The wisest course, it seems to me, is to get the President out of here before anything else happens."

"That's your recommendation, then?"

"Yes."

"Then I concur," said the Secretary.

"Now it's up to you," Cartwright said, "to get Nikolayev to lift the secrecy and to spring us immediately."

"Easier said than done."

"But now you have a card to play," Cartwright reminded him, "from our brave friend here. Harry," he turned to the agent, "you acted in the best traditions of the Service. You are going to be a hero, and your picture will hang in—"

"Want a sawbones from home," Harry told him.

"There's a surgeon on the way, complete medical team, including equipment," Cartwright assured him. "Just before we came to you, we got through the only communications the Soviets permitted us. To Bethesda Hospital. We rendezvous with a medical team at the Azores. An eye doctor and one or two others come back with us to the States, and the rest of them come here to you. They're on the way now."

"Eye doctor?"

Dr. Abelson put in, "The President has a problem there, Harry."

After a silence, the agent said something that seemed curious to Nurse Kellgren: "Better get Hennessy."

"Odd you should say that," said Cartwright. "Those were the very words the President spoke soon after he regained consciousness. Mark Hennessy will be on the plane with the medical men."

"If Furmark's alive," Harry added, "he should take over the detail."

"He already has. The nurse is shooing us out, but I want you to know that I intend to recommend that the Secret Service name its target practice range, where you spent so much of your time so valuably, the Harry Bok Target Range."

"Counterfeiting," Harry whispered, which the nurse thought was evidence that he was losing consciousness. Then his voice came back strongly, "Herb, he needs his picture taken now and then."

"I know," the doctor said. "I'll see to that, too."

In the hallway outside the ward, Nurse Kellgren told Dr. Abelson that he should not be sure that their conversation went unheard by the Russians, since the acoustics in the ward were unusual. The doctor, distracted and upset, said he would pass the information along.

The Secretary of State

"We are leaving right now, Vasily."

"Not right away."

The Secretary of State felt a wave of fury surge in him and said nothing until it had passed. They were in the hospital administrator's office, originally a waiting room on the ground floor of the Czar's palace, which the Foreign Minister had taken over as his command post. Upstairs, the President of the United States lay, alive, conscious, unable to see, in need of the best medical attention in the world. Down the hall from the President's room, Agent Bok occupied a huge ward, his condition unknown, but paralysis likely; he was sedated now, out of pain, but in need of a surgeon they could all trust. On the top floor, being photographed now, were the bodies of Soviet General Secretary Kolkov, his guards, and his Chinese assassins.

George Curtice looked at his watch again: 12:30 P.M. Yalta time, three solid hours since the aerial ambush, one hour and a half since the President opened his eyes and said his first shattering words, "Am I alive?" To have him lying there attended by a couple of unknown Soviet doctors and his own half-competent personal physician was an impossible situation. Almost as bad, a mile or so down the road, the world's press corps was sitting, many sunning themselves on the beach, totally unaware of the murder of the leader of the Soviet Union and the critical condition of the leader of the United States. As far as they knew, the two leaders had gone off to have a pleasant lunch, and were not expected to come out in public until the 4:30 photo session.

"You cannot keep this bottled up for five more minutes," Curtice said, his voice under control. "The President's life comes before any other consideration."

"I completely agree," said Nikolayev, seated behind the desk, making no move toward the telephone. "But there are logistical difficulties. You said yourself that he cannot be transported by car over these roads, that a helicopter would be needed—"

"You have those helicopters at the airfield, I saw them when we got in," Curtice insisted, knowing the Russian was deliberately dragging a foot. "Delay is dangerous. You—and I hold you personally responsible for this—you are endangering the life of the President."

Nikolayev rose. "Do not say what is not true. I have ordered the helicopter. I have ordered the airport sealed off and secured. But I must make absolutely certain that the men we use to fly the plane are loyal, and not allied with the Chinese assassins."

"How long will that take?"

"If it protects your President's life, the time is well spent."

"Unacceptable." Curtice knew exactly what Nikolayev was doing, and might have done the same in his shoes: freezing the situation, blacking out all news reports, until his fellow leaders in the Politburo could be informed and an immediate policy decided upon. Nikolayev was under enormous pressure: The slightest omission, the failure to act precisely as the men at the center would expect him to act, would open him to charges of misfeasance at a crucial moment.

"Your formal protest is noted," said the Russian.

"For Chrissake, Vasily," Curtice almost shouted across the desk, "this is no formality, this is—" he groped for the words, and ended weakly with a banal "life and death." More than that, Curtice's reputation rested on his ability to negotiate them out of here posthaste, with the news blackout lifted. Every action, every movement, every moment's delay, would be analyzed by reporters and historians for years, and the blame, he was determined, would not be laid at his door. He felt a twinge of conscience at thinking of how he would look in this situation later, and returned to the pressure: "Every moment you sit on this powder keg, the worse the explosion will be when the story breaks. Don't you see? You're making it worse."

"The General Secretary is dead," said the Foreign Minister. "What could be worse?" Curtice thought it best not to make a quick reply, and Nikolayev answered his own question: "It could be worse if your President were dead, I know. But he is not dying. In terms of his own life, which as you say is paramount, the needs of security are greater at the moment than the need for medical specialists."

"We're not sure we're safe right here," Curtice pressed, a sense of helplessness mounting in the face of Nikolayev's rigid line. "What about an attack on the hospital? It could happen. They could burst in any moment, you don't have twenty men guarding this place." It was hopeless; this was fencing, Curtice knew. The Russian was operating on a timetable of communication; after he knew the initial power lines were laid, the story would be made known, the President permitted to leave. The delays were "unavoidable," any objections would be politely listened to but not heard. And Nikolayev had an edge: America's first black Secretary of State, new in the job, had to show himself to be calm and cool, with no bombast, in his first crisis. The explosion that might be allowed a white would be criticized in a black; a subtle edge, but one the Soviet Foreign Minister was ready to exploit.

"The hospital is secure," Nikolayev said. "The airport is in the process of being secured."

"How long a delay?"

The Russian shook his head. "Not a delay. The logistics require at least four hours."

Curtice seized on that detail as something to work with, a basis for negotiation. He let himself flare up: "Four hours! Do you realize what you're saying? That's past the time they're scheduled to make a joint appearance. You want to lie to the press? You don't understand the American press corps, they'll—"

"Understand my problem, too, George." Nikolayev was trying to build a personal bridge, which Curtice welcomed at this stage. "People have to be prepared for this information in the Soviet Union. It will be a tremendous shock. There will be some hotheads who will want to strike at the Oriental powers without waiting. The delay, as you call it, the necessary time, is in our mutual interest."

"You're wrong, Vasily," Curtice said. His own mention of the reaction of the American press, which he had brought in as an arguing point, was beginning to sink in to himself as well. "Every minute that goes by is a lie. After the story breaks, then they'll want to know what happened after the ambush, in the news blackout. We will be accused of a cover-up, or being part of a conspiracy, there'll be all kinds of suspicion." A note of panic crept into Curtice's voice, not put there intentionally. "You may not worry about that here, but we do. And Lucas Cartwright, he's worked in the White House forever, he has a feel for these things, he says we have to get the hell out of here right away. Four hours!"

"Four hours would be four-thirty, when the picture was to be taken. We can announce it then."

Curtice tried an out-of-my-hands gambit. "If I tell Cartwright we have to sit here, with the President in critical condition, for four hours, he will go to the President and I can guarantee that the President will be furious with you and me. He won't forget, Vasily, if he lives—and I will have nothing to advise except to say that Vasily Nikolayev could not assert his authority at a crucial moment."

The Russian shook his head angrily. "Four hours. If you explain my situation to the President, he will understand. He will see the whole picture, which evidently you do not. Nothing is more important than establishing order, preventing rash mistakes."

Curtice smashed his fist on the desk in frustration. He came around to Nikolayev's side, opened a couple of drawers, took out two sheets of paper and a piece of carbon. "You want an official note? That's what you'll get." As the Russian coldly watched, he wrote in his bunched-up longhand: "To the Government of the U.S.S.R.: At this moment, 12:35 P.M. Yalta time, which is over three hours since the attack upon Secretary Kolkov and President Ericson, the United States protests the deliberate"—Curtice thought of adding "unconscionable" but did not want to chance a spelling mistake—"delay by the Soviet Foreign Minister—"

Nikolayev stopped his hand. "Tear it up," he said. "Three hours. If you don't tear it up, four hours."

Curtice did not tear it up, but left the note unfinished. Lying on the table in that state, it was neither a diplomatic note nor a nonexistent scribble; it was a threat, as far as he could go. Nikolayev, he knew, would not be pushed further, but three hours would not satisfy Cartwright or the President, and he was beginning to worry more all the time about how he would be savaged by the American press for concealing the biggest news event of the generation. Curtice could think of no other way out. He told himself that he was acting in the interests of getting the wounded President adequate medical care, and of making public the facts. He played his hole card.

In a different, quieter voice, he said, "I have just come from the bedside of the injured Secret Service agent, Bok." Curtice walked to the window and reminded himself that his words were probably being recorded, so he chose them with care. "Agent Bok is not sure of his memory of the moments on the ground, when the attackers charged his position. His uncertainty is understandable, since he was bleeding from the grenade wounds, and everything was happening so fast." Curtice paused to let that element of uncertainty sink in.

"Go on," said Nikolayev, betraying an uncharacteristic nervousness.

"He is not sure," Curtice said slowly, "but he indicated that he thinks he remembers Secretary Kolkov crawling over to the President, who was unconscious in the ditch. He thinks he recalls the Secretary lying on top of the President, shielding him with his own body."

"He remembers that?" Nikolayev was apparently weighing the possibilities in his mind.

"His memory is hazy—after all, the agent is in pain, partly sedated. When he's better, it could be he will remember that Secretary Kolkov died a heroic death saving President Ericson's life. Or"—Curtice shrugged—"he will remember that the General Secretary just died."

He let the Russian think it over. Curtice knew that the offer he was making was attractive to the Foreign Minister. If Kolkov died a hero, then Nikolayev, Kolkov's chosen successor, would be strengthened inside the Soviet Union. The American Secretary of State could not know what machinations were going on in Moscow at that moment, or the relative weight of the need for time against the introduction of the fact of Kolkov's heroism. Maybe, Curtice allowed himself to worry, Nikolayev wanted to discredit Kolkov, that no heroism was desired.

"Two hours," said Nikolayev.

"Immediately," snapped Curtice. He had won.

"Thirty minutes."

"Done." He extended his hand, Nikolayev shook it, and picked up the telephone. He gave some orders in Russian, presumably to doctors, and placed a call to Moscow.

"Tell your President," Nikolayev said, "that his bed

will be moved to the front lawn of the palace in exactly one half hour. A medical ambulance, a helicopter, will pick him up and take him to *Air Force One,* which will be cleared for take-off upon his arrival."

"And the press?"

Nikolayev waved that off. "Talk to your press man, have him talk to Mishnikov. I have better ways to spend the next half hour." Curtice picked up the copy of his draft note, crumpled it, and put it in his pocket, hurrying down the hall to the staircase and up to the President's room. The halls were silent and echoed his footsteps; somehow, he thought, crowds should be milling around, barricades up, passes needed. Did news become news when it happened, or not until it was released? A lone guard stopped him at the President's door; in a second, an American came out.

"Furmark, acting head of the White House detail, Mr. Secretary," he said, and waited for Curtice to say what he wanted.

"Can I go in?"

"I'll ask, sir."

"It's important."

"Of course. I'll ask." The agent went inside and closed the door. Curtice took a deep breath, let it out, said to himself that it was good to have security tight around the President, but for God's sake, he was the Secretary of State and he had just negotiated the President's release.

Lucas Cartwright came out. "Did you spring us, Mr. Secretary?"

"I'd like to tell the President, Mr. Cartwright."

"He—um, I know he wants to see you, but he asked me to come out and find out from you—" Awkward. The President did not want to see him. The Secretary of State took that to mean he was an instrument, an appendage of power, with no place at the center. His good news soured in his mouth.

"It's not a time for visitors," he conceded. "Lucas, the ploy worked. Nikolayev wanted to freeze everything for the rest of the day, but the possibility of the agent remembering that Kolkov was a hero turned him around. Tell the Secret Service that the doctors will be moving the President down to the front lawn for the helicopter at two thirty-five."

"Great work, George," said Cartwright with sincerity. Curtice hoped the chief of staff's enthusiasm would transmit itself to the President. "Can you wait here a moment?"

Curtice had no place else to go. He paced the hall as the chief of staff consulted the President. He went over the reasons why he might have been shut out. Because he was black? No—if anything, that was an advantage. Curtice had been appointed to the job because Ericson not only wanted a black in his Cabinet, but a black at State, so he could be tougher in his dealings with the demands of African nations. Because he was not a long-time Ericson intimate? Not that, either—Cartwright was in there with Ericson, and Curtice had seen how Cartwright was put down by the President's desire for the presence of Mark Hennessy, his lawyer. When it became difficult for Curtice to think of Cartwright interposing himself between the Secretary of State and the President, Curtice's pique subsided. The only reason left for his exclusion from the President's hospital room was the President's desire not to see him, and Curtice was not willing to face that directly; most likely, he thought, Ericson was lying there, blinded and confused, and did not want any other presence to deal with.

The Secretary of State stopped pacing, folded his arms, and leaned against the wall opposite the door to the President's room. It occurred to him that he could be most useful not as somebody tagging along on the return trip to the United States, but here in the Soviet Union, at Spaso House, the U.S. embassy in Moscow. The U.S. ambassador there was a foreign service officer who did not have the President's trust. Just as important, remaining behind during Nikolayev's most delicate time of trial might cement a relationship that could be useful. And—after the initial briefing to reporters here, in a few minutes—he would be out of the flow of news. The first press reaction would be wild, to file the story; the second re-action, which he would just as soon miss, would be to turn on those who kept them from the story for so long.

Cartwright came out. "The President is personally very grateful, Mr. Secretary. His exact words were 'I knew we could count on Curtice.'" The Secretary, despite himself, was proud to receive those second-hand remarks, possibly made up by the tactful aide. "By the way," Cartwright added, "I didn't think this was the time to go into the business of Bok's story, and the leverage it gave you, and all. We can brief the President when he's up and around."

Curtice would have preferred to have had presidential approval of his idea to encourage Bok's memory along lines that would make Kolkov heroic, but he could not really insist on any decision from an injured and distraught President. He told Cartwright of his plan to remain in Russia during the postassassination crisis, provided Nikolayev wanted him there.

"Good idea," said Cartwright, who was evidently making the decisions. "You're the senior American present." Curtice liked the way Cartwright repeated that, which was only formally true. "Whatever you say on that, goes."

"What about the press?"

"I feel like a big, heavy, dark cloud," sighed the white-haired Cartwright, "that hasn't been allowed to rain. Let's use the phone in Nikolayev's office."

"Who's with the President?"

"Melinda. And the agent, Furmark, who took Bok's place."

They trotted quickly down the stairs, received permission from an aide of the Soviet Foreign Minister's to use the phone for a call to James Smith, the press secretary, with the caution that a press conference could be called, but no information given out about what until 1:30. The Soviet aide openly picked up an extension to make sure his guidelines were followed.

"Smitty? Listen carefully." Cartwright was crisp.

"Call a press conference at the hotel for one-thirty, that's fifteen minutes from now. No, sorry about the lid, they'll just have to scramble back, this cannot be delayed. I can't tell you. No, I'm under a restriction. The Secretary of State will brief. No, I won't be there. The photo session? That's off. Sorry, you'll find out why at the briefing. Look, Smitty, I know exactly how you feel, and you know the faith I have in your discretion, but this is the way it has to be. Wait." The staff chief covered the phone. "Should he tell Mishnikov that Nikolayev will be there, too?" Curtice motioned him to wait, went into the office where the Foreign Minister was speaking in fast Russian into an ancient telephone, and interrupted with "You want to join me in the briefing?" Nikolayev, still talking, nodded yes; Curtice smiled tightly at the Russian's desire to make sure the Kolkov heroism story would be put out, but was relieved that he would not have to bear the questioning alone. Curtice went back to Cartwright, who was patiently explaining why he could say nothing to Smitty, and nodded his head.

"In conclusion," Cartwright said, "the Soviet Foreign Minister will join the Secretary in the briefing. One-thirty sharp. And have some buses there. As a private note, Smitty, I hope you have not unpacked. Yes. Look, Smitty—get set for something. Okay? Good-by."

Curtice left him to go back to Nikolayev. "The President has asked me," he said to his Russian counterpart, "to indicate my willingness to stay in the Soviet Union, if it will be helpful to you, for the next few days."

"Why should he want to be helpful to me?" Nikolayev was evidently not anxious to appear to owe the Americans a favor.

"Forget it, then."

"It is a good idea of the President's," said the Foreign Minister, "to show that our two governments are working closely together to find out who did this and why. And it is an expression of personal confidence in me." He choked out the last words: "I'm grateful,

George. You'll come to Moscow in my plane after the President leaves here."

By "my plane," Curtice thought, Nikolayev meant Kolkov's plane. The power had to pass somewhere, and it was in the United States' interest that it passed to somebody the Ericson Administration knew. He nodded and went back to Cartwright. "I'm staying behind," he told the chief of staff. "The Foreign Minister needs me here."

"The President will be grateful," the staff chief said. That was true enough, Curtice knew—Ericson did not especially want his Secretary of State nearby—but the better reason was that Curtice could probably be more useful in helping the Nikolayev faction with his presence. Between the veteran Cartwright and Defense Secretary Preston Reed, the President would have the necessary foreign-policy advice in Washington; with the national security adviser's post dispensed with at the start of the Ericson Administration, much of the bureaucratic rivalry had receded temporarily.

"You mustn't allude to this possibility in your press conference," Cartwright was saying, "but if the President should have to step aside, temporarily, I'll try to get word to you first."

The thought that the President might have to step down as disabled had occurred to Curtice, but he had put it aside after Ericson had regained consciousness. Was the President really functioning? He had only Cartwright's word to rely on. The thought of a government in the hands of the Vice-President, Arnold Nichols, dismayed him.

"God save the President," Curtice told Cartwright, and meant it fervently. He went to get Nikolayev to break the news of the ambush to the world.

The President's Physician / 1

Seven hours out of Yalta, as *Air Force One* began its descent toward Lajes Field in the American Azores, Dr. Herbert Abelson gave a nervous start when the buzzer on his wrist watch went off. He had promised Sven Ericson he would wake him a half hour before arrival, and only with that promise had the President taken the sedation he needed.

He jammed at the buzzer until it shut up. They gave the President's doctor a fancy watch that tells the time all over the world, that glows and buzzes and counts heartbeats and measures blood pressure. They gave the President and his staff the world's softest landing, the pilot trained to touch the flying power center down on concrete as if on a field of soft-boiled eggs—and he'd better not commit the sin of bouncing this time, with Ericson's head still in semiconcussion. And they gave men like Abelson either ulcers, or hemorrhoids, or a tic in the eye, some physical reminder that the pressures of this job are too much for normal people to handle without some tangible evidence of deterioration. With Herb Abelson, it was hemorrhoids; he shifted his position and groaned.

He had been wrong to take this job, the next thought followed on. This was exactly the kind of life he had decided not to live, the reason why he had set aside the practice of medicine a few years back for the more orderly life of medical editor. He should never have let Ericson talk him into the political life in the first place: "C'mon, Herb," the candidate had said, "it's just for the campaign. You'll see the play of power from the inside, and it's fascinating." And the

56

campaign manager, that bastard Leigh, had assured him, "The only thing you'll have to hand out is aspirin and cold pills." Like a dope, Abelson thought, he had gone along for the ride.

An editor of a successful medical monthly should never let himself be put in the position of having to deal with flesh-and-blood human bodies, especially— Abelson shook his head slowly—the eyes. Sven Ericson, his fraternity brother, his roommate, had been a cool cookie even in college, using his classmates with the greatest of ease. Now Ericson was still using him, and he in turn was performing a disservice. The President of the United States is in trouble, Abelson accused himself, because he has had inadequate medical attention. He shifted in his seat again. He had to keep his promise to wake up the President in time to let him get his bearings before the medical team boarded.

The most intolerable part of the situation to Abelson was the knowledge that only he, of the people around the President, knew of the worst part of the problem. Not the medical part, the political part. With Harry Bok flat on his back in Yalta—poor bastard, he'd walked his last—only Herb Abelson carried the weight of guilty knowledge around with him. He had to share it; he would not bear it alone. That was why he was looking forward to seeing Hennessy, along with the doctors, at Lajes. He would give the political secret to Hennessy and then the responsibility would be out of his hands. Then he would give the medical secret to the Bethesda team, so that the medical responsibility for the patient would be where it belonged.

The doctor went forward to the President's sleeping quarters to find Ericson already sitting up in bed. "You're awake," he said, then thought that was a pretty dumb thing to say, then thought it wasn't so dumb because it announced his presence to a man who could not see.

Ericson was in pain, brow furrowed, eyes staring ahead, his fingers lightly touching the bandages around his head to find out how bound up he was. "I'm a little dizzy, and I feel sick, and my head hurts," he reported.

He was lucid, the doctor noted; the complaints were differentiated. "You're lucky to be alive, Sven."

"You're right. How's Harry?"

"He'll be okay." Abelson did not think it was a good time to suggest paralysis: the President had enough on his mind. "We left him in the hospital there, along with the big blond nurse, and we're sending doctors." There was a silence.

"All right, Herb, what do you think?" the President asked. The doctor passed his hand across the patient's eyes, back and forth a few times. No blinking. "You're stirring up a wind in front of my face, Herb, what do you think?"

"Can you tell light from dark—I mean, the window's to your left, there's a lot of sun, but over here it's darker. Can you tell the difference?"

"I can't see a thing," the President said. "Not a goddamn thing."

"We'll be landing in the Azores in a minute," Abelson said quickly, "and the ophthalmologist from Bethesda is there waiting for us. He'll give us a diagnosis, we'll know a lot more. Concussion like this, could be a couple of days, you'll be good as new."

"How long was the last time?"

"Forty-one hours."

"The second time lasts longer?"

"Jesus, Sven, I wish I knew," said the doctor. "The way it was such a big secret, I was afraid to ask around. That's a very specialized field, a whole different branch of medicine. . . ."

The President closed his eyes and nodded. "This eye doctor coming aboard, can he be trusted?"

"I don't know him from Adam. He's the one Bethesda sent out, he must be good."

"Discreet?"

"Who knows? You mean you want him not to say you can't see? I suppose we could shut him up for a while, but when we fly an eye doctor all the way out here to see you, what the hell, word gets around. And I had to do that, because maybe there's something that has to be done. I still lose sleep over the last time."

"That's not what I meant," the President said. "We'll have to tell the truth about my condition when we land at Andrews. In a calm way, just the temporary effect of the concussion. And in a couple of days I'll be out of it. That's not the problem. The problem is the last time."

"You mean you don't want to tell the eye doctor about the last time?"

"Not unless I absolutely have to, Herb." He reached for the fresh-air jet, fumbled with it, directing the air at his face. "What I need to know from you is this: How important is it to the diagnosis that he know about the last time?"

Abelson was the first to admit he did not know enough about medicine, but he knew enough to know the value of a patient's history to a doctor unfamiliar with the case. "It's goddamn important that we tell him that this happened before, only six months ago, under similar circumstances, and that you came out of it in forty-one hours. It could affect his treatment. Otherwise, he's flying blind"—Abelson started to say "if you'll pardon the expression" and stopped after "if."

"I'll pardon the expression, Herb. Christ, my head hurts."

"Let me give you a painkiller."

Ericson started to shake his head, which made him wince, and he said, "No, not now. I can't be doped up when they talk to me. How much does the press know?"

"Not a hell of a lot. You have a concussion, and a problem with your eyes. We left it very vague—it may be a problem focusing, or whatever. That's what Cartwright told Curtice to tell them."

"Good. Less the better."

"They're really pissed, Smitty says, at not having a pool on this plane right now. The press planes are following along, and will get here in about a half hour, when we should be ready to pull out again and head for Andrews." After arrival at Andrews Air Force Base in Washington, Abelson promised himself, he would go home and collapse for a week.

"Send Curtice in."

That was troubling to the doctor; the President had forgotten that Curtice had stayed behind with Nikolayev. Abelson reminded him, adding his misgivings about not telling the medical team about Ericson's previous experience with blindness on the campaign train less than a year before.

"Not a word, Herb. I know what I'm doing. No hints, nothing. Ever. Let's go over who else knows."

"Buffie was in the compartment with you. She knows, and she's been very good. You and I know. And Harry Bok. And that bastard Leigh knew. That's all." Then he went over the people who probably should have been told but from whom it had been kept. "Not even an eye doctor was told. Cartwright, Hennessy, Smitty, Melinda—not one of them knows. I haven't said a word."

"Keep it that way," the President said, in a presidential-order voice. "I'm going to tell Hennessy about the last time. Second thought, you do it, when Hennessy comes aboard now. And Herb"—he reached behind him for a pillow, and the doctor moved to give his head the support he wanted—"if you have any questions ever about what to do, and you can't reach me for any reason, work with Hennessy." The President took a deep breath to fight back his nausea. "He's my honcho on this, nobody else. Where's the girl?"

Abelson swallowed. "She's on the press plane. I guess Buffie hasn't said anything yet about the last time, or we'd have heard about it on the radio. Smitty's here with us, in touch with them."

The President said, "Nobody knows I'm blind yet." It was the first time he used the word, the doctor noted, and it did not seem to distress him. "First chance you get, Herb, tell her to keep the last time graveyard quiet."

Abelson nodded.

"Will you?"

"I will, Sven," the doctor said aloud.

The Special Counsel

Hennessy bounded up the steps of the ramp ahead of the medical team, and spotted Melinda McPhee.

"Never thought I'd be glad to see you," she said tersely.

"The Boss?"

"He can't see."

Hennessy's chest contracted. "Blind?"

"He can't see, is all." Her voice, like her face, was rigidly controlled. Hennessy looked behind him; the medics were showing their Bethesda passes, one by one, and Furmark was carefully matching up the pictures with the faces. As each man cleared, he was sent upstairs on the jumbo jet to the conference room, rather than to the President's bedside. That meant the President's condition was not critical. In mid-Atlantic, Hennessy and the others on the medical plane had heard the first reports of the ambush in Yalta, of Kolkov's heroic death, and of Ericson's injuries, the extent of which were not known. It had been announced that *Air Force One* was flying back to Andrews, but the brief stop in the Azores to pick up the medical team had not been mentioned, presumably for security reasons.

During the two hours waiting for the President's arrival at Lajes Field in the Azores, Hennessy had paced the airport tarmac, a small radio in hand, trying to figure out what was going on. The phrases used by Secretary Curtice at the press briefing were "scalp wound . . . lacerations . . . regained consciousness . . . possible concussion . . problem with the eyes." If the "problem" were not serious, it would not have been mentioned; the fact that it had to be mentioned was evidence to Hennessy that Curtice was downplaying an important fact, and that was the reason for the ophthalmologist. What was the reason for Hennessy? The lawyer reasoned that he was the man who carried the Letter. All Presidents had written agreements with the Vice-Presidents about the transfer of power in emergencies, to be used before anything so drastic as the Twenty-fifth Amendment was even examined. If they wanted Hennessy, they wanted him with the Letter, to make sure he did not prematurely deliver it; he patted the bulky original, signed by Ericson, in his breast pocket, walking up and down the edge of the airstrip, looking sourly at the bleakest array of rocks and boulders he had ever seen anywhere in the world, angry that he had not been invited along on the President's trip in the first place.

Herb Abelson, the President's doctor, came up behind Melinda, took Hennessy by the arm tightly, and pushed him toward the stairs leading to the conference room up in the bulge of the forehead of the jet. "First I tell the doctors all I know," Abelson said, "and then I have to see you alone right away."

"I'd like to see the President while you're briefing the doctors, Herb—"

"Stay with me!" Abelson half-shouted, on the edge of hysteria. He gulped a breath, and said, "I have to tell you some things before you see Sven. I don't know what the hell to do. You're here for a reason, and you have to stick very close to me, you hear?"

Hennessy, worried now about the medical attention Ericson had been getting—or not getting—ever since the ambush, let himself be guided up into the room where the medical team was assembling. Problem one was to calm Abelson down so he could brief intelligibly, and not to let a watching world know that the

President's doctor was a nervous wreck. "Melinda says you've been terrific, Herb," he whispered to him, as if to a witness. "Now just be calm and give them the facts. They'll take all the responsibility after that."

"Got my goddamn hands tied," replied the harried doctor. He took a deep breath, looked around at the dozen doctors and nurses crammed into the room with Melinda, Smitty, Cartwright, and Hennessy, and appeared to get hold of himself. "The ambush took place at 9:19 A.M. Yalta time, that's 2:19 last night Washington time, or nine and a half hours ago." All the pencils started scratching, Hennessy observed sourly, as each of the doctors began his memoirs for some medical journal.

"As near as I can reconstruct it," Abelson went on, "in the crash the President suffered a blow on the upper right temple a half inch from the hairline, and began to bleed profusely from a three-and-a-half-inch scalp wound. As he was dragged out of the helicopter by Agent Bok, he received minor contusions on his hands and legs. A grenade explosion caused a piece of shrapnel to embed itself in his right leg lower calf." He pulled out a dozen photocopies of a one-page document and passed them around. "Here's a report by the Soviet doctors, the longhand portion on the top. Translation typed on the bottom, we just got that in from Signal. Describes the removal of the shrapnel, the stitching of the scalp wound, the time that the President regained consciousness, which was eleven-forty, two hours and twenty-one minutes after the crash."

"X ray?" said one doctor, probably the one, Hennessy figured, who brought along all the X-ray equipment.

"I have them here," said Abelson, putting three long celluloid negatives on the table, which most of the doctors closed in on. "There's no mention in the report of the primary problem that the President faces now, which is that, he, uh, cannot see. I guess they left that out for security reasons."

"No penetration of the skull, or any fracture, shows in these," said one of the doctors.

"Blood pressure?" asked another. Hennessy felt like shouting at them that he was in pretty good shape except he was blind, and why don't they focus on that? They went on, infuriatingly, taking down notes on temperature, blood pressure, even a urinalysis taken at the hospital. Abelson, in the minutiae, steadied; he had the answers.

Finally, the eye doctor that Hennessy thought was a prissy type asked, "Any light perception?"

"He says no," Abelson answered, "but he may not know what to look for, you'll have to determine that."

"Difficulty hearing?"

"No."

"Any previous history of concussions?" the eye doctor asked. Abelson stifled a sigh and looked through his folder, finally answering, "We never had a blind President before, that's for sure. You want to see him now?"

The senior man in the medical group, in a captain's uniform, said, "We've worked out a sequence of examinations. Brain first, then heart, then eyes, then the others. No more than three of us in at a time. The test results we can transmit to Bethesda, which should give us a good head start when he arrives." The group rose and followed Abelson down the spiral staircase to the President's quarters. Hennessy, lagging behind, heard the eye doctor say, "Known this, would've brought a neurosurgeon." The President's lawyer started to go to Cartwright, to get "up to speed," in White House jargon, but Dr. Abelson, coming back from the bedroom, latched on to Hennessy's arm again.

"You have to know something," Abelson said urgently. They looked for a spot to talk in privacy, but their seats were in a cabin with other nervous aides and agents, and a few of the medics were still in the conference room. Abelson pulled Hennessy into the forward galley and chased the steward out. "The President has a problem," Abelson began strangely, and stopped.

"It's this blindness business," said Hennessy, helping him along.

"No. I mean, God knows that's a problem, but there's something else that wasn't important before that makes everything worse. You remember the campaign train back in September, that great idea of that bastard Leigh to go back to politicking in the old style?"

Hennessy remembered it well: In an era of television spots, jet stops, and reaching the people through plastic tubes, it had been considered "colorful" to hearken to the more traditional ways of political campaigning. The train ride would provide fresh material for the television spots and something the candidate could talk engagingly about on jet stops. Arthur Leigh, the campaign manager, who was widely called "that bastard Leigh," termed it "my change of pace." He had chosen Ohio, a swing state with good communications facilities, as the backdrop for the "Ericson whistle-stopping." The experience had been incredibly wearing on everybody: Fourteen hours on a special train, rattling and lurching down a poor roadbed, with most of the staff cramped into compartments smaller than the airplane cabin or the local hotel room of the usual campaigning, got on everybody's nerves. The whole phony business had been a waste of time, Hennessy thought; the television crews had difficulty filing their film from places like Lima, Ohio, and the writing press—spoiled by the constant availability of facilities throughout the campaign—ripped into the day on the campaign train for the gimmick that it was.

"You remember how we canceled the last stop of the tour," Abelson was saying, "some excuse about laryngitis?"

Hennessy thought back to that period, less than a year before, but in a different lifetime. That bastard Leigh, who covered up his lack of intelligence with what Hennessy always considered an exaggerated reputation for street-smarts, had insisted that the folksy gimmickry was needed. Ericson, he said, was presenting too slick and detached an image: "We've got a hoity-toity professor of economics," Leigh would growl, "a divorcee, a governor who got in by a fluke and looks like he's riding his luck, and a man who expects folks to understand big words. We've got to go against that grain now and then, show he's not a jet-setter." When this was challenged by Hennessy, who objected to a false folksiness on practical grounds that it would cost Ericson votes in his areas of greatest strength, Leigh had a more subtle response: "It's a matter of respect. He can be a sophisticate, so long as he isn't proud of being sophisticated. He can screw every broad in sight, so long as he doesn't flaunt it. A lot of people like a leader smarter than they are, luckier than they are, richer than they are, and who gets laid oftener than they do, but the people want respect from him. They want him to admit they're the boss, and their proprieties have to be kowtowed to. Most of them know it's phony when he rides on an old-fashioned train, most of them know it's a way that an upper-class smoothie kisses the ass of the populace. But the fact that he kisses their ass is important to them, it's sorta democratic." Hennessy had considered that to be crap, and said so; when the campaign was over, he had made certain Ericson knew that Leigh had some questionable dealings in the past that might embarrass an Ericson Administration. He had shot Leigh out of the saddle, and expected to slip into the top spot himself, but Ericson wanted an inoffensive soul with Washington Establishment savvy like Cartwright. All these thoughts flooded the lawyer's mind on cue from Abelson; Hennessy could not see how it was relevant at a moment like this, and said so.

"It's relevant as hell, counselor," the doctor said. "You remember how we canceled the schedule for the next two days while the candidate recuperated from his laryngitis?" Hennessy nodded, and figured if Abelson was going to take him down memory lane, he might as well have a drink. He began to look into the small compartments in the galley, finding only small packages of nuts. "Well, it wasn't laryngitis, and

it wasn't a slight fever, the way I told the press because Leigh made me. Hennessy, this is important."

"I'll settle for one of these little bottles of booze,"
said the lawyer, on his knees now, looking through
the lower drawers. "From the sound of what you're
about to tell me, I'll need it."

Abelson crouched down beside him, speaking urgently: "What happened was that Ericson was in his
upper berth with Buffie, the photographer, humpin'
away between stops. When the damn engineer
slammed on the brakes, Sven smashed his head into
the end of the berth. Buffie started hollering and waving a naked arm through the curtains of the berth—
maybe she couldn't get out from under, I dunno—
but Harry Bok was right there, in the corridor, and he
shut her up and got her out and came for me."

"So?" Hennessy couldn't get aggravated about the
beginnings of an Ericson affair.

"The candidate was unconscious for about an hour,
and Leigh and Bok and I just sat around, they
wouldn't let me call a hospital."

"Nobody else knew?" asked Hennessy, who had
found the supply of little scotch bottles. He saw where
Abelson's story was heading, and was all ears, but
affected breeziness.

"Leigh insisted everybody freeze. He wouldn't even
tell Smitty, he said he didn't want him to have to lie.
Me, he let lie. Finally the spirits of ammonia got some
results and Ericson came to. But he couldn't see. We
thought he'd gone blind."

Hennessy opened a little bottle for the doctor and
another for himself. Abelson needed no encouragement: "We bundled him in towels around his neck
and walked him off the train at the terminal into a
car and then into bed in Cleveland. Ericson wouldn't
let me consult with anybody; he said I was the only
doctor he trusted. He said it had happened before,
when he was a kid, and he came out of it. So I went
to a medical library and looked up concussions, and
their effects on optic nerves, and I figured the
only thing to do was to wait, no harm could come

from it—I mean, there wasn't a danger from not treating it immediately."

Hennessy drained the small bottle, handing Abelson another. "Did he get his sight back gradually, or all at once?"

"The first day, he could tell light from dark, and the second day, the pressure came off the nerve when the swelling went down, and he could see as well as ever."

"Then, aside from the story getting out," Hennessy said soothingly, "you're not worried about his eyesight."

"This time he can't tell light from dark yet. And when these things happen more than once, it's not good. That's why I said the hell with it, this time I'd get an eye doctor before anybody stopped me. Cartwright passed the message on to Bethesda without arguing; he didn't know the background. Doesn't, even now. The President said you were the only one to know, that youw ould be the honcho on this."

"He likes those words. 'Honcho' comes from the Japanese, it means 'squad leader.'" Hennessy's asides were intended to bring the doctor's worries down to scale, but this time did not work.

"Acting all cool and professional is well and good, Hennessy, but this is a bitch of a spot we're in. We're going to have to tell the world when we get back to Andrews that the President is blind, and that this is the second time it's happened."

"We have to look at this thing with a detached retina," said the lawyer. The doctor closed his eyes and shook his head in frustration. "No," Hennessy continued, "there's no problem about making full disclosure about the current state of the President's health when we arrive in the United States. He is in complete possession of all but one of his faculties, and you and the specialist will be able to suggest that his loss of sight is probably temporary. Not from any past history," he added carefully, "but from your general knowledge of optic nerves and concussions."

"Why can't we just tell the whole thing? What the

hell, he's President now, and people know he likes girls, he's not married—"

"I don't think you quite understand the worry on the President's mind, Herb." Hennessy had grasped the real problem immediately, and it worried him more than he wanted to show. "As you suggest, the girl-in-the-berth angle is relatively unimportant. But the fact that he did not volunteer the nature of his ailment during the campaign could cause an unfavorable reaction."

He watched Abelson think about that. The lawyer was not telling the doctor what to do, but was leading him to make the decision the lawyer wanted him to make. "So there would be a flap," Herb said, not comprehending. "Won't there be one sooner or later, anyway?"

"I have not even spoken to the President about this," Hennessy said, "but from what you tell me he told you, it seems that he is concerned that his enemies might use the campaign incident to try to drive him from office. The previous blindness was unimportant then, but it becomes important now, as you said at the beginning. Very important. I'm not suggesting what you do, only that you think about it." He looked for another handle to help Herb shut up about this. "Think about the medical ethics, of telling outsiders more than your patient wants you to tell them about confidences vouchsafed to you under the doctor-patient relationship."

Abelson nodded dubiously. "I want you to hold my hand all through this, counselor. I have the feeling I'm in something over my head already."

"Then the first thing you should do is stop swilling booze while on duty." Hennessy smiled, handing over three more tiny bottles. "Actually, 'vouchsafe' is one of my favorite words. Don't be a vouchsafecracker." He squeezed the doctor's shoulder and went down the corridor to meet with Cartwright.

Moving down the aisle, looking out the windows at the piles of rocks, fences of rocks, and fields of rocks that made up the island, Hennessy felt the enormity of the President's triple problem beginning to grip him. The threat of upheaval in the Soviet Union, or the threat of vengeance against the people who would be blamed for the assassination, had to be foremost in the mind of the man elected to protect the nation's survival. The U.S. intelligence agencies knew little about the internal dynamics of Kremlin power, or its relationship with the Oriental powers. Perhaps Ericson had some idea of how to deal with Nikolayev, and putting Curtice in his lap had been a good idea, but who really knew how much tension was really in the air, or at what point the tension might resolve itself into the spasm of war? And that was only the beginning of the problem for the President, Hennessy thought, putting himself in Ericson's shoes. He was blinded—temporarily, probably, judging from the previous experience—but even for a few days, he would have to grope around physically as well as mentally, giving the appearance of disability, even paralysis, at a time when the situation cried out for the appearance of supreme ability.

And then the complication: the concealment of the previous blindness. Hennessy turned that over and examined it: At the time, on the campaign train, it would have seemed vital to hide the fact that the President was playing around with a girl between whistle-stops. The word "whistle-stop" would have taken on a whole new meaning, offering the opposition an instrument of ridicule at a moment that a political campaign could least afford it. The lawyer could readily understand that bastard Leigh's need to hush up the accident, to sit tight for a couple of days and hope for the best. But that innocent concealment of the affair was now a suspicious concealment of a "previous blindness," inviting the charge that Ericson had failed to fully disclose his health before the election. That was no peccadillo, to be brushed off as fuel for gossips, but a substantive complaint about a false basis for assuming the reins of power.

That reminded the lawyer of Roy Bannerman, the Treasury Secretary, who had been Ericson's rival for

power in the party. If Bannerman were to learn of
the previous blindness, perhaps he would be inclined
to mount a challenge to the President while he was
still blinded, getting him to step aside, invoking the
terms of the Letter to the Vice-President, or even invoking the Twenty-fifth Amendment.

Hennessy smiled out the window at the rocks. He
felt the thrill of being the man needed to contain the
situation, so that a President could get about his business of exercising his intellect and power to maintain
the peace. The highest stakes. Exactly what he had in
mind when he joined Ericson in his quest for the
presidency. He had been disappointed in the first few
months, and sore about not being taken on the journey
to Russia, but now he was being happily drawn into a
power vacuum. Ericson trusted him, and needed him,
and that, Hennessy freely granted, was mothers' milk
to him. Just as Ericson needed power to be a whole
man, and needed a good-looking young thing to control from time to time as a symbol of his ability to flex
that power, so Hennessy needed to be wholly trusted.
And he was worthy of that trust, he told himself—not
like the Cartwrights of the world, who were loyal to an
institution of the White House; or the ass-covering
Smittys, who were anxious to build a reputation they
could cash in on after this was over; or even the
Melindas, who had an ancient, perverse Pygmalion-
Galatea thing going with Ericson, neither one knowing
who was shaping the other. Hennessy was certain he
would prove to be the most important support to Ericson: He saw the man as friend, compatriot, leader,
power-sharer, and most important, client, a relationship that nobody else had with the President.

Hennessy ran his stubby fingers through his short
red hair and allowed himself to lick his lips. Lucas
Cartwright, the man who operated from the corner
office of the West Wing where Hennessy belonged,
who was now holding together the United States
Government in pretty good style—and Hennessy was
thankful for that—did not know of Ericson's previous
blindness. When the moment of truth—actually, of

71

necessary falsity—had arrived, it was Mark Hennessy and not Lucas Cartwright, or the hot-shot Attorney General, Emmett Duparquet, that Ericson had turned to. Hennessy could fairly taste his opportunity, and was thankful that Ericson was of sound mind that could make the right choice. Ericson's eyes could be a problem, and an episode in his past could be a big problem, but his judgment was good, and that was half the battle. Heartened by the Truman-like scrappiness of his leader, and reminding himself that Cartwright was not to know of the previous blindness, he made his way to the cabin of the chief of staff.

The Chief of Staff

Lucas Cartwright had read somewhere that celestial beings on a star some two hundred light-years away, observing the earth at this moment, would be seeing the American Revolution and its aftermath. In that situation, what would "now" mean—when it happened on earth, or when it could be viewed by an intelligent mind? Cartwright often thought of himself living in that never-never time between the world of decision and the world of announcement, between event and perception, between happening and interpreted fact.

The dramatic case earlier that day had been the withholding of the news of the ambush, but the elderly staff chief had seen so many other, less dramatic cases in his White House service. Most news had its lead time, an event-producing process even more inexorable than the decision-making process; the duality caused him to live with bifocals on, partly observing the reported events and partly watching unreported events marching to public knowledge.

"Make the desk turn into a coffee table," Hennessy told the chief of staff. "I like to see the play of power."

"I never play with presidential buttons," Cartwright replied. "It is tempting fate. And what is more, you would probably put your feet up on the coffee table, which is a habit of yours that the President asked me to talk sharply to you about." Cartwright, the Old Man of the White House staff, felt almost contemporary with the forty-five-year-old Hennessy; more so, say, than the press secretary, in his mid-fifties, who operated in a world of black and white, able to carry responsibility because he did not feel its weight as Cartwright and Hennessy did. Cartwright was at a seeming disadvantage because he had signed on to the White House staff during the interregnum, while most of the others had come to know the President during the campaign or in his state capitol office, but that was actually an advantage: He had been through no power struggles, he owed no loyalties other than to the President, and—best of all—he was unfamiliar to the "Ericson people." He was a White House person, a relic in a way from the mellow past, nobody's competitor, nobody's friend. The chief of staff's job has traditionally out-lonelied the "loneliest job in the world," Cartwright knew, but he was happy to take it on. No martinet, not even a terribly efficient manager, he knew he suited Ericson's needs at the beginning of his Administration, when the new President wanted some experienced judgment, sophisticated press respect, restraint. The chief of staff did not mind in the least being called "courtly" by trendier aides, and his style—excessively polite, circumlocutious, time-consuming—was as good a mask as any for deliberation.

Cartwright knew that Hennessy wanted his job; it did not bother him. Hennessy might get it one day—if he learned to control his temper—meanwhile, he could wait.

Hennessy laid the Letter on the table. Cartwright

picked it up, read the admonition: "For the Vice-President's Eyes Only," opened it, and read it through slowly twice. He thought it excessively detailed, but did not convey this to Hennessy, the probable author. "I had not seen this before, Brother Hennessy, although the President made me generally familiar with its contents. He told me as soon as he regained consciousness that he wanted you and the Letter by his side, not half a world away. I took that to mean that he feared you would panic and deliver it prematurely."

"I've always dreamed of leading a coup d'état." Before the badinage got worse, Hennessy broached the subject: "Why have I been dragged out of bed?"

"The President cannot see," said Cartwright. "This fact will be announced as soon as we get home. Who announces it, in what forum, at what time, will be the subject of discussion as soon as the doctors are satisfied. But what I would like to anticipate with you is not the immediate reaction—relief that he's not dead, sympathy, shock, all that—but the subsequent reaction, that the President's disability may be so great that he cannot function as President." He returned the Letter to Hennessy, its custodian. "If the doctors say he's going to be fine in a few hours or days, we have no problem. If they say he is permanently blind, then we do have a problem we must be prepared to cope with. If they say what I think they'll say—that there's no way of knowing yet, they need more tests, wait and see—then we're in that gray area of uncertainty that could cause enormous trouble for the country."

"A President is disabled," said Hennessy carefully, "when he asserts he is disabled, or when he is unable to communicate whether he is disabled or not. But if he says he is not disabled, then he is not disabled, period."

"—unless he is insane, which is not our problem here, or unless he is wrong about his disability."

"He's the sole judge of that," the lawyer said firmly. "The people elect a man and trust him to do what's right, or at least what he thinks is right. If he's mistaken, or wrong, the burden of proof is not on him—first it's on his Cabinet, and then it's on two thirds of the Congress."

Cartwright nodded. His colleague had exhibited his familiarity with the obvious, although he was misusing "burden of proof" for "remedy," perhaps intentionally. He wondered what the President's real purpose was in sending for Hennessy. Protecting against premature delivery of the Letter? Ludicrous. The feeling of confidence in having a long-time associate with legal training around? More plausible. Having Hennessy ready to take over the chief of staff's job in a tight spot? Always possible. Still, it had been Cartwright's observation that the President, in tight spots, tended to tighten the circle around him rather than expand it. Time would tell; Ericson was not his first President, and he had never found previous ones to feel an obligation to tell chiefs of staff everything.

"Counselor, you need to have available a legal definition of blindness; a medical definition of blindness; and to be able to cite some authorities that show how the inability to see does not affect judgment. I would not go as far as 'blindness is good for you,' " Cartwright continued, "but some evidence of its noncatastrophic nature would be helpful, at least as shown in case law."

"Are we using the word 'blind'?"

"It is a harsh word." When Cartwright pushed a buzzer, Melinda McPhee appeared. He asked for a dictionary, which she brought in quickly, and he asked her to stay. The staff chief put on his glasses and searched up the page for the word: "Blind drunk, blind date, blind alley—here, blind. 'Sightless.' Sven Ericson's that, all right, but it has a connotation of permanence, doesn't it? 'Having less than one tenth of normal vision in the more efficient eye when refractive effects are fully corrected by lenses.' "

"That sounds legal," said Hennessy. "Melinda, for Chrissake, what's bugging you? You keep chewing your lipstick."

The secretary shot him an angry look. "You two,

figuring all the angles, do you know what he's going through in there? It's the most frightening thing that can happen to a human being. He's lying there and he's scared. I've never seen him scared before, and it scares me, and I'd be a little less scared if you two showed some understanding of the agony he must be in."

"Thank you, Melinda," Cartwright said, "it's always good to be reminded of the human considerations."

"Now straighten up and fly right," Hennessy snapped. "The last thing the Boss needs is a hysterical staff at a time like this."

"I am not hysterical," said the President's secretary coldly. "I am not callous, either."

"Then in a manner neither callous nor hysterical," Cartwright stepped in, "would you inform the captain of the medical team that this aircraft leaves for Washington in exactly ten minutes. Thems that is staying on board for the flight back, stay; thems that handle the transmission of data from Lajes to Bethesda, get off now, along with the group that is going on to Yalta to take care of Harry Bok." Melinda moved out quickly. Cartwright admired the woman; Hennessy, he noted, did not get on with her at all, perhaps competing for Ericson's attention or affection as "closest in." At the time of Cartwright's first White House stint, he used to think that sort of jockeying was foolish and time-wasting; now he regarded it as normal, human, and sometimes useful.

In a moment, she returned: "The medics want a meeting, all of them, with you and all of us right now. Press secretary, too. And they want twenty minutes to take-off, to give the electroencephalograph operator time to finish."

"That's a mouthful, that word," said Hennessy. "How come you—"

"Brain waves," she dismissed him. "Lucas?"

Cartwright had figured on the request for a delay; its shortness was good news. He could still take off just as the press planes were arriving and avoid the renewed demands for a press pool coming aboard. He rose to go to the meeting room up the stairway with a heavy feeling on his chest, however; the staff chief was not as hopeful as Herb Abelson seemed to be about President Ericson's eyesight.

The room atop the jet filled with the doctors, looking brisk and important, as doctors do as a part of their professional demeanor, along with the President's aides: Cartwright surveyed Melinda, with a notebook, Hennessy trying to look bored, Herb Abelson trying to keep from wringing his hands, Smitty glowering, and Jonathan, the young speechwriter—Cartwright could not recall his last name, and never liked to ask —looking tense and alert, holding a small tape recorder in his hand. The chief of staff nodded at the writer that it was all right to tape the meeting. He might as well have an accurate record for an angry press corps.

The head of the medical team wearing the captain's stripes began the meeting with the good news. "The President's life is not in danger. Let's begin with the brain."

"Mild concussion," diagnosed the brain specialist. "No penetration of the cranium. We don't have the EEG yet. Hairline fracture of the optic channel, the ophthalmologist will address himself to that. In laymen's terms, the President's brain is undamaged."

"Heart."

"Sound," the heart man said. "Normal for him."

"Internal."

"No internal bleeding," repeated that specialist. "The Russian doctors applied the proper first aid to the contusions of his extremities, and the shrapnel in his leg was removed cleanly, no complications."

"Now to the problem area," the captain said. "Dr. Lilith, the patient's eyes."

"Why don't you tell us about the President's condition in laymen's terms. Dr. Lilith," added Abelson. Cartwright nodded; he did not want to have to depend on the President's personal physician for interpretation, either. Lilith cleared his throat, nervously looked at the speechwriter's recorder and the secretary already making notes, and began.

"The President has suffered a concussion, which is an injury to the brain resulting in the disturbance of cerebral function." He paused a moment. "The function of the brain that is disturbed, as you know, is his vision. At this moment, ten hours after the injury, he is totally blind. No light perception—he sees black, or dark colors.

"The cause is the—the probable cause is—" He began again. "One possible cause is the blockage to the cortex of the synapses leading to the optic nerves. The injury has caused a swelling which might be temporary; in that case, he could regain his sight in a few days. Other possibilities exist; of permanent damage to the brain, which would mean either partial blindness or total blindness. It's too soon to tell. The eyes themselves are fine—no damage to any part of the eyeball. The message, or picture, that the eye is sending is just not getting through to the brain."

"Isn't it a little early, Doctor," interrupted Hennessy, "to use the word 'blind'? I mean, wouldn't it be more accurate to say that the President's injury has temporarily affected his sight?"

"I would go along with that," Dr. Lilith said carefully, "except that it may not be temporary. We try not to use the word 'blind' at this stage because it is a scare word. I'd say 'loss of sight, perhaps temporary, maybe caused by the swelling from the concussion.' Frankly, I'd be more optimistic if he'd had some history along these lines, and had come out of bumps on the head after a brief period of sightlessness."

The other doctors questioned the ophthalmologist more closely on the details of the President's blindness, but Cartwright found nothing usable in the technical analysis. His task now was to get the President back to Washington, to let the world know that he was functioning and that United States decision-making was in good order, and to avoid alarm about Ericson's blindness. Also to reassure the President that all this was being done.

The senior medical man looked at his watch, and true to his word, concluded the meeting promptly with assignments to the medical team: four to continue on in their own plane to Harry Bok in Yalta, two to supervise transmission of the data from Lajes, the other six to return with the President on *Air Force One.*

But the meeting did not seem to want to break up; Cartwright sensed the cause of the awkward pause, and called for the President's photographer to make a record of the moment. As Buffie started clicking, the doctors, who had up to then seemed most professional, assumed their most worried looks. When her thank-you dismissed them, Buffie shot a knowing look at Cartwright, and murmured, "We all have our roles to play." The chief of staff nodded.

"Herb," Cartwright said to the President's physician, "would you sit down with Dr. Lilith and Brother Jonathan here"—he motioned to the young speechwriter—"to write out the medical statement for the captain to review. I think Dr. Lilith should be the one to read it to the press, since it is a specialized ailment, don't you, Captain?" The senior medical officer could not have been happy about that, but nodded. "Meanwhile, Smitty, let's have your ideas on when to break the news and how."

The doctors separated into their subgroups, departed, and the aircraft engines started. "We follow the Hagerty rule," said Smitty, "tell 'em everything twice a day. The press plane will be at Andrews when we get there along with live television. Doctor reads the statement right there and answers all questions. We'll have another press conference late in the day— live, in time for the evening news shows—from the hospital press center."

"That's just dandy," said Hennessy. "Convince the country and the world that the President of the United States is blind as a bat and unable to function."

"Look, Hennessy, you weren't with us in Yalta," Smitty flared. "The press corps is sore as hell, and they have every right to be. The Russkies put a news blackout on the ambush, and nobody knew anything for close to three hours. At least we can blame the Russians for that. But not having a press pool aboard *Air Force One* on the way back—that was Cartwright's idea, and it sent everybody right up the wall. You just cannot manage the news of an assassination attempt."

Cartwright said mildly, "Not all my ideas are Divinely inspired." That particular one had been inspired by the President, with the staff chief designated to take the blame. "At the time, what with the need to pick up medical personnel and the like, I thought we might need the space allotted to the press pool. That's why I overruled your rather vehement objections, Smitty, although I acceded to your demand that you be aboard." Cartwright felt no compunctions about making up this little story. The President himself had forbidden the presence of a press pool soon after regaining consciousness in Yalta. The chief of staff took the rap in such an unruffled manner that he was sure he would have passed a lie detector test; President-protection came with his job.

"You were wrong, Lucas," the press secretary pressed, "and one day you'll admit it. They'll never forgive us for this: A press pool has a right to be aboard this plane right this minute."

Melinda McPhee put in a word: "Smitty, maybe you'd be earning your money by telling us how you're going to make the headline read 'President Alive and Recovering' instead of 'President Goes Blind.'"

"Do I tell you how to take shorthand?"

"For Chrissake, Smitty," Hennessy said, his voice rising, "you're the President's press secretary, not the press's press secretary. You made your point, you can write your goddamn book with a clear conscience, now stuff it long enough to do your job. If you don't lean against the natural tendency of the press to play up the worst, the goddamn world could go up in smoke."

The chief of staff stepped in to reiterate Hennessy's point in a gentler way. "There is that national security consideration. The Soviet Union could be in a state of upheaval—Kolkov assassinated, the Politburo meeting, the news suppressed on the inside and coming in from the outside—we really don't know who'll pick up the phone if we have to use the hot line. Secretary Curtice thinks it's in our interest to help Nikolayev calm things down, but we're not even sure of that. The one thing we do know is it is not in our national interest to spread alarm about the President's condition. Just the opposite. We should assure the world that no disability exists that lowers our guard—"

"But we cannot lie," Smitty warned.

"Nobody has suggested lying," Cartwright said with as much sincerity as he could muster. "What we are obliged to do is make sure the truth comes out, not some exaggeration that would distort the truth. Fact number one: The President is alive and the doctors say he is out of danger. Number two: He is conscious and in contact with his advisers, and will soon put out a personal statement about the heroic act by Premier Kolkov that saved his life. Very important that we stress that, according to the Secretary of State, who has remained behind and needs all the help he can get.

"Number three," Cartwright continued, "and only number three, not number one: The President cannot yet see, but has been told by his doctors that a good chance exists that he will recover his sight completely when the swelling goes down. All it means at the moment is that the President will get his news on the radio rather than on television." He hoped the press secretary would accept that way of minimizing the fact that the leader of the free world was crippled in a way that no President had ever been.

"That's reasonable," said Smitty. "I can handle it that way in the briefing. But you can expect the blindness will be right up there in the lead."

"His inability to see yet," amended Hennessy.

"Instead of the airport statement and press conference," Smitty continued, "we could announce now that the statement will be made at the hospital tonight. The eye doctor could read his statement and beg off questions, saying it's too soon to tell and he refuses to speculate; another doctor could say how great the President's heart is, or whatever, and I could brief about the details of the ambush, that's still red-hot. That'll hold the overnights, with the question about the eyes building up for tomorrow morning."

"Then we should have three other specialists consulting," said Melinda, whose judgment Cartwright respected, "and it will still be too soon to tell. By that time, he may be better, or at least the world may be cooling off a little."

"Or maybe tomorrow the President could make a brief statement on radio," mused Hennessy, "about Kolkov. Keep the focus on the heroism, and show the Boss still has all his marbles. And we may get a break, there could be some slight improvement in his eyes tomorrow."

"You sound like Scarlett O'Hara," the mollified press secretary said. " 'Tomorrow is another day.' "

"I would regard the arrival of tomorrow," said Cartwright, "as a victory in itself." He concluded the meeting and walked down the corridor to report to the President. The Secret Service man, Furmark, said he was resting, and Cartwright turned to go back, but the President's voice called out, "Is that you, Lucas? I want to see you."

The chief of staff sat next to the bed and quickly summarized the way the plans were shaping up. "Unfortunately," he felt he had to add, "the eye doctor's report is a big, fat question mark; we can't make any plans based on it."

"Make the assumption," said Ericson, "that I'll be seeing again in two or three days." He seemed sure of himself; Cartwright marveled at the natural optimism of Presidents. "Minimize it every way you can for the next forty, forty-eight hours, to give Nikolayev a chance, so the kooky faction in the Kremlin doesn't get any ideas about now being the time to take out China. You'll have to lean on Smitty very hard, he'll want to show my X rays on television, but you'll have to give the impression I'll be fine soon. Make that assumption yourself, Lucas—I'm sure it's true."

"So am I, sir." He wished he could be as confident of that as he was sure he was not completely in the President's confidence. "You want to see Hennessy? We flew him out here to come back with us on the last leg, as you wished."

"Yes, just for a minute. I was worried that he might go off half-cocked and deliver that letter to Nichols, but that was foolish, I guess. Lucas, as soon as we get back, I want you to keep an eye on Bannerman. If we have any internal trouble, it'll probably come from there." The Secretary of the Treasury, a powerful opponent of Ericson's candidacy within the party, had been brought into the Cabinet against Cartwright's advice, on the old Lyndon Johnson theory that it was better to have an old opponent "inside the tent pissing out."

"I think you're exaggerating your disability problem," the staff chief offered. "Nobody's going to say anything but 'Thank God he's well' for the next few days, and by then you'll be on the mend. I wouldn't dwell on it if I were you." The hell he wouldn't; if he were in Ericson's shoes, Cartwright would be thinking nonstop what it would be like to be a blind President, or if the public interest called for a prompt resignation. But he hoped he would be served by a staff chief who would tell him to forget it for a few days.

"You're right, Lucas. And you'll see, in a couple of days—good as new."

The Personal Secretary / 1

In the Bethesda Naval Hospital tower, down the hall from the room where Defense Secretary James Forrestal had jumped out a window, the President listened to the television news. Melinda McPhee was there to tell him what the screen showed, if the picture became important, which it seldom did.

"From the CBS News headquarters in Washington, this is the CBS evening news." The picture showed a bunch of people moving around a newsroom, handing each other messages. It was phony, Melinda observed. Those people knew they were on camera and were being actors handing each other messages.

"Five days after the President of the United States survived the ambush at Yalta," the anchorman reported, "the nation is coming to the realization that for the first time in history, it is being led by a blind man. For the latest word on the condition of President Ericson, to the Bethesda Naval Hospital." A reporter came on standing in front of the hospital. A phony use of a backdrop, Melinda muttered to herself. He could just as easily have reported from the studio, but a show biz need for the appearance of reality placed him in front of a giant prop. The more she worked in the White House, Melinda decided, the less she liked television news.

"The President's doctors continue to emphasize that their patient is in excellent physical and mental health," the reporter said into the camera, "but for one defect that has not improved in five long days: He cannot see." The reporter pretended to consult his notes, so the viewer would not know he was reading a teleprompter reflection in front of the camera eye. "The blindness of the President becomes more ominous with each passing day. A panel of leading eye specialists met with reporters a few moments ago and Dr. Perry Lilith gave this pessimistic report:"

"Picture of Lilith at the blackboard downstairs," Melinda told the President, who was sitting, dressed in sports clothes, in an easy chair.

"Although it is still too early to tell, and there may yet be marked improvement possible, we can give no assurance that the President's sight will return."

Reporter's voice: "That means you think he's likely to be totally blind for the next four years?"

Doctor: "I would not want to speculate, based on the information we have now, as to how long or how total the President's blindness will be."

Cut to live reporter: "For the first time, the President's doctors stopped tiptoeing around the hard word they have avoided using all week: blindness. It's a fact that the President—and the nation—will have to face up to, in the days to come."

Back to the anchorman: "For a reaction to the possible permanent nature of the President's disability, first to the Speaker of the House, Republican Mortimer Frelingheusen, who thinks all such speculation is premature."

The Speaker, sucking on his pipe in his office: "Too soon to tell. Let the man get on his feet again, and see how he can cope with this new situation. Blindness is a terrible thing, but a lot of blind people lead useful and productive lives. Let's just be thankful the President wasn't killed."

Anchorman's voice over a film of Treasury Secretary T. Roy Bannerman coming out of Bethesda Hospital, after a brief meeting with the President: "We can't minimize blindness. It's a disability that deeply concerns the President, not only for himself, but for the nation. The presidency is a big job, and this is a big drawback. Let's pray it's temporary."

Melinda breathed, "Thanks a heap, old buddy."

The President smiled: "About what I expected from Roy. Frelingheusen was good, though."

She flicked to another network, in the midst of live satellite coverage of Kolkov's state funeral in Moscow. "—of State George Curtice, who is President Ericson's personal representative to the funeral and who has remained here in the Soviet Union ever since the fatal ambush of the legendary Ukrainian. Western observers here, looking for a clue to the succession, have noted that the three chief pallbearers are Georgi Mendeyev, the aged President of the Soviet Socialist Republics and a figurehead; Mihail Voroshilov—you see him there, closest to the camera—the fiery young party ideologue, a leader of the hard liners in the Kremlin; and Foreign Minister Vasily Nikolayev, a moderate, someone the West has come to know well over the past two decades, but whose Communist party base is not the strongest. . . ."

"Wrong," Ericson commented to Melinda. "That's what everybody says, but Kolkov told me Nikolayev was solid in the party, and Voroshilov was the one with the troubles. Make a note to tell the CIA about what Kolkov told me in the chopper before it went down. Stick the note in my diary, too."

"Speculation here in Moscow is that the Politburo will select a troika, perhaps these three leading pallbearers, to head the government in a period of transition, or a time of upheaval. And now the Soviet state orchestra has begun to play the anthem. . . ."

Click to a third network, which was reporting on the shutdown of the last large American shoe factory because the Administration had made what the commentator sternly called a "conscious decision" not to protect shoe manufacturers from foreign competition. Melinda heard the President murmur, "That used to be called 'free trade,'" and then, in a more commanding tone, "Hell with the rest of the show, Melinda—read me the News Summary."

As she flicked off the set with a remote-control switch in her hand, Melinda was ready with the President's News Summary, a forty-page typewritten publication put together each night by a crew of five researchers—"the gremlins," they were called, because the daytime staff rarely saw them—with a circulation of only twenty White House staffers. The operation cost about $100,000 a year, but it was worth it: The President was kept informed of not just the flow of the news but the play of the news. The purpose of the summary was to show not only what was going on, but how events were being perceived by the daily press, television, and even the small magazines of opinion. The midnight gremlins of the Executive Office Building did a good job, Melinda knew, by the way the President kept sending them little notes of commendation. The value of those little notes, scrawled in his own hand, was discovered by Ericson soon after his Inaugural, when he read that a personal note he had written years before to a fellow professor had been sold at auction for three hundred dollars. Ever since, he had sent commendations in handwritten form to whoever did anything out of the ordinary in the White House. "On presidential stationery, it's worth at least five hundred dollars—not that they'd sell it, but it's nice to know," he had said delightedly. "It's like giving a five-hundred-dollar tip, and not having it cost you a nickel." For a tightwad like Sven Ericson, that was one of the presidency's better fringe benefits. She wondered what he would do now for his "tips"—could he still write, or learn to? Would he send little Dictaphone tapes? Maybe she could type the notes and attach the tape of his voice.

"The President's News Summary Number 146," she read aloud. One hundred forty-six days in the Presidency, she noted, plus three years in the Illinois Governor's Mansion, plus four years at the university, drifting with this man from job to job as he had floated to the top. She was pushing forty now, and had watched Ericson unhappily married, happily divorced, and making casual liaisons with women she penciled in on his calendar, and she had passed up most of her own chances at a successful second marriage. The two of them had experienced their moment together, about three months after she had begun working for him, but she had said she would be damned if Melinda McPhee would be anybody's penciled-in interlude, and they had agreed that there should be no bed for an office wife. He had put it in an inelegant army term: that it was never wise to build your latrine near your mess hall.

"I'll skip the television rundown, you're ahead of that already," she said, "here's the press play. Two-column head in the *Times,* one column in the *Post,* three columns in the L.A. *Times,* all leading with hospital report yesterday on the growing concern that the President may be permanently disabled. World financial markets very unsteady in wake of Soviet uncertainty and Ericson uncertainty, danger of war. Bannerman says President will do the right thing, whatever that may be, and counsels calm. Prospective stories second lead on Kolkov funeral and speculation on successors. Good sidebar in the *Times* on Vice-President Nichols' activities during tragic week.' "

"Nichols sat on his ass and posed for pictures," Ericson said. "That's what I told him to do. I want everybody to be reminded of the alternative to me—Arnold Nichols is my secret weapon. For my private information, Melinda, get Cartwright to check on whether Bannerman and the Veep have been spending any time together."

She wrote that down on the margin of the News Summary, which later would become her agenda for calls. He was unduly worried about being pushed out of office, she thought. That was the insecurity from the blindness coming through in a mild form of political paranoia, which would pass, if she knew Ericson, who could adapt to anything. Living with changes, using changes to his benefit, turning minuses to pluses, playing the breaks that seemed always to come his way, that had been his life since she went to work for him. "Here's one you won't like," she said and read: " 'One column below the fold in *Post,* with jump to full page inside, on question: What does the President's signature mean now? Story begins: Presidents sign a flock of documents every day, some important which turn bills into laws, some ceremonial which appoint political cronies to commission sinecures. But constitutional scholars are asking in the light of the President's blindness whether a man can be held legally responsible for signing something he demonstrably has not seen, and more specifically, if a blind President's signature is valid on a law. After all, they point out, he may be signing a document that has been misrepresented to him by aides. . . .' "

"Hadn't thought of that," said Ericson, hunching a long leg over the arm of his chair. "Son of a bitch. That's why Cartwright hasn't been sending me the daily bundle. Give me a pen and paper, Melinda." He took them, signed his name three times, and held the paper out for her to take. "Does that look like my signature? Is it any different?"

"It isn't as sloppy as usual," she said. "You were being careful. When you loosen up, you'll see, they'll even pass your checks at the bank." That wasn't the constitutional problem, she knew—was he focusing?

"It's important the signature look the same as before," the President said. "I want you to kick back to me anything I sign that looks wrong, because I can just see the comparison in the news magazines, 'the old Ericson and the new.' Now for the basic question of law"—she relaxed, he was focusing—"get a memo from Hennessy on that. On some documents, the Secretary of State countersigns, it's been that way for centuries. Find out why commissions—you know, the appointments you hang on the wall—have two signatures, and why laws have only one. Maybe there could be a verification statement on each document I sign, by the Secretary of State, saying something like 'I read this to him myself.' Tell Hennessy that. We'll turn Curtice into a notary, if need be."

She started to continue the News Summary but he cut her off. "What am I doing in the hospital anyway? They're not doing anything for me. They can set up all the eye-testing equipment in the White House, if they want to. I want to get out of here, now." He picked up the telephone. "Abelson," he said, knowing that the White House operator would be on the line in the split second it took to get the receiver to his ear. Ten seconds of grumbling to himself, then, "Herb? I want to go home right now. Any good medical reason why not?" Melinda pushed the "dead key" on her extension and listened to the reply: "No medical reasons, Sven. Public-relations reasons. You wanted people to worry about your being sick, remember? Not just your eyes, your whole physical set-up after the ambush. We got a lot of questions on that, first couple of days."

"That's over now," the President said. "Anybody from our staff here at the hospital now?" Smitty was in the press room, along with Marilee Pinckney, his deputy. "Get 'em both and bring them with you now, here, to my room." To Melinda, he said, "Keep reading."

" 'Chicago *Tribune* feature on the President's Eyes and Ears—how the top White House staff functions in this emergency.' " She slowed down to let him enjoy this. " 'Mild-mannered Lucas Cartwright doesn't crack the whip the way past staff chiefs have done in the White House, and is said not to have the necessary "take-charge quality" the moment requires. Special counsel and old Ericson crony Mark Hennessy has been moved in close to the power center to handle troubleshooting assignments, a sure sign of Cartwright's imminent fall from power, but Hennessy—abrasive, hot-tempered, and wisecracking—is hardly the man to inspire staff confidence. And there is no national security adviser, since Ericson returned those functions to the Defense and State departments. Of the senior staff, the man emerging as the one the President looks to most is tough-minded, experienced James Smith, fifty, former news executive and now press secretary to the President. Like James Hagerty during the illness of Dwight Eisenhower, the press secretary is not only the public's window on the presidency, but the President's chief contact with the world, and Smith has risen to the occasion. Some insiders think, and many reporters hope, that Smith's influence will continue to rise after the hospital emergency ends. It was Smith, many remember, who crossed swords with Cartwright and Secretary of State Curtice in Yalta, when they wanted to go along with the Soviet news blackout. Smith's insistence on some press consideration led to an earlier-than-planned end of the blackout, his presence on *Air Force One,* and his informed briefings since that time. . . . Smith's deputy, economist Marilee Pinckney, whose good looks belie her seriousness of purpose, has also impressed the hard-to-impress press . . . most of the President's time has been spent with his doctors, Herbert Abelson and Perry Lilith—down-to-earth medical men—and his long-time personal secretary, severe and protective Melinda McPhee. . . .' "

Melinda paused. The President did not react. "Skip to the opinion section," he instructed. "What is Zophar saying?" As she was flipping the pages, he asked, "Who wrote that crap?" and she was ready with the answer: "Evelyn Benn, she's a buddy of Marilee's. I don't think Smitty planted it." The President grunted.

"Samuel Zophar's column. Here's the way the gremlins boiled it down: 'Concern for the President's eyesight has obscured a much more fundamental concern to world leaders: the ominous competition between the Third and Fourth Worlds. The sudden paralysis of the Soviet and American superpower alliance gives the other superpower alliance—China and Japan—an unexpected opening. Here is the order of battle:

" 'The Third World—Arab wealth bolstered by Israeli technology, buttressed by the manpower and atomic arsenal of India—has had as its main support the Soviet-American Western superpower alliance. Will that remain the same with Kolkov gone and with Ericson's future uncertain?

" 'The Fourth World—the hungry, volatile, less-developed nations of Africa, Latin America, and Southeast Asia, combined with the surprisingly militant Canadian-Mexican entente—has been supported at the United Nations and elsewhere by the Far Eastern superpowers. Its power and influence has been growing until it is now nearly a match for its wealthy target: the resource-rich Third World.

" 'It is to the advantage of the two superpower groups,' Zophar writes, 'that the Third and Fourth Worlds compete, but it is to everyone's disadvantage if one side or the other "wins," or goes to war—then the precarious balance, so carefully maintained for close to a decade, would be tipped and the world order upset.

" 'A decade ago, it was unthinkable that the Arabs and Israelis would ever be able to work together. Now they do—only too well. A few days ago, it was equally unthinkable that the Western superpowers could be suddenly paralyzed, and tantalizing—perhaps false—opportunities placed in front of the Eastern superpowers. Will the Chinese and Japanese leaders take advantage of this chance to combat what they call "the white peril"? Will the Western superpowers stick together, or will the Soviets go it alone with an attack on the Orientals? That is what concerns the men and women in the chancelleries of the world in a time of testing that could be prelude to disaster.' "

"Sam's usually a little on the glum side," the President observed, "but this time he isn't glum enough. He doesn't know the half of it. And I should turn it all over to our Throttlebottom Vice-President? He's just what the world needs now."

Abelson knocked and looked around the half-open door. Melinda motioned him in, and the doctor was followed by Smitty, Marilee, and Jonathan Trumbull, the speechwriter. Why were speechwriters such certified good guys, usually named Jonathan?

"Is he all right?" Jonathan asked Melinda.

"I'm right here," said the President, "you can talk to me direct." Melinda could have told the writer that more than anything in the past five days, Ericson would be irritated by visitors speaking to third parties, as if he were not there. "And I'm fine, which is why I wanted to see all of you." To Melinda, Ericson said, "Get Cartwright on the speakerphone, he should be in on this."

When the chief of staff came on the line, the President said to him, "Is this 'mild-mannered Lucas Cartwright'?" Everyone had read the News Summary; Smitty winced. "I want to go home," Ericson stated. "What's involved?"

"When you get to the White House," Cartwright cautioned, "business begins. You will have to have a Cabinet meeting—do you feel you are ready for one? You will have to prepare a speech to the nation, or a televised press conference—is that what you want to do now?"

Melinda frowned. The hospital, while offering no special health benefits, did offer protection from the normal duties of the presidency. In seeking the security of familiar surroundings, Ericson would have to cope with normal activities that would be suddenly unfamiliar, without eyes.

"Who says?" the President challenged. "I'll be recuperating. Nothing on my calendar for a week. I'll be upstairs in bed, never come to the West Wing. The bill-signing business you and Hennessy can figure out, and the Attorney General."

"Pressure will start building right away for you to speak," said Smitty, siding with Cartwright.

"Which I can't do with a thermometer in my mouth," said Ericson. "Any other negatives?"

"Mr. President," said Cartwright, "the nation will be cheered by your return to the White House." Sensible fellow, Melinda thought; no use arguing with Ericson in his let's-get-out-of-here mood. "The press secretary has put together an excellent memo on the movement when it takes place."

"You've been thinking ahead, Smitty," the President said approvingly. "Since I read in the papers that you're running the country, that's a comfort."

"I had nothing to do with that sumbitchin' story, I swear," Smitty protested. "It's a reverse hatchet job.

You know I wouldn't knife anybody that way, really, I saw it and I was sick." He glared at his deputy, Marilee Pinckney, who lowered her eyes. Melinda didn't blame her a bit for planting that story: She was building up her boss, not at the President's expense, and her boss needed the lift at this tense time. And if Cartwright slipped, or stepped aside, and Smitty moved up, then Marilee would be the logical choice for press secretary. She'd be good, too; infinitely better educated and more intelligent than Smitty, more skillful with reporters, more sensitive to the public-opinion needs of the President. She already propped Smitty up on issues, briefing him before his press briefings. She was a lady, too, Melinda acknowledged, not a slut like the photographer; if the President were having an affair with Marilee, Melinda told herself, she would tolerate it. Then she told herself that was a lie.

"That *Tribune* story was my fault, Mr. Cartwright," Marilee said toward the speakerphone. "I apologize, I mishandled the reporter."

"I don't have the faintest idea what story you're all talking about," said Cartwright, "but Miss Pinckney —your good looks belie your seriousness of purpose."

President Ericson threw his head back and had a short, loud laugh at that. Melinda felt good to see him laugh that way again, and suddenly felt sadder than ever. "Smitty, tell us what's in your memo about high-tailing it out of here."

"Three ways to go," said the press secretary, "recognizing that your departure from the hospital is the major news story of the day. Option one: the full, Marryin' Sam two-dolluh weddin', departure with handshaking and posing with doctors, statement by the President before the cameras, camera setup at the White House being welcomed back at the front door, happy staff, the works." Smitty awaited comment.

"The trouble with that," said Melinda, "is that the President could stumble and fall. Or that he would be seen being led by the hand, or groping around."

"Not only that," agreed the press secretary, "but the

cameras would all go for close-ups of his eyes at his statement. Intense close-ups. All in all, the full two-dolluh weddin' is not the option I recommend. On the other extreme, there is option three—"

"No fair, Smitty," came Cartwright's voice over the speakerphone. "Don't set up the decision so that the President's only choice is the mid-course between extremes. I have the feeling that if we do that once too often, he'll pick an extreme just to cross up the staff."

"Very well, Lucas. Mr. President, there's a less formal way of handling it. We'd pick a press pool to shoot the departure; no statements; a walk from the side entrance of the hospital to the car, which is about ten steps; a wave from the President to photographers thirty feet away, no time to really zero in on the eyes, no dark glasses needed. Slow pull-away, with shots of you waving through the window as usual. Needless to say, I think that way makes sense.

"The other alternative," Smitty concluded, "is to sneak out of here like a thief. Just go, and announce to the press, at such-and-such a time, the President felt like going home, and you can reach him at his forwarding address on Pennsylvania Avenue."

"That last one is the one I like," said the President. "No chance of a stumble, no morbid fascination with pictures of my eyes, a whole week more to get used to handling this. Say that with the assassination attempt still only a few days old, the Secret Service insisted on a quick and quiet movement." He added, "They will, too, if you ask them."

"It does seem a wee bit like skulking about," the chief of staff's voice opined. "Melinda, you of the severe and protective nature, how do you feel about it?" Cagey old bird: She was neatly set up to disagree with the President, and her opinion would then carry the day. Smitty would love her, Cartwright would enjoy his use of her, and the President would respect her independence of judgment. What the hell; she was trapped into saying what she believed, anyway.

"The fifty-cent weddin'. The one with a little wave, and then zoom off. No big hello at the White

..., straight upstairs for a few days at least, and let's for God's sake get the best people in the world in to teach him how to cope."

The President made an exaggerated shrug of resignation, and that's the way his return to the White House went.

The Vice-President

Above all, he was determined not to make a mistake. To be too slavish a follower of the President would be a mistake. To veer from the Administration line on a matter of substance would be a mistake. To appear uninformed only because he did not know would be not merely a mistake, but a blunder. To appear knowledgeable on matters of campaign finance or other untouchable topics would be what newsmen liked to call "a gaffe of major proportions."

Every interview, every dedication speech, presented new opportunities to the Vice-President to commit a blooper, every tie-breaking vote in the Senate a chance to make a misstep. Arnold Nichols was conscious of his ability to blow it all every time he opened his mouth. He would be careful and he would someday be President. Let others play to win; all he had to do was to play not to lose.

Consequently, the Vice-President knew, he would be accused of being an other-hander, a middle-road man from a border state. Fine with him. In his late sixties, Nichols would be too old for renomination if the President ran again, as Ericson surely would. This Vice-President had one chance at the brass ring: to be there, steady and ready, incorruptible and uncontroversial, should the President die.

If the President were to die, Nichols reasoned—and not to reason along these lines was foolish, that's what Vice-Presidents were for—it would be better for the country and for him for the event to be early in the term. The "accidental President" could then establish a solid base for running and serving another term in his own right, especially if age were considered a handicap.

The ambush at Yalta was not It, he told himself, looking out the bay window of the Massachusetts Avenue home that was taken from the Chief of Naval Operations some years ago. Could have been It, but It was not to be. Now the possibility of succession after an assassination was remote, because Ericson was not expected to go out in crowds any more. The Secret Service could get away with being especially protective, and the President did not have to prove his manhood by overruling them. The Vice-President, on the other hand, would have to be especially visible, working every damned fence at every airport in the country. Nichols was prepared for that; not to take up that end of the job would be a mistake. Still, he was certain that fate did not bring him this far for nothing; he would succeed one day, in both meanings of the word.

Bannerman's limousine swung up the driveway. The Vice-President never looked forward to these weekly briefings on economic affairs by the Treasury Secretary because Bannerman was an impatient pedagogue, just as he was an incautious politician. More important than the information conveyed was the regularity of their get-together. It showed that Arnold Nichols was being kept closely informed, and not by any mid-level assistant, either, but by the man who mattered in financial circles around the world. T. Roy Bannerman had been one of the three most important investment bankers in the world before his appointment to head the Treasury, and he never let any of his new colleagues forget it. His renown was not the quick celebrity of the appointee, but the family-name fame that lay just at the subsurface of public attention. Gains ill-gotten so long ago that they could be used to purchase unassailable respectability. Big man, big reputation, big ideas. Good for the Administration, Nichols thought, and smart enough to pay the Vice-President more respect than most; their informal alliance would pay off for both.

Curiously, Bannerman had drawn him aside after a meeting of the Cabinet committee on economic policy to ask when they could talk privately. Curious because the only really private talk that men at the top in Washington could have was at a public gathering; every other meeting was just that, a meeting, and known to whoever really needed to know. The Secret Service might be part of Treasury, but its men were loyal to the President, whoever served in the office. If Bannerman wanted a meeting private from the President, that was not in the cards. But the regularity of these tedious economic briefings was a solid cover for whatever he wanted to discuss. The Vice-President decided that today's visit probably had to do with the division of responsibility of international affairs after the ambush attempt. In the Ericson Cabinet the old National Security Council system was scrapped. The President ran international affairs himself, with a black Secretary of State considered by Nichols to be a front man; Bannerman ran international economics, and brilliantly, everyone agreed; and Secretary of Defense Preston Reed was in the process of absorbing the covert part of CIA to centralize security matters. On the domestic side, the country pretty much ran itself; that is, the governors were riding high with their revenue-sharing funds and had moved into the administration of the weak cities. As Bannerman liked to drill into him, "The only national economic responsibility we have is to keep the dollar sound and the business cycle flat."

Roy Bannerman was not talking economics today. Abruptly, he began: "Mr. Vice-President"—that was a formal salutation, giving Nichols a feeling that the meeting was momentous—"you and I have to discuss a matter that nobody else seems willing to face up to."

"The President's illness," suggested the Vice-President.

"The President's blindness," said Bannerman. "Everybody's pussy-footing around, pretending it's all just an ailment that's going to go away in a few days, but it's not. And what we've got right here, right now, is a national crisis."

The Vice-President made soothing sounds, but Bannerman barreled ahead. "I have it on the best authority that the President is permanently blind. You know I don't jump to conclusions, Arnold. But this was too important a matter to be left to one mortal man and a handful of sycophants who like to ride around in flight jackets, with presidential seals embroidered over their hearts."

"What's the best authority?" Nichols' interest quickened.

"The head of New York Hospital," Bannerman told him. "I was chairman of the Board of Trustees for years. Their man is the one the naval hospital brought in for expert advice. And he said quite clearly, that with no previous history of this sort of thing, the odds are that the President is blind for good. That's bad news, tragic news. But it won't go away, and it's malfeasance to go around as if we don't know what our responsibility is."

The Vice-President did not know if this was a subject that it would seem proper for him to be getting into. "Do you believe, Mr. Secretary"—Nichols could get formal, too—"that this is a matter in which it is correct for me to play any kind of role—I mean, any kind at all?"

Bannerman started to brush that aside, stopped, and considered for a moment. The Vice-President was pleased; Bannerman might be the most ferocious tiger in the forest of economics, but when it came to constitutional niceties, the Vice-President had read the book.

"I know what you are getting at," Bannerman said more slowly. "You cannot ever be in a position that might be construed as being anxious to usurp power.

99

But a discussion of the President's disability is right and proper, because you have certain responsibilities to discharge—that is, if you think he is disabled."

"Look, Roy," the Vice-President said quickly, "I cannot be a part of any cabal. That's the word they'll use, a 'cabal.' If you think the President is permanently disabled, and if you really think he can't discharge his duties, then it's up to you to discuss it with him. He'd thank you for being honest with him. He might not get such frank advice from his staff. Deal me out, though."

"I think I know Sven Ericson," said Bannerman. "We've had a few battles in our time. He's an intellectual, and a theorist, and a darling of the Georgetown crowd, and all the columnists love him, because he looks Lincolnesque. But he's not. He'll hang in there no matter what it does to the country, because he has some kind of messianic complex."

"You're being unkind," the Vice-President demurred.

"He thinks you're a horse's ass, Arnold," Bannerman continued, "and you know that. He's said that on a dozen occasions, ever since the convention when I insisted that you be his running mate. He'll use you as an excuse to hang on."

The Vice-President swallowed. Bannerman was right on his facts, but wrong to drag him into this, and unnecessarily blunt. Maybe someday he would have to testify to a congressional committee about this; Nichols did not want to have to talk about a discussion of disability that he might have had today.

"But set aside the personal stuff," Bannerman followed up. "Think of the country. You think we can afford a Woodrow Wilson in the last year of his life, practically a vegetable, with his wife making the decisions? Or a Roosevelt at Yalta, too sick to cope with Stalin and too stubborn to admit it?" The Vice-President knew there was logic in all Bannerman was saying, but wished he would stop saying it to him.

"For God's sake," Bannerman nearly shouted, "the President of the United States at the moment—

and for the foreseeable future—can't find his way across the room! Stop feeling sorry for him, feel sorry for the country—if he can't bring himself to do his duty, somebody will have to do it for him."

"Please remember my words, Roy," said Nichols. "The words are 'Tell the President, don't tell me.' I'll repeat, so we both never forget: 'Tell the President, don't tell me.' "

"Your response is quite proper," Bannerman allowed, ignoring it as the Vice-President knew he would, "but you're the one who will have to call the Cabinet meeting if a blind President won't resign. The Secretary of State never will—he's in Ericson's pocket, and now he'll see his chance to act like a real Secretary of State—and he out-ranks me. But you call the meeting—"

"Do I have the authority?"

"You have the Nixon precedent during the Eisenhower illness. Have somebody research all that." Nichols nodded. "Don't trust Curtice," Bannerman warned, "he sees this as State's big chance, to be a big shot while the country limps along with a President who cannot legally sign his name. Watch out for the Attorney General, too, he's a down-the-line Ericson man."

"I'm talking to nobody about nothing," said Nichols. "It's not going to come to a confrontation. You should tell the President what you think, Roy, he'll do what's best for the country. But don't push him too hard, you know? If you talk to him like you did to me, that would be, uh, unproductive—counterproductive."

"I'm not asking you to say one word, Arnold," said the Treasury Secretary, rising to leave. "I just want you to know that when the chips are down, I'm counting on you to be a patriot. Even if it means taking a chance."

"Don't rush into anything." Nichols wondered how to put his next point so it wouldn't appear later that he had a hand in the situation. "The President faces some terrible difficulties in the next few days. I mean, simple things, which he may not realize now, will cause him great trouble. His first reaction—yours, mine—is to fight back. But he knows the country comes first. When he sees what it's like to be blind, how it hampers the presidency, then, who knows? We may have to do nothing but applaud his sacrifice."

"Good sense," said Bannerman, and Nichols wished there were not a note of surprise in the comment. "I hadn't thought that through, the human element. I'll buy that. We'll wait a few days. But if nothing happens then—"

The Vice-President shrugged, and repeated his catechism: "Tell the President, don't tell me."

The Therapist / 1

"The President wants you to know," Dr. Abelson told him, "that what he needs now is immediate operational help, not psychological help."

"He needs to cope with everyday situations," added Melinda McPhee. "How to move around, how to get dressed, how to organize himself."

The therapist nodded, and added, "Yes, I understand." He always verbalized after a silent signal in case there were any blind persons present. He understood, too, the primary cause for concern of the President's aides: Hennessy had told him on the telephone the day before that they were taking a big chance in bringing a psychologist into the White House. "God knows this is a happy hunting ground for a shrink," Hennessy had said, "but the American people would flip their lids if they thought their leaders needed somebody to keep them from flipping their lids. So you cannot come as a psychologist. You have

to be identified publicly as a blind man who has offered to help the President adjust to the physical requirements of not being able to see, even temporarily.
The ABC's, so to speak—walking with a cane, reading
braille, whatever."

"You needn't introduce me as 'Doctor,'" Dr.
Fowler said mildly to the President's doctor and secretary. "The name is Hank, Hank Fowler, and I'm just
here as a man who's been blind for a long time, to
teach the President a few tricks of the trade."

Abelson breathed his relief. "They said he was the
best in the business," he said to Melinda. "He catches
on quick." There was the third-person blunder, talking
in the presence of a blind man as if he were not present, and Fowler wondered whether he should correct
the President's staff immediately. He decided to wait.
He could teach the staff how to deal with a blind man
later; now he was more interested in getting to The
Man himself. All these protestations of nonpsychology
were necessary not only to conform to presumed
stigma in the minds of the public, but to that of the
patient as well. Just learning to work a long white
cane.

"He has certain advantages," said the woman's
voice—a resonant, warm voice, unusual in a person
whose forte was efficiency—"that you can work with.
The Secret Service is constantly with him, and can
move him anywhere. The telephone operators, the
permanent staff, are always right there to get whatever or whoever he wants. The whole government
is at his fingertips."

"Uses the phone like a crutch," Dr. Abelson
added. "He used to prefer face-to-face meetings."

"He has an edge over most blind people," the therapist agreed, then ventured into a subject more useful
to him. "How is he taking it? I know this makes me
seem like a shrink, and I don't mean to, but it may
help to know before I meet him—is he more irritable
now? Or strangely quiet? How does he seem to you
that's different?"

"He really has adjusted remarkably well," the

woman began, and the man pacing around the room cut her off.

"Melinda, for Chrissake, the man's a doctor. He's here to help. He'll play our game to make this all purely physiological, but we have to level with him. Ericson's a different man."

"If he weren't different," the therapist said, "he'd be crazy."

"Okay," the woman's voice said, "he's secretive. He's reluctant to say what he thinks. Look, he was never a confiding soul, but to us, in private, he'd let his hair down. We're all in this Presidency together, you know? Now he's frozen everybody out. He's scared, and he doesn't want us to see it."

"Deeper than that," said the man's voice. Abelson kept changing his position. Fowler would have to warn him about that. A blind man likes people to stay where they are or at least to speak while they are moving. "He is a totally independent man now facing dependency. It makes him sore, which is irrational, he knows, and he is angry with himself for letting it get to him. Ericson is a very, very cool customer, too much so, and he's never let himself become vulnerable, to anybody or any situation. Now he's totally vulnerable. He's worried about losing everything. Who knows, it could do him some good, in a way, but it means he's a different man in a different world."

Melinda added, as if as an afterthought: "He doesn't want to lose his powers. That's always been important to him, and now more than ever."

Fowler had the impression that both people he was talking to were animatedly working out their own roles in relation to Ericson. Abelson seemed to particularly feel the elation one experiences at the edge of hysteria, with a hint of pleasure at getting his own back from a man whose previous invulnerability had irked him. The woman seemed more serene, responding well to being more needed, but he would reserve judgment about that. Her observation about the President's loss of power—powers?—interested him. "May I touch your face?" he asked her. He reached out and went over her face with his fingertips: smooth complexion, high cheekbones, sharp nose, full lips, strong jawline. He thanked her, having done that partly for his own curiosity, mostly to implant a sense of awe at possibly eerie powers of the blind person. A mystique never hurt a psychologist. He asked if it would be possible to see the President; the woman made the call and cleared the way.

"Dr. Abelson," said the therapist, rising, "let me take your arm and let's move out. Please walk quickly, I'll stick with you. When I'm with the President, if you could find a way to excuse yourself and leave us alone, I'd be grateful." They moved quickly enough, out of the doctor's basement office in the central White House residence, to an elevator, ten seconds up, into a high-ceilinged room that echoed footsteps. Courteously, Abelson described the room for Fowler: the center hall, a long corridor running the length of the residence, wide enough to be decorated as a room. He was led left, and Abelson described the Oval Sitting Room on his right, then the Queen's Room on the left, then to the small Lincoln Sitting Room, where Abelson announced him to the President. Fowler stuck out his hand and said, "Herb, how about setting up a handshake?" Abelson moved his hand over to the President's extended hand. "At this point," Fowler, turning the large, knobby hand in his own, said, "somebody usually says something about the blind leading the blind." Abelson tittered nervously and guided Fowler to a chair, telling the President, "Hank here is the world's leading expert in helping people who can't see become operational in a hurry. He has a few doodads with him. I'll take off now; Furmark is right outside the door, as usual."

The therapist waited for the President to speak first.

"I understand you bring some firsthand experience to your job," Ericson said, and Fowler said only "'Yes." The last thing blind people wanted to hear was the problems of other blind people. The newly blind also did not look forward to meeting new people, whose voices could not be connected to known faces.

"Let me describe myself, sir," he said, keeping his voice low but speaking rapidly. "I'm a little guy, square-built, round face. Fifty-two years old, liberal, hair thinning on top, striking black mustache."

"You trim it yourself?"

"I do everything myself, Mr. President. Not because I have to—my wife could do it for me—but I run my own life because it makes me feel cocky, and I need that." His contact made, the therapist induced the patient to perform a simple task: "This is the famous Lincoln Sitting Room? Could you describe it to me?"

"Sure." Presidents would like describing parts of the White House, Fowler imagined; it established their connection with all that went before. "This easy chair, where I am, belonged to President Buchanan. He was an old man when he got to the White House, and he said, 'All my friends are dead, and all my enemies are now my friends.' Good line, I wonder who wrote it for him. To my left, your right, is a bookcase, used to have Sandburg's life of Lincoln, and the complete set of Lincoln's works, but I put them downstairs in the official library because I need the space here for books I'm reading now." He paused. "I guess they can put Sandburg back. Only thing that's Lincoln in his sitting room now is a bust, the Volk bust, on the desk, here on my right."

"Put yourself at the center of a clock," said the therapist, "like in those Air Force movies, and say I'm twelve o'clock. Where's the desk?"

"Three o'clock."

"The phone?"

"There are two in here. One on the desk, say two o'clock, the other at my right hand, toward five o'clock."

"Window?"

"Behind me. Six o'clock."

"Bathroom?"

"Three o'clock, a john, no shower. My bathroom is down the hall, off my bedroom."

"Ready for lesson number one? Take me there."

Very slowly, the President rose, touched his visitor's shoulder, and led him out of the Lincoln Sitting Room. Fowler could visualize him, arm outstretched, working along the walls he thought he could remember. The President passed through the Lincoln Bedroom, telling the agent not to help or to say anything. As they reached what Fowler judged to be the central hallway that was his route in, the President moved ahead more confidently until his hand jabbed into a wall.

"That's a wall," Ericson announced. "That's a new wall, it's never been there until today."

"Is there a door over to the right?" Fowler remembered coming through one, and it was logical to assume there was an entrance to the central hallway. Ericson led them through the doorway and into the central hall, down toward where Fowler had first stepped off the elevator.

"We turn left here," said the President. "Try not to knock over any antiques. Jackie Kennedy went to a lot of trouble." They walked into a couch, backed away, and through a door into the President's bedroom. The President went to his bed, familiar to him, and sat on it. "The bathroom," he said, with some strain, "is seven steps from where I am. If the head of the bed is twelve, the bathroom door is four o'clock."

Next to him, Fowler said, "Seven of your steps should be about ten of mine. Remember that picture of Romulo following MacArthur ashore?"

"If you don't really want to use the can, I may kill you."

"Right back." Fowler crossed the room, sensed the doorway, quickly touched the shower curtain, sink, toilet, and towel, and proceeded to take a pee, flush the toilet, rinse his hands, humming all the while, as if he were familiar with the bathroom. He was well aware that Ericson must have spent agonizing moments there making sure of his aim, groping for a towel, breaking bottles. He made a mental note to

107

tell Abelson to change all the bottles and glasses to plastic and to install a grip for the bath.

Fowler came out to hear the President quietly chuckling. "What strikes you funny, Mr. President?"

"I know that old song you were humming. That's got to be pretty funny. You're a cornball, Fowler."

That pleased the therapist; not many of his clients caught or appreciated "I Only Have Eyes for You," as hummed by a blind psychologist; it meant Ericson could be kidded, which was most useful.

"Now let me lead you back to the Lincoln Sitting Room," he said briskly. "Grab my arm firmly and let's move quickly." He took the President out into the hall, through the doorway, and back to where they had started, confidently, easily.

"Good trick, Doc. Now tell me how you did it."

"Step count, obviously," Fowler told him. "Six steps out of the door, twenty-seven steps down the hall, doorway, twelve steps to Mr. Lincoln's room, nine through it to the sitting room. Now you want to know how to keep from banging into walls. We have a new gimmick for that." He produced a round, thick object on a watch band and pressed it into the President's hand. "That's a wrist sonar, not commercially available yet, but you can use it instead of a cane. You've heard the expression 'blind as a bat'? Bats may be blind, but somehow they don't run into things, because they have this built-in echo device. Same principle." As the President delightedly strapped the device to his wrist, Fowler began the training, bringing his hand close to the sonar, starting a slight vibration. "It detects obstacles in front of you. Performs the function of a long cane."

"I was worried about having to use a cane," said the President. "That would have made me an object of pity. This electronic gadget is much better, Hank."

Fowler decided to give him a dash of cold water. "It's not nearly as good as a cane, Mr. President. Skillful use of a long cane is still the best way for a blind person to go anywhere. The sonar watch is just a gimmick for you to use until you stop being self-conscious about arousing pity. Let me give it to you straight: A watch looks better, a cane works better."

"At this point," said Ericson, "I am infinitely more interested in the way it looks. If I go stumbling around, or act like a man who can't get from here to there without a blind man's cane, there will be those who will hand me a tin cup and tell me to change jobs."

The therapist had a few other electronic gadgets to give Ericson a quick boost of morale. For the President's other wrist, he produced a watch that told time by touch; in five minutes, Ericson had mastered that simple operation, but that brought up another subject: braille.

"You could get the rudiments of braille in less than six months," Fowler told him. Silence. "If you're shaking your head, Mr. President, that doesn't help me."

"I'm sorry," Ericson said hastily, "I forget. I mean I don't have six months to devote to learning a new language. I'm better off with Melinda reading to me."

"Tell you what I'm gonna do," Fowler imitated the pitchman. "I have a tape recorder here, size of a pack of cigarettes, and a simple system to bring your hearing input up to your reading input. If you read fast, you read about 225 words a minute. When people talk fast, they talk about half that speed. Now, here is something we do for blinded executives who need to absorb information at least as quickly as they used to read. I've just been taping myself. Now I'm going to rewind, and play it back at double rate—not fast enough to be gibberish, just fast enough for you to grasp the meaning."

He played the speeded-up tape of his last minute's talk and waited for a reaction.

"That even beats your suitcase full of wrist watches, Doc." He could hear Ericson smiling. "Right now, it takes a good forty minutes for Melinda to read me the News Summary. She could tape it and I could cut the time in half."

"More than that, you could fast-forward where you get bored and want to skip."

"Now we're talking," the President said excitedly.

"The business about moving around, counting steps, the way I look, all that is important in re-establishing public confidence. It's not important in doing the job —agents can steer me around. But the problem that's been nagging me is the ability to cope with the job. Can I absorb all the information that comes to me? Can I organize data for a decision? You're showing me that there's more hope than I figured."

Working more slowly now, getting into more difficult areas of training, Fowler showed the President how to accomplish a feat that seeing people took for granted: making a list. On the blank blackboard of his mind, a blind man could write, and see his own writing. Fowler tried him out on a few numbers and symbols, and was pleased to see he had an apt pupil; not all executives took to this training. "In a couple of weeks, you'll think you are beginning to cope," he said, "and in a couple of months, with intensive training, and with your staff getting trained as well in programming your somewhat different mental computer, you will actually be able to cope. I'm assuming, Mr. President, that you were able to cope with this job when you could see." After some more of this kind of banter, respectful but not obsequious, the therapist felt the time was ripe to slip in a question: "Have trouble when you wake up in the morning?" He could feel the President's chill in the silence.

"What do you mean, Hank?"

"I went blind in my thirties, result of an accident, same as you, and what used to bother the hell out of me was waking up in the morning. Before, you woke up, you opened your eyes—that was part of waking up. Not to see when you woke up—it was like not knowing you were up, or still dreaming, or what. Then I used to dream I was up when I wasn't and that made waking up worse. Eerie sensation. Started my whole day in a sweat."

"That doesn't happen to me," said the President. "I'm fine in the morning."

He'll be a tough one to open up, thought Fowler. And he won't adjust to the operations of his new job until he comes to grips with the reality of being a blind man. A lot was riding on this therapy; not just the smooth operations of the presidency, but the hopes of 20 million handicapped people in America. Fowler would handle his patient with care. The President may be euphoric now, with his discovery of electronic aids and mental gymnastics, but he would soon slip into the inescapable depression of the newly blind, which Fowler remembered vividly.

"You think I can bring this whole thing off, Hank?"

"Any man who thinks he can run this country," said Fowler, "has to have an ego a mile high. Let's start with that. If you think you can run it at all, then you probably can convince yourself that you can run it with a handicap, like loss of speech, or sight, or hearing, or legs. So it's safe to say you have the motivation." The therapist wondered how far he could go at this early stage, and felt his way. "Mr. Hennessy told me to give you my opinion about whether you are able to discharge the duties of your office. Look: I'm going to walk out of here, get a cab to the airport, fly home to Atlanta, pack for a month's stay here, and come back—all with no help from anybody who can see. Then I'm going to do a job of occupational therapy on you that will make me a hero with every psychologist in the country. That's because I'm proud and I'm tough and I'm awfully good at what I do. I don't know if you are able to discharge the duties of your office, or ever will be, but if we fall on our ass, it'll be your fault, not mine."

The President stood up, moved over to the desk, pushed some papers out of the way, and sat on the desk top, Fowler following every motion with his ears. "Now I want to ask you something as an American, Hank, and not as a psychologist, or a blind man: Do you think it's right for me to make the try?" Fowler knew what the President wanted to hear, but he decided to give him a taste of what life was like on the blind side:

"Never ask a blind man not to think like a blind man."

FULL DISCLOSURE

The President's personal physician made known his presence at the door to the sitting room at that point, summoned, Fowler judged, by a button close to the President's hand. "That's interesting," the therapist piped up, "what's the code for your buttons to call people?"

"Most of the time I use the phone," the President said. "On the phone, I'm anybody's equal, so I'll be using that a lot. Trouble is, I can't make notes of a conversation—well, I suppose the memorecorder's the answer to that. On the buttons, the signal corps beat you to that, Hank"—he passed over a gadget about the size of a television remote-control switch, with six buttons—"the top one is Melinda, my secretary; the second is Furmark, the agent at the door; third is Herb, here; fourth is the White House operator, to ring me in case I can't find the phone; fifth is Cartwright, the chief of staff."

"The bottom one?" the therapist asked, fingering it.

"Blows up the world," the President said. Even at the joke, Fowler took his finger off. "Actually, that's for the man with the black bag, in case of a need for a retaliatory nuclear strike. Starts a process that has all kinds of cross-checks and safeguards built in."

"How do you get a cup of coffee?"

"That's two buzzes to Melinda, and she sends in the waiter. Three buzzes is the diet soda."

"And two buzzes to Dr. Abelson says, 'Come and get this guy out of here using some kind of medical excuse,'" Fowler surmised.

"You got it," said Abelson. "We're working things out. I'm putting a bunch of talking books from the Library of Congress here on the desk, along with the machine that plays them. That was a good tip, Hank, the Librarian there was waiting for a call—they have a huge setup for compressed-speech books."

"What books did you pick out for me, Herb?" the President asked.

"*Moby Dick*, for one," said the doctor. "You wrote a paper on that in college, remember? You can hear the whole thing again, every word, in six hours. And

Sandburg's Lincoln, because it goes in the room, and the book you had at your bedside last month and never read, Professor Lord's *Raising Keynes*. Here's one that was Hennessy's idea"—it made a clunk on the desk—"the latest trashy best seller about a couple of sensitive lesbians. I listened to it last night myself, quicker than having to read it."

"It always amazes people," Fowler offered the President, "when a blind person makes a reference to a current novel. Good trick when you want to show you're ahead of people with eyes."

"I'll use that. Herb, what's the latest on Harry Bok?"

"Spoke with him this morning. Not good. Flat on his back, no sensation in his legs. Our surgeon is over there, and may operate tomorrow, says it's touch and go on paralysis."

The President called the agent at the door, skipping the buzzer, and made an odd request: "Get me a counterfeit twenty-dollar bill and a red crayon." Furmark had an odd answer: "If a counterfeit ten will do, sir, I happen to have one on me. A lot of us carry them for souvenirs." Ericson took it, and a pen with red ink, and wrote a message on the bill: "Can you read it, Herb?" The doctor read: " 'Help me fight the phonies, Harry! Gratefully, Sven Ericson.' " The President asked: "Does it look like my handwriting?" Abelson replied: "Close enough to make this counterfeit tenner worth a hell of a lot of real money. I'll get it to him on the courier."

"Five hundred bucks, at least," said the President, adding, "See that they take care of Harry. Is Curtice still over there? Have him visit Harry before the operation, send a message quick. Besides," he added in a different tone, "it's better if the Secretary of State stays there awhile, they'd need him to call a Cabinet meeting here."

"Harry turned over to me the job of arranging the photographic sessions," the President's physician added, Fowler thought irrelevantly. "Let me know when you want some pictures."

"Soon," Ericson answered. "Let's make that three long buzzes." Fowler shook his head in wonderment at the vanity of a public man who wanted a photographic record of his most trying times. He did not yet have the handle on his new patient: now cold, now generous, now deceptive, now incisive, now persecuted, now confident. Hell of an opportunity, though, which the therapist was determined not to miss.

The Official Photographer / 2

"Hiya, Potus. Miss me?" Ordinarily, she would have struck a stunning pose against the doorjamb leading from the West Wing hallway to the Oval Office, dangling her three cameras and leaning on a tripod, but The Man couldn't appreciate it any more, so she just stood there, delivered by Herb Abelson at eight in the evening acutely conscious of her most important function in the Ericson Administration.

"Buffie. What are you wearing?"

"Feel and see." She slipped into his lap for him to dig his fingers in her back and down along her flanks, remembering, as he must, the green jumpsuit he had seen her in so often. Herb told her to wear something the President would remember, and not to try any different perfume, and not to act different—they were programming people to handle Ericson like a machine with a part missing that would operate perfectly if only it didn't know a part was missing. His big hands were the same, though, molding her fiercely, then putting her off. She sat on the rug, arms across his knees, as he sat in an easy chair in front of the Oval Office fireplace. "They wouldn't let me near you since the ambush. Cartwright said no photos, and there was no

Harry to get me through to you. You're really in a cocoon, you know, more than I ever figured." Still, she knew that if Ericson had wanted her around, he would have found a way to bring her in. He wasn't fair, insisting she be exclusive and then keeping her on ice like that, but he had been through a lot in the last week. She told herself to be more considerate; maybe he couldn't get it up and was embarrassed. She gave his legs a hug. Herb Abelson was right, it was different being around him when those eyes weren't ricocheting cool glances off you, when they were open and focused on nothing. "I gotta get you some shades, Potus," she told him, because it made no sense to hold it back. "I want to think you're still giving me the eye."

"You think I ought to wear dark glasses?" The question had obviously been in his mind. She couldn't blame him for not wanting to look like a blind beggar —dark glasses, cane, tin cup, sign around his neck, mangy dog—playing for sympathy.

"Not 'dark' glasses," she amended it. "Maybe one of those snazzy one-way mirror outfits that the motorcycle types wear."

"I'd look great in a leather jacket and those silver glasses," Ericson murmured. She shook her head; he never used to give a damn about his image, unless not caring was part of his image. Now he would probably bring up their age differential. "You miss the swinging young set, Buffie?"

"Tell me again about how many centuries you've been High Lama of Shangri-La."

He smiled, but not a real smile. She hoped to have a chance to get to him, through the night, to show him how she felt—a kind of follow-the-leader love, but still a love—and to draw some of his strength to her, because she was shaken up by the turn of events, which could affect all her plans for an exciting future. She hoped he had sent for her to have a real get-together, not a quickie in the office before he went back to work or into one of those long bull sessions with Hennessy. The telephone booth could be fun—it was she who had taught him the kick of sudden sex in office surroundings—but at this point it would only be his way of showing himself he was still the boss, and it would be good if he didn't have to prove that.

"What do you hear, Buffie? Around the press room?" His favorite question—what do you hear?—the same question all worried politicians ask.

She pretended to be exasperated, he liked that. "You sent Melinda on some phony errand. You cleared most of the Secret Service agents out of the West Exec entrance to the West Wing. You got your doctor thinking he's some kind of pimp—I mean, the poor bastard's embarrassed as hell—all to get me here at your feet, and then you want a public-opinion survey? What's with you?"

That loosened him up, she was glad to see, and she rubbed the inside of his leg idly. "Actually," she reported, since he asked and since she had noticed, "they're all getting hot for a press conference."

"They always are."

"Ah, but not this way. They want to see if you've turned into a helpless invalid they can feel sorry for." She touched the rising lump in his trousers. "You haven't changed all that much. I'll pass the word."

"You haven't mentioned anything about the other time, have you, Buffie? In the train?"

As if she'd blurt out a thing like that. There were times when The Man was so sharp, so far ahead of her, just being near him was a high, and there were times when he put her down like a dumb broad he kept around as a handy receptacle. "I don't even remember another time, Potus," she replied. "But now you mention it—that's a hopeful sign, isn't it? I mean, you snapped out of it before, you can do it again."

He smoothed the hair away from her forehead, cradled her face in his hands, bent down and gave her a long, tender kiss, then leaned back again, far away in the wingback chair. "Last time, on the campaign train, it was only two days, remember? It's been five days now I can't see, Buffie. I expected to come out of it long before this."

"Second time," she said, as if in touch with some

gypsy medical wisdom, "takes longer. Two weeks, maybe. Then you'll see again. But let this be the last warning—no more banging your head, you hear?"

"The reason we have to be quiet about the last time," he said, coming back to the subject as if she did not understand, "is not that you and I were making love on the campaign train. That was only the reason then. The reason why we have to keep it quiet now is because we did keep it quiet then."

"You don't wish we had told the world about what happened then, do you?"

"No, we couldn't. I wish we had, actually, but we couldn't. There's nothing wrong with tearing off a piece between campaign stops"—he caressed her hair as if to show he meant no disrespect—"but it's kind of insulting to people. People expect a candidate to make love at night, in bed, to his wife, in a sensible position."

"But that's not what they do," she insisted. "You've got no idea the screwing that goes on in offices, in darkrooms, in the back of cars, in the front of planes. That was always the trouble with you," Buffie added. "You were such a stiff till you met me." Talking about this had an effect on him; she touched him again. "You're getting stiff, stiff." Time to go upstairs, make love, have dinner, talk, play around.

"The problem now," he said, "is that keeping it a secret then has become sinister." Potus was not usually this anxious to get his message across, it must be awfully important to him. "It's not just that I didn't want to admit having sex between stops. It's now become that I misled the public about the state of my health before the election. It was only a little deceit, back then, about the sex—but now it seems to be a big deceit, about the lost eyesight. You see?"

"I see," she said, wishing they could get out of the office and be together in the residence. "Do I get dinner tonight, or are you going to be cheap?"

"Not hungry," he said. That was not true, Ericson was ravenous by this time; maybe it was the blindness, that he was still learning to eat what he couldn't see.

117

Maybe he did not want to show the weakness of a man having to be fed.

"You can use your fingers," she assured him. "Be like a picnic." She looked at his pants and could tell the conversation was coming to an end.

"You're the picnic," he said. "Time for the telephone booth."

She sighed, took his hand, leaned back hard to pull him out of the chair, and led him to the half-concealed door to the left of the door to the West Wing hallway. On the afternoon of Inauguration Day, Potus had shown her the little room, six by nine feet, off the Oval Office, where Presidents went to retire or whatever. It was originally the telephone booth, when the West Wing was first built around the turn of the century, where Presidents went to take their infrequent calls. Potus had said that when Warren Harding's mistress, in her memoirs, had written that she had made love to the President in a telephone booth, everybody thought she was making it up, but this telephone booth was just the right size. Even for the gangly Ericson, who sometimes lay diagonally across the bed.

She pushed him back and rubbed his long legs. "So you think we should have told the truth at the time," she teased, knowing she could continue the discussion without danger of it continuing.

"Morally speaking," he said, unzipping his fly, "it would have been right to own up to the whole thing. The headline would have been 'Banging a girl between stops, the candidate cracked his head and was temporarily blinded.'"

"You'd have picked up brownie points for honesty," she said, idly taking his erection in her hand.

"We would have lost the election fair and square, and I wouldn't have had this little eyesight problem today."

She dipped her head into his lap, thinking how the telephone booth had been used before, and by such awesome men. For straight intercourse, probably—she wondered if the girls of the past gave head the way they did today. She kissed him lightly, then pulled back. "Hey, Potus, do you suppose that you and me are the first ones, right here—?"

"Everybody wants to be the first," he said, a good laugh in his voice, almost making him limp. "Probably not, chum. You want a historic first? Okay—this is the first time in more than two centuries of American history that a blind President has been blown by his lovely official photographer so close to the Oval Office. Nobody'll challenge that."

She shrugged and went back to her task, amused but not so amused—after all, it wasn't her patriotic duty—thinking that one of these days, when Potus could see again and didn't need to prove he could dominate her this way, she would ask him about moving their relationship onto a fairer give-and-take thing. That would be a mistake now, though, when he was worried about so many of his powers. She enjoyed pleasing him like this, she told herself, and suddenly stopped and looked up, thinking of his last remark. "You know what I'm doing?" she asked, and answered proudly, "Going down in history." He didn't even smile. There were times when Potus lost his sense of humor.

"Potus," she said afterward, "you gonna be all right?"

"I think I'll see again, Buffie."

"I know that, I mean you—I don't get the right vibrations, ol' buddy."

"I been sick."

"You've been through hell, and you were almost killed, and you're worried somebody like me will blab, and you're blind and you can't tell anybody why you're sure you'll be all right again, I know all that. But ease up, will ya? It's me. Trust me. Relax." She had to tell him. Nobody else was going to tell him. "You're thinking about losing your grip, and it's making you lose your grip. I hooked up with Sven Ericson, not this guy. Come back."

"That's a disability I never knew I had." He patted her head; she was being dismissed. Hell with that.

"Why do we have to play this game of skulk

around?" she demanded. "You're single, so'm I. You think the American people expect their President to live like a hermit? Why don't I just move in upstairs? We don't have to get married, and I don't have to be your official hostess. We could just live together, like people do."

"You know I'd like that, but we can't. We have to be discreet. The President can do almost as much screwing around as the ordinary guy, as long as he's discreet. The people will let me get away with anything so long as I just don't flaunt it."

"That's being a hypocrite."

"Right, Buffie, that's the word—hypocrisy, 'the payment that vice makes to virtue.' But there are still certain standards, and the public expects the Chief Executive to uphold them in public. No matter what he's doing in private."

"Balls," she commented.

"I know you hate to sneak around, or have to arrange through Harry or Herb to get sent in to see me. But appearances count."

"A whole lot?"

"Sometimes," he said heavily, "appearances count more than realities, because realities come and go but appearances linger on. One appearance that counts is that nobody is ever shacked up in the national museum called the White House."

"So I wouldn't be First Lady," she said, ignoring what he said and indulging her fancy. "I'd be First Piece of Ass." She put his penis back in his pants and zipped up the fly. "Centerfolds everywhere. I'd even shoot 'em myself, long cable release, f/8 at a hundredth, available light right here in the phone booth." She went to the door.

"What's got into you?" he asked. She said nothing. "Buffie?" She did not breathe, watching the sightless eyes in the tortured face look through her. "Buffie, you still there?"

She went to him with a sudden rush of feeling that was more than he had ever shown her. She was not unhappy when he dismissed her in a few minutes, because, she felt, if that was what he needed, she would give it to him. And in his present state, he was not all that easy to be with.

The Press Secretary

When a President begins to prepare for a press conference, the executive branch convulses. Smitty reveled in these moments. The Office of the Press Secretary is the fount of anticipated questions, proud of its reputation inside the White House of coming up with a far nastier and more exhaustive set of questions for the President than are ever asked at a press conference. The likely questions are sprayed across the federal bureaucracy, drawing responses in position papers submitted by department heads to bolster or summarize their views, or slipped past department heads by adroit staffers who want a pet policy enunciated by an unsuspecting chief executive.

Smitty delegated to the News Summary chief the task of collecting the questions, from press clips, reporters' queries, and the news staff at the Voice of America, along with submissions from the official spokesmen at State, Defense, Treasury, and the Council of Economic Advisers. Smitty's deputy, Marilee Pinckney, would remind him of areas left unexplored by these sources, and Smitty would send memos with questions far and wide, with twenty-four-hour deadlines for responses. These White House deadlines were never ignored; each department knew that if its response were not incorporated in the "black book," somebody else's response would be inserted instead, permitting the remaking of policy by default.

FULL DISCLOSURE

Smitty enjoyed flaying the government with savage questions because he saw his job as the White House resident conscience. He was determined that the truth come from his briefings twice a day, and the reputation he had built over the years in newspapering would not be demeaned, as had that of so many of his predecessors. Looking back, Smitty admitted to himself that he had cut a few corners as a reporter, excessively buttering up a source, kissing an editor's ass, abusing an official who would not leak, and stealing a few stories from competitors' carbons, but he had come out of the business known the way he wanted to be known: tough, straight, incorruptible, skeptical. He had worked on his personal public relations, gravelly voice and all, and had been bitterly disappointed when his newspaper chain passed him over in the selection of a top executive. Ericson's selection of Smitty as campaign press aide came at a perfect moment in his career; after making an appropriate fuss torturing himself over "crossing the street," he jumped at the opportunity.

Now the "black book" was his. The President's Briefing Book, in loose-leaf binder, was on the press secretary's desk at all times except when it went to the President before press conferences. When long-winded answers came in from the departments and the White House staff, Smitty was an editor again, sending most of them for shortening and toughening to the speechwriters, writing a bright lead or concluding "snapper" on some himself. He prefaced each edition of the black book with his own estimate of the flow of the questioning, and he was usually right, astounding his colleagues and the President with a sandpapered-fingertip sensitivity to what was on the minds of his former press associates. As a matter of fact, with Marilee's help, it was easy. Best job he ever had, once the Decision was made.

The Decision was the moral dilemma put to him during the interregnum by Hennessy. "Before you take this job, Smitty, I want you to tell me how to handle the following situation: Let's say the dollar has to be devalued. That decision has to be protected; any admission that the government is considering devaluation will trigger massive dollar dumping by speculators, and would be directly contrary to the public interest. The Treasury Secretary, the way he always has since Alexander Hamilton, will flatly deny devaluation right up to the minute it is announced. Now let's say you call me up and say, 'Hennessy, they're asking me if we're thinking of devaluation, what should I tell them?' Tell me what you want me to do, Smitty. Do you want me to say, 'We are, but you cannot tell them that, you have to deny the truth'? Or would you prefer that I tell you to fuck off, it's none of your business?"

"I will never consciously tell a lie," Smitty had said. He was proud of that stand, and would have to quote it in a book one day. "Why couldn't I just handle the devaluation question by saying, 'I won't answer that'?"

"But that would be answering it—in that case, if you don't deny, you confirm, and the public would suffer."

"Then I guess, Hennessy, you might be within your rights to tell me to fuck off. I will not deny what I know to be true; if I did that once, I'd blow my credibility and would be no further use to the President."

"Are you taping this?" Hennessy had replied in his wise-guy way. Smitty wished he had. It was a crucial decision for a press secretary, and it meant that Smitty would be an outsider on some of the key decisions. Sometimes he even wondered if he had been wrong—that he might have done more for the cause of revealing the truth by working on the inside, even if it meant the rare official lie—but that decision was long past. He was smart enough to know that Hennessy—and silky old Cartwright, who probably put the lawyer up to the question—had maneuvered him into the outer inner circle right at the start, despite the President's protestations that he would be at the center. So be it; it was better than torturing yourself with moral complexities. Smitty hated to look dumb, but sometimes it was smarter to look dumb than venal.

In his sunny West Wing office, he sipped his coffee and perused the morning's wire copy before his 11 A.M. briefing. He would win this morning's briefing because he would not have his back to the wall, swatting down questions, but would lead with an announcement that would be welcomed. Smitty went over it in his head: He would pull his ear a couple of times—a signal to the cameramen to roll, this next bit was important—and say, "Ladies and gentlemen, I have an announcement. The President has decided against making a speech this week about the state of his health and about the current international situation." Pause for groans and grumbling. "Instead, two days from now, on Wednesday at nine P.M. Eastern time, six P.M. Pacific time, which is two weeks to the day since the ambush at Yalta, the President will hold a live televised press conference from the East Room of the White House." That'll change the negative atmosphere from "Who helps him get dressed?" and "Might he take a leave of absence?" to an upbeat "How is he studying for the conference?" and "When does the President officially go back to work?"

That's when he would spring Hank Fowler on them; the blind therapist would make a positive impression, play a few tricks like tying names to voices—he'd been listening to a few briefings over the loudspeaker in the press secretary's office—and announce a two-week "orientation course." Not just for the President, but for his staff, in "aural organization" so that it would be possible to run this country with your eyes closed. Smitty made a note of that phrase. If public reaction to the Ericson blindness could be changed from a fear of terrible disability, to a newsworthy kind of game of "How will he overcome this obstacle?" then those ugly questions about disability and resignation would be stilled.

Zophar's piece in this morning's *Post* brought the vague doubts to a head, and Smitty glumly looked at his column again:

"A nation thankful for the survival of its President from a brush with death is also a nation concerned with the ability of the President to discharge the incredibly difficult duties of his office.

"The time has come to ask: Ought not the President, unable as he is at the moment to address the people, step aside temporarily under the provisions of the Twenty-fifth Amendment?

"He need not resign. It may be, as all hope, that his sight will be restored and he will soon be able to assume his familiar, vigorous leadership. But in the interim, while he is so patently disabled, and while he makes those painful adjustments to darkness that fate may require, the Government of the United States need not be paralyzed. He has it in his power to be the first President to step aside temporarily, to appoint his running mate in the recent election as Acting President while he recovers or adjusts, and then—at a time that Sven Ericson alone determines—to resume the office by declaring himself able to discharge his duties."

The Zophar column went on to recount the episode of the long terminal illness of Woodrow Wilson, when the country went without an elected leader capable of functioning. Sam Zophar liked to show off his grasp of history, Smitty said to himself, noticing how the op-ed page editor had picked up the idea and ran pictures of Mrs. Wilson—who had run the country from her husband's bedside—and Thomas Riley Marshall, the Hoosier Vice-President who never got the chance to step up, and was only remembered for his "What this country needs is a good five-cent cigar" remark made during a dreary Senate debate.

Marilee Pinckney was standing in front of his desk, not interrupting his train of thought; he motioned for her to sit down and asked her what questions were likely to come up in his briefing about the press conference.

"Is he going to wear dark glasses?"

"That's a stupid question." Smitty enjoyed beating up on Marilee, because she was so rich and smart and good-looking and secure that it never seemed to bother her, and she was so obviously after his job. "God help the country when you push me out of here," Smitty added. "You know your economic lingo, I'll grant you that, but this place will be grinding out releases on how well the President looks, how his eggs were cooked this morning, all that jazz. 'Is he going to wear dark glasses?' Jesus!"

"You're trying to be a male chauvinist, but you're not," Marilee said. "Most men are, but try not to be. That's why all the women in the press office are your slaves."

"You hired 'em, I didn't. I figured if you picked out the staff, we'd have some bright young fellas in here, but all we got is the dregs of Vassar and Smith."

"And your press office is the envy of the White House staff. By the way, Buffie says he'll be wearing dark glasses." She looked at the clock, showing five minutes to eleven. "Do you want to chase me around the desk or get ready for your briefing?"

He wanted to chase her, all right, Smitty admitted, but she was not only a different generation, but a different social class; the one real lever he had on her respect for him as an executive was his respect for her as a woman executive, and he was not about to throw that away on a series of passes doomed to failure. Besides, he was looking forward to the briefing.

"Word from Harry Bok?" he asked. "Be good to show the President cares."

"President spoke with him on the telephone," Marilee reported, "right after Harry came out of the after-effects of the operation. That was last night. Prognosis is not good. Abelson says the doctor tells him Harry may be paralyzed from the waist down, but you're not to say that yet, just that he is recuperating slowly from the removal of the bullet from his spinal column, and it's too soon to tell anything definitive."

"That's a bitch," Smitty said. He would have no trouble holding back part of that story: That wasn't lying, only protecting the privacy of a medical patient. He picked up his phone and dialed Melinda

McPhee on the intercom to ask what she knew of the President's conversation with Bok. She said she had not placed it or listened to it; Ericson was making a lot of calls on his own these days.

"Nothing special on the wires this morning," said Marilee, flipping through a batch of white AP and yellow UP sheets. "Inflation down to nine per cent, we say that's not good enough but a big improvement. The balance of trade figures will be announced this afternoon, expected to show the United States strong, despite oil and grain purchases from China—that'll make 'em sore in the Fourth World, you have to watch that and bounce those queries over to Agriculture."

Smitty had tuned out. "You know that sonar wrist watch he wears?" he asked her. "You like that?"

"It's much better than a long white cane," she replied. "If it works, it would do a great deal to dispel the image of a blind man. Show he's modern, electronic, capable of coping, all that."

"How does a Seeing Eye dog grab you?"

Marilee looked genuinely shocked. "That's just an obvious play for sympathy. That's all wrong, not like President Ericson at all. I hope you're not serious."

"I haven't suggested it. Boss would get sore, I know. But I dunno, Presidents always have dogs, Ericson doesn't like 'em. Seems wrong. I have in mind a mutt—"

"A mongrel?"

"Your grandfather," Smitty reminded her, "—the bootlegger who made all the money?—was an immigrant. Yes, m'dear, a mongrel, a mutt—no pedigree at all. Just a smart dog trained by the Seeing Eye people to help a President. Become a very famous dog in a hurry."

"If you want the tin-cup image."

"Has its drawbacks, I know. But the electronic thing may be wrong, too, in a way." He pushed himself out of his chair; she would leak to her boy friend at a network that a dog was under consideration, which was all Smitty wanted for the time being. "C'mon, the

stars are blinking." The signal lights in the press briefing room were flashing press conference, calling the
moths to the flame.

"Fala was a purebred Scottish terrier," Marilee said
on the way down the hall, "and Johnson's beagles
could have been champions. Liberty, Ford's golden
retriever, made that breed the most popular in the
States for a while." He enjoyed her irritation. "Even
Nixon had a pedigreed Irish setter, I think. Smitty, I
know you're only doing this to get me thinking what
kind of dog, and not whether or not a dog, but
really—" She would leak it as an idea that had already been rejected, he assumed. All the better. Get
all the dog owners pushing for their breeds.

"You just better be sure everybody breaks their
asses on the black book," he told her, nearly running now. "It's never been more important. How it
goes from the book into his head is beyond me, but he
better have a way."

At his 11 A.M. briefing, after Smitty dropped his
announcement that the President would hold a press
conference, the first question was "Will he wear dark
glasses?"

"Of course," Smitty snapped; he was ready for that
one.

"Any limitation on subjects?"

"None. The President is hopeful that questions on
his health will be asked in the first ten minutes so that
he will be able to move on to many matters of domestic and foreign policy. But if you guys are not interested in what's going on in the world, that's up to
you."

"Is he aware of the talk among some Cabinet members that he should step aside?"

"Which Cabinet member and what did he say?"
Smitty wasn't having any of those phony probes. "You
know I don't react to unattributed dope stories."

"Can he tell light from dark, or does he just see
black?"

"Beats me," said the press secretary. "Ask him
yourself, Wednesday night."

The incipient presidential news conference took the heat off the spokesman; he could duck questions without really giving offense, since the prime target would soon appear. Smitty cut the briefing short, which meant the TV nets would have to use his statement about the press conference as their leading news clip that night. Also, he did not want to face one question sure to come up if he hung around: "Does this mean the President is unable to give a speech?" Ericson could not give a speech because he could not read one. To ad-lib a half-hour talk, live, would be an enormous strain; taping it in short takes was out of the question, if the primary purpose of the television appearance was to show the President able to deal with reality.

Smitty worked over the briefing book in his office with Marilee for a couple of hours, then walked to the downstairs through the basement to the President's living quarters. He did not take the incomplete black book, since Ericson liked to be handed the complete job, and Fowler, the therapist, was working out a way with Melinda to funnel the questions and answers into the President's head. As he went into the Lincoln Sitting Room, the briefing officer from the Defense Department was leaving; that was good.

"I told them you'd wear dark glasses," he said to the President, "maybe you'd better get used to wearing them."

Ericson felt in his smoking jacket pocket for the glasses and drew them on. Smitty thought Ericson seemed depressed, or at least was not trying to seem cheerful.

"We're going to have a tough time writing the lead we want on this one, Smitty." That was Rule One of press conferences: Always go into them with your news lead in mind, or else you'd get trapped into providing them with a lead of their own making. Your lead was good news; the media's lead was bad news, badgered out of you or the result of a slip or a trap. Smitty was not going to fall into the President's downcast state; The Man had to be up for this appearance.

"Got any good news about your eyes? If there was

any way of getting the word 'improved' in your answer, that would play."

"They're the same," Ericson said soberly.

"All you see is black."

"No, I wouldn't say that." The President motioned to the window. "I can make out that there's a window over there, with a blob of light, and I can vaguely tell when shapes are moving around."

"You mean you're not totally blind?" Smitty let his excitement show through.

"The eye doctor and the lawyers say I am totally blind. Being able to tell light from dark doesn't mean you're not blind."

"Hold on a minute. Have you always been able to tell light from dark, since you woke up from the ambush?"

"Sure, I—well, now, let me think." Smitty waited while the President gave the matter some thought. "Last week," he said finally, "it was all pretty black. Dark colors, really. In the past few days, there's been some improvement. Nothing dramatic, but I would have to say it's encouraging. Here, I'll show you." He got up. "Take me out of here, bring me back, and turn me around a few times." Smitty did so, facing the President toward the wall away from the window. Ericson turned around and pointed to the window: "The light comes from there."

"That's our lead. 'An improvement.' The opta-whatsisname will back that up?"

"You bet he will," Ericson said determinedly, "and so will Fowler. I'll discuss it with them later today."

"Some of the questioning is liable to get pretty personal," Smitty warned. "Like how you shave—"

"—White House barber shaves me, same as before." He was tensing.

"—and how you brush your teeth—"

"Jesus!" Ericson covered his lips with his hands, as he did when furious. Smitty waited. "That's a bitch," the President said finally. "That particular one happens to be a bitch." He tried to compose himself. "You get into the bathroom," he said in a rush of words, "and you knock over the glass with the tooth-brush in it. Then you feel around the broken glass on the floor to pick up your toothbrush. Then you take up the toothpaste and you wonder if it's the toothpaste or the shampoo in the tube. Then you try to squeeze the goddamn toothpaste, if that's what it is, onto the tiny little area that is the end of the toothbrush, and you miss and it falls in the sink. And so you do it again, squeezing the paste into your palm, and picking it up with the brush. If there is ever a time you feel so—so helpless—it's when you try to do a silly little automatic thing like brushing your teeth. Thank God for Fowler, he taught me how to brush my teeth."

Smitty didn't know what to say, but he remembered some of the therapist's advice, so he toughed it out. "You're making me cry, Mr. President. Now when a reporter who wants to see you come apart at the seams asks you how you brush your teeth in the morning, what's your answer?"

Ericson took a deep breath and replied sweetly: "It's surprisingly difficult at first, Mr. Smith, but after a while you get the hang of it and do a better job than ever before. See?" He grimaced toothily.

"They'll want to know about the validity of laws signed when you can't see what you're signing."

"That concerned me, too," said Ericson, still using his stagey press conference voice. "But thanks to the splendid co-operation of the legislative and judicial branches of government, I think we've worked out a method that will fully satisfy the law." He resumed his normal speaking voice. "Cartwright says that it's all set. Whenever I sign a bill, it will be countersigned by the Secretary of State, the Speaker of the House, and a federal judge, under a statement swearing they were present when the bill was read to me. We'll get some-body with standing to start a lawsuit the first time we do it, take it up to the Supreme Court. The Solicitor General—a good lawyer, no politics—says they'll rule on it right away, and it's in the bag." Smitty noted that the President had snapped back quickly from his emo-tional moment. "I should call the Speaker to lock that up," Ericson added, lifting the phone and telling the White House operator, "Speaker Mortimer Frelingheusen, and put Melinda on a dead key." This was a formal call and required some record. To Smitty, he said, "Thank God for Mort at a time like this. He's a Republican and his economic ideas are antediluvian, but he's played it straight as a string for the past two weeks, which is more than I can say for Bannerman." In a moment, "Mort? I'm sitting here with Smitty working over some dirty questions at the press conference Wednesday." Smitty picked up an extension and made his presence known. Ericson said: "First, I wanted to be sure you tuned in."

"You'll get a good rating," the Speaker allowed. "Lot of people want to make sure you're *compos mentis*."

"And then I want to thank you for the signature-attesting thing. That'll be a chore, I know, at least a couple hours every week, but maybe you can delegate it after a while."

"No, I'll be glad to sit there and listen to them read it aloud," the Speaker, in his New Jersey Middle America monotone, observed. "It might even cause us to shorten some of them, which would be a net gain. While I have you, Mr. President"—that was how Frelingheusen conducted most of his business, Smith knew, at the tail end of calls initiated by others— "the International Relations Committee and the Defense Committee are both concerned about the breaches in the arms control agreement by China-Japan. The Chijaps have been selling nuclear missiles to Zaire and Uganda. If the Africans use them against the Arab-Israeli alliance, then we're all in the soup. The Secretary of State is still in Russia and the Secretary of Defense is ducking us. We could use a statement from you at your press conference that the Administration will consult with the Congress on this very soon, and not just the Senate, either."

"I want to hear what Secretary Curtice says when he gets back from Moscow at the end of the week, Mort." Ericson did not want to give the Congress too much oversight. "He advises that Nikolayev seems to be taking charge there, and their intelligence system is a hell of a lot better than ours when it comes to the Far East. I'll say that we'll consult, if you want, but I'd hate to give a date."

"Why not say you'll send your men up here some-time next week, then?"

Ericson was not in a position to resist. "That's a fair compromise, Mort." Not much of a compromise. With a warm farewell, the President hung up. "Tough bird," he said to Smitty. "He's doing what I'd do."

"You going to be able to get all this stuff in your head in two days, Mr. President?" The normal black book contained eighty questions and answers, running between one and two minutes each, with backup fact sheets on some matters the President knew little about, like emergency flood relief in Alabama. Of these, only twenty would be asked at a half-hour press conference, even fewer if the President rambled on his answers. But you never knew exactly which twenty, so The Man had to be ready for them all.

Ericson took off his dark glasses and spun them around in his hand. "You just get me the black book by nine tonight. Fowler and Melinda will tape it and compress it, and I'll run through it three or four times tomorrow. You'll see, it'll sink in. Then we'll rehearse walking around the East Room the way I did at my wedding."

It occurred to the press secretary that the President's wedding had ended in divorce. He said only, "The press may come at you pretty hard, Mr. President."

"You think they have a legitimate grudge, don't you? You think I deserve a few shots for cutting them off right after the ambush."

Smitty was wary. "What makes you say that, Mr. President?"

"Easy. When you're on their side, you call them 'the press.' When you're on my side, you call them 'the media.'"

"Do I do that?" Smitty hated to be so transparent.

He recalled how the White House in the early seventies changed the nomenclature from "press conference" to "news conference" to shift the emphasis from the press to the news the President would generate. "Anyway, you're better off with a press secretary than a media secretary."

"I guess so," said the President, and Smitty knew he thought the opposite was true.

The Television Set

The televiewing arrangement in the press secretary's office is a four-screen affair, taking up most of one wall, playing four networks simultaneously, with the sound speakers controlled from the viewer's chair. During press conferences, all four speakers remain on low volume, since the regular viewer is absent and his office is left empty. The press secretary can be seen on all four screens when the directors choose to go to the "pool" equipment inside the East Room of the White House. Accompanied by his deputy, the press secretary stands on the platform facing the four hundred reporters jammed in on little gold chairs, in view for over-all shots, out of range for shots of the lectern with the presidential seal.

"Ladies and gentlemen, the President of the United States." The sound of the military aide's voice could be heard on all four speakers. All four screens showed the press rising as the President walked down the middle aisle toward the podium.

Unaccompanied, walking briskly, the President took eighteen steps straight ahead, paused, took one more, made a half-left turn, took five steps to the step leading to the platform, made a half-right. Still alone, he aimed the back of his wrist at the floor. All four speakers began murmuring variations of "President Ericson is using his sonar watch to determine the location of the steps." He walked up the two steps, made a right turn, walked four steps forward, reached to his right and touched the rostrum. He held the wooden stand firmly with both hands, then struck a familiar Ericson pose, leaning on it with one elbow, long legs crossed in back, one toe on the ground. He broke out in a broad smile and the standing press corps broke out in enthusiastic applause.

"Please be seated," he said as usual, and as usual pointed down to the senior wire service correspondent in the center front row. "Sir, you're entitled to one soft ball," she said. "Here it is: How do you feel?"

The President shook his head and said, "There's always one question you haven't prepared for." Laughter. Then, soberly, the image on the four screens said: "Physically, I feel well. The bumps and bruises are pretty much healed. Emotionally, I've begun to adjust to the shock—and it is a shock—of not being able to see. I have to absorb information through my ears rather than my eyes, and that takes a little getting used to. But I'll manage.

"When you ask how I feel, I have to tell you how bad I feel about the tragedy of two other men. Of General Secretary Kolkov, that brave man who dragged his wounded body over to me and who saved my life as he gave up his own. And of Harry Bok, of the U. S. Secret Service, who absorbed shrapnel that was intended for me. I spoke to Harry in a hospital in Yalta earlier today, and to his surgeon after the operation, and the outlook is not good—his legs may be paralyzed. So when I think about General Secretary Kolkov, and about Harry Bok, somehow I just don't feel sorry for myself."

The usual jumping up, waving, and hollering for attention to the next questioner did not take place; the press corps had evidently decided on a more orderly process, and the junior wire service reporter asked:

FULL DISCLOSURE

"Mr. President, what's the latest on the condition of your eyesight?"

The man in dark glasses on the podium turned slightly in the direction of the voice and replied: "I may have some cautious good news on that. When I first regained consciousness, I couldn't see a thing—just black, with some dark colors. In the past week or so, I've begun to be able to make out the difference between light and dark—for example, I can see a strong source of lights over there, where the television lighting is always set up. Now that's no guarantee that my eyes are on the mend. But it makes me hopeful. I'd put it this way: At the moment I'm officially blind —let's use the hard word, blind—but my sight seems to be improving."

"Don't you think it would be in the best interests of national security, sir, if you stepped aside under the provisions of the Twenty-fifth Amendment until such time as you were fully capable of discharging your duties?"

"No," said the President. He said nothing more, and there was a pause. The camera panned the face of the press secretary and his deputy, who looked grim.

"To follow up—with all respect for your courage, sir, don't you think that your blindness calls into question your capacity to serve?"

"No. A lot of people thought I couldn't handle this job when I could see." The half-joke did not get a response.

"Could you tell us how you know what you're signing?"

The President was evidently ready for that and went through the procedure of countersignatures at some length, praising Speaker Frelingheusen and hoping for an early Supreme Court test.

"Sir, do you think the Vice-President would make a good Acting President—do you have confidence in him?"

Nettled, the President took off his glasses for a moment; the screens instantly showed an intense close-up of his eyes, which looked like normal eyes. He put the glasses back on.

"I have every confidence in the Vice-President. As I said when I chose him, if I were to die in office or become disabled, he could be expected to carry on. But I'm not dead and I'm not disabled." The pool camera picked up some of the disturbed expressions of the reporters and flashed them on the screen. The press secretary was looking at the floor.

"There are some fairly important matters going on in the country and the world," said the President. "If you're prepared to ask questions on other subjects, I'll take them now."

The next questioner, a gray-haired gentleman from the *Christian Science Monitor,* said in his well-known voice: "We don't tell you what your answers should be, Mr. President, and I don't think you ought to tell us what our questions should be. My question is: What is your definition of the phrase 'ability to discharge the duties of his office'? Second—"

"One at a time," snapped the President. "If you want a legal definition, I'm sure the Attorney General can draw one up. But as I understand it, the President is the one who is elected by the people and trusted by them to decide on his ability or disability, and I've made that decision. Next?"

"Second," the same voice continued, "did you ever consider stepping aside as an option, or did you rule it out automatically from the first?"

"It's not in my philosophy to ignore illness, Mr. Harley, or to seek a cure in pretending it does not exist. I thought about it as an option and rejected it and that's behind me. Let's look ahead." The camera picked up a reaction shot of the press secretary shaking his head; all four screens displayed James Smith's headshaking at the President's derogation of Christian Science.

"Are you concerned, sir, that the sale of nuclear missiles by the Far East powers to the African nations is a unilateral abrogation of the arms control agreements?"

The screen showed the President squaring his shoulders and moving into the foreign-policy question with relief. "As you know," he lectured, "one of the main reasons for my meetings with General Secretary Kolkov was to explore our mutual reaction to the arming of the Fourth World by the Far East powers. I believe we had a useful exchange of views on that. Secretary of State Curtice has remained in the Soviet Union to find out what the successor leadership thinks about that. Tension between the Third World of the Mideast and the Fourth World of Africa and Latin America could spread to the two superpower alliances very quickly. The central problem of the eighties is to avoid that.

"Speaker Frelingheusen has been after me to send the Defense Secretary to the House to testify on the arms sales to, uh, Nigeria, and I have assured him that his request will be granted by the end of next week."

The President reached for a glass of water on a table next to the lectern. As the camera closed in, his hand moved eighteen inches from the corner of the green felt table along the edge, then twelve inches in toward the center of the table, closing confidently on the glass. Extreme close-up of the glass of water moving to the President's mouth, being returned to the small table. Ericson's hand released the glass, and moved back, but his sonar watch caught the green felt cloth, pulled it back, and the glass crashed to the floor. The camera remained in the silence on the broken glass.

"It's the little things that get you down," the President cracked. "Next question?" Mundane domestic questions dominated the next ten minutes of the conference, with Ericson handling them in a somewhat shaken way, but holding answers to ninety seconds and finishing each with a memorized summarizing tag line. After the "Thank you, Mr. President" from the wire service reporter, the screens showed a sudden glare and then blackening; an old-fashioned flash bulb had gone off at the President and caused a reaction in the sensitive lens.

"That came from over there," the President pointed, half off-microphone. "Did I pass your test?" The sound picked up some of the edge of bitterness in his tone as he felt for the step with his foot, walked down the two steps off the platform, and made his way—accompanied this time by the press secretary and two Secret Service agents—through the crowd and out of the East Room.

The sounds of the four-screen set intermingled: "After a good start, the President's performance in this crucial press conference went downhill . . ." ". . . granted the tension he was under, his mood seemed almost mercurial, from the gracious and witty man we've known to a waspish and somewhat embittered man that we have not seen before . . ." ". . . most glaring error was in confusing the recipient of the nuclear missiles in Africa, certainly not Nigeria, the least militant of the Fourth World nations . . ." ". . . though frankly I cannot blame him for showing a little temper when a photographer broke the rules of the press conference to shoot a flash bulb in his face. The President interpreted that as an insulting test of his truthfulness, after having said that he could tell light from dark, but frankly, don't you think the way he indeed passed the test worked out to be a net plus . . ." ". . . fact remains that from an atmosphere of sympathy, an atmosphere of hostility soon developed, whosoever's fault it was . . ."

An hour later, when a secretary turned off the lights and the sets in the room, the murmuring ceased and the pictures converged into four white dots which vanished into a blank.

Hennessy tore into Cartwright's corner office after the press conference the way he remembered Ensign Pulver ripping open the door of the captain's cabin in the last scene of *Mister Roberts*.

Smitty was there, along with a depressed Melinda and Fowler, and the press secretary was announcing, "He blew it. He had it right in his hands and he blew it."

Hennessy didn't trust himself to speak. To lose your temper when it served a purpose was one thing; to blow up to no purpose or as a personal indulgence was another. He sat and listened to the playing of the dirges.

"They didn't ask one question that wasn't in the briefing book," Smitty insisted. "I edited 'em. Melinda recorded 'em. Fowler compressed 'em and poured them into Ericson's head time and again. And he had 'em down pat—I heard him rattle them off this afternoon. What in hell got into him?"

Lucas Cartwright, ignoring the direct question, said to Fowler, "He certainly moved in and out of the East Room, and up to the platform, with great authority, thanks to you. That was remarkable, Hank."

"My heart sank when I heard that glass break," the therapist replied. "I could have sworn he was ready for that."

"Not your fault," said the chief of staff, "nor his. Accidents will happen. And to compensate, we had that flash bulb incident. Nothing we could have said would have made the point more dramatically that the President can see a source of light."

"Little bastard," said the press secretary, switching targets, "he popped that bulb just to see if the President was lying. Be a long time before that photographer ever gets off the zoo plane."

"I guess the strain was just too much," said Melinda McPhee. "We knew the way he always used to massage the press, we just assumed he would do it again. It was a mistake to let him try it so soon—he can't be sure of himself yet."

"Nah, it's more than that, Melinda." Smitty was acting, it seemed to Hennessy, like an outside observer come to a family post-mortem. "That shot at the *Christian Science Monitor* man was mean, vicious—I never saw Ericson do that before. And the flub about Nigeria —that was no slip of the lip, he just had his facts screwed up. Hennessy, I suppose you think your blue-eyed boy did everything right tonight?"

"I watched it on television," Hennessy said slowly. "I wasn't in the East Room. And I never saw a more disloyal, disgusting performance by a press secretary in all my life."

"Now, Mark—" Cartwright began, but Melinda cut the staff chief off with "Don't 'now, Mark' him— he's got a point. Smitty was worse than the President."

"Every time the President made a mistake," Hennessy went on, "the camera went to you, Smitty, and you gave them just what they wanted. Shaking your head. Looking down at the floor in disgrace. You put on quite a show, buddy. You saved your own precious credibility again, and you stuck a knife in the President's back."

"That's a lie."

"You go get the video tape played back for you," said Hennessy, keeping his voice low. "You'll see how you looked, how the media used you to emphasize every mistake. It's a wonder you didn't go over and shove the President off the platform."

Smitty looked for help to Cartwright, who let Hennessy have his say.

"It'll be a cold day in hell, Smitty," Hennessy went on, "before you ever stand up there again on national

141

TV, mugging away and protecting your own ass. From now on, your assistant can stand there, at least she knows how to keep a poker face. You can watch the conference on that snazzy TV set in your office, on all the screens, and you can moan and groan to your heart's content in private."

Now Cartwright stepped in. "Let's consider the ways to mitigate the damage. The religious slur seems to me to be the immediate item to handle."

"If you want a new press secretary," said Smitty, doing a slow burn, "you've got her right there, ready for the job."

"Just like you to jump ship now," said Hennessy, switching direction. "You ever think about any reputation but your own?"

"Cut it, Hennessy," Melinda told him sharply. "You made your point, now drop it. Let's move on."

The lawyer noted how Fowler was taking all this, seated in a corner, cane at his side, smiling slightly. The whole thing must seem to him like a radio program out of the thirties.

"The press conference will be covered in the late city editions of the morning papers," Smitty said, glancing at Hennessy, "too late for editorial comment. The columnists won't hit for two or three days. The evening news shows tomorrow are the first place for major reaction, so we've got to do a few things I can talk about at tomorrow morning's briefing. And we have to set up some reactions from friendlies so the commentary on TV won't be all about how the President can't cope."

"Why doesn't the President invite the *Monitor* man in for an exclusive later this week?" Melinda suggested. "He can do it first thing tomorrow morning, and you can take the sting out of the Boss's shot at your briefing. I'll get the Boss to make the call. Religious slurs are bad. They have to be apologized for immediately."

"The Nigerian thing," said Cartwright, "was just a slip of the tongue. Of course he meant Uganda. How many Americans are going to condemn a man because he substitutes Nigeria for Uganda? Same continent and everything."

"Take a different tack on that photographer who flashed the bulb," Hennessy put in. "Tell the press corps you'd like a blowup of the picture for the press room, since it proved our point. If there is a picture, we'll show how relaxed we are about the whole thing, and if there isn't, everybody will know that little prick never even had film in his camera."

"Miss McPhee," said Cartwright, "I would like to apologize for the language used by some of my colleagues in the presence of a lady. They must be under great stress."

"That's a put-down, Lucas. I don't mind it at all—it shows that they accept me as one of the boys."

"I will never think of you as 'one of the boys,' Melinda." Hennessy had to admire how the staff chief was taking some of the poison out of the atmosphere with his exaggerated charm. "Smitty," Cartwright continued, "do you suppose it would be possible for your deputy to inveigle her inamorato—the one who works for television—into calling the Speaker of the House for a reaction tomorrow?"

"Her what?"

"The guy she's banging regularly," Hennessy translated. "The one you're jealous of."

"I'll get the message across," the press secretary said. "It'll be good having Frelingheusen come in with a strong statement. The foreign-affairs thing is a worry —they could really go after the Chief for not having his head screwed on straight about that."

"This is the only administration," announced Hennessy, "in which an eyeball-to-eyeball confrontation is impossible." That even got a groan out of the gentle Fowler. "You don't like black humor?" the lawyer asked him. "You a racist?"

The telephone rang, and a panicky light insisted it was from the President. Cartwright answered, and replied, "Reaction here is mixed. Smitty would have preferred if you had stuck to the deathless prose in the briefing book. The reference to Kolkov and Bok went over very well. On foreign affairs, Hennessy here has just made the most tasteless joke I have ever heard in my entire experience in the federal employ, which he will want to repeat to you himself." The chief of staff listened awhile, then put in the negatives gently: "Your remarks to the *Monitor* man will certainly be topic A in all the Christian Science reading rooms across the country, Mr. President. You might want to do something to smooth that over." He listened, then nodded, satisfied, at Smitty: "I'll tell Smitty to set that up for Friday, and to tell the press about it in the morning." Pause. "It happens that Mrs. Cartwright watched the press conference at a dinner party at which the Bannermans were present, and I'll find out what the Secretary said. It's been a long day, sir, why don't you have a glass of warm milk and go to bed?" He listened to the President's final comments, said only, "A glass of that, then," and hung up.

"The leader of the free world would like to see you in his sitting room before he retires," Cartwright said to Hennessy, and then turned to Melinda: "Did he really throw up all over you the last time he had a glass of warm milk?"

The special counsel to the President hurried through the West Wing, down the colonnade to the residence, nodded to Buffie, the photographer, who passed him silently in the hall—that surprised him, she usually had a cheery greeting—and continued on up to the Lincoln Sitting Room.

"You blew it," Hennessy said to the President as he came in the room, nearly out of breath, "you stupid bastard, you blew it."

"I know," Ericson said. "Stop trying to keep from hurting my feelings."

"But you had them eating out of your hands when you got up there. All you had to be was yourself. What got into you?" Hennessy knew he would not have been summoned if the President did not want a frank, even a harsh, assessment. There sat Mr. Cool himself, feet crossed languidly on the ottoman in front of him, indulging in a little self-criticism from an alter ego. Detachment was a fine thing, Hennessy thought, but Ericson carried it too far at times. "There you sit," he tried a line out for a second time, "looking at life through a detached retina."

"Was that the joke Cartwright said was tasteless? Not bad. Not tasteless, anyway."

"I dumped on Smitty pretty hard for shaking his head when you kept screwing up. The cameras caught him doing it. You'll want to tell him it didn't matter, that I'm too intensely protective."

"I'll do that," Ericson nodded. "What was worst?"

It was hard to begin. The President already knew each specific instance of error. "You weren't in charge, was the worst. The real President Ericson never blows his cool, never loses his sense of humor, never drops his sense of style. So who do they see? Some blind guy who takes offense, lashes out. That was the worst."

"Yeah," said Ericson. "Damn."

"Look, we haven't talked over something yet." Hennessy had been waiting for the right moment to throw a hard one at his client's head. "Forget all the previous stuff, or what could happen if anybody finds out. Just the cornball question: You think you're doing the right thing?"

"Right thing in what?"

"About not quitting, for Chrissake. Can you handle this job?"

"How the hell do I know, Hennessy? I've never been President before. You know for sure you're going to be a great intimate adviser?"

"That's what I'm being right now." Hennessy thought it would be better to switch to curve balls. "I am sitting in a little room that is graced by the ghost of Abraham Lincoln. I am talking with the forty-first President of the United States, who must have enjoyed one of the quickest post-press-conference pieces of ass in American history. And I am bringing up the subject of morality with a capital M, and asking if he really in his heart believes he is capable of discharging the duties of his office. What the hell else is an intimate adviser for?"

Ericson grinned. "You ran into Buffie?"

"She had that radiant look on her face—conspiratorial, womanly, satisfied, dazed." Actually, she had looked worried or angry, but Hennessy could afford to flatter his long-time client on this. "You're still a swordsman, Sven, but are you still a statesman?"

"Okay," the President said, getting serious, "let's go into the pros and cons. Cons first."

"That means the pros are going to win," Hennessy predicted.

"Damn right, but I have thought this through. The cons are, first, that I am substantially less able to do this job than I was before. Nobody, including me, knows how much less, or will know for a while.

"Second, the Far Eastern powers could take my blindness to mean that our government is paralyzed, unable to respond quickly to a power play. So whether or not I'm capable of discharging my duties doesn't matter—if the Chijaps think I cannot, it's just as dangerous as if I really could not. That's the big argument against going on.

"Third, there's the psychological problem in the country. The American people want a leader, a strong and confident person at the helm, somebody they can beat up on, who won't crumble. A blind man, or a cripple, can't be that—in a television age, not even FDR could have gotten away with it—he would have been seen and pitied. That's bad for the leader, bad for the led.

"Fourth—well, I forget the fourth," the President said irritably. "What's another con?"

"Simply that you could be spending so much of your time learning how to cope with blindness that you won't have the time to run the country. Just plain bad management, missed opportunities, mistakes. You could be a relatively lousy President."

"That's the fourth," Ericson agreed quickly. "Now to the pros. First, it's never a good idea to rush into a big decision. I don't have the information yet. Can I cope, discharge my duties? Who knows? Maybe I can. I gave a bad press conference—maybe I'll do better next time. Let's give it a month, then we'll see. But we can't say that, because that's a show of weakness, and it would get everybody having fun with what life will be like in the next administration. I want to make that decision, I don't want it made for me."

So Ericson must act as if there were no chance of his stepping aside; makes sense, thought Hennessy, provided he was not kidding himself. Possibilities in Washington take on lives of their own, becoming likelihoods and then certainties by a combination of hope and dread and mass communication.

"Second," Ericson went on, "this business of 'stepping aside' is a lot of crap. When you're out, you're out—nobody could run the country with other people's men, without being able to plan for the next year. And the idea of returning to power when you think you're capable—that would only generate a lot of mischief at the center. Big disagreements, Cabinet fights, uncertainty about who is in charge for how long. That's dangerous, that's real paralysis. So 'stepping aside,' as Zophar put it, is the nice way of saying —'get out for good.'

"Third—you making notes, Hennessy? Please do. The presidency is not a job you quit in a hurry. It's instability when you do. When you're elected, it's for better or worse all the way—and once people get the idea that Presidents they don't like should resign, or don't think are doing the job should resign, then the four-year term starts crumbling at the edges. Unless he is absolutely sure he is incapacitated for a long time—really out of it, and for a really long time—a President's duty is to stay in office.

"Fourth—this is a practical one—we happen to have a Vice-President who is an amiable jerk. He was not chosen because he would be a good President, he was chosen because he would be a good Vice-President. That choice wasn't mine—it was the party's and particularly Bannerman's choice. Operating at twenty per cent of capacity, I would be a better President than Arnold Nichols operating at one hundred per cent of capacity." Hennessy allowed as how that was true.

"Fifth—there are a lot of handicapped people in this country who are pinning their hopes—" the President stopped when Hennessy started humming "Hearts and Flowers." "Okay, I won't use that one unless I have to.

"Sixth, or fifth, or whatever—and Hennessy, don't write this one down—I want to be President. It's been a bitch getting here. I lost my eyesight because I'm President, it owes me something. And it's not going to be as hard being blind, if you can imagine it, so long as I have the most important job in the world. That's selfish, I know—"

"Not selfish," Hennessy interrupted, "irrelevant. What happens to you shouldn't be part of your decision. What the hell are you, anyway, a man or a President?"

"I want to be a President."

"Then stop acting like some kind of human being. You're the Chief of State, you may face decisions about who's to live and who's to die. You make your decision for reasons of state, and whether it wipes out a city or makes you personally unhappy the rest of your life is irrelevant."

The President did not say anything for a while. When he did, it was banter: "You suppose FDR had to put up with this sort of shit from Harry Hopkins? Or Wilson from Colonel House?"

Hennessy took the cue to back off. "We intimate advisers," he said, "fulfill the functions of court jesters. We can say anything as long as we say it with a smile."

"That's what I need, an honest-to-God court jester. Nobody around here has a sense of humor. You're a good intimate adviser, Hennessy, but you're a drag when it comes to laughs. All right—what do you think?"

Hennessy tried to be judicial, keeping in mind his own prejudice at wanting his friend to be President and wanting to linger himself at the center of action.

"On the con side, you're right, the big one is the invitation to the Chijaps to probe a weak spot. And you left out that this is the beginning of your term—three and a half years is a long time to play blindman's buff." He looked at his list, wondering how Ericson could visualize a list. "On the pro side, you made a big deal out of stability and the four-year term. I don't really think that has much traction. Look at the Nixon resignation, the presidency is not all that weaker. A selling point, not a deciding point."

"The Nichols comparison? Bannerman in the saddle?"

"That's a good practical point for deciding, but not for selling. The biggest pro, in my book, is that there is no need to rush into an irrevocable decision. No President ever decides something before he absolutely has to. Since we know the 'step aside for a while' suggestion is bullshit, we should postpone the decision until the facts are in. Coupla weeks, maybe coupla months, we'll see."

The President relaxed, sliding back into his chair. "You call that a standard to which the wise and honest can repair? I'd hate to try to rally support on a slogan like 'Let the Dust Settle.'"

"You'd be surprised," Hennessy told him, the advocate replacing the judge. " 'Go Slow' has an appeal. The burden of rallying support isn't on you, at least not yet. If Bannerman tries to push—let's call it a 'putsch,' that has some nice, Nazi connotations—make him make his case completely before you start to knock it down."

"No more temper tantrums," Ericson promised. "I'll massage that *Monitor* reporter like you never saw. Get me a rundown on Brigham Young."

"That was the Mormons," said Hennessy, not quite knowing if the President was kidding. "I'll get you a rundown on Mary Baker Eddy. Tell me one thing, though—how'd you and Buffie get that photographer to flash that bulb in your face?"

Gleefully, Ericson sailed a slipper in Hennessy's direction, and the President's counsel pretended that it

had hit him. After he had said good night and taken
his leave, it occurred to Hennessy down the hall that
they should plot some follow-up to the report Cartwright was to get from his wife about Bannerman's
reaction. He spun around and came back to find the
President on the telephone, looking bleak, saying,
"You're certain you tried the right number, Herb?
Where the hell could she be? Who saw her after she
left here? Hennessy said he ran into her in the hall,
she looked radiant." The counsel turned silently and
left.

The Speechwriter / 1

The reason Buffie was unreachable was that she was
spending the night in the apartment of the President's
junior speechwriter, Jonathan Trumbull.

She had showed up at his apartment door a couple
of hours before and announced, "You've had eyes for
me for months, now's your big chance, I want to stay
with you tonight. Is anybody else here?" As it happened, there wasn't—he wanted to write a memo on
the press conference—and in rapid succession there
occurred a drink, a savage first kiss, a tearing at
clothes, and a bout of sustained sexual acrobatics that
he had not experienced since his teens. Then the
girl's tears, her revelations, the soothing, and now he
lay in bed, pillows propped up so he could look out
the window of Columbia Plaza at Kennedy Center.
He tried to sort it all out, numbering the items as he
knew Ericson did.

One, I am twenty-seven years old and this is my
first job out of graduate school. Two, I have just laid

the President's mistress. Three, I am on a collision course with disaster.

That was not an acceptable scenario. Jonathan tried again. One, I am the third-string speechwriter and until recently spent most of my time on the bench, writing the "Rose Garden rubbish." Two, lately my career has accelerated, largely because the two other, infinitely more experienced and older men who write for Ericson, have been giving him what they thought he should use, while I have been giving him exactly what he says he wants. Although this has caused the rest of the research and writing group to call me "Young Round-heels," it has meant that I have suddenly become the President's favorite wordsmith. Three, my pleasing of the President has given me a bird's-eye view of history in the making, just as I had hoped when Ericson remembered a freshman who had taken economics from him and wrote a passionate defense of the theories of David Ricardo, and sent for me to be a staff aide. Four, President Ericson is a terrific guy and a pleasure to work with, and Mr. Cartwright has hinted that I may soon be a Special Assistant with more money and with equal standing with the other speechwriters, who talk a lot about integrity and adviser status but who just can't seem to give the Old Man what he wants. Five.

He touched the sleeping girl, who drew the covers tighter and moved away from him. Five, the President's blindness was a personal blow to me, not anything like the magnitude of the blow to him, but if a man cannot read, then what use does he have for a speechwriter? And does this mean that I will be reduced to rewriting messages to Congress and letters for the President's signature, which will keep me far from the center of power and make it impossible to write a valid and meaningful book of memoirs later? Shouldn't use "meaningful," the President hates that word, and "viable" and "relevant" and "ambivalent" and "life-style." Six, then this strange and lovely girl busts her way into my life, which is very busy at the moment. Not just in terms of girls is it busy, because there is no other walk of life·in which there is half as much preoccupation with sex as politics—the aphrodisiac of power, and all—but busy in absorbing ideas and spewing them out in usable form, making copious notes all the while which were ultimately to be turned into the stuff of history.

He was attracted to Buffie; the two of them felt the tension in the staff office on *Air Force One*. Not only because they were contemporaries, but because they were the acknowledged free spirits, who had read and tasted of Paris, youth, night, and the moon. Life in the White House is—he happily faced it—a romance, and a yen soon develops to share it with another person, or two, or three. People change so quickly in that crucible. Maybe you go back to your real self later in what cynical Mr. Hennessy calls "real life." So the attraction between them was there, but it was generally known that Buffie was the President's girl, and out of bounds for anybody else, and Jonathan Trumbull was certainly not going to make a move that would not only be stupid and disloyal, but dangerous.

So here she was, strawberry-blond pubic hair, long, lush figure and all, incisively sexy, a free-and-easy courtesan in the sack. Yet in unburdening herself afterward she had burdened him.

"He's changed," she had said. "He was changing even before the ambush, but now it's going much faster." When you worked in the White House, there was never a need to say who "he" was. "I don't like it," Buffie told him. "I'm not a receptacle, I'm not a whore. In the old days, in the campaign, we had our quickies, of course, and I always thought that was kind of a turn-on, while everybody was waiting for a speech or something, but there was a feeling then. It was fun. We got something from each other. We didn't have to be together a lot, because we were so close when we finally made it. He had his life, I have my life, and when we got together—sparks. And tender, too, which is nice once in a while."

"Are you sure you want to tell me all this?"

"Is it boring you?"

"No, I mean, it's—personal stuff, you and him." He suddenly had a thought of Buffie in bed with the President telling him about his third-string speechwriter. "You've got to be discreet, Buffie."

"I gotta be discreeter than you'll ever know, Brother Jonathan. Why does Cartwright call you 'Brother Jonathan'? He's an upfront old coot, isn't he? You like each other." She was right. "I had that generation-gap thing with Potus, at first, and I thought it was going to be a hang-up, but he was good about that. He said he would always be old enough to be my father and I would always be young enough to be his lover. You guys with the words."

"So how is he changing? You said it started before the ambush."

"Possessive. In the old days, he kinda played me loose, and I was free, so I didn't screw around. Then a couple of months ago he started acting like The President, and I had the feeling Harry Bok was keeping tabs on me. So I balled a few guys, not because I specially wanted to, or anybody who I felt something for, like you. Just a couple of the reporters— and I got a big lecture. He doesn't want any playing around. Maybe I'll blab state secrets or something. On the other hand, he can play around."

"Does he?"

"Why shouldn't he? Doesn't bother me, so long as I don't know who. But you know how all the movies say, 'I want to be needed'? Like that's some big thing for a woman, to be needed? That doesn't do a thing for me. I want to be not needed."

"Now, of course," Jonathan had said, "you're needed more than before. And that upsets you."

"What's driving me up the goddamn wall is the guilty feeling I get at the horrible way I feel right now. Why am I hurting him? What kind of person am I becoming?"

"You worry about losing it all, ever?"

"I used to." She stretched. It killed Jonathan to watch her stretch. "I don't now, because I have a handle on them, which I'll never use, but they don't

153

know that, so the pressure that way is off. So I just bite down on my toothache and come to you."

"You got a toothache?"

"That was a figure of speech, Jonathan. I got it from Hennessy. You're a writer, you should know those things intuitively."

Sometimes she threw him like that. He was her superior in education, in a grasp of world events, and was prepared to accept some superiority from her in experience of relationships, but not in his own field: Snips of understanding or use of perfect words would occasionally become part of her way to surprise him. Not a pigeonholable pigeon, this girl. Jonathan went to sleep, pleased that she did not like to snuggle close and spoil his customary thrashing around.

In the morning the President's junior speechwriter was stroked awake cunningly, and dreamily went along with an arousal he would never forget, starting the day with triumphant intercourse, finding a woman even more demanding and delighting in the sunlight. She had no taste for oral intercourse, but surprised him by pulling him into the shower with her and making the suds fly. Buffie's body melted into him when he toweled her dry, and then she took the towel —it was his last one, that was embarrassing—and instead of tying it around her waist, made a turban for her wet hair. No shame, he started to think, and asked himself what the hell was there to be ashamed of?

"You prepared for something really intimate?" she asked, looking at him in the bathroom mirror.

"There are no boundaries left," he replied.

"Got any deodorant?"

Borrowing somebody else's deodorant seemed to him the ultimate in intimacy. He opened the medicine cabinet and gave her free rein to all his sundries. She poked around the shelves, getting to know him. Quickly—and, he noted, shyly—she used his roll-on deodorant under her arms, two quick wipes. "You ought to meet Secretary Bannerman," she said, smelling his bottle of aftershave, making a face. "You'd learn a lot from him."

"Economics isn't my bag," Jonathan shrugged. "I once conned the President when he was teaching with an off-the-wall study of some dead economist. I don't want to press my luck."

"I was thinking of something else."

Jonathan was thinking of something else, too, looking in the mirror at her turbaned head and scrubbed face. They left the bathroom and went back to bed. He never knew he had it in him. Later, he fixed breakfast as she sat on the floor, cross-legged, still in her towel turban, and meditated with her transcendentist, or whatever they did. He was glad he had plenty of cereal; she was a vegetarian and made him feel guilty about bacon and eggs.

With her mouth full, she somehow brought Bannerman's name up again, and he said, "I tend to let the speeches to the Chamber of Commerce go to the other guys. And on the black book answers, I buck that to Marilee, she's up on money and interest rates and the balance of everything." That was not the right thing to say, he immediately sensed; her brow clouded.

"Jesus, don't you get started on Marilee, too. The Perfect Woman. No, I was thinking how Bannerman's a good man to know for the future, I mean, after we all go home."

The speechwriter had to shake his head. The future was here, now, with four years stretching out ahead, maybe eight, and this girl was talking about the future's future. "When you showed up here last night, Buffie, I didn't figure you for a long-range planner." He didn't like her look. "Meaning no putdown," he added. Mercurial, he decided, was the word for her moods.

"The guy has all the money in the world," she said, munching noisily, "and he means to use it to do good things. Like start magazines. Or buy book publishers. His family already owns the biggest movie-tape distribution outfits, and that's just a drop in the bucket."

"If he's so rich, why is he"—Jonathan had in mind to say "sucking hind teat" but he instantly changed that to—"playing second fiddle in politics. Money can buy happiness, but it can't buy power." That line was original with him, and he used it often, but he had never before tried it on this girl and in such an apt usage. He was disappointed that she didn't notice it. Buffie seemed determined to make her point.

"Think ahead," she pressed. "Might be fun to work on a magazine together, hunh? Maybe own a piece of it? Like *Rolling Stone,* or the *Voice*—look, someday we're gonna be thirty."

"You, maybe," Jonathan laughed. "I'm Peter Pan. But if you say I should get to know Bannerman, fine with me. I get turned on by your devious mind."

She cleared the dishes and came back from the kitchen as if she had never had a devious thought in her head. She had a tomato in her hand. "Let's take a day off," she said, biting in deep, letting the juice and seeds run down her chin into her—his—T-shirt. Rather an obvious come-on, he thought, as he felt himself coming on.

He called in sick. The umpteenth message to the Congress about the energy conservation program could wait another day.

The Treasury Secretary

Looking out his window across East Executive Avenue, T. Roy Bannerman could see the Secretary of Defense coming out of the East Wing of the White House and crossing the street to the Treasury Department. Downstairs, the Treasury Secretary's private elevator was being held in readiness; his fellow Cabinet member would be up in a moment.

The rest of his office windows faced south, toward the Washington Monument, in the long shadows of a late June evening. A well-laid-out city, thought Bannerman, if you liked parks and vistas and monuments; clean, at least. But the soaring spirit of New York was not to be felt here, nor could Washington offer the clubbiness of London. His visitor, Defense Secretary Preston Reed, had been Ambassador to the Court of St. James's a few years ago, and they had come to know each other on some of Bannerman's frequent trips to the United Kingdom, as he tried to shore up the financial markets of that former financial capital. Bannerman respected Reed: Wall Street lawyer, good mind, independent judgment, a foot in nearly every establishment. The Defense Secretary could pick his way through the no-man's land between State and Defense without setting off the mines and springing all the leaks. Kept his people strictly out of international economics, as he had assured Bannerman he would; trustworthy. Tough, too, as he exacted from Bannerman budget support for specific defense projects, as well as channels to political support on the Hill that few of the new men in the Ericson Administration knew existed.

He and Reed had known the loci of power long before Ericson came along, and would remain there after Ericson was a memory. In or out of government, no matter who controlled the Executive or the Congress, their hands rested comfortably on at least some of the levers. Alexander Hamilton, first of his predecessors, whose portrait hung on the wall, would have approved; Bannerman was a progressive and an activist, and accustomed to being derided as a limousine liberal, but he was certain that the country was well served by an aristocracy of responsibility. There was a class bred to govern or—if not govern—at least gently but firmly guide the governance. The judicious use of money helped, but the critics concerned with superficialities were wrong: Bannerman's power, and

Reed's clout, did not come from money, but from the lifelong assurance that money was not a problem, and from membership in the web of friends and associates around the world who bore the burden of making financial systems and governments work.

A Secret Service agent ushered Reed in. Small, slender, gray; his own man. When Bannerman indicated a chair near the fireplace, Reed shook his head. "Roy, I've been indoors all day and the first whiff of fresh air I took was when I just crossed the street. Why don't we try Bernard Baruch?"

Bannerman smiled his assent and together they left for Lafayette Park, across the street from the White House, to a place where they had conversed before. It was a plain park bench near the statue of Andrew Jackson, with a plaque: "The Bernard M. Baruch Bench of Inspiration," where that elder statesman, hated by Harry Truman, liked to advise Truman's Cabinet members after World War II.

"Good place to speculate," Bannerman cracked, knowing that Reed would be one of the very few to catch his allusion to Baruch's self-description as a speculator before the long-forgotten Pujo Committee. Good place, too, he knew, for Reed to be certain they were not being overheard or taped in the office of the Treasury Department, parent of the Secret Service, and for both men to feel on equal footing, neither visiting the other. Bannerman judged Reed to be his equal in intellect, prestige, and savvy; his inferior in long-term power, because he had little family backup; and his superior in selflessness, because he had no personal power goals.

"I wanted to talk to you," the Treasury Secretary began, "because I am convinced that Ericson has to go."

"If you're planning to overthrow the government by force and violence," Reed said dryly, crossing his legs and looking at the play of water in the fountain in front of the White House, "I would have to muster the armed forces to resist."

"I want to save this government," Bannerman said

too slowly, "by all constitutional means, from a man whose arrogance and pigheadedness will not let him see that he is physically incapable of running it."

The Defense Secretary thought that over. He said, "Roy, suppose you were President, and you went blind. Or had a stroke that impaired your speech badly. Would you resign?"

Bannerman had already wrestled with that. "I would step aside without hesitation. And so would you, Preston. The President must always put the country first—it's an article of faith—and if you are unable to function with all your faculties, you have the moral obligation to step down. Or at least to step aside."

"Moral obligations," said the Defense Secretary, "are usually cited by people who don't have a legal leg to stand on. Your legal position is weak, Roy." Bannerman took heart; his colleague had evidently done some research into the Twenty-fifth Amendment about the transition of power. Reed was thinking down the same lines, in his own way, and might well come out where Bannerman came out. He would probe for the Bannerman rationale, disagree with it, and put forth his own thought process, but chances were at least fair that the conclusion would be the same. Different approach, same character mold; Bannerman would let Reed arrive on his side by himself.

"According to the Twenty-fifth Amendment," Bannerman intoned, "if the President is unable or unwilling to declare himself incapable of discharging his duties, the Vice-President and a simple majority of the Cabinet can make such a declaration to the Congress, at which point the Vice-President becomes Acting President."

"Close enough," said Reed. "But the key is the word 'inability.' The amendment deals with the '*in*ability' of the President to act, not the *dis*ability— most specifically, not the disability. Any good lawyer can point out that the legislative intent was to cover a President who is in a coma, or has been captured by an enemy, or has gone out of his mind. Not one who has suffered a physical disability. If he's able enough to argue about it—unless you think he's crazy, which he's not—then he's fit to sit."

Bannerman conceded the legal point. "But you have to admit that there is some gray area here— where the President may or may not be wholly capable of making a sound judgment on his own ability. We saw, in the press conference, how Ericson was not himself—he can't even keep his foreign countries straight in his head. The remedy of forcing him out against his will would not have been put in the Twenty-fifth Amendment unless there had been a recognition of that gray area. The sick man is not the best judge of his own inability—the Cabinet is. And in case of disagreement, the Congress is."

"Weak," Reed pronounced. "You wouldn't get my vote in the Cabinet on that argument."

"What argument would get your vote?"

The Defense Secretary stopped fencing. "Whether Ericson is able or unable to discharge his duties is beside the point. The gut of the matter is whether the Far Eastern powers, and the Soviet Union as well, *think* he is able to discharge his duties. If they assume, however wrongly, that this government may not react immediately to a nuclear threat, then our deterrent means nothing. It ceases to be a deterrent. And that is the situation we're in right this very moment."

"You think we're in danger of attack right now?" Bannerman appreciated the support, but too strong an argument would give an alarmist edge to the Twenty-fifth Amendment thrust. Odd; Reed was normally a coolheaded fellow.

"The painting in your office," Reed answered obliquely, "is of Hamilton—Federalist papers, strong central government, governing class, a solid banking system. In a real sense, no rhetoric, that's the heritage of your office and yourself." He waited a moment. "The painting in my office at the Pentagon is of Forrestal, the first Secretary of Defense. Wall Street law, investment banking, War Department, cold war. The pressure drove him out of his mind, and he jumped out of the tower at Bethesda. So the heritage of my office, without getting all dramatic about it, is to try to live with the threat of destruction. It's my sworn duty to demand that the President blow up half the world if I judge enemy missiles to be coming in. I don't want to exaggerate, Roy, but living with this is a bothersome thing."

Bannerman said nothing. Reed had never talked this way, and was not finished. "See that man on the corner, next to your Secret Service man?" Reed indicated with his hand. "That's the fellow who is wired in to the War Room. Comes the big moment, I have less than ten minutes to make a decision, get to the President and obtain his decision, and order the retaliation. Roy, I have never been an indecisive chap, but that has consequences that could drive a man to indecision.

"President Ericson's blindness has raised the chances of having to make such a decision. The Defense Intelligence Agency has made this estimate: that the Far Eastern powers think of themselves right now as being in the best position for a strike. The timing would be right, with a man that *they think* is incapable of deciding to retaliate in time. A blind Sven Ericson is that man. Now, Vice-President Nichols is no Dwight Eisenhower, but at least he gives the appearance of capability, and that very *appearance* reduces the risk of war." He stopped.

"And so, as Secretary of Defense—" Bannerman urged him on.

Reed picked it up reluctantly, "As Secretary of Defense, I have already urged the President to step down. Not aside, down. And in a Cabinet move such as I presume you have in mind, I would vote accordingly."

That's two of us, Bannerman said to himself. If his colleague wanted to base his decision on such parochial grounds, that was his business.

"There is something else that worries me," the Defense Secretary added, steepling his fingers in front of his face and murmuring quietly, as if concerned anyone would pick up his lip movements or sound by long-distance camera or microphone: "Our friend Vasily Nikolayev. It is not impossible that he may have engineered the ambush; certainly he's come out on top. We have some evidence it was his doing, to be blamed on the Chinese—"

"Hard evidence?"

"No. But it will have to be shown to the President, even if it is misleading. That could sour our alliance with the Soviets in a hurry—the President might be a touch suspicious of a Soviet leader who tried to kill him. And that personal equation could throw certain other balances out of whack, as in our joint satellite program. As I say, it may not be true, but the possibility introduces a personal element into our alliance that is a weakener. If it is true, then we would be better off if both Ericson and Nikolayev were to remove themselves." He looked sharply at his benchmate. "What's the matter, Roy, you look a little sick."

Bannerman, who had expressed rhetorical shock often enough in his life, felt a genuine sense of shock. Abstract references to nuclear deterrents were one thing, but a serious suspicion that the head of one superpower was the attempted murderer of another was of a different degree. "Hits home," was all he said, and after a while added, "I would hope you check out your intelligence as carefully as possible before showing it to the President. It could be the sort of thing to get him to dig in his heels all the more."

"I'm waiting to see if we can resolve it with the CIA. And to talk it over with our peripatetic Secretary of State."

"Curtice is coming back tomorrow," Bannerman said, focusing on a vote count. "You think we can get him with us?"

"Unlikely," said Reed. "He's Ericson's man, no other base of his own, and he would be out on his can in a Nichols Administration. I wouldn't trust him yet with the Nikolayev-as-assassin possibility. The Secretary of State thinks he now has an inside track to the Soviet leadership."

"Neither of us should approach him then." Ban-

nerman, consciously folding Reed in "us" as he re-
viewed the rest of the Cabinet, suggested: "Maybe I
can find a handle, through somebody else, for at least
an abstention. Next is Human Resources, Andy Frangipani." Cabinet reform, which had taken place in a
previous administration, had made it easier to nail
down a majority in a situation like this. The old
Interior, Agriculture, and part of Commerce Departments were melded together in a Department of Natural Resources, and HEW, HUD, and most of Labor
and Transportation were fused into a Department of
Human Resources, reducing the Cabinet from an un-
wieldy eleven to a manageable six departmental members: State, Defense, Treasury, Justice, Natural, and
Human.

"If there is any Cabinet member with a vested interest in voting with the President, it's the Big Flower,"
Reed observed, and Bannerman agreed. Frangipani,
former mayor of New York, now headed the health-
elderly establishment, and any move that could be
taken to seem to demean the disabled was anathema
to him. Jobs for the handicapped was a favorite cause;
blindness in a President was, to that interest group,
a plus. His institutional and personal rival in the
Cabinet, Natural Resources Secretary Mike Fong, was
likely to be inclined the other way, Bannerman knew.
The Democratic party had forced Fong on Ericson,
partly at Bannerman's behest, just as it had rammed
through the vice-presidential choice.

"Figure Fong in with us," said Bannerman. "And
the Attorney General will stick with the President."
Bannerman reminded himself that he would have to
start calling the President "Ericson" and not "the
President" from now on.

"That's three to three," said Reed, "not enough. The
amendment requires 'the Vice-President and a majority' of the Cabinet. We'd have to pull one over. I take
it you have the Vice-President—this whole discussion
is academic if he uses his veto."

Bannerman nodded, "If I have a majority, I have

him. Could we knock the A.G. out on a conflict of interest?"

"Not a chance. Duparquet will want to milk this for all the publicity it's worth, because he knows he has the law on his side."

"Then Curtice is the weak sister. I'll have to get to him. Guarantee the job, like that."

Reed got up, took a deep breath of the evening air, contemplated the White House, illuminated, fountains dancing, flag flying on the roof, in the sunset. Continuity. "Curtice might go for a straddle."

Bannerman grinned. He could hear the Secretary of State now: "Although I, personally, believe the President can and should continue in office, I will not cast the vote that denies to the Congress the right to work its will. I cast my vote for putting it up to the Congress."

They walked down the brick path toward the corner of the park where their aides were waiting. "That's Rochambeau," Bannerman said, pointing to one of the park's four statues of foreigners who had helped George Washington. "He headed the French troops aiding Washington, but Lafayette got all the credit."

"Washington could have used a decent G-2," the Secretary of Defense replied. "His intelligence community was abysmal."

"You're right, Preston." He decided a hint would be in order: "I have somebody in very close, and a strong possibility of a second source. It's important to know Ericson's thinking. He must be suffering fits of depression. We can play to his moods. Maybe avoid a confrontation and have a sensible transition."

"Won't happen. Ericson's a President, he'll hang on like a bulldog. But the intelligence you pick up could make a difference."

Bannerman nodded. Ericson was indeed a President, with all the obduracy that went with the word. That was the pity; at this moment, a less stubborn man would have been better for the country. Bannerman raised his hand in a farewell to Reed and informed the Secret Service driver on the corner that he would not be needed that evening. Whenever the Treasury Secretary did anything like that to protect his privacy, Bannerman knew the men of the Service leaped to the conclusion that he was playing around. He never did; he admired—loved—his wife of twenty-five years, would never do anything to hurt her, or to compromise himself. But the guilty assumption within his organization suited him. He had already told Susan Bannerman that he was planning a clandestine meeting with the President's girl friend and the President's speechwriter that night at a dreary Chinese restaurant in Bethesda.

This suborning of loyalty was not the end of the business that gave him any pleasure. The girl he considered to be a cheap opportunist, a quick and easy purchase with promises of editorships; he was surprised that a man like Ericson, who could have had almost any woman in the country, would have become so deeply involved with her. Male menopause, perhaps, an affliction that Bannerman had successfully avoided, could cause an otherwise careful political figure to make it possible for others to erode his power base. Ericson was strong in some ways—admirable, really—weak in others. Knowing when to quit was not a weakness in Bannerman's eyes, but a strength. The greatest pity, he thought, was that the nation had to suffer because Sven Ericson lacked that strength.

II

The Twenty-fifth Amendment

The Chief of Staff / 2

Lucas Cartwright was no sooner in the White House car than the mobile phone rang. The WHCA operator cautioned him: "This is an insecure communication, sir, the President is calling."

"Lucas? You up and around?"

"This is an insecure communication, Mr. President. At seven in the morning, I feel especially insecure."

"Read the News Summary yet?"

"I'm just starting it. It may be the low point of my day."

"Melinda just read it to me." The President's voice was worried. "It's about as bad as we thought. Have breakfast with me, family dining room, when you get in. See if you can figure out the sources for the columns, and let's also talk about the *Post* editorial. Was your wife a good reporter?"

"As always, Mr. President. I'll tell you about that when we're not broadcasting all over Washington on this insecure device. And for all you folks that are tuned in, this is the Landon School drama society signing off."

Not going to be an upbeat day. Thirty-six hours after the Wednesday night press conference, and the reaction storm was breaking. This was Friday, its negative headlines to be followed by the curious calm of summer weekends, and then on Monday—with the appearance of the news magazines—the whole thing would be rehashed, once over heavily, fresh incentive for the dailies and television news to dig up new angles, covering the weekly coverage of the daily coverage. Congress, thank God, would soon conclude its business and go home for the summer.

Mrs. Cartwright—he liked calling his wife "Mrs. Cartwright," and she called him "Mr. Cartwright," it was their little code of intimacy—had reported to him all she had been told about the Bannerman reaction to the press conference after a Georgetown dinner party. The Treasury Secretary had refrained from any overt head-slappings or groans during the President's ordeal, saying solemnly at the end, "We have to stand by him, no matter what, until he's himself again." Then the men, accompanied by a token woman reporter, had withdrawn to the study: Bannerman, Zophar, a senator from Georgia, a Washington editorial writer, and a lobbyist-lawyer. The lawyer's wife related to Mrs. Cartwright the next day all that had been said "not for attribution": that Bannerman and unspecified others in the Administration were deeply worried about the President's ability to cope. That the President was afraid to hold a Cabinet meeting. That Ericson was the captive of the staff, especially "hatchetman Hennessy." That the Cabinet members had been hoping that the press conference would prove that Ericson was able to discharge his duties with his handicap, but that hope had been dashed.

Cartwright nibbled one end of his reading glasses, looking at but not seeing the passing McLean greenery leading to Chain Bridge. Bannerman was wise in the ways of Washington; he would know nothing was unattributable for long; he would know his reaction was certain to get back to the President. Didn't he care? Was he willing to take a chance? Was he bluffing? The staff chief slipped on his reading glasses and took a look at some of the results of the President's rancor and the Treasury Secretary's knifing:

President's News Summary: Includes Fri AMs
TV: All three commercial nets led with clips from news conference, highlighting Nigeria slip and broken-glass bit, with ABC and NBC concentrating on exchange with *Christian Science Monitor* man,

following it with a protest reaction from *Monitor* spokesmen. Only CBS added comment from *Monitor* reporter that he had date with President at White House Friday. Fourth net did feature on the reactions of the press secretary, unflattering. TV commentary, which has been sympathetic up to now, has turned negative. Most Democrats interviewed for reactions say the President should consider stepping aside temporarily. Most Republicans say it's a matter for the Democrats to work out among themselves (taking cue from Speaker Frelingheusen, who told NBC: "When it comes to press conferences, I've given a few clinkers myself. The President had a bad night, that's all." "Mr. Speaker, do you think he's able to discharge his duties?" "Read your Constitution. If he's able to say he's able, then he's able.")

Cartwright skipped through the television section to the columns.

The Altman-Peterson Group reports "insiders say the White House staff is dividing. Stick-with-Ericson diehards, led by the mysterious Mark Hennessy, the President's crony and former divorce lawyer, include influential Melinda McPhee, Ericson's executive secretary, and the President's new therapist, Dr. Henry Fowler. Another group, putting the nation's needs ahead of personal ambition, seems to be forming behind straight-shooting press secretary James Smith and the President's personal physician, Herbert Abelson. The chief of staff, Lucas Cartwright, a retread from the Eisenhower generation, has not yet indicated which way his cat will jump. . . ."

"Gorge, stop rising," Lucas Cartwright said aloud. The driver looked back quickly: "The river isn't flooding, sir, it's just a little muddy from the rain last night."

"That's good," said the chief of staff, reflecting that

such "insider" columns often contained a grain of truth grown wild. The source? The notion of Smitty being less than loyal would spring from his woebegone expressions during the conference, and was mistaken; the Hennessy and McPhee guesses were just that, and obvious, drawn from Hennessy's call to fly back on *Air Force One* and Melinda's reputation for personal devotion. The nailing of the President's physician was not obvious, however, and indicated some insider was talking. Abelson did seem to be a weak link; Cartwright wondered how the reporters found out about the doctor's misgivings. Abelson himself? Not likely. And the man-in-the-middle item about Cartwright: That was either an unsure columnist or a source planting an item to sow doubt between the President and a man he had to trust. That source could easily be Bannerman.

Zophar's column was predictable: He had staked out his position first, and in his ornate style was determined to make the rest of the story his crusade.

"In the aftermath of the unfortunate President's ill-advised, too-early press conference, a wave of Byzantine intrigue is bound to inundate the White House. The President is deeply wounded, perhaps worse than some of us had feared; the young lions are beginning to stir.

"At a moment like this, with all the mischief that uncertainty and instability can bring, the President's doubters ought to pipe down. All urging of him to step aside is counterproductive, since it will only harden the famous Ericson resolve. On the contrary, this is the time for a 'creative pause'—a moment to hope for an act of genuine statesmanship from the President.

"It is no easy thing for a man as energetic, ambitious, and idealistic as Sven Ericson, to step aside. To admit 'defeat,' even defeat by an act of an assassin. His decision is excruciating.

"And yet Presidents are elected to make the painful decisions, at great personal cost. Let the cacophony of sychophants cease. Let the President think it over. He will conclude, as a patriot must, that the welfare of the country comes before any other consideration. . . ."

The *Post* lead article, Cartwright thought, was sympathetic, less cloying, and more subtly effective:

". . . not forget that less than four weeks ago, President Ericson was a healthy, exuberant leader, determined 'to shape events to fit our visions of the good society.' He is injured; he can be thankful, as are his countrymen, that he is not dead. The issue of his disability—and there is no blinking away the issue—is for him to resolve or to dispel. That issue is not 'Can a blind man be President?' but 'Can this blind man, at this moment of history, be a good president—or would the country be better served if he stepped aside under the provisions of the Twenty-fifth Amendment?'

"This is a serious, soul-searching time. The disability of Mr. Ericson is not the 'inability' of the coma, as the amendment's writers were most concerned about. The decision is the President's, the first great decision—and perhaps the last—of his presidency. As he ponders whether to set aside the powers and duties entrusted to him, his countrymen —who ardently pray for his complete recovery— venture to hope that he will place the welfare of the nation before any notions of pride or . . ."

The trend appeared to have set in. After next week's news magazines gave it the delayed push, the poll results would start to come in. So much depended on the way the questions were phrased. "Do you think the President should step aside until he is better able to function without his eyesight?" Answer: 80 per cent yes. "Do you think the President's blindness should cause him to be forced to resign?" Answer: 80 per cent no. Cartwright made a note: Get our own pollsters out with the right questions.

FULL DISCLOSURE

He stopped reading. How must a President feel, reading this about himself, or in Ericson's case, having it read to him? Ericson's surface was rough-textured in a civilized way, like a Scotch grain leather; inside, there was a gentleness that surprised and delighted men who worked with him; and inside that was the core toughness expected when one originally looked at the surface. Perhaps toughness was the wrong word, popularized in the cool Kennedy days; maybe it was strength. Or obstinacy. Whatever was at the center of Ericson, strength or cold void, the crucible of the White House would render it pure and unalloyed before the end. That was what Cartwright liked most, and sometimes feared most, about working there.

But the press play puzzled and distressed him. In the Eisenhower days, only a generation ago, the press would have joined in a tacit protection of the White House, minimizing the danger of indecision when the President was incapacitated. Later—months, years later—historian-reporters would recount how the country had been run from the hospital or from the Cabinet Room. Not any more. To expose incapacity at the first sign of weakness was the newsworthy thing to do. But such haste for the hard truth seemed unpatriotic to old fuddy-duddies like himself. The clinical probing was realistic, he admitted, but unkind. Cruelty—even savagery—in the pursuit of news was now considered acceptable. If he had a choice, Cartwright hoped to be tough enough to err on the side of kindness.

The car stopped at the West Basement entrance. He nodded at the guard, spiraled up the narrow staircase to the first floor of the West Wing, which he considered good exercise for an old man, and started for his corner office. He needed a couple of moments to look at his telephone messages before going to breakfast with the President.

In the anteroom a young man, Jonathan, the President's new favorite speechwriter, lay in wait for him. Cartwright wished he could remember the lad's last name. Ordinarily he would be pleased to chat with him, but not now. "You shouldn't work so late," Cartwright told him. "Go home and get some sleep."

"Sir, there's something I need to talk to you about." Humorless young fellow. Cartwright hated to appear hurried to anyone, but the President was waiting, and he could see two dozen little pink telephone message slips arranged in chronological order on the table in his office.

"You know my door is always open, Jonathan," Cartwright said, making a mental note to tell his secretary to close his door when she left at night, "but El Número Uno requires my presence. Would after lunch be all right? Three-ish?" The young man, obviously distraught, mumbled yes and went away. Cartwright looked at the display of phone messages, selected three from the tableau like an experienced fruiterer, and put those in his wallet; the rest he scooped up and dropped on his secretary's desk. When she came in at 7:45, she would hurriedly return all the calls. She would tell those callers who were already at their desks that Mr. Cartwright wanted to call them back—and was tonight soon enough? She would tell the secretaries of the ones who had not yet arrived at work that Mr. Cartwright had returned their call. This procedure gave the illusion of an efficient chief of staff anxious to get back to people, and placed staffers who worked normal hours on the defensive.

Breakfast with the President, when the man could see, was a familiar event; but today Cartwright did not know how it would go. Did somebody feed him? Did he grope around for his food? Should one try to help him? He should have asked Hank Fowler about the proper procedure. From his corner office, Cartwright walked past the Oval Office with the guard in front, past the press secretary's office with the machines beginning to chatter, down a ramp, past the Rose Garden into the basement of the White House residence where the portraits of the First Ladies were displayed. He nodded to Mrs. Coolidge, an aquiline beauty with a Scott Fitzgerald look and a white wolfhound at her side, then trotted up the marble stairs to the State Dining Room. Each of the guards had alerted the next, who nodded to him politely, all appearing hard of hearing, with tiny receivers in their ears. The downstairs Family Dining Room was one third as big as the State Dining Room, giving it a comparative sense of intimacy that such a forty-foot-long room rarely had.

A butler was removing the President's plate as Cartwright entered. Melinda announced his presence and her own departure, carrying the taped, compressed-speech News Summary. Ericson pushed his chair back from the table and sipped from a large mug of coffee. Cartwright sat at the table that had, a century before, served as President Grant's Cabinet table, and ordered his regular hot cereal.

"Nobody else orders oatmeal, Lucas," the President said. "I think they cook a pot every day just for you."

"White House oatmeal has a smooth consistency hard to find anywhere else," Cartwright said mockseriously. "I think they put the oats in cold water, and then bring it to a boil. Mrs. Cartwright tends to throw the oats into already-boiling water, giving it a lumpy consistency. That's why I have breakfast at the White House so often. It's cheaper, too."

Ericson smiled into his coffee mug, warming both hands around it. "That tells me more about oatmeal than I want to know."

"What about your taste for food, Mr. President? I've heard that when you lose your sight, your other senses become sharper—"

"Malarkey," Ericson said, slicing the air with his hand. "Compensation, it's called, and it doesn't happen. You're supposed to be able to hear better, or improve your touch or smell or taste. The truth is, you concentrate more. Like when you listen to music, do you close your eyes? I used to. You cut out distractions, so you seem to hear better. Nope, nothing gets better when you can't see, you just use your other senses more. Hank is teaching me how to eat, so I won't act like a slob at a state dinner. Wait'll I send back the wine. Who was the column source on the Abelson thing?"

The man had a way of suddenly veering to the heart of the matter. "That was the part that troubled me, too," Cartwright answered. "Your physician has been looking a little sickly of late, taking your ailment to heart."

"Herb is the only one around here who wants me to quit," said Ericson. "I don't hold it against him. But he's not a blabbermouth, he wouldn't say so outside. Somebody in here passed the word. Who?"

"I'd rule out Melinda, who's a recluse when it comes to press. Wasn't me. Smitty is a possibility, or Marilee, who gets a lot from him secondhand, but both of them are fairly careful of the gossip columns." Cartwright then explored a subtlety: "It's so obviously not Hennessy, who gets clobbered as a 'hatchet-man,' that it could be Hennessy." Not likely, but possible. "Maybe Fowler, he's unsophisticated when it comes to answering questions. Or a secondary source could leak—Herb's assistant, or Melinda's secretary, like that. Then there is the worst leaker in every presidency—"

"The President," said the President.

"You cannot trust the man. A veritable fount of leaks, conscious and unconscious, in the office, on the phone—"

"I'll think about that. You keep your ear to the ground. Now what poop do you get from your wife—forgive me, Lucas, her name slips my mind."

"Mrs. Cartwright."

"That's the one." Ericson smiled over his coffee mug. "You know, if you get married a lot, it's a good idea to call 'em that, could save some embarrassing moments." The smile disappeared. "What did Bannerman say?"

Cartwright gave him the fruit of the grapevine, about the back-stabbing at the dinner party. "Millionaire bastard," said Ericson, satisfied, as if relieved to learn his suspicions were accurate. "He's going to come at us. My own fault, I was too cocky, shouldn't have had a press conference that fast. No, I wasn't confident enough, I should have told everybody to go to hell for another week. Well, that's past."

Cartwright was pleased; the President had never ruminated so frankly with him before. Ericson carefully put his coffee mug down on the table, rose and stood behind his chair, running his fingers along the top of the wood.

"Let's war-game this, Lucas. First they send somebody to see you to appeal to my patriotism."

"Yes. When that doesn't work, another emissary will come—possibly through me, since there seems to be some thought that I'm not one hundred per cent behind you—to show how you cannot possibly win in a Cabinet showdown."

"The pressure will mount in the press to 'step aside,' " the President picked up, "and there will be a series of stories about choosing up sides."

"And then—?" Cartwright did not want to make the decision in the next step.

"Then we show them," said the President, "that we're not taking all this lying down, and mount a counterattack."

"You are then charged with arm twisting," said Cartwright, feeling better, "of abusing the power of the presidency by making crass promises and dire threats to specific Cabinet members to support you in a crisis of the Cabinet."

"That's the headline," Ericson agreed. " 'Crisis of the Cabinet.' A diagonal line across the corner of the news magazines. Then all the attention is focused on convening a Cabinet meeting without me."

"It becomes a foregone conclusion that such a meeting will be held," the staff chief carried it forward. "The question becomes not if, but when. There will be agitation to make this the first televised Cabinet meeting."

"Maybe we should encourage that agitation," said the President. "Scare hell out of a couple of the guys." The war-gaming stopped as both men paused to reflect on where the projection of developments had led them. "I don't like it," the President said finally. "Best way to win this fight is to avoid it. Let's do all we can to block that meeting before it's ever held."

"We have the White House as a forum," Cartwright said. "We can keep trying to dominate the news."

"See if you can resuscitate that improvement story, Lucas. Needle Smitty on that, how my eyes are getting better, seeing light from dark. It got swallowed up in the hollering about my boo-boos in the rest of the news conference, but it's worth a try."

Cartwright decided to take a chance. "Strictly for my own planning purposes, Mr. President—and I hope you won't take this the wrong way—how much of an improvement is it, really?" That was more felicitously phrased than "Is it true?"

"A little," the President said. "Not a hell of a lot. I could make out shapes from the start, but I didn't want to say." Ericson leaned forward on the back of the dining room chair. "You asked me that to see if I trusted you, Lucas, and I do. Now—no more tests. What have I got on today?"

"The nine A.M. national security briefing, which will be handled today by the Army chief of staff, General Lawton. Tall, skinny fellow from Alabama, lives for football. Then at ten, the Council of Economic Advisers, all three, informational, next week's figures, no decisions required. At eleven-thirty, still in the Oval Office, the *Christian Science Monitor* reporter. He's disposed to be kind. Be ready to dwell on Africa, he once worked in Accra, in Ghana."

"Jesus," breathed the President, "I hope General Lawton knows his stuff on the Fourth World. Any handle on the reporter?"

"He's a bird watcher. On that score, the White House gardener reports that two birds frequent the Rose Garden outside your office, a blue jay, who sings incessantly, and a rather quiet cardinal. Neither very rare, but would show how you have always taken a deep interest in birds."

"They're probably beautiful to see," Ericson added

quietly. "Never bothered to look at them. So it's a jay that's making all the racket. What else?"

"Four appointments with me and other staff members, listed to make the schedule look jammed, but really nothing else of consequence until five. That's when Secretary Curtice reports in from Russia."

"Why so late? That means he'll be too late for the evening TV."

"That's when his plane gets in at Andrews, and we chopper him right over."

"Get his plane in a couple hours earlier," the President directed, "then he meets me and comes out and says how on top of things I am. They interview him on the porch at four, and the nets have a foreign lead."

He was right. Cartwright had made the mistake of planning the President's schedule on the basis of somebody else's schedule. Curtice's time of arrival could easily be changed with an international call, and the Secretary of State could be produced in the President's Oval Office in time to be properly exploited. "I goofed," the staff chief admitted. "Curtice at three-thirty for a half hour, with his impromptu press conference on the porch at four."

Ericson shifted the subject. "Will Curtice be the one Bannerman uses to call the Cabinet meeting?"

"I think not," Cartwright said. "He's out of touch, for one thing. We've seen to that. And the Secretary of State could be with us—certainly he has no other political base except with you. Bannerman will promise him the moon, but you're more of a known quantity to Curtice."

The President asked: "Who else can call it?"

"Any member of the Cabinet, or the Vice-President, can call a meeting of the Cabinet to consider the inability of the President." Cartwright had been studying the Twenty-fifth Amendment.

"And they're all in town and healthy."

"Regrettably," Cartwright answered. "But their task is not easy. They need the approval of the Vice-President, plus a majority of the heads of the principal departments—that's the six Cabinet members. Which means the initiators of an inability motion would lose on a three-three split. They need four to win."

"Or three and an abstention."

Cartwright nodded, then realized a nod meant nothing to Ericson, and said, "Of course."

"It's not really that hard for them, Lucas. These things develop a momentum. I haven't been in this town much—it's more your town than mine—but there is a packlike quality to the thought and the movement here. We had it going with us, remember? There was the honeymoon, then the month when everybody complained, and then the surge when we moved hard into foreign affairs. Mood and momentum are important. It's picking up steam against us."

"You could be wrong." It would not do to have the President depressed. "Nobody likes to rush into grave constitutional matters. There are some cool heads around, especially in the Congress."

"I don't want it to get to the Congress," the President said sharply. "We have to nip it in the bud, before it even gets to a vote in the Cabinet. If we fail, and the meeting is held, then that's where we lance the boil, and that's an end to it. Then I can start all over."

"You'll need a campaign manager."

"I'm ahead of you, Lucas. The Attorney General's my man. I can trust him, and he's good. I'll call him first thing."

"Why? You'll only get him all steamed up, and that will contribute to let's-have-a-meeting fever. Back off. Don't assume this will go any further than the talking stage. It takes considerable"—Cartwright reached for the word—"temerity to assemble a team for an assault on the presidency. There'll be accusations of usurpation—treason, even."

"The more talk like that, the better." Ericson seemed to perk up. "That's the word, Lucas—'usurpation.' Nope, I'm not about to turn this country over to the likes of T. Roy Bannerman. Here's the strategy: We'll play it cool. I won't call the A.G. until we hear a plot's afoot. On second thought, at the right moment, get him to call me. I'll stay busy, stay here in the White House, no Camp David or anything, and we'll ride this out."

"Grand, that's grand." Cartwright let himself be enthusiastic. "Couple of housekeeping matters before I go. You want to see the President of Uganda next week? He'd like to come."

"Nah, why remind everybody about my flub. Seeing the *Monitor* man is enough."

"Your official photographer left a message late yesterday, she would like to photograph you at lunchtime today."

"Not today, tell her. Where's Abelson, anyway?" asked the President, irritated.

"He went home with a cold yesterday," Cartwright said. "Diagnosed it himself." It struck him as odd that the President noticed the absence of his personal physician so quickly. "Said he expected to be back on duty tomorrow. Meanwhile, his deputy is here."

"It would be good if Herb stayed home and didn't answer the phone. Abelson is with us, and I trust him completely, but he worries a lot, and it shows."

"The rest will do him good," Lucas Cartwright said, and rose. He saw Hank Fowler standing at the doorway to the larger dining room. "Come in, Hank, I'll turn the President over to you now." He watched in admiration as the therapist walked seven steps forward, his cane in front of him, reached out and tapped a chair, then moved into it and sat down confidently, holding his hand in a way to allow the butler to fit in a mug of coffee.

Hank Fowler's voice stopped him from leaving. "You were in the Eisenhower Administration, weren't you, Mr. Cartwright?" He acknowledged he had been an aide to Ike's chief of staff, Sherman Adams, and the therapist asked: "Did you have a chance to observe any Eisenhower disability? He had stomach problems, and a heart attack." Fowler was introducing a conversation they had planned to have in front of the President, as if spontaneous.

"I did see the President once, not long after his

stroke in 1958," Cartwright reminisced. "I've never told anybody about that. It was in his hospital room, and I had taken some paper in to sign. Ike pointed to a thermometer on the table next to his bed and said, 'Give me that.' I said, 'You mean the thermometer?' And he said, 'That's the word.' The President sat up in bed for a while, just holding it in his hand, not saying anything, and then he told me he was having a terrible time remembering words to describe common objects. Eisenhower was never a despairing man, but I won't forget the look on his face that day when he couldn't find the word, and when he must have been wondering if he would get the use of all his brain back. That lasted about ten days, and Governor Adams wouldn't let anybody in to see him until it was certain that he wouldn't be groping for the words. When Ike recovered, we never talked about that time at the White House when he wasn't functioning completely."

"At the time, during those ten days," said Fowler, on cue, "Eisenhower must have been torn."

"Bleakest look I've seen on a man's face," Cartwright admitted. "Lucky nothing much was going on in the world at the time, and he pulled out of it, so no decision had to be made." He excused himself and left the dining room. The staff chief did not feel in the least queasy about doing a little play acting in front of President Ericson, to remind him that others had faced his dilemma in other ways; the Eisenhower hospital visit was true.

The White House day crowded in on Cartwright; the more telephone messages he answered, the more he received. The calls he was most scrupulous about returning were from the Hill; President Ericson could not afford noses out of joint there, in case watertight door number one (holding the meeting) gave way, and watertight door number two (voting to declare the Vice-President to be Acting President) followed, which Cartwright thought could well happen. At that point, Ericson would challenge the take-over, and Congress would be the last watertight door.

Peaches and cottage cheese at the desk reminded him of the delicious breakfast that morning—dining at the White House was a genuine pleasure, always had been—and he was surprised by the appearance, three o'clock sharp, of the young speechwriter, Jonathan whatsisname. Cartwright had neglected to put the appointment on his calendar, and then to tell his secretary to postpone the date until the following week. So here the young man was, looking too forlorn to be put off.

"You're the only person around here I trust, Mr. Cartwright," Jonathan began. The older man nodded; younger people had a tendency to trust him, and he them, which was a mistake, since trustworthiness was not a function of age differential. He held up a finger, and said to his intercom, "No calls for ten minutes, except the President." That told the visitor how much time he had, in a nice way.

"I think there's going to be an attempt, sir, to drive the President out of office," the writer said, swallowing. "I mean I know that's a hell of a thing to say but that's really what I think."

Very calmly, as if it were a job of college counseling he was engaged in, the President's chief of staff asked: "And what has caused you to think that, Jonathan?"

"It's liable to take more than ten minutes, sir, to tell from the beginning."

"I have plenty of time," said Cartwright. Not true; at that moment, the sound of the chopper heralded Secretary of State Curtice's arrival on the lawn; the President wanted Cartwright in that meeting, but it would have to wait. Also, Hennessy was calling with something he considered urgent, and Smitty was objecting to the impromptu news conference coming up in a half hour, and Herb Abelson was not at home or at his office, which could be troubling. "It's a slow day," he lied easily, "just a lot of damn memos to read. Tell me what's on your mind."

"Buffie the photographer, who sleeps with the President, came to my apartment the other night, after the

184

press conference," the speechwriter blurted. At first haltingly, later with avid articulation, he recounted his temptation and fall from grace, until here he was sharing a girl with the President at great personal risk to his future.

"Jonathan, if it has made you feel better to tell all this to another person," Cartwright said, "then I'm glad to have heard it. This may surprise you, but even in those dull, staid years, a generation ago, when I worked in the White House last, there was a remarkable amount of hopping from bed to bed that took place. You are carrying on what can only be called a grand tradition, although nobody can protect you from the consequences of this particular liaison."

"I wouldn't take up your time just to tell you I scored with the President's girl friend, sir. It's what happened after that, that I came to see you about. The take-over plot, I guess you could call it." Cartwright did not permit himself to react, just kept listening. "Well, you see, after we got to know each other pretty well, Buffie suggested I meet the Secretary of the Treasury, Mr. Bannerman. I said economics wasn't my bag, and she said it was nothing to do with speeches, but that we had to look at careers after we left the White House, and Bannerman could be very helpful, bankrolling magazines and like that. So I said yeah, maybe, one of these days, and she said, 'How about tonight?' That was last night, and we met in the North China restaurant out in Bethesda, that hot Hunan food, tears your throat out."

"Very spicy," said Cartwright, an oatmeal man.

"At that point, I began to feel that I was maybe being used. I mean, when she showed up at my door, I figured she just had the hots, and that's not all that out-of-the-ordinary around here. Mr. Cartwright, I don't know how it was in the Eisenhower days, but believe me, everybody is banging everybody in this place, it's a wonder we all get through the day. Anyway, Buffie does more and does it better than anybody I ever saw, and I was kind of shaking my head, when she comes on strong with how I should meet Bannerman. Too soon, you know? And right that night. He's the Secretary of the Treasury, a busy man—how did she know he'd be available so quick unless she had a date with him? And unless I was part of the date from the start?"

"Good deduction," the older man said, nodding. "You were obviously being used, or set up."

"So we have this godawful meal, the three of us. I was all fucked out—excuse me, sir, I was really bushed, physically and mentally—so I just listened with a sappy look on my face, must have seemed like pretty much of a dope to Secretary Bannerman. He buttered me up at first, or soy-sauced me up, by saying how he'd heard of the fine job I'd been doing for President Ericson. Wanted to know how close I really was. So I exaggerated, the way I always do, that I was the President's favorite writer."

"You are," Cartwright interjected, "on the Rose Garden, uh, remarks."

"Rose Garden rubbish, is the phrase, sir. Anyway, then Secretary Bannerman started asking me how I felt about the President's blindness, and I said it was awful, and he couldn't read a speech any more. He began a pitch on how the men who thought most highly of the President should rally round him now in spite of himself. By that he meant that the true test of loyalty to Ericson was loyalty to the country, which comes first, and nobody denies that. Then, maybe a half hour later, and I'd had a few drinks, he said that a small group of Ericson loyalists were banding together to help the President make the right decision about stepping aside, just for a little while, until he could learn to cope with the job. I said, 'You mean snatch the presidency away from him?' He almost dropped his teeth, and Buffie kicked me under the table. No, he said, the idea was to help him help the country at a critical moment, to help Ericson see his duty, which was of course to step aside temporarily. This way, he could come back—but, he said, if the President stayed on and screwed up, it would not only be bad for the country, but Ericson would wind up out on his ass. So to speak."

"So to speak," Cartwright repeated. "Did Secretary Bannerman ask you to do anything?"

"To stay in touch through Buffie, to stand by for what may be the most important assignment of my career, whatever that is, and to pass on to him any poop that indicated the President was losing his marbles, or falling on his face, or whatever."

"Brother Jonathan, did you ask him what his plans were?"

"No, I figured that would make me look nosy." The young man was not as dumb as he tried to sound, Cartwright decided; a born double agent. "He did say that there would be a Cabinet meeting to ask the President to step aside pretty soon, maybe early next week. Said he and all the other Cabinet members were getting 'pressure from Natural Resources' to move fast."

"Secretary Fong?"

"Guess so. Didn't ask."

"Good. In all this, Brother Jonathan, listen for who and when, but never push anything. Anything else?"

"I kept drinking water and beer to put out the fire in my mouth, so I had to keep interrupting to go to the john, which made things a little disjointed. But then he pledged me to secrecy, and hinted as how I was going to make my fame and fortune sticking with 'President Ericson's only true friends,' and we got in my car and I dropped him off and then I dropped Buffie off. Buffie didn't want me to come in, said she was worried about being watched by the Secret Service, which was all right with me, I don't think I could have made it again. She's really something."

"She certainly must be," Cartwright allowed. He was convinced that the young man in front of him, already a combination stud-speechwriter-spy, could be of great value in the campaign to keep the President president. Not only in what he could learn, but in what he could pass back to the take-over group. Stupid of Bannerman, taking a chance like this on a stranger.

But perhaps the Treasury Secretary had found that everyone had a price, and considered it unlikely to find anyone in the White House who did not have the customary values; or perhaps Buffie had exaggerated to Bannerman her hold on the young man. Cartwright continued to treat Jonathan—he would have to find out and remember his last name—with respect. "What do you think we ought to do now?"

"I figured you would know, Mr. Cartwright. Tell you the truth, I'm in over my head. This is not my line of work."

"Make a good book someday."

"Yeah. Is it possible for the President not to know I'm banging his girl?"

"That is an inelegant expression," Cartwright chided. "If you wish, I will keep your identity as our informant to myself. The President need not be apprised of the interest that you and he seem to share."

"It's just you and me, then? I'd like that."

"A promise. If I have to reveal your identity, Brother Jonathan, I'll ask you first. Just go along as you have; your instincts in this are good. And stop worrying, you're doing the right thing, the moral thing, if you will forgive an absolutist word."

They talked for a while about morality, about coups and takeovers, about the Constitution and the intent of the framers. Cartwright had plenty of time. He gave the young man his private telephone numbers in the office and at home, and walked him slowly to the door and then out to the elevator. When the elevator door closed, the staff chief spun on his heel and bolted for the Oval Office, to catch the last moments of the meeting with the Secretary of State.

Before going in—the staff chief had the right to enter any official meeting of the President's, and in this case, Ericson had wanted him there from the start—Cartwright paused to sort out how much he wanted to reveal of what he had just learned. To Secretary Curtice, he would raise only the likelihood of the move to meet coming from Fong, with Cartwright's source covered as a newsman's tip. To the President, after Curtice left, he would add the imminence of the take-over meeting on Monday or Tuesday, three days hence. What about telling Ericson the sad news of the unfaithful Buffie? She was probably the source of the information to the columnist about Herb Abelson's misgivings. And Abelson was her contact with the President, to make arrangements for her availability, which was why—when Abelson went home sick—she had to come to Cartwright.

Light dawned: That was why the President asked him about Abelson the moment after he learned that Buffie wanted to take his picture today. With the President's physician still home and out of the picture, Cartwright had control of Buffie's access to the President. She would not likely end-run him by going to Melinda, who despised her, probably. And in her official photographer's role, Buffie could have little other information of value to the take-over group.

Taken together, these strands of information led Cartwright to decide against telling the President today about Buffie's two-timing. Some of the information from the speechwriter could be passed on without revealing the source immediately; that was good. He would have the chance to talk the whole matter over with Mrs. Cartwright tonight, and the President would be spared for at least twenty-four hours the certain knowledge of his cuckolding, to use an old-fashioned term. At the doorway, the staff chief asked himself once again: Is there any information Buffie could have, or could obtain in the next day, of value to the take-over group? Unlikely. Did she know anything about the condition of Ericson's eyes that the President's chief of staff did not know? Of course not. Cartwright went into the meeting.

The Secretary of State / 2

This was the first time George Curtice, Secretary of State, had spent any substantial amount of time alone with the President. At other meetings, a third person had been present—Cartwright, or a speechwriter or secretary making notes, or another Cabinet member— as if President Ericson needed some other witness to their conversations to protect himself in the eyes of history. To keep Curtice honest. Perhaps that was unduly sensitive, the Secretary acknowledged, but a certain hypersensitivity was bred to the bone in blacks who rise to positions of genuine power in a white world.

In their twenty minutes alone together, Curtice experienced a strange satisfaction that he would admit to no other, and not enter in his personal journal: The President, who could not see, could also not be even subconsciously affected by the color of a man's skin. To be truly color-blind, one had to be totally blind. But this stray thought was swept aside in the rush of observations Curtice was making of the man who had chosen him to be the nation's principal agent of foreign policy.

Ericson seemed to concentrate more, now. Not superficially, as might be expected, but profoundly: He listened closely to what Curtice had to say, sometimes asking that a point be repeated. Nor was his human concern perfunctory, as Curtice had always suspected it was in the past. The questions about Secret Service man Harry Bok were neither formal nor idle; Ericson obviously cared for the other surviving victim of the ambush. And—this was the difference, more than anything—Ericson was not as damnably cocky and detached as before.

Lucas Cartwright opened the door and looked in. Curtice had been briefed quickly by Melinda McPhee and a blind therapist on how to operate now with the President, and he followed instructions: "Here's Lucas," Curtice said to the President. "It's been a long couple of weeks since I've seen him."

"Come in, sit down," the President said, indicating the couch; he and Curtice were sitting on the wingback chairs near the Oval Office fireplace, which meant that pictures would be taken before they left. "Please don't feel left out, Lucas, but I wanted some time alone with the Secretary of State."

"I didn't really mind," said the chief of staff. "Got a little backache from peeping through the keyhole."

"George here says that Harry Bok is paralyzed from the waist down," said the President sadly. "Getting the best of care and all, good spirits, but damn. I want you to see what the Service can do for him in its counterfeit division. A man doesn't need to walk around to look at phony bills."

"He'd appreciate that," Curtice said, looking at Cartwright, with whom he had planted the idea of the Kolkov heroism at Bok's bedside. "The country owes him a great deal." He wondered if Cartwright had told the President of the slight alteration of emphasis concerning the ambush: It was not vital that Ericson know that, and Curtice would not bring it up if Cartwright did not. The supposed Kolkov heroism helped spread calm at a frightening moment, sped the wounded President's departure, and helped Vasily Nikolayev solidify his position as the logical Kremlin successor. That white lie helped the cause of peace and the alliance between superpowers, and the smaller the circle, the better. Bok, Cartwright, and Curtice would have a lifelong bond.

"Give Lucas a quick fill on the aftermath of the ambush," the President said. "The summary will help me, too." The Ericson of a month ago would never have added that.

"Vasily now has effective control," the Secretary of State reported. "He tells me the ambush was staged by the Far Eastern powers, in an attempt to split the Soviet-American alliance. Meanwhile, they'll encourage the Fourth World to attack the Third—"

"One world at a time," said Lucas, shaking his head. Good staff work; appearing to be confused, so that the briefer would slow down and let the President digest it all.

"The First World, that's the Soviet-American alliance," Curtice began again, "was intended to be split by the assassination of the American President in the Soviet Union. Then, the Second World—that's the Far Eastern powers, Japan and China—would be the dominant superpower. It would be in the Chijap interest to have the Third World—the Middle Eastern powers, Arabs and Israelis, and India—under attack from the Fourth World, the have-not nations of Africa and Latin America. Not just economic cartels on raw materials, either—military pressure, nonnuclear."

"Don't forget the good neighbors," Ericson said.

"Within that world strategic situation," Curtice expounded, "we have an immediate problem on our borders, as you know: Both the Québecois and the Mexicans are aligned against us, leading the Fourth World, along with Nigeria. That makes all the more necessary a solid Soviet-American alliance to keep the world from flying apart."

"Other than that, Lucas, nothing new," said the President.

"Did the President mention to you a few of the events that have been taking place at home while you were gallivanting around?" Cartwright asked Curtice.

"We hadn't come to that," the Secretary of State replied. First things first, he thought: On the way in from the airport, glancing at the newspapers, Curtice had been appalled at the lack of attention to the dangerous international situation, and the media preoccupation with the President's physical difficulties. With the survival of the world at stake, the only thing the American press seemed to be interested in was the poor performance of the President at a press conference. Ericson's blindness was a distressing matter, of course, and a personal tragedy, but in the scale of human concerns, minuscule compared to the danger of war.

"The Secretary of the Treasury," Cartwright said in a slightly bored tone, "has been trying to convince the Vice-President and a few other Cabinet members that the President is practically in a coma. He wants to call a Cabinet meeting to declare the President's inability to function, and to appoint Nichols Acting President. Then, when President Ericson challenges this, Bannerman thinks he can get two thirds of both houses of Congress to agree that the elected President should be deprived of his office. Crazy scheme, never happen."

"Bannerman is serious?" Curtice had gotten wind of this while abroad, and a cursory update from his aide on the chopper to the White House, but it seemed like a lot of newspaper talk to him. More like the maneuverings at the Kremlin than at the White House.

"Maybe he is," said Cartwright. "Bannerman pretty much controls the Vice-President—you know how Nichols is—and he'll use a cat's-paw to take the lead in the Cabinet. Secretary Fong will be the one who'll probably sound you out, George."

"Mike Fong's with them?" said the President, surprised. "Son of a bitch, I saved him from total obscurity."

"I'm the ranking member of the Cabinet," the Secretary of State pointed out. "Absent the President, isn't the convening of a Cabinet meeting up to me?"

"Not in this case," said Cartwright. "Any member can call it for the purpose of declaring an inability, and you all must go. Bannerman and Fong will probably shoot for early next week, to catch public opinion at its fever pitch."

"Don't lobby George here on this, Lucas," the President said. "If he thinks the nation's foreign policy would be in better hands under Vice-President Nichols, with an elected President challenging a usurper's legitimacy every few months and no foreign leader knowing who to deal with—hell, that's Secretary Curtice's decision and I wouldn't want to influence it."

"Secretary Bannerman is going to lean on you," Cartwright told him quietly. "Obviously, the President is not. I would not presume to give you my own opinion unless asked."

"What's your opinion, Lucas?" Curtice admired the Cartwright technique: Though his proximity to the President gave him more real power than any Cabinet member, he always deferred to Cabinet members, which buttressed his power.

"A coup—and that's what this would be, no matter what amendments to the Constitution are cited—would never succeed. An abortive coup, which is what would happen at such a Cabinet meeting, would make the United States look like a banana republic in the eyes of the world, and might even invite some international mischief. For that reason, I think it would be disastrous if such a Cabinet meeting ever took place."

"I strongly doubt that it will ever come to that," Curtice said, not making any commitments before he had to, but leaving the impression that he was loyal to the President. "Now should I speak to the newsmen out front, or put them off for a day and have a press conference at State?"

"Entirely up to you," said the President. "They're right there, dying to talk to you, and you have plenty to say—I suppose you could do both, if you wanted to, a brief comment here now and a longer press conference at Foggy Bottom tomorrow."

"I'll do that," Curtice said. Two bites at the apple. He left the Oval Office with Cartwright, who added on the way to the press secretary's office, "The comments I made to you about the political scuttlebutt, of course, were not part of your report to the President."

"That matter was never raised," the Secretary of State assured him. "My meeting with the President took place before you arrived, and that's the meeting I'll be talking to the press about." Cartwright delivered him to Smitty, who walked him into the press briefing room. A State Department aide handed him a note before he mounted the platform: "Secretary Fong called to say he hoped you would turn aside any questions on constitutional domestic matters until you and he had a chance to talk." Evidently Cartwright's suspicions were well founded; it was a good subject to avoid until he learned the lay of the land. Curtice reminded himself that this was the rough and sassy White House press corps, interested in domestic affairs, and not the more urbane press corps that covered the State Department.

"The last time I saw the Secretary," Smitty said to the assembled reporters by way of introduction, "was three weeks ago, when he was fighting for the rights of the United States press corps in Yalta, trying to get the whole story out as soon as possible. He'll brief you on his report to the President, and take a few questions, and then will be available for a full-scale press conference at ten tomorrow in the big room at the State Department. Secretary Curtice."

The Secretary of State ascended the podium, the lights came on, the cameras in the far end of the room blinked their red lights. George Curtice gave them two minutes of generalities about his talk with Ericson. As he was rolling toward an end, a questioner impertinently broke in: "Did the President seem to you to be able to properly discharge his duties?"

"That's a strange question. Last I saw him, he was flat on his back in Yalta, lucky to be alive. Today he was up and around, listening to a briefing. That's quite a gain in a little more than three weeks." From the back of the room, shouted: "Do you know anything about a Cabinet meeting called to discuss his inability?"

"No."

"Your answer to the first question, Mr. Secretary, was a lot of smoke," said the first questioner. "Do you think he's capable of carrying out his duties or not?"

"You're not the first one to be dissatisfied with one of my answers," said Curtice smoothly, "and you won't be the last. But you have my answer." When they give you a hard shove, he had found, it was best to stonewall; then they treated you with more respect.

"Sir, have you been in touch with any other members of the Cabinet, or with the Vice-President, since your return?"

"I haven't spoken to a one." He did not respond to the "in touch with," imperceptibly changing it to something he could truthfully handle. "My first task was to brief the President on some extremely important foreign developments. I was prepared to evade your questions about them, but it seems that I won't have to until tomorrow." That got a smile.

"Is there gonna be a war?" came a voice to his left.

"I'll treat that question with the seriousness it deserves," Curtice responded, making a moment's preparation to answer, which indicated to the film cameramen that here was the part of the conference to roll on, and perhaps use. "We have entered a period of heightened tension in the world. There is reason to believe the ambush was aimed at President Ericson as the primary target, Premier Kolkov as the secondary target. It would suit some powers, or some factions within some powers, to drive a wedge in the Soviet-American alliance. We must not permit this to happen, because that alliance is the fundament of peace in the world today."

"Whodunit, Mr. Secretary—do you know, can you say?"

"We are not yet prepared to make any disclosures about who the assassins were, or who directed or hired them. The Soviets are conducting an extensive investigation. We are in touch with that, and we have many lines of inquiry out ourselves. But this is an extraordinarily sensitive subject, and a difficult moment. I'm not an alarmist, by any means, but I informed the President in a preliminary way of my lengthy discussions with Vasily Nikolayev, and President Ericson and I will be having further consultations this weekend."

"By the nature of his questions, sir, did you get

the impression that the President fully grasped the significance of all you told him?" The terriers were not about to abandon their favorite bone.

"I've already responded to that, but I should add that the President was most concerned with the progress of Harry Bok, whose legs appear to be paralyzed. I regret I had no good news to convey about that very brave man." Good, touching moment for escape. "I have to go, but I'll be available tomorrow at much greater length." With reporters who have a considerably different outlook, he might have added.

In his limousine—State still had the long Cadillacs, to keep up with the diplomatic Joneses—Curtice grumbled to his aide, a foreign service officer of indeterminate age, sex, creed, and national origin. "What is it about this city? Only thing they're interested in is politics, power, who's up, who's down, who's next. The President is blind, that's terrible for him, but in the context of all that's going on in the world right this minute—it's nothing. If Nikolayev can really pin this thing on the Chinese, the consequences are enormous. Or if it was the Arab-Israeli bloc, worried about the oil deal we are making with the Soviets, that's a convulsion in another direction. Every chancellery in the world is holding its breath, and what are they talking about here? Ericson's eyesight. God!"

"Secretary Fong has asked if he can come over to your house before dinner, sir. Says it is a matter of the highest moment."

Curtice looked sharply at his aide. "Highest moment—was that your expression or his?"

"Actually, mine. I think he said it was urgent as hell."

"Sounds more like Fong. I'll go home now and get a little sleep—it's past midnight for me on Moscow time—and see him at eight. He can have dinner with us."

"If he can't make that?"

Curtice gave a little smile. "Mike will want to make it when I can make it."

After a nap that was restorative to Curtice, the two

Cabinet members dined at the Secretary of State's residence and talked for three hours. Secretary Fong's argument seemed far more cogent than Curtice first thought: Ericson had lost the ability to govern, the people were beginning to lose confidence in him. That loss could soon begin to hemorrhage. Three and a half years remained in the term, which would be an interminable stretch with no real leadership, and the President was too obstinate—or worse, too confused—to take the necessary action to step aside temporarily. If the Cabinet set the precedent of failing to act in the face of such obvious inability of the President, then the Twenty-fifth Amendment was worthless, and no future Cabinet would be inclined to move out a stricken leader.

Curtice wanted to know if the group that wanted Ericson out—the President called them the "take-over group," Fong picked up a newspaper phrase that identified them as the "Twenty-fivers"—was likely to succeed. Did they have the Vice-President's vote? Mike Fong's answer was that the Vice-President did not consider it appropriate for the man who would take the President's place to influence the Cabinet's decision, and he would not veto any action of the majority.

The two men walked out on the patio, on a hill overlooking a school. "You must be exhausted, George," said Fong. "There's no need to decide tonight." Mike Fong, former governor of New Mexico, was the right man to make the opening, Curtice acknowledged—soft sell, low key, a man most people liked. Bannerman was too domineering and was more effective operating from afar.

"Of the six votes, Mr. Secretary, how many do you have?"

"The only one we are sure we do not have," said Fong, "is the Attorney General. He will want to stick to the strictest interpretation of the law, defining 'inability' as a lingering coma in some terminal illness. Bannerman and I are one hundred per cent. The Secretary of Defense is leaning our way. The Secretary of Human Resources—well, Andy Frangipani has plenty of political reasons for sticking with Ericson all the way down, but he may surprise. He'll vote his conscience on a matter of this importance. So it looks like this: for removal of Ericson, two sure ayes, one sure no; one likely aye, one could-be aye. And then you."

"Of course," Curtice said carefully, "it does not matter to me, on a matter of this kind, which side has the most votes. As you say, this is a matter of conscience, and if I felt that the President were unable to function, or if his blindness made others think we had become vulnerable, then I would vote to remove him even if that vote was doomed, and if it were to cost me my political career."

"Naturally," nodded Fong. "Same with all of us."

"If I say no, and it looks like you'll lose, will you drop it?"

"We're going to go ahead with the Cabinet meeting Monday, George, and it's my judgment that a majority will vote for Ericson to step aside. It would be better for the country if it were as nearly unanimous as possible. That's why your decision is so important. Sense of unity, continuity, all that."

Curtice pondered that. Two approaches had been available to Bannerman's group: to act as if the Curtice vote was crucial and deciding, and they desperately needed him; or to pretend they had it in the bag, and he'd better come along if he wanted to stay in Washington for the next three and a half years. They had chosen the latter, the band wagon. Either they were bluffing, or they had the Defense Secretary locked up and the Secretary of Human Resources likely to bolt from Ericson.

"I won't decide until I have to," he told Fong. "Tell Bannerman I'm keeping an open mind."

"Talk it over with the Secretary of Defense," Fong suggested. "You're the two senior officials in the Cabinet, and Reed hasn't finally decided, either. He looks at it from a different angle, I think, and your foreign concerns and his overlap."

Curtice said he would do that. After Fong had left, he walked out into his small back yard in the Foxhall

Road section—the neighborhood was still nearly Lily-white, but for economic reasons—and stood by himself in the balmy Washington summer night.

So they were serious. Fong was a good man, sincere, wanted to do right. Inclined to be dominated personally by Bannerman and ideologically by that wing of the party, but on the whole his motives could not be challenged. Bannerman was another story: the power broker tired of being a power broker all his life, and anxious to become the power wielder. Curtice judged that, in terms of policy and the exercise of power, Bannerman, for all his overbearing ways, might be better than Emmett Duparquet, the Attorney General, who was certainly the Cabinet member that Ericson had in mind for a successor. He did not quite trust Duparquet, a Southerner, a wealthy Jew, contemptuous of Fourth World aspirations. And when he peeled the onion down to the place where there the tears were, Curtice had to admit he did not trust Sven Ericson, either.

But he owed President Ericson a great deal. The appointment of Curtice as Secretary of State was all Ericson's, no domestic political pressure or gratitude involved. How would it look if the first black Secretary of State returned that trust by turning against his President in an unsuccessful grab for power? On the other hand, how would it look for the first black Secretary of State to hang on, like a grateful Uncle Tom, when serious men, patriots, successfully invoked the Twenty-fifth Amendment and removed a stubborn but physically incapable man from the presidency?

Curtice was reminded of the story of the corrupt judge who called a couple of lawyers in his office and pointed out that one had offered him five thousand dollars to decide for the plaintiff, and the other had offered ten thousand to decide against. When Curtice told the punch line at dinners, it always drew a laugh: "Now what do you say, boys, the first guy gives me another five thousand, and we decide the case on its merits?"

He would think about this, with all the solemnity it

deserved, and discuss it with the Secretary of Defense. Curtice had a great deal of respect for Preston Reed's cool judgment. Vasily Nikolayev's judgment was important, too; he seemed to have great respect for Ericson. The American Secretary of State would do best, he decided, to wait and see; it was always possible that no decision would be required.

The President's Physician / 2

The White House Mess, two staff dining rooms in the basement of the West Wing—windowless, wood-paneled, off-limits to press but open to guests of staffers —seats about fifty people. The food is plain but good; no liquor is served in the daytime except a margarita at lunch on Thursdays with the Mexican special. Inexpensive, prestigious, a fringe benefit for underpaid senior staff and a small bonanza to overpaid junior staff, and most impressive to a luncheon guest brought past the "Situation Room" across the hall. On Saturdays no tie or jacket is required because a staffer's presence in the nation's pressure cooker, on what is to most people a day off, entitles him to a privilege of relaxed attire.

Dr. Herbert Abelson, cold-ridden and irritable, dressed in jeans and an open shirt, slouched into the Mess at noon and sat at the Dutch-treat table reserved for staff who came in alone. He should not have come in at all, the doctor told himself; he was spreading the germs of a miserable summer cold. But the television news the night before spoke of a "fateful weekend at the White House, when so much hung in the balance," and he supposed the President's physician should be around. Waiting for the "C" lunch, the diet special,

Abelson depressed himself by reading the News Summary. The Curtice statement was the lead, which was okay—at least it reminded the people that the rest of the world was in bad shape—but dope stories were everywhere about a "Cabinet revolt" and secret studies being undertaken in the Justice Department about the Twenty-fifth Amendment. *The off-lead in the* Post *quotes the* Monitor *reporter who had an exclusive with the President Friday as saying—*" Abelson picked up a nearby copy of the *Post* to see what an "off-lead" was. The second most important story of the front page carried a dreary headline: "Monitor Reporter Says Ericson 'Not Himself.' " Not even that attempt at smoothing ruffled feathers had worked, and the President had supposed it to be a snap.

He picked up the phone near the table and asked the operator for Melinda McPhee. "How's the Chief today?"

"I think he may have your cold," she said. "He's blowing his nose and growling and kickin' the cat."

"We got a cat?"

"If we had a cat, he'd be kicking the cat. We don't, so he's beating up on me. Why don't you look him over and give him a knock-out drop?"

He arranged with her to examine the President at one o'clock. When he hung up, the White House operator called back and said Buffie Masterson had been looking for him that morning, and did he want her to put the photographer on to him. He said yes, and wished Harry Bok were back; this middleman end of the job did not appeal to him.

"Hey, Herb," came the breezy, reedy voice, "shouldn't I be shooting up a storm on the 'fateful weekend'?"

"I'm seeing him in a little while, Buffie, I'll ask if he wants to be preserved for posterity."

"What I mean is—hey, where are you, in the Mess? I'm right around the corner, I'll be right there." She appeared within thirty seconds—the photo files were also in the West Basement—and the sight of her made Abelson's heart sink even lower, she was so fresh and carefree. She sat next to him, stole three little to-matoes from his salad, and said in a voice too low for the Filipino waiter to hear, "What I meant was tonight. All night, if he wants—anyway, tell him that's what I want. Do you mind it when I'm frank with you? You're a doctor."

"Buffie, you're not a refillable prescription."

"You look awful. How can you come to the White House without shaving?" She put her hand on his arm. "You really were sick yesterday, you weren't just ducking me and cutting me off."

"I had a mild grippe. The President may have it, too. And I take it you're willing to run the risk of contagion." She had a strong hand, no nail polish, insistent fingers.

"I want to see him. Please tell him that. I think he wants to see me. I'll be in the office, or the switchboard will know where I am." She took a wedge of cheese off his plate, stuffed it into a roll, and winked as she slipped through the door.

Abelson ate what was left of his lunch, signed his chit, and walked upstairs to the anteroom between the Oval Office and the Cabinet Room, Melinda McPhee's domain. She was on the phone and he was early, so he walked into the Cabinet Room. Hank Fowler was sitting alone, in the President's Cabinet table chair, running his fingers lightly around the blotter on the table, the President's agenda book, and the buttons and telephone equipment just under the table.

The President's physician had made no sound step-ping into the room—the door had been open—but Fowler looked up in his direction immediately. "Caught me," the therapist said sheepishly. "Who is it?"

"Just your friendly country doctor, making the rounds of his patients." Abelson decided the hell with it, he would stop trying to be cheerful. "How you hold-ing up, Hank? This place gets on my nerves."

"Help me get the feel of this room. You're used to it, Doctor, but it's all fresh history to me."

Abelson motioned to the guard at the door. "Officer, give this man sixty seconds on the Cabinet Room."

FULL DISCLOSURE

"The West Wing was built during the administration of Theodore Roosevelt," the officer began, as if a button had been pushed, "and this room was first used as the Cabinet Room in the Taft Administration. There have been at least ten Cabinet tables; this one, of American walnut, was the gift of President Ericson's predecessor. The walkway outside, leading in through the French doors to the Rose Garden, was built to accommodate President Franklin Roosevelt's wheel chair. Each Cabinet member has his designated chair, with a small brass plaque on the back with his name and the date of the appointment. The President traditionally buys that from the government and presents it to the Cabinet member on his departure.

"Where you are sitting, sir," the guard droned on, "is the President's chair, and you really shouldn't sit there." Fowler got up and stood behind the chair. "Across the center of the table is the Vice-President's chair, to the President's right is the chair of the Secretary of State, to his left the Secretary of Defense's. Since the reorganization of the executive branch, there are only eight chairs at the table, four on each side, none at the ends. When the room is used for bipartisan leadership meetings, some of the chairs along the walls are pulled up to the table, which can then seat eighteen."

Fowler started moving around the table, touching each of the chairs. "Paintings?" he asked.

"Each President chooses three Presidents. Over the fireplace, President Ericson has chosen the portrait of Woodrow Wilson, and at this end of the room, Grover Cleveland and Herbert Hoover."

"We took a razzing at that choice of Hoover," Abelson said. "Thank you, officer. Can we use this door to the terrace? Let's sit on the stoop here, Hank, you'll like the Rose Garden." They sat on the steps leading down to the formal garden. "The trees have finished blossoming. You should have been here in the spring, Hank." Not that the sightless psychologist could have seen them, Abelson realized; when you were feeling down, the presence of a blind man tended to make you count your blessings.

"You seem a little low today, Doctor."

"Does it show? Feel like hell. Grippe, I think." That was silly, trying to fool a professional psychologist, and one with a sixth sense to boot. "The fact is, we're all a bunch of zombies around here. Sven Ericson is dead and he doesn't know it."

Fowler said nothing. "You got a good technique," Abelson told him. "You don't say anything, and the person you're with feels awkward, and he talks to fill up the gap. But does it work with other blind people?"

Fowler smiled. "I use a different technique on the blind. You want to unload, feel free. Professional courtesy, no bill."

Abelson felt the frustrated fears well up in him. "He's an old buddy of mine, the poor son of a bitch in there. He doesn't know what hit him even yet. All the people around here, they keep telling him he can make it, it's just another challenge that he can rise to, but they don't know he isn't a whole person any more. You know what I mean?"

Fowler nodded. "Good way of putting it. It's true, he's not a whole person any more."

"Cartwright likes the White House life, he's good at it, he's happy as a clam at high tide to be back. Hennessy is fascinated with power, with the interplay of personalities, with the publicity—he laps it all up, he's having the time of his life. Melinda lives for the Chief, and she puts him first, but even she is locked into this you-can-make-it crap, because she thinks he'll come apart if he can't be President. Smitty is gathering material for a book, he needs more memories before he can write his goddamn memoirs."

"You?"

"I'm scared. You know what we're screwing around with? War, peace, millions of lives. This is a job for a whole man, and it may be too big for any one man even when he's in perfect shape. But it's more than eyesight. It'll take Sven a long time before he can put things together in his head the way he used to. And we could all be a party to botching up the world."

"The President—" the blind therapist began, but the doctor cut him off.

"You think of him as 'the President,' with a capital P, because that's what he was when you met him." Abelson shook his head in frustration. "And all the people around here, 'Assistants to the President,' 'Special Counsel,' Secretary of this or that. They're not. They're guys like you and me, who put on offices, and all of a sudden they're very, very big. You should've seen them in the campaign. Scared, awed, all excited, like I am now. You ever see a play in rehearsal? My wife Barbara was an actress. In a rehearsal an actor walks around in a T-shirt and he's playing a king. All the others, the courtiers, they're dressed the way I am now, in jeans and whatever. You look and you ask, 'That's a king, this is a court?' And afterward, when they're all dressed up in costume and the make-up and the lights are on, you try to get in the spirit of the thing but you know it's all play acting. It's hard to believe the actor you saw in the T-shirt is a real king."

"But the President is really the President," Fowler said. "You know that."

"He's the guy in the rehearsal in the T-shirt, and now he's got the role of the President, and okay, he is the President—but he's also just a guy, just Sven Ericson, he's not superman. He's hurt, he can't do the job. Why do all of us try to keep propping him up? I'll tell you why, because we all have a vested interest. You too, Hank, you'd like to see a blind man overcome his handicap, and you'd like to play whatshername to Helen Keller. Don't let it get to you, friend. Think of your patient."

"He's not my patient, he's my student."

"Horseshit. We all pretend you're only teaching him how to feed himself and walk around, but you're a professional shrink. You have a responsibility that isn't technical. I'm not much of a doctor, Hank, but as one doctor to another, isn't this guy riding for a fall? And what the hell happens if he's in a depression and an international crisis hits?"

Fowler gave the matter some thought and Abelson shut up. "It's a fact," the therapist said finally, "that in most cases of sudden blindness, a period of courage and determination is followed by a loss of will, a letdown that is sometimes described as a depression. That has not happened to Ericson yet. It may not. It probably will, and fairly soon. Who's that?"

Melinda was standing behind them. "Which one of you can fix a cold? The President will see the one that can."

Abelson went in the Oval Office, told his patient to roll up his sleeve, and took Ericson's blood pressure, which was on the high side but normal for him. He stuck a thermometer in the presidential mouth, and as he was taking the presidential pulse, said, "I saw Buffie in the Mess at lunch. She's got the hots for you and wants to know why I've been keeping you two apart."

"Mpf," the President said.

"So if you want, I'll deliver her to the third floor around ten tonight. Your calendar says you're having dinner at seven with the A.G. Up to you."

Ericson took the thermometer from under his tongue, said, "Bring her around," and put it back.

"Do you good," the doctor agreed, as he pulled down a lower eyelid. "You got a cold, or what?"

"You are the personal physician to the President of the United States," Ericson said, taking the thermometer out again. "You get paid sixty thousand dollars a year by the taxpayers to keep the closest possible tabs on the President's health. What would they say in the medical schools of this nation if they knew you just said, 'You got a cold, or what?' "

"Ah, but can they edit a medical magazine?"

"If I could see, Herb, I'd read this thermometer for you. You want to send it to Bethesda?"

"You got ninety-nine and a half. That's a little temperature. You sound like you got a cold. Maybe what I've had the past couple of days. I'll come by every four hours with aspirin and an antihistamine. Here's for starters." The President took his pills. "Take it easy today, Sven. Save your strength for tonight."

Abelson left the Oval Office; Cartwright was waiting for him in the hall and asked him to step into his corner office.

"Doctor, I'm speaking to you in your capacity as the President's physician, about a matter that could affect your patient's health," Cartwright said formally.

"The doctor-patient privilege is thereby invoked," Abelson replied. "Take it to my grave. What's up?"

"I'm at a loss as to how to put this, Herb," Cartwright said uncomfortably. "I've learned a few things that the President must know. I'm going in there now to tell him that Bannerman is making his move. Secretary Fong has called a Cabinet meeting for noon on Monday, that's forty-eight hours from now, on the subject of the President's inability to discharge the duties of his office."

"Do they have the votes?"

"Bannerman's one, Fong is two, Reed is three. They need a fourth. Frangipani is solid for us, as is the Attorney General, who will make our case in the Cabinet meeting. Secretary Curtice was with us until this morning, but he has just had a disturbing session with the Secretary of Defense, and he could be wavering. I think he'll stick with us and the move will be defeated, but nobody really knows."

"The fact that they've called the meeting is a defeat in itself, isn't it? I mean, that's what we were trying to avoid."

"Well, you fall back to your next position. But that's not the problem I want to burden you with."

"How can I help?" Abelson wished the President would step down before the meeting ever took place, but now that the battle was shaping up, the President's physician would be a good soldier.

"Your relationship with the President," Cartwright began, "is close and personal. Mine is professional only. There is a personal matter that would be better for you to discuss with him than for me. It has to do with the young lady with whom the President is having an affair."

Abelson waited: What business of this was Cartwright's? "The young lady," said the chief of staff, "is a source of concern only because she is a potential leak."

The doctor made a face; if Cartwright only knew how discreet this particular lady had been, he would not worry about her as a risk to pass secrets. The episode on the campaign train, the accident and the previous days of blindness, the hushing up and the deception that hung so heavy on him when the second, permanent blindness struck—all this was tucked away in one girl's head, and had never been revealed.

"You don't agree," said Cartwright. "I am informed, reliably, that the President's official photographer had dinner in a small Chinese restaurant the night before last with Secretary Bannerman. The purpose was to recruit another member of the White House staff into the conspiracy to remove the President from office."

Abelson felt his heart constrict. He sat down, numbed. If Buffie worked for Bannerman, then Bannerman knew everything. It was all over. In a way, it would be a relief.

"Now, it is not a matter that should give us great concern," Cartwright was saying, "but it's something the President should be aware of. Either to cool the liaison, or to continue it knowing where the girl's real sympathies lie. Are you all right, Herb?"

The doctor nodded. Then he shook his head, he was not all right at all. Would they give Ericson a chance to resign honorably, or would Bannerman insist on disclosing the President's "lack of candor" during the campaign?

"Don't overreact," said Cartwright, who did not know the background that Abelson knew. "But I would be grateful if you found a propitious moment to warn the President about the security risk before he sees the young lady again. Frankly, though it is none of my business—and I recognize the emotional implications of this—it might be useful if he did not let on to her that we know she is betraying the President. It could be a useful way to send back misinformation."

Abelson had to see Hennessy. "I got to see Hennessy."

"He'll be here in a moment," the staff chief replied. "We're going to break the news together to the President about the Cabinet meeting. After that, I'd be grateful if you told the President about the private matter."

"No, I got to see Hennessy first. Alone. Please."

"If you wish," Cartwright said coolly. "Use this office, I'll just go and check the news tickers, see how the take-over attempt is being played."

When Hennessy came in and saw the jean-clad Abelson seated on the couch, he said: "What kind of outfit is that to wear to a fateful weekend?" Then he saw the gray look on Abelson's face and added: "Look, we're in a fight, we're gonna win, cheer up. Lucas told you about the way the voting is touch and go?"

"That's not the problem, Hennessy. Cartwright doesn't know the problem, either. I'm the only one in the world who knows the problem."

The special counsel sat down near the doctor. "Apprise me of the problem. I'm the lawyer, my privilege is like yours."

"Cartwright says not to worry about it or anything, but Our Girl Buffie is working for Bannerman. Tried to recruit one of the staffers to go to work for him the other night." Abelson let the ramifications of that sink in.

"Shit," said the President's special counsel. "That's a problem. You were right about that. Good, sweet Christ."

"Hennessy, you know what that means? That means Bannerman's got the President by the balls, doesn't it? It means there's no use fighting any more."

"Have you talked to Buffie about this?"

"No, I just this minute found out. I saw her in the Mess at lunch, I'm supposed to take her to the Chief at ten o'clock tonight."

"How long has Cartwright known?" Hennessy asked.

"Beats me. He doesn't know the significance of what he knows, about Buffie knowing about the previous blindness. Serves us right for not trusting him."

"That's a chance you take. Pull yourself together, Herb, this may not be the end of the line."

The doctor looked at him bleakly. He thought of a cartoon of two men chained to the wall of a dungeon and one saying, "Now here's my plan." Abelson sighed and said, "Okay, Counselor, where's the silver lining?"

"I wonder why we haven't heard from Bannerman on this, is all," Hennessy said. "If I were Bannerman, and I had Buffie's affidavit, I'd come in and ask for the President's declaration of inability on the grounds that he failed to disclose his potential for blindness before the election. I wouldn't horse around with Cabinet meetings."

"Too much for me," said Abelson. Much too much. Yet it was a weight off his back, in a way, with the end in such clear sight. "You tell Ericson, Hennessy," he said brokenly. "I haven't got the stomach for it."

The Special Counsel / 3

"Let me go in alone first," Hennessy said to Cartwright. "Herb doesn't want to tell him about the girl, so I will, and it might be better if it's just him and me."

"Of course," Cartwright said, "but can't it wait? We have this official notification from a member of the Cabinet that the President might be removed from office, and it's the sort of thing he should know about without any delay."

Hennessy did not feel that it was up to him to widen the circle of those familiar with the story of the previous blindness. That was Ericson's decision to make, whom to trust and how far. And he felt the President should know about Buffie's possible defection to Bannerman, so he could roll with that punch, before he was hit with the other. First Ericson had to cope with the unexpected, then he could handle the expected.

"Lucas, the thing with Buffie is not a casual affair. The Chief treats it casually, but she has a hook in him, and in his present state, it may affect him badly. Trust me on this, it'll only take a few minutes, and then he'll be better able to focus on the Cabinet meeting."

Cartwright nodded. "I shall be sitting by my telephone."

"One thing he'll want to know," Hennessy said. "Is Bannerman making it with Buffie?"

Cartwright looked puzzled. Hennessy put it another way: "I know this seems far-fetched, but are Buffie and Bannerman having an affair?"

"Oh, no. No, no." The staff chief stopped shaking his head and added: "Not to my knowledge. I believe their relationship is one of mutual interest, with him promising her the moon in the future."

"And who's the one she tried to recruit on the staff?"

"I gave my word I wouldn't say."

"Man or woman?" Cartwright was silent, and Hennessy did not press. The lawyer walked to the Oval Office anteroom, nodded to Melinda and Hank Fowler, and went in to see the President, who was on the couch in the small room off the Oval Office, the "telephone booth," alone, listening to the News Summary on earphones. Hennessy tapped him on the knee and Ericson removed the phones.

"It's me, the special counsel and intimate adviser, and I didn't come with a whole lot of good news. As a matter of fact, if this wasn't Saturday, it would be Black Friday."

The President shook his head. "I could have sworn

I handled the *Monitor* reporter perfectly. Maybe I'm losing my touch."

"How you feeling?"

"I've got a cold, and antihistamines always get me down."

"That's the least of your troubles," Hennessy said. "I have to give you a fill on something, and it's a shaker-upper. No time to ease into it, so brace yourself."

"It's something about Buffie." The President had been worrying about her. That, Hennessy thought, was not good.

"How'd you guess?"

The President smoothed his hair back, then literally braced himself on the arms of his chair. "Out with it."

"Cartwright has information that she's in cahoots with Bannerman. They had a little tête-à-tête night before last. She tried to get another White House staffer to leak stuff on you to them."

The President digested that. "Buffie and Bannerman," he said finally. "You suppose it's strictly business?"

"They're not making it together, if that's what you mean," Hennessy assured him, as if that had not been his own first concern, knowing Ericson. "But that's not the important thing. C'mon now, focus on this. She knows you were blind during the campaign, and we covered it up, and that's enough to get everybody very mad now. And here she is playing footsie with the man who's trying to dump you."

"That wasn't my first reaction," the President said numbly. "You're right, I'm not focusing on what's important."

"It's a strong possibility that Bannerman knows, and he's waiting to bomb us with this tomorrow or the next day. It's also possible that she hasn't told him yet, since he hasn't come to us to get you to step aside quietly."

"If she's on his team," the President wondered, "why shouldn't she tell him?"

"Let's go down the list," Hennessy said, doing what

he did best. "One: She's just a dumb broad and doesn't know how important that piece of information is. Two: She's a shrewd cookie and she's feeding out a little at a time. Three: She's playing both ends against the middle, doing something for him, keeping a secret for us, so she comes out on top no matter who wins. Four: She's developed a thing for you that makes it hard for her to really kill you."

"Run those past me again," Ericson said. Hennessy did, and the President said, "I like the last one best, but I have a hunch it's the third—both ends against the middle." He allowed himself a deep sigh. "Oh, Hennessy, that's a hard one to take."

"Don't tell a divorce lawyer about women," Hennessy snapped, hoping to dispel the ravaged look crossing the President's face. He tried a different tack: "As Dorothy Parker used to say, the screwing you're getting is not worth the screwing you're getting."

"That's a funny line," the President said mirthlessly.

"What has to be done now is this: First, we have to find out if she's blabbed. You're sleeping with her tonight, Herb tells me. So—find out." Ericson nodded automatically. Hennessy had the feeling that the President, in this state, would do whatever his counsel advised.

"Next, Cartwright is outside, wants to come in now to tell you how your loyal Cabinet is after your hide. He's with us, Sven, and I think we ought to fill him in on the previous blindness."

"No," said the President firmly. "Enough people know already. He'll tell his wife, who's a one-woman CIA. Keep it to those who know or need to know." Hennessy quickly revised his judgment about the malleability of Ericson in this state. Ericson picked up the phone. "Tell Mr. Cartwright to come in," he said to the operator, "Melinda too." To Hennessy, he said. "Let's go into the Oval Office for this, it's like a formal ceremony. Historic first. The revolt of the Cabinet." He shook his head. "It's one goddamn thing after another—they're going to go through with it."

He took Hennessy's arm and was steered to the

President's chair behind the President's desk next to the President's flag. Cartwright came in the hall door as Melinda McPhee entered from her office, and as they sat around the desk, the President said easily, "I hear Buffie has turned out to be a security risk. Good detective work, Lucas, we'll all have to watch what we say to her."

"We could actually turn that to our advantage, Mr. President," Cartwright said cheerily, "and pass back misinformation at an appropriate moment. A turned-around agent, that's what it's called in the movies. I imagine the CIA has a more bureaucratic term."

"Sex with extreme prejudice," said Hennessy.

"Melinda, I always told you not to trust that girl," Ericson kidded himself, "but you kept insisting she was a great photographer, a fine artist, would do wonders for my image."

"I'm sorry I forced her on you," Melinda said wryly. Hennessy walked away from the chairs drawn up around the President's desk, seating himself on the couch, observing the tableau. There they were, talking about a piece of ass, Melinda perversely delighted at the fall of somebody she cordially hated, Ericson heartsick at the political defection of the woman he needed to keep his pecker up at the moment, and whom he had an affection for besides. Melinda had probably guessed the big secret long ago, but she kept that knowledge to herself. Cartwright did not know the significance of Buffie's defection, only the details of it; but he was keeping a secret of his own from the President, the fact that Buffie was banging a particular White House staffer who had come running to the chief of staff with the news. Hennessy was certain of Buffie's sexual infidelity the moment Cartwright would not say if his informant was a man or a woman. Cartwright was not telling the President about the promiscuity of his mistress because he had given his word to his source, probably a friend of his. Hennessy was not telling the President of this deduction because that was the kind of elemental shock that might send a blinded man off the deep end. Tangled web-weaving at the

West Wing, the special counsel thought, among people on the same side. Surely the other side was being as deceptive to one another. And this little byplay going on as a prelude to the formal notification of presidential inability. Pay attention, Hennessy told himself, here comes the history.

"Melinda is making notes of this meeting, Mr. President," the chief of staff informed the blind executive, "and if there are any comments you want off the record, say so." Beats a tape anytime, Hennessy thought.

"At ten-thirty this morning," Cartwright stated, "I received a telephone call from the Secretary of Natural Resources, Michael Fong, to say that he intended to call a meeting of the Cabinet to discuss the President's inability to discharge his duties, as set forth in the Twenty-fifth Amendment. The purpose of his call, he said, was to ask if the President was aware of his inability."

Ericson said nothing. He slowly swiveled his chair back and forth.

"You will recall, Mr. President, that you anticipated such a telephone call or visit to me, and we discussed what my reaction should be in our meeting at five forty-five yesterday evening. You directed me to inform any member of the Cabinet who made such an approach that you had no intention whatever of declaring any inability, and on the contrary, no inability existed and you would vigorously resist any attempt to usurp your powers."

Ericson nodded, still swiveling. Cartwright continued: "I delivered your message to Secretary Fong, and the memorandum of that conversation, which the Secretary and I agreed to be recorded, is attached herewith." He handed a paper to Melinda. "As that memorandum shows, I did not seek to persuade him not to call the meeting. I made clear you were certain you had the ability to handle any charges that arose on the subject of inability. I transmitted your message that you were sure he was acting out of patriotic concerns but was profoundly misguided."

"You used the word 'misguided'?" the President asked.

"That was the word we agreed upon yesterday," Cartwright replied. "He then said how sorry all this made him, and that he hoped you would reconsider, but that he was sending a notification of the Cabinet meeting on inability to his fellow Cabinet members and to the Vice-President. He said that a copy of those letters, with a covering letter to you, would be delivered to me by hand by one P.M. today, Saturday."

"It's one-thirty now," said the President, feeling his watch dial.

"And I have the letters in hand. The meeting is called for ten A.M. Monday, here in the Cabinet Room. I assume there is no objection to letting them use the Cabinet Room."

"Be my guest," waved the President. "Sorry I can't be there."

"It would be an interesting constitutional question if you insisted on attending," Cartwright said. "I spoke to the Attorney General after Secretary Fong's call, and he said there was nothing in the Twenty-fifth Amendment that precluded your attendance. But he thought it would be inappropriate and undignified. He also said that upon receipt of his invitation at one P.M., he would write both Secretary Fong and you to say that he considered the convening of such a meeting to be in accordance with the Twenty-fifth Amendment, and intended to oppose the motion with every argument at his disposal. Then the A.G. said, as an aside, that he thought it would be a 'piece of cake'— that this was a power grab and a perversion of the intent of the framers of the amendment."

"At least some people have their heads screwed on right," muttered Melinda.

"Some piece of cake," Hennessy interjected. "You're seeing the A.G. tonight at dinner, Mr. President, you better let him know that this is very thin-sliced cake. He's in a real fight."

"Read me Fong's letter," the President said.

"It's an artful dodge," said Cartwright. "It's a letter

217

to me for you, not a letter to you. They don't want to admit you're competent to understand a letter to you. Here—'Dear Mr. Assistant to the President.' Never saw that salutation before. 'As a courtesy, I enclose copies of letters to the Vice-President and to my fellow Cabinet members convening a meeting of the Cabinet at 10:00 Monday June 17 in the Cabinet Room on the subject of the President's inability to discharge the duties and powers, pursuant to the third paragraph of the Twenty-fifth Amendment to the Constitution.' Here's the jab—'I would be grateful if you would seek to communicate the content of these letters to President Ericson, with the assurance that I, with every American, look forward to the day when he can once again assume the duties and powers of the presidency upon his recovery.' "

"The prick," said Hennessy. " 'Seek to communicate,' my left nut. That's a mistake, people won't like that. Lawyers' tricks don't go over with juries."

"You should answer this, Mr. President," said Melinda, "not Cartwright."

"Good idea, Melinda," Hennessy said. "Like 'My chief of staff was successful in communicating your message to me, and now would you please tell the Secretary of the Treasury, who is pulling your strings, to take the Twenty-fifth Amendment and shove it up his ass.' "

"Not in those words," Cartwright said. "But the thought has merit. A short handwritten note from you would be perfect—can you work it out on a piece of paper? Give that paper-guide of Dr. Fowler's a try."

"Nice thinking, kid," Hennessy added to Melinda from deep in the couch. "If you could only take pictures."

"The day we don't need you any more, Hennessy," replied the President's personal secretary, "will be a happy day for me and a great day for the country."

"Cut it out," said the President, too sharply, digging a handkerchief out of his pocket and blowing his nose. "That's just what I need now, on top of everything, a goddamn cold in the nose."

"Is there anything else you need to tell him?" Melinda asked Cartwright, making a high sign that they should all leave.

"I'm right here," the President said, "I'm not 'him.'"

"We used to call my father 'Himself,'" Melinda shot back.

"Easy, kiddo," Hennessy said, "Ericson here is not Himself."

"Okay, okay." Ericson was irritated. "It's just that everything is crowding in. I want to be alone. Send in Fowler."

Melinda led the group out of the Oval Office and sent the blind therapist inside. The two men stood near her desk looking out the french doors, as if unwilling to go to lonely offices. "Funny he should say that," Hennessy said. Melinda looked up: "'I want to be alone, send in Fowler'?" Evidently she had been turning that one over too.

"I never thought the day would come," said Cartwright, changing the subject, "when I couldn't pass on to the President an important message from the director of Central Intelligence." He held up one of the papers he had taken in and out of the President's office.

"It can wait," said Melinda.

"It'll have to," Cartwright agreed.

"What's it say?" Hennessy was cleared for everything.

"Up to now, the CIA position on the ambush has been that it was probably inspired by the Far Eastern powers, to break up our alliance with the Soviets. Now the Defense Intelligence Agency wants to object to that evaluation. They say the evidence points to a coup engineered by our friend Nikolayev. If that's true, the President will have to look at the world differently."

"So what does the director of Central Intelligence want?"

"He wants the President to know that Defense Intelligence has appealed the CIA evaluation, and that the possibility exists that their minority view is correct. In case a missile comes flying in, it's the sort of thing a President has to have in his mind."

"The rest of the world can just lay off for a couple of days," Melinda decided. "We've got problems of our own."

"Sorry, you're wrong," Hennessy told her. "Lucas has got to get to the President with that in the next hour or so, even if the Boss bites his head off."

Melinda shook her head. "The Boss is right at the edge. All that news today, and that stupid cold could be the last straw—no, back off. Tomorrow you can brief, part of the morning national security wrap-up."

"You're right, but you're wrong," Hennessy said, explaining: "From now on, we all have to operate as if the Cabinet has stripped him of the presidency, and the matter has been put to the Congress. They have three weeks to decide who's President, and we'll all be called as witnesses." Hennessy walked around to the side of the desk and faced them. "We're under oath, and the committee counsel says, 'Here is a vital communication from the CIA delivered to the White House at such and such hour. When was this given to the President? What do you mean, it was delayed twenty-four hours? What do you mean, he was over-loaded? What do you mean, he had a cold? Was it your decision at the time that the President was unable to handle such crucial information? Isn't that an inability to discharge his powers?' "

"You're good on the questions," Cartwright said.

"You better be good on the answers, Lucas. You better be able to say, 'First I discussed this at some length with the President's special counsel, asked the CIA for clarification on such and such a point, and then took it directly to the President, who ordered the intelligence community to re-evaluate everything or whatever the hell they do in a case like this.' "

"The son of a bitch is right," Melinda said in a weary voice to Cartwright. "I'll run you in right after he's finished with Fowler. It's not just what we do, but how it would look at a trial."

"And since we'll be challenging the Vice-President's assumption of power," Cartwright said, "we won't be able to claim privilege. I suggest we all keep only the kind of diaries we would be willing to turn over to the Congress."

"You guys look like you need a drink," Melinda announced. She went to the liquor cabinet and poured three stiff bourbons on the rocks. They drank without a toast.

The Therapist / 2

"The flower gimmick doesn't work when you've got a cold," the President said gloomily as Fowler made his way into the Oval Office to sit at the side of the large desk. Two days before, as part of training in the development of other senses—to help Ericson locate himself in a familiar room—Fowler had ordered a bowl of roses placed on the coffee table near the fireplace. The source of the scent became a landmark to the President, and strict instructions were left never to move the bowl from the coffee table; but as the man said, it was not helpful when the blinded person's sense of smell was blocked by a cold.

"Can't win 'em all," Fowler said in his soft voice. "Did you find the clock trick useful in orientation?"

"Yeah, that's a gimmick that works. As long as my hearing holds up, or nobody forgets to wind it." The patient was in a negative frame of mind. The "clock trick" was the use of known sources of sound as landmarks. On the President's desk, center back, was a pen holder with a small, fast-ticking clock. Across the room, near the hall door, was a freshly installed antique grandfather's clock, with a low, slow tick. At any time, even coming out of a nap or being turned around, Ericson could hear where his desk was and where the hall door was, and gauge his distance from each. If he wanted to greet someone coming in from the hall, he would move toward the right of the source of the slow tick; if he wanted to go to the bathroom, next to the telephone booth. he knew it was the doorway to the left of that sound. And when he wanted to sign something, he could hear his pen. To a visitor, the ticking was unnoticeable, part of the general background. Good, simple aids to help a blind man orient himself.

"How's your friend in the garden?" Fowler asked, since they were on the subject of sounds. The day before, the President made a point of listening to the blue jay in the Rose Garden; the bird argued with itself incessantly, like the jay in a Mark Twain story, and it added a dimension to the "regular" sounds.

"Damn birds didn't impress the *Monitor* reporter," Ericson muttered. "I thought I had that guy in the palm of my hand, but I lost him. I didn't like the way he kept asking questions in a loud voice as if I couldn't hear and maybe that put me off."

"That shouldn't have been a surprise," the therapist said. "You know sighted people do that. It was one of the first things I told your staff about, to keep their voices normal."

"It worked too well on Hennessy," the President observed. "He's a little guy with a big voice and he used to fill up the room with his booming. Now I can tell he's holding it down, and it's unnatural."

Ericson did not want to go to work on his daily training, the therapist knew. That was a switch; up to then, the President had plunged into the training exercises, concentrating on the tips and mental crutches that could get him through the beginning of blindness. Ericson had offered no opening for introspection, and Fowler was not about to push. The President knew he was being helped in rehabilitation by a professional alienist, and might come to use Fowler's nontechnical talents in his own good time.

"As part of the training in the identification of sounds," Fowler began, "I brought this tape player with me. I've been going around the White House recording the sounds you might hear in the course of a normal day. The slap of envelopes on a table, the air conditioning, the sound a Secret Service agent makes when he's walking compared to the sound of a secretary walking. You'll be surprised how—"

"Not today, Hank. Let's just talk." The therapist listened to Ericson's wheezy breathing for a while until the President said: "Lookit, I'm thinking of chucking the whole job." Fowler waited. "I haven't discussed this with anybody yet, and you have to treat it as graveyard, but maybe I ought to say the hell with it. I get the feeling everything is closing in at once."

"Gee, it's about time you started into a depression." Fowler reassured him. "I was beginning to think you were some kind of nut."

Fowler waited in the silence that followed for the President to follow up.

"If you could see, Hank, and if I could look at you, then you would see me looking at you suspiciously. What the hell does that mean?"

"The thing that worried me most at the press conference, and even in the briefing book getting ready for it, was your talk about your eyesight improving. If you believed that, you were in big trouble." The President used the silence technique on him, which showed he was learning, and Fowler continued: "I mean, most blinded people cling to the notion that their sight is coming back soon, that the solution is just around the corner. They won't face the fact that they won't ever see again. I wondered if that was what you were doing, running away from reality."

"I had not realized," the President said evenly, "that most people think that being blind is seeing black. I could detect some light and different colors from the moment I woke up after the ambush. So I called it an improvement, to give the public some hope and buy a little time for myself. I was lying, but I wasn't lying to myself."

"I figured that, when the ophthalmologist didn't know what to say." Fowler smiled at the memory of the eye doctor's puzzlement. "It's a shattering time for most people, when that realization sinks in."

FULL DISCLOSURE

"It's sunk in," said the President.

"Has it really? Here's a test: How long are you going to be blind?"

"How the hell do I know, am I an eye doctor?" The President's chair made the sounds of a man shifting in it: "How long are you going to be blind, Hank?"

"I'm going to be blind the rest of my life." The words hung in the air.

"I see what you mean. It's a hell of a thing to get formed in your mouth."

"Well?" said the therapist.

In a firm voice, the President said, "I'm going to be blind for the rest of my life."

"And productive, too, if you want to be," added Fowler quickly. "In case you're wondering why you prefer the sonar watch over the Hoover cane, or why you don't want to get a Seeing Eye dog, that's all part of your natural rejection of the idea of being blind. You don't want to wear the badges. When you've fully confronted the idea, you'll want to use all the help you can get in becoming more mobile."

"You may be right on the cane, but I've always preferred a cat to a dog, if I had to have an animal around. Answer me this, Hank—what scares you most?"

"Losing my hearing," the therapist replied. "If I couldn't hear, I might as well be a vegetable."

"Yeah," said Ericson. "That was the first thing I thought of, right after the clock gimmick worked. What else scares you?"

"President Ericson," Fowler said gently, "that doesn't come under tricks and gimmicks. You're asking me questions in my capacity as a professional psychologist, a specialist in the mental adjustment of the newly sightless. That's exactly what all the people in the White House tell me to forget. I'm here strictly as the fastest cane in the West."

"C'mon, I don't have time to lie on a couch and tell you the story of my life. I once could see, and now I'm blind. This morning, I thought I could bring this

whole thing off, and this afternoon, I think I may resign the presidency. Can you help me or not?"

"Sure, try me." Fowler would be able to ask his
own questions in time; his patient needed immediate
support.

"This feeling I have, it's not a depression, it's like a
desolation. I'm standing on a trap door. You say this
is a normal reaction, that it'll pass? I'll be my old self,
and all that crap, in no time?"

"I didn't say that," Fowler answered. "All I said
was that after the realization comes the depression, in
most cases. Then the blind person makes it back part
of the way, or he doesn't. Either way, he's never himself again, the way he knew himself to be. His self-
image has to change."

"Don't start with the jargon," snapped the President.
"Why can't I sleep at night, and why do I need to take
a nap in the afternoon like an old man?"

"You haven't adopted the habit of sleeping to time,
you're still sleeping to light. That's nothing. Night
watchmen learn to get sleepy in the morning and not
at night in a matter of weeks."

"Why do I feel so generally shitty? I've recovered
physically, I exercise every morning, still I never felt
so over-all lousy in my life."

"Emotional strain, constant, results in loss of body
tone," Fowler answered easily. These were the standard questions. "When you get over the strain in your
head, you'll feel better in your body. You never completely get over the strain, by the way—you always
have to be more on the alert than anybody. You have
to work your other senses, and it takes something out
of you."

"This is good," said Ericson, "you're making sense.
When this happened to you, when you went blind, did
you have trouble making decisions?"

Fowler decided the time was ripe for some firmness.
"You're not talking to just another blind person, Mr.
President, sharing a common experience. You're talk-
ing to what is called a shrink, who is a pro, who

charges fifty bucks an hour, who knows the reactions of thousands of people in these circumstances."

"Excuse me, Dr. Fowler," the President said, "but why are you having difficulty answering that question?"

Fowler quickly decided that the time was not ripe for firmness, and it might be better to supply the President with answers.

"I had trouble making decisions at first," the therapist said, "partly because I had been destroyed and didn't trust myself, and partly because my family and friends moved into making all the decisions for me. They had been dependent on me, and always resented it a little, and now I was dependent on them, and they enjoyed it. I started to slip into letting them do what they wanted with my life. Until I rebelled, and got some psychiatric help, and built up my ego and decision-making ability again."

"Is that what's happening here? Hennessy and Melinda, they've been terrific, but I have a funny feeling they're getting a perverse kick out of it, and I don't like that."

"That brings you to your next question," Fowler said, having overheard some of the conversations going on around the Oval Office by people who assumed blind people do not listen, "which has to do with sex. The answer is, for the next couple of weeks at least, sex is more important than at any other time of your life."

"Thank God," said Ericson. "I thought I'd lost all sense of priority. If there's one thing a President must have, it's an idea of what comes first. Just a few minutes ago, they were telling me about a Cabinet meeting to throw me out of office. I kept telling myself that the most important thing to keep in mind was the long-range welfare of the country, and second most important was the stability of the presidency. But I kept being reminded of a girl, and was she running out on me, and would I be able to be myself with her. And she's really not all that important to me, Hank. She was something to play around with, to be young again with, you know. Now she's important. Maybe she was important to me before and I didn't know it, but I doubt that. And there's a lack of priority even within my lack of priorities."

Fowler went "Um," to show he was still there. Ericson was beginning to direct the questions at himself instead of the therapist, which was a good sign.

"This particular girl—she's Buffie, the photographer, that's no big secret—happens to have a political significance, something she knows and something she's doing. But I'm not even focused on that. I'm worried about her screwing some other guy, or changing toward me—which would tell me I'm not Sven Ericson any more, but just a forty-eight-year-old blind man who has stopped not needing her any more. I know that girl, and I'll admit this to you, which I've never even admitted to myself—I get a kick out of controlling her life, and our relationship. One of the holds I had on her was that she thought I never needed her, that there were a dozen others anytime, smarter and prettier. I need her now, and if I let her know I need her, I'll lose her, and if I lose her—"

"—you'll have lost all your sex appeal? Your manhood? Come on now, that is such a predictable reaction you should be able to set it aside with no trouble."

"I am going to participate in more sexual intercourse than ever, right in the middle of all sorts of crises, and I am not going to feel guilty about it," Ericson announced, with a kind of carefree determination.

With Ericson's spirits on the climb, Fowler put in the question he felt was central to the situation: "Do you need this job?"

"The job needs me," the President answered too quickly. Evidently he was not prepared to explore those sensitive areas of his own power needs, and the way they had become amplified during his sight loss. "Flying blind, I can do a better job than Nichols and Bannerman. The job needs me a hell of a lot more than I need the damn job, don't ever forget that, Hank."

He sent in a shaft. "Your words are telling me one thing, Mr. President, but your hostility is telling me something else."

Pause. "Okay. What am I really thinking?"

"This isn't a mind-reading game, sir. What is important is that you know what you are really thinking."

"Hank, enough of my friends have been to psychiatrists, including my wife, who I don't intend to talk about—" Fowler knew from Hennessy that Ericson's divorced wife had committed suicide soon after the decree became final, and even though it had been duly reported it was not a subject Ericson ever discussed with anybody. "The trick is the patient keeps talking until he makes all these amazing discoveries about what went wrong in his play pen. Sudden flash of insight, and the problem is solved only because you've worked it out for yourself. Is that the pitch? Well, I just don't have time for it in this situation. If you have something to tell me about myself that I can use, spit it out, because now is when I need it."

"They'd throw me out of the union," Fowler said, lightening it up. Ericson was working his way into some serious self-examination, in a fairly normal process of denying it with great specificity, and the analyst was pleased. "So have you decided to chuck the job or not?"

"You crazy, Hank, or what? I only threw that out to see what you'd say. That's how Presidents stimulate free discussion. Actually, Dr. Fowler, I'm glad we had this little talk. Come to me with your problems anytime. See if you can cheer up some of the droops in the other offices around here, and have a heart-to-heart with Herb Abelson." He pushed a button under his desk: Melinda put her head in the room, and asked what he wanted. Fowler noticed that Ericson preferred to deal on the telephone with everyone else, but tended to summon Melinda in person. "Tell Hennessy I'd like him in the meeting at dinner with the A.G. tonight. And send Marilee in here, fast."

Fowler could sense the frown on Melinda's face. "Cartwright needs to see you right away."

"Okay, right after Marilee." The President swiveled toward his therapist. "These depressions that you say are normal—how long do they last?"

"In somebody with a strong ego, a couple of weeks. Then a substitute personality is formed to cope with the new circumstances. The old self-image dies—" No, this was losing him. "You'll have moments of euphoria, too, like right now."

"You're a good shrink, Hank, but this is no euphoria. Forget those momentary misgivings a little while ago. I sometimes get a little cranky when I get a cold."

Marilee, Smitty's deputy, appeared. Nobody ever knocked when entering the Oval Office, Fowler noted. The theory was that if you were not expected or invited in, you would not be there. But staffers entered in different ways: briskly, like Hennessy, or respectfully, like Cartwright, or reluctantly, like Melinda, or reverentially, like Marilee.

"Do me a favor," the President told her. "Get a hundred bucks from Herb Abelson. Go to Garfinkle's, or someplace, and buy an ounce of Ma Griffe perfume. Then buy a good silk scarf and wrap the perfume in it, and when she's not looking, drop it on Melinda's desk. It's her birthday."

Marilee made a properly simpering "ah . . ." and went off on the errand. "That's a nice gesture for Melinda," Fowler said, "but isn't it a bit of a put-down for the woman who's the deputy press secretary?"

"It's impossible to put down Marilee," the President said admiringly. "She knows I like her, but not how much. Neither do I." Fowler remarked that he was surprised the President knew which perfume to order, and Ericson surprised him back: "I'm an expert in perfume. When I was a kid, in the Army in Korea, I figured out a way to make money. I bought every top brand of French perfume cheap at the local PX and shipped it back to a friend in the States, Army mail with no duty, and he sold it for about twenty per cent less than the stores. Made a few thousand dollars when I needed it most, and became an expert in all the different perfumes along the way."

"You can differentiate?"

"Of course, it's just a matter of training your olfactory sense, Doctor. And I use a mnemonic to remember: 'Ma Griffe' means 'My Clutches,' and that's Melinda."

Fowler released his own tension with a laugh.

"You probably wonder why I fiddle around with trivialities when some people think the world is coming to an end," the President said. "My using Marilee in this way cements her relationship with Melinda, which gives me tighter control of the press operation. Being nice to Melinda when she least expects it makes her my slave for a month, and this is a time when a feller needs a slave. It's also evidence, if the time comes to show that evidence, of my thoughtfulness, and the kind of evidence that would hit home with every woman in the country."

"I was mistaken," Fowler said, "I thought you were being a nice guy."

"Now here's something for the book you're going to write someday contrary to all medical ethics, about how you saved the President. Trivialities are very important when big things are afoot. When nothing is happening, you tend to think big thoughts; when everything is happening at once, you tend to think about little, insignificant things. It's a way of keeping in touch with the familiar. Put that in your chapter about ways of establishing security."

Fowler shook his head. "I'm shaking my head," he reported. "In return, I wish I could give you political advice, but I can't think of any."

"You will. Probably be good—politics is the art of looking confident while you feel your way in the dark. Look, let's skip the sound training for today, huh? Cartwright's got something important. You keep collecting all the noises and the creakings and the things that go bump in the night on your handy recorder, and we'll go over them tomorrow. After church. Yes, this is a good Sunday for church. You better not tape anything else, though, the last guy who tried that got into trouble."

The telephone on the side of his desk made three bleeping noises and Ericson picked it up. "Yes, Hennessy. I can listen." After a pause, "Isn't that a little melodramatic?" Another pause. "I like it, too. Let's do it. You get to Herb Abelson and have him deliver her at nine sharp. Sharp, and then Herb goes immediately. My bedroom connects to the Oval Sitting Room. Tell the butler I'll take dinner there." Pause. "Tell the A.G. now, so he can plan, and we'll remind him at dinner that he's to be overheard starting at nine. You're a conniving bastard, Hennessy. What's the second item?" Pause. "You don't have to remind me, I'll do everything I can to find that out. Third?" Long pause. "I didn't know that. No, I don't think we should, that's a sucker play. They must know about the firing possibility, and they must want me to panic. But tell the A.G. we'll think about it, and that may be one of the things to talk about after nine o'clock. Okay, just make sure Herb delivers her on time." He put the telephone down and told Fowler part of the conversation, which the therapist took as an effort to show he was trusted. "The A.G. and Hennessy have been looking at the law. Seems that I have the power to fire any member of the Cabinet, or all of them, between now and the time the meeting takes place. The Twenty-fifth Amendment didn't think of that."

"I would have thought that the take-over group had thought of that," Fowler said. "They could have called the meeting in a hurry."

"That's why I think it's a sucker play," the President agreed. "They'd like me to try that. That would be directly against the spirit of the amendment—proof that I wanted to hang on to power at all costs. And the American people don't like a shady trick. If I pulled that, it would be called the 'Sunday Night Massacre.' There'd be a move to impeach—no legitimate grounds, no high crime committed—but it would add to the momentum. No, I have to let that Cabinet meeting go forward, but I can confuse the hell out of Bannerman in the meantime." Fowler could sense the Ericson smile. "Oh, that Hennessy's a bastard."

Lying in the President's bed, Buffie could hear muffled voices in the Oval Sitting Room—the "yellow room"—next door. She could also hear the ticking of a clock on the night table with the telephone, which struck her as odd—she thought all clocks were electric now—and a portable radio on low volume across the room next to the easy chair. Herb Abelson had taken her into Ericson's bedroom, and said uncomfortably: "He's having a dinner meeting with the A.G. and Hennessy in there, but don't worry, that door is always locked, the only way you can get into the bedroom is from the hall door. He doesn't know how long the meeting will last, but he said to stick around, he may drop in and out."

She smiled, slipped out of the bed to look in one of the drawers for his long cashmere cardigan. Dangling it from a finger, she posed naked in front of the full-length mirror, and then shook her head in annoyance at the idea that the man couldn't see a thing. Didn't even need a light in the room. The lamp was for the use of guests.

This was not the first time they'd used the sitting-room dinner routine. When the Administration was forming, and late meetings were going on almost every night, he'd hold a meeting there, come in to see her for a twenty-minute sex break, then go back into the meeting relaxed, refreshed, under no pressure, finally coming back to find her asleep and willing to be awakened. Those were high times, with excitements melding; you never knew whether you felt high because of what you had just done, or what you were doing, or what you were going to do.

She shrugged his sweater on and wondered what it was like for him now, in bed. He used to take pleasure in looking at her, and she had made the most of that, moving in absolute freedom, striking graceful, sometimes acrobatic poses, helping him produce an album of mental pictures. That was out now, and she hoped he kept those old pictures vivid in his mind. The mirror wasn't needed any more; she frowned, remembering how he would position her so that he could be a doer and a watcher at the same time. Did being blind mean he would get different pleasures? They say your sense of touch improves: Would he feel more through his fingertips?

The voices. Buffie had a moonlighting job to do, and maybe she could pick up something useful. Turning out the lamp, she sat cross-legged at the door to the breakfast room, and through the half inch of space at the bottom of the door could make out most of the conversation.

". . . no reason why we can't do it," Hennessy's voice was booming. "We fire 'em before they have a chance to meet. Nip the whole thing in the bud. Look. We wait till the last minute. Monday morning, Bannerman comes to the White House for the meeting, and Cartwright slaps an envelope in his hand that says he has been discharged and his deputy has been nominated Treasury Secretary. What's Bannerman gonna do? He'll scream like a stuck pig, but he's got no right to go into that meeting. Does he, Emmett?"

A deep, slightly southern voice Buffie did not recognize said, "There would be no doubt about the ruling. The amendment calls for the 'principal officers of the executive departments.' If a man's been fired five minutes before the meeting, he has no part to play in the proceedings. The job would be vacant and the seat taken by the acting head of that department, who would then be the one to cast that vote. But the fired man is out."

"Let's not decide until the last minute," said the President. "Hennessy, have the envelopes ready and

I'll tell you what to do when Bannerman and Fong come in Monday morning."

That would be something for Secretary Bannerman to know. Buffie listened to a lot of legal talk that was hard to follow, and then they got down to personalities she knew.

"Bannerman thinks he has the Secretary of Defense in his pocket," said Hennessy. "We know that's wrong. The boys in Wall Street are working on him, and he's beginning to weaken. Maybe Bannerman can put on some Wall Street pressure to shore Preston Reed up, but unless he does, the Defense vote will swing over to the President."

"I don't know why you guys are so worried," said Ericson's voice. "The Vice-President will be there. Even if we lose in the Cabinet, which we won't, he has the power to veto the Cabinet's decision to have him take over. And Vice-President Nichols has personally assured me that he would veto any attempt to take over unless it were unanimous. He hasn't told Bannerman that, though. Roy Bannerman is in for a big shock even if he thinks he's won."

"What are the three points we should take away from this meeting?" Hennessy asked in his loud, court-room voice. Buffie could hear him near the door, and concentrated on the review: "First, we're ready to surprise Bannerman with dismissals when he walks in Monday morning. Second, we're going to keep the pressure on Reed, and Bannerman isn't daring enough to apply Wall Street counterpressure. And third, we say nothing to anybody about the Vice-President, who's set to double-cross Bannerman if necessary at the end." There was some more talk after that but it made little impression on Buffie, who repeated the three points to herself so she would not forget. When she heard the chairs in the breakfast room scraping the floor, she took off Ericson's cardigan and inserted herself into the sheets.

He knocked once and opened the hall door, closing it quietly behind him.

"Hullo, Potus. Just taking a break?"

"No, the meeting's over. I have the night off."

"I left the light off," she said, " 'specially for you."
She saw his form move to the easy chair where he laid
his coat and after a moment, his shirt and pants. He
sat on the edge of the bed to get his shoes off and
then came to her.

"You know your way around this room," she said.
"I'd have stubbed my toe by now."

"When the lights are out, we're even." He flipped
the sheet back and ran his hand over her breasts. Then
he ran both hands over all of her, and she had the
feeling of being studied in the darkness.

"Potus, you worried? They gonna throw you out?"

He rolled her over and climbed into bed. "Sure I'm
worried, but not so much about Bannerman. Hennessy
and the A.G.—that's who I was with just now—have
it in hand. There's some foreign stuff that's kind of
serious, though. I think you're gaining a little weight."

She decided she must be growing a conscience because she did not like the feeling she had. In the past,
Ericson had used her, and played with her, and taken
all a man could want from a woman, but he had never
abused her or deliberately put her down or tried to
impose his ways on her. She had a nagging feeling
that he did not deserve what was being done to him
—at least, not from her. She had never double-dealt
anybody before; maybe she would never do it again.
She wished she could make it up to him.

"You've been holding out on me, Potus. Got another girl?" He never answered that, and she never expected him to, but she knew it pleased him to think
she was jealous. He circled his palm on her nipple,
which always got her going, she reached under him
and responded first tenderly, then savagely. For forty
minutes by the luminous dial of the old-fashioned ticking clock on his night table she rolled on him, bounced
on him, writhed under him, gentled him, and unexpectedly, because she intended to bring him to climax
first, she cried out in release: a long, thin, twisting wail,
as if from the third person between them. She didn't
know whether he finished or not; she started to ask,

then lay back again, knocked out. For a change, he didn't make some cool observation about the performance. She was hoping he might kiss her but he didn't have it in him, so she kissed him.

"That never happened to me before," she told him. That was a lie, but it was in the parking lot of the ball park of truth. She wanted it to be true. He said nothing and she could tell he didn't believe that. "Actually it happened four times before," she said clinically to recoup, "but never to me in our nation's capital." Ericson arranged her the way he liked, across his lap as he leaned back against the bedboard, where he could touch her nakedness when he wanted to, just as he used to enjoy looking at her when he wanted to. She knew he still didn't believe her about her orgasm. "If you want the truth, I always come like that with you blind guys," she added, and that got a chuckle out of him.

She found the curve of his jaw that fitted the curve of her forehead and nose, and slept for a while pressed close to him, an act she did with Ericson and no other; generally, when she finished making love, she turned herself into an armadillo, all turned-away backbone and protective elbows. She knew that pleased him, sleeping close, leaving her legs open and herself vulnerable, and that he often stayed awake while she slept a half hour or so.

She woke in a little while as Ericson extricated his arm and left the bed to get a drink of water in the dark bathroom. He came out, moving easily in the shadows, around the bed, to the window, then seating himself in the easy chair. Buffie got out of bed, too, stumbled around looking for his sweater, put it on and sat on his feet, holding his legs. "You're becoming a night person," she offered. "Moving around in the dark like a cat. You have an edge at night."

"I don't get to sleep until late," he said, hand in her hair. "Tonight should be better, though."

"You mustn't think about losing your job," she said. "If it happens, it happens, and it wouldn't be for long, you'd be back soon."

"Nope, once you're out, it's all over. There's no coming back. Would you stick with me, Buffie?" He asked that with an edge of sarcasm in his voice she did not like. She sat cross-legged, took one of his bare feet, and began slowly massaging it, separating the bones, making each toe feel like an individual and not part of a foot, not answering. She spent about five minutes on that long, knobby foot, getting into her work, and then rested it on her shoulder as she took the other foot in her lap.

"Defeat," he said after a while. Long pause. "Not many people know how to handle de feet." How long had he been working on that stupid joke? Was that what he had been thinking all the while she was freezing out her own thoughts? She gave a hard twist to his big toe. "Ow," he said, probably with a silly grin in the darkness, "but how do we turn defeat into victory?"

"You don't appreciate what I'm doing," she said. "I'm giving you this fantastic pleasure not because you want me to, but because I want to. It's a mode of expression that you'll never understand."

"Keep expressing," he said, "makes me feel like a king. Should a President feel like a king? Guess not. So what we're doing is wrong."

His toenails, she noticed, were getting long. "When was the last time I gave you a pedicure?" He had never had a pedicure before she gave him one, the second or third night they spent together last year. Few men did, and the sight of a free-spirited woman carefully clipping their toenails gave most men such feelings of dominance that they could easily be controlled.

"Right after the Inauguration, right in this chair," he recalled. "You cut right into the flesh of my little toe, remember? Blood all over the place. No more pedicures." He fell silent. He was probably thinking what crossed her mind as well, that cutting toenails now, while unable to see, could be difficult for him. "Well, no more amateur pedicures."

"Always think of me as an amateur," she smiled. "A professional photographer, of course, but an amateur everything else."

"Where the hell were you the night of the press conference? I could have used you then."

She stopped working on the second foot, and took the other off her shoulder. "Don't lean on me, Potus. I'm free, you know? When I'm with you, you'll always know it's because I want to be with you." She might as well be kind, she thought, adding, "There are times when I have to be alone. I take long walks, you know that."

"Dangerous around here."

"Nobody's gonna rape me, I have a long hatpin." They said nothing for a time. "When Harry Bok was here," she said, "there was an agent assigned to watch me at night. I didn't like that at all, Potus. That wasn't for my protection, that was for yours. That was keeping tabs on your property."

"Harry did that? And he never said a word."

She picked up his first foot, pulling gently on the big toe until it gave a satisfying pop. That was something-to-remember-for-Bannerman number one, the letters firing the Cabinet members when they walked in Monday morning. She popped his second toe, that was the Wall Street pressure on Reed, the Defense Secretary. She pulled the third toe, which would not pop, so she gave it up and went to the fourth, which popped, and that was a possibility of a double-cross of Bannerman by the Vice-President after the Cabinet had voted. Three pops, three points to tell Bannerman when she called him tomorrow. She was feeling better about disloyalty now.

"Can I trust you, Buffie?"

"Not completely. When you crowd me, I get a yen to play around. The next agent you put on my tail, I'll make a gift of my tail. I'll ball him and send him back to you with a great report. Some of those agents are super guys, Potus."

"You're picking a fight," the President said. "You want to be sore. Why do you want to be sore?"

She said nothing back. He had picked the fight, and when she responded, he accused her of picking a fight. Good trick, it made her defensive, even when she knew exactly what was going on. She had plenty to be defensive about, more than he knew, which made her doubly determined not to be defensive.

"I did such a great job of relaxing this foot," she observed idly, "and now it's gone all tense. Wasted effort. A perfect picture screwed up in the developer."

"Aah," he said and took his foot back and went to bed. She stayed at the easy chair.

"You don't mean 'aah,' " she said in the night. "You mean 'arrgh!' " She tried again. "Arr-aggh!" She made more guttural, leonine sounds and finally came to him in the bed and shouted "Ar-ragghrrorwr!" in his ear, bit his neck, plunged her head between his legs, and devoured him.

Afterward, tightly held, close in to his chest, she murmured, "We were in bed, how'd we wind up back in the chair?" She had not followed all that happened as clinically as usual; in the chair with him, completely in his lap, she had not remembered how they got there. "You're only treating me so good because you pity me," she told him. "I can't stand to be pitied."

"It's not that I pity you," he said, playing a game of reversing roles which they had used before to flush out what was suspected of being in the other's mind, "it's just I think it's right for a blind girl to have a lot of good sex."

"I need you desperately," she whispered. "Need, need, need. If I can't see, will I still be able to enjoy a good fuckin'?"

"You're better than ever, you don't need anybody." Ericson stroked her hair. "Your handicap is a turn-on."

"You won't laugh at me when I take off my arm?" she asked.

"Just show me the socket." He was getting good at this game. "I'll do anything you like as long as you never get possessive."

"But you must promise that nobody else will ever use that socket."

"Hell with that," he snarled, "I gotta be free. Only if you tell me I can bang anybody will I ever be faithful. Then I won't have anything to rebel against."

"Why won't you let me trust you?" she-as-he said. "I got this great big need to trust somebody, why won't you let it be you?"

"Because I don't ever want to be trusted," said he-as-she, "to be trusted is to be controlled. That's why I'll betray you every time."

"Not every time," said Buffie, "not on the big ones. You may let me down on the little things, but on the great big secret you'll protect me, but you know you're not a total shit, not on the big one . . ." Buffie caught herself; the game had sucked her in to saying more than she had intended. But it was not so bad for Ericson to know that even if she ratted on him a little, she would not ever speak about the campaign train incident and the hushing up of his blindness then. Passing a little poop to Bannerman was like balling a Secret Service man, a little fun, and a way of getting even or ahead in life, but it was not going all the way, like having an all-out love affair with somebody else. Some leaking, some screwing, okay; real betrayal, no, that was not in her. She figured Potus would understand.

After a while, he said, "The guitar still in the closet?" Long ago, during the campaign, he had discovered she could pick at the guitar and had a pretty fair voice. She left the instrument in his bedroom closet—couldn't lug it back and forth, it looked like a huge machine gun in its case—and she would play when she felt like it, usually after making love, and most often when he left her unsatisfied.

She always thought the guitar was something he put up with, because she was only learning the instrument and never put in the time required to play well. This was the first time he had asked her to play, and the idea pleased her.

"You King Saul, me David?" she asked from the closet, reaching behind the suits.

"You know your Bible," he smiled.

"I know my Bible movies," she said, leaving the closet light on to see his form, as she sat cross-legged on the floor. "Gregory Peck was David, strummin' away. Soothed the hell out of the old king."

"Soothe me," said the President.

She didn't know what to sing, but the talk of the Bible reminded her of the hymn so many folk singers used as a crowd warm-up, so, slowly, she began, concentrating on the chords rather than the words:

> *"Amazing grace,*
> *How sweet the sound,*
> *That saved a wretch like me."*

She found the right chord and continued more confidently,

> *"I once was lost,*
> *But now am found—"*

She stopped abruptly, dreading what she had almost done. She did not trust her voice.

"Why'd you stop?"

"Wrong song," she choked.

He came off the bed to her, touched her hair, felt her wet cheeks, and thumbed her eyes. He kissed her gently, and said, "Sing it through. Gimme that old-time religion."

It was more of a test for her than for him, so she did it sweetly and perfectly, not missing a chord.

> *"Amazing grace,*
> *How sweet the sound,*
> *That saved a wretch like me.*
> *I once was lost,*
> *But now am found,*
> *Was blind, but now I see."*

She swallowed a couple of times and laid her fingers across the strings.

"Everybody knows that one, huh?" He looked thoughtful.

"Just about everybody, Potus," she answered, her

voice steady now. "All the churchgoing Baptist types know it from singing on Sunday morning, and all the young people know it from the folk singers. It was number one seller for a long time. People kind of come together on that song from different places."

"Carter's favorite hymn," he recalled. "Like FDR's 'Home on the Range' or Truman's 'Missouri Waltz'— it's a good idea to pick out a popular song as your favorite."

"You do know it, then."

"I only know its politics," he smiled ruefully, "the way I know that 'The Battle Hymn of the Republic' became Bobby Kennedy's song for a while when it was sung as his funeral train passed through. But I don't know all the words to that, either." Ericson was seated in his easy chair, the deep one, his long arms along the arms of the chair, hands gripping the ends the way the statue of Lincoln did in the memorial. "I may be the only person in America," he mused, "who doesn't know the words to 'Amazing Grace.' I ought to —teach it to me, Buffie."

She taught it to him, easy enough, and afterward asked him why he wanted to dwell on stuff that reminded him and everybody of blindness.

"You must never run away from it, chum," he said. "People are afraid of being blind. It's the worst fear there is, deep down—except when you're already blind, and then the worst fear is losing your hearing. But if a blind man runs away from the thought of being blind, or if he winces at expressions like 'seeing eye to eye' or whatever—then he makes people even more fearful. That's a show of weakness. Fowler handles it right, and Hennessy is best of all—he looks for plays on blind words, and uses them, and we all laugh, or groan. That's best, to force the fear out in the open. Confront it."

She climbed on the bed with the guitar and sat close to him. He attempted to fondle her shoulder, but she knew he was thinking about "Amazing Grace," making sure he had the words memorized.

"Everybody knows that hymn," he said as if to

himself. "I can use that someday. The idea in it, too. Funny it passed me by, all these years."

"Blind spot?" she offered.

"Atta girl," he approved.

"Why you feelin' up my guitar, Potus?" That brought him back; he had been stroking the curve of the instrument rather than the woman next to him on the bed, which was ludicrous enough to cause him to turn his attention to the present and to the person happily cast in the role of teacher.

Ericson gave her what she could only think of as an affectionate hug. In the past, he had squeezed her, or touched her, or caressed her, or savaged her, but she could not recall a single affectionate hug. Buffie was not sure she liked it, either; it was paternal, out of place for a couple of lovers between sexual bouts.

"The little leaks can't hurt," he said. "You're right —just hold on to that big one and never let it go."

"You're beginning to mature, Potus," she said. "And someday you'll understand that it's no reflection on what we have together, for me to have a little something on the side, nothing serious, just some fun."

"No," said Ericson. "I'll never like that. A little screwing around is wrong, because it bugs me. A little leaking is wrong, too, but I'll live with it, because I have to." Only as long as you have to, she thought, and only as long as you make your girl feel a nagging guilt, because then she has to make it up to you. Now and then she loved the man, she decided, fingering the strings and reminding herself of the three items she would have to tell Bannerman in the morning.

The Treasury Secretary / 2

T. Roy Bannerman's Washington home was small but ostentatious, a brick dwelling on Massachusetts Avenue's Embassy Row, about halfway between the White House and the home of the Vice-President at the Naval Observatory. Mrs. Bannerman considered her sojourn in Washington to be a temporary exercise in public service by her husband and would not bring down from their New York home any of their art treasures or antiques, which was just as well with her husband, who had grown tired of them.

Sunday of the "fateful weekend"—that cliché was becoming locked into the political language—the Treasury Secretary spent the morning on the telephone, walking up and down the shaggy white rug of his long den, dragging a thirty-foot extension cord behind him. His clandestine White House source—that despicable little opportunist, Ericson's photographer/girl friend —had called after breakfast with three items of intelligence. First, the possibility of dismissals as Fong and Bannerman entered the White House Monday for the Cabinet meeting on the President's inability. Next, the need to shore up Reed at Defense with Wall Street pressure. Finally the potential double-cross by the Vice-President.

He ticked these off to Susan Bannerman, who responded seriatim: "The President would be a fool to play a trick like firing you. And you'd be a fool to lean on Preston Reed, or to have anybody else do it for you. About the Vice-President, I'm not so sure— he's the sort who'd go with the last person who spoke to him."

Bannerman appreciated his wife's good sense, and ordinarily gave weight to what she said, but in this case, the source of his information was too close to disregard and the tips too timely to dismiss. Besides, he had been distrustful of the Vice-President all along—the man was what Bannerman's father used to call a trimmer—and it would be just like Nichols to let the Cabinet go ahead, lay its collective head on a block, only to cross them up and veto their decision.

"Nichols could kill us," he explained to his wife. "The Twenty-fifth Amendment calls for the President's inability to be declared by 'the Vice-President and a majority of the principal officers of the executive departments'—that is, the Cabinet. So if we are able to swing over Curtice's vote, and win by four to two, that's a majority of the Cabinet. If the Vice-President doesn't veto, he becomes the Acting President at that moment, no matter what the President says. If the VP vetoes, then the action of the Cabinet becomes one huge embarrassment, and means nothing—because without the Vice-President willing to go along, the President remains President."

"I hadn't realized Ericson could be deposed, if he put up an argument, without the Congress in it somewhere."

"Don't use the word 'deposed,' " Bannerman said uncomfortably. "Ericson would still have the title of President, he would still technically occupy the office of the President. But the 'powers and duties' of the presidency would devolve—that's the word, 'devolve'—on the Vice-President as Acting President."

Susan Bannerman opened her saccharine pillbox. "And when Ericson says to hell with all that?"

"Then it goes to the Congress to decide the issue. If we get two thirds of the Congress to agree that the President is unable to function, within a three-week deadline, then he's out and Nichols remains Acting President."

Susan Bannerman poured some coffee. "The line spoken by Lady Macbeth comes to mind. 'If we should fail'—?"

" 'We fail!' " Bannerman quoted the next line, "and I must say, Susan, you pick the goddamnedest literary allusions. There will be no blood on any hands. If we fail, or if Nichols double-crosses us, then Ericson will see to it that all those who tried to remove him are ridden out of Washington on a rail."

"Why should Nichols turn down the presidency? He wants to be President."

"But he wants to be President for more than three weeks," Bannerman replied, "and he doesn't want to go down in history as a would-be usurper that Congress slapped down. On the other hand, if he turned down the chance the first time, he would be proving his loyalty to Ericson in the most dramatic way. Then maybe he could get Ericson to declare his inability himself, without a fight. Or maybe, in a second challenge, the Congress would be more likely to back the Vice-President up."

Bannerman's sensible wife shook her head. "But your old friend Arnold Nichols doesn't think that deviously. You do, Roy. Ericson does. Not Nichols."

"I put that nonentity where he is today," Bannerman said, allowing himself a slow burn, "and now, with the country's welfare at stake, he's thinking of double-crossing me."

"Somebody says he is."

"The President of the United States says he is."

"Do you believe him?" she asked. That stopped Bannerman: Maybe Ericson was lying about having a deal with Nichols. A possibility. One could not trust Ericson on this at all.

The butler announced Secretary Fong. When his colleague walked in, Bannerman wasted no time on amenities but went directly to his intelligence report. "Mike, we could be fired the minute we walk in there tomorrow morning."

"Not going to happen," said Fong. "He'd be inviting impeachment."

"That's what I said," said Susan Bannerman, pleased.

"We'd be better off with an impeachment proceed-

246

ing," Fong added. "To impeach, you need a simple majority of the House, two thirds of the Senate. But to declare inability, you need two thirds in both houses. I think we could get a majority against Ericson in the House, but not two thirds—not unless the Speaker went along, and he's not sympathetic at all."

"So Ericson would be well advised to fight us on his second line of defense," Bannerman said slowly. "Well, we'll come to that later. First let's be sure we win in the Cabinet."

Bannerman told Fong of the need to pressure Reed; Fong was ill at ease about that, but went along, "since you know how to read Wall Streeters better than I, Roy."

The Treasury Secretary went to the phone to begin operations in the field he knew so well, calling one lawyer, one retired banker, the current ambassador to the Court of St. James's in London, and the only living former Defense Secretary. With these persuasions under way, Bannerman reached the board chairman of New York Hospital, and asked that old fund-raising friend to have his doctors on tap in Washington that night.

"What about Curtice?" Fong wanted to know. "The only person who can deliver the Secretary of State is the Secretary of Defense, and we're not even sure of the Secretary of Defense."

"The best thing to do," said Susan Bannerman, "is to get Preston Reed working on George Curtice, and as he convinces Curtice, he'll convince himself. That's a lot better than pushing Reed. He's the kind of man my father was, who does not like to be pushed. All right, Roy, now I'll shut up."

"She makes sense, you know," Fong said to Bannerman.

"She was responsible for this rug," said Bannerman. "Did you ever see a rug more inappropriate for the home of the Secretary of the Treasury?"

"Pretty interesting carpeting," Fong said noncommittally. "Must have cost a fortune."

"The white shag rug is a disaster," she asserted

freely. "I admit my mistakes. Good luck with Reed, but I can't help thinking of my father. Now shall we listen to *Meet the Media?* They have a special on this fateful weekend."

The wall screen came on and they watched a panel of newsmen zero in on a pair of constitutional scholars:

Q: First of all, what is "inability," in the eyes of the Constitution?

Scholar: The Constitution leaves it vague. The word is used in Article II, Section 1, Clause 6, which reads: "In case of the removal of the President from office, or of his death, resignation, or inability to discharge the powers and duties of the said office, the same shall devolve upon the Vice-President . . ." and then later it changes "inability" to "disability" when it says "until the disability be removed."

Q: What did the Founding Fathers intend by "inability"?

Scholar: The vice-presidential clause was just added in at the end of the Constitutional Convention, kind of an afterthought. There's no definition of inability to guide us. And the legislative history of the Twenty-fifth Amendment isn't much help, either. The framers of that amendment thought it would be a mistake to tie the hands of future Cabinets and Congresses with a specific definition of "inability": They left it up to us, so to speak.

"That's good," said Bannerman. "The word 'inability' is what this Cabinet says it is. No precedent. We can create the criteria ourselves."

Q: Well, then, what do you think "inability" means?

Scholar: I think it means "inability to govern." In the debates on this amendment, the case of James Madison was brought up—he was nearly captured by the British in the War of 1812. If a President were taken by a hostile power, or kidnapped by some revolutionaries, the Twenty-fifth Amendment clearly intends for the Vice-President to assume the powers and duties. I would interpret that as meaning that the actual physical condition of the President is only one element in determining "inability." Especially in a nuclear age, we have to make a broad construction of that word, to encompass any eventuality in which the President is unable to govern. A combination of a physical disability such as President Ericson has, blindness, plus a feeling in the country that he cannot cope with the immense responsibilities of his job, would be grounds, in my opinion, for a Cabinet decision on inability.

Q: Do you agree, Dean McAllister?

Scholar II: No, I would put a much narrower construction on "inability." This amendment was not put in the Constitution to encourage usurpation. Once we start down the road of "inability to govern," we start saying an unpopular President can be brought down in mid-term because the people don't like him any more—and that is certainly not in the spirit of the Constitution. No, I would say "inability" is most specifically a physical ailment that is demonstrably, provably, and unarguably disabling —a coma, or obvious insanity, or something that is not in the gray area. When a President insists he is able to perform his duties, only the most unassailable proof of inability, by an overwhelming testimony of medical experts, should be used to challenge that assertion.

"You better have a strong medical lineup," Fong said to Bannerman. "Ericson will have his personal physician, and the blind psychologist, primed to say he's fit as a fiddle."

"Doctors will always disagree," said Bannerman. "This is not a medical decision, it's a political decision —not inability to walk and talk, but an inability to govern. That's the key."

Q: Isn't this all pretty fuzzy? In a "government of laws, not of men," aren't you saying that the Constitution still doesn't give any guidance to the Cabinet about ousting a disabled President—that it's strictly up to the men, and not the law?

Scholar I: Sure it's fuzzy—it was intended to be. The Constitution has to be flexible. That's why the amendment gives us an alternative to the Cabinet: It talks of "the principal officers of the executive departments or of such other body as Congress may by law provide." That's in case the Cabinet idea doesn't work out so well, and maybe another generation would prefer the decision to be made by a group of doctors, or by the Supreme Court. After all, there wasn't any Cabinet when the original Constitution was written—it may turn out to be a fly-by-night institution, or one incapable of making a decision.

Scholar II: As a strict constructionist, I would like to call your attention to the legislative history on this very point. The House Judiciary Committee recognized its inability to define "inability," and said, in this case, that we would have to rely on a government of men. Here it is in their 1965 report: "The final success of any constitutional arrangement to secure continuity in cases of inability must depend upon public opinion with a possession of a sense of 'constitutional morality.' Without such a feeling of responsibility there can be no absolute guarantee against usurpation. No mechanical or procedural solution will provide a complete answer if one assumes hypothetical cases in which most of the parties are rogues and in which no popular sense of constitutional propriety exists. It seems necessary that an attitude be adopted that presumes we shall always be dealing with 'reasonable men' at the highest governmental level."

Now, that puts the responsibility squarely on the Cabinet to act with a sense of "constitutional morality"—to seize power from an unwilling President in only the gravest case of obvious inability.

Q: Do you agree?

Scholar I: I think the passage just read by my colleague shows just the opposite—that the Cabinet has extraordinary leeway to do what they think is right for the country. Not to act according to the letter of a deliberately vague law, but to do what is right in their judgment. That's what morality is, a sense of what is right. . . .

"Perfect, perfect," said Bannerman. "They'll be arguing all day long, and when you come right down to it, it's entirely up to us. Turn that noise off, will you, Susan—Mike and I have to work out our strategy for tomorrow."

The Secretary of Natural Resources started to pace across the room, nearly tripped on the shag rug, came back, and sat down. "You ought to mow that lawn," Fong murmured, and then came to the reason for his visit:

"It's all going to hinge on George Curtice, Roy. You'll run in your doctors, and I'll make all the historical points I've been studying, and we'll put up a respectable show for the memoirs. But what goes on in that room ain't going to change any votes."

"So the question is—what heat can we put on the Secretary of State, remembering his particular sensitivities against being told what to do?"

Fong nodded. "There's something weird going on in our relations with the Soviet Union. Reed told you what the CIA thinks, and how Defense Intelligence disagreed—the minority view is that Nikolayev was behind the ambush. If that's true, Curtice is way out on a limb, since he's Nikolayev's buddy. This morning, Reed is telling all this to Curtice, and it's going to scare hell out of him."

"That's part of the plan," Bannerman nodded. "Reed is to assure the Secretary of State that we'll stand behind his necessary actions after the ambush, whatever they were, and that Ericson might not."

Fong shook his head, worried. "Curtice is really going to be torn. I'll see him tonight, and again first thing tomorrow morning, and I'll tell him that his only safe haven is with us. I'll remind him of the Lansing episode—"

"What was that?" Susan Bannerman, halfway out of the room with the coffee tray, seemed to recognize the name.

"When Woodrow Wilson was flat on his back in 1919, and his wife and a couple of close aides were making his decisions, the Secretary of State—Robert Lansing—tried to get the President to step aside and turn his power over to Vice-President Marshall. As soon as Wilson could make an appearance, the first thing he did was to fire Lansing."

Bannerman's wife smiled grimly, recalling the aftermath in family terms. "And that was the end of the Lansing family influence for more than a generation, until his nephews—Foster and Allen Dulles—came back under Eisenhower. When a President drives you out for disloyalty, the stigma lasts a long time." She marched out.

"She has a point," Bannerman noted.

"No, Roy, that's not the point," Fong said. "The point is that if you strike at a king, you have to kill him—that was Oliver Wendell Holmes, I think. None of us can afford to lose, or there'll be a hell of a bloodletting—we'll all be ruined, and our names mud."

"Curtice must be made to understand," Bannerman said with deliberation, "that if I go down, Curtice will not reap any benefits. I'll make it my lifelong occupation to see that he is ruined, that the first black Secretary of State will be remembered as a coward and an ignominious failure."

Fong took off his shoes so that he could pace around on the rug. "I'll be sure Curtice knows that, but I'll be sure it's not in the nature of a threat. That'll be the trick of the week. Before I forget—you got that abstention opinion?"

Bannerman had asked the dean of Yale Law School for a letter on the subject of abstention at the Cabinet meeting to consider presidential inability. Could a member of the Cabinet refuse to vote, or did it mean that the next man in his department could be called upon to cast the vote? Did the Cabinet member have the franchise personally, or did that vote belong to the department, with the requirement that it be cast?

"I'll try to have the opinion in hand," the Treasury Secretary said. "Curtice should be able to abstain, if that's what we need for a majority."

"We'll need it, all right. The Vice-President will have to so rule, if the A.G. objects, and if he's smart, he will. And Duparquet is one smart cookie." Bannerman agreed; the Attorney General, Emmett Duparquet, was both resourceful and skilled—a good advocate for the President, a tough adversary for them.

"Don't you worry about Vice-President Nichols, Mike. He's with us all the way."

Fong smiled. Bannerman knew that as a former governor and long-time politician, Fong was aware of the Vice-President's reputation for vacillation; for credibility's sake Bannerman added: "All the way, as long as he thinks we'll win."

"The VP is your responsibility," Fong said, putting on his shoes to go, "and the Secretary of State is mine. Win or lose, I'll have a clear conscience, because I think Ericson is wrong to try to stumble through this way. But Roy, I'll tell you the truth, I don't have your resources to fall back on in case we don't win."

"We'll win," Bannerman said firmly. "In the Cabinet, and then if need be, in the Congress. But win or lose, ours is a lifelong alliance, Mike. The Bannermans never forget a friend. We learned that from the Rothschilds, the Kennedys, and the Rockefellers."

"Good company," said Fong. "And as for you, remember Robert Lansing."

The Attorney General

As always, he came to court early. When Emmett Duparquet practiced criminal law, he liked to sit in the courtroom an hour or so before anybody else arrived, getting a sense of the scene, absorbing familiarity with a case through familiarity with a locale. In his mind, he would people the jury box, cast the empty chairs in the dock and on the bench, and try out his opening argument in silence long before the bailiff's cry.

The Attorney General had arrived before the camera crews were ready to take statements, and only the radio and pencil press caught him on the way into the West Wing. "I saw the President over the weekend, I spoke to his doctors, I am convinced no inability exists." When he was asked if the move was a disloyal act by a "cabal," he would not take the bait: "The Cabinet has a duty to discuss this matter frankly and fully. That's what I'm prepared to do."

Duparquet was not as prepared as he would have liked to be, but there had been no time for the exhaustive analysis and preparation that a historic case like this deserved. At his direction, the Solicitor General, a respected and nonpartisan former law school dean, had whipped together a memorandum of law for the Cabinet members, which had been distributed Sunday night. Essentially, the memo spelled out the procedure to declare inability, stated how the Vice-President would become Acting President the moment he cast his vote with a Cabinet majority, and set forth the method the deposed President would have to challenge that decision. The Vice-President would continue as Acting President until Congress decided one way or the other within twenty-one days.

In the empty Cabinet Room, Duparquet stood behind his chair, to the right of the Vice-President's chair, across the table from the President's chair, which would be unfilled. The morning summer sun streamed through the french doors; twenty steps away, the President was working in the Oval Office, and would continue to be there, ostensibly being briefed on foreign developments, throughout the morning. The Attorney General, who had been given command of the campaign to keep the President in office, had decided it would be best for Ericson to make a show of carrying on normal business. Nobody would believe he was not secretly listening in, but symbolism counted in the stage directions for great events.

The Attorney General walked slowly around the room, as he would later, looking at the phantoms in the chairs, forming his defenses. For a defense it would be: The burden of the argument was on the prosecution, on the members who wanted to declare Ericson's inability. But the prosecutors had an edge here that did not exist in the criminal courts where Duparquet had spent his life first as counsel, then as judge: They did not have to prove their case "beyond a reasonable doubt." He would insist they do that, of course, but they could insist—with equal force—that if enough of a doubt existed of the President's inability to function, then the Cabinet members would be obliged to vote to remove him. No body of law to draw upon; virgin legal territory.

He was not addressing a jury, the tall Floridian reminded himself: The metaphor of Cabinet as jury was not apt at all. Most of the votes had already been decided. The empty chairs were filled with ghostly Red Queens: Bannerman and Fong, with Reed probable, in favor of removal; Frangipani and the Attorney General, firmly against. The sixth vote was that of Secretary of State Curtice. Duparquet moved behind that chair, to the right of the President's. If Curtice held firm against removal, there could be no majority; if he went with the Bannerman group, Ericson was deposed, or at least until the matter went to Congress. If he sought to abstain, the Attorney General would fight against his right to do so, because that would give a three-two majority to the removal forces.

The case, then, was not to be decided by a jury, but by a single judge—one man, George Curtice. The presentation had to be made to him, remembering his wish not to be the one to have to make the decision. "If you think you're going to lose," Lucas Cartwright had told Duparquet when he came in a few moments ago, "call a recess before the vote. I may have a handle on Curtice. I would hate myself for using it unless I absolutely had to."

In a sense, the appeals judge was present: The Vice-President, who would chair the meeting and undoubtedly say very little after calling it to order, was Duparquet's second line of defense. From the Secretary of State's chair, the Attorney General looked across at Nichols' place at the table: Perhaps he could be swayed by argument. The Attorney General would have to present his defense in a way that—if he lost Curtice and the Cabinet—he might still win with the Vice-President's veto. Not easy: Curtice would resent the certainty and firmness to which Nichols would respond favorably.

The Attorney General strode out of the Cabinet Room, through the connecting office to the Oval Office, where Ericson sat, coffee in hand, talking to Hennessy. In olden times, when political cronies were Attorneys General, Hennessy would probably have had the job Duparquet now held.

"Here comes the star quarterback," said Hennessy to Ericson, "for final instructions from the coach before the big game. Punt and pray, sez I."

The President did not look well. He had evidently spent a bad night: a gray cast soured his face and he kneaded the knuckles of his large hands. Duparquet was glad he would not have to use him as a witness. Ericson said anxiously, "See the papers, General?

Lousy stories. And all the television this morning, everybody's all keyed up like they're going to a good hanging."

"We're going to win," said the Attorney General, and meant it, though not as decisively as he said it. "I'll bet my job on that."

Hennessy snorted. "You already have. If you win, you have the next Supreme Court seat all locked up, and if you lose, Bannerman will make you ambassador to some country where they boil ambassadors in pots."

"I hadn't realized the stakes were that high," said Duparquet. "I thought this was only for the presidency." He did not like the way Ericson was reacting; he could tell Hennessy did not, either.

"Mr. President," the Attorney General, standing before the President's desk, said formally, for whatever leaks Hennessy would leak or memoirs the President would write, "the Cabinet is about to meet on the subject of declaring your inability to discharge the powers and duties of your office. It is my view, from my personal observation of you these past few days, that such an action—if taken by the Cabinet and the Vice-President—would be the first usurpation of presidential power in our nation's history. I intend to resist it with every resource at my command. Is there anything you want me to know, beyond all you've told me, before I go in?"

"Don't lose Curtice," Ericson said, "and remember that Bannerman put a lot of heat on Reed. Preston might not have liked that." Those tactical tips were not the sort of historic advice Duparquet had in mind. He shrugged and turned to leave.

"Win it for the Gipper," said Hennessy.

"General—" Ericson called after him. He stopped at the door. "You're not acting in the interests of one President this morning. You are serving every President who follows—and one of them will be another Lincoln, under the most savage attack. Think of him."

"I will, Mr. President. And that was spoken like a President."

It was five minutes to ten, and all the other Cabinet members were in the room. The Vice-President, per protocol, arrived last, and took his seat; Duparquet and the others followed.

"Before we get started," Vice-President Nichols said to nobody in particular, "I wonder if the Cabinet thinks this meeting ought to be recorded, or verbatim notes taken, or what."

"I would have no objection," the Attorney General stated, "to having the entire proceedings recorded by the White House Communications Agency. Certainly there is a public interest in what is said here on such an occasion, and a complete record might obviate any misunderstandings later."

"This is a Cabinet meeting," Bannerman put in. "Cabinet meetings are never recorded. We get a page of minutes and that's all."

The Vice-President looked around for other comments. Secretary Fong said, "I think we should conduct this Cabinet meeting just as we do the others. We can all speak more freely if we know that every word is not being taken down."

"I would have no objection to that, either," the Attorney General said, being agreeable. "No legal requirement exists for such a record. Since there is no staff present, Mr. Vice-President, you might wish to assign the job of taking the usual minutes to a member of the Cabinet."

"Andy, would you do that for us?" The Vice-President chose the Secretary of Human Resources, Angelo Frangipani, who nodded. The Vice-President cleared his throat. "It is now 10:05 A.M. Monday, June 15, and the Cabinet is in session. The meeting was called at the request of Secretary Fong for the purpose of discussing the possible inability of the President to discharge his powers and duties." Nichols sat forward, concentrating, the picture of a man being eminently careful and fair. "This is a sad occasion, that the need for this meeting has arisen. In the light of the seriousness of our meeting, I would like to go back to the Eisenhower Administration's tradition, and begin this Cabinet meeting by asking you all to join me in a moment of silent prayer."

Good touch, Duparquet thought; uncriticizable, and Nichols could hardly put his foot in his mouth during a moment of silent prayer.

"I am advised," said the Vice-President, breaking the silence, "in this excellent memorandum of law prepared by the Solicitor General, that for the purposes of this meeting, the Vice-President is not a member of the Cabinet. The Twenty-fifth Amendment says that I sit 'with' the principal officers of the executive departments in this meeting, and I understand that I have the power to veto any action you may take. Mr. Attorney General, is my understanding of the law correct?"

His understanding was slightly off, the Attorney General knew, but he would correct him without seeming to do so: "That's right, Mr. Vice-President. If a majority of the Cabinet votes to declare the inability of the President, and to invest you with the powers and duties of his office, you have the power to veto that action. I should add that there is no specific direction in the Constitution as to who chairs this meeting, although it is my opinion that the intent of the authors of the amendment was that it ought to be chaired by the Vice-President. For the record, I think the Cabinet should now elect you as chairman of the meeting."

Bannerman so moved, Frangipani seconded, all voted aye, and the Vice-President said, "I intend to have very little to say at this meeting. Secretary Fong, you convened the group, the floor is yours."

"Let me begin," Fong said solemnly, reading from notes, "with the question that was asked at the Constitutional Convention, August 27, 1787, by John Dickinson of Delaware, on the subject that faces us today. Mr. Dickinson read the clause about the Vice-President taking office upon the 'death, resignation, or inability' of the President to act as President 'until the disability be removed,' and he asked: 'What is the extent of the term 'disability' and who is to be the judge of it?'

"I submit that the first part of that question has never been answered. We are bound by no definition, constitutional or historical, of the word 'disability' or 'inability.' All attempts to define it specifically, to tie our hands today, were rejected by the authors of the Constitution and the Twenty-fifth Amendment.

"The second part of that question of Mr. Dickinson —Who is to be the judge of disability?—has been most clearly answered in the amendment. At this stage, this Cabinet is the sole judge of that. It is our solemn responsibility, and ours alone, to make certain that the presidency is always filled by a person who is capable of fulfilling its functions. We cannot escape this responsibility. Considerations of friendship, of gratitude, of sentiment, must all be set aside before the single consideration of our duty.

"Therefore," said Fong, making his first point plain, "there is no definition of 'disability' to guide us and we are the sole judges, at this moment, of whether or not there is a President in office able to carry out his duties. Mr. Attorney General, in your capacity of the nation's chief law officer, and not as the advocate of the particular President in office, do you agree with this interpretation of the Constitution?"

"You go ahead and make your case, Mike," Duparquet said in a relaxed voice. "I'll take it apart later. But you're doing fine." He was not about to get involved in a point-by-point legal argument with the Bannerman group at this stage. He knew it was harder to make a case alone, and he would let them alone. Nor would he adopt the formal attitude of a court proceeding, or the stiffness of an inquisition. This had to be treated as a group of friends gathered together to chat about overthrowing the President.

"Since the Attorney General prefers to keep his legal opinion to himself," Bannerman said, picking up the case from Fong, "I would like to say that the Twenty-fifth Amendment could not be any plainer than it is on this point: We have a duty to perform, painful though it may be. I've fought against Ericson for the nomination, as you all know. I've fought on his side during the campaign, and you know that too. I consider him a friend, and if fate had not decided otherwise, he could have been a damn fine President. But the ambush took place, the tragedy struck, and now he's incapable of making the decision he has to make in the best interests of the country. We have to make that decision for him."

"But what if we're wrong?" asked Frangipani. "That's a helluva step to ask us to take, to strip the presidency from a man the people elected and give it to somebody else. Especially when he insists he's capable of carrying on." Duparquet wished Frangipani would shut up, but said nothing.

"If we're wrong," Fong said, well prepared for the point, "the amendment has made it possible for Congress to set it right. If only one third of the Congress agrees that the President is not disabled, then he gets the presidency back, and no harm done. But if we're right, the President is disabled—and we fail to do our duty—then there is nobody to make the right decision. If we fail here, right now, then we deprive the Congress of the opportunity to give this urgent matter the consideration it deserves."

Score one for them, the Attorney General thought, although it might have been a point better made at the end.

"Besides, Andy," Bannerman added, talking at Frangipani but talking to Curtice and Nichols, "we're not 'stripping' him of his office. We're seeing to it that the other man elected by all the people as his running mate steps into his office until Ericson's well enough to come back. And there is a procedure for him to declare his regained ability, and if the Vice-President agrees, he gets it back without further ado. If the Vice-President doesn't agree, he can go back to the Congress, and if one third—just one third—agree with Ericson, then he gets his presidency back. The presumption that he is *not* disabled is always on the President's side. If his eyesight improves, or his—well, say his head clears, and he can operate without these terrible mistakes—then it becomes our duty to say so publicly and help him get back his job."

Score one for us, the Attorney General thought. That was a point he would use on the Defense Secretary, who looked uncomfortable, probably contemplating the congressional challenges and the danger of having the presidency in doubt for an extended period.

"Now let's get to the heart of the matter," Fong said. "Is the President disabled or not? To help us decide, I refer you to page 309 of the Legislative History, after it says that we, the Cabinet, are best able to decide. 'It is assumed,' it says, 'that such decision would be made only after adequate consultation with medical experts.' I would like to make a motion, Mr. Chairman. In view of that specific direction by the framers of the amendment—"

"Mike, why don't you hold off on the motion?" said George Curtice. "And let's just talk about what you have in mind. Maybe it won't need to come to a vote."

"Good idea," said Bannerman.

"Okay, the point is this," Fong said. "The only medical advice we presently have access to, or who have access to the President, rests with three men. One is the third-string eye doctor at the local naval hospital. Another is the President's personal physician, who is a nice guy and an old crony, but who we all know is in that job because he is the President's buddy and not because he's any kind of doctor. And the other is a 'psychologist,' whatever that means, but it does not mean he's a psychiatrist with an M.D. after his name, and he was hired to teach the President how to work a long white cane and things like that. Now, that's not much of a medical team for the President of the United States. If we're to decide on his ability to function, we need the best advice from the most prestigious doctors in the country, in both the physical and the mental areas, as called for in that legislative report I read."

"So what's your idea?" Curtice asked.

"To have the President examined today, now, by a

panel of the leading doctors, who Secretary Bannerman and I have arranged to be in Washington and available. The very top men, unassailable credentials. They won't make our decision for us, but we can at least make an informed judgment—if the President will permit himself to be examined by them. If he won't"—Fong threw up his hands—"then he's pretty much admitting his disability."

The Attorney General shook his head in wonderment, and kept shaking it until all eyes were on him. "The President is blind," he said quietly. "I'll stipulate that—he's totally blind. He cannot see. Certainly, he can tell the difference between light and dark, we all saw that proven most dramatically, and the improvement may continue—but nobody is suggesting he is not totally blind, in any legal definition of that term. Now let me see if I understand you correctly, Mike— do you propose to march in a couple of dozen of the leading eye doctors in the country to tell us, over and over again, that he really is blind? We already know that, Mike. You think that this Cabinet is going to know that any better if a parade of doctors comes in here and each says, one after the other, 'Man, is he ever blind! He's *really* blind!' Is that supposed to panic us, or something?"

"You don't understand, Mr. Attorney General," Bannerman said. "Some of the President's close advisers, who want to cling to power at any price, have been spreading the word in the press—and indeed, have gotten the President to go along—saying that Ericson's eyesight is improving. That raises false hopes. That falsehood ought to be demolished, and your reluctance to subject your client to expert medical examination shows just how false and misleading it is."

"First of all, Mr. Secretary," Duparquet replied, "perhaps I'm oldfashioned, but somehow it strikes me as—good taste—as we sit here in the Cabinet Room of the White House, to refer to the President of the United States as 'the President,' and not as 'Ericson.' "

"I stand corrected," Bannerman conceded immediately.

"Second, I consider it a personal affront for you to talk of the President as my 'client' in this matter. It betrays a certain misunderstanding of constitutional roles. I am here as a member of the Cabinet—the Ericson Cabinet, if you will—and I sit in my own right, and not as advocate of another. Like you, I have one vote. I make no secret of my position, but I deeply resent your impugning my motives by saying I act not as a member of the Cabinet, but as a lawyer for a 'client.'"

"Come on, General," Fong said, "don't get on your high horse—"

"Third," continued Duparquet, "you can bring every single eye doctor in America in here to hold up his hand and swear that the President is blind as a bat, and I will ask them each one question and one only. That question will be: 'Doctor, will you stake your professional reputation on the *im*possibility of this patient's eyes improving in the months and years to come?' You want to see some fast backtracking? Then, if you feel like a little more cross-examination, I'll ask, 'Doctor—four weeks after an accident, just how certain can you be that a blinded person's eyes will or will not improve? Ten per cent? Forty per cent? Sixty per cent? And you want us to throw a President out of office on that kind of a fuzzy possibility?'"

"He has a point, Roy," said Defense Secretary Reed. "He's stipulated that the President is blind—totally, legally blind. I think we can all agree that the possibility of his improvement is a matter of pure guesswork. It's today we're thinking about. He's blind right now. If he sees again tomorrow, then he has a remedy in the Constitution, he can recover the presidency. We're not really in disagreement about eye doctors. Let's move on."

"Now as to his general health," the Attorney General went on, not waiting for any counter to Reed's suggestion, "Mike here has suggested that the President's personal physician is incompetent."

"I didn't say that—"

"You suggested it, we all heard you and got the point."

"I suggested that many more competent doctors exist."

"Sure," the Attorney General said. "Mike, I'm sure it was inadvertent, but without meaning to, you pulled a fast one on us. You remember your quotation from the Legislative History? How about reading it again, and this time, finish the sentence—don't cut it off."

Fong was uncertain. "What I read is what I have here. I didn't bring the original document."

"I'll finish it for you," said Duparquet, who had memorized the line that was sure to come up at this meeting: " 'Such decision would be made only after adequate consultation with medical experts'—now here's the part you were not given—*'who were intricately familiar with the President's physical and mental condition.'* " The Attorney General let that sink in: The Bannerman group had been caught playing an out-of-context trick, and it had to concern Curtice, who was the judge. Then he added, "That changes the meaning, of course. We're not talking about the greatest world experts in medicine, we're talking about the doctor who knows the President's health best. 'Intricately familiar'—"

"I suppose they meant 'intimately familiar,' " the Vice-President said, and then looked as if he wished he had said nothing.

"You're right, Arnold," said Frangipani. "Read 'intimate' for 'intricate.' We're talking about a human being, not a machine."

Duparquet rolled with the change in mood; it would not do to hit hard when the group wanted some relief from tension. "You know," he said conversationally, "there's a mistake in this Twenty-fifth Amendment. The only typographical error in the Constitution. And it's about us." He picked up a copy of the amendment, which they all had in front of them with the memorandum of law: "Look at Section 4, line two. It says 'the principal officers of the executive departments'—plural, that's the Cabinet. Then look down to the, uh, fifth line of the next paragraph. It says 'the principal officers of the executive department'—singular, that could mean the office of the President. Obviously, the framers meant the plural—but after it was ratified by the states, they couldn't change the damn mistake without amending the Constitution again."

"Ten years they were slaving over the language of that amendment," Frangipani marveled, "and they wind up with a typo. I am reminded of the remark by one of my predecessors in New York City, 'When I make a mistake, it's a beaut.' ".

"My point about the President's general health," said the A.G., slipping back into his argument, "is that the President's physician is the only doctor to have treated him over the past year. He has been with him constantly in the past month. His familiarity is, to use that word, 'intricate.' Now, I submit to you an affidavit from Dr. Abelson, drawn up this morning after an examination of the President, attesting to the good general health of his patient." Duparquet dealt out a sheaf of papers, which Bannerman took glumly. "For the examination this morning, Dr. Abelson drew on the resources of the Bethesda Naval Hospital, as well as a blood-count specialist from Johns Hopkins. All the facts and figures are here, drawn up by six of the most qualified men in their respective fields. Mike, if you have somebody who will challenge this report on the general health of the President, you'll start the first public disagreement between such doctors in the history of the American Medical Association."

"Learned counsel is twisting my argument," said Fong. "It isn't the President's blood pressure and pulse that's at issue here. His physical health may be fairly good, other than the fact that he is totally blind. But it's his mental health, the trauma from the shock of the new blindness, that makes him incapable. That's what I'm getting at, General, not his goddamn temperature."

"And how do you propose to determine his mental incapacity?"

"We have a panel of psychiatrists. They're standing by, in the waiting room of the West Wing."

Duparquet rose from his chair, leaned on his knuckles on the Cabinet table. "You would suffer the President of the United States to be examined by a panel of psychiatrists to see if he's fit for office?"

"Damn right!" Fong almost shouted.

"Gentlemen," said Bannerman, the soul of reason. "I direct your attention to the portrait that stands in the place of honor in this room. In 1919 Woodrow Wilson suffered a severe stroke. He was surrounded by his White House advisers and his wife, who determined what he would consider and what he would not. The decisions about the League of Nations were pressing on the country, and some twenty-eight urgent pieces of legislation became law without his signature. For all we know, Mrs. Wilson was the Acting President. President Wilson's actions were—in the light of present psychiatric knowledge—obviously paranoid. When his Secretary of State, Mr. Lansing, suggested that he step down, the head of the White House staff at the time—Joseph Tumulty—reproached him, and saw to it that Secretary Lansing was soon dismissed." Bannerman looked from the portrait to Secretary of State Curtice: "You sit in the chair of a great and courageous man. I say this to you, gentlemen: If the Wilson Cabinet had the power that we now have, President Wilson would have been examined by competent psychiatrists and he would have been forced to resign. No harm can come from such psychiatric examination; only good can come from it."

"No harm?" asked Duparquet. "What does it do to his capacity to govern if he has to sit and be judged before a supreme court of shrinks? Forcing a President to have his head examined—that's demeaning the office as well as the man. And are we to abdicate our judgment to a handful of psychiatrists? Isn't it hard enough for him to be blind—do we have to implant the suggestion in the public mind that he's crazy, too?" That argument was getting nowhere, Duparquet knew; scorn worked before a jury, seldom before a judge. But he knew, as Bannerman must know, that Ericson's pride would never let him hold still for a public psychiatric review, especially since such a report would contain language that the layman might find alarming. The Attorney General had no decision to make—Ericson had made clear that he would not set the precedent for psychiatric examination of Presidents who were not actually raving mad and chewing the rug—so he sought to reduce the impact of the refusal on Curtice. He had to show that Ericson's adamant refusal was not unreasonable. Suddenly, he asked Fong, "Who's your top shrink?" He deliberately chose the slang derogation.

"Dr. Paul Whitney, president of the American Psychiatric Association, would be considered a logical choice to head the panel."

"Bring him in," said the Attorney General. "Let's talk to him."

Bannerman looked alarmed, Duparquet was glad to note; their strategy was to turn the psychiatrists away unconsulted, and present that as evidence that an unstable President would brook no examination. Bannerman had not thought through what an experienced criminal lawyer could do to any psychiatrist's credibility.

Dr. Whitney came in, was seated at the end of the table; the Vice-President swore him to secrecy and thanked him for his patriotism in coming. Nichols then looked to Duparquet, who said to Mike Fong, "He's your man. You want him to make a statement, or what?"

Fong looked uncertainly to Bannerman, who said, "Dr. Whitney, would you tell the Cabinet what would be required, in terms of time, to give us a report on the President's mental health?"

"Assuming time is of the essence," the psychiatrist said, hands folded calmly in front of him, "two days of tests and interviews. A third of consultation and writing the report. I think it would be similar to urgent courtroom expert testimony."

Secretary of State Curtice turned to Defense Secretary Reed, sitting next to him across the President's empty chair. "If that were known, what would it mean to our deterrent?"

Reed gave a thin smile. "If a hostile power thought our President were crazy, our deterrent would be that much stronger. Sanity, human concern for lives, weakens a deterrent—a sane man is less likely to launch a retaliatory strike in time."

"Then an examination wouldn't trouble you?"

"No."

Bannerman followed up: "Just from what you have been able to observe on television, Doctor, and from your own experience with patients who have suffered a shock like the loss of sight, what would you say the effect of the ambush at Yalta has been on the President's abilities?"

The rest of the Cabinet looked not at the doctor, but at Duparquet, to see if he would object to such a question. He did not.

"I would never attempt to make an individual judgment from afar," the doctor replied. "Speaking generally, and not about President Ericson, I would say that a traumatic shock like the sudden advent of blindness would have a measurable detrimental effect on the average person's ability to—well, to make decisions."

"What would you say, Doctor—may I, Roy?—" Duparquet broke in smoothly, as if helping the examination, "if a person were blinded suddenly, physically shaken up and unconscious, escaped from a bloody assassination attempt at which a man died on top of him—and after all that, the man suffered no mental aftereffects at all?"

The psychiatrist was careful. "That would not be a normal reaction."

"Put it another way. If a person came through all that completely calm, absolutely in command of all his wits, the very soul of equanimity—would you say that would be abnormal?"

"If you take 'abnormal' to mean not the average person's reaction, yes."

"In other words," the Attorney General summed up, "you'd have to be crazy not to be upset—quite upset."

"I would never use an imprecise word like 'crazy,' sir. But I understand your point, and it's well taken. I would like to—"

"Dr. Whitney, to move on"—Duparquet did not want to let the other side's witness make a speech— "I would like to explore with you the terminology used in psychiatric reports. Forget about individuals, let's talk generally. Can a person have manic-depressive tendencies, or schizophrenic tendencies, without being psychotic?"

"Of course. Such words, used by laymen, are frightening, but when used with some precision by doctors, they are necessary to understand a patient's mental make-up."

Duparquet nodded, the doctor's friend. "Such words are often pulled out of context by laymen, aren't they?" The psychiatrist nodded. "What about words like 'psychotic' and 'neurotic'?"

"Psychosis is severe mental disorder and withdrawal from reality," replied the psychiatrist, "and neurosis is any one of various functional disorders without any visible effect, such as undue anxiety."

"Do many people have neuroses?"

"Most do, in some form or other, but they're manageable."

"So if I were to get a report on myself, say, it might say that I have this or that neurotic tendency, and inclined to depression at times, and certain relatively modest schizoid manifestations."

"I know what you are getting at, Mr. Attorney General," the psychiatrist began, but Duparquet pressed him back to the specific question: "Please, sir, let the Cabinet decide what I'm getting at, you just be our expert witness and answer that specific question."

"Terms that indicate normal behavior patterns to doctors often sound frightening to laymen. But—"

"Thank you, Doctor."

"Let him finish, for Chrissake," Bannerman snapped. "Go ahead, Doctor, you're not on the stand."

"What I wanted to point out was that in a sensitive situation like this, doctors would, of course, avoid using any terminology that might be misunderstood by the general public."

"Of course," said the A.G. "And when a television reporter sticks a microphone into the face of a member of the panel and says, 'Is the President neurotic or not?' the doctor will reply, firmly, 'Absolutely not!' "

"Well," the psychiatrist hedged, "you couldn't expect him to say that—"

"On a different subject," Duparquet said, "what's your feeling about psychologists? Would you put them in a class with chiropractors, or quacks, or what?"

"Qualified psychologists often make excellent therapists. They are not doctors, as psychiatrists are, and sometimes some unqualified people call themselves psychologists, and these cause great harm."

"Would you say that someone who has a doctorate in psychology from Harvard Medical School, and is a member of the board of directors of the American Psychological Association, and whose articles on the special psychological difficulties of the blind have appeared in the *Journal of the American Medical Association*—would you call him 'qualified'?"

The psychiatrist nodded. "Dr. Henry Fowler is one of the most brilliant psychologists in the country, and President Ericson is fortunate to have his services. He is not, however, a psychiatrist."

The A.G. decided the moment had come to get the witness out of there. "Does any other member of the Cabinet have any other questions? Then I want to say how grateful we all are for your willingness to help, sir." He put the knife in gently, almost imperceptibly. "When I was on the bench in Tallahassee, I very much admired the work you did on identity crises,

Dr. Whitney. And I know that my colleague here is proud that it was financed by the Bannerman Foundation."

"It's good of you to remember," said the psychiatrist, pleased, evidently glad that his former patronage was no secret. "And I've always wanted to thank you, Secretary Bannerman, for the great assistance your family has been to many of us in this field."

"You're very welcome," Bannerman said dryly.

When the psychiatrist had left, Mike Fong said, "You can still muddy up a witness' testimony, General, I'll grant you that. But you know damn well that President Ericson is a sick man, sick in the head as well as blind, or he wouldn't be clinging to power the way he is, against all reason. And you know that a serious psychiatric examination would show that, and that's why he will not permit it."

Curtice was the target, Duparquet reminded himself; not the rest of the room, not the record, not "history." As a famed Secretary of State used to say, "Show me a good loser and I'll show you a loser." If he lost Curtice, he lost Ericson's presidency, so he could not afford to make idle points.

"You happen to be wrong, Mike," the A.G. said, "and I'm glad that your man testified to Henry Fowler's credentials. Here is an affidavit from Dr. Fowler, again dated this morning, containing his analysis of the mental condition of the President. Very frank and full, and highly confidential. It states without equivocation that the President is in control of his faculties, and that he is adjusting satisfactorily to one of the most devastating traumas a person can go through." The men in the room paused to look at the Fowler affidavit, which was not quite as unequivocal as Duparquet had characterized it, and he quickly went on: "Moreover, we have now discharged our duty in this meeting to seek and study the expert medical opinion of doctors 'intricately familiar' with the President. We know he is not mentally ill. We know he is not physically ill. And we know that he *is* blind. The only question before us is: Does blindness make it impossible for a man to discharge the powers and duties of the presidency?"

"I will not accept that," said Bannerman. "You're framing the question much too narrowly. Ericson— President Ericson—is confused. He's scared. He's indecisive, he's certainly not himself. The blindness is not something he's learned to live with. Maybe a man who was born blind, and knew how to cope, could run for President and be elected and be able to serve. But this is sudden, stark, shocking blindness, and the man is literally staggering. He cannot do his job properly."

The Attorney General saw an opening. "Did I understand you to say that a man who was born blind could be an effective President?"

"Don't twist my meaning, General. We're discussing a subtle point, and you're not playing to the grandstand."

"Please forgive my lack of subtlety, but if blindness is not an ipso facto cause for declaration of inability, you don't have a leg to stand on." Mixed a metaphor on that one, Duparquet admitted to himself, but maybe this was a break.

"My point is this," Bannerman said slowly. "We're not talking about blindness alone, we're talking about inability to cope. Hank Fowler is blind, but he can cope—it's taken him years, maybe most of a lifetime. A suddenly blind President does not have time. He has to be able to cope now, this afternoon. And you know Ericson cannot."

"Fowler wasn't even born blind," Duparquet said, "he only went blind a few years ago. You say he could be President?"

"Goddamn!" Bannerman exploded, slamming his open palm on the Cabinet table, as Duparquet had hoped he would. But the Treasury Secretary quickly capped his anger: "General, there are none so blind as those who will not see, as the saying goes. You refuse to see the difference between the American people electing a blind man, and having a suddenly blinded person thrust upon them. There's all the difference in the world."

"Back off, General," Preston Reed said. "If a blind man ran for President, and was elected, there would be no discussion of inability. That would have been the people's decision. This sudden onset of blindness is a wholly different situation—the people did not elect a blind man."

"It's not as if Ericson wore thick glasses," Bannerman added, "or had a history of eye trouble. If that were the case, and the people knew the risk and went ahead and elected him anyway, then you could say the people knew what they were doing, and a blind man could serve."

"Ericson had no such history," stated Duparquet. "He never had a moment's eye trouble in his life. This happened in the line of duty. Accidental handicap is a chance we take in the election of any man." He wished now he had not been drawn into this area, and was glad when Frangipani came to the rescue, with an irrelevancy.

"I wouldn't mind having a psychiatric test for all candidates for President," said the Big Flower, a conversation behind, out of sync, but sensible. "It'd give a Cabinet in a situation like this something to go on, to measure against."

"That would have made it impossible for Abraham Lincoln to be President," Duparquet suggested.

"Then it may not be such a hot idea," said Frangipani, turning on a dime, and then looking at Fong. "Mike, see it my way. You pretty much agree that the President isn't nuts, he isn't falling apart or in a coma, and that blindness itself is not a surething cause of removal. What the hell you got left? He knocks over a few glasses? We're up to our ass in glasses. He calls Uganda something else? I do that all the time. He gets pissed off at a snotty reporter? Big deal."

Nobody interrupted Frangipani. "Now the way I look at it," he went on, "we're all thinking about our own constituencies. The A.G. here, he's worried about the legal precedent, making it easier to steal the presidency. Curtice, he's got to think about how we look in the world's eyes. Me—hell, I had to cross a picket line in front of the Human Resources building this morning, of the lame, the halt, and the blind—people saying that if we throw the President out, we kill the chances for a decent life for twenty million handicapped people. What I mean is, we all of us look at this through our own eyes, and we're all 'right'—we're sure as hell we know the right thing to do, even when we come out on opposite sides of this. But I say, when you don't know what to do—do nothing. We're pretty much split on this, so let's stay loose, let's hope the President gets better, and if he doesn't, let's try to talk him into voluntarily stepping out. Then, if worst comes to worst, a month or two from now, if we have to, we meet again. That's the way I see it, and I think a hell of a lot of people in the country will agree with me."

"That's a cogent statement, Andy," said the Secretary of Defense. "You're right that we look at this terrible situation, each of us, from our parochial point of view. But I submit that there is only one 'right' thing for us, as a Cabinet, to do. Let me pose the problem from the Defense point of view. Maybe you will think it is overriding. Mind if I walk around?"

Preston Reed got up, walked to the empty chair at the President's place, and leaned against the back of it. "The most important trust we hold is the survival of the United States. All of us—President, Cabinet, perhaps later Congress—have to keep that uppermost in our minds. There are no really 'safe' times, but the nuclear scientists have a way of measuring international tension, using the hands of a clock. At one point in the sixties, we were 'two minutes to midnight.' Then, as the Soviet-American alliance took hold, the danger receded—by the end of the seventies, the scientists' clock said we were twenty-five minutes to midnight. This year, the danger has risen again, as you all know. The Second World of the Far East is fomenting trouble between the Third and Fourth Worlds, perhaps in the belief that a surrogate war can be fought, drawing in the First World, and leaving the Far East with the upper hand.

"We are back, then, to two minutes to midnight. The Yalta ambush could possibly be this generation's Sarajevo. We think we know why the Yalta ambush took place, who was behind it—but we could be wrong. If we are wrong, and the primary target was the Soviet leader and not the American President, then it is possible that the Soviet-American alliance is under great stress, and a war could be imminent." Curtice frowned. The Vice-President swallowed. Frangipani whispered loudly to Fong, "Who was Sara Jevo?" and got no reply. Bannerman remained impassive and the A.G. emulated him. "At such a time," Reed continued, "the survival of the United States would be strongly aided by the appearance of stability and continuity. The potential for survival would be badly harmed by the appearance of instability and uncertainty. Please note that I say 'the appearance of.' In this situation, where we are dealing with the plans of other powers, how we appear to them is even more important than how we really are. That's a strange thing to say, I know. But it's important to grasp. We all know that there is that constitutional morality rooted in America's national being, that makes us stable when other democracies tremble and fall. We know that—but others do not know it. We feel our stability in our bones, but they cannot feel what is in our bones.

"If we *look* paralyzed," Reed drove home, "it is as if we *are* paralyzed. That in itself encourages the more militant elements in the Far Eastern alliance, and perhaps in the Soviet Union, to take charge. We are then open targets for a nuclear strike. The crisis thus feeds on itself.

"Some of you have that look on your faces," Reed continued, "that people get when a Defense Secretary talks about Armageddon. I'm not an alarmist. But please believe me when I tell you that I am very, very worried at this moment. And I think that unless we take action that will end this impasse, that will end the appearance of paralysis, we will be inviting catastrophe. And catastrophe will come.

"This is what I think. The President, if he is the patriot I think he is, should be prevailed upon to step down. Not step aside, let's be realistic, to step down. We should send you, the Attorney General, as our messenger from the Cabinet to say it is the sense of this meeting that he would serve his country best by resigning. Surely he and you are thinking about the stability of the presidency, which is entirely worthy of you both. But you must put the survival of the nation ahead of that, even that. Do it, General—it's the right thing to do. Don't force us to strike the President down."

They had three votes, thought Duparquet, to our sure two. If Curtice were to abstain, and be successful at it, they would have a majority. "Preston," he replied from his chair, "you remember that line of Lincoln's before the Civil War, when he told the Southerners that they did not have an oath registered in heaven to destroy the Union, and that he had taken such an oath to preserve it. The burden of starting the war was theirs. The burden of precipitating this crisis is yours, not ours."

It was the Attorney General's turn to rise and walk the room. "Roy Bannerman here told us how Woodrow Wilson, perhaps unable to discharge his powers, was isolated by his staff. Is Sven Ericson isolated? Is he unavailable to see any one of you?" Wrong word; he recovered by going back, "unavailable to meet with any of you? President Garfield, when he was wounded by an assassin, lay in a coma for eighty days while his Cabinet debated whether or not to have Vice-President Arthur take his place. Is Sven Ericson in a coma? Is he unconscious and dying?"

Curtice, Curtice, Curtice, and he also must not forget the Vice-President's possible veto. "We are both a government of laws and a government of men. The framers of the Twenty-fifth Amendment, who wanted to make sure the dangerous times of Garfield and

Wilson did not happen again, assumed that the men of a future Cabinet would not be rogues, but would be reasonable men. They did not foresee, perhaps they could not foresee, that there need be no rogues for profound disagreement to break out. I do not accuse anyone here of attempting to seize power—although, God knows, there will be cries of usurpation raised throughout this land if you overthrow the President.

"But if your essential point, Preston, is that the nation not appear to be paralyzed—then why do we not come together and say that we've done our duty, and we've found the President to be able to carry on, and then unite behind him and urge the country to follow our example? That would resolve the matter. That would remove the danger that the Secretary of Defense so rightly warns us of. You have no oath to overthrow the President—but the President has an oath to do his duty as he sees it. When you rally behind him, you underscore his ability to govern."

"This is leading nowhere," said Bannerman. "Mr. Attorney General, I consider your use of the term 'overthrow' especially offensive. I am not a traitor, we are not contemplating treason. Secretary Fong, let's move the question."

Fong took up a piece of paper and read: "I move that the principal officers of the executive departments, acting under the authority vested in them by the Twenty-fifth Amendment of the Constitution of the United States, declare the present occupant of the office of President of the United States to be unable to discharge the powers and duties of said office, and that the powers and duties of the office of President devolve upon the Vice-President as Acting President."

"A sadder moment has never taken place in this room," said Andy Frangipani.

"Mike," added the Attorney General, "you will rue those words for the rest of your life." He turned to Bannerman. "At least Mike Fong believes what he says. You're out for the brass ring, Bannerman, same as you've always been, and God help this country if the likes of you ever seize power."

"I second the motion," was Bannerman's reply as he looked straight at Duparquet.

"The motion has been made and seconded," said the Vice-President, adding lamely, "is there any debate?"

Secretary Curtice raised a finger. "Point of information, Mr. Chairman. Before any of us vote, I would like to know whether each of is required by law to vote, or whether abstentions are in order."

The Attorney General sagged inwardly, and compensated by sitting up straighter. The Vice-President looked at him and said, "Can the Attorney General give us a ruling on that?"

"He should be the last person in the world to be asked for a ruling," snapped Bannerman. "He's the President's advocate first, last, and always. A ruling from him would be a blatant conflict of interest. The ruling must come from the chair, Mr. Vice-President."

"Of course the ruling will come from the chair," said the Attorney General, "but the chair is entitled to ask the man that the Senate has confirmed as the nation's chief law officer for an interpretation of the law." Get a recess, Duparquet thought; let Cartwright do whatever he could with Curtice now, throw anything he had at the Secretary of State to get him to vote with the President. No worry now about any pressure backfiring—persuasion had not worked. "As a matter of fact, a point of information of that importance deserves some research, and consultation with the Solicitor General. I can get a solid answer in twenty minutes."

"A twenty-minute recess is granted," said the Vice-President. "May I request that you all remain in the general area of the Cabinet Room and Roosevelt Room across the hall, so that we can reassemble quickly."

The Attorney General rose with the rest, went to the telephone under the Cabinet table at the President's seat, and stentoriously asked the operator for the Solicitor General, the man at Justice who handled most of the arguments before the Supreme

Court. "Seems a question has come up of abstention. Look in the Legislative History—testimony in the House, I think, and then repeated in the committee report—that deals with that, and call me in fifteen minutes in the Cabinet Room." The Solicitor General started to tell him he didn't need fifteen minutes, he knew the answer, but Duparquet said loudly, "Has to be in fifteen minutes, ol' buddy," and hung up.

He walked out into the West Wing hallway, saw Lucas Cartwright standing out in front of his office at the end of the hall, and followed him to his corner office. "Curtice wants to abstain," he reported. "I'll force him to vote, but he'll vote aye, to remove the President, unless you have a way of turning him around."

"I will drop a ton of bricks on him," said Cartwright quickly and sadly, "since his sensitivity is no longer a factor. Any luck with Preston Reed?"

"He's killing us," said Duparquet. "Tell you the truth, he even scared hell out of me."

"Strange. Mrs. Cartwright reports that Mrs. Reed says he was furious at all the anti-Ericson heat he was getting from Wall Street."

"May have irritated him, but he's a principled bastard. The appearance of stability is everything, and his vote goes on that one point alone."

Cartwright thought about that, and suggested: "Then hit him with instability."

"What do you mean?"

"If Ericson is thrown out, he will go to Congress to get the presidency back. Twenty-one days of debate. If he loses, he keeps going back every two weeks, declaring his ability, and they have to debate and vote again. Twenty-one days every time. He could tie the country in knots."

"He wouldn't do that."

"How can you be sure? And if you say that is the President's intention, can Preston Reed be sure you're wrong? If you want dramatic proof, send out for a message—we'll be ready."

"I'll try it. Look, there's not much time. Clobber Curtice with anything you've got."

The Attorney General walked down the steps toward the White House Mess, stepped into the room with the bank of vending machines, and bought a doughnut and a carton of milk. The milk was for his ulcer, the doughnut was a treat for his psyche. Alone, at the stand-up counter, he sucked at the straw and leapfrogged past the likely Cabinet vote to oust the President to the moment when Vice-President Nichols had to make his decision. Duparquet planned to intercede at that point with an appeal, reminding Nichols of the restraint shown by all previous Vice-Presidents, and suggesting that the first use of the Twenty-fifth Amendment should be a non-controversial one, where the President acts voluntarily, or at least is unconscious and cannot oppose it. Or else the amendment itself might be repealed, as inviting usurpation. Might work. Nichols might be scared off by a threat of looking like a usurper, and being violently hated by loyal Ericson men. Duparquet made a quick assessment of his own feelings: At that moment, part of him was the analytical advocate, working out the strategy of the cornered rat; part the gut-fighter, calling in Cartwright with whatever pressure could be brought to bear; part of him was the partisan, hating to be defeated, and loyal to the man who put him where he was; part the statesman, defending the office of the presidency from wrongful if lawful seizure, and enjoying every moment of participation in a historic scene; and the last part was the observer, sifting all this when he should be back upstairs in case some slight edge could be added to his cause by his presence. He put the doughnut down, half eaten, and went back to work.

"Let us serve our country," the Attorney General opened, after Nichols had reconvened the meeting, "by declining to make history. The first time the Twenty-fifth Amendment should be invoked, in all its majesty and solemnity in the transfer of the greatest power on earth, should be at a time when an overwhelming majority of Americans can agree to its necessity. Not when men of good will can differ so strongly as to cast doubts on the legitimacy of that transfer." To avoid looking at the Vice-President, he looked toward Bannerman: "I include you, sir, in the men of good will, and withdraw my impassioned comment as to your motives."

"Accepted," said Bannerman, jowls set, his face cold. "Let's get on with the voting. Did the Solicitor General go along with your position, or have you found somebody else at Justice to support your opinion?"

"Oh, there's no doubt about it," said Duparquet cheerfully. "The Solicitor General confirms my initial reaction. The Legislative History is most specific that each of the executive departments is expected to cast a vote. If the head of that department is ill, or is not willing or able to vote for any other reason, then the acting head of the department casts the vote of that department." He turned to the Vice-President. "The formal opinion of the Justice Department, Mr. Chairman, which you requested: If any member of the Cabinet wishes to abstain from voting on the inability of the President, he is at liberty to do so personally, as an individual; but the vote of his department would then be cast by his deputy secretary. As there are six departments, then there must be six votes counted. That is, of course, if you want to force what appears to be a deadlock to a vote. Personally, I think that in the absence of a clear majority either way, which would mean the President would not be removed, that the country and this Cabinet would be better served by withdrawing the motion entirely."

Fong said, "No, thanks. I think we might just have a clear majority." He looked to Curtice, who gave a slight nod, Duparquet's heart sank; Cartwright's pressure had not worked. The Secretary of State looked harried, but determined.

After a pause, the Vice-President said, "Well then, on the advice of the Attorney General and the Solicitor General, my ruling, Secretary Curtice, is that individuals may abstain but departments may not. Each of you, or your immediate subordinate, must cast a vote, if Secretary Fong does not withdraw the motion." Nichols sighed his reluctance to be drawn into the proceedings at all.

"Before we vote," said the Defense Secretary, "since there is not much doubt which way the vote is going to go, can't we prevail on the Attorney General to persuade the President to do his duty? It would surely be better for the country, and in the interests of peace, for the President to invoke the Twenty-fifth voluntarily, and not insist on being pushed out."

"President Ericson is not doing any insisting or any pushing," the Attorney General replied, sadness in his voice. "He is serving in the office to which he was elected by a majority vote of a democratic people. You are doing the insisting and pushing. He is obligated to resist a wrongful seizure of presidential power."

"You are absolutely certain, then," said Defense Secretary Reed, "that the President intends to push this to a constitutional crisis."

"You, and not he, are precipitating this crisis." Duparquet grasped at the straw that Cartwright had suggested. "And what is more, you have not stopped to consider the national security consequences of your act."

"What do you mean?" said Reed.

"If," said the Attorney General, "—and I think your certainty about the outcome of a vote is misplaced—but if the Cabinet should vote to oust the President; and if the Vice-President does not prevent you from making him Acting President, which of course he has the veto power to do; then President Ericson has made absolutely clear that he intends to take this to the Congress to decide the issue."

"We know that is his present intention," Reed said, "but surely, when he considers—"

"I know the man," said Duparquet. "Sven Ericson will fight this wrongful seizure as long as there is breath in his body. And don't forget, he will still be the President. He will occupy the office of President —only the powers and duties of the presidency would be stripped from him. And you know what? He has told me that he will take that word 'office' literally, and continue to live in the White House, and continue to use the Oval Office in his campaign to recover his powers and duties if they are stripped from him. Then you go tell the world, Preston, that the United States is in a stable position. And you tell the world, George, that the business of state can be conducted with assurance."

"Surely he would not do that," said Reed. "The idea of the Twenty-fifth Amendment was that the Vice-President would become Acting President, and that he would remain Acting President through the twenty-one days of any challenge by the removed President. That was to avoid a question of legitimacy, or a switching of power back and forth. Now you're saying President Ericson would conduct some kind of a sit-in?"

"People who become President," said the A.G., feeling he was getting some traction with Reed, "are very strong and determined fellows. They fight very, very hard. Now let's take the consequences of your action further. Let's say you win here. Let's say the Vice-President makes the greatest mistake of any Vice-President in our history and plonks the crown on his own head. And let's even say the Congress puts a two-thirds majority together to agree to it. You know what will happen then?"

"Tell us," said Bannerman, unruffled.

"Read your second paragraph of Section 4." The A.G. picked it up and read: " 'When the President'— that's Ericson, he keeps the office of President—'When the President transmits . . . his written declaration that no inability exists, he shall resume the powers and duties of his office. . . .' You know what that means? That means that if an inability is declared, President Ericson has the right to go back to Congress, again and again—there's no constitutional limit on the number of times—and demand they vote on the restoration of his powers."

Bannerman waved his hand impatiently. "That's stupid. He would lose by a greater majority each time. He'd be seen as a fool and a pest, and as a matter of fact, his mental capacity would come into question even more."

Frangipani broke in. "On the other hand, he might be seen by a lot of people as the conscience of the presidency, knocking at the door of the Congress every couple of weeks, demanding and getting a vote. Be a moving thing in a way, like King Lear or something."

"That would be disastrous," said Reed coolly. "That would be an engraved invitation to adventurism by our enemies. No man who put his country before himself would ever do that."

"If you don't believe me, ask him," said Duparquet.

"Let's vote," said Bannerman.

"Wait, Roy, this is important," Reed said. "What are you getting at, General?"

"Let's push that button under the President's place and get his secretary in here. I'll put the question of his intent to President Ericson, and you can see for yourself."

"Yeah," said Frangipani, "maybe Emmett's bluffing."

Without a word, Defense Secretary Reed leaned across the President's empty chair and pushed the button; in a moment, Melinda McPhee entered, notebook in hand.

"Miss McPhee," said the Attorney General, "would you sit there for a moment and take this message to the President from me." He did not pause to deliberate for fear Bannerman would break the momentum. "Sir: Would you please write out, in your own hand, any action you intend to take in the event—which I consider unlikely—that the Cabinet, the Vice-President, and the Congress declare your inability? I would like to show your written answer to my fellow Cabinet members as soon as possible." Melinda did not pause to read it back; she turned and left the room.

"That was a big mistake," Bannerman said. "You're foreclosing your options. You're also accepting the inevitability of defeat. Mr. Attorney General, I think you'll regret the hastiness of that action."

Duparquet decided Bannerman did not understand high-stakes political poker. When you're sure to lose, you raise the ante; when you verge on bankruptcy, you borrow more, making it impossible for your creditors to close in without harming themselves. Of course it was a gamble; that was what the game was all about, to play upon the certainty of others that you would unhesitatingly use all the strength you had. And no options were really foreclosed; if the gamble lost, the President could always change his mind.

A few moments passed in silence. Melinda McPhee opened the door, marched around the table to the Attorney General's chair, and laid the piece of green-tinted stationery firmly in front of him. Quite a woman, he permitted himself to think; trustworthy, authoritative, well put together, handsome features. He watched her shut the door before he picked up the paper, which Ericson and Cartwright must have started working on before the recess ended.

"It's obviously the President's writing, and the ink is still wet. Here's what he says: 'Mr. Attorney General—I'm not the pessimist you are. But if I have to return to the Congress to assert my ability, I would do so, if necessary, again and again and again.'"

Frangipani broke into a broad grin. "That's the old Franklin Roosevelt line—'again and again and again.'"

Duparquet went straight at Reed. "I wasn't bluffing. Ericson means this. If you wish to plunge this nation into three and a half years of bitterly disputed leadership, then the responsibility is on your head."

"That is a rotten thing to say," said Reed. "And that is an evil, rotten, corrupt thing that the President has just done. Sven Ericson is no patriot, General—he's a man who puts his own personal political ambition ahead of his country's interest." Even as the Defense

Secretary began his excoriation of Ericson, Duparquet felt his flicker of hope grow stronger. "I'm ashamed of Ericson," said Reed, "I'm ashamed to serve in his Cabinet. The man is filled with a consuming lust for power, and totally devoid of principle."

At Bannerman's glance, Fong said, "I move the question."

Reed glanced at him sharply: "Are you crazy?" Fong looked puzzled. "Don't you understand?" said Reed. "He has us over a barrel. If he does what he threatens to do—and the son of a bitch just might— then the nation is paralyzed. Not only the appearance, but the reality, of paralysis. And that means we're begging for a war. I can't vote for that."

"Let me get this straight, Preston," Fong began.

"If you bring this to a vote," snapped the Defense Secretary, "I'll have to vote against his removal. The Secretary of Defense has no other choice. In terms of war and peace, better one blind Ericson as President than two Presidents."

Fong, dazed, looked to Bannerman, who said, "Let's vote."

"But there can be no majority to remove him," Curtice broke in. "The General, and Andy, and now Reed will stick with him. What's the sense of forcing a vote?"

"He's right," said Fong, slumping back in his seat. "Let's just say we had a worthwhile discussion."

"Let's vote," Bannerman repeated, glaring at Reed. "I want it on the record that at least some members of this pusillanimous Cabinet wanted to do their duty." The Attorney General looked at Bannerman, a hard and uncompromising man. Reed had steel in his backbone, too, and had been ruthlessly consistent throughout. Duparquet's eyes swung to Curtice, who had shown surprising strength in withstanding whatever it was Cartwright put to him, and had signaled his willingness to put his career on the line. Frangipani had stood firm; poor Fong was in a box, and Bannerman was holding the box and his feet to the fire. Not a gutless Cabinet, as Duparquet weighed it: extraordinarily strong, in fact. Pity it would soon be split up.

"The motion has been duly made and seconded," the Vice-President said wearily. "Roy, you really want to go through with this?" Bannerman, jaw tight, nodded. "Then you will vote in the order of precedence. On the removal of the President, how do you vote? State?"

Curtice looked at Bannerman, shrugged, said, "No."

"Defense?"

Reed said, "No."

"Treasury?"

"The Treasury Secretary votes yes," Bannerman said.

"Justice?"

Duparquet said, "No."

"Natural Resources?"

Fong said, "This is the first time I ever voted against a motion of my own, but I see no purpose in it any more. And Roy Bannerman should have the honor of standing alone. I vote no."

"Human Resources?"

Frangipani boomed, "No!"

"Five to one, the nays have it," said Vice-President Nichols. "Mr. Attorney General, is it possible for me to cast a vote for the record?"

"No," said Duparquet; no free rides. "For this purpose, you are not a member of the Cabinet. You may, if you wish, say whatever you like about how you would have voted if the matter had come to you."

"Then I would like to say, simply, that I would have voted no. In my view, the President is both able and courageous and the Cabinet and the nation should unite behind him." The right thing for the Vice-President to say, Duparquet acknowledged; he wondered how true it was, whether Nichols would have really stayed the hands that offered the presidency.

"Amen to that," said Frangipani. "Who gets to break the good news to The Man? General, you were the hero."

The Attorney General shook his head; "I think it would be most appropriate for the Vice-President to do that. Andy, why don't you go in with him?"

"While you're at it," said Preston Reed bitterly, "you might tell him to take the job of Defense Secretary and stick it in his ear. He'll have my resignation on his desk in an hour."

"The wrong thing for the right reason," Bannerman commented. "That's the story of your life, Preston. God save this nation from men who are afflicted with the need to remain foolishly consistent."

As the others made their way out, Bannerman and Duparquet remained behind, seated diagonally across the table. "I admired your insistence on a vote," said Attorney General. "Wish you good luck in private life."

"You won the first battle," said Bannerman. "The war's not over. That selfish incompetent will not serve out his term."

"Come on, Roy, give it up. Reed had the best point of all: One blind President is better than two Presidents."

Bannerman shook his head. "One able Acting President is better than a disabled President who won't admit his disability." He looked at Duparquet for a long time. "You're an attractive personality, General, and a proven vote-getter. You play to win. You come from the only southern state that Northerners trust. You're young enough, you could go all the way. I, on the other hand, look like the stereotype of moneybags, and my family name is a liability in politics. I have to deal through others, and who knows, the day may come when I will deal through you. But I know what's best for this country, General. Perhaps someday you'll find that out."

"I believe you think so," said Duparquet. "That's what makes you so dangerous." He got up and left Bannerman sitting there. What was it that Cartwright had on Curtice? And wouldn't Cartwright be a good replacement for Reed? The Attorney General wished the Vice-President and Andy Frangipani would get through with the post-mortems. He had a lot to talk to the President about.

III

---

*The Goddamn
Speech*

The Personal Secretary / 2

She had been in the President's bedroom once before, on a tour with a few other White House senior aides, but this was the first time Melinda McPhee had been there at 7 A.M., seated at the President's bedside, with Ericson propped up by his pillows, sipping his coffee, chortling at the play of the news. The night before, he had called her to say, "I don't want you to put the News Summary on tape this time, and have it speeded up. I want you to read this one to me slowly. There may even be some items I want to hear twice."

She felt awkward. Reading to him in bed in a hospital room was one thing, a proper function for a staff person to a boss in need; but being part of breakfast in bed was demeaning. She said so: "Hey look, Mr. President, why don't I do some underlining in the sitting room next door while you throw on a robe and then join me?"

"What's the matter, Melinda?"

"I have a lousy bedside manner. And you shouldn't be doing business in here if you're not sick, which you're not."

"You're embarrassed," the President said, amused, "and you're crazy. The door is open, Furmark is standing there with a gun, you're completely safe. It wouldn't even cause any talk if everybody knew you were here."

True enough, she agreed grimly. It had been eight years since she and Ericson had spent a morning in a bedroom together, and she did not like the contrast in circumstances. "You want to hear the News Summary, or you want to horse around?" She made paper-rustling noises as she headed for the door. "I'll be organized on the dining table in a minute."

Ericson emerged a moment later, coffee mug in hand, using the long cane. First time he had done that, she noted; he must be getting less self-conscious. "Read me Sam Zophar first," he said, "the son of a bitch, yesterday's meeting must have been a blow to him."

She turned to the opinion section. "His column is headed 'Curtice's Mistake' and leads, 'At Monday's extraordinary Cabinet meeting, called to examine the President's obvious inability to discharge his duties, the crucial vote to keep Sven Ericson in office was cast by Secretary of State George Curtice. As the historic discussion developed, it became evident that the Cabinet was split, 3–3. Curtice first asked if he could abstain, thereby allowing the anti-Ericson forces to have a majority. The political Attorney General, after a recess spent pressuring the professionals at the Justice Department to back his already-made decision, said no. Then Secretary Curtice, on the theory that a prolonged fight for the presidency would be harmful to the country, reluctantly cast his vote to support the President, taking the Secretary of Defense along with him. At that point, even Secretary Michael Fong, author of the resolution to replace the President, beat a retreat, leaving the only vote to be cast with honor in that room to belong to T. Roy Bannerman. Not since the time of Salmon P. Chase has there been a Treasury Secretary who—'" She broke off. "He's way off base, that's not the way it happened."

"How do you know?" asked the President.

"Andy Frangipani told us that Curtice hung tough, even after Cartwright worked him over, and didn't come over to us until after Reed turned around. And the Attorney General confirmed that. This Zophar column is a whole lot of, of—misinformation."

"What is truth?" Ericson mused, still in his good mood, not awaiting an answer. "It may not have been the truth before, but now that Zophar has written it, the pack will follow, and it will become the truth. And Melinda—who knows? Maybe we have been given misinformation, and Curtice was our real savior."

"You don't believe that."

"No, I don't." He hung his cane on the back of the chair. "What happened was that George Curtice gave the story to Zophar shaded the way he wanted it, knowing that Zophar would rap him and tout Bannerman. Now everybody thinks Curtice had been on my side, and Curtice's head is not on the block. Smart play. Give George credit, he's trying to cut his losses."

This was a side of Ericson Melinda was not at all sure she liked: the detached politician, the quasi-realist, trusting nobody, professing to admire technique and setting not much store in right and wrong. "The Sanders-Bennet team has it right on the button," she commented, and read: "President Sven Ericson's political hide was saved by the powerful advocacy of Attorney General Emmett Duparquet, with an assist from New York's 'Big Flower,' Angelo Frangipani. Washington now awaits the purge: Defense Secretary Preston Reed has already quit. George Curtice at State is a question mark, and power-grabbers Bannerman and Fong are sure to go. As for Florida's Emmett Duparquet, his star is clearly on the rise. The sun-belted savior of the President with the prematurely silver hair is now the second most powerful man in the staggered Ericson Administration. . . ."

"Good, good," said Ericson, "build the A.G. up. Who was the source on that?"

"Smitty said he spoke to Sanders, and Marilee spoke to his partner."

"Tell Smitty that was good. That's just the line we want out."

Melinda was not so sure. "I hate to see anybody become a knight in shining armor. This is the Ericson Administration, the spotlight belongs on the President."

"You're loyal to a fault, Melinda," the President

said cheerfully. "I like to spread the credit around. You smell good, though."

"Thank you for the perfume," she said, embarrassed she had not thanked him before. "That was the first time you remembered my birthday, and it threw me. Who reminded you?"

"Marilee, I think. Anyway, the date is now burned into my brain. The reason I want to see Duparquet built up, chum, is that he's my boy. Nobody can outshine the President unless the President wants him to, and for now, I want to show what a great team I have. He's the main jewel in my diadem. And he's no threat—the way the Vice-President would be, if he were any good."

"Duparquet's an ambitious man," Melinda said. She was attracted to him in spite of herself, and distrusted him for that.

"Could be the next President," said the President, "or the one after that. Okay with me. Every Cabinet needs at least one potential President, like Hoover in the Harding Cabinet."

"What is it with you and Hoover?"

"Great President, much misunderstood," said Ericson. "Both he and Wilson wound up broken and hated, the way I will, but history will resuscitate us all." That was a melancholy thought, spoken in a tone of light irony; she could not tell if he meant it. "Now start from the top of the News Summary and read it all. I'll only interrupt to give you notes."

The summary took them forty-five minutes to complete. He wanted to hear the texts of the editorial and congressional comment on the Cabinet meeting. The other item that concerned him, Melinda knew, was this: *Times* reports the intelligence community torn in disagreement on who was behind the Yalta ambush—some say the Far Eastern powers, but a minority insists that Soviet strong man Nikolayev arranged the assassination himself to seize power. To the obvious question 'Whodunnit?' we must add this question: Which leader was the real target?"

"Three days ago," the President dictated to her for

Cartwright, "the notion that Kolkov was the primary target was the biggest secret in town. Tell Defense Intelligence I don't like the way they're playing the game. I heard them, they didn't have to go outside—as far as I'm concerned, their leakage adds credence to the opposing view. Make sure they know that. It's the only way to shut them up."

Melinda left the President and walked through the Rose Garden to her own office. She went back out with a scissors and cut three flowers, a procedure she had cleared beforehand with the White House gardener—a stubborn, surly man—for placement on the coffee table in the Oval Office. When she came back, holding the pink roses carefully to avoid the thorns, she found Hennessy sprawled on the couch. "Early for you," she said; Hennessy liked to think of himself as a "night person."

"I hear you had breakfast in bed with the President," he observed. "The times they are a-changin'."

"I'd hate to have a mind like a divorce lawyer," she replied. Trust Hennessy to notice that. "You look at life through a keyhole."

He put his feet on the coffee table to annoy her, so she refused to act annoyed. "Kiddo"—Hennessy got to her with "kiddo," they both knew that—"I'm the only one on your side, you'll realize that someday. The more blind he gets, the better you look."

Melinda slowly arranged the roses in the bowl, gathering her thoughts for the right level of response. "Do you know why you don't have any friends, Hennessy? It's because you're so vulnerable and sensitive and scared. You strike out at people, you think offense is the best defense. You're afraid somebody would get to like you otherwise, and then you'd have to tell them the truth about how hateful you really are."

"Another shrink! And to think, just a few months ago there had never been a psychologist in the White House. Well," he sighed, "be happy, Melinda. Enjoy the big victory. Let The Man do the same, until this afternoon. I have to see him this afternoon."

"The afternoon's blocked out for Hank Fowler, you know that."

"Intimate adviser says," said Hennessy.

"Why don't you take your intimate advice," she began, and stopped herself. This was banter, not argument; this was letting off steam after a crisis, between friends and allies, and the intimate adviser and the personal secretary were on the same side. Someday, long after it was all over, she would drive him crazy by refusing to put him through to the former President, and she comforted herself with that thought. "Why don't you go over to the play pen"—she referred to the sauna designated as the "health unit"—"and sweat some of the poisons out of your system."

"That's a good idea. Melinda, you're a good woman. Fine figure, and you're wise to call attention to it by covering it up. Pretty face isn't everything. I had a lot to drink last night, thinking the crisis was over, and today I don't feel very well."

"Somehow, I guessed that." She was irritated by the casual way he exposed the truth about the way she dressed.

"Arrange for me to see the President around three. He'll have a chance to savor his victory, and I'll get a sweat and a sleep and a look at the paintings in the Fenwick. Then if he wants to know what I want, tell him I heard from an old friend from the campaign, and you will see the President's face fall. Tell nobody else, though."

Melinda went to her own desk, called in two secretaries who worked for her, and plunged into the stack of telegrams and letters that had come in wishing the President well over the "fateful weekend." Most of the mail was screened routinely across the street in the EOB computer, with computer-typed "personalized" replies sent back by return mail. Names on the President's "friends" list, or VIPs on a master list, were passed to Melinda for truly personal treatment. She checked her card file for first names and wives' names —"love to Maxine and little Charley, S.E." made all the difference—and Melinda alone was entrusted with the Ericson autopen, the impersonal touch that signed his name, in ink, thousands of times each week, a presidential timesaving tradition started by John F. Kennedy.

Smitty came in as she worked, kibitzed a bit, and drifted into a meeting going on in the Roosevelt Room, considered a Cabinet Room for staff. At the same time a meeting of the Cabinet committee on antitrust reform, an Ericson favorite subject, was going on in the Cabinet Room. Upstairs, the Domestic Council was listening to a delegation of consumer advocates. Down in the Situation Room, the White House Fellows were having their seminar on federal administration, which was hardly a dramatic use of the most dramatic room in the White House, but conference-room space was at a premium. If one more group had wanted to meet that morning, the bomb shelter under the residence would have been pressed into service. Melinda relaxed into her activity; after the past month, a normally hectic day was a relief.

"I understand that you are the only one able to arrange for a table at the Sans Souci." Smooth, confident voice. She looked up to see the deeply tanned face of the Attorney General.

"It's after noon now, General." She smiled. "You really ought to plan ahead. For how many?"

"Just the two of us," he said. "You need to get away from the fan mail, which is probably turning abusive, and I need to get away from the defenders of monopoly. I hope you will forgive my brashness and will accept my invitation."

The "Tallahassee Charmer," they called him, and they were right; Melinda was more pleased than she liked to admit. She said to the White House telephone operator, "Would you please make a reservation for two at Sans Souci in ten minutes? Ms. McPhee and guest."

He feigned resignation. "My name means nothing there, you're right. I rarely eat out. The Justice Department is in the low-rent district."

At the restaurant, they were seated along the balcony overlooking the pit action. A White House staffer did not rate a booth or banquette in the pit, and the maître d' had not expected the Attorney General, but Melinda knew the elevation would be useful to Duparquet in observing the phenomenon of the Washington lunch. She was pleased by the way he freely displayed his fascination, and was confident that no gossip would come of her taking lunch with a married man: He was a Cabinet member, she was important in the Administration, they were political allies, and nobody came to Sans Souci if they were doing anything that required skulking around, unless they were employing the theory of Poe's purloined letter.

"There was a television commercial for a home heating system," Duparquet said, surveying the crowd, "that showed, in color, the waves of heat that flowed through a house, and how they could be controlled with a newfangled thermostat. Same thing right down there, where you can see the shimmering waves of power."

"Show me one shimmering wave of power."

"Right there," he pointed. "Look now, so they know we're looking at them. That's the director of the FBI, McCoy, with the chief counsel of the Senate Oversight Committee, politely trying to scare hell out of each other. And in the booth over there, next to the stairs, that's the undersecretary of State trying to convince somebody that his bossman George Curtice really did support Ericson in that meeting."

"It's the bureau chief of the Los Angeles *Times*," she said, wanting to help Duparquet make his point, but not wanting to top him.

"Good, good," he said, "I took the right woman to lunch. Miz McPhee—"

"Melinda." She could not tell if he had picked up her "Ms." or was pronouncing "Miss" southern-style.

"Good. Call me 'General,' I always hated my first name. Down there, who are those three bitties?"

"The well-dressed one facing us is Mrs. Cartwright. The President thinks she's a one-woman CIA. On her right is Susan Bannerman, who's probably very happy about going home to New York. Neither one's a 'bittie,' General. The third I don't know." That one looked more like a bittie, she had to admit.

He reached in the breadbasket, ignoring the cellophane-covered sesame crackers for the French bread, and tore off a chunk. Melinda liked that; she kept herself on a permanent diet, but if the man she was with wanted bread, he should not fiddle with the niminy-piminy diet crackers. She wished she had worn a different outfit that day, with a cowl collar, but who knew she would be asked to lunch by the man she had been thinking about? With Ericson blind, she had little incentive these days to look her best.

"Hard to figure," Duparquet was saying. "Cartwright was one hundred per cent against Bannerman in the fight, and there are their wives, bosom buddies. Sorry, I didn't mean that to sound sexist."

"Not so hard to figure," she said. "Connective tissue. Lucas always likes to keep the channels open, in case somebody wants to send a message, or a feeler. Matter of fact, he gave the President a note about his wife having lunch with Mrs. Bannerman today."

"You tell your boss we were having lunch?"

"You think I'm insecure?"

"I think I'll tell my wife we had lunch. I'm not as secure as you."

She asked him why his strategy was to let George Curtice get away with rewriting his role in the meeting, partly because she wanted to know, mainly because—with this man—she wanted to stay on the firm ground of political intrigue.

"He'll have a dirty secret, and we'll know it," Duparquet explained eagerly. "That'll keep him in line in the next few months, when Ericson needs it most. Also I don't want that vote to look as close as it actually was."

"Who should get canned?"

"Bannerman and Fong. And Reed's already resigned. I'd be willing to take a chance on Curtice, but that's all."

She agreed, and would have gone further—dismissing the two-faced Secretary of State as well—but she

301

baited Duparquet: "That's retaliation for speaking their minds. Will it look good for the Boss to seem to want a bunch of rubber stamps?"

"Screw 'em. President can't afford to show weakness, not now, when he's weak."

She leaned back in her chair. "I think I was just hit by a shimmering wave of power."

"Hey, I like you," he said. "You don't take any baloney, and I don't have to watch what I say. I wish I had somebody like you." He did not say for what.

"You might, someday," she said, choosing to take it professionally, "President Ericson thinks you'd make a damn good President."

"He said that?" The Attorney General seemed a little too eager, but then recouped with that flash of honesty that so often took him out of trouble. "Melinda, I'm eating out of your hand—did your boss really say that?"

She enjoyed giving him the good news: "He said that every Cabinet should have a potential President in it, and you're it for this one." She did not go into the Harding-Hoover comparison. "He's also not worried about your standing in the limelight, but I'm not sure he's right about that." Now he could tell himself the lunch was worthwhile; she would let him pick up the check.

"Why isn't he right?" Duparquet came at her straight; it was part of his charm, to eschew the charming indirection. The captain came for the order and she started to order a salad, but the Attorney General said, "Why a chintzy li'l ol' salad? You're a healthy woman, you work hard, eat a proper meal." She went along with gusto, ordered the blanquette of veal and added to the captain, "Ask Paul to find out who's dining with Mrs. Cartwright and Mrs. Bannerman."

Duparquet nodded in appreciation and said: "Okay, Melinda, who's in and who's out?"

"Now we get to the real purpose of the lunch," she said.

"The real purpose of the lunch," he said right back, "is for me to lay the basis for making a serious pass at you. Since we don't know each other well enough, and since I hate to be rejected by somebody I respect, I have to stick to the business of politics, at least in the beginning. Okay? Now—who's in and who's out?"

"You're in," she shot back, tapering off with, "the Cabinet, that is. Cartwright's in, as you had suggested last night, replacing Reed at Defense. Reed, by the way, told the President he didn't know what had made him more furious—the President's threat, or Bannerman's uncalled-for pressure from mutual friends on Wall Street."

"Oh, that's good." Duparquet smiled. "Then a lot of silly play acting was not all for naught. Keep going —Bannerman?"

"Out. Cold turkey, tomorrow morning by phone from the President. It's something the Boss is looking forward to. Hennessy says that there will be an investigation on the Hill about the connection between Treasury decisions and the Bannerman real estate empire, but the President is not officially aware of that. Hennessy's playing pretty rough."

Duparquet nodded, and raised his shot glass filled with sippin' whiskey. "The U.S. attorney in New York has been looking into that, too. There'll be a thorough investigation."

"You're all alike."

"We're not," Duparquet said sharply. "Man goes for your throat, you clobber him as hard as you can, Ericson and I agree on that. But if I were President, and suddenly went blind, I'd resign. No temporary stepping aside, either—resign."

"Then how can you—"

"Because that's a President's decision to make, nobody else's. If you say he cannot make the wrong decision, then you say he cannot make the decision. The far greater danger is the threat of usurpation, turning the country into a banana republic."

Melinda did not hide her surprise. "Does the President know that's the way you feel?"

"No, and I hope you don't tell him." By placing his trust in her hands, he took her into camp—Melinda knew that trick and was not about to fall for it. "I think the President should have the power to decide," he said, "and Ericson is clearly mentally competent to make that decision. Then when he does, we should all move to shore him up. Cut down the opposition. He's elected to make that decision, not you or me or the Cabinet. I have no difficulty defending him."

"Fong stays in," Melinda continued, as she had been instructed to—before going to lunch, she had excused herself to wash her hands, and had called the President to see what he wanted told to Duparquet—"because without Bannerman he's no trouble. And he was the author of the motion to declare disability, so keeping him shows that the President is not retaliating."

"Makes some sense," Duparquet said grudgingly. "Who's in for Bannerman?"

"His deputy, I forget his name, the one we put in under him to represent the President's interests. Hates Bannerman more than ever, but that makes the deputy aces high in our book."

"And what was it that Cartwright had on Curtice?"

She looked at him, irritated. "What do you want for one lousy lunch, all the inside secrets of the Republic?"

"I'd spring for dinner, for that."

"Tell you what—you find that out from Lucas Cartwright, and tell me, and I'll pay for the dinner."

Duparquet seemed to veer off. "Interesting, the President doesn't know. Lot of ass-covering going on. That's half the fun, I guess."

Melinda kept her face in neutral. His supposition that the President did not know what Cartwright had on Curtice was based on his assumption that if the President knew, Melinda would know, and since Melinda said she did not know, then the President did not know. But of course, the President did know—Cartwright had briefed him quickly on Harry Bok's Curtice-instigated creative memory about Kolkov's heroism—and Ericson had delightedly confided it to Melinda. If Melinda now allowed herself to look

knowing, always good for the ego, then Duparquet
would hook what he had been fishing for—whether
the "ton of bricks" pressure on Curtice had come directly from the President. That was why she went in
the opposite direction, acting irritated that Cartwright
had not told her—or the President. That drew the Attorney General to the wrong conclusion, as he swallowed his own bait. Melinda enjoyed that.

The captain came to the table and said quietly that
the name of the third lady at Mrs. Cartwright's table
was Mrs. Arthur Leigh. Melinda frowned.

"Who's she?" the Attorney General asked, not all
that interested.

"Wife of the old campaign manager, the one without a first name—'that bastard Leigh,' we all called
him. Alienated everybody, didn't get a job after the
election."

"He's got an FBI file as long as your arm," the Attorney General said. He looked at her arm on the
table, adding, "Nice long arm."

Melinda could not decide whether his banter was
only kidding around, or kidding with a purpose; nor
did she yet know what her response would be if he
followed through. She toyed with that throughout the
sturdy lunch; on the way out, she turned down his
invitation to a ride, since the White House was only
two blocks away. "What is it you want me to put in
the President's ear, General?"

"Tell him the old Tallahassee Charmer pulled out
every stop, tried every trick in the book, and couldn't
get to first base." Duparquet smiled.

"I would never consciously mislead the President,"
she replied ambiguously. Let him chew that over. She
shook hands gently, not trying to show she had
a strong grip, and walked down the hill, across the
street, past the old Executive Office Building, toward
the West Basement entrance of the White House,
thinking about her boss and his best new political
friend. The differences: Ericson forty-eight, seeming
older; Duparquet fifty-four, seeming more boyish, at
once more openly rural and more smoothly urbane.

Ericson, introverted, man of thought, deliciously complex, with the ability to convey a genuine warmth when he wanted to; Duparquet, extroverted, man of action, a gambler, a winsome smile with the ability to project a chilled edge of cruelty in his voice. The President was an Episcopalian, a born insider, who anticipated good fortune, or at least used to; and the Attorney General, a Jew, a talented outsider, who anticipated trouble. Ericson was more interested in government and "the people," and Duparquet more interested in politics and real people. The similarities, Melinda judged, were striking, too: the constant calculation, the self-flattering flirtation. Both loved the play of power, and found joy at being in the center of action, using their friends, letting their friends use them, telling themselves so often that they were idealists underneath the cynicism that they actually became fairly idealistic. She knew one too well, the other not well enough, but enjoyed the way the two men respected each other with the warmth unique to political figures who could help each other and who were not likely to come into competition.

Would Duparquet, if blinded as President, really quit? She stopped before the entrance. Of course not; the Attorney General was saying that—as Ericson would say if their roles were reversed—to titillate and intrigue a woman who might be useful one day. To be roughed up in a world of smoothies happened to too many personal secretaries, Melinda knew. She was more concerned with her own need for such intimacy with men who all too often confused the power of their sex with the sexiness of their power. As she stepped off the tiny West Wing elevator, she slipped back into the job she was hired to do, and went to a telephone to tell Hennessy about that bastard Leigh's wife being in town.

The Campaign Manager

A double room on the park side facing the White House was what he wanted. When the room clerk at the Hay-Adams had said none was available, Arthur Leigh waited a couple of hours, called the manager, and without wheedling or blustering, finally came up with the right room with the right view. That was because Leigh knew how to persevere, neither to wait impotently nor to wait angrily, but to wait purposefully. After campaigns were over, he would sport the only political button he would ever wear—"Great Job, Kid, Now Get Lost"—and he knew the difference between hanging around with high hopes and waiting with specific goals.

After the Ericson victory the preceding November, he had not hung around. Ericson had expended Leigh in that campaign, using him to bear the brunt of most angriness, and it was understood privately between the antipolitical candidate and the superpolitical campaign manager that the pay-off would be further down the road than usual. In salary, Leigh had been paid handsomely—fifteen thousand per month for ten months of political campaigning—but his tacit understanding with Ericson was that a win would merit a bonus, to be determined later. An IOU for a target of opportunity.

Few outside the inner circle of the Ericson campaign understood that. When "that bastard Leigh" did not get a government job after the victory, newsmen took it to mean that he and Ericson had fallen out. Hennessy, in particular, made that point in backgrounders during the interregnum, recalling the bitter fight between newly elected Woodrow Wilson and his

New Jersey campaign manager in 1912. Leigh was the lightning rod for the flashes of anger at the Ericson campaign, the "abominable no-man" who grounded the resentments—and then, the battle won, he was apparently shunted aside by a candidate who agreed with those who disliked the no-man. More important than that, Leigh had made hundreds of vague promises during the campaign and had become the contact point for a great many little debts; if Leigh was not in the White House, nobody was there to remember. People who thought they had a handle on Ericson would be unable to find the handle. In November, Ericson had shucked Leigh like an old snakeskin, and slipped into the White House with praise for his political independence. Innumerable annoying IOUs were canceled by the metamorphosis.

Seated at the window of the Hay-Adams parkview room, looking across Lafayette Park at the play of the fountain in front of the White House, Arthur Leigh waited. He read the *Star* and he leafed through the *Post*. He read the news magazines that had held their deadlines to get the "ticktock" account of the "fateful weekend," and he waited some more. He sent his wife out to lunch, he made his presence known to Hennessy, and he stayed put.

His paunch hanging over his belt, worn slippers hanging from feet extended across an ottoman, Leigh read about the resignation of T. Roy Bannerman and was pleased. He disliked the kind of fat cat who could not be taken advantage of. He read about Ericson's surprise retention of Mike Fong, puzzled it out, and gave the President credit: showed confidence he would no longer be challenged.

After a couple of days, the patient Leigh read of the appointment of Lucas Cartwright as Secretary of Defense, which made sense to him, and of the appointment of Hennessy to replace Cartwright as chief of the White House staff, which made less sense to Leigh— unless the President were still worried about holding on to his presidency.

Leigh knew the reason for running a tight, secretive White House staff under Hennessy: the possibility of leakage of the President's late-dirtied little secret, his previous blindness. Only a month ago, Leigh was aware, the year-old episode with Buffie on the campaign train was only to be a minor footnote in a couple of memoirs. Now the episode assumed all sorts of sinister implications, as evidence that the people had not voted for a President while fully informed of his potential disability. Leigh was frankly surprised that the girl had not blabbed already, or that some newsman had not ferreted it all out, but that was a plus for the old manager: It gave him a bit more leverage in case he needed it.

"The smoking gun," he said aloud. His wife, accustomed to non sequiturs from her aging husband, looked up and said only, "How long are we staying in Washington, Arthur?"

"Day or so. Maybe another week."

On Friday, three days after they had checked in, the call came from the White House: Melinda McPhee was on the phone to ask the Leighs to attend a small reception and dinner on Sunday night if they were in town. Leigh's wife, on the phone, repeated the invitation aloud, and her husband growled, "Leaving tomorrow, sorry."

Mrs. Leigh made their excuses and hung up. "I don't know why we couldn't stay over one more day, Arthur," she complained. "We don't get invited to the White House all that often. The last time was in the Eisenhower Administration."

"We're not here to get our hands held," Leigh told her. "Hennessy'll call in a little while, after Ericson's girl tells him we're about to leave."

"Secretaries don't like to be called 'girls' any more."

"That McPhee dame wouldn't mind being called a girl." Leigh smiled. "She never liked the way Ericson treated her like one of the guys."

The phone rang. "I'll take it this time," Leigh said. "She must have called from Hennessy's lap." He picked it up and growled, "Yeah?"

"This that bastard Leigh?"

"I can see you now, Hennessy, but I haven't got all day."

"Cut the shit, Arthur, you haven't got another appointment scheduled for a week."

"You may be right, but that next one's a beaut."

That caused Hennessy to pause, as Leigh knew it would. Hennessy could intimidate anyone he could irritate, but Leigh had his number: the amused contempt of a real bastard toward a would-be bastard. The stories in that day's papers called Hennessy "the second most powerful man in America" but that wasn't true; the redheaded lawyer's power was totally derivative, and Leigh knew that Hennessy knew that Leigh knew it. The new chief of staff was a man in a big job, not a big man in a job.

"I could meet you in the bar downstairs at your hotel," said Hennessy, "or I can pour you some of Cartwright's leftover bourbon here in this snazzy corner office, whichever you like." Leigh chose to go to the White House, ambling across the park on a warm afternoon, thinning gray hair disheveled, thinking about what he wanted to come away with. This was Leigh's last chance at substantial money. If he could get his man appointed highway commissioner in Tennessee, he could expect a sensible decision on a highway access road to property he held an option on, and then a sale to a developer. The man making the appointment, the patronage man for the Tennessee governor, wanted the word from the White House, so that Ericson would then owe the governor a favor. "Honest graft" as George Washington Plunkitt would put it; the man to be appointed highway commissioner was capable and would be grateful, the access road belonged on or near Leigh's option property, the deal did not injure the public interest. And the campaign IOU would be honored.

At the West Gate, the guard had his name and nodded a welcome, buzzing the gate open. Leigh walked down the roadway to the new portico outside the West Wing, past a television commentator posing for a camera crew with the President's office as backdrop. Leigh hoped that Hennessy would not mention the episode on the campaign train—that would be amateurish, the most derogating word in Leigh's vocabulary—and he hoped the new staff chief would not take him in to see the President, which would be an embarrassment for Leigh and a mistake for Ericson. One did not see the President on a matter as minor as this. Nor did he want or need to see Ericson, who he remembered only as an inept but lucky candidate who concealed his love for the people in his distaste for crowds.

Leigh gruffed his name to the receptionist inside the West Wing, a pretty former campaign worker encased in hair spray, who recognized him and pretended not to. While he waited, he looked around at the antiques, heroic paintings of American views, and pewter in breakfronts. He experienced the feeling of a theatrical producer who casts a play but then is expected not to come to see it. Leigh had populated this place with its current residents, he told himself, and he would not be impressed with its occupants, who were all so terribly impressed with themselves. Hennessy was the old woman who lived in a shoe, who had so many children she didn't know what to do, but Arthur Leigh had been the necessary shoehorn.

A knockout of a young woman in jeans with a camera in her hand came into the reception room, looked at him levelly, and said, "You're the one they call 'that bastard Leigh.'"

"Only my friends call me that."

"I'm Buffie Masterson, the official photographer, and I heard you were here. You're a legend and I wanted to meet you. I don't understand—why does everybody hate you so?"

She was so fresh and radiant and young and sassy that he decided to shake her up. "You're the broad we dragged out from under the candidate after he smacked his head in the wall."

Buffie lost her color. After a pause, she said in a

smaller voice, "Now I understand why everybody hates you so."

"Honesty ain't lovable."

"You know, Mr. Leigh, um"—she stepped closer to him, conspiratorially—"we don't talk about that incident a whole lot here, y'know?"

"I haven't shot my mouth off," he said, enjoying this, "have you?"

"Never told a soul," she said, raising her right hand, with the camera clutched in it. "Never will. Will you?"

"Who sent you to me just now?"

"Hennessy, of course. I was supposed to soften you up and bring you in. So you gave me a shot in the mouth, just because I asked you why everybody hates you."

Leigh decided he liked her, she was calculated in her spontaneity. "The answer is, they hate the kind of people they're becoming, and they see themselves in me."

"You the ghost of Christmas future?" The girl read Dickens. Not just a pretty body. Leigh watched her chewing over what he had said, and then she commented, "That's off the wall. Did you just make that up, or is it something you always say?"

"Some flack gave it to me long ago," he shrugged, which was the truth, but he knew she would not believe it. He enjoyed telling the truth in such a way that it would be construed as a lie.

"If a flack like that existed," she said, "he'd be a speechwriter here."

Leigh decided the President knew where to go slumming: The girl made you want to grab her, hold her, and talk to her for hours, letting her rape your mind. "Why don't you tell Hennessy you softened me up like you were supposed to," he growled, "so I can poke my head in and be on my way."

"Almost right," she admitted. "After I got your heart all melted, I'm supposed to run you past Hank Fowler, for further working-over."

"The blind shrink?"

"You'll like him. Hennessy's in with the President, it's better than you waiting out here frightening everybody."

Leigh grinned and followed her down the hall past the Oval Office—the hall door was shut—to a tiny office containing a small man wearing earphones. Buffie came up behind him and put her hands over his blind eyes and said: "Guess who?"

Fowler took his phones off. "Just listening to the News Summary, Buffie. Mr. Leigh?"

Leigh grunted hello. The girl smiled at Leigh, offered to take his picture, was firmly turned down, and ducked out.

"We only have a couple of moments," the psychologist said, "so I'll come to the point. Do you have advice for me?"

Leigh narrowed his eyes, realized facial expressions were useless with a blind shrink, so he narrowed the eyes in his tone of voice. "Advice about what?"

"Sven Ericson. What drives him. What his weaknesses are. What his hidden strength is. You deal in mass psychology, that's your business—you ought to be able to help me."

Leigh was amused. First the woman, now the flattery from an expert presuming to ask what made Ericson tick. Hennessy was pulling out all the stops for him. He decided to let them have the truth in a short couple of bursts that they could think was baloney and could conveniently disregard.

"As long as the man needs the power, the power does not need the man. You with me so far?"

"Uh-huh."

The hell he was, that was too profound for the likes of this amateur to grab right away. He went on: "Think of power as a great thoroughbred horse, the strong neck clothed in thunder, like they say. That horse, that power, has to have a rider. So he looks over the jockeys.

"Jockey number one has a need to ride that powerhorse. He's not a whole man unless he can climb on up. That's a weakness, that need, and the power-horse knows it—but that weakness can be tolerated as long as the jockey has good hands and acts confident. Jockey number one needs power, and can handle power—so the power-horse will consent to be ridden. That was Ericson before the ambush.

"Jockey number two also needs to ride the horse, to make himself a whole man, but he can't handle the reins, he acts lost. The horse will throw him, the power-horse won't put up with a double weakness. That's Ericson now." Leigh started to rise, his little lecture over, but the blind man seemed to sense his movement and motioned him to stay.

"Keep going," Fowler said. "Jockey number three. He does not need the power, he does not have that weakness—but he doesn't have good hands, either, doesn't know how to handle power. Will the power-horse let number three ride?"

Leigh grinned. Smart little cookie, this shrink. "You shouldn't talk about the Vice-President of the United States that way," Leigh told him. "Nichols would kinda like a ride, but he doesn't need it in his gut. That's a strength, in a way; the horse will let him climb on, but somebody like Bannerman better be there to grab the bridle."

"Jockey number four," Fowler pressed on, "who does not need the power, but can handle it. No inner weakness, good hands."

"Ah," said Leigh, "now you're talkin' about an Eisenhower, kind of guy who could get elected forever. The power-horse will even walk slowly for the likes of one of those."

"Now the crucial question," said the psychologist, making Leigh feel uncomfortable, but unable to escape the extension of his own analogy. "Can jockeys change, and will the horse know it?"

"Ericson has already changed from jockey one to jockey two," Leigh said slowly, "from a man who needs power and can handle it, to a man who still needs power and cannot handle it. Sure, he could change some more—to a man who doesn't need power and cannot handle it, jockey number three, like

Nichols—but what the hell good is that? Do you want Ericson to just stagger along?"

"No chance for him becoming jockey number four, you think." Fowler made it a statement.

Leigh agreed: "That would mean he'd have to change inside, and then change outside. Never happen. Well, never say never, but not soon. Not in this term."

Leigh got up, frowning. He had been drawn into saying too much, which was not like him. He had intended to stop at jockey number two, because he had never handled a candidate who did not have that gaping hole that cried out to be filled up. He would not know how to manage a man who was so damnably secure that he could ride the horse or leave it alone; Leigh was just as glad he never met jockey number four. Buffie appeared at the door and took him around to Hennessy's office.

"Here's that bastard Leigh," she announced, "all softened up."

"All hardened up is more like it," he growled at the lawyer. She waved good-by and closed the door.

Leigh and Hennessy then participated in a forty-minute minuet. Campaign recollections, discussion about the "fateful weekend," who on the campaign staff was succeeding on the presidential staff, Hennessy's stomach acidity, an apology for not being able to bring him in to see the President, who was resting in the residence—that was a relief—and Leigh rose to take his leave.

"You may get a call from Tennessee," the politician mentioned on the way out, "checking on a guy named Kerr for highway commissioner. I think he helped out during the campaign. Good guy."

Hennessy nodded noncommittally, as he was supposed to, and walked his visitor to the small elevator. "You want to remind me of anything?" Fishing for pressure; Leigh suspected Hennessy might be heavy-handed in these matters.

"No," said Leigh, "I don't want to remind you of a thing. I don't remember anything special myself." He hoped Hennessy would leave it at that, which he did; the campaign manager wasn't some kind of blackmailer, for Chrissake. This was the favor he was owed.

When Leigh opened the dark wooden door of the Hay-Adams room, his wife had a message: "Susan Bannerman called, not two minutes ago. Says why don't we have dinner tonight, just the four of us."

"What'd you say?"

"That you might have to be at the White House till late, but I'd call back."

"Good." That was fast of Bannerman; evidently he had somebody in the White House to keep track of who the President's men were seeing, and had not given up the fight.

"Arthur, can we go to the Bannerman's? Our only other offer is to eat alone in the room, and it's costing us plenty as is."

Leigh had to assume first, that Bannerman did not know of the President's previous blindness. He also guessed that Bannerman did not know why Leigh had contacted him in the first place, and guessed further that Bannerman thought Leigh had something on the President. Next, he had to assume that Hennessy, who had probably been told of the campaign train incident, was worried that Leigh was a potential leak. Hennessy would know soon enough, through the Secret Service, that the Bannermans and the Leighs were dining together. That's why Leigh had sent his wife out to eat at Sans Souci in the first place. That would induce Hennessy—and the President—to keep Arthur Leigh happy and quiet. No blackmail; just positioning.

"Let's take him up on it," he said to his wife. "Least Bannerman could do for us—I helped him make his dopey buddy the Vice-President."

"If everybody in this town owes us something, Arthur, how come we're back home and they're all here?"

"Because they hate the kind of people they're becoming, and they see themselves in me."

She gave him a look as if she intended to take his temperature. "What did you say?"

"Nothing." That line had sounded better when he said it to that knockout of a girl photographer. He looked out the window at the White House and indulged himself in daydreaming about Buffie for a while.

The Acting Premier

The three black Zis limousines squeezed through the narrow gate in the Kremlin wall, gunned their engines, and thundered across Red Square. The few tourists and drunks wandering around at 3 A.M. watched the show of bureaucratic power: a three-car motorcade, with no flags or motorcycles, driving at top speed with blinds drawn in the dead of night. Impressive to some, frightening to others.

Vasily Nikolayev sunk low in the right-hand back seat of the middle car. He was Acting Premier, having temporarily replaced Kolkov in one of his two jobs—significantly, not as General Secretary of the party, a post that was left vacant for the time being. That night's meeting of the Politburo had gone badly for him. Nikolayev had been confronted with evidence—nebulous, hard to decipher, but evidence—that Kolkov had not been the hero he was being made out to be. The story of Kolkov saving the American President's life was said to be a Nikolayev fabrication, designed to help him inherit the Kolkov mantle. The irony was that the accusation was untrue.

"I'm surprised at you, Vasily." The man seated next to him, Slovenski, was neither friend nor foe, but chosen to make the trip with Nikolayev because he was accepted as neutral by all factions. "You knew the hospital room had microphones."

FULL DISCLOSURE

Of course Nikolayev knew the Secret Service agent's room was wired; a domed room had been chosen to make possible surveillance from afar. But he had been told nothing out of the ordinary had been overheard, even when the agent, Bok, was visited by Secretary Curtice and the President's man, Cartwright, in those terrible hours after the ambush. Nikolayev had taken Curtice's report as true, or at least as not untrue— that Bok had indeed offered the possibility that Kolkov had died protecting President Ericson. But the tape was ambiguous, with portions that could not be heard, and the Politburo could only entertain suspicions. Nothing was yet certain.

"We will ask, we will listen, we will find out," he replied. They drove the rest of the way to the military airport in silence.

The Tupolev supersonic aircraft put them in the Crimea in under two hours. At the Yalta hospital, the KGB had preparations in hand: The American medical corpsman in Bok's room had been drugged, as had the nurse. The doctors in attendance from the United States were lodged ten minutes away, and drivers had orders to bring nobody to the hospital without clearance.

Nikolayev and Slovenski, with a recording engineer, were taken to the room where Bok had been taken for the interview. The American Secret Service agent was in a deep sleep. The sodium pentothal with clarifying booster was administered, and Slovenski asked the questions.

"Your name."

"Harry Bok."

"Is that your real name?"

"Bokstansky, Harold."

The agent was taken through the hours of the ambush up to the point in the gully. Nikolayev, his heart sinking, was becoming convinced that the Curtice-Cartwright story had been induced, and could be shown to be fraudulent. Nobody would believe that he had not been a party to the concoction.

"And at that point, was General Secretary Kolkov alive?"

"No, he was dead. Grenade. And he must have had a dozen slugs in him."

"And how did General Secretary Kolkov's body get to be on top of President Ericson?"

"I dragged him over and put him there. No harm to him, he was dead."

"And when did you first think up the idea that General Secretary Kolkov saved President Ericson's life?"

"Here in the room, with Cartwright. Curtice I don't know, but Cartwright's a man you can trust. That was what Curtice and Cartwright wanted to hear. I never say I'm sure, either, I only say it's my impression and I can't swear to it."

The interrogator went back over the questions and drew the same general responses. Nikolayev tuned out. He could see what Cartwright and Curtice had been doing, and it was the kind of expedient he would have used had the roles been reversed: offering a good cover story that would help the local man in charge—at that time and place, Nikolayev—to gain an advantage, to be traded for immediate safety. The Americans' mistake was to leave their man behind, alive.

Perhaps the situation could still be salvaged; the tape of the conversation between Curtice and himself was available, and Nikolayev knew it left room for differing interpretations. And perhaps the Politburo could be convinced that a great advantage lay in having the Americans compromised. That was a good countercard to play, the Russian thought: the secret knowledge that the Americans had falsely maintained that Kolkov saved their President's life. It could be saved to play at some critical point, and at least until then, it would be wise for the Politburo to retain Nikolayev as Premier. And with time—

"Let's catch a nap in the plane to Moscow," Slovenski said. "Or at least I will. You will want to plan what to say at the eight A.M. meeting."

Nikolayev had a thought. "Ask this final question of the agent: Does President Ericson know the truth about Kolkov?"

When put to Bok, the question brought an uncertain reply: "I didn't tell him. I guess Curtice or Cartwright would have told him by now."

"Will you tell the President the truth when you see him again?"

"Sure I will. I got no secrets from the President."

Good man, Nikolayev thought; it was important that Ericson know that the Kolkov "sacrifice" was a fraud, and that his Administration had conspired with Nikolayev in its perpetration.

Next afternoon, in Moscow, Nikolayev looked over a query from an angry U.S. ambassador about suspicious activity at the Yalta hospital the night before. The American nurse and medic both insisted they had been drugged and could not account for a four-hour period. Bok did not remember anything. Nikolayev directed the Foreign Ministry to put a plane at the Americans' disposal in Yalta immediately, provided they took responsibility for Bok's safety in transit; he would not permit any such suspicion to poison the diplomatic atmosphere. The American ambassador backed off; he would seek instructions.

"We were planning to give him a medal," was Nikolayev's indignant message, "but if you want Bok home right away, we will put the medal in the mail."

The important thing, Nikolayev made clear to Slovenski, was that there be no deliberate leak of information gathered from the truth-serum interview with Bok. Such a leak could be used to embarrass the Ericson Administration, which was tottering, and a fresh scandal might just topple it. The Soviet interest, he insisted, would not be served by the downfall of Sven Ericson.

"Why not?" Slovenski was, as always, noncommittal.

"Because I have what Churchill would call a 'special relationship' with Ericson," said Nikolayev.

"He needs me, to stay in power in Washington. We can use that."

"You sure it is not the other way around, Vasily?"

Nikolayev knew that was true, too, but waved it aside: "Ericson's presidency is in our interest. No leaks about the agent's lie."

Slovenski shrugged. Nikolayev assumed that if it suited the dominant faction in the Politburo to let the truth of the duplicity in the attack on Kolkov and Ericson be known, then the leak would be leaked. If not, if the secret were kept, it would be—along with Nikolayev himself—a card to play.

The Acting Premier was well aware that his future was now closely linked with the American President whom he had regretfully condemned to death only a few weeks before. Ericson's continuance in office was necessary to Nikolayev's consolidation of power.

The Russian tried to think of ways to ensure that the opposing faction in the Kremlin did not leak anything from the Bok tapes that would weaken Ericson's position. The dam was as big as the one at Dnepropetrovsk, and it was hard to tell where the crack might develop.

The Secret Service Agent / 3

"Bok's back!" Harry smiled at the red-lettered sign carried by a delegation of the children of Secret Service men marching out toward the ramp, as his wheel chair was being carried down by two medical corpsmen. This was the returning-hero treatment, and Harry thought that was kind of nice. Come to think of it, he deserved it, and it was a good thing for the Service, too, to let the world know that its men were ready to lay their lives on the line. All the times the aging agent had wondered if he would do the right thing when the time came—those doubts were dispelled now. He was equally certain he would never put his life on the line again.

The new Treasury Secretary, Zack Parker, the one who stepped up to take Bannerman's place, was there, since the Secret Service was a division of the Treasury Department. The Secretary made a little speech for the cameras, the chief of the Secret Service shook his hand, and the agents' families clapped. Very nice; Harry hoped it would help him get a job in the counterfeiting branch—you could do a desk job from a wheel chair. He was determined not to spend the rest of his working days on a disability pension.

Harry rekissed his wife for the photographers and accepted the hugs of his two sons, fourteen and twelve —they were hams, looking at the cameras as they welcomed their father—and was wheeled into the VIP lounge for film interviews. He had been briefed: The chief had TWX'd him copies of what had been said about the ambush by the President, by Curtice and Cartwright. Nobody told him exactly what he should say, other than a general hint to stay fuzzy. Even Smitty, the press secretary, sent him a message saying, "Save something for your memoirs, the offers are already coming in."

"Would you tell us in your own words, Mr. Bok, just what happened in the gully during that last assault on the President?"

Harry didn't like that "in your own words" stuff. It smacked of the sob sister, or of a put-down of somebody who had no command of the language. But he did not let himself get testy; heroes, if they want to stay heroes, stay modest.

"Everything was happening at once," he told newsmen, "and I can't be too clear about the details. It seemed to me that General Secretary Kolkov was reaching out toward, or crawling toward, the President. I can't swear to that, though. At any rate, a lot of the bullets and flak that went into his body would have hit the President if Kolkov's body had not been protecting him. But the details are still a blur, I'm sorry." Nothing untrue; people could take it any way they wanted; fairly close to the Curtice description, but not as specific.

Two days later, after he had taken all the adulation and fussing over him at home as he was ever going to take, Harry got the call to come to the Oval Office.

An agent wheeled him in; the President, in dark glasses, was half-seated on the edge of the old Hoover desk. Another agent took the President's arm and brought him to Harry's wheel chair, where the hands of protector and the protected made contact. The President asked the other agents to leave, and moved over to an easy chair, nimbly avoiding the coffee table loaded with flowers.

"Good to see you again, Mr. President," Harry said, and then wondered if he should be avoiding the word "see."

"I'm alive and kicking, chum, thanks to you." The President seemed strong and cheerful to Harry; different with those glasses, of course, and the awkwardness of the handshake moment could not be set aside, but other than that, Ericson seemed to be comfortable in the Oval Office. "And thanks to Kolkov, I suppose."

"Well . . . maybe."

"Cartwright told me there was some confusion about that, and you all decided to give Kolkov the benefit of the doubt."

"Um." If the President wanted to know the story, Harry figured, he would ask; if he wanted to know only what he knew, Harry Bok would keep his trap shut.

"Level with me, Harry."

"Kolkov's body was lying there," Harry leveled, relieved, "and I threw it on top of you. The idea about his saving your life started when Curtice and Cartwright came into my hospital room."

"No chance of it being true, then?" A plaintive note was in the President's voice; if he needed some comfort there, Harry could give it to him.

"Sure there's a chance," he backpedaled. "He had

his arm out toward you, which could have been the way he fell, or maybe he was crawling over. Maybe I helped him over to you, he could have been alive, I dunno, I didn't stop to take his pulse. It could even be true, I won't swear either way. That's why I didn't fight Curtice's idea."

"Good," the President said. "I noticed the way you handled it in your interview at the airport, Fuzzy. Harry—" Ericson stretched out, feet on an ottoman, taking his glasses off. "Never lie. Remember I told you that for your memoirs. What I said was, 'Never lie.'"

"Not even about the broads?" Of course he would never write anything about the women in Ericson's life, but he liked kidding about them, and knew Ericson liked being kidded about them.

"Write all about the women," said Ericson seriously, "but remember they were never 'broads.' Say nothing while I'm alive, but after I'm gone—remember, first, my good taste. Interesting women. Buffie's giving me a hard time, by the way, I want you to look into that" —Harry was surprised; had the President forgotten his former chief of detail was now a cripple?—"and second, decorum. I never flaunted it, or let any woman offend the American people by living in. I kept up appearances. And never any adultery, single girls only. Highly moral, slightly oversexed—Hank Fowler thinks that's no contradiction in terms."

"Who's he?"

"I forget you've been so far out of it. Fowler's my psychologist, the best blind shrink in the world. We say he's here to help me learn the tricks of getting around, but he's more than that. Don't tell him I said so, he'll get ideas. You want to talk to him, too, about life in a wheel chair."

Harry could not help thinking about how recently —only a few weeks before—Ericson's eyes had missed nothing and his own legs, which had been slowing down, still worked. The President read his mind: "I'm a blind man and you're a cripple, Harry. At least for a while, and maybe for life. You'll find it depresses the hell out of you at first, and then you snap out of it."

"You've snapped out?"

"Nearly. Bannerman and Fong, and I think our loyal Vice-President, tried to throw me out a week ago today, you heard about that. I didn't let on to anybody, except Fowler a little, but I damn near came apart that weekend. Fowler, Duparquet, Hennessy—they held me together. And when I got sore and wanted to show everybody I couldn't be pushed, then I was okay again. So now I'm riding high. The atmosphere of this place has changed. Duparquet is on the cover of *Time* and *Newsweek,* even Melinda is falling for him, I hear, and I'm thinking about making a speech soon."

"How you gonna read a speech?"

"A prompter in my ear. But the point is the momentum is on my side. Well, to be accurate, the momentum to get me out is stopped, and things are kind of at a hinge. But now I can take whatever they throw at me, even falling on my face in public. The hopeless feeling is sort of in the background, and I can push it back. It's not gone, but I can cope."

Harry nodded. By the time he remembered what Melinda had told him, that the President couldn't hear a nod, Ericson was talking again. "So the reason I'm telling you this, and I haven't said any of this to a soul—well, there are two reasons. One is that you're a good listener, always were—only now you'll have to get in the habit of grunting occasionally—and I know you won't ever let anything leak. Except what I want leaked. The second reason is that I know what you're going through, in spades, and I can help."

"You'll help me with that job?"

"Bok, you're pretty thick at times." The President got up, evidently thought about pacing around, then thought better of it and sat down again. "Counterfeiting can wait. I want you around here. Right in close. There are three people I really trust—Hennessy and Melinda and you. I can't afford to lose you. Besides," he added, to take some of the sentiment out, "Herb Abelson's got no taste."

"Not going to look good," Harry warned, feeling safe enough to argue against his own interest, "the lame leading the blind."

Ericson waved that off. "You saved my life, I want you as a companion and a sounding board. Who can criticize?" He shifted suddenly: "You think the Russians got you to talk when you didn't know it? There was a complaint from the medic and the nurse who were watching you that they were put to sleep the other night?"

"Could be." Harry had not known of that. Was it true, and what did he tell them? He had a lot to tell, if the Russians knew what to ask, about Secret Service procedures, codes. And the President's habits, the women—everything. "I better talk to Furmark, to start changing things around, just in case."

"You don't remember anything about being interrogated, or bothered in the night, or anything like that?"

"Nope. The American nurse used to sit by me till I went to sleep. I liked her around. Kind of a blank face, but she's got a helluva build."

"Which reminds me," Ericson said. This time he did walk over to the french doors, opening them to breathe some sultry summer air, letting a bit of humidity into the air-conditioned office. "Look around for me, Harry. I'm a little hung up emotionally on Buffie, and that's not good—I need an escape hatch. Nothing complicated. Know what I mean? You do know what I mean, because Herb tells me your life is not affected by the paralysis in your legs. I worried about that for you."

"It's going to be tricky, but where there's a will." Harry meant about himself, but the same applied to providing for the President's needs.

"Whenever you guys want to call a halt," said Hennessy, rapping on the doorjamb, "you could bill yourselves as 'the maimed, the halt, and the blind.' Make a fortune in the record business."

"You think we've got the sympathy vote, Hennessy?" The President acted pleased; that must take some practice, Harry gloomed.

" 'The Song of Bernadette' should be your first smash hit. This place looks like a busy day at Lourdes." Hennessy squeezed Bok's shoulder. "Cheer up, bright eyes, better you than me. Look—I brought you a commission." He produced a large, framed document that included, in hand lettering: "Harold Bokstansky, of Illinois, Special Assistant to the President for liaison with former Presidents."

Harry swallowed. "That's quite something." A thought occurred: "But there are no former Presidents alive."

"Leaves you a lot of time for your other work," Hennessy snapped, "and besides, Sven Ericson is the closest thing you'll find to a former President, after last week. You're on leave from the Secret Service, accumulating pension rights and seniority."

"I wish, Hennessy, you'd talk these things over with me first," Harry began, but the new staff chief cut him off with "This pays fifty thou." Bok said, "I'll take it."

"This is not the place for housekeeping details," said Ericson. "This is the center of power, the Oval Office. What's happening that's important?"

"Haven't you been listening to your speedy whizbang News Summary?" Hennessy said. He looked down at Harry: "You ought to hear it, the goddamn thing sounds like a newscast for chipmunks."

"Now that you mention it," the President said, "you might read Harry the part about the Bannerman committee. We might as well bring him up to speed."

"Cliché," said Hennessy, about the old radio turntable figure of speech.

"Touché," said Ericson.

"Hey," Harry interposed, "if all this phony gaiety is being put on for my benefit, you can skip it."

"Read," the President said to Hennessy. "You're carrying the page in your pocket, torn out of the News Summary." He knew his aide.

327

" 'Two nets led'—led, mind you—'led with the announcement of the Committee to Replace the Disabled President,' " Hennessy read, " 'with former Treasury Secretary T. Roy Bannerman as national chairman, and a distinguished board of industrialists, bankers, and doctors, located mainly in the Northeast. Bannerman said it would be nonpartisan and would launch a nationwide membership drive in two weeks. "We're not against Sven Ericson," said Mr. Bannerman, "we're pro-the-Presidency . . ." The White House press secretary, James Smith, declined comment, but Attorney General Duparquet denounced the committee as "a bunch of sore losers, and the American people never like sore losers." ' "

"Good line," said Harry.

"Damn right," the President said, walking to his desk and sitting on the edge again, "I gave it to the A.G. myself." He walked back to the french doors and started fiddling with the handle. "Let's get some sun, it's not too hot today."

Harry signaled the agent at the hallway door, who alerted the agents in the Rose Garden. Hennessy and the President went out and sat on the steps. Bok moved his wheel chair to the top of the steps. Ericson put his face up toward the sun, not squinting.

"Melinda has her face pressed against her window looking at us," Harry said. Hers was the only other office that overlooked the Rose Garden.

"Tell her to come out," said the President. Bok motioned her urgently and she joined the three men.

"No bathing suit?" Hennessy started to tease Melinda, but Harry, who knew the President had something on his mind, cut him silent with a gesture.

"This is the family," Ericson said. "Just the four of us. A divorce lawyer, a spinster, a cripple, and a blind man, and we're running a large part of the world. We have to trust each other with everything. We have to trust nobody else." Ericson's voice was low, and Harry figured that the President had given this talk some thought. "Let me explain first about trusting each other. Trust is always a risk. In this situation, the greater the risk is for us to develop gaps in information that could kill us. Look at Lucas Cartwright. He's a trustworthy man, and a patriot, but he's not one of us. So when he found out about Buffie making contact with Bannerman, he couldn't put it together with something he did not know, which is about my previous blindness and the incident on the train with Buffie. So he waited a couple of days, and the whole presidency could have gone up the flue in those two days. Wasn't Cartwright's fault; it's just that I didn't trust him with everything, and I had to pay the price.

"So my point is that we four have to share our information about everything. We cannot afford gaps. Hennessy, you don't know that Melinda knows about me going blind that day on the campaign train; well, I'm telling you now, Melinda knows. Melinda, you don't know that Hennessy knows you spent last night with the A.G. at your place at the Columbia Towers; well, Hennessy knows. Harry, you don't know that Hennessy and Melinda know about the Russians truth-seruming you; they know. No secrets within this group or we're going to get run right out of here."

Ericson wasn't finished; Harry knew he didn't need questions. "Now about trusting other people: don't. Hennessy, find out who Cartwright's contact was, the one that tipped us about Buffie and Bannerman, but don't tell Lucas about the previous blindness. Melinda, work as closely as you want with Duparquet—enjoy yourself, I hope you become his First Lady someday —but only tell him what we want him to know, and I have to decide what that is. For example, I want you to tell the A.G. about Harry and Kolkov and the ambush, because he can't sit on the National Security Council with Lucas Cartwright and George Curtice as my top man without knowing that—but Duparquet has no need to know about the incident on the campaign train.

"Harry." Bok watched the President turn on the steps and face generally toward his wheel chair, grab the wheel and pull the chair closer to him. "I'm counting on you to have the agents unofficially keep a close watch on the Vice-President, in case any funny stuff is going on there. Also Buffie and Bannerman. And Arthur Leigh, the bastard. The chief of the Service cannot know of my interest, because it's all officially none of my business, and the Secret Service is not a spying arm of the President, but Harry, you're their boy and you can work on the back fence. Got it? Don't nod, speak up."

"I got it."

"Now let's recap who doesn't know what, and who knows what," the President said quietly. Harry liked the way he was completely in charge. "Besides us four, the only people who know about the campaign train blindness are Buffie, Leigh, and Herb Abelson. I'll take care of Buffie. You, Hennessy, take care of Leigh. And Melinda, you shore up Herb when he needs it, and tell me when I have to help."

The President thought a moment. "On the other matter. The only people who know about Harry's little story about Kolkov, besides us, are Curtice, Cartwright, and soon the A.G., Duparquet."

"And maybe the Russians," Harry put in.

"And maybe the Russians know all about the blindness on the campaign train, too," Melinda added.

"How?" the President asked sharply.

"If they got it out of Harry," she suggested.

"Highly unlikely," said Hennessy. "We can't make our plans on that remote a possibility."

"Let's keep the possibility in the back of our heads," the President said. "Okay—no secrets from each other, no information to anybody else that I don't know about."

"And I'd just like to say," said Hennessy, the lecture over, "that I think the Attorney General of the United States is a very lucky man, whom I personally envy."

Harry watched Melinda fight against reacting, which made her redder. "You'd be pleased to know, Mr. President," Harry told him, "that your secretary is blushing. It's nice to know somebody around here can still do that."

"You take a lot of abuse, Melinda," said the President, "but I couldn't do without you. Hennessy I could do without, but not you."

"What are we going to do now," she asked, getting up, "sit around and tell dirty stories?" Harry noticed that the President's revelation of Melinda's affair did not go down as easily as the President, in his all-for-one pitch, might have hoped it would. Melinda was probably not sore about Hennessy knowing—or Harry, who always knew these things—but about the President knowing, and not caring, or not seeming to care. Harry marveled at the complexity of Melinda's relationship with her boss, but he had to admit that the President could not have avoided dealing with it in the family.

She pushed Harry's wheel chair into her office, leaving the President and Hennessy on the stoop facing the Rose Garden. She closed the french doors behind her to conserve the air-conditioning and remained behind his chair, her fingers tightly gripping the handles.

"I think I know what the trouble is," Melinda told him when she was ready. "I think the trouble is I'm frightened."

Harry waited. In the campaign last year, she would sometimes share her feelings with him, and he had learned that questions never drew her out.

"Frightened isn't the right word," she continued. "I was frightened last week, just before the Cabinet meeting, and then that was over. Now I've got this heavy weight on my chest. Dread. I dread what's going to happen. I find myself sighing all the time. I haven't sighed since I was a kid. Harry, you understand?"

The agent knew the feeling. Harry remembered covering a crowd in a ball park, opening day, and a President was throwing out the first ball. His back was to the President and his eyes were flicking back and forth between two possible sources of danger, but he worried that there was some other place he should be watching. Nothing had happened; the President threw out the ball, watched the game for a couple of innings, and slipped out. His wave of anxiety ebbed, but it never really disappeared after that. Made him feel on the edge of helplessness, and he could understand Melinda's need to sigh, to fill up her lungs with fresh air in hope it would displace the dread.

"You think somebody's going to blab," said Harry, "and then everybody will turn on us?"

"No," she said, still behind his chair, "when I think that, I worry, but it's not the same. Even if the time in the train comes out, we'll tough it out and we'll win. Ericson's just not a loser, you know that. He'll come up with a Duparquet at the right moment, or he'll make a Checkers speech, or a Houston ministers speech, and he'll turn it around, I believe that. So should you, Harry."

"Thanks for the pep talk," Harry said. "So what is it you're mooning about?"

"It'll never end," she said. "It'll only get worse. And the more we thrash around in the quicksand, the more impossible it is to get out. What I dread, I guess, is he's going to fail, and the only thing the Boss really has now is that he's never failed. You know how I feel about him, Harry, and I wish I could help but he has me tucked away in a pigeonhole. Loyal secretary. I can't reach him, never could, but now there doesn't seem to be a hell of a lot of hope."

Harry caught himself starting to sigh and cut it short. "Maybe it's a good idea to have a man like Hennessy around," he said. They all needed a stinging astringent.

"Hennessy learned a lot of that nasty ramrod stuff in the last campaign from that bastard Leigh," she said, finally letting go the handles of his wheel chair and moving around to her desk. "Hennessy bitched once about something and Leigh carefully wrote out a message on a slip of paper and handed it to him, and told him to keep it in his wallet forever. Said it sustained him in politics through all the wars. Hennessy still has it, I bet—it says, 'It's Tough All Over.'"

Harry watched Melinda tuck in her blouse, riffle through a stack of letters, make a show of getting busy—which slipped her into getting busy. Her telephone light flickered. "Brother Jonathan," she said crisply, "it's about time you went to work for the tax-payer's dollar. The Man would like you to work with him on a speech. His note says 'foreign affairs, fifteen minutes and no longer, I want Jonathan working with me directly and no drafts from State.'" Reading up-side down, Harry saw that the noted transcription from a dictabelt said, "Get Jonathan whatsisname, I want somebody who will take down my ideas and not try to sell something of his own."

Harry wheeled himself to the door of the West Wing hallway. Furmark, head of the detail, was standing near the statuette of Nathan Hale, and came over to help. "I don't want you," Harry told him, "I want Lieutenant Kellgren, my nurse. I like the way she pushes, very gently but firmly."

"She's in the agents' lounge," Furmark said, push-ing him to the elevator. "She's a quiet one. The guys think she's too tall and bosomy for you, but they've accepted her."

"That's nice," Harry said. "Tell them to look but don't touch, I have plans for her. And get me the scuttlebutt on Bannerman and Leigh. And Buffie and the Veep. By the way, whoever gave you the poop on Melinda and the A.G.—tell him to shut up and not be such a goddamn busybody."

"Got it," said Furmark. "Any trips in the works?"

"No trips," said Harry. "Ericson sits tight right here. He likes the White House."

The Columnist

"I write like a pompous ass," Samuel Zophar told his daughter, who had kindly brought him a cup of tea. "Have you noticed that?"

"Not true," said the young woman, who should

have been married by now, but who the columnist realized was a hopeless perfectionist about men and words. "You write like the best of writers write, seated at a typewriter. It's just that what you write comes out as if it had been written by a pompous ass."

"It's not easy," said Zophar. "Anybody can write good, clean, lucid English prose. Not everybody can lard in the pomposity in a way that intimidates politicians and readers alike."

"That's why I call you 'Father,'" she agreed, "and not 'Daddy' or 'Papa' or 'Pops.' Or by your first name, as so many daughters now do. One of the reasons we all love you is that you strive so hard to be a pompous ass, and we feel we have to help."

"If any daughter of mine called me by my first name," he bloviated, "I would disown her on the spot. That's the trouble with the American family today, there's not enough disowning."

"You have to be rich to disown somebody, otherwise it doesn't count."

"Ah, but your legacy has more value than money, my dear. Power. The name of Zophar sends a chill into the hearts of the mighty. Three hundred newspapers, a hundred sixty-eight television stations. And all founded on my pretended pretentiousness." He took off his glasses and looked at her fondly. "You understand, of course, that nobody who is only pretending to be a pompous ass can ever really be one in his heart of hearts."

"Not so," his daughter contradicted him again, as he had taught her to, which he was beginning to regret. "You used to only pretend you weren't pompous. But you played the pompous role too well for too long, and now the image has become the man."

"You're thirty years old," Zophar pointed out. "Why don't you find a husband to badger with your amateur psychiatric poppycock?"

"I have a pompous-father fixation," she said, kissing his head, "and I'm what they call 'plain.' It's hereditary, but I don't blame you."

"Looks don't count any more. Or do they?" Zophar made a note on his pad, and dropped it in his "column ideas" drawer. "Are people afraid of good-looking politicians—worried they'll be taken in by a pretty face? Or are they still charmed by the good-looking Hardings, who fit a casting director's idea of a President?"

"Harding was the only newspaper publisher to become President," his daughter said, closing the door gently. Zophar stared at the blank wall in front of him. The blank wall was his best "source." He would get a tip now and then, a confidence or an insight passed along at a party, but he did not do a lot of reporting. Scurrying around for news did not befit his self-portrait of the Washington columnist. The contribution he had to make was to detect or set trends, to shine or tarnish reputations, and to introduce a note of wisdom—wisdom was not too strong a word—to the chatter and nervous news making at the center of politics. The blank wall was his partner. Downstairs, in the dining room where he bedazzled the preening transients in power, he decked the walls with signed pictures and notes of the great or notorious. Here, at his typewriter, no distractions; just a pretentious blank wall.

Looks did count, Zophar decided. Not good looks, but comforting, reassuring looks. Movie-actor looks might be a negative, but cragginess was next to godliness. Ericson had the look of a President: older than his years, tall and slightly stooped, lots of character-giving wrinkles, bushy, tousled hair, strong jaw, penetrating eyes. Used to have penetrating eyes. Bannerman, on the other hand, was close to a physical likeness of the caricature so often drawn of him: imposing, stolid, too big to be good. "Mere size is no sin," President Taft had said, all three hundred pounds of him, but nobody trusted a man that size. Zophar did not trust Bannerman either, but for a less superficial reason: The former Treasury Secretary was unaware of his own arrogance. The financier had convinced himself that he was acting in the public interest at all times; it did not occur to Bannerman that he enjoyed, even lived for, the play of power. Zophar, who often deliberately assumed an Olympian role, found it hard to understand how any man could actually believe he lived atop Olympus.

Ericson and Bannerman. Might be a good book in the relationship between those two, the way the gifted Stewart Alsop contrasted Nixon and Rockefeller. The removed-from-voters Bannerman was no Rockefeller and the coolly ironic Ericson was a far cry from Nixon, but the presence of a cobra and a mongoose on the same side of the political street was instructive. Zophar judged Bannerman to be right about Ericson: The President was wrong to cling to power when he obviously could not do the job—but would Zophar be more comfortable with Bannerman running the country through his cipher, Vice-President Nichols? Talk about a Harding. On the whole, the columnist decided, a manipulated Nichols would be better than a helpless Ericson.

His daughter knocked and looked in. "Man on the phone named Gregor," she said. "No other name. Must think he's Garbo. Very mysterious-sounding, possibly a crackpot. Shall I tell him to write?"

Zophar had an unlisted telephone number, which was taking a chance for a journalist—like the joke about the unlisted number of the Beverly Hills Fire Department—but he was not the type to get unsolicited tips. Nor did he allow a telephone extension in his study, because it might tempt him when he should be writing. He had intended to take no calls today.

"He's a Russian," he told his daughter, "I'll take it." Gregor was a fairly good source, semiofficial, useful not only in what he imparted but in the fact of his imparting it. He had never called Zophar at home before, nor had the columnist ever given him the number. Downstairs, in front of the Karsh portrait of George Marshall, Zophar picked up the receiver, listened to a request for a rendezvous, and agreed to the time but changed the place to the bar of the Hay-Adams Hotel. Public places were best.

Late in the afternoon, Zophar put on his Homburg —nobody since Eisenhower's Inaugural wore a Homburg—and stepped into his Checker Marathon. Nobody who counted had one of those roomy taxicabs, either. The chauffeur took him from his Wesley Heights residence to the television studio near the White House, where he cut a two-minute video tape on the likelihood of a split in the Semitic world. "Deep down, Jews and Arabs still distrust each other," he always believed, and still could not accept the startling fact of their recent alliance, coming as it had against his frequently expressed judgment.

Zophar was early for his Hay-Adams appointment, but a rumpled man with a familiar face and a sloppily spilling paunch said hello in the lobby. "That bastard Leigh," the columnist said cheerily, and invited the politician for a drink. Straight bourbons in hand, they discussed the state of the Ericson Administration, and Leigh—to Zophar's surprise—had no ill will to spread. The columnist had heard from Bannerman that the anti-Ericson forces considered Leigh to be in their company. But Bannerman was a loser these days, and Zophar judged that losers have no allies, only former friends. He idly tried a few probes on Leigh, admired the man's noncommittal parries, and finally spotted Gregor, his Soviet contact, looking at him from a seat across the dark room. "Arthur Leigh," he raised his glass in farewell, "I salute you with Shakespeare's classic line—'God, stand up for bastards!' " Zophar enjoyed that kind of punctuation. He took leave of Leigh, and joined the man he had come to see.

"Please come directly to the point, Gregor," he said, "without your usual reminiscences of luncheons we have had in 'space needles' overlooking Moscow."

"I had forgotten about that lunch," the compact Soviet agent observed. "You made a wager that our lovely waitress was Swedish, and I said she was Russian, and you paid up the moment she said *'Pajolsta.'* "

"Why are we meeting?"

"I have a very big lead," Gregor said. "It may be

the biggest story I have ever been able to impart. For some reason, my sources want you to be the one to have it."

Zophar said nothing. The flattery and the promotional line was par for the course, although Gregor seemed more excited than he usually permitted himself to appear.

"The ambush at Yalta," Victor said, "was set up by Vasily Nikolayev and President Ericson. The target was Kolkov. He was the only target."

Zophar held back a reaction, then gave the Soviet agent a look of contempt. "And President Ericson agreed to be blinded just to make it look like an ordinary ambush."

"I realize it is a hard thought to grasp right away. No, Ericson was not supposed to be injured. The story was supposed to be that he was saved by the heroic action of Kolkov, who was to die as he saved Ericson from the ambushers."

"Go on," said the columnist. He was surprised that any Russian agent had been given the go-ahead to plant this kind of story. It could mean that Nikolayev was under attack in Moscow right now. That was of far more interest than the cock-and-bull that Gregor was peddling.

"Nikolayev and Ericson agreed that the ambush would take place," the Russian went on, "and that Kolkov would be killed. Kolkov was killed instantly, just as planned, as soon as the helicopter was forced to land. Why else was the aircraft not destroyed in the air? The American Secret Service head of detail, Harry Bok, threw Kolkov's dead body over Ericson in the gully, as had been arranged. Then, on orders of your Secretary of State, he came up with the story that Kolkov had died trying to protect Ericson, making Kolkov a hero. Ericson was not supposed to be injured—his concussion and blindness could not be foreseen."

"The purpose of all this?"

"Kolkov was thinking of a pre-emptive strike at the Far Eastern powers. Nikolayev, who we all thought was a loyal Kolkov man, wanted to stop him and take his place. But Nikolayev's strength in the Politburo came from Kolkov's men, so Kolkov had to be a dead hero with Nikolayev the natural successor. Do you follow me?"

Zophar nodded for him to continue.

"The deal was set up with Cartwright and Curtice, representing Ericson, and the American in command of your end of the operation was Bok."

"How come the Soviets have said nothing, and Nikolayev is Acting Premier?"

Gregor shook his head vigorously and took a sip of his drink. "Nikolayev is no longer in power. He is in the process of being replaced. The story of the terrible thing the Americans did should come from the Americans, part of your investigative tradition. That is why I was told to pass this along to you."

Zophar was guarded. He had a lot to lose if what Gregor said was partially true and he pooh-poohed it. He had more to lose if he went with it and the story turned out to be a smear, or an abortive power play by an anti-Nikolayev minority in the Kremlin.

"I need corroboration from someone higher than you, Gregor. The ambassador?"

The Soviet agent shook his head. "The ambassador is a Nikolayev man who will soon be replaced. He may even have been in on the plot with Cartwright and Curtice. He will laugh at you."

"Evidence," said Zophar. "You undoubtedly have evidence to convince me of this. Before I use any particle of it, I must see the evidence." The purpose of the Soviet agent's probe, Zophar calculated, was to get a powerful columnist asking questions on the American side at the highest level, perhaps provoking a reaction here that could be useful to a clique trying to oust Nikolayev in Moscow. That is, if he had not already been ousted—one never knew. "I will be damned," Zophar said, "if I'm going to get the whole White House in a tizzy on the basis of your flimsy theorizing, without a single scrap of hard evidence. What have you got?"

"I have nothing," said Gregor. "Only the truth. And it will come out, if not through you, through somebody. It is only a matter of time."

Zophar shrugged; he would not be stampeded. "How do you know it's true, Gregor, and not just an anti-Nikolayev fairy tale? I'm sure you wouldn't be taken in, or try to take me in, on the basis of an overseas phone call. What have you got in hand?"

The Russian shook his head. "I have control of this tip for three days, then they will use somebody else or another technique entirely. You do your checking, and I will do some of mine to see what can be given to you from my side. How long do you need to get an answer from Ericson?"

"I am not saying what I will do or will not do," said the columnist. "Where, physically, is Nikolayev at this moment? Under house arrest? In Moscow?"

"I don't know."

"Give me one detail that is checkable—that if your story is true, the White House will know I have it."

The Soviet agent hesitated. Zophar assumed he was trying to appear dramatic. Finally, Gregor said, "Bok may have talked without knowing it. That's why Ericson pulled him back here so suddenly."

"Without knowing it?"

Gregor shook his head; that was as much as he was going to give. He picked up the remainder of his drink, gulped it, and said, "I'll let you pay for the drinks. Just don't put my name down on your expense account. Let's meet here, tomorrow, for breakfast. Nine o'clock. If you cannot show me how you have developed the story, then I will be disappointed and generally uncommunicative."

Zophar walked briskly out of the Hay-Adams, signaling the driver of his Checker Marathon, climbed in, and then was embarrassed to admit he did not know where to tell the driver to go. "Wait here," he snapped, and ran back into the hotel. From a telephone booth, he called the Defense Department and asked for Lucas Cartwright. The former chief of staff, now Secretary of Defense, was in Alaska. The columnist thought about calling the State Department but decided George Curtice would only mislead him. This had to go to the President for comment, and come back to him directly, without spilling all over town. The deputy director of the CIA was a lifelong friend, but Zophar had a feeling the CIA had been cut out of this. If any of this had happened at all, he added to himself, checking his inclination to treat Gregor's story as partly true. At the very least, the tip meant that a faction was at work in the Kremlin that thought seriously of a strike at the Far Eastern powers, and might be trying to enlist some pro-Kolkov men on its side. That should be brought to the President's attention.

Zophar had met Hennessy at parties, did not trust him at all; he was out. The Attorney General? No, it had to be the White House, and someone who would protect the story. Why not the press secretary? Ordinarily, it might be against the columnist's code to go to the press secretary, where all the rest of the press went, but absent Lucas Cartwright, James Smith might be the man. Zophar called the White House.

The press secretary was not there. Trust Smitty to go on that same idiotic trip to Alaska just when he was needed, Zophar fumed, leaving the presidential press office in the hands of some young ornament from Vassar. What kind of government was supposedly in charge of running the United States? Mostly people he did not trust, or people he did not know, or people he knew and trusted who were out of town. Zophar had no alternative; he left word that he would be paying a call immediately on Marilee Pinckney.

Into the car, around Lafayette Park, dropped off at the Pennsylvania Avenue gate, flashing the seldom-used press pass, into the office of the press secretary, occupied by a tall, dignified young lady in a prim sweater and skirt with whom the columnist shook hands.

"I will only take a moment of your time," he said, meaning that he would only spare her a moment of his time, since he wanted it known he was unaccustomed to dealing with underlings, unless they were bringing him useful information. Miss Pinckney, he noted, did not fuss or flatter, simply folded her graceful hands and awaited his pronouncement. "I have come into possession of some information," he continued, "which—if true—could be a source of embarrassment to the President and the nation. As a responsible journalist, I want to verify the facts before rushing into print."

"Of course, Mr. Zophar," the young lady said respectfully. "I'm at your disposal. What is the story?"

"Since it is a matter of such direct, personal concern to the President, I would prefer to discuss it with him alone."

She shook her head. "I don't see how I could even ask for an exclusive interview with the President in your behalf, without knowing what the story was."

He rose. "Do not take it upon yourself to say no, without checking with the President himself, Miss Pinckney. Please tell him first that this is a matter of great personal concern to himself and his presidency. Next, tell him that I expect, naturally, to be protected in my exclusive."

She hesitated. "Can't you just give me a hint? Otherwise, I'll look inexperienced or untrustworthy, and neither of us wants that."

He acknowledged her need. She was evidently a capable woman, not on the level he wanted to deal with, but she could be useful in getting to the top quickly and quietly. It occurred to him also that this handsome and intelligent woman might have a direct channel to the President.

"Let me choose my words carefully," he said, and was pleased that she took up a pencil. "It is a matter that a certain Secret Service agent talked about without realizing it." She waited for more. "That's all I'll say," he said.

"Got it," she said, tearing the note off the pad, "I'll be back to you tomorrow."

"Tonight would be better," he pressed. "I am not

the melodramatic type, Miss Pinckney, but this is not a matter that brooks delay of any kind. If you have access to the President, take it to him directly; if not, take it to someone who does, and impress upon him the urgency I am trying to convey to you."

"You can rely on me, Mr. Zophar," she said, "and I know the President will appreciate your sense of responsibility in coming to us first." Well said. Zophar hoped she had an intimate relationship with the President, for all their sakes.

The New Chief of Staff

"No big deal," Hennessy assured her. "I think I know what he's driving at."

"Samuel Zophar is the most pompous journalist I ever met," Marilee said, perched on the Queen Anne visitor's chair in the office formerly occupied by Lucas Cartwright, who had moved to the Pentagon. "He's a marvel. Intimidated the hell out of me. I thought it was the end of the world." She smiled warmly at Hennessy. "You're a real comfort, you are. I was ready to panic and go running to the President. Where is The Man, anyway?"

"In the Lincoln Sitting Room," Hennessy replied soothingly, "where Presidents hang out. Jonathan whatsisname the writer is with him, they've been fiddling with a foreign-affairs speech all week. Get that out, if you like, at tomorrow's briefing."

Hennessy watched Marilee slide down in her chair, nibbling a pencil tip and regarding the fancy chandelier. Most genuinely beautiful, most unself-conscious woman in the Ericson Administration, it occurred to Hennessy, that neutral thought mingling with the panic-induced constriction in his chest cavity. Christ, he thought, the first cave-in has begun, the news coming out of the mouth of a babe.

"I should get back to Zophar tonight," she said. "Why did I promise him that?"

"You want to show you work at night," Hennessy told her, "that you're not chasing around with guys, and you're ready to push Smitty into the gutter."

"Not true. I want Smitty to succeed. Somewhere."

"When the press secretary calls in from the North Slope," Hennessy put in casually, "don't go into this with him—Smitty would want to handle it himself, and it's something the President would want you to have the chance to do." The first panic that had gripped him when she had passed along the message was easing. "Tell Zophar around ten tonight that you reached me, and I said I'd get together with the Secret Service man first thing in the morning."

"Will you?"

"Yeah, I think it was Harry Bok talking in his sleep or something in Russia, and he might have spilled one of those Secret Service codes or passwords. No big deal, they can learn to mumble something different or wear different buttons. What was it Zophar said again?"

She read from her notes: " 'A matter that a certain Secret Service agent talked about without realizing it.' "

Hennessy nodded, as if it confirmed how minor the matter was. "Treat it seriously with Zophar, he thinks he has something big. You want to cultivate him anyway. I'll tell you what to tell him in the morning." How much of the story did Zophar have? Had Buffie talked? "Get your ass out of that chair and tell Melinda to poke her head in on your way out."

Marilee drew herself up in languid self-possession. "You've sure crossed the street from Intimate Adviser to Executive, Mr. Bossman. There's a real exciting whipcrack in your voice now."

He smiled, feeling sick. When the door closed behind her, he picked up a phone and said, "Tell Bok I need to see him right now, and to make those wheels burn rubber." He poured out a tablespoonful of thick white antacid, swallowed it, made a face, put his hands on his stomach a moment. Who had leaked to Zophar? And how much had leaked?

Hennessy told himself to get organized, beginning with the evidence at hand. Six or seven people, outside the Secret Service, knew of the possibility of Harry Bok having talked to the Soviets under hypnosis or truth serum that last night before being brought out of the Soviet Union. Anybody else who knew of the previous blindness of the President would also be able to put two and two together from the hurried way Harry had been snatched back. One possibility: that the Russians were leaking what they had learned about Ericson's previous blindness from Harry Bok. Another possibility: that Buffie, or Herb Abelson—who was still shaken up, and more worrisome all the time—or Leigh, had dropped a hint that reached Zophar. Maybe one of them had told Bannerman, who tipped Zophar. Stay calm, Hennessy said to himself, this may be one of those fishing expeditions, and when you're the fish it looks like the ocean is full of hooks, but when you're the fisherman it looks like the ocean is very large with very few fish.

Melinda and Bok arrived almost simultaneously. "Marilee briefed me," Melinda said, "just some minor matter about a columnist knowing that Harry blabbed something to the Russians."

"Goddamn," said Bok, slumping in his wheel chair, "they got something out of me, and God knows what."

Hennessy made a note on his memo pad to find out from Hank Fowler if it was possible to put somebody under hypnosis or a truth serum and find out from him what he had already told somebody else under the same technique or drug. It would help to know how much the Russians knew.

"First we have to find the leak," Hennessy said, being suitably calm. "It's probably something that was passed within a matter of hours, because Zophar is worried about being scooped and he's moving fast. Harry, what's with Buffie?"

The Secret Service agent picked up the transmitter

in his lap, spoke briefly, and tuned up the receiver in his ear. In a moment, he reported, "Last night she was with the writer, Jonathan Trumbull. In the photo lab this morning. This afternoon, right up to now, on assignments here in the White House. No calls to Bannerman lately, nothing out of the ordinary. She came over to me about an hour ago, wants to be with the Boss tonight, but I have something better for him and I told her no."

Hennessy couldn't stand looking calm. He let himself pace the room. "Abelson?" He didn't like the mopey way the President's physician was acting. Bok shook his head: "No, Herb's in Camp Hoover, still fishing. I got a couple of guys to buy live trout and stock the stream from up the mountain, and Herb catches about a third of the ones that go by. He's pretty glum, they say, but there's no phone, and he's had no visitors."

"Leigh?" Hennessy was not worried about Leigh; two days ago, a call had come in from Tennessee about a man recommended for highway commissioner, and Hennessy had personally given the order to the governor's office to hire him. The IOU was paid, and Leigh was a pol; Hennessy anticipated no trouble there, since keeping the secret was Leigh's bread and butter.

Bok worked his communications gear, frowned, asked for verification and repeated: "Leigh's been seeing Bannerman here in Washington, at the Bannerman home last couple of days."

"Today, this afternoon?"

"This afternoon," Bok said, "Arthur Leigh had what the agent said 'appeared to be a chance encounter' in the lobby of the Hay-Adams with columnist Samuel Zophar. They had a drink for about ten minutes, then Leigh went to the home of Vice-President Nichols, where he is now."

"The cocksucker," Hennessy breathed, "the double-crossing bastard. And I thought I took care of him." Hennessy had not ever raised the possibility that Leigh might be getting a better offer. "What time was this drink with Zophar?"

Bok checked. "Five-twenty to five-thirty."

"Immediately after which Zophar called Marilee," Melinda put in.

Hennessy closed his eyes. "And he was in her office at six, and she was in here before six-thirty. That's it. That bastard Leigh, I never thought the leaker of the previous blindness would be him."

"Don't jump to conclusions," Bok cautioned, "we'll get a report on that dinner at the Bannermans tonight."

"I'll wait for that," Hennessy replied, looking back up sharply. "Need to know who was there, all they talked about. Pull out all the stops on this one, Harry. If you have to take a few chances, it'll be worth it. Careful about Zophar, though, I don't want to get caught keeping an eye on him, and he's probably looking over his shoulder right now."

They were silent a moment. "It had to come," Melinda said. "Ever since that one-big-happy-family routine the other day, I knew it had to come."

Hennessy shot her a hard look, he didn't want her coming apart or getting sloppy. This was going to take some toughness of mind and some willingness to gamble, and they all needed their nerve. He hoped Ericson was up to a big decision. Bok had said he was running somebody other than Buffie into the Boss's bed that night, which was good; Ericson had a hard-to-figure emotional thing with Buffie—no accounting for taste— but what was needed tonight was something satisfying and uncomplicated. Bok's nurse with the big tits would do fine.

The President was in the Lincoln Sitting Room with Jonathan, the speechwriter, who Hennessy had figured out was screwing Buffie also. The kid was probably scared that the President would find out. Neither Bok nor Hennessy had mentioned the Buffie-Jonathan liaison to Ericson yet, out of kindness. Maybe it was a good idea to keep it from the President, because he was going to need that writer badly, and soon. No wonder the kid wanted protection from Cartwright as a source—he was shooting the President out of the saddle; anybody else would want the President to know all about his loyalty. Hennessy decided not to share that particular insight with Melinda or Bok yet.

"So what happens now?" Bok asked. "You deny the story and hope it will go away?"

"We could wait for Smitty to get back," said Melinda, "and he could deny it. He wasn't on the campaign train, he'd be telling the truth."

"Wouldn't work," Hennessy stated, "and it would be morally reprehensible. No more lies, no more living with a horrible secret. From now on, we tell the truth."

Hennessy enjoyed the way they looked at him. "No, this is not being recorded," he said. His idea was only half-formed, but he tried it out on them. "Scenario number one is if we wait to get hit. Zophar, and Leigh and Bannerman and Nichols, they get all their ducks in a row, and they clobber us. Figure they orchestrate it pretty well—first the column goes on the wire, then everybody covers the story on television. We issue some lame excuses and say we're sorry we didn't say the President was blind before, and the shit hits the fan in Congress. 'The President lied to us! He didn't fully disclose! He's been lying all along while we sympathized with him'—all that, and there's a move to impeach, and everybody screams for him to resign."

"You got another scenario, Hennessy?" Melinda asked.

"Yop. Pre-emptive strike. Let's assume our assumption about Leigh and Zophar checks out, and tonight the VP and Leigh are plotting the succession. We'll know by eleven o'clock, Harry, right?" Bok nodded. "Okay, we turn out a ring-a-ding speech confessing the previous blindness. That takes us all of tomorrow. Then Fowler works out that cockamamie speech-audio-feeder that he's been talking about, which we planned for the foreign-policy speech, and we quick ask for prime time and we go on the air forty-eight hours from now."

Melinda was dubious. "And Zophar will hold still that long?"

Hennessy waved the objection aside. "We'll string

him along, promise him an exclusive with the President, all that, and then let him holler afterward. He'll be sore—let's face it, it's unethical—but more important that the President put his case about the previous blindness to the people than some blowhard commentator get credit for Leigh's leak."

Melinda nodded. "Marilee can do it. Smitty being gone is a good break."

"I like it," Bok said, "a helluva lot better than sitting around while everything goes down the drain. And who knows, the speech might lance the boil. Never can tell the public reaction."

Hennessy liked it better now that he heard himself aloud. There was something about detailing a plan out loud that gave it shape and reality. He looked at his calendar for the President's activities in the next day and shook his head grimly. "Tomorrow is going to be a pisser. Tonight, about eleven, I'll tell the writer to stand by and I'll brief the Boss. If Ericson agrees, we'll put scenario two into effect. I'll brief the kid, Jonathan, and he can work all night on a draft. Meanwhile, you, Harry, get the Boss serviced and asleep by one. He and I and the writer can get to work on the speech at eight A.M., and have it whipped into shape by tomorrow night. Then we bring Hank Fowler into it, to pour into Ericson's head."

"The Boss will go along," Melinda said. "He has no other choice. Never say die. And maybe it's better to have the previous blindness out in the open, where we can fight it out once and for all."

"You just make sure your buddy Marilee comes through for us," Hennessy told Melinda, "and I don't care what she has to do to stall Zophar."

"You never do."

Hennessy said he'd talk to them later, grabbed a News Summary, and went down to the Mess to eat. "The usual," he murmured to a waiter. Hennessy's "usual" consisted of a melon, a minute steak, and a bottle of 1966 Château Lafite Rothschild, a leftover from a state dinner. The entire lunch cost five dollars, a fringe benefit.

Alone, the former divorce lawyer flipped through the News Summary, lest he fall a day behind. He forced himself to read the foreign news: Nikolayev missed a big reception and there were rumors he was ill. He marked that with red pencil to see if CIA had anything new. The Chijaps denounced the Semitic powers for interfering in the internal affairs of India, which had become an economic basket case but had a sizable nuclear arsenal, and was making warlike sounds about rich Kuwait, within grabbing distance. Nothing new about that. Hennessy stopped; he remembered that he had meant to ask the President what his foreign-affairs speech was all about. He wrote that in his "ask the Boss" notebook. Whatever it was, that speech would have to wait.

After dinner, back in his corner office, with its view down the Ellipse in the lowering darkness, the new chief of staff tried to shoot holes in his own analysis.

Could the leak have come from someplace else—inadvertently, from one of the family, from himself? Always possible, which was why he was taking his chances and having Harry Bok checking with an agent's girl who was Bannerman's waitress.

Could Zophar have developed the story totally independently? Wasn't like him—columnists were fed, they did not go foraging.

Was Zophar still ignorant of the previous blindness story, and after something else? Maybe a different story entirely? Hardly likely, it seemed to Hennessy—especially since Zophar's hint was at what Harry had told the Russians, and the Soviet advantage was in knowing the President's secret weakness—his hidden history of blindness. Hennessy could think of nothing else that Harry could have told them.

Self-doubt was dispelled by a call from Bok. "Bannerman and Leigh talked about a Nichols Administration, and about Arthur Leigh as the chief patronage dispenser. They were always careful to say it would be after the Ericson Administration, three-four years from now."

"They don't trust each other, and they're both

350

right," said Hennessy, convinced that Zophar could have no other story but the previous blindness. "Bannerman probably has the place bugged. Anybody else there?"

Harry said no, just the Leighs and the Bannermans, and added that it appeared Hennessy's hunch was accurate: Leigh was in their camp. Zophar's name had come up, as part of the general conversation, as far as the waitress could make out.

The new chief of staff called the President, who was still in the Lincoln Sitting Room with the speechwriter. "I need to see you for a half hour right now, and I'd like for the writer to stick around, but not with us. I'll need to see him after I see you."

"What's up?"

"A problem," Hennessy hedged, "but I have a way to handle it. I'll be right over."

He hurried down the hall, through the colonnade along the Rose Garden, into the residence basement to the elevator. The guard, expecting Hennessy, took him to the second floor, where Jonathan whatsisname was seated in an easy chair in the central hall wearing the radiant expression of a young man who had been high on a mountaintop. Hennessy told the writer to stick around, not to move, while he saw the President in the Lincoln Sitting Room.

"Cough, cough," Hennessy said to Ericson, "I'm here." The President was in an open shirt and a pair of slacks, no glasses, eyes looking blankly ahead, long frame draped along the sofa. "What you been doing, Sven?"

"Being President," Ericson said. "Interesting job. Foreign affairs was never my strong suit, except for the economic side, but I think I'm getting the hang of it."

The former professor had enjoyed being with a bright young student again, Hennessy figured, and you could learn a lot by teaching. Jonathan would be the right writer for tonight.

"Let me give it to you straight," Hennessy said, "and if you really like the job, you may want to put up a fight for it. First, we need a drink." He poured out a couple, put the President's in his hand.

"There's been a leak?" Ericson put it in question form, but it was a statement of an event he had been expecting.

"Arthur Leigh, the bastard, was seen with Sam Zophar this afternoon. Half hour later, Zophar was in the press office, asking Marilee for an interview with you on a big story."

"Um. I thought you said you were taking care of Leigh."

"I thought I did," Hennessy told him. "I won't go into details, but I took care of an item for him, nothing earth-shaking. But evidently it wasn't enough, or he got a better offer. Anyhow, he sold out."

"Can't be sure," Ericson cautioned, leaning forward, rubbing his temples. "What did Zophar say?"

"Said it had to do with something Harry Bok had said without knowing it. A bunch of people know how fast we pulled Harry back home, Mr. President. It wouldn't take a hell of a lot of imagination for Arthur Leigh to figure out that Harry told the Russians about your accident on the campaign train."

"Maybe, maybe not. Marilee sitting on Zophar?"

"No problem tonight. As I see it, we have two options. One, to sit tight and let the storm break, or two, to take it public ourselves. You must have known this moment would come, we all did, and I've been planning for it."

Hennessy went over the alternative scenarios in detail, Ericson resisting every inch of the way his new chief of staff wanted him to go. "I don't know if I could do the best possible speech so quickly, Hennessy. And I don't know for sure that I can get any speech delivery system worked out so soon. In a couple of weeks, maybe, not in forty-eight hours. I could screw it up."

"That you could," his lawyer told him. Hennessy did not want to press—indeed, knew that pressing would sit badly with Ericson—but there came a time when you had to be decisive. "If you make a speech telling how the previous blindness happened, and how you're on the mend now and more and more capable of doing the job, you'll be ahead of the news curve. If you don't, we'll be reacting, and we'll be apologizing, and we'll get the shit kicked out of us."

"What do the others say?" Ericson, not like he used to be, seemed to need a consensus.

"There's just Melinda and Harry. They think it makes sense. Melinda thinks you'll find it a relief to get it behind you, clear the air."

"She's wrong," the President said. "I'm happier with everything just the way it is. This is the wrong time to go rocking the boat. I need time."

Hennessy shut up awhile to let Ericson think. After a few moments, the President said, "Tell Marilee to squeeze Zophar for what he's got. I don't want to take the plunge unless I'm sure. Maybe he doesn't have the story at all. It could be something else— but no, not if it came from Arthur Leigh."

Hennessy capped his temper; this was a hell of a way for a President of the United States to act, pussy-footing along when he should take charge of events. Well, Ericson was new. So was Hennessy at the staff chief's job, and he allowed as how a little caution could be a good idea.

"Why don't we do this," he suggested. "I'll put Marilee to work messaging Zophar—thank God Smitty isn't here—and I'll arrange to see him myself tomorrow afternoon. Meanwhile, let's get our ducks in a row in case we decide to go the speech route. Let's brief the writer, Jonathan, tonight, and get him to do a draft of the speech for tomorrow morning. We'll get Hank Fowler in then, if you like the speech, and begin to feed it to your head. We can abort anytime. If Zophar only has a little piece of the story, or has it all wrong, then we can sit tight and do nothing. All we would lose is a day's work."

Ericson shook his head, no. "That would open it up to two more people, neither one with any particular loyalty to me. You know how it is when you get into a speech preparation, you get so you want to give it—

there's that momentum, too, that could carry us right off the goddamn cliff."

"You want to sleep on it?" Hennessy figured he had lost.

"Yes. Come back in the morning, early."

Hennessy leaned on the doorjamb. He could see the writer in his chair in the yellow oval living room, twenty yards away, making notes about some foreign-affairs speech that would never be given. "Sven, you want advice from your former intimate adviser, now chief of staff?"

The President did not answer right away. "I know what the advice is, and I won't like it." Ericson hesitated. "Okay, Hennessy—what do you think?"

"The kid out there is loyal to you. I think he's Lucas Cartwright's source, the one who told him about Buffie and Bannerman."

"How does the kid know?"

"He's your brother-in-law."

The President looked puzzled, so Hennessy gave it to him hard. "He's banging Buffie." That hung in the air as the blood went out of Ericson's face. "The kid didn't want you to know," Hennessy continued. "That's why Lucas was so mysterious. Jonathan is loyal —he blew the whistle on Buffie and Bannerman. We can count on Jonathan to keep his mouth shut, at least for a couple of months."

"Then he can write his memoirs," Ericson nodded. "I don't care what he says. That's not so—I care what he says, that's why I talked with him for hours tonight, with his pencil scratching, so he'll have a side of me for history that not a hell of a lot of people know. You're sure about him and Buffie?"

"No," Hennessy let the sarcasm show. "I'll go ask him."

"Stay," Ericson said, reaching a hand out in Hennessy's direction. "I don't want the kid to know I know. Hennessy, that girl has a hold on me, especially now, and I'm annoyed with myself about it. God, you pay for everything."

"You developed an attachment with a woman half

your age, Sven," Hennessy said quietly, no longer the chief of staff or even the official intimate adviser, but the old friend and former divorce attorney. "It happens to a lot of guys. And you're right, you eat your heart out after a while, you pay in blood. But there comes a time you finish paying. Something new comes up. Time wounds all heels."

"Puns, that's all I need."

"Look," Hennessy said briskly but as gently as he could, "the best news I heard about your state of mind is when Harry Bok told me you wanted a different girl for tonight. That means you're trying to shake your dependence on Buffie for emotional and sexual support, because it's gotten too strong. Good for you. You cannot let yourself need her, it's a weakness."

"How many shrinks we got around here?"

Hennessy smacked the doorjamb. "I dunno who Harry came up with for tonight, ol' buddy, but if it's that nurse of his, the tall one with the fantastic legs and the big tits—then you're better off than I am, Gunga Din." If Ericson needed a little ego massage for his machismo, Hennessy figured, it was easy enough to provide.

"They say her face isn't all that much to look at."

Hennessy's spirits sagged; here was the President of the United States, a newly blinded man under attack, with his secret leaking and the leak desperately needing to be plugged, worrying about the attractiveness of a face he would never see in order to shore up his battered ego.

"Reminds me of Ingrid Bergman," Hennessy lied. "Wears no make-up, that's why some jerks can't see her good looks. But you never went in for heavy make-up."

Ericson stood up and changed the subject. "Bring the writer Jonathan in," he said firmly. "We'll brief him together about the previous blindness. Leave out the part about the accident on the train happening with Buffie and me in the sack, that's not to come out publicly anyway. Maybe we can make a case,

Hennessy—at least, we'll see how it reads in the morning."

"I'll alert Fowler, too," Hennessy said, delighted that the President had decided to take the matter in hand.

"No, we'll only take one step at a time, and each one only if we have to. Maybe," Ericson added, "we can work some of this foreign-affairs stuff into the speech, too, looking ahead and all that. Nothing's wasted."

"You're stepping up to the situation, Mr. President," Hennessy said proudly. "Hats off, and all that."

"I just wish to hell," Ericson said one last time, "that we could be sure we're not overreacting to what we think Zophar has."

"That's behind us now," Hennessy told him. It was not presidential to have second thoughts right after a decision. The new staff chief waved Jonathan into the room and the three of them went to work on the speech.

The Speechwriter / 2

Woodrow Wilson, that's who Ericson is like, Jonathan thought, only more human and less austere. Same idealism, same reach for greatness, but without the arrogance. The shattered dream. For nearly three hours, he had been alone with the President as Sven Ericson expounded on his dreams for the people of this country and his vision of freedom throughout the world. Unabashedly corny in some ways, too; not the cool and detached participant-as-observer he was perceived to be. Ericson had opened up to him, to Jonathan Trumbull, who was lucky enough to be on the spot with a pencil in his hand and the ability to tell it to history. There had been moments when Jonathan had been too moved to write; he could reconstruct those.

Range was what Ericson had, the writer concluded. The eye for the minute detail, the ability to sense weakness in one foreign leader and the hidden strength in another, the understanding of the human foibles that made great men real men. At the same time, Ericson displayed the broad scope of his strategy: how to bring forth the under-currents that motivated the Far Eastern powers, how to play that against the forces that agitated the Semitic powers, and a certain fatality that seemed to say that a President was only given a small arena, mainly economic, in which to manipulate men or guide events. "Brother Jonathan," as they called him, had written it all down, Ericson at his most unguarded and best; in years to come, he would incorporate some of that vision into drafts of speeches, which was a way that he—a relatively inexperienced kid—could have an impact on the world, make his contribution to the action and passion of his time. Even if only a little, and that secondhand.

What a night, Jonathan marveled, in the back seat of the White House car that was taking him back to Columbia Plaza. First time he had a car assigned to him, but the President and Hennessy evidently didn't want him driving around Washington on this night by himself. What a night: first the hours with the President, the intimacy of discussing his dreams, then the blockbuster, after Hennessy had come up, about the previous blindness. He shook his head in worried wonderment at what the President must have been going through, the past few weeks. Finally, now, it was up to Brother Jonathan, his typewriter and his way with words, to lay out that story in a way that would minimize the terror in judgment, and accentuate the President's desire to take the American people into his confidence, because he refused to live a lie.

"No sob stuff," President Ericson had directed. Tell what happened in sequence during the campaign: how he lost his sight temporarily after a shock; how nothing was said for a day while his aides wondered if he would regain his sight; how it was felt mistakenly afterward that the condition was purely temporary and would not be repeated. That mistake was to be admitted forthrightly, in retrospect; let the people with twenty-twenty hindsight get their full satisfaction. Remember that, the writer told himself; twenty-twenty hindsight was a nice play on sympathy.

Jonathan had the beginning of the speech shaped in his mind when the car drew up to his door and the driver said, "I'm to wait here until replaced, so you don't have to call the pool for a car. You're a big wheel tonight, Mr. Trumbull—enjoy it."

He put the key in the door of his apartment and noticed it was not double-locked. The lights were on. Buffie was asleep in a chair in front of the television. Jonathan's heart sank; he should never have given her the key. Of all the nights he needed to be alone, this was the one.

And the secret; she must not know what he was to write. No, he was painfully aware that this was not the night for Buffie. He touched her shoulder, and then thought about the car outside. The driver would see her. Should he send her home in the White House car? God, no, it would surely get to the President. He couldn't keep her here, not if he had to turn out a speech in seven hours, and he could not send her home. Jonathan did not quite know what to do, so he shook her shoulder until she woke up.

"I was lonely so I came over." She stretched. "Then I got the sleepies. Mad at me? You don't have another girl out there in the hall, do you? If you do, bring her in, I'm not—"

"No, no, I'm glad to see you." She was adorable in half-sleep. "It's just that I have this speech to finish and I gotta write all night."

"Big drama," she whispered. "I'll keep bringing you coffee and massaging your back. We'll save the world, the two of us." Speculatively, she touched his leg.

"No, look, seriously, Buffie, I've got to get to work. If I'm late with this, it'll be my ass."

"What's it about?"

"Foreign affairs," he half-truthed. "You know, I been working on this all week and now they need it right away. Hennessy isn't like Cartwright, with him it's got to be immediately." Working on the President's speech, possessed of the President's secret, in the room with the President's girl, and a dawn deadline looming, this was a lot. Jonathan needed a little time to sort it out. "You go in the bedroom and go to bed," he suggested, "and go to sleep. That way you won't be lonely, I'll be right here." If she came out to look at the speech, he had drafts of the foreign-policy stuff he had been working on, he would leave them all over, she wasn't interested in that. The secret of the previous blindness—which would be so useful to Bannerman —that, Buffie must not see.

"Okay," she yawned. Deliberately, not provocatively, she took off all her clothes in front of him, lumped them under her arm, and kissed him. "Everybody's so busy, a girl can't even get laid any more," she said, turning. At the bedroom door, she added, "Last chance."

"Buzz off."

"Oh, you're so masterful. You Tarzan, me Jane. You Samson, me Delilah. You Sam Spade, me— what was her name?"

Jonathan gave her a sudden, blank look. "That's a thought."

"What's a thought? You going to use Tarzan in the speech? I know"—she put on a deep speech voice— "as a special show of respect to our African allies, I have decided to take on a Seeing Eye chimp. And here he is now." She took the hand of an imaginary chimpanzee and pranced around the room, calling "Wait for me, Cheetah!" After a moment, she stopped. "That wasn't your thought?"

"Samson," Jonathan said. "Bible. Kind of reference I need."

"You really going for that Bible-totin' jazz?"

"Samson lost his sight, but it didn't stop him. Obvious. And you're right, Buff, the Bible story's the

359

wrong place." He went to the telephone in the bedroom and called his researcher. "Sally? I got a challenge. You up? Well, rise and shine, chum, the night is young. Lookit, I need you to find a poem by John Milton, long poem, called *Samson Agonistes*. It's a little late for the Library of Congress, but I don't tell you your business. Just get it, read it, find out some passage that can apply to President Ericson, and get back to me in a couple of hours. If you need a White House car, use my name, it'll work for once, tonight. Okay, move."

"You're a terror," Buffie told him. "I'd sure hate to work for you." She still had her clothes in a bundle in her arms. "You want to order me around a little? Crack the ol' whip? I wouldn't say no. The New You is kind of a turn-on."

Jonathan had more important things to do. "You've made your contribution," he snapped, enjoying it, "now get out of my hair." She inclined her head respectfully and closed the bedroom door.

Problem postponed. Now he had the most important speech of his life to do. He would handle that, too. Jonathan felt unexpectedly confident, partly because he always knew he could do it, mainly because he had the beginning in his head: "There is a matter on my conscience that I feel I must share with my fellow Americans," was the way to open. Start with the strong vote of confidence of the Cabinet. Then flash back to the campaign. How insignificant the temporary loss of sight seemed at the time. Then the second blindness, and the question—what to say now? The President's initial confidence that he was going to see again soon, same as the last time. Then the mistake—admit it, disarm everybody—of covering up. The dilemma, his struggle with conscience, his decision to tell all. Hit hard Ericson's new ability to cope, open up a little on the problems with Moscow and the Far Eastern powers, then his vision of peace—can a blind man have a vision? Good image. Jonathan, who liked to do the easy parts of a speech draft first, wrote the opening and the peroration, and was hammering out some loose lines for later insert when he heard the telephone ring.

The telephone was in the bedroom. His researcher couldn't be that fast—who was calling at this hour, half past midnight? He opened the door, suddenly remembered the girl in his bed, and was stunned to see the nude Buffie sitting up in bed, holding the receiver, saying "Yes, he's here. Who's calling?" Buffie smiled and handed it out to him: "It's the President," she said.

Jonathan closed his eyes in horror. Buffie chuckled. "It's the White House operator, lover, not Ericson. I wouldn't do that to you."

"Hullo?"

"The President is calling, Mr. Trumbull. Would you stand by?" Buffie made room for him in bed. He sat on the edge, facing away.

"All finished yet?" The President's voice was relaxed and cheerful, no sign of strain, no forced cheeriness either.

"I've got the first page in the typewriter," Jonathan said.

"I'm kidding, Jonathan. Take your time, you have all night. And there's a chance, too, that I might not give it for a couple of days."

"The urgency's gone?"

"Well, you know how Hennessy is, everything has to be done yesterday." Jonathan had just made the same observation; obviously, the President and his writer were on the same wave length. He reeled at being taken into Ericson's confidence on a matter as intimate as a knock at the chief of staff. "We'll see. Look, I just spoke with Herb Abelson, who's all upset, so would you put in your draft that I kept all this quiet against his better judgment? He'll like that, and it won't cost me anything. I didn't tell Herb about the speech, of course, nobody but you and I and Hennessy know that, and we have to keep it that way."

"The foreign-affairs speech," Jonathan said, thinking of Buffie behind him.

The President paused. "That's the one," he said

finally. "Well, I was feeling good, and I wanted you to know I have every confidence in you, and I won't need the draft before nine o'clock. Go to it." He cut off.

Jonathan turned around. "Well, that was the President, and he didn't send you his best, thank God."

"He was up, was he? Feelin' good?"

He nodded. She thought about it for a while, sleepiness slipping away, and observed moodily, "He does that after he's knocked off a piece. He likes to call somebody up and talk business. I don't know who the hell he thinks he's impressing."

"You jealous, Buffie? Not like you." It occurred to Jonathan that Buffie must be thinking of another woman in her place next to the President tonight, with him doing what he did when she was there. But Buffie was wrong, assuming President Ericson only did that to show off, or have a private joke—the call was for a purpose, to add the line about Dr. Abelson.

"I hate the bastard sometimes," she answered, wide awake, "because he's so important to me. He has a hook in me." She put her finger inside her cheek and pulled, to illustrate.

"You love him?"

"Of course I love him, and he's crazy for me."

"Then why are you spying on him for Bannerman, who only wants to ruin him?" Jonathan had a lot to do, but this was worth finding out.

"There's no future for Ericson and me. We started coming apart the minute we got together." Buffie moved out of bed to the window, breasts too firm to sway, holding her hands out, as if to warm them, in front of the air-conditioner. "To him, I'm a piece of ass that got out of hand, and now he's emotionally involved and he's sore at himself for it. For needing any woman in particular, and especially for needing one so obviously not in his set."

"Come on, he's not a snob—"

"Of course he is! He doesn't have anything to talk to me about that interests him. When he talks to me, he's only trying to find out what young people think, or women think, or how we talk. I know that. He's a user, but I mean a complete user, nothing is wasted.

He manufactures memories, you know? Whenever I'm with him, I know that he's thinking of how he'll remember it when I'm long gone and he's dealing with people in his own world. And his own wrinkled, decrepit age group."

"Doesn't the blindness change anything?"

"Yeah, it puts the whole thing on my head, which is what he always wanted. Now I'm the son of a bitch for pulling away, now when he needs me most, all that jazz. I got to look out for myself, because he'll never look out for me, blind or not." She ran her fingertips along her huddled arms. "When I'm not with him, I don't miss him. It's when I'm with him that I miss him most."

Jonathan told himself he would have to pursue that one day, but now he had a dawn deadline—nice alliteration, dawn deadline. "You get some sleep," he said, extricating himself, but Buffie was not ready for that.

"How important is a goddamn speech? So you'll be a few hours late, I don't open up like this on cue, or to anybody. You afraid to look inside me, too?"

Jonathan shook his head firmly. "Sorry, this is an important goddamn speech, and the needs of the nation come first."

"Is he gonna spill the big secret?"

"What big secret?"

"You're a good security risk, Jonathan," she said, with a disconcerting smile. How much did she know, he wondered—and how much did Bannerman know through her? She was not going to get anything out of this speechwriter, though.

"He's telling all about the time on the train," she continued, "and you've got to put it together so it all comes out innocent."

She knew. "You know," he said stupidly. But if she knew, why didn't everybody know? Why hadn't Bannerman used it to drive him out of office? "I thought it was the most tightly held secret in the world," he said aloud, to himself, "and the first person I run into knows all about it."

"So Potus really is laying it on the line," Buffie said. "Good for him. Gutsy thing to do now."

"Have you told Bannerman?"

"Course not. What kind of person do you think I am?"

"You're a double-crosser," Jonathan enumerated, "a fink, a girl who loves one man and informs on him to his worst enemy——"

"But not on the big thing. Small change, sure, a chance at a leg up in a career." She crossed to the bed and got under the covers. "But I don't go for the jugular. I'm not a shit."

"How did you know? Did the President tell you, Buffie?"

"About his not seeing before?"

There it was, in plain words, from one who knew. "Yep, that's it, his previous blindness."

She grinned. "He didn't tell you how it happened?" Jonathan shook his head.

"You'll want to put this in the speech," she said in mock seriousness, "for color. A little anecdote to liven up the picture caption. Well, you see, he was fucking me in an upper berth of the campaign train, humpin' away like crazy, and I was right on the edge of coming——"

"Oh Jesus," Jonathan breathed. He wished he were not hearing this.

"——when, *wham!* the brakes are slammed on, and he's on top of me like this, and my legs are up like this, and *crash!* goes his head into the steel headboard. He's like a dead weight, but still stiff, and still in. I couldn't breathe, I couldn't get him off me, so I hollered bloody murder until Harry Bok came to the rescue. Then——"

"These are private matters," Jonathan interrupted firmly, "between you and the President of the United States of America, and you really ought to keep it to yourself. I wasn't told about it. And it sure as hell isn't going to be in the speech."

"Pity," Buffie sighed. "He'd get a lot more sympathy.

What are you going to have him say, that he bonked his head into an economic adviser?"

"I don't go into that kind of detail. He bonked his head, is all." He had a thought. "And it's a good thing for you nothing is said about how it happened. If that gets out, and Bannerman knows you knew about it and just strung him along and never told him, then he'll have you on his shit list for the rest of your life. That wouldn't help your career."

She nodded, and nibbled a nail. "I hadn't thought of that. Forget I said it. It was all a lie."

"Buffie," he said, "why do you have to play both ends against the middle? These are powerful people you're fiddling with."

"I figure if I'm a little loyal to everybody, everybody'll be a little loyal to me. And I can't be one hundred per cent for Ericson—I'd fall in a trap and never get out." She sat up and looked plaintively at Jonathan. "I'm happier with you, right here and now, than I ever would be with him, even in Mr. Lincoln's bed." He saw her mood change at that thought. "I wonder what bimbo Harry lined up for him. Probably Silent Sam, the Swedish nurse with the big tits and the zipped lip."

"You're a phony," Jonathan told her.

"But not a real phony," she parried.

"A genuine phony. You give me all this horseshit about your career, and how we have to look ahead, and cozying up to the powers that be after we're out of the White House—and it's nowhere in touch with reality. You're not gettin' ahead, you're gettin' your kicks—this whole thing is a huge ego-trip for you, and you won't admit it to yourself. Laying the President, laying his writer—you laying Bannerman too?"

That question had been in the back of his mind ever since she introduced him to Bannerman, and he immediately wished he could call back the words because he was afraid of the answer from a girl with such fidelity to unfaithfulness. Jonathan was more deeply involved with her than he wanted to admit, and was even beginning to resent her affair with the President.

"He's a terrifying man in a lot of ways," she said,

not answering. "I sure wouldn't want to cross him. I better shut up about the train, my part in it. You too, huh?"

The undenied possibility that the gross Bannerman, too, was enjoying Buffie's favors suddenly infuriated Jonathan, who wanted to see her as a free spirit and not as some kind of slut, as a talent in a conniver's masquerade, and as a woman who could be his own. The speechwriter, with his dawn deadline, ripped the covers back and looked at her fresh but too-well-used body curling in surprise, pulled off his clothes, and tore into her the way a dangerous multimillionaire or a candidate on a campaign train might. He satisfied himself, pulled away before she had a chance to reach a climax, took a cold shower, and went back into the living room, jeans and no shirt, to finish the speech.

The writing went well. The fierce, punishing interlude might have been just what he needed, Jonathan thought. Fresh start. Strange girl. He wrote a transition into the peroration, added the line the President had wanted about Dr. Abelson advising full disclosure from the start, and began stapling paragraphs in sequence on clean white sheets. He worked this way, in bits and pieces. It sometimes made the first draft choppy, but such was his method. He looked at the electric clock: 3:15. Not yet dawn. He started from the beginning on a second draft.

What he could see of the Potomac River was turning from black to gray when the telephone rang again: 4:35. He moved quickly this time to keep Buffie from grabbing it again, but she lay spreadeagled, uncovered, and fast asleep; when she slept, she slept. He picked up the receiver.

"I have Mr. Hennessy for you, Mr. Trumbull," the operator said. "Sorry to disturb you at this hour."

"You got it done?" Hennessy said. His voice was flat.

"It's not in bad shape," Jonathan said. "I need a couple of hours yet, to cut it down to a half hour." The writer had been tired a half hour before, but the drained feeling passed and he had his second wind and would be functioning well until two in the afternoon, when he would surely fall apart.

"Look, we got a problem," Hennessy said. "Herb Abelson took too many pills and he's dead."

"Suicide? The President's doctor?"

"Maybe, maybe an accident. I'm going to Camp Hoover now, it's about a two-hour drive. If there wasn't any note, there wasn't any suicide."

"The President talked to him tonight, called me and said—"

"Yeah, I know," Hennessy said, "I got the phone log. In the speech, put him in the past tense, call it an accident—better still, don't put him in the speech at all, one thing's got nothing to do with the other. If the President wants to maunder over it, don't let him."

"You think the strain of the secret, and maybe the thought that he helped to mislead the eye doctors, might have gotten to Dr. Abelson?"

"I think he was upset about something, maybe his own personal life, and maybe he forgot how many pills he was taking." Hennessy's voice was cold and controlled. "Don't overdramatize this, don't go jumping to conclusions. I'll look at the evidence, I'll talk to the forest ranger there, I'll bring back the body. This may just be a coincidence. The reason I'm calling you is to make sure you have the goddamn speech because we're going to have to go with it sooner than the President thinks."

"I have it."

"Good. I should be back around ten this morning. You get it to Melinda in her office at eight. She and you and the President will start going over it right away. I'll tell her to get Hank Fowler in on it right away. Say nothing about Abelson until I get back. That specifically includes the broad in your bed." He hung up.

"Have a good trip." Jonathan put the phone down. The draft speech was all right, he knew, but he was not so certain it would be well received any more. The pressure on Ericson to come clean must have been intense, and the President's decision to make a clean breast of the matter would not seem so much an act of conscience as an act of necessity. "Foreboding," he said aloud at the girl on the bed, to lessen the feeling he had by identifying it. She didn't stir. "Gloom and doom," he tried. Perhaps the heavy feeling on his chest was only the result of a sleepless night, and maybe the exhilaration of working directly with the President on a speech would soon return. But he knew a few things could not, even for a Candida, be glossed over: the death of the President's doctor, the controlled fear in Hennessy's voice, the creepy suspicion that Hennessy's crack about the broad in the bed was based on surveillance, not conjecture. "Enlightened trepidation," he said to Buffie's form, and as if in response, she rolled over.

The Therapist / 3

"I thought I told you to have a heart-to-heart with Herb Abelson, Hank," the President said, voice cold.

"You did, sir, and I never got around to it." The consequences of his failure oppressed and frightened the psychologist. "It always seemed that there were more important things to do. I failed you, and I failed Herb." Hank Fowler checked himself for having his priorities confused; his failure to Abelson had been considerably greater than his failure to the President.

"Not your fault. Mine, more than anybody's—I didn't size up the situation last night when I talked to him. Herb sounded bad, irritated as hell and nervous, but not on the brink of something drastic." Fowler heard the faint sound of a fingernail being bitten. A silence, a sigh, then: "What did you think of the speech?" the President asked. The writer, Jonathan Trumbull, had read it to them moments before, and then had been sent back to his typewriter.

"The speech itself, or the contents?"

"React to everything, Hank. I need to know where you stand before we go into today's activities, which may turn out to be a little hectic."

The psychologist, an elbow on the President's desk in the Oval Office, resisted the temptation to react as an individual blind man, reminding himself that he was dealing with a patient in trouble. "First, about the speech itself. It ran about twenty minutes, which I think could be cut to about fifteen. That would make it about the right size for you to handle."

"Agree," said the President.

"I would have to hear it again a few times," Fowler said, gaining confidence from the details, "but I think it separates naturally into five segments, of—let's say —three minutes each. We could break it down and you could handle it that way." The nuts and bolts would help reinforce the President's confidence as well as his own, Fowler knew; the therapist was proud of his method of segmenting a speech, summarizing each segment with a recorder that could be received in a small earpiece. It enabled a blind man to appear to speak extemporaneously—from aural notes, promptings in his own recorded voice.

"You know how I work," the President said. "How soon could I learn to do it?"

Ericson was a quick study, Fowler reckoned; with this patient-student, the preparation could be speeded up. "I'd say you would need about six or seven hours. If you decide what the speech should be by about ten this morning, you could deliver it tonight." Fowler preferred that same-day delivery; overrehearsal or memorization would remove the necessary spontaneity.

"Good, I may have to," the President said. He started to crack his knuckles. There would be five cracks, Fowler knew; three knuckles on one hand, two on the other. At the sound of the fifth, the psychologist broached the content of the speech, the more difficult part of his reaction.

"On the matter of your previous blindness," he began, "I think you were wrong."

"Always glad to have a moral judgment," said the toneless voice, "from somebody who wasn't there."

"No, I'm not judging the business about whether you should have made public the two-day blindness on the train before the election." Fowler paused, allowing himself a bit of judgment: "I guess you should have, but what with all the confusion, I can see how"—he reached for the phrase—"your saying nothing would appear to be part of the semiconsciousness associated with the postconcussion period." Well put. "That's not the problem."

"A lot of people will think that's precisely the problem."

"Yeah, well, that's something that can be argued, or explained." Fowler decided to press the point with the President, since it bore on a danger Ericson evidently did not know he faced. Discussing it might contribute to Ericson's feelings of guilt about Abelson's suicide, but that would have to be confronted quickly anyway. "I think you were wrong not to tell your doctors about your previous blindness after the assassination attempt in Yalta."

"That's easy to say, Hank," the President said, not so coldly this time, "but I didn't want to rush into any decision. And since I had been through something similar before on the campaign train, I figured it would clear up again. You have to understand, the doctor-patient relationship would not have protected me—the story would have come out. In all probability, I would have lost that disability vote in the Cabinet. I needed time."

Fowler shook his head and said automatically, "I'm shaking my head no. You're thinking politically, tactically, Mr. President. I'm thinking medically, as Herb Abelson must have been thinking—a doctor concealing relevant medical evidence from a specialist, perhaps causing the wrong treatment. I can see why it got to him."

The President waited, and Fowler laid it out. "I'm not a medical man, but I have made it my business to know something about the causes of blindness. The first time you were injured, in the train, it may be that you cracked the optic channel—the housing for the optic nerve that goes between the eye and the brain."

"Herb had some X rays taken," Ericson replied. "He put some staff member's name on them and had them read at Bethesda. He said they didn't report any permanent damage."

"Um," Fowler acknowledged, "and it could be there wasn't any. But the second time it happened, at Yalta, and blindness ensued, it could be that the treatment should have been different."

"What do you mean?"

"I'm not a medical man," Fowler cautioned again, "but it could be that knowing of a record of previous blindness, an ophthalmologist—looking at your symptoms after the ambush—might have called for a neurosurgeon."

"Come on, come on," Ericson snapped, "get to the point."

"It could be," said Fowler, not rushing, "that a neurosurgeon might have decided—knowing of the previous blindness—to go in and lift the top of the optic canal, to relieve the pressure on the nerve. An operation might have helped." Fowler let that sink in, then moved to soften the blow: "Of course, he might not have recommended that at all. And an operation might not have helped. I'm only suggesting that the procedure might have been different if the doctors had all the facts."

"So if I had not decided to keep this quiet," the President said, "I might not be blind today."

"That's putting it very dramatically," said the psychologist. "Don't, for God's sake, start treating a remote possibility like a solid fact. It's nothing more than a possibility. I only raise it now so you'll understand something of what Abelson was going through."

"Christ," said the President. "He was telling himself that because he listened to me, and didn't tell the eye doctor, that he'd caused my blindness."

"Um. And that's what a lot of other doctors are going to think."

"And say." The President's chair squeaked faintly as he leaned far back. "Ericson, with his penchant for secrecy, brought it all on himself. Not the doctors' fault, the patient's fault—a whole new field of malpractice. Don't waste your sympathy on the bastard, his own lust for power was responsible for his blindness. And the moralizers will have a field day—see what happens when you cover up? God strikes back." After a pause, Ericson added, "And maybe that's what God does."

"No doctor would go so far as to say that an alternative treatment would have prevented your blindness," Fowler protested.

"They don't have to, in so many words. Just give Bannerman the opening—and come to think of it, Bannerman owns a few doctors who will say just that, in righteous indignation." The President sighed, and said lightly, "Just this morning, I said, 'It could be worse,' and sure enough, it is."

Fowler looked for a way out. "A lot depends on how your ophthalmologist reacts."

"Uh-huh." The psychologist noted, not all that relevantly, that the President had picked up the habit of articulating a nod in the presence of a blind person. "Hank, after the speech tonight, I'd appreciate it if you had a talk with the commandant at Bethesda Naval. He might be able to counsel with the eye people, suggest that they might have done the same thing no matter what, operation might have been dangerous in my condition, whatever. Would you do that, tactfully?"

Fowler hesitated.

"You there, Hank?"

"I'll talk to him, Mr. President. Maybe I'm just anticipating trouble where there is none."

"No, no, you were good to point it out, maybe we can avoid some hotheaded ass-covering by the eye doctor."

Fowler gave a little laugh.

"What's funny?"

The Goddamn Speech

"I was just thinking of an eye doctor's hotheaded ass-covering."

The President picked up a phone and said, "Get me the press secretary, James Smith, up in Alaska, or wherever. Track him down." To Fowler, he added, "I better get Smitty into this now, it's developing more angles than I figured."

"I thought Smitty was practically unreachable."

"These operators reach anybody, anywhere. They'll pull him out of an igloo and bring him to a phone by dog sled, you'll see. I need him now. I wonder if I really have to go on television tonight. Maybe there's a way to stall Zophar."

Fowler did not understand the President's reference to the columnist, but felt Ericson could use his team around him in the preparation of a speech. Since delivering the speech was an act of conscience—a confession, to clear the air and give the President a solid moral footing—going ahead with it was something to be encouraged. But Fowler wondered why Ericson was impelled to break the news of the previous blindness now, today, and in such a seeming hurry.

The President seemed to read his thoughts: "There's some urgency to this, Hank, because we suspect somebody has leaked and the news is about to break. I was going to lay it out to the public one day, in my own good time, but now we don't have a lot of choice. I may abort the speech, may postpone it indefinitely, but I want you to prepare me in case I decide to make it tonight." To the telephone, the President said, "Tell Marilee to come in, if she's back from breakfast, but don't track her down." He pushed a buzzer that Fowler could hear buzz on Melinda's desk just outside the Oval Office, and the secretary was in the room in an instant. "Tell Jonathan to come back in, and get Harry Bok in too. Find a notebook, Melinda, and we'll see if you can still take short-hand."

The psychologist liked the way the Chief Executive could clear his mind of self-doubt and concentrate on

373

the matter at hand—in this case, a speech. Ericson assembled his troops, directing each where to sit around his desk, then told the speechwriter to read his speech aloud again all the way through. As Jonathan proceeded, the President murmured his comments to Melinda: Fowler built a five-part structure of the speech in his own mind.

"Okay, step one is to cut," Ericson said. "The long paragraph about how sorry I am that I didn't go into this sooner can be put in one good sentence. Contrite, quotable, and then let's get off it. The twenty-twenty hindsight reference is too cute, I don't want to strain for effect, so cut that. Boil down the campaign train incident to half the time you give it now, and beef up the circumstances around the decision after the ambush. Melinda, read off my specific running comments." She did; Fowler saw the President was shaping the speech to a more matter-of fact presentation, making more of a clarification than an apology, with an emotional uplift at the end, appealing to the people over the heads of the commentators.

"It's nine-thirty now," Ericson said, tapping his watch. "See how fast you can make those changes, Brother Jonathan, and then use Melinda to retype— neatness doesn't count, Melinda, I can't see it anyway —but I just want it in shape so you can read it to Hank, who can set it up in sections for me."

"Marilee is here," Melinda said. "Would you like her to come in?"

"Yes, everybody clear out and go to work. Harry" —to the Secret Service agent—"you put in your two cents whenever you like. You have a feel for the way these things go over. Hank, stay here with me."

The cast shifted, and Fowler greeted Marilee as she took the seat Melinda had been in.

"What's with Zophar?"

"He is not susceptible to charm, Mr. President. I gave him the full treatment, and he wasn't buying. He wasn't even as pompous as usual. He's like a reporter nervous about his story." Her voice was strained; Fowler could hear long fingernails tapping nervously on the President's desk.

"What does he have?" A clinical interrogation by Ericson, the psychologist observed—that was good.

"Information in considerable detail, he wants us to think, about what Harry Bok told the Soviets under a truth serum, or hypnosis, the night before we grabbed Harry back. Zophar says it is genuinely scandalous—"

"That's the word he used? Scandalous?"

"He used that word," Marilee said. "He said he's a responsible journalist, and he does not want to exaggerate or play into his source's hands, or allow himself to be used. That's why he wants to see you personally, Mr. President. He said that if every member of the Cabinet had known about it, the vote to declare you disabled would have carried."

"Were those his words, 'every member'?"

"Yes, Mr. President."

In the silence that followed, Fowler put in, "That story surely would have an impact on some of your supporters. The Attorney General, for example, made a big point about there being no indication before the election that anything like this would have happened. He told us about that—"

"Not now, Hank." When the President cut him off, the psychologist realized that Marilee was not yet privy to the contents of the speech. "Marilee, the exact wording here may be important," Ericson said carefully. "Did he say, 'every member of the Cabinet had known about it,' or are you paraphrasing? Did he say, 'If the Cabinet had known about it'?"

"Every member," Marilee reported. "It was just a few minutes ago, and that's why I can still hear his words in my head."

The phone buzzer sounded and Ericson picked it up. "Smitty? I want you back in a hurry. No, right now. There's a story breaking that you don't know about, and I may have to go on the air with a speech tonight." Fowler could hear the crackled expostulations for a moment until the President interrupted: "I want you here fast, in a matter of hours, and you can help decide whether we go on or not, but meanwhile explain to Marilee how you get air time on the networks on short notice. I can't get her to do a thing without your say-so." That was a lie but a sure mollifier to the press secretary. "Call her from the airport, Smitty, don't make any calls from the plane, it's not secure. You got any pull with Sam Zophar? Good. Come back in a hurry." He hung up.

"I told Zophar he could see Hennessy this afternoon around five," Marilee said. "Hennessy could stall him further with a promise to get him to see you tomorrow. And speak of the devil, here's our chief of staff now, looking a little the worse for wear."

"Been a long night," said Hennessy from the doorway.

"Are you all right?" The new note of concern in Marilee's voice drew a picture of the staff chief in Fowler's mind: rumpled, harried, red-eyed.

"We're eyeball to eyeball," said Hennessy, "and it doesn't matter who blinks, because you guys could never tell."

"He's all right," said Marilee.

"Buzz off, good-lookin'," Hennessy said wearily. "I'll come to see you in a few minutes about Zophar, you'll give me a fill."

"And Smitty will be back late today," she told him, her voice fading into the hallway.

"Who the hell sent for Smitty?" Hennessy was evidently not pleased with the prospect of the press secretary's return.

"The elected leader of 250 million Americans sent for him," the President replied.

"There was no note," Hennessy reported. "Either Herb didn't commit suicide at all, which is the position I'll take—or he mailed a note to somebody, his wife maybe, from the post office box a mile and a half down the road, which is unlikely." With an exaggerated moan, he collapsed on the couch.

"Where, uh . . ."

"In a funeral home near Adas Israel synagogue,"

the staff chief said. "He was Jewish. Melinda can break the news to his wife, she knows her."

"Overdose of sleeping pills?" Fowler asked.

"Yes, which does not automatically mean suicide," cautioned Hennessy.

"Most people think of it that way," Fowler volunteered. He did not want to encourage anybody to lead the President away from reality.

"No note, no suicide," said Hennessy doggedly. "Let the insurance company prove suicide. Until then, his wife gets whatever he's insured for."

"Oh," said Fowler. He kicked himself for forgetting that angle. Good that an experienced lawyer was involved, who could protect the family. Fowler was chagrined at having thought that Hennessy only wanted to save the White House from embarrassment.

"Could have been an accident," growled Hennessy. "There was a whiskey bottle nearby, I showed it to the forest ranger. Herb could have been depressed, and drinking, and forgotten what he took. Let's not jump to conclusions. Nothing's official unless it's official. An accidental overdose of pills sounds fishy, I know, but it won't be easy to turn it into a hard fact of suicide without at least a note."

"Poor Herb," the President said, in a voice Fowler could hardly hear. "We went to school together." After a moment, in a normal tone: "Hank, tell Hennessy what you think Herb was depressed about." The psychologist briefed the staff chief on the possibility of opening the roof of the optic canal after a second injury, and how not undertaking such surgery might have troubled the doctor that Herb Abelson had almost been.

Hennessy moaned, but not about Abelson. "That little fag of an eye doctor might just wander off the reservation about this."

"Hank said he'd talk to the commandant at Bethesda about that," the President said.

Fowler nodded, adding "Um" for Ericson, not too happy at that assignment, but accommodating a patient. And it was probably the truth—the odds were strongly against alternate treatment making all that difference.

"Let's focus on the central matter," the President went on, "whether or not to go on the air tonight."

"Will you have him ready, Hank?"

"Don't worry about that," the President interrupted. "I'll be ready for a speech if I have to be. The question is, do I have to be? Talk to Marilee, Hennessy, and see what Zophar knows. She says he said it was a scandalous thing that would have meant a different vote in the Cabinet if—and here's the exact wording —'if every member of the Cabinet knew about it.' Now what the hell does that mean?"

"Turning it around, it seems to say that one or more of the Cabinet members did know about the previous blindness. Which they did not." Hennessy paused. "Did you ever tell Duparquet?"

"Never," the President said. "The people who know now are the family—and we have to include Hank here in the family—and the speechwriter, Jonathan. Marilee doesn't know." Fowler felt, and was not ashamed of, the thrill of being at the center of power, fully trusted. They could not avoid trusting him, but it was exciting nonetheless. The flow of events seemed to be picking up speed and Hank Fowler was being carried along.

"I'll crack Zophar this afternoon," said Hennessy, "with Smitty, if he gets here. And if Smitty doesn't come apart under pressure, the self-righteous bastard. I think the nets need a three-hour notice, so we could make the decision at six for a nine o'clock broadcast." He stretched and groaned, the sleepless night reaching out for him. "Only three more years to go. You want a second term, you get yourself a new boy. I'll send Melinda over to Herb's wife."

"Send her in with the speech first," the President said.

When Hennessy had gone, Fowler used the moments before the return of the speechwriter to see how the President's mind and mood were interacting. No tricky questions: "How do you feel?"

"Like I'm making a mistake," Ericson replied evenly. "I'm doing the right thing, morally, in telling the truth about the previous blindness. But I'm being rushed into it, and that's bad. I don't like jeopardizing everything unless I absolutely have to. So in owning up to the truth, I'm right, and in doing it now, I may be wrong. Premature. Mixed feeling."

"No relief that it's finally coming out? You must have been all bottled up inside," Fowler said, thinking also that the President had been quite guarded with his psychologist up to now.

"I'm not looking forward to this, Hank. It's too soon—it's not good to have too many shocks in a row, not good for the people. It's important that I hold on to this job."

"For you? For the people?"

"For both." The chair squeaked back, and Fowler heard the thump of the President's feet on his desk. "Consider the alternative: Nichols would be a disaster. He would be a puppet on a string for Bannerman, and Hank—you don't know this as profoundly as I—Bannerman is not a man of good character." That phrase hung there, until Ericson added, "I know what you're thinking. Who the hell am I to be talking about character, having misled people about the blindness? Well, I did nothing venal, nothing out of a motive to lie or cheat or steal, but only to stabilize a situation until I could deal with it intelligently. The full-disclosure thing was not important before the election. It only became important after the ambush, in retrospect, but by that time there were other things, more important." He got out of his chair and walked to the french doors, turned his back to them, and talked directly at Fowler across the room. "I got into this shape because I was trying to do something, for the country, for peace in the world. I mean that, you know I do. And if I can hang on, if I can ride this out, I can do the job well—not only well, but infinitely better than our Vice-President and Bannerman, who could botch it up tragically. So I'm sorry I made a few mistakes in tactics. But I might have done the same thing if I had it to do over—I'm not sorry for the compromises, Hank, because that's what you must do to get in and stay in. And you can't do any damn good if you're not in."

"You're not just rationalizing your feelings of guilt?"

"Of course I'm rationalizing," Ericson rasped. "Don't be a jerk—that's the only way you can live with guilt. The one biggest nagging item on my conscience goes back to a year ago July, at the convention, when I bought my way in by agreeing to take Bannerman's choice for a running mate. That was the big one. Good sweet Christ, man, I cannot let this country suffer for that mistake, not while I have breath in my body. So I'll connive, and I'll plot, and I'll cut a few corners, the way every man who ever worked in this office has had to do. But I'll keep this place out of Bannerman's hands if it's the last thing I do, which it may turn out to be. And better than that, I'll be a good President—you'll see—better than I would have been with eyes. I'm not quite as cool as I used to be, or as objective, and maybe that's good, maybe I shouldn't have been looking down my nose at a little honest passion all my life. I like it here. I belong here. I'm going to stay, and I'm going to do one hell of a job. You hear that, Hank?" He turned toward the door leading to his secretary's office. "Melinda, where the hell is that speech?" He strode across the back of the Oval Office toward the doorway and Fowler could hear the crack of a head against a door that should not have been closed. The psychologist crossed the room in an instant, reaching the President's side just as he hit the floor, cursing and crying more in frustration than pain. Fowler could feel the sticky blood on Ericson's temple. It would worry the psychologist later that the first thought that came to his own mind at that moment was that the cut could be covered by make-up for the television appearance.

"Just a scratch," Hennessy insisted. "He bonked his head, came up on the count of four. The new doctor saw him, put a piece of flesh-colored tape on his forehead, and with the television make-up you'll never see it."

It occurred to Smitty that Hennessy was minimizing everything. After a six-hour supersonic ride from the North Slope oil fields, the press secretary arrived at the White House to be hit with five separate jolts of information. First, the impending Zophar revelation. Then, Smitty's own first knowledge of the previous blindness, gained from being shown the speech draft in advance, a copy of which would not be handed out. Next, he had learned of the Abelson suicide, which had been announced as a probable accident, which was slicing the truth thin. And then there was the possible public reaction of "he brought it on himself" that Hank Fowler was concerned about. Finally, there had been the news of an impending speech, to beat the Leigh-to-Zophar leak, which the President might make later that evening.

"According to you, everything is a piece of cake," Smitty said to Hennessy, at the table in the chief of staff's office, "except when you add it up, the plate is pretty goddamn full."

"Too much for you, Smitty? I know flying's a strain for a man of your years."

"Mr. Zophar will be here in a couple of minutes," Marilee changed the subject. "What's the strategy?"

The press secretary did not appreciate Hennessy's crack about his age—an older man could make an excellent chief of staff, as Lucas Cartwright, nearly seventy, had shown, far better than the abrasive divorce lawyer the President had chosen—nor did Smitty like the way Marilee had moved in on his preserve during a short trip to the north country. "Been too damn much strategy here the past couple of days," he grumped. "We could have saved ourselves a lot of grief by telling the truth."

"I knew it," said Hennessy, bounding out of a chair and over to the window, where he stood, jingling the keys in his pocket, "we should have left him up there flacking for Eskimos. I told you the first thing he'd say is 'I told you so.'"

"I never told you so because I never knew," Smitty reminded him. "And why did you want me back here if you didn't want to listen to me?"

"The President insisted you be here in the crisis," Marilee said soothingly. "And I'm damn glad you're back. So is Hennessy, too, but he's finding some difficulty in expressing it."

Hennessy turned, his mood suddenly changed. "She's right. Sorry, Smitty, maybe you'd have been better in this job, but I've got it for a while at least. Want to help?"

"I'm here, I'm here," Smitty said, feeling better. Maybe he could turn this thing around; as it stood, the situation could hardly get worse, and he did know Zophar from long ago. "The first thing Sam Zophar will ask is what the President has been reading lately."

"Huh?" Hennessy gave him a weird look.

"That's Zophar's style," Smitty explained. "No matter how urgent his question, or what he really wants to discuss, he begins with what books the President is reading. Been doing that for as long as I've known him, which is about twenty-five years."

"But the President's bli—" Hennessy caught himself. "No, he's reading books. We worked out that thing with the Librarian of Congress, where he sends over those talking books, the tapes. Marilee—" he pointed to the telephone on Smitty's desk, which she took up to see what requests the President had made. "You want her here for this, Smitty?"

"We don't need Marilee," Smitty began, eliciting the sought-after look of despair from the woman on the phone, "but she might as well stay, since she started this with Sam Zophar. I want her ready to step in the minute I move up to your job."

"How should we proceed," Hennessy said deferentially, "never not telling the truth." Smitty noticed the double negative, which was a shade different from "always telling the truth."

"I'll be the nice guy, you be the heavy," said Smitty, and Marilee covered the phone to add, "He'll never guess the truth." Smitty grunted, and went on: "I'll see what he wants, and how much I can get out of him; you clam up, we'll argue a little, you soften up and say he can see the President later. Then I'll see what more we can pry out of him."

"If he's got the previous blindness story in any detail," Hennessy said carefully, "then I tell him the President is planning to speak on television tonight. I'll say it's too bad his exclusive is shot, but maybe we can give him some exclusive details after the speech."

"Hate to do that to a journalist," said Smitty. "It's a double-cross—they'll never bring us anything for verification again if we don't protect an exclusive." This had all been decided before he returned from Alaska, he added to himself.

"You know that if we didn't break it ourselves, we'd be dead, Smitty. Let that decision be mine, over your objection, all right?" The press secretary was glad Hennessy got his message. The staff chief continued: "Now what if Zophar doesn't have the story at all? The President suspects it's all a probe—he's just fishing, got a tip, not a real briefing from Arthur Leigh. Maybe he's got a different story, something unimportant. That means we can wait a day or so, maybe scrub it for a while—"

"The President has to make this speech," said Smitty firmly, "and the sooner, the better. I won't be a part of a cover-up." He saw Hennessy wince at that point, but drove it home: "I'm not saying you all covered up a crime. Honest men could differ on when to reveal the whole story. But it could be played as a cover-up by Bannerman and the rest, and we'd all look terrible, especially the President."

"Especially you, you mean."

"Damn right!"

Hennessy visibly checked his temper. "You were certainly in favor of full disclosure the moment you heard about it, Smitty, and Marilee's our witness." The staff chief sounded as if he were making a statement for the record. The blond head with the telephone in it bobbed.

"Is this the whole story?" Smitty felt he had to ask that; for the record, too. He didn't know if he wanted an answer.

"I am still the President's special counsel," Hennessy said. "There's an attorney-client relationship that he and I have, which could be the reason for my getting the staff chief's job. There may be another matter involved here, and I suppose I'd have to tell you if you pushed me to the wall, but you'd have to pretend you didn't know the first thing about it."

"I'm not a lawyer," Smitty said, and was relieved when Hennessy took the hint and was silent. Marilee hung up and read from her pad: "He ordered three books in the last week, and Melinda says he's played them all. One is the current nonfiction best seller, *Partners in Pain,* the dual biography of Jacqueline Kennedy and Pat Nixon, and the others are oldies, fiction: *Billy Budd,* by Herman Melville, and *The Man that Corrupted Hadleyburg,* by Mark Twain."

"That's what he does at night?" Even Hennessy was surprised.

"Respectable enough titles," Smitty allowed.

"I took a course in Melville," Marilee offered. *"Billy Budd* is about a young sailor who gets hanged for killing a vicious mate. Guilt and innocence, good and evil—"

"What the hell are you babbling about?" Hennessy

looked astounded. "We're up against the goddamn wall, the President of the United States is waiting for our signal about whether he has to make the toughest speech of his life tonight, and you're giving us a Vassar freshman literature course."

"Zophar should be in the west lobby now," Smitty said, looking at 5 P.M. on his watch. "Marilee, bring him in." When she went for him, the press secretary and the chief of staff could not think of anything to say to each other. In a way, Smitty wished he had not been called back.

"Gentlemen!" Zophar, pompous as ever—more so, Smitty decided, now that he had a paunch—entered the office of the press secretary, waved rather than shook hands, and proceeded to study the pictures on the walls. "Here's Jim Hagerty, Smitty—whom you'd like to think of as your prototype, but press secretaries were more powerful in Eisenhower's day."

"Hagerty had to handle a genuine disability," was all Smitty said. But then he calculated how his long-time association with this pretentious old coot might be played to the President's advantage, and added, "You've seen 'em come and go, Sam."

"I don't think you'll be in this job much longer," the columnist said matter-of-factly, "unless you want to stay on under Nichols. I don't know if you read my column"—he waited for them all to nod, which Smitty dutifully did—"but I've taken the clear position that the Ericson Administration is to be short-lived." Smitty thought at first the columnist had mispronounced "short-lived" with an "eye" sound, but then figured Zophar had it right and was showing off.

"What makes you think that, Sam?"

The columnist waved the question aside; he came to ask, not to be asked, the imperious hand seemed to say, and certainly not to rush his questions, or to discuss matters of great import with flunkies. Smitty had to remind himself that he was to play Mr. Nice Guy.

"I would ordinarily begin by asking what books

the President has been reading, Smitty, but that would hardly be in good—"

"Melville, I think," said Smitty casually. "Marilee, you were checking into those talking books from the Library of Congress and Recording for the Blind before I left, weren't you?"

"His taste is fairly eclectic," she reported quietly, and Smitty was pleased she used a fifty-dollar word. "Some Melville, some Twain, and the new Kennedy-Nixon biography. And some William Blake."

"What Melville?" Zophar was wary.

"Billy Budd."

The columnist smiled. "God bless Captain—what was his name?"

" 'God bless Captain Vere' were the sailor's last words," Marilee replied evenly. Smitty felt a surge of pride: The James Smith press office was not without a college education. But what the hell was Ericson doing, reading these old novels, when there was so much presidential homework to be done?

"We don't want to take too much of your time, Mr. Zophar," Hennessy said.

"I don't want any of your time," the columnist replied. "I would like to see the President on a matter of the utmost gravity."

"Marilee told us just a little of what you wanted to know, Sam," Smitty said, "could you expound a little further?"

"No," said Zophar. "I respect you, Smitty, which is why I am here; but it is only preliminary to seeing the President."

"That's not impossible," the press secretary said, "and I want to assure you that we all realize that you would not ask for the appointment on a minor matter. We're grateful, too, for the chance to check out a story. In case your tip turns out to be wrong, it avoids embarrassment all around."

"I do not deal in 'tips.' My information is solid, I am not in danger of being embarrassed, and I did not come here for more of a runaround."

Smitty kept cool. "I flew six thousand miles to be

here at this meeting, Sam, and I'd look a hell of a lot better to my boss if I had some inkling—"

"That's the number Miss Pinckney played for me yesterday, and I've had quite enough of it. Whether you look good or bad is of no concern to me. Am I going to see the President now, tonight, or am I going to run the story as I have it?"

"If I were you, Smitty," said Hennessy, his voice tightly controlled, "I would first boot this gentleman's ass out of the White House immediately. I would then tell him that the three or four tipsters we know to be his sources in this Administration—including Lucas Cartwright—will be asked to stop being his sources. And he can forget all those invitations to state dinners and columnist's intimate backgrounders he likes to go to. I would tell him, in Thomas Jefferson's immortal words, 'publish and be damned!' "

"Fortunately, you're not the press secretary," Smitty told Hennessy with a severe look. "Mr. Zophar is doing us a favor by being here, and if you can't treat him civilly—"

"Oh, for Chrissake," said Zophar. "Cut out the good-guy bad-guy routine. I've seen it played right here in this room a dozen times, and much better than you two do it. Are you going to stonewall me or not?"

Hennessy surprised Smitty by smiling warmly at Zophar. "You're like an old judge I knew in New York. He used to be a divorce lawyer before his appointment. I could never get a nickel out of him. Speaking of old-timers, what do you hear from that old bastard Arthur Leigh?"

"Just ran into him the other day," said the columnist innocently, "quite by accident. Seems fine, but kind of out of it." Smitty admired the way Zophar protected a source—acknowledging the meeting with Leigh, in case they'd been seen, but dismissing him as unproductive.

"Look, Sam," Smitty said, seeming to capitulate, "why don't you just tell us as much of the story as you're going to, and then we'll see where we go from there."

"The Soviets have squeezed some information out of Harry Bok," said Zophar. "Information, which if known at the time of the disability session of the Cabinet would have resulted in the declaration that the President was disabled and the naming of the Vice-President as Acting President. That is because the information squeezed out of Mr. Bok was nothing short of scandalous."

"One quick question," said Hennessy. "You told Marilee that a couple of the members of the Cabinet already knew it?"

"Did I tell her that? Must have been befuddled by her charms. Now do I get to see the President or not?"

"Stay here with Marilee," said Hennessy. "Smitty and I will be right back."

Smitty listened to Hennessy's points in the hallway between the press secretary's office and the Oval Office, then went in to the President, who was waiting with Melinda and Harry Bok.

"I sure hate to bust a man's exclusive, Mr. President," Smitty told Ericson, seated behind his desk steepling his fingers, "but I think he's got the story and you would be better off telling the American people your way."

"Hennessy with you?" the President was not happy with Smitty's news.

"I'm right here. That opening about a couple of the Cabinet members knowing—Zophar backed off it, it may not be so. He hit the word 'scandal' pretty hard. I think you'd be crazy to wait, unless you're having trouble getting the speech delivery worked out."

"He just ran through it for us," Melinda said. "Needs some work, but he's nearly ready."

"Mr. President," said Smitty painfully, "I don't think about this the way Hennessy does. I don't think it's important to know what the hell story Zophar has. Even if it were something else entirely, you have to tell the truth about your blindness. It's the only right thing to do. I for one couldn't work for you, out there in that den of wolves, knowing that you were living a lie."

"You want a gun to hold to his head, you shit?" Hennessy hissed. To the President, he added, "He only said that for his memoirs, that's no fair. Decide on the basis of what's the practical thing to do right now."

"If I had a choice," the President said, after some thought, "I wouldn't make the speech now. In a couple of weeks, under the right circumstances, I could do it better." Pause. "We're panicking, on the basis of too little information, and I don't like that, either." Another pause. "You know why I'm going to do it? The reason I was afraid of all along—because the speech is done, I've got it in my head, and I'm up for it, and I won't easily be able to get up for it again. Also, I've never been much of a gambler, but I'd kind of like to roll the dice, after shaking them in my hand all day." Ericson had not finished, and Smitty did not move for the phone. "All that, and then—it would be as difficult as hell for me to go against what all of you advise. There's just nothing pulling me back from the brink of this, and the momentum is kind of carrying me over. That's not the way I like to make a decision." Everybody in the room was uncomfortable, Smitty knew, but sometimes a man had to be pushed into doing what was right. "But I don't always get to do what I like to do. So we'll go. Everybody go do what has to be done to set it up, and I'll perform. Hank and I will work on it here."

Smitty thought that Ericson was lucky to have a chief of staff—even Hennessy—who could engineer a decision when the top man was reluctant to make it. He was certain Ericson was going to rise to the occasion, and he hurried out to tell Zophar that his story was beaten. Sorry about the exclusive, but the President had previously decided to go on the air.

The Television Set / 2

The television set with four eyes, one on each network, looked into the press secretary's office that night carrying the same image: the floodlit White House, from the fountains in the front lawn. The voice-overs were different, babeling different versions of the same wonderment.

". . . only three hours ago, when the President's press secretary requested this time for what he described as an 'important personal address.' This will be the first prepared speech made by President Ericson since the ambush at Yalta six weeks ago. . . ."

". . . no advance release of a text, indeed, there may not be a prepared text, as this is the first speech by a President who is unable to read. The President has been in relative seclusion for the past few hours. The only staff members to see him were Dr. Henry Fowler, the blind psychologist helping him to prepare his presentation, and his official photographer, Buffie Masterson, who recorded some of the historic moments before this historic 'first.' . . ."

". . . only speculation, but there's been plenty of that. Some say the President has been deeply affected by the apparent suicide of his personal physician, Dr. Herbert Abelson. The White House has been suggesting that the death might have been the result of an accidental overdose of drugs. Why would the President's doctor take his own life, if that is what he did? The question is on the lips of the press corps assembled here tonight. There is speculation, too, that this may be the moment President Ericson has decided to step down, under the provisions of the Twenty-fifth Amendment, now that the pressures to remove him from office have abated. The theory is that, having successfully resisted being pushed, he may now be ready to go of his own accord. . . ."

". . . and gentlemen, the President of the United States."

The four tracks melded into one sound, of the voice of Sven Ericson saying, "Good evening, my fellow citizens." The four heads of the one man, each with slightly different coloring, were in the familiar setting of the Oval Office, behind the desk and in front of the drapes, flags left and right, no pictures of family or other distractions, as Ericson had no family to show.

"This is the first chance I have had to talk things over with you since the assassination of General Secretary Kolkov six weeks ago.

"Since that tragic day, I have been recuperating from the attack. I have been adjusting to the blindness that the attack has brought about. I have held a press conference to answer the most pressing questions. And I have been fighting to protect the presidency from an unprecedented seizure of its powers.

"Now, at last, I can come before you to discuss a personal matter in the past, and to reveal a new initiative affecting the future.

"Let me explain first how I'm making this speech. This little device in my ear is not a hearing aid—there's nothing wrong with my hearing, thank God—it's a tiny headset attached to the tape recorder here on the desk. From time to time, I'll press a button that will play to me a record of my own voice, made earlier today, outlining what I want to say. I'll pause a few seconds, listen to my speeded-up notes, and then go ahead and speak extemporaneously. Nothing fancy, but I'm doing it this way so that I don't leave anything out that I want to say or you need to hear. So when you see me pause, it's to listen to my notes."

The pool camera showed the tape recorder on the desk, and the President's finger pushing it for a three-second interval. In the press secretary's office, Smitty said, "That's good, he's involving everybody in the business of making the speech. He's not hiding a thing."

His deputy, watching with him, shook her head: "Appeals for pity. Not like Ericson."

"First, and briefly, the bad news. Many of you have sent me letters, and recordings of prayers, for which I will always be grateful. But my doctors tell me that there is no evidence to give me hope that I will regain my sight. Like a million and a half other Americans, I am blind and expect to remain so for the rest of my life.

"I have come to grips with that. I don't pity myself and the last thing I ever want is for anybody to pity me. It will be a test of my own character to learn to live with blindness, and it will be a test of the national character for the American people to learn to live with a blind President. Together, we will pass those tests.

"There was a moment when I may have flunked that test, however, and I want to tell you about it. It shows how important it is to face the facts, no matter how unpleasant those facts may be. I learned a lesson from that episode that served me in good stead in recent weeks, and I want to share it with you."

In the office, Smitty said, "Here it comes." Marilee breathed, "Jonathan set it up just right."

"During the election campaign last year, I made a whistle-stop tour of Ohio on an old-fashioned railroad train. It was a publicity stunt, the way you do in campaigns—like the rail that Lincoln's supporters said he split, but he never did. Clean fun, traditional —but there was an accident on the train. As some of you may remember, and we announced it at the time, when the train jolted to a stop near Lima—excuse me, that's pronounced Ly-ma—I was thrown against a bulkhead and suffered a mild concussion.

"It was announced that I was sick in bed, which was only partly true. The whole truth was that for about a day after I banged my head, I could not see. It did not occur to me that I had been temporarily blinded—it just seemed to me as if it was taking a long time coming all the way back to consciousness.

So we said nothing about it, waiting to see—actually, waiting to see. And sure enough, in a day or so, my eyes were fine again."

Smitty: "What do you think?" Marilee: "Jesus, I didn't know that. The poor guy."

"In retrospect, I suppose my managers should have put out the fact that I had lost my eyesight for a matter of hours. But frankly, I refused to face up to that fact. I refused to believe that it was not a part of the process of being knocked out, and seeing stars. And I waited, and said nothing more about it when my sight returned.

"Well, I've learned my lesson. With the benefit of twenty-twenty hindsight, I can say this: It's important to face the fact of blindness, to tell the truth about it, and then to triumph over it. And that's why I'm saying to all of you tonight, who may be supporting me in the hope that my eyesight will return—set that hope aside. I've learned to live with blindness, and so should you."

The camera took a picture of the President's hand pressing the recorder for his notes. Smitty looked at Marilee: "He turned it all around. It's no scandal, it's a lesson. Oh, that kid writer, if it was his idea, he's a pisser. It wasn't that way in the draft I read, it started out as a confession." Marilee, moist eyes on the screens, motioned him quiet.

"After the ambush at Yalta last month, while I was unconscious, my staff told the Soviets nothing about my loss of sight. This made good sense, since their primary goal was to get the presidential party out of the danger zone and back on American soil as quickly as possible.

"After I regained consciousness, in *Air Force One,* I realized that I could not see. I directed my staff to keep my blindness a secret for the time being. I did not want any foreign power thinking the United States was in any way incapable of responding to a threat. I was right to do that. I may have been wrong, in retrospect, not to take my doctors into my confidence regarding last year's concussion. But—at the time—the previous blindness did not seem all that pertinent. My staff and I were concerned, first and foremost, with making certain the nation and the world knew that the President of the United States was well enough to make certain decisions, and if necessary, to repel any attack.

"In those crucial moments, the nation and I were fortunate to have two great public servants assisting me: George Curtice, the Secretary of State, and Lucas Cartwright, who was then my chief of staff and who is now our Secretary of Defense. Both these men were towers of strength at Yalta; they are the nation's senior Cabinet officials today." He pushed the recorder to listen to his notes.

"After consultation with them, I have this afternoon directed that an invitation be extended through normal diplomatic channels to the new Premier of the Soviet Union, Vasily Nikolayev. The Government of the United States is prepared to resume negotiations where they were tragically broken off at Yalta. It is our suggestion that these vital talks take place in Washington in the near future, possibly around Labor Day. Let me add this to my fellow Americans: The Ericson Administration is ready, willing, *and able* to conduct those negotiations." He pushed the recorder playback again.

Smitty shook his head, worried: "He's crap-shooting. The Russkies haven't responded to the feeler yet, he only made it this afternoon. He needed a lead."

Marilee shrugged it off: "No big deal. Nikolayev will come, one of these days. The President wouldn't take a chance like that, not knowing." The moment with the recorder ended.

"Let me come now to a personal word, if I may. I had to ask myself a most serious and profound question not long ago. The question was this: Which would be better for the American people—my stepping aside or my going on?

"Many well-meaning and wise men and women pointed out to me that no person is indispensable.

The Goddamn Speech

Certainly I have no delusions of grandeur, or lust for power. I was elected to do what is best for the nation, not what is best for myself. And I gave careful consideration to the argument that some other person with all his faculties, would be more capable as President than I, missing the faculty of sight.

"While I was thinking about this, there was a movement to unseat me—to usurp my constitutional authority, making unprecedented use of a new and untried amendment. I had no doubt that the right course was to resist this attempted coup. As President, I could not allow myself to be pushed out of office—thereby weakening this office for all time. I was not elected for that.

"But now that the crisis is past, I had to consider it again. Without pressure, without coercion—what's best? Some lines from John Milton, in the epic poem *Samson Agonistes,* were recounted to me. The blinded Samson, in the agony of his imprisonment, cried out for some way to still be able to serve his people." He listened to his notes, then said:

> *"Now blind, dishearten'd, sham'd, dishonour'd,*
> *   quell'd,*
> *To what can I be useful, wherein serve*
> *My Nation . . .*

"God answered Samson's cry, and gave him back the strength to confront his enemies, to make his sacrifice, to free his people.

"I'm no Samson bent on destruction. And I don't have the genius of a Milton. But I do know that the American people elect a man, a human being, as President. Not a computer, with an infallible memory; not a manager, with some supremely efficient method; not an eagle, with an eagle's eyes. You elect a man, with his faults and weaknesses, and his character. Most important of all, you elect a man who can—we all hope —grow into the job that is too big for any man who has not yet filled it.

"I believe—I'm not certain, but I believe—that I

may be well on the way to becoming that man. The ambush at Yalta cost me my sight, but it might have given me a vision—a vision that I might never have been graced with otherwise.

"That is why I am going to go on. This office, this White House, has been occupied by troubled men, by crippled men, by men who overcame great handicaps in their lives.

"In looking back over the past few weeks, I can see now that my blindness—my permanent blindness—was not my handicap. My greatest handicap was my own uncertainty—not quite knowing whether or not staying in office was the right thing to do.

"I may be sightless, which is a technical problem, but I am handicapped no longer. With God's help, with your help, I now know I can do the job you elected me to do. And I mean to see it through.

"Thank you and good night."

The President took the earpiece out of his ear and laid it on the desk alongside the recorder. He took off his glasses and laid them down on the desk as well, leaning far back in his big chair. The four pictures of the television sets cut away from the President and closed in on the props on the desk, holding them in the frame, in silence, for nearly thirty seconds.

Smitty blew his nose. "Goddammit, he carried it off. I knew he would. I knew it was the right thing to do."

Marilee used her thumbs to press the tears out of her eyes and then fumbled around for her handkerchief. "I'm just so proud," she said. "I've never been so proud."

Smitty turned up the sound on one of the channels, cutting off the others. The newsman giving a summary of the speech, recognizing its emotional content, used a respectful voice:

". . . mixed the bad news of the permanent nature of his blindness with the good news of a continuation of the negotiations with the Soviet Union, probably early this fall. He also put forward a fact we had not been aware of before—that during the election campaign last year, an accident blinded him for a matter of a

couple of days, and that the fact of that previous blindness was concealed." He turned to a couple of analysts,
who began dissecting the possibilities of another summit: "These are not suggestions which are lightly
made," said one. "A summit invitation is never extended publicly unless it has been accepted privately."

"Hmf," Smitty grunted, switching channels. Everywhere the reaction was muted, as if the television set
were waiting for a cue from the morning newspapers
as to how to play what news. Politicians reached for
comment were playing it safe, too, hailing the President's courage but reserving judgment on the "campaign train episode," as it was beginning to be called.
Reporters said they heard only no comment from the
Committee to Replace the Disabled President, "which
had evidently been caught unawares," and T. Roy
Bannerman was said to be in London on business. A
network's White House correspondent said he had
heard the President's chief of staff, Mark Hennessy,
had opposed making the revelations in the speech, but
that "at least one member" of the President's staff had
threatened to resign unless the truth were made
known. The sets filled with other cautious comment
until nine-thirty and went back to normal programming.

In the room with the four darkened sets, the President's official family unofficially assembled to match
reactions. Melinda McPhee was the first to join Smitty
and Marilee, followed by Hennessy.

"He brought it off," Melinda said in wonderment.
"It didn't sound so bad. Am I crazy?"

"You do the right thing," said the press secretary,
feet on his desk, "you can't go wrong. Even Hennessy
will agree on that tonight."

The staff chief was elated, but not carried away:
"You come up with a good excuse for not saying anything for six weeks. You get your audience hooked on
the way you're delivering the speech, with speedhearing gimmicks, and they don't quite catch what
you're saying. You fuzz up a decision not to say he was
blind on the campaign train and, quick like a bunny,

top it with a foreign-affairs announcement. You play hearts and flowers about being blind all your life and use that as the counterpoint to brushing off the failure to disclose before the election. You do all that, Smitty, and you can't go wrong."

Marilee shook her head. "That's not the same speech I heard."

Smitty waved it off. "We hit a home run. Come in, Buffie, we ought to record for posterity the happy picture of the President's staff at the moment of his greatest triumph." Buffie moved around the press secretary's office, catching some self-conscious candid shots as they talked.

"Where's Brother Jonathan?" Melinda asked somebody. "Somebody ought to give the kid a pat on the back." Marilee picked up the phone to have him tracked down.

"Sam Zophar must be turning purple," Smitty said. "To have a world beat snatched away from him."

"I liked the Samson business," Hennessy admitted. "A blind President quoting a blind poet about a blind biblical hero—that was a grabber."

"Sure beats a Seeing Eye chimp," Buffie muttered irrelevantly.

"If you've finished your blubbering," Smitty said to his deputy, "go out in the press room and tell 'em we're being flooded with telegrams and the White House switchboard is jammed."

"But telegrams were discontinued last year," Marilee protested.

"Oh. Well, lean hard on how the switchboard is really tied up."

"I better check the operator—"

"Jesus H. Christ, Marilee," Smitty exploded benevolently, "there has never been a presidential speech since FDR started using radio that was not followed by the switchboard being jammed. The bloody White House switchboard is built to be jammed after a speech. Go out in the press room and say the switchboard is being jammed, or else they'll think nobody watched."

Marilee went to do her job, passing Harry Bok in

the hallway being wheeled along by his tall, quiet nurse. Harry directed her to Smitty's office, looked in at the silent screens and laughing group, and asked, "Who's with The Man?"

"I thought you were," said Hennessy. "We better tell him how great he was, he'll think he flopped again." The lawyer took off down the hall. Harry Bok looked at Melinda, smiled lopsidedly at Buffie, who was photographing him, and motioned to Nurse Kellgren to push him after Hennessy to the President's quarters.

The Columnist / 2

Samuel Zophar pressed the remote switch that snapped off the television set. He rose and placed the switch on top of the set, where he could find it again without his glasses, and wondered why he used the device at all if he had to walk back and forth to the set. Must have something to do with holding the programming decision in one's fist.

Ericson was turning into a President, he had to grant that. Not every man who was elected President became a President, but Sven Ericson had the requisite character and guile, lion and fox, to qualify. The speech seemed to the columnist to have been crafted with extraordinary care, delivered with halting skill, and was an example of the powerful use of mass communication in political leadership. But when Zophar worked on a column with such care, the craftsmanship was usually to conceal what he did not know, or to plant an idea casually that he could come back to months later and be able to claim he had beaten the rest of the fraternity with his insight. Zophar suspected there was something to the Ericson speech that did not meet the ear.

The columnist was irritated with the President for

not having seen him, but he set that aside; obviously the man had been planning this speech for the past few days, and if Zophar had been in the President's shoes, preparing a domestic blockbuster, he would not have seen any columnist about a foreign-affairs story. But an element of falsity lurked in Ericson's moment of truth—he jotted down that phrase—and he could not quite get a handle on it.

To Zophar, the campaign train episode seemed of relatively minor importance. A flap might be kicked up over failing to fully disclose the state of the candidate's health before the election, but only fools would get worked up over that. Ericson's dubious claim about not knowing when he became conscious, true or not, covered the President there—isn't opening your eyes part of waking up? No, the phony part must have to do with great events, with the new initiative to the Soviets. That was the coin a skeptical mind would have to bite.

He took up his white lined pad and put down the facts he had.

From Gregor, the Soviet agent, he had the hard fact —or convincing allegation—that Harry Bok of the U. S. Secret Service had revealed a fantastic deceit by the Americans on the Russians, that Kolkov was made into a hero he was not, and that Vasily Nikolayev was part of the American plot to portray Kolkov as sacrificing his life to save Ericson's.

Next, from his own deduction, Zophar had the soft fact—or promising surmise—that a faction in the Kremlin was actively seeking to topple Nikolayev right now, and had sent Gregor with the story to the Western press.

Third, from Ericson's speech, he had the contrary fact—deduced from long experience—that the Soviets had informally agreed to send Nikolayev to the United States to continue the negotiations, which meant that the former Foreign Minister was firmly in the saddle.

Zophar drew a line under that and looked at the page a long time. No. There was no way those facts could be fitted together, if Gregor's story had any truth in it at all. He turned to a fresh page and wrote out some questions.

Why had Ericson gone out of his way to praise Curtice and Cartwright? Cartwright had been loyal during the Cabinet crisis, but Curtice had not—there had to be something linking the two men outside domestic affairs, which made Ericson want to bind them to him.

Why was Gregor unwilling to show him any hard evidence? The Soviet agent had some evidence, of that the columnist was certain—it needed to be blasted out of him. The likely item was a tape recording of Bok's revelations under hypnosis or drugs.

The columnist drew another line. What could he do to check what facts he had? First, he could make certain that the Soviets had agreed to send Nikolayev around Labor Day, and perhaps also find out why there was such a long lead time between announcement and conference. Next, he could lean on Gregor.

Zophar consulted his address book, a bulging leather loose-leaf binder crammed with numbers, facts, anecdotes, and reminders of wives' names, and dialed the home of a former Secretary of State. The old boy would be able to find out quickly, that night, some of what Zophar needed to know; and the ex-Secretary owed the columnist a few. After the call, with his request in work, Zophar turned to Gregor.

"I need to see you right here, right now," he said urgently into the receiver at the Russian. "Your professional reputation rests on it. You know the address. Come." He hung up. Let whoever was tapping Gregor figure that out.

The first of his castings to produce a nibble was from the former Secretary of State. "Samuel, there seems to have been just a tiny bit of a snafu on the summit invitation." Nothing agitated the old gentleman, the columnist knew; six years in office and he had seen it all. "Customarily, or at least in the absence of a national security adviser, our man in Moscow sounds out his counterpart on an invitation, to be sure it will be favorably received. Seems that didn't happen here, and nobody at Foggy Bottom knows what the devil the Russians are going to say. Either Ericson jumped the gun, which is unlike him, or he had a semiprivate talk with Nikolayev on the hot line."

"In that case," Zophar said, "the NSA would know and would inform the Director of Central Intelligence."

"Right. Say, you chaps are well informed. I checked that out and the DCI doesn't know about any hot-line calls in the past couple of weeks. Could be the President is bulling it through, or he just assumes his invitation will be accepted based on some unofficial intermediary's message."

At half past eleven, about two hours after Ericson's speech had ended, Gregor showed up at Zophar's house. The columnist slowly poured a brandy, glowered, lit a cigar, glowered some more, and in an ominous tone, stated: "It is a damned lucky thing I didn't trust you."

Gregor did not flinch. "My information is accurate."

"The President of the United States," said Zophar, rolling the syllables, "has just gone before the world and demonstrated that your information is so much bilge water. The counterrevolutionary faction you evidently represent, Gregor, has been crushed. Nikolayev is so securely in charge he can afford to leave the Kremlin and come to America. Only my good sense, and my natural skepticism of unsubstantiated information, has kept me from using your misinformation. Which means that I keep my reputation and you keep breathing."

"You are so certain you are right," Gregor said.

"Prove me wrong."

"At this moment," the Soviet agent said slowly, "Nikolayev is in Lubyanka Prison. He has been stripped of all his powers and is being prepared for trial."

Zophar felt the pounding in his chest at the sudden possession of exclusive information, followed by the relaxation of considering the likelihood of it being wrong. He put on a bored look. "You spin some fantastic yarns, my friend. I wish you could give me something to go on."

"Did you not check this out with the President? You were at the White House twice today—what did he tell you? Didn't he admit that the story of Kolkov saving his life was a hoax?"

"The President—" Zophar pretended to catch himself. "I am not at liberty to say what he told me, other than to say that all you have told me is a lie. It does not check out. I will never believe you again, my good man, and neither will—"

Gregor caved, or pretended to. Nothing dramatic, no slumping shoulders or hung head, just a perceptible blink and a small smile. He went into the hall, where he had put down his raincoat, and brought out a small tape recorder.

"I have two tapes here. You are familiar with the voice of the agent Harry Bok?"

"I am not."

"No matter, it is not the important tape, he is drugged and who knows what a man can say when he is drugged. The tape now in the machine is of the hospital room of Agent Bok as he is being visited by your Secretary of State and by Lucas Cartwright. You are familiar with their voices, of course."

"Of course."

"Use the earpiece," Gregor said.

"I don't like those things, just turn the machine up loud."

"Use the earpiece, it's not easy to hear otherwise." Zophar knew that Gregor assumed the room—this room—was bugged, and did not want a recording made of the recording. Despicable man. He put on the earpiece, grimacing at the music in the background, listened all the way through once, and asked for a replay. The second time, he could make out not only the voices but many of the words:

Bok: Then I dragged him out of the wreck . . . set up a perimeter . . . Chinese face, right between the eyes . . . guy with the burp gun caught it . . . grenades got me, killed Kolkov, and I dragged his body over the President's. . . .

Curtice: Might it not have been possible that Kolkov, while still alive, tried to protect the President with his own body?

Bok: Dead, I think. Dragged him over.

Cartwright: So the Secretary is looking for something that might help ameliorate the situation. Like some heroism on the part of Kolkov.

Curtice: Something that the Russians can be proud of. . . .

Bok: Okay, coulda been that Kolkov crawled over. . . .

That was all. Zophar put down the earpiece, feeling the flush of excitement at the news in his hands, and the sick sensation of exposing American deceit which would benefit the Soviet Union. "That was what may be called 'leading the witness,' " the columnist said.

"You recognized the voices of Curtice and Cartwright?"

Sadly, Zophar said, "I couldn't swear to Curtice, I don't know him that well, but that was Lucas Cartwright, unless you've got a helluva mimic working for you." He told Gregor to play the second tape, of Bok reciting what had happened; as he had hoped and feared, the drugged voice of the agent corroborated what had been eavesdropped-on in the hospital room. The evidence was as firm as any Zophar was likely to get on any story, and he was now prepared to accept more of what Gregor had to offer.

"How long has Nikolayev been at Lubyanka Prison?"

"Four-five days."

"And we didn't know? Nobody knew?"

Gregor smiled. "An intelligence failure on your part. Looked at another way, nobody leaked, for a change. Until we were ready."

"Will the Kremlin accuse the President of conspiring with Nikolayev to murder General Secretary Kolkov?"

"No, there have been second thoughts on that. Ericson approved the lying, but was not in on the planning. It is in our interest to stick to the truth on this."

The columnist shook his head and rose. "I regret that I insulted you earlier, but it was the only way to get you to be serious."

Gregor shrugged. "You think Ericson knows about Nikolayev, that this invitation in his speech tonight is a very clever trick?"

Zophar, with the information received earlier from the former Secretary of State, had good reason to doubt that, but was not about to give Gregor anything the Soviets could use. "It's possible," he replied. "With Ericson, you never know."

Gregor gathered up his raincoat and recorder and stepped out into the Georgetown street. Zophar, at the window, watched the car pull away. Intelligent little man, the Russian, adept at survival; not despicable, as he had too quickly condemned him before. Gregor lived in an atmosphere rife with the routinization of deceit, with half-truth the half-norm. Zophar's thoughts turned to Lucas Cartwright, whom he had known and trusted most of his adult life. What motivated that honorable man to engage in this kind of business? The pressure must have been enormous. "Perhaps it just seemed like a good idea at the time," the columnist said aloud, and went upstairs to his blank wall and his typewriter.

The Secret Service Agent / 4

Bok pushed his wheel chair into Hennessy's office to hear the gray-faced lawyer say, "You've just been elected to bell the cat."

The agent looked at Melinda McPhee, Hank Fowler, and Hennessy seated around the table in the southern-exposure corner of the West Wing, and nodded. Harry had figured he would be the logical candidate to read the Zophar column, and the wire service stories breaking around it, to the President. At that moment, Bok hated himself; everything had been going so well, a whole day of good reaction to the President's speech thirty-six hours before, and now this sudden shot from the blind side—on a different subject —perhaps as a result of some mistake Harry Bok had made, a leak he had been an unwitting participant in. He was a bit player, a face in the background of the news pictures, suddenly thrust to center of stage. Why him? Harry Bok didn't want it; he was no good at it. He belonged in counterfeiting.

It was not yet 8 A.M. on a glowing, low-humidity summer's day that made the gloom in the White House all the more stark. Harry took a sweet roll off the table and waited while Melinda poured him a cup of coffee. He dropped a couple of saccharine tablets in and inhaled another sweet roll.

"When all of this is understood," Hank Fowler said softly, "it will be seen that Harry was only doing his duty, in what he thought was the country's best interests."

Melinda was not so kind. "No secrets between the four of us, remember? That's what the President said. You should have told us about the Kolkov heroics being a phony, Harry—maybe there was a way of getting ready for this. Did the Boss know?"

Harry did not know whether he should answer that. "Sort of," he hedged. "Frankly, I didn't see it the way it's coming out at all. This sumbitch columnist makes it all look like a conspiracy between the two countries, or a plot by Ericson to help maneuver the power in the Kremlin. I never saw it that way." He went further. "That's not what happened. I don't think so." He couldn't be sure—what had Cartwright done? Or Curtice? Or for that matter, what had Ericson done, after he found out that Kolkov was not the hero he had been cracked up to be? "I better go read the President the stuff before he turns on the radio."

"Take the News Summary, too," Melinda said, handing him the recorder along with the cassette for the President's speedhearing. "As of four o'clock this morning, when the summary was finished, it was a lot of good news. I even had a good night's sleep. Listening to it may make him feel better, after you read the column to him."

"Tell him I'm on the way." Harry wheeled himself out into the corridor. He had given Nurse Kellgren the morning off, and an agent pushed him along the colonnade into the residence. The President was in his underwear in the bedroom, being shaved, and his radiant good spirits made Harry feel worse. While the barber was there, he played the News Summary for the President; when that aide left, Harry stopped the recording and said, "And now for the bad news. It seems that what we were worried about we shouldn't have been, and what we weren't worried about we should have been."

"You mean Zophar didn't have the previous blindness story?" Ericson had a grim, I-told-you-so set to his mouth. "All right, Harry, give it to me straight."

"Today's column by Zophar takes up most of the top of page one," Harry said, giving it all too straight: "Here's the headline: 'Soviet Leader Reported Ousted; Nikolayev-Ericson Collusion Charged.' "

"Huh?"

Harry read the headline again, and the first few paragraphs of the column: "Vasily Nikolayev, who replaced the assassinated Alexei Kolkov as Soviet Premier one month ago, has probably been deposed—and possibly jailed—because his Politburo colleagues suspect him of conspiring with President Ericson to consolidate his Kremlin power."

"Jesus," Ericson said. "Read that over."

Harry did, and continued: "Tape recordings in the possession of Soviet authorities, which this reporter has heard, show that General Secretary Kolkov did not heroically save President Ericson's life. This was a story concocted after the ambush by Secretary of State George Curtice, and then-Chief of Staff Lucas Cartwright, and obediently parroted by Secret Service agent Harry Bock.' " Bok stopped. "He spelled my name wrong."

"Don't worry, Harry," the President assured him, "you'll be a household word in no time. But not as a hero any more. Keep reading."

Bok went through the entire column, to the conclusion: " 'We do not yet know if the President's invitation this week to Nikolayev was a desperation maneuver to save the Soviet leader's life and job, or whether—mind-boggling though it is—the Ericson Administration does not yet realize that an upheaval is going on in the Kremlin. What we do know is this: The President, in his praise of his aides in this week's speech, put his seal of approval on the Curtice-Cartwright deceit—and joined in the attempt to mislead the people of both the United States and the Soviet Union."

"Keep reading," Ericson said, picking up the phone and telling the operator to put Hennessy on. As Harry went on reading, the President said, "Tell the DCI, if he's awake yet, that I want to know what CIA knows about the status of Nikolayev, if he's in jail or in power. Now give me your thinking." He listened for a moment, then shook his head: "No, Smitty will just have to skip the eleven o'clock briefing because he can't have anything to say until I tell him, and I don't know what to tell him until I know what cooks with Nikolayev. I mean, what the hell do we have a CIA for? Fifteen billion bucks a year and we don't know who's running Russia, for Chrissake? Um." He listened, then cut in, "If they can't come up with a damn good idea in an hour, I'm going to pick up the hot line and ask for the man in charge and see who the hell answers. We're not helpless. Get Curtice in my office in a half hour and tell Cartwright to get his ass back from wherever, and they should both shut up on the way. Right." The President's tone was malevolent; Harry sensed his helplessness in not knowing whether the central assertion of an urgent problem was true, and in not being able to react until sure that it was a real problem that called for a reaction. "Just put a freeze on everything," Ericson snapped at Hennessy, "until I find out how much of this is true. Then I'll decide. Nobody else is to make any decisions, or put out any statements. If you can find out where Zophar got his stuff, that would be helpful, too. He sure didn't get this from Arthur Leigh."

Ericson went to the area where his clothes were laid out and proceeded to dress quickly. He reached confidently for each garment, not thinking about the drill, bitching to Bok all the while. "I straighten out the whole goddamn previous blindness thing, I get the mountain off my back, and then this. Harry, nobody ever told me we plotted with Vasily to cook up a story making Kolkov a hero."

"If you say so, sir." That was a possible way out— Harry could truthfully say he never spelled the plot out in so many words to the President. He could say he had "indicated" it. "Indicated" was a fuzzy word, it didn't mean that he was sure what he had passed along had been understood.

Buttoning his vest, the President paused. "Maybe that would seem worse, me not knowing. Maybe it would be better if I had known, and had ratified the action in the national interest."

Harry frowned; he was having trouble figuring out where the truth was. Did he tell the President? Did the President understand him, that Kolkov was not the hero? Did the President just get the message now, and was he reacting to the politics of the problem? Did the President want Harry Bok to tell him something else?

"You see," the President thought aloud, "when the story about Kolkov was being cooked up, I was unconscious, half dead. The motive in cooking up the heroism story wasn't venal—hell, Lucas and George just wanted to prevent a furious reaction, maybe a war. And they wanted to get me out of Russia in a hurry. Then, when I was informed, I thought it would be the better part of wisdom to say nothing for the time being."

"In the press conference you said Kolkov was a big hero," Harry reminded him, still not knowing if Ericson was working out a scenario or recounting what he actually remembered.

"I wasn't fully informed then," Ericson answered tentatively. "No, that wouldn't wash." He tried another tack: "I thought it best to back up the battlefield judgment of my top advisers." He liked that better, and Harry watched his expression relax, then harden again. "I wish I hadn't invited Vasily over here in the speech, last night, but I needed a lead, and it never occurred to me that the CIA wouldn't know of a big switch in the Kremlin. Should've run it past State, dammit, to feel out Moscow first. I'm culpable on that. The other thing —the cooked-up story—that was a Curtice and Cartwright idea, which I might have been right or wrong in ratifying, but I was shaken up, and it may be defensible. But inviting Vasily over was my idea, and I knew it took State by surprise—Defense, too." He pulled on his jacket and checked with his hands to see if his hair was combed.

"What's so bad about inviting him over?"

"Harry, you're not thinking. If I knew Vasily Nikolayev was finished and I invited him here, it looks like I was gambling on influencing the Kremlin to keep him in power. If I did not know Vasily was out, and invited him over—and just found out this morning he'd been canned—then it'd look like I was the dopiest President since Warren Gamaliel Harding. At this stage, I cannot afford to look stupid. Not on the big things."

Harry rolled his wheel chair to the door. "Give me a push," he asked the President. Ericson took the handles and pushed, guided by Harry's braking. The agent tried working out Ericson's alternatives in his head: whether to look tricky, lying to the world, or to look confused, admitting he was never really in control. Tough choice.

Ericson seemed comfortable pushing the wheel chair, and Harry signaled to his fellow agent at the elevator that the odd couple needed no other assistance. With "half-left" and "bear right," Harry had the President take him to the main floor, out of the residence, past the Rose Garden.

"Buffie's taking our picture," Harry said, as they went along the colonnade. "She's over by the steps near the entrance to the Cabinet Room."

"Let her," Ericson said. "Shows I'm kind, I go out of my way to help the handicapped."

"We both could use a little sympathy today," Harry said.

"Wish to hell you were a Seeing Eye dog," the President responded, jiggling the wheel chair. "A dog would know how to handle a press conference. He'd sit up there and howl till they stopped twisting his tail."

Harry hmfed. That was Ericson's way of telling him that Harry Bok would be facing the press today, with no help from Smitty, who would be protecting his own reputation.

"Sharp left, driver. Here's Buffie, blue denim dress, dripping cameras. Hullo, Buffie."

Ericson stopped pushing, and Harry watched Buffie come up to them. He was reluctant to give the President more of a description because it would have been cruel. "That's a good situation," she said. "Shows you got a good heart, Potus."

"I'd be better off with a good intelligence agency," said the President.

"Here's a kiss for Harry," Buffie said, stooping to give Harry a swift, noisy kiss on the mouth, because they were in view of a half-dozen people, and the agent had to be the proxy. "I got a good heart, too," she said. Ericson pushed the wheel chair again, and Buffie said, "Luck today."

"Everybody deals with you through me," Harry remarked. "Three more steps, the french doors are open, and here we are. There's Melinda, looking dependable, and Hennessy, looking all stern, like he's God and he's sore at me for slipping Eve the apple."

"You should've told me, Harry," said Hennessy, speaking through Harry to the President. "You can't keep the facts from your lawyer. I didn't know we were only foolin' about Kolkov. Maybe if I knew, I could have planned for this morning."

Ericson took his seat behind the Hoover desk and said, "Gather round and sound off." Hennessy, Melinda, and Harry spoke up so the President would know their positions in the room. They were joined around the big desk by Smitty, Marilee, and Hank Fowler. "Curtice coming?" the President asked.

Hennessy, voice disgusted, said, "The Secretary of State refuses to be summoned in such a brusque manner. I got that from his persnickety aide—Curtice won't even talk to me on the goddamn phone."

"I see his point," Ericson said mildly. "Melinda, get George Curtice here for lunch about noon, ask him nicely. Lucas coming back?"

"Cartwright's on his way," Hennessy said, "be in tonight."

"A lot of good that's going to do me for the press briefing this morning," Smitty said. "What the hell am I going to say? Is Nikolayev in or out? Did Kolkov save your life or not? If Sam Zophar is right, why the hell did you—"

"Shut the fuck up, Smitty," said Hennessy, to Bok's relief. "We'll get around to the press in a minute."

"No, no," Ericson said, still mildly—he had cloaked his fury and wasn't offending anybody this morning, it seemed to Harry—"Smitty, tell me the reaction to the column."

"It's bad," said the press secretary. "And it's getting worse every minute we stonewall 'em. Frankly, I never saw it so rough—Marilee was out in the press room, you tell him."

"They're milling around getting each other riled up," said Marilee quietly. "The other day, with the speech, there was a different feeling. They weren't so sure what was right or wrong, or how it would be interpreted. But there are a lot of hot-eyed people in the press room this morning. Talk about lying, disability, the works."

"Um," said Ericson, revolving his chair toward Melinda, who was standing next to Bok's wheel chair.

"Let's hear from Ma Griffe." The secretary was wearing more perfume than usual, Harry noted, and the President could spot it easily.

"The calls are worried," she said. "I told the DCI of your wish, and he sounded—well, calm and helpless, I guess. The Attorney General called to register his hope that there would be a clarification issued immediately. Your Aunt Flora called"—that was the President's nearest living relative, often used as a loyalist public-opinion weather vane by the White House staff —"and she said the commentator on television this morning ought to be shot for what he said about you, unless the commentator was right, and if so then you should be the one to be shot."

"The Hill?"

"Usual jumping up and down," Melinda reported, "but Speaker Frelingheusen called to say he would withhold comment until he sees your statement, and I should tell him when you plan to make it. That's his way of leaning on you a little."

"Here is what we will do," said Ericson. "Smitty, postpone your morning briefing until—oh, two this afternoon."

"That's not fair to the afternoon papers—"

"Life is unfair, as they say. But you can announce that you will produce Harry Bok for them this afternoon to question at will. Harry will tell the truth about Kolkov—that he can't really be sure, shrapnel was flying all around, he was soon to be in shock himself, and that he thinks the report of heroism might be true, but of course there's the chance he got the idea while he was in shock. Harry's testimony, as he outlined it to me, is ambiguous, fuzzy. Like the truth usually is. By the time he's talking with the press this afternoon, I'll have instructions for you, Smitty, on what to say about Nikolayev." Bok liked the way Ericson was functioning in a tight moment. "Melinda, get my Russian translator over here right away, and hook up the video tape for the hot line. Okay, meeting over, I just want Hennessy now. Everybody walk tall, no glum looks except for

Smitty, who's normally glum. It's going to be a long day. Stick it out."

The staff filed out, Harry wheeling his chair into Melinda's office next door via the porch, where the path had been made generations before for FDR's wheel chair. He looked at her, in her trim black skirt and full white blouse, make the call for the translator and alert the White House Communications Agency for the hot-line call. The recording facilities required a signed order from the President countersigned by Hennessy, which Harry watched Melinda prepare. Ericson buzzed; Melinda flicked up the listening switch to hear him say, "Be sure George Curtice says nothing to any press until he sees me," and then, looking at Harry Bok, she deliberately failed to lower the intercom switch.

"Stupid bastard," they heard Hennessy say. "You didn't need this. This was avoidable."

"Right you are, Brother Hennessy," Ericson's voice replied. "This whole flap could have been avoided if you knew what the hell you were doing." Bok had not heard Ericson use that whiplash tone of voice before; evidently Melinda had.

"My fault? You're blaming me? I was ten thousand miles away—"

"Not the Kolkov business. The prior blindness."

"What is this shit, Sven?"

"I never had to make the goddamn speech!"

Hennessy was silent, and the President, coldly angry, went on: "Zophar didn't have the prior blindness story. He had the Kolkov story. I kept asking you—are you sure he knows? You kept saying yes. It turns out he knew something, all right, but not what you thought. You panicked, and you panicked me, and then I had to make the goddamn speech, and now we're in one hell of a pickle."

"Sven, I didn't even know there was a Kolkov story. I was a good-natured schnook along with the rest of America. I figured you and Harry and Curtice and Cartwright were telling the truth about him being a big hero—"

"Bullshit, Hennessy, you knew we were cooking something up on that. I don't have to spell out every detail for you. But you had your head all fixed on the other big guilty secret, the prior blindness, and the minute somebody started asking questions about something—something else—you jumped to the wrong conclusion. Harry didn't tell the Russians about the blindness, he told the Russians about the phony story on Kolkov—but you were so sure. Oh, were you sure. I never"—here Hennessy's voice joined Ericson's, finishing the sentence—"had to make the goddamn speech."

"Okay, I blew it," said Hennessy. "You want a new lawyer? You want Cartwright back? Or Smitty?"

"I need Cartwright in the Cabinet and I don't trust Smitty so I'm stuck with you. But stop being so goddamn sure of yourself, it's costing me the presidency."

"Have you considered the possibility, Mr. President, sir, that my erroneous assumption might have been the biggest break you ever had? Can you imagine where we'd be today if the story had just broken of how you and your buddy Vasily have been fucking around with the facts—and we still hadn't come clean on the previous blindness?"

"I never had to make that goddamn speech," Ericson repeated.

"Making that goddamn speech was the luckiest thing that happened around here in three months." Hennessy had moved from a possibility to a certainty. "It's behind us now, not hanging over our heads. We thought the roof would cave in, that the Cabinet would reassemble and retry the case with new evidence—you remember how Duparquet made a big deal out of not knowing before the election of any likelihood of blindness? We thought they'd kill us on that—but they haven't. You owned up to it, you were great, you got away with murder. Don't you see?"

"If I didn't have to make the goddamn speech, I wouldn't have had to grab for a lead, and I wouldn't have made that mistake about Nikolayev. Now I'm boxed in. Get off the defensive, counselor, and try to understand the way the walls are closing in on us."

"You know why you act so calm in a crisis?" Hennessy's big voice boomed. "You're calm because you're scared shitless. Sure, it gives Melinda an orgasm, and Marilee too, to see you cool and collected, but the truth is you're paralyzed inside. You wanna repeat your catechism? Let's go—'I nev-er had to make that goddamn speech.' "

Silence for a couple of minutes. Harry Bok looked at the squawk box on Melinda's desk and was afraid to say anything for fear it was two-way. Melinda twisted a coffee mug and waited.

The President's voice broke the pause, "Aah, maybe it was for the best."

"Christ, Sven, I'm sorry. I thought I had it all together, and all the time I was running over the cliff. I let you down. Cartwright would never—"

"You're laying the *mea culpa* on a little thick, Hennessy."

"Think so? There's a catch in my voice I haven't even used, tears up a jury. Tough-guy lawyer breaks down, it's a grabber."

"Funny how the previous blindness didn't cause an explosion." The anger had dissipated, and now the President was looking at the ironies. "I was sure that was all they needed to take my powers away, but after we broke the story, the reaction just sort of hung out there, not this, not that. And now this Kolkov-the-hero thing—which I didn't think was a big deal, I never really focused on it—may get out of hand. Hard to figure."

"Let's get through one day at a time, Sven. It'll pass."

"I'm beginning to allow for the possibility that we may not be so good at this line of work."

"You're getting better all the time," Hennessy assured him. "Staff work's been a little sloppy lately."

"I wonder. If I'm not good at it—" Ericson's voice trailed off.

"Compared to what?"

"True. Never should have let Bannerman sell me Nichols."

"Your crying jag over, Mr. President?"

"Don't blame yourself for everything, Hennessy, even though, God knows, it was all your fault. You think I had to make that speech?"

"You nev-er had to make the goddamn speech. Now let's get our translator and put a person-to-person hot-line call into whoever. Ask him how the weather is in Moscow, and would he please spell his name."

Melinda flipped the squawk box switch and waited for Hennessy to come out. The staff chief stopped, sat on the edge of her desk, and put his hand on the silent squawk box. "Get an earful, doll? Did you like the part where I said you had an orgasm when he acted calm in a crisis? Did you blush?"

"What do you mean?" She tried to play dumb; Harry was glad Hennessy did not look at him.

"The light was on his squawk box on the side of the desk. He couldn't see, but I could, and I knew you were copping a listen. Tell me—when he's banging a broad in there, do you get your kicks by looking through the keyhole?"

Shaken, Melinda looked at Harry. "You still carry a gun? Give it to me, I'll kill him." She was not serious about that, Harry knew, but there was real menace in her tone. Harry knew she hated Hennessy, in a way, at times; and she hated the part of Ericson that turned to a Hennessy.

"Which reminds me"—Hennessy turned to Harry —"no more Buffie, not even if he wants her—just too big a risk. We've never been more vulnerable. Any-time he gets horny, run in that nurse of yours, or who-ever you use." Harry did not like the way Hennessy enjoyed talking about this in front of Melinda. "Keep him pooped, Harry. Use the telephone booth. Buffie doesn't have us over a barrel any more—most of the secret's out. Now the trick is to keep her from finding out how groggy we are, and telling Bannerman to move in for the kill. I'm right about that, you two—

keep Buffie away. Who else should we be worried about?"

"Herb's dead," Melinda said flatly.

"You handled his wife?"

"I gave Barbara the news." Melinda added, "She's with friends."

"Our friends?"

"What the hell do you mean?"

"I don't want trouble from there," Hennessy told her. "I don't want any stuff about Ericson driving her husband to suicide."

"Barbara Abelson is a good soldier," Melinda said.

"More than you can say for her husband," Hennessy muttered, and Melinda flared back with "Herb wasn't tough, but he didn't make huge, stupid mistakes." Hennessy seemed to enjoy the opening for savagery: "Look, Old Faithful, you didn't just spend the night mopping up after a suicide with a cop on your back while you tried to find a suicide note that could have blown everything. You didn't come back with a body in a bag. You didn't get blamed by the Boss for being an idiot, when all you did was make it possible for him to hang on to his job, and when your biggest handicap was not knowing what some foreign-affairs geniuses were screwing up. And you didn't have to take a browbeating from Papa, like a little kid who was caught jerking off, while you knew your respected colleagues were eavesdropping and lapping it all up. So kiss my ass, Melinda."

Bok decided it was time to step in. "I got something to say," he said, and Melinda and Hennessy broke the lock of their glares to look toward him. "I'm sorry about listening in. That was wrong. It wasn't something we did consciously, Hennessy, it just started coming over the intercom and we didn't stop it."

"Don't apologize," Melinda said, voice trembling. "He's probably got a bug in your wheel chair."

"I got to thinking just now how it was in Russia," Harry continued, not just to break up their argument, but because he wanted to say this, "where you have to watch everything you say. Somebody's always listening, or making you talk when you don't know it, or like that. And there's no guarding against it, sooner or later they get to you. I should have thought of that when we started listening, but all I thought was 'Gee, this is interesting,' and then 'It's important we know that.' That's crap. We can't do that, ol' buddies, we got to give each other as much respect as we can."

"Don't give me Brandeis on privacy," Hennessy said, and barked his laugh. "Melinda and I like to tease each other, Harry, we're never serious. Get Hank Fowler to explain it to you: It's a love-hate thing."

There was a pause in which they all avoided hurting each other any more.

Hennessy hitched his pants up and said, "Back to work. We make the hot-line call from the Situation Room. The translator should be there now. I'll take the Boss, Melinda, you shove this cripple. Remember, Harry, keep Buffie a mile away, and run a broad in and out whenever he's got a minute. It's better he gets laid than gets worried."

"I am not one of the boys," Melinda said firmly. Hennessy appraised her bosom insolently, shrugged and went back into the Oval Office. Melinda closed her eyes, took a deep breath, and held it; slowly, she exhaled.

"Look at it this way," Harry offered. "Somewhere in all that, he used the word 'love.' " It might have been a bitter divorce lawyer's way of saying it, but Harry noticed the love-hate reference and didn't want the event unrecorded.

"I have never been so mortified," Melinda snapped, opening a drawer and snatching a couple of tissues angrily out of a dispenser, holding them to her eyes now that Hennessy was gone.

"He was just being vicious—"

"Harry, I'm mortified at myself, don't you see?" When she took the tissues away, her eyes were still hot with tears. "I did something hateful, I watched him when he was absolutely naked. He'll never forget that, and I can't blame him. What is this place doing to us—"

"Wait a minute," Harry said, a half-development behind.

"And I hooked you into it, the eavesdropping," Melinda said bitterly. "The way Cartwright and Curtice did in Yalta. Wasn't your fault, you just went along with what I was doing. Then when you made your little speech, I swear I never felt so small in my whole life."

True enough, Harry thought, his sins were mainly in going along with people he trusted. "We all make mistakes," he said.

"Lame excuse," she said, unthinking, and then winced at the double meaning. "Christ," looking at the ceiling, "you have to watch everything you say around these guys. Come on, I'll 'shove the cripple,' as Hennessy says when he wants to be compassionate."

She pushed his wheel chair down the hall and into the elevator to the basement, out and past the agents' lounge, down a ramp to the Situation Room. By the time they arrived, she had composed herself; pushing a wheel chair was probably a kind of therapy.

Harry was always disappointed in the Situation Room. Couple of maps, some electronic equipment, a television screen; a likely place to come in a crisis, but the drab layout of the room did not support the drama the way he always thought it should. The agent at the door nodded him in and smiled slightly at Melinda. Now that Harry thought about it, the new version of the hot line—a television telephone, in constant satellite contact—would be especially helpful today. In this situation, seeing Vasily Nikolayev was as important as hearing his voice; a telephone voice could be imitated.

When Ericson took his place at the table, the WHCA corpsman said into his mouthpiece, in English, "The President of the United States is calling the Premier of the Soviet Union." The American translator repeated the message in Russian to one of the microphones on the table. A voice answered in Russian, and a Russian voice translated: "Your communication is received. Please stand by." The communication, Harry knew, was not a complete surprise to Moscow; the operators had signaled each other about a hot-line call a half hour before. They watched the black screen to see whose face would appear.

Vasily Nikolayev's Slavic face filled the screen, and Harry Bok let out his breath in relief. Then it occurred to Harry that the President did not yet have the information that eyes could see, and he whispered to Ericson, "It's Nikolayev," as the Russian's voice said, "Mr. President, it is good to talk with you." After the translation—Nikolayev could speak English, but hot-line protocol required official translation for monitoring by other officials in both capitals—Ericson said: "This is not, repeat not, a military emergency." That also was standard; alerts were expensive.

"The purpose of this call," said Ericson, as if the purpose had not already been largely served by seeing Nikolayev in office, "is to expedite my public invitation for you to visit this country and continue our meetings. It was not possible for internal reasons, to make a private approach first, which we would normally do."

"The timing is not good," said the Russian. "I regret that it is not possible to give you an answer right away. The Presidium will have to consider it carefully."

"Please give my compliments to the members of the Politburo whom I met during my visit, before Yalta," said the President. "Is the composition of that group the same as when I was there?"

"The Presidium will take your kind invitation under advisement," said the Russian, looking straight at the camera, "and will be pleased when I tell them that your recovery appears to be continuing." Very formal, quite unresponsive.

Ericson's voice became equally formal. "A personal word, Premier Nikolayev. I have taken note of the careful medical attention you so kindly gave my Secret Service aide, Mr. Bok, who has recently returned."

Harry did not know whether to be glad or to worry.

Was Ericson telling Nikolayev he knew about the drugging, and if so, would the Russian catch it?

"Agent Bok is considered a hero," said the Soviet Premier, "and one day, when he can come to accept it, we will give him the highest award for bravery that we present to a foreign national. He is a worthy product of your Marines. All members of the Presidium will be informed of your expression of thanks to our hospital staff." Harry figured he caught it and chose to hear only Ericson's word, "kindly." In a slightly impatient tone Nikolayev concluded, "Is there any other communication in this emergency channel, Mr. President?" That was a rebuff.

"Thank you and good day," said Ericson, and the corpsman clicked off. To those in the Situation Room, the President ordered, "Hennessy, Bok, McPhee, CIA, stay." The others left. "CIA," said the President.

"Let's play it back," said the head of the CIA's Soviet desk.

The playback only took a minute. Harry watched Ericson this time, rather than the screen; the President looked weary, and was rubbing his temple.

"Nikolayev is evidently in trouble," said the CIA analyst. "He said that the Presidium, the large body, was considering the invitation—that's abnormal. You picked that up, Mr. President, asking about the Politburo, and he repeated 'the Presidium.' As you know, the Politburo, the small body, has always been in charge during transitions—if it's not, and the much larger Presidium is the forum, the power is all diffused and nobody knows who is in charge.

"Two, his not being able to give an indication about coming over is nothing less than ominous, in my book, sir. That's an admission of impotence, unlike Nikolayev, unlike—unlike any Russian leader with any power.

"Three, the way he did not answer your question about the composition of the Politburo, and the way he cut you off at the end, was insulting—unless he had no alternative. I would assume he had no room to maneuver—that he was there with specific instructions to say nothing, and nothing was what he said." The analyst looked at his notes. "Four, there was some byplay in your reference to Harry Bok that I didn't fathom. What was that about?"

Harry wondered about that, too. The President had good reason to believe that the chief of his Secret Service detail, in the Yalta hospital, had been drugged and interrogated—Ericson's use of "kindly" could only have been sarcastic.

"I wanted to give Vasily an opening to tell us something," Ericson said slowly, still rubbing his forehead. "He told us that Harry is still considered a hero, which means that they're going to stick with the story that Kolkov was a hero, too, at least for the time being. I guess they're waiting to see which way the cat will jump."

"The reference to Bok being a Marine seemed gratuitous," the analyst said. "Anything there?"

Harry shook his head. "I was in the Navy when I was a kid, I was never in the Marines."

Hennessy's head snapped toward him: " 'Tell it to the Marines.' "

"You think that's it?" the analyst asked tensely. "Would Nikolayev be aware of the meaning of an Americanism like that?"

"Yes," said Ericson, sitting up. "I used it in Moscow, passing a Marine guard at the embassy, and I told Vasily that it came from an ancient Army feeling about dumb Marines. I told him 'Tell it to the Marines' means 'That's bullshit.' He knows it, and—more important—he knows I know he knows it."

"Then reverse his previous sentence's meaning." The CIA man looked at his notes. "He says, 'Agent Bok is considered a hero.' The truth, then, is that Bok is not considered a hero, and neither is Kolkov probably—that is, if we're not jumping to a conclusion about the Marine reference."

"Don't jump to conclusions," said Hennessy, with a hard look at Melinda.

"Vasily may have had it," concluded the President. "He could be finished, and he took one hell of a chance telling us that. Somebody over there thinks he can keep us at a disadvantage by not making public the shift in power, or trying to get us to go for the Presidium stuff. I don't believe that, it's not the way they operate. They know I'm in a bind with my invitation, so they're letting me have a little more rope. They don't confirm the Zophar story, that Nikolayev and his clique are out—they make it possible for me to deny it, and be wrong, and get in deeper."

"Which you won't do," said Melinda.

"Not if I can avoid it," said the President. After a silence, he added, "No, I can't, no matter what. I'll have to take the bath on this and get it over with. We can't have the Russians thinking they have me lying to the world."

"You'll be confirming Zophar's story, then?" Hennessy asked. "Admit you invited Nikolayev, not knowing he was deposed?"

"Thank you, Frank," the President dismissed the CIA man. "You brief your associates, tell the DCI to look at the film." When the analyst had gone, Ericson said, "Who's here, just us?"

Melinda said, "Hennessy and Harry and me. Just the family."

"I'm going to look terrible," the President told them. "Like a man who does not know what the hell he is doing in relations with another superpower. Incompetent, disabled, the works. But I have to take it, you know? I can't let the sons of bitches over there think they've got me under their thumb."

"You lost me," said Melinda. Harry was glad she said that.

"The men in power in Moscow today—whoever they are—think that Ericson and Nikolayev conspired to put Nikolayev in power," said Hennessy slowly. "So what they're offering now is kind of half-assed cover for us to deny the Zophar story. They'll keep Nikolayev in the job for a while, to keep the President from looking like a real dope—but we'd be beholden to them, and they could put out the whole truth anytime." To Harry, it seemed as if Hennessy admired the technique. "They're trying to do to us what they think we tried to do to them."

"Well put," said the President, adding, "I never had to make that goddamn speech."

Harry was moved by the unfairness of the criticism to come. "You're going to do the right thing for the country, and you're going to get clobbered. That's a bitch."

"It evens up," the President said. "I got away with murder on the previous blindness. I had to do the wrong thing there all the way down the line, just one wrong thing after the other, and only admitted it because Hennessy likes me to make speeches. And what happens? The damn thing blows over. The mistake about Nikolayev, though, I have to own up to, and I'll pay and pay and pay. Bannerman'll see to that."

"Back to work," Hennessy said. "You have lunch in the office with Secretary Curtice, then—"

The President interrupted: "I'll say I'm sorry he didn't come over earlier, I had wanted him here when I made the hot-line call."

"Yeah." Hennessy grinned wolfishly. "Then I'll tell Smitty what to say to his piranhas, and he can go into the press briefing with Harry here and with Curtice, too. Let ol' George take part of the rap. Kolkov-the-hero was his idea in the first place. We'll get through the day. I'll tell the gremlins not to prepare a News Summary, it's too depressing."

"I'll tell Speaker Frelingheusen myself," said the President.

"Answer me one thing," Harry felt he had to put in. "This suspicion the Russians have that you and Nikolayev were in cahoots, to help him get the top job —was that true?"

"I have to leave you some reason to read my memoirs, Harry," the President said, rising.

As Harry was being wheeled out to the steps, he caught Melinda's question to Hennessy: "You suppose this is another one of those times we expect the worst, and it doesn't happen?" And Hennessy's reply: "For the next few days, kiddo, this place is going to seem like Hitler's bunker."

IV

_____

*The Sparks Fly
Upward*

"You're a nip-flicker," Buffie said, on her back, hands behind her head, as Jonathan built up the tension between his thumb and middle finger, and every ten seconds, like a reliable geyser, flicked her nipple. "Worse than that," she offered, "you're a preoccupied nip-flicker. You're thinking you're writing a book, and the hero says,"—she deepened her voice to that of a hero—" 'I frowned thoughtfully, flicking her nipple, just fooling around, not caring how I was driving her crazy-wild with passion, making her crave me with my unconcern.' "

"Words like 'preoccupied' and 'unconcern' are not used by real people," he said, turned on by her mind, his eyes on a pile of Buffie's ink sketches on his desk. They captured more in a few intuitive lines than he would ever be able to catch in prose. "But go on, what does the heroine say?"

"She says nothing, but writhes passionately," Buffie mused. "Actually, she's not the heroine, she's just a minor character you put in there to spice things up, or to show that the need for sex and the need for power are alike. She knows her place—everybody's favorite lay, when they're not too busy."

"You're shooting mental pictures of all this," the writer countered, as his middle finger flew to its target again. "You not only want to be a character in my book, you want to be the illustrator."

"What's in my frame?" she smirked, making a good imitation of writhing passionately.

"Handsome, virile man," said Jonathan, "mature beyond his years, lying naked across the frame, idly fingering a slim, lithe body with its knee lifted and toe pointed for maximum sex appeal. Your picture is deliberately out of focus. Morning light, the afterglow of appetite, the impotence of satiation."

"That's the picture," she nodded. "Backlit, to disguise the faces, but the body whose nipple is being flicked cannot be disguised, there's not another one like it in the world. Grainy print, black and white. Lotsa mood, perfume ad." She sighed happily; he imagined she was happiest at dreams of success.

"How come you never wear perfume, Buffie?"

"I'll tell you if you make me, but you don't want to know."

"I asked because I want to know," Jonathan said. "I can take pain." He couldn't, all that well, and wondered whether he was straying into one of those areas where she would make him feel a twinge of jealous fear.

"I don't wear perfume because Sven Ericson is tuned in on scents and odors," she said. "He always was, but more than ever now. He knows that Melinda smells of Ma Griffe, and that debutante press secretary Marilee smells of Femme. Silent Sam—Harry Bok's nurse with the floppy tits—smells of some cheap Lily of the Valley. He classifies women that way. He gave me a perfume, which I bet Melinda picked out, and I'm supposed to wear it so I fit in my category. But I don't wear it. Or anything else."

"So how does he know you're around?" Jonathan was impelled to track this down, even though he suspected he did not want to get to the reason.

"I smell of me," she said. "When I get near him, or touch him, I get excited. I get wet, you know? And somebody with a nose that's really sensitive can tell when a girl like me has the hots."

Jonathan tried not to show the ache that went through him. Here she was, ready to make love to him at a nipple's flicking, yet willing to describe her excitement for another man to him as if he were her brother or conspirator. Jonathan well knew that musky odor; it would cling to him all day after he had luxu-

riated in Buffie, and he hated to take the shower that
would send her woman-scent away.

"Lieutenant Kellgren does not have floppy tits," he
said, to wound her in return. "She has a firm, full
bosom that would make any woman proud. Carries
herself well. You're right, she doesn't say much, but
she's not cheap."

That got to her. Buffie rolled out of bed and took
a position on the window seat. "Not going to flick my
nips and think about those floppy Air Force tits," she
announced. After her pique passed, she came back to
him and started massaging his foot. "You haven't been
to work in the past two days," she said. "Ever since
the speech you wrote. Nobody misses you at the office, God knows, but I do." She had a point; a speechwriter's presence after a speech was as keenly desired
as a floozie's after a sex bout.

Jonathan had no desire to go back to the White
House that day. He had seen the pictures of the angry
picket line, the demonstrations in Lafayette Square, the
nose-to-nose buses around the Ellipse keeping that
area inaccessible. He had read, first, the tepid reaction to the speech he was supposed to have written,
and the next day, the stories about the deception at
Yalta. He had watched television last night with its
long session deploring the way the President was fum-
bling our relations with the Soviet Union. The writer
felt doubly betrayed: The draft speech he had submitted had been revised—twisted—by the President
into a tricky evasion of issues. On top of that, he had
not learned until after the press corps did of the lying
in high places about the Yalta ambush. There had
turned out to be a dark side of Ericson he had not
perceived: duplicitous in personal matters, deceitful
in affairs of state. Jonathan was not prepared to quit,
or even to express his disgust—and certainly not to
defect to Bannerman—but neither was he prepared to
go back to work at the Ericson White House right
away. Nobody missed him, anyway.

"The speech Ericson gave was not the speech I
wrote," he told Buffie. "I wrote a speech that owned

up to a campaign deception and apologized for it. No wonder he couldn't give it, he had a bigger lie about Yalta waiting to explode in his face any day. But I didn't know about that. I only had a little information to work with."

"Never heard you call him 'Ericson' before," Buffie observed irrelevantly, he thought. "You always said 'the President,' even when you talked about him getting into me."

"The President is still the President," he said irritably, "and I am a true-blue member of his staff. When he gets 'into' you, as you put it so romantically, he represents himself, and not 250 million other Americans. When you put out for him, Buffie, you are putting out for one individual man—and you are not putting out for your country. A cock is not a flagpole." Jonathan was surprised at himself; that was not what he had started out to say. Striking metaphor at the end, though, entirely spontaneous, even if it was not the sort of image he could ever use.

He watched Buffie walk across the room to his closet, select a tie, and stand in front of the full-length mirror, naked, slowly tying the tie around her neck. She pulled a belt out of his pants, and tied it around her waist—the holes were too far out to fit the buckle, but she faked it. Wearing only his tie and belt, she then slipped on a pair of his shoes, and came to the side of the bed, kneeling to reach for his penis. She stroked it, squeezed it, and toyed with it until he had a quivering erection, and then she stood back suddenly, saluted, and started to sing "The Star-Spangled Banner." When he started to laugh, he lost his erection, and she snapped off her salute.

Some kind of woman, he laughed to himself, taking her back in the antic hay. The only girl he had ever met who was nuttily sexy, or sexily nutty, and at the same time resolutely untrustworthy. "Adamant for drift," in Churchill's phrase. He had to remind himself not to unload his frustrations and disappointments in Ericson on her, because they would surely be transmitted to Bannerman. The thought of Buffie in Ban-

nerman's hands—or worse, Bannerman in Buffie's—
wiped the grin off Jonathan's face.

He flicked her nipple again, which he had discovered helped him think. Who could he talk this over
with? His friends, mostly principled conservatives, had
withdrawn their confidence when he went with the
centrist Democratic President. The girl he loved was
a kind of double agent drawn to danger and luxuriat-
ing in duplicity. The new chief of staff was a mercurial,
opportunistic divorce lawyer. The old chief of staff?
Lucas Cartwright, who Jonathan always felt offered
some solid footing for probity and idealism at the
White House, had returned from Alaska the day before, to be savaged in a press conference. Feet of clay.
But was it fair to hold feet of clay to the fire?

"Going to work?" she asked, as he began to dress.
"As your one true love, I'm sorry, but as a taxpayer,
it's good to see." He thought of telling his one true love
that he was headed to the Pentagon to see Lucas
Cartwright and get a piece of the truth out of him, but
decided to keep it to himself: It was just as well she
didn't have anything interesting to report to Bannerman about his whereabouts this week. Could be, too,
that Bannerman was not the Bad Guy, but was a Good
Guy in a terribly effective disguise.

"You snapped me out of my depression, Buffie," he
said in a way to make it seem like a lie. "When you
leave, clean up the bathroom. I get a lot of complaints
when you leave your stuff all over the sink." That
meant he would come home to a message from Buffie
lipsticked on the mirror, which would cheer him up
again, provided he did not know she was sleeping with
the President or being manhandled by a President-
breaker.

In parting, Jonathan said; "Buy me some aftershave, I don't want the President making a pass at
me." He had been working on that exit line for ten
minutes, and felt better about lying in wait for Lucas
Cartwright.

At the Pentagon, the guard at the desk was
unimpressed with Special Assistant to the President

Trumbull's fancy White House pass. He had no appointment with the Secretary of Defense, and his secretary would not clear him for waiting in the E-ring waiting room. A brigadier general came on the phone, and Jonathan heard himself saying, "I am a special assistant to the President of the United States, and I am going to see the Secretary of Defense at the first possible moment. You will fit me in between appointments, General, or you will find yourself with an implacable enemy at the White House." It worked; like bird colonels at the Pentagon, special assistants might be nothing much around the old Executive Office Building, but out in the departments the title swung some weight.

Lucas Cartwright, who looked drawn after his long flight and two-day media ordeal, was cordial as ever. "You will be pleased to know," he said in his courtly way that relaxed Jonathan, "that you left the one-star general you spoke to with a small puddle of pee under his desk. I take it you identify with the enlisted men?"

Jonathan nodded, slumping in the corner of a leather couch, facing the Secretary's desk, under the portrait of Forrestal. Cartwright, he knew, was under as much strain as that predecessor, so he came to the point: "I'm running a little low on heroes, Mr. Cartwright."

"You ought not to be depressed, Brother Jonathan. Your speech the other night was brilliant. I heard it in a little shack at the air base on the North Slope, and I was deeply moved. You ought to be proud, at a relatively young time of life, to have been—"

"I didn't write that goddamn speech."

"Ah," Cartwright blinked. "I was told you had."

"Oh, I wrote a draft speech, all right. Good speech. Forthright, no play for pity, right on the line. But that was not the speech the President gave."

"He tampered with your prose?"

"No, no. He gave a different speech entirely. Covering up what happened on that campaign train was morally wrong—the people had a right to know that a candidate for President went nearly two days unable to see. In my speech draft, I admitted that, I was frank about it—but the President twisted it all around. He made it seem like nothing. It wasn't nothing, it was wrong."

Cartwright removed his glasses, wiped his eyes, and put the glasses on the coffee table, next to a newspaper with a headline that read "Protesters Circle White House." He said, "I hadn't really focused on that, Jonathan, I've been so busy with the other story, which the press like to call 'the Yalta Deceit.' In the President's speech, the reference to the blind Samson—"

"That was mine," Jonathan said quickly. "The Samson bit was the only part that was mine."

"I thought as much. That was very moving."

"I can't make him understand," Jonathan said to the coffee table. "That only helped the fraud. It was all a fraud."

"All?"

"The main thrust. President Ericson conned everybody back in the election, he conned them in his speech, and nobody's focusing on it. Instead, everybody's up in arms about your Yalta Deceit."

"I wish you wouldn't join in that general characterization, Brother Jonathan," Cartwright said with a pained look, and the speechwriter gave him an accusatory glare. "You make me feel like Shoeless Joe Jackson." Here comes one of those time-consuming Cartwright anecdotes, Jonathan thought, and waited as the Secretary of Defense recounted: "1919, I think it was, the Black Sox baseball scandal. Shoeless Joe Jackson, the great slugger, was accused of throwing the World Series so some gamblers could clean up. And a young fan came up to the heroic Shoeless Joe, tears in his eyes, and pleaded, 'Say it ain't so, Joe.' Shook the nation." After a pause, Cartwright said, "I can tell from your rather saturnine expression that my recollection of Shoeless Joe is not conveying the perspective I had hoped for. Well, no matter."

The telephone interrupted them. "Senator, you— yes." Long silence. "Senator, your tone distresses me.

FULL DISCLOSURE

We have known each other for many years, and this is the first time you have ever questioned my integrity. I shall chalk it up to the heat of the moment and shall not remind you of it when the storm passes." Jonathan noted the mixed metaphor, unless it referred to heat lightning. Cartwright heard the senator out, assuaged his anger as best he could, which was pretty well, and turned back to the young man in his office. "That was from one of our ardent supporters and most articulate defenders. Some of the other calls are not so kind."

"I don't feel guilty about feeling guilty," Jonathan said, "or about being here bugging you when all you really want is blind loyalty. I want a good reason for sticking with Ericson. I can't talk to Hennessy, because I think he is a genuinely evil man, and Smitty is pretty much of a lamebrain, and I don't know most of the others. That leaves you as the one I can turn to for some reason why I shouldn't join the rush to the lifeboats."

"There is a saying in the Navy," said Cartwright ruefully, " 'When the water reaches the upper level, follow the rats.' " Jonathan scowled.

"Your understanding, and your willingness to hang in with the President," said the older man with evident sincerity, "is more important to me than you know. Ask me anything, and I will be frank with you, and I will trust you completely to keep my confidence."

"Why did you cook up that story in Yalta?"

Lucas Cartwright did not flinch. "It was urgent that we get the President and his party out of there. We had a fear that the ambush was just one part of an effort to kill him. It was an idea that George Curtice came up with to trade with Nikolayev for our immediate departure. On sober second thought, it may have been a mistake, but at the time it seemed like a white lie—a story that would not harm anybody's reputation, only enhance it. And a story to cool the passions that might have flared up between the United States and the Soviet Union. That white lie may seem like the Yalta Deceit today, but it seemed like a damned good idea at the time."

"That was then," Jonathan said. "But after you got back, there was no need to continue the lie. Did the President know?"

Cartwright hesitated. "It would not be right to discuss with anybody, even you, what I told the President. Nor should you, if anybody asks a similar question about your own talks with the President. But remember that President Ericson for the past two months has been in shock, newly blinded, and under enormous—unbelievable—strain. The responsibility for not clarifying the situation is mine and Curtice's, not the President's."

"If you've made a horrible mistake," Jonathan pressed, "shouldn't you resign, take it all on yourself, you and Curtice?"

"That would be my inclination. But I won't resign, because I want my loyal derrière firmly planted in that Cabinet seat if another attempt to oust the President is begun."

"Is that in the works?"

"Could be. Mike Fong is still there. If this public opinion fire-storm gets out of hand, there might well be another usurpation move."

Jonathan shook his head; he wanted to get away from tactics, to get to the root of the rottenness. "Why didn't the President tell you about the previous blindness—didn't he trust you?"

"Evidently not—no, I can't even say that. He did trust me, and still does, and is right to. He thought I had no need to know about that train incident, and knowledge was limited to those with a need-to-know, like poor Herb Abelson. Once you start breaking the need-to-know principle, start making exceptions, you really do insult everybody else."

"But you did need to know. The previous blindness was important to the decisions you took in Yalta, after the ambush."

"Ah, so true. Not letting me in on the secret was, in retrospect, a terrible mistake."

"Mr. Cartwright," Jonathan insisted, "it was wrong." He wanted to hear the word from the Defense Secretary's lips.

"No, in error. Not 'wrong.' It was a tactical judgment, not a moral question of right versus wrong." He softened: "I was profoundly offended, up in Alaska, when I listened to that speech, and heard for the first time of the prior blindness. It had been my belief that I was in the President's total confidence, and that I deserved to be. I'm human, I sulked about it, and would undoubtedly have bitched for years to Mrs. Cartwright. But these are affairs of state; great men have great reasons for keeping their own counsel, and no aide can insist on being privy to a President's every secret. That's why he has different aides for different duties."

"Like Hennessy?"

"Mark Hennessy is not the venal man you think he is."

If Cartwright was going to defend Hennessy, Jonathan thought, he was going to buy himself a big credibility problem. "Mark is more inclined than you or I to put ends before means," Cartwright said, "which is not automatically immoral, if the good ends are urgent. Paul the Apostle was quite proud of being 'all things to all men,' as he put it, because he found such tactics sometimes necessary to save all men. I'm not saying that murder or arson is permissible as a means to a good end, but cutting a few corners has been done in the White House, to serve good ends, for many a year. To the nation's benefit."

"Hennessy puts his loyalty to one man, Ericson, above everything. That's wrong."

"True, loyalty can grow into a vice, but it is a quality rooted more in virtue than in vice. Was Hennessy the one who changed the emphasis of your speech?"

"I think so," said Jonathan. "It couldn't have been Hank Fowler, and I know it wasn't Melinda."

"Possibly the President had something to do with it," Cartwright offered tentatively, quickly adding, "though it is always possible that he was caused to swerve from your straight-and-narrow by Mr. Hennessy's ultra-loyal judgment. At any rate, if the editing culprit was Hennessy, then your dedication to the President need not be all that impaired. Cartwrights and Hennessys come and go, you know."

Jonathan did not bother to challenge that don't-blame-the-boss argument because he had his next question carefully framed: "Why are the papers jumping up and down about the Yalta Deceit when they didn't react to the bigger deceit on the train? Why is everybody, including you, missing the point—that the real venality was not so much tricking the Russians at Yalta, but at tricking the American electorate by covering up the previous blindness?"

Cartwright shook his head. "Venality, cover-up. Those are loaded words, you know that. We have to deal with the crisis at hand, not the crisis you think ought to be at hand. If you feel that the Yalta decisions were defensible, as you seem to be saying, then you should be helping convince people that the President and the nation were not so badly served. At least we meant well. Later, if you wish, you and I can go into the morality of the prior-blindness episode at length."

Jonathan was not having that. "Tell me straight: You don't get up in the morning these days feeling sick at heart? You don't reach for your morning paper wondering what new bomb is going off? You don't ever ask yourself if what you've been doing is wrong—deeply immoral, really rotten?"

Cartwright indulged himself in a profound sigh. "Yes to all of those. And then I ask myself—how could so much have gone so wrong with an upright patriot such as myself right there on the scene? But all is not what it seems. 'As ye sow, so shall ye reap,' the Good Book says. We didn't sow this. Or if we did, we sowed it unconsciously over a period of a year, and now it's all getting reaped in one week, which distorts the crop. The way everything is coming out, it seems like we all sat around and conspired to deceive the world on everything. But it did not happen that way. Different men took different actions for different reasons. And we did everything with the best interests of the country and the President in mind. On balance," he added.

"The ends don't—"

Cartwright held up a silencing finger: "—justify the means, you were going to say. I have committed to memory a quotation from Charles de Gaulle on that subject, which I have from time to time quoted to various Presidents. 'Every man of action has a strong dose of egotism, pride, hardness, and cunning. But all those things will be forgiven him, indeed, they will be regarded as high qualities, if he can make of them the means to achieve great ends.' "

"Power corrupts," Jonathan quoted back.

"Power tends to corrupt," said Cartwright, correcting the quote, "but there is no guarantee that it corrupts. Sometimes men corrupt power. And the ends do not usually justify the means, but sometimes they do. Perhaps that proves the rule. If there is anything I have learned in the service of three Presidents, it is that absolutism leads to disaster." He amended that: "Sometimes. Sometimes what leads to disaster is an absolute absence of absolutism. Is that a quotable quote?"

"Pragmatic," said Jonathan, with what he hoped was the right degree of sarcasm.

"From the Latin *pragmaticus*," Cartwright instructed, "which means 'an affair of state,' and has only recently come to mean 'practical.' "

Some of the wind went out of Jonathan's sails. "And another thing is I wish to hell the President would stay away from my girl," he blurted. It was true and he was happy it had come out, ridiculous though he knew it sounded.

"There can be no *droit du seigneur*," Lucas Cartwright agreed sternly. "You are absolutely right about that. I take it, then, that the young lady you refer to also wishes that the attentions of the President would no longer be directed to her?"

"Oh, hell no. Every time he gets near her, she creams in her jeans," he said. And not just figuratively, he might have added. Cartwright seemed to restrain a smile with some difficulty, and said, "If you can take care of her, some of us can take care of him. But I can't fight your battles for you with the young lady."

"Aah, I should never have brought it up. I'm sorry, forget it."

Another call. "Yes, Hennessy. Yes, Jonathan was right here in my office a moment ago. He has some ethical questions, but I would say he's dependable. Um. Sorry, I never knew he was acquainted with the young lady. Anything else?" Hennessy, the sneaky bastard, was checking up on him; probably someone in the Pentagon informed the White House that a presidential speechwriter was seeing the Secretary of Defense, and Hennessy promptly wondered why. He was right to be suspicious.

"If I were you, Mark"—Cartwright was the only one to call Hennessy by his first name, which was his way of being formal—"and as you know, I am not you at all, I would check on the general good cheer of our blue-eyed boy, the Attorney General. The reservation wouldn't be the same if he wandered off. Like you, I was mainly concerned with the reaction to the Yalta Deceit, as it has been charitably named, but Brother Jonathan has suggested that the jury may still be out on the revelation of the previous blindness." Hennessy must have made some reference to pipsqueak speechwriters, because Cartwright continued: "But the young man's moral sensibilities could well be more closely tuned to those of the general public's than yours or mine. That means Attorney General Duparquet will be embarrassed. He made quite a point at the Cabinet meeting of there being no way of knowing at Yalta that the President had been blind before, remember? In a sense, the A.G. won on a foul, because his client lied to him. Embarrassment could make a man like Emmett Duparquet do strange things." Hennessy evidently disagreed; Cartwright deferred with "Well, you're there on the scene in the White House and I'm not. One other thing—really?" He looked surprised. "I have a ticker here. I'll go look, too. Speak to you later." Cartwright pushed a button calmly and said to his secretary, "There appears to be something coming over the AP ticker—that's the machine down the hall with the yellow paper, not the white—about a group of reporters meeting with Dr. Abelson's widow, after the funeral. Would you tear it off and bring it in here? And then keep looking for follow-up 'adds,' they're called, and bring those in, too."

Jonathan sat up. "Got a radio?" Cartwright nodded, and took a transistor radio out of his desk drawer and found an all-news station; before the ticker copy arrived, the bulletin was on the air:

"The widow of the President's physician said after his funeral today that Dr. Herbert Abelson took his own life because—quote—he couldn't live with a lie —end quote." Jonathan moved to Cartwright's desk and stood beside the Defense Secretary, who cradled the bad news in his hand. The announcer recapped the details of Abelson's death three nights before, caustically read the text of the next-day White House statement which suggested it might have been caused by an accidental overdose of sleeping tablets, and interrupted himself to switch to his network's correspondent at the Abelson home.

"The grief-stricken widow has just released copies of the letter from her late husband, the President's doctor, that came in the mail this morning, the morning of Herbert Abelson's funeral. Apparently Dr. Abelson wrote the letter in Camp Hoover, a rustic set of cabins some two hours from Washington, and walked to a mailbox about a mile up the road from the isolated retreat. In a deep depression, he then returned and took the fatal dose of sleeping pills. Here is the text of the letter—I'm reading from a photocopy some friends of the widow, Mrs. Barbara Abelson, handed out moments ago. A few paragraphs have been deleted, probably of an intimacy that Mrs. Abelson prefers to remain private, but most of the text follows."

Cartwright sorrowfully sank into his chair and set the transistor radio on the desk. Jonathan remained standing, visualizing the face of the dead man whose words were being read:

"Darling Barbara—I can't stand it any more. I can't live with myself. I've always been a coward and now I'm taking a coward's way out.

"Because I'm a weakling, the President of the United States is blind. Because I'm a weakling, there's a horrible secret in the White House eating at the vitals of our government. I'm sorry if this sounds over-dramatic but you're allowed to get dramatic in a suicide note.

"After the accident on the train, when Sven Ericson regained consciousness and could not see, I wanted to get an ophthalmologist in immediately for consultation. But Sven said no, and his campaign manager, that bastard Leigh, told me I had no right to alarm the people. So I did what no self-respecting doctor would ever do—I went along with my patient on a medical decision.

"I thought it would be all right when his sight returned the next day, but I was wrong. There must have been some hairline crack in the optic channel. His sight was vulnerable because I put politics ahead of medicine, because I let Mr. Tough Guy push me around.

"After the ambush at Yalta, I knew I had to tell the doctors of his record of previous blindness. But the President leaned on me, and I was in the deception up to my hips already, so I went along. I didn't tell the eye doctor what he needed to know to make a proper diagnosis. If I had, he would surely have called in a neurosurgeon, and maybe Ericson would have had his sight restored.

"What got into me? How could I have let these guys, especially Hennessy, stop me from fulfilling my duty as a doctor? They all kept reminding me that I was a lousy doctor, that the most important item in my black bag was the phone number of a real doctor at Bethesda, and they were right, up to a point. But a lousy doctor is like a bad priest, he can do some things right, and have it count. I failed my patient, I failed my country, I failed myself, and I'm sick of failing. I'm sick of the way Sven talked to me tonight, patting me on the head and telling me not to worry. He used to be my friend. I gave up a lot for him to work in his damn pressure cooker, and I think he's gone crazy for power. Anything to stay in office, no matter how disabled he is, no matter who has to lie for him."

The announcer, his voice changing tone, said, "Next there are several paragraphs deleted, probably personal good-bys to his wife and children. A final paragraph:

"I'm going to walk to the mailbox, which is God knows how far, in the middle of the night, and mail this. If I get cold feet, and don't go through with it, I'll stay home a few mornings and intercept the mail before you get it. If I can stay with it, I'll come back and take a dozen Seconal. I love you. I can't take it. Good-by. Herb."

The transistor perched on the desk prattled on a few minutes, telling of the scene in front of the Abelson house, the black-draped mirrors inside, the coming of children and relatives, and then: "Mrs. Abelson is going to face the microphones and cameras now, we have word that she is going to try to talk about this—"

Cartwright cut off his transistor and turned on the television set in his office. Barbara Abelson's puffed, ravaged face came on the screen. The voice-over said she was going to read her husband's suicide note.

"Oh Christ," said Jonathan, "she's going to read it and it will be on five times today, on the evening newscasts, on tomorrow morning, like Ruby killing Oswald." He knew it would be hammered into the American psyche, repeated over and over again, until most viewers would be able to recite the words and never forget the face. Sure enough, as the widow began reading the letter aloud, the camera cut to the photo on the dining room table of her dead husband, then panned to another photo of the family together, back to the widow, then to the campaign memorabilia that the President's physician had proudly collected, his framed letters from Ericson, his parchment commission, and finally back to the grieving, bravely persevering former actress reading his last words.

Jonathan decided he must still be on the President's side because he was upset at the devastating impact of the television presentation. The writer was not thinking so much of Abelson, or his widow, as of the effect that the tear-jerking performance would have on the viewing public. He thought he should feel bad about his emotionless outlook, but he was satisfied that he was on a side. He studied Cartwright's face, looking at the screen, jaw slack and eyes moist. The man was more deeply affected than he; Jonathan felt good about that.

The Ex-Treasury Secretary

"Turn that off," Bannerman told Mike Fong, who switched off the announcer's breathless recap of the performance of Abelson's widow. Bannerman, who had returned the night before from London, had been furious at the way the Committee to Replace the Disabled President had been bungling the attack on Ericson. He assembled Fong, Vice-President Nichols, and Marty Quinn—the press agent who had just been hired to run the staff of the committee—to a meeting at his home. Fifteen minutes before the news broke of the Abelson broadcast, Bannerman had taught them something about striking down a President.

"You missed the big one, the moral turpitude," he told them, "and you made a big fuss over the one that you'll never bring him down on. Why can't I trust strategy to anybody? It should have been obvious. I just hope you haven't blown the whole thing."

"There are pickets marching all around the White House, Roy," the Vice-President pointed out. "That was the committee's doing."

"A bunch of kids and rowdies that you can turn out for anything," Bannerman snorted.

"But it's getting enormous coverage," Quinn, the press agent, put in. "Television, editorials—the phrase 'Yalta Deceit' is already part of the language."

"Forget your inconsequential press clippings!" Bannerman did not try to hide his frustration at the inadequacies of his confederates. "They said Roosevelt betrayed America at Yalta, what did that do to him? We're not looking to hurt Ericson in the eyes of history, or beat him in the next election. We're out to force him out now, marshaling all the rage of the American people and the fury of the news media."

"Ease up, Roy," Secretary Fong said. "Marty's doing a good job. The Zophar column was a bombshell, and we followed it up with all the organization—the telegrams, the letters, the marches, the statements in Congress, the works. Ericson's on the ropes."

Bannerman told himself he could not afford to offend Fong or Nichols, to cool down, but their stupidity upset him. He explained it slowly, as if to children: "We are not going to win on the battleground of foreign affairs. We'll see a big fuss, and a lot of noise, and the graybeard editorial writers clucking and tut-tutting to beat the band. But what will the man in the street think? He'll think he had a President who had a staff that made some tough decisions after an attempted assassination, for the good of the country—"

"He tried that in his speech, and it flopped," said Quinn.

"Who did it flop with?" Bannerman sneered. "Zophar made him look like a fool, but the great unwashed is going to rally to their President if it's him against the Russians. What have you got? Ericson tried to pull a fast one on the Soviets? The average guy is going to say, 'What the hell's so bad about that? So Ericson blew one, at least he's on our side.' "

"You really believe that, Roy?" The Vice-President was worried.

"Not only that." Bannerman could not resist putting it to them hard: "I happen to think Cartwright and Curtice did the right thing to get him the hell out of danger in a hurry. When you're President, Arnold, I only hope your staff serves you as well. That Harry Bok, he's not a liar, he's a hero—that's what I think. And if Ericson decided to exploit that, to help put a man in power in the Kremlin who was beholden to the American President, then I say hats off to him for that. And after the smart-ass crowd stops huffing and puffing about deceits, you'll find that most of the people in the country will feel that way, too. And then go try to get Ericson to quit. Mark my words, your whole damn orchestration about the Yalta Deceit is going to turn, unless we get off it and get on to the basics right away."

"What are the basics, Mr. Bannerman?" The press agent was malleable; he had been hired to carry out orders. Bannerman had hoped for more good sense from Fong, who had at least been in politics for a long time, or even Nichols, on whom some judgment might have rubbed off over the years. No. Bannerman would have to run the whole show himself. No more leaving the country for any reason.

"He cheated the people in the last election, that's the basic basic," he told them. "The people have a right to know—remember that phrase, 'a right to know'—if their presidential candidates have been in a crazy house, or been communists in their youth, or were blind at one time. Ericson covered it up. He lied. He failed to fully disclose his disability, and his disability is now crippling the nation. Not by the nation's choice—the people never knew. They had a right to know, but the danger was deliberately, corruptly concealed from them. That's wrong, immoral. God struck Ericson for it, and now he must be pushed aside."

"The Constitution doesn't provide for that," the Vice-President grumped. "It doesn't say if you don't fully disclose, you must step aside. You can't be impeached for it, it's not a high crime. We have to show he's disabled and cannot function."

Fong joined Nichols on the defensive: "The Yalta Deceit at least has people thinking he doesn't know what the hell goes on in Russia. That's evidence of disability. But Roy, I guess, is right, people might flock to his banner on a foreign-affairs matter."

Bannerman closed his eyes. Was it worth it, toppling Ericson, to put in people who did not understand the molding of opinion and the play of power? He answered his own question in the affirmative, because he would be able to use them to run a country well.

"First we have to get clear what route we are taking," the former Treasury Secretary said. "The avenue of impeachment, or the avenue of the Twenty-fifth Amendment. If it's the avenue of impeachment, we would have to have a high crime, an obstruction of justice or an abuse of power. We don't have that yet. So impeachment remains a threat, an alternative, not our main thrust. We have to go the Twenty-fifth Amendment route—create a storm of public opinion so severe that even a rubber-stamp Cabinet has to throw the matter into the House, for fear that failure to act would cause the Cabinet itself to be impeached."

"Isn't that why we should concentrate on Ericson's not knowing who was running Russia?" Nichols still did not see the picture.

"We will make some use of that, certainly," Bannerman told him, "but it's only an intellectual argument. You're right, Arnold, it goes to the question of ability, but a blunder is not enough. The only force that can move this Cabinet to do its duty is an infuriated public opinion. And the public will get good and sore when it realizes it's been had. Then the Twenty-fifth Amendment route will be a convenient way to carry out the will of the people. Get it? The excuse will be disability—but the real reason will be that he stole the election by failing to fully disclose his blindness. And we don't have to go through the whole process—just up to the point when he resigns."

They got it. The impact of Barbara Abelson reading her husband's suicide note was excitedly discussed by the other three; Bannerman sat silently, his judgment justified, trying to think of a logical way to follow up, to keep the White House in its state of siege.

"The eye doctor," Bannerman said at last. He thought of the young and indecisive physician, out of his depth, who looked weak at the press conferences, and who shielded himself with medical jargon. "He's the next link. Put the heat on him. Mike, you know my connections in the medical world, first we have to have an uproar about the self-sacrifice of Dr. Abelson"—damned weakling, he thought, what was wrong with Ericson, surrounding himself with people who would crack under pressure?—"whip up the AMA types, all that. But get the eye doctor, have a press conference tomorrow—not tomorrow, the day after—about how differently he would have treated Ericson if he had known about the previous blindness. All doctors like to dump on their patients, blame them for the medical failure. He should go for it in a big way."

"Military might try to keep him in line," Quinn said. That was the first useful comment by any of his associates, Bannerman thought.

"We have friends who will guarantee the doctor a future in private practice," Bannerman said. "If there's pressure on him from the top brass at Bethesda to shut up, we can exploit that. But get cracking on that right now, through the medical press. Abelson was an editor there, they ought to be up in arms." That gave Bannerman an idea: How would Ericson have tried to hush up the previous-blindness scandal? The cover-up is always more troublesome than the original act—it involves more people, it seems shabby, its exposure keeps the pot boiling. Perhaps the President's young writer was asked to do something on the shady side. Buffie, the photographer-bed partner of everybody in the White House, was the key to him. Perhaps Arthur Leigh, who was mentioned in Abelson's suicide note as "that bastard Leigh," would recall how the cover-up was conducted and be ready to tell.

"Mr. Vice-President," Bannerman said formally, "the meeting is about to get down to nitty-gritty, and there is no need for us to hold you here." Nichols took his cue and was happy to depart. Bannerman told Quinn to bring Buffie and Leigh to the house in a hurry.

Leigh was first to arrive, pleased with the limousine pickup and the new notoriety. "Reporters following me around like I was a bitch in heat," he drawled. Mike Fong put it to the former campaign manager directly: What other details did he have to contribute to the cover-up of the previous blindness?

"There's a sex angle," he volunteered. "Ericson sure didn't say so in his speech the other night, but when the campaign train jolted to a stop, he was in the sack with his girl, the photographer, banging away between campaign stops. He was right in the saddle when he hit his head. Bok had a hell of a time pryin' 'em apart, with her hollerin' bloody murder in the upper berth while we were trying to keep it all quiet. That ought to add a little sauce to the story."

The bitch. Bannerman's eyes slitted; this meant that Buffie knew about Ericson's previous blindness all along, and had said nothing. With possession of that information two weeks ago, he could have turned Ericson out of office. The slut had held it back, letting him think she was betraying the President, but only passing along useless little tidbits. Perhaps a double agent. Bannerman had underestimated her, underestimated Ericson's use of her; his surge of anger was first directed at the girl, then at his own unforgivable overconfidence. But he had an advantage now; Buffie did not yet know that he knew all she knew. He would use that to break her and use her.

Bannerman forced himself to remain calm and turned his attention to Leigh: Why had he been so quickly forthcoming? The politician, one of those unproductive middlemen with whom one had to deal on the path to power, would ordinarily bargain for his information. Bannerman had expected Leigh to extract some advantage, or promise, or consultancy; but here he was, freely providing vital information. Why? One reason was that Leigh did not know what his "sex angle" really told Bannerman—that Buffie had been holding back vital information. Another reason could be that, late in life, Leigh was learning how to deal with men of substance: To Bannerman, a gift, no strings attached, called for repayment with a bonus, and would be of greater value to the giver than any emolument called for in a contract. A Bannerman could not afford to be indebted to a Leigh for anything. A third possibility occurred to him, that Leigh had something else of far greater value—possibly embarrassing, or shady—to reveal, in his own good time. The sex angle might only be an appetizer.

Bannerman took Leigh away from the others, so the two could talk more freely. On the patio, looking down the long sweep of lawn, away from any likely electronic surveillance, he made the offer abruptly. "Arthur, what's your ambition? What do you want in life?"

"You mean, what's my price?" Snide bastard, thought Bannerman; the world would be better off without such crassly political intermediation.

"No, if I wanted your price, Arthur, I would have asked you what your price was. I'm not bashful. But I've been told that you are a man of parts, and it occurs to me that the way to enlist you in the cause is to find out directly what you want. Power? Position? Money? Fame?"

"I'll take the one from column three," Leigh said. "Money. I'm tired of politics. I put a President in the White House, and there's nothing you can do to top that. So it's time I made myself comfortable."

"Done," said Bannerman, relieved it was a simple

matter. "I'll make you a loan, tell you where to invest, and guarantee you against loss. In six months you'll be a wealthy man. We'll pick out the target figure later."

"I won't let it slip my mind."

"Be serious now," Bannerman commanded. "We're alone, I'm under the gun, now is the time for you to come forward and tell me what Ericson did to conceal the fact of his previous blindness." Leigh was bought; he would stay bought, as Henry Clay Frick used to say. Until a higher bidder came along.

"It could get me in a lot of trouble," Leigh said tentatively. Bannerman judged he was not being coy, but was worried about involvement in a corrupt bargain. He tried to wait him out. Leigh was good at waiting, too, and Bannerman finally said, "You will be well paid for your trouble, and well represented to ameliorate any difficulty your telling the truth might cause you. The best lawyers in the world will cost you nothing."

Leigh made up his mind. "Hennessy tried to bribe me. He thought I was going to blab his big secret—which, frankly, I would never have done. So he asked if there was somebody he could appoint back home who would be helpful to me."

"Was the appointment made?" That was important, Bannerman knew, because unkept promises were not venal—on the contrary, they were evidence of political purity.

"Yes, over some local squawks. The heat came from the White House, though, and the governor of Tennessee couldn't say no."

"What could the appointee have done for you?"

"Highway stuff, zoning, that kind of thing. But nothing was done by the appointee. Or asked for, yet." Only Hennessy had acted corruptly; Leigh had not yet tried to cash in.

Bannerman walked to a low stone bench, looking out over it down into the lush park. Probably Leigh had extorted the appointment from Hennessy, threatening to expose the secret, and the President's aide had consented to make an innocent-looking appointment.

Now Leigh was offering to turn it around into a bribe offer. Would such a charge stick? Could it be made to reach Ericson himself? Sam Zophar would be the man to break the story, Bannerman decided. "Call Zophar, tell him everything. Don't try to absolve yourself totally, everybody knows you're a big boy."

"It's running a risk," Leigh said. True enough; Hennessy would probably countercharge extortion, or dredge up other misdeeds in Leigh's shadowy past.

Bannerman came to the point. "How much did you stand to make?"

"Couple million, on the land alone."

"That's a million and a half net after taxes, at the most optimistic," Bannerman said. "Your. former target figure, which you won't let slip your mind. Let's make the new target two million net." He dismissed him then, an expensive employee doing a distasteful job. "Today's Wednesday. Don't waste this on Saturday's papers—arrange it for Monday morning publication. Call your friend Zophar."

Bannerman walked down the patio steps to a telephone in his bedroom and called an aide in New York. He spelled Buffie Masterson's name—he did not know her real first name—and requested an informal FBI rundown on the girl and her immediate family, by telephone, within the half hour. He called his wife, Susan, in New York to ask her to keep tabs on Mrs. Arthur Leigh for the next few days.

Bannerman debated whether to tell Fong and the staff man, Quinn, about Leigh's coming bribery charge against Hennessy. He shook his head; they had no need to know. Back in the living room, he told the staff man to start focusing medical association pressure on Andy Frangipani of Human Resources, posing the question: Should a man who will not trust his own doctor be trusted with the fate of the nation? Until now, the pressure on Human Resources had all been pro-Ericson, by the lobbyists for the handicapped; the Abelson suicide ought to be made to turn that around.

He sent Fong and Quinn away and concentrated on how he would break the girl. Downstairs, in his bedroom-office. Bannerman took the call from his contact with the FBI. Curiously, unhelpfully, the girl had never been in trouble, and the only FBI reports were related to the full field investigation undertaken when she went to work in the White House. The agents' reports tsk-tsked about her morals—that was nothing new—but no arrests. No derogatory information at all; only records of prizes won for her photography and a couple of art show awards.

"Give me the points of leverage," he said to his man, making neatly written notes about her family and friends. "Who was her protector before Ericson?" He wrote down the answer, which was, coincidentally, up to the minute: A call made from New York to check the advertising agency where Buffie's previous lover was located had found that he had been laid off that morning, in a general agency cutback. "Get the line of credit, and the bank, for the health-food store in Fond du Lac, and any financial vulnerability." He hung up without saying good-by. Years ago Bannerman had discovered how much time could be saved, and how many subordinates reminded of their positions, by the simple procedure of never troubling to say hello or good-by.

He recognized that he needed the satisfaction of proving to this girl and to himself that nobody crossed T. Roy Bannerman. He also recognized that his satisfaction in punishing her must not conflict with his continuing need for a set of eyes and ears in the White House. He needed her undivided loyalty, which, if it could not be obtained by hope of future reward, would come from fear of immediate retribution. He would not underestimate her again; nor would she, him.

"I washed my fayce before I come," Buffie said, in a nice reference to Shaw's Cockney flower girl in strange, luxurious surroundings. She was dressed in a brief halter and skirt, White House photographer working clothes, but with no cameras. High heels drew attention to her long legs, and Bannerman could calculate how she could exert her influence: not only the pugnacious good looks, or the lithe figure, but the easy way of carrying herself, the lift she seemed to want to give others. Too many others, he knew, in too many camps.

"You've been holding out on me, Buffie."

She put on a puzzled look, then laughed nervously. "Gee, I never thought you were interested in me that way, Mr. Bannerman."

He motioned for her to sit down in the straight chair facing his bedroom desk. His face was normally impassive, and he kept his voice flat, devoid of feeling. "I am not interested in your capacities as a whore, I am interested only in your worth as a source of information."

She paled and stood up. "Hey, I'm nobody's whore, ol' buddy, and I don't have to take any shit from—"

"Sit down." He did not raise his voice. She sat. "You have been having a fine old time," he continued, "playing both ends against the middle. It's been like a game with you. You're everybody's friend, everybody's confidante, everybody's betrayer."

She said nothing, appearing to Bannerman to be suitably frightened. Fright would not be enough.

"You knew about the President's previous blindness," he went on. "You didn't tell me. Instead you told me little bits of useless information, with the President's knowledge, just stringing me along. Stupid old Bannerman."

"How do you know I knew?" she breathed.

"You were flat on your back with your legs around him when it happened."

"He knows I knew," she said, as if to herself. She picked up the canvas bag she had laid next to the chair and placed it carefully in her lap, containing herself and her possessions for the next development.

"I wonder if you realize," Bannerman told her quietly, "how important it was to me, how important to the nation, to know about the previous blindness weeks ago, when the Cabinet was meeting."

After a while, she said, "Pretty important?"

"Don't play the dumb blonde with me. You made

the decision to con me, gambling on a big pay-off if you played your cards right. You did not. You lost. Now I'm going to tell you what you lost."

He took out a piece of paper with his notes and looked it over for about a minute. She broke the silence with "I guess that magazine editor idea is out, huh?"

He looked at her as if she had spoken in a foreign language. "You don't seem to understand, Buffie. You double-crossed me. I cannot permit anybody to double-cross me and get away with it. If I did not react vigorously, the word would get out that I could be double-crossed with impunity. I cannot let that happen. You are going to pay for what you did. You are going to regret it for as long as you live."

"Lookit, sir, I know you're sore, and you've got a right to be, I wasn't a hundred per cent with you. But I never lied. The information I did give you was useful, wasn't it?"

Bannerman drew his lips back over his teeth, he hoped ominously. "You told me what Ericson wanted me to know. You thought you could handle me the way you handled every other man you have come in contact with. Now you will discover how wrong you were."

"You hit me, I'll scream. I don't go for this sado-routine, I won't let you hurt me."

"I'm not going to touch you," he assured her, relishing the moment. "I'm just going to destroy your life, and the lives of those you love. It's not something I enjoy, but it's what I have to do. Do you want to see how it's done?"

"No. I want to go. Can I go?"

"The door's open," he said. "You're free to go anytime." She rose, two hands tightly on her canvas bag. "Fond du Lac, Wisconsin," he mused. "I'm in the banking business, Buffie, and I have a great many associates in that field. Masterson's Health Foods, it says here, has a fifteen-thousand-dollar line of credit, on which it owes some eleven thousand today. Now, overnight, that credit is going to be withdrawn, and not be reinstated. There are going to be hard times for

Masterson's Health Foods, and the two people who own it."

She shook her head. "You're playing a role," she said, unbelieving. "The mean old banker going to fore-close the mortgage on little Nell. That can't happen any more, not in this day and age."

He nodded matter-of-factly. "I understand. You want something more sophisticated. What else is on the list, here—chap named Stanley Marcowitz, you lived with him in New York for nearly three years, a long liaison for you. Parted friends, it says. Okay, as a sort of free sample, a preview of things to come for you and yours, last night I spoke to a friend who has a friend who spoke to a client who called an advertis-ing agency. And something happened today to affect your former lover's life adversely."

"Nobody can do that," she said. "You think you're God, and you think you can scare me, but you can't. You're bluffing."

"Call my bluff. There's the phone. Do you have the number of the agency?"

She did. She direct-dialed, said, "Hiya, Sally, is Stanley there?" In a moment, her face fell, and then turned panicky. She put down the phone without speaking.

"You can get him at home," Bannerman said. "You'll be able to get him there for a long, long time, because no other agency in New York will be inclined to hire him."

"He worked there for ten years," she said, sitting down again, benumbed. "His whole life. You can do that?"

"I'm just getting started," Bannerman said, all busi-ness, looking down the list. "There's your sister in Milwaukee. She's on probation after that drug arrest. In about a week, she's going to be found with her 'stash,' as they call it, whatever that means, and the law will be strictly enforced. The federal facility she will likely be taken to is in Joliet—"

"You win. Stop. Turn it all off." Buffie curled for-ward in her chair, her head pressed to the bag in her lap, and Bannerman watched her body heave with a dry sob, then another. She straightened up after a long moment and—pluckily, Bannerman conceded—whispered, "You sure know how to hurt a girl."

Bannerman, halfway to his goal, heaved his bulk out of the chair and walked to the window. She had been shaken, more than impressed, but more remained to be done. "You probably think you can get your friend, the President, to block these efforts. You will find he is powerless at such a low level. He can order the most godawful atomic strike, but he cannot order a local bank to make a loan, or a magazine to hire a photographer, or a local cop to not make an arrest. Or an advertising agency from firing a good man whose mistake it was to associate with a woman who later turned out to be a traitor to her country."

"Hey, lookit, I'm sorry. Let's be friends. What do I have to do to keep the roof from falling in on everybody? Name it, Mr. Bannerman, I'll do it. No more funny business, I promise."

Not nearly good enough. "I made a mistake in trusting a prostitute," he said evenly, looking at the landscape. "I won't make the same mistake again. You seem to think your apology is all that's necessary. You don't understand: You betrayed your country. What you did, in withholding vital evidence, is—to my mind—nothing less than treason. You deserve to be destroyed. And you will be, along with your parents and your sister and your friend. I have no further need of you. Good-by." He turned to look at her, and for the first time saw the flicker of fear that he wanted. She began to twist the bag in her hands.

"I could tell you some stuff about Hennessy," she offered.

He was not interested. "Hennessy will be out of a job in seventy-two hours," he said. "He is corrupt. You have nothing of value to me. Good day."

"You want a great body?" She stood up to show him. "All yours, whenever you say. And I do crazy things, anything—I'm not a whore, really I'm not, but there's nothing I won't do for you—"

He shook his head. "I figured you'd make that offer before long. It's always worked for you, hasn't it? Thank you, but I'm not interested. You're too frequently used."

"Christ, mister, there's got to be something—" She got on her knees. "I'm on my knees, Mr. Bannerman, I'm sorry, I'm sorry, I didn't realize what I was getting into—" She began to cry at last, which soon turned to a hysteria satisfying to observe, and his slap smashed her halfway across the room.

Buffie reached for the bed, pulled herself up, and sat for a while, breathing deeply. She rose, slowly took off her clothes, and lay on the bed, propped on an elbow, rubbing her cheek.

"If you want to hurt me, go ahead, I'll scream in the pillow. Nobody can hear. I bruise easy, but Potus'll never see it."

He studied her carefully. She was striking no false pose, like the whores in girlie magazines. The tears did not mar her eyes. Her body had a natural grace, the classic coloring of the natural reddish-blond enhancing the flow of her movement, the blush of the lips and nipples worthy of one of his Bouchers, perhaps even the Titian he had once bid on. A beautiful nude. It occurred to Bannerman that one of Ericson's tortures must be the knowledge that he could no longer see beauty like this. The examination over, he made no move toward the bed. Ericson's girl returned his stare, her eyes fearful that her final chip might lose, and she made a final, inviting gesture, pitiable but not in the least awkward.

"I have been happily married for thirty-three years," Bannerman told the young woman offering herself to him, "and I have never been unfaithful to my wife. I am not about to begin now, with a slut who is also a traitor."

He did not watch her dress, because he found himself wanting to. When she finished, she picked up her bag and gathering some dignity about her, addressed him without tears.

"I may be a slut in your eyes, Mr. Bannerman, but

not in mine. And I'm not a traitor. I was just trying to help everybody a little, and I got a little out of my depth."

"You can go now," he dismissed her.

"I am terrified, Mr. Bannerman," she said, not sounding terrified at all. "I'm scared you won't give me another chance. I'll do anything you say. I'm your slave. Anything."

As if reluctantly, he nodded. "Anything," she repeated, and he had the feeling she meant it.

The Therapist / 4

"In the morning, every time I go to the front door and pick up the paper," said Hennessy, "I get a klong."

Hank Fowler was unfamiliar with the term. "You get a what?"

"Tell him what a klong is, Hennessy," said Melinda. The three of them were on the small patio outside her office, next to the Oval Office, facing the Rose Garden.

"A klong," said Hennessy, savoring the definition, "is a sudden rush of shit to the heart."

"The feeling you get," Melinda explained, "when you're out to dinner someplace and you suddenly remember that you invited a dozen guests to your house for dinner, for an hour before."

"Or you're sitting at your desk," said the former divorce lawyer, "happy as a clam at high tide—that's when clam diggers can't get 'em—and a kid comes in and says, 'Weren't you supposed to be in court right now for the final argument this morning?' That's a klong. Kind of a sad little panic, about something all your own fault, and cruel and heartless on your part, that you didn't mean but nobody will ever believe that."

"All you can say is 'Oh, my God,' " Melinda added. "I know the feeling, but I never knew the word for it until Hennessy used 'klong' one day."

Fowler smiled, making a mental note to try that word at a seminar for psychologists; the helpless, self-blaming mini-panic was common and could use the nomenclature. It applied both to the sighted and to the blind. "You both had a klong yesterday," he said to them, "when Mrs. Abelson had her press conference."

Both accompanied their nods with "Um," as he had taught them. Melinda, Fowler knew, was upset with herself for not paying more attention to Hennessy's warning about Mrs. Abelson's "friends." Perhaps, surrounded by different people or in seclusion, the widow might not have turned on the President and made the suicide note public. Hennessy had refrained from rubbing it in; he felt guilty, he had told Fowler, at not doing the job at Camp Hoover he had set out to do: finding and destroying the suicide note. "Would have meant fifty grand to the widow, and would have stopped nutty Herb from doing real damage. I had a hunch the note was in that mailbox up the road. I should've figured a way to get it out." Fowler had his doubts about that; more likely, Hennessy, who delighted in savaging Melinda McPhee on occasion, was trying to share her vulnerability in this case. Perverse man, the psychologist thought, who found satisfaction in swimming against whatever current of blame or credit was running.

"Where's The Man?" Hennessy asked Melinda; it was nearly lunchtime, and the President had not appeared in the West Wing as yet. Fowler slept up there, in a room once occupied by Harry Hopkins, but was downstairs for breakfast each morning at seven.

"Lincoln Sitting Room with Harry Bok," she replied. "He's pretty low. Barbara reading that letter really got to him. He listened to the damn thing half a dozen times. I couldn't get him to stop, he just kept rewinding and playing it back."

Fowler asked what the President was doing at that moment, and was puzzled when Melinda told him that Ericson was speedhearing parts of the Bible.

"Don't noise that around," Hennessy said, "too cornball. Not Ericson. People will think he's all shook up. What chapters?"

"Book of Job, I think. Goes pretty fast on those tapes."

"Hank, how's he holding up?" Hennessy sounded worried.

"Surprisingly well, considering." Fowler did not want to discuss his patient's mood in detail with anyone, but Melinda and Hennessy were extensions of Ericson. They were his antennae for incoming signals, his tentacles for manipulating others. Fowler told them he was cheered by the way Ericson was rolling with the punches of this week: Abelson's suicide, then the supposed need to confess the previous blindness, then the Yalta Deceit charge, then the second and far more serious wave of reaction to the suicide. The President occasionally bitched, but generally he sustained the people around him. One reason for that, Fowler surmised, was the pace of events—every day a new blow or counterblow—permitting little time for introspection. Next week, when Ericson might have time to worry, would be a time to worry about. Meanwhile, the hectic nature of the activity brought along its own therapy.

"I want to get him off the defensive," Hennessy said, "book him into an event next week that's controversial but presidential. Domestic affairs. Something that involves your boy friend, Melinda—what's he hot about these days, besides you?"

Fowler appreciated the way Melinda slid past the intended irritation: "The Attorney General, who is a friend but not a boy, has been nagging us to have the President accompany him to the two-hundredth anniversary of some big constitutional deal down in Colonial Williamsburg. Law Day. You said no way. He tried an end run through me, but"—she caught herself before Hennessy picked up the double meaning—"he asked me to intercede, but I wouldn't."

"We may do it. Next week we'll be very pro-Constitution. Hank, could you get The Man up for a platform walk-on, and a speech?"

"He'd probably like that," Fowler replied, as a soft voice at his shoulder told him of a telephone call in his office. He picked up his cane and moved back through Melinda's office to his own cubicle, which had been assigned to him by Hennessy with the crack, "You're the only staffer who won't complain about an office without a view. If you like, tell your friends you have a window."

A worried commandant of Bethesda Naval Hospital was on the phone. "I really can't be held responsible for this, Dr. Fowler," the voice said in agitation, "I was following orders." Gently, Fowler asked what it was about, and was not upset to learn that the ophthalmologist, Lilith, was about to "go up the flue," in the commandant's phrase. The blast from the eye doctor who had been kept in the dark was to be expected, and Hennessy had already arranged for other eye doctors and neurosurgeons to counter the blast with expert testimony that would effectively confuse the issue.

"Admiral, what form will Dr. Lilith's protest take?"

"He's calling a bloody press conference at the medical association this afternoon. Can you imagine, a doctor? It's all the attention he's been getting for the past couple of months, it's gone to his head, damn fool thinks he's a celebrity."

"Did you suggest to him that medical ethics, and naval tradition—"

"Of course I did, Fowler, and that's part of the problem. He was all a-twitter—you know, he's a reserve officer, not Annapolis—and I reminded him of the doctor-patient relationship. He said I should have told the President about that. So then I got a little hot under the collar and I told him that if he popped off like some kind of crybaby I'd ship his ass off to the sick bay of a mine sweeper in the Aleutians."

Hank Fowler sighed. "He didn't react well to that, I take it?"

"That's when he started howling about his duty to the country and the respect of the medical profession and God knows what-all. I got good and pissed off, and I'm afraid I broke our confidence in trying to get him to come to his senses."

Fowler felt a small sense of terror at the possibility of his own involvement in Ericson's ordeal, not as a respected psychologist but as a criticizable participant. "Go on, Admiral—you told him about our talk?"

"Sorry about that, yes, but only to impress him with the fact that he could expect no White House help when we lowered the boom on him."

"Admiral, the only thing I asked you to do was to remind him of the medical ethics—"

"Well, as I recall, you went a little further than that, or I did and you concurred"—the naval officer was covering his ass—"but anyhow, he got all upset at what he called White House pressure to deny him his free speech. Cover-up, he said—that kind of stuff. He's just not a reliable officer, and it's one of those damn twists of fate that our top man at Bethesda was ill when the Yalta ambush took place."

"Did you think I wanted you to pressure him?"

"Look, Dr. Fowler, we're in this together. I don't know exactly what the President, who is my commander in chief, told you—but the message I got, reading between your lines, was that he wanted this man to be a good sailor. I gave it all I had to carry out the President's wish, and I'm sorry it's turned out to be, uh, counterproductive."

Fowler thanked him and hung up before he got the White House into any more trouble. He went out to Melinda, waited until she was off her phone, and asked her to accompany him to Hennessy's office—the chief of staff, too, had taken a call in the last few minutes. They were both already aware of Dr. Lilith's coming press conference.

"I got a klong," Fowler said to them, and related his call from the Bethesda commandant. "I have a hunch I may have worsened the situation." Even as he told the story of his initial call to the admiral, he found himself minimizing the main point of that call, as he stressed the medical ethics he had mentioned. Fowler had felt a twinge of conscience when he first called the admiral, but he had not thought his action in trying to restrain the ophthalmologist was all that bad, and it surely had been in a good cause.

"It isn't your fault, Hank," Melinda said.

"It is all your fault," Hennessy said. "Yours and the President's for trusting that dumbhead admiral at Bethesda with a job that required some finesse. I knew that Lilith was a fag. Now we're gonna catch it—welcome to the club, Dr. Fowler."

Fowler could observe himself wondering how anything like this could be happening to him. "I'm frightened," he said truthfully.

"Don't be," Hennessy ordered. "It'll be a big deal for one day, and then it'll be over and forgotten." Cold comfort. "Cheer up, kiddo, at least you won't be able to see the black headlines—'Blind Shrink Terrorizes Brave Naval Fag.'"

Fowler was glad Hennessy was around at a time like this. "If it's all right with you," he said, pulling at his mustache, which was a signal to himself that he was agitated, "I'd just as soon not listen to the press conference. Put yourself in Dr. Lilith's shoes, Melinda —the admiral threatening you, saying the White House psychologist got him to twist your arm. I empathize with the eye doctor."

"Empathize with yourself, Hank," Melinda said. "Don't start looking through the other side's eyes in this. You'll drive yourself up the wall."

"C'mon, c'mon," Hennessy hurried up, "we have things to do. Hank, sit down and dictate your recollection of what you said to the admiral, and if the idea to lean on the eye doctor was yours, and not

Ericson's, jot that down too. I'll get the doctors on our side to give Lilith a blast for looking for alibis, and making the wrong decisions. Melinda will brief The Man."

"Right," Fowler said, an inept team player. "Tell the President I'm sorry."

"Stop for Chrissake being sorry," Hennessy snapped. "These flaps come and go. I fucked up on the need for the goddamn speech in the first place, and now that's past. Melinda fucked up on the handling of Abelson's wife, the actress, and that's past. You fucked up on the handling of the fag eye doctor and in twenty-four hours, that'll be past."

Melinda's voice added under her breath, "Lot of fucking up around here." To Hank, she said, "That's the first time I've used that awful word out loud in my life, truly it is. Hennessy must be corrupting me."

"Let the Attorney General corrupt you," Hennessy said, "Lucas Cartwright says Duparquet is the one to stay close to, in case there's another putsch in the Cabinet. Hank, have a good cry if you like, but don't let if affect the way you help The Man as a shrink."

Fowler went out and worked on his memo-for-the-file with his recorder. When he heard the television on in Melinda's office, he was drawn to the doorway to listen to Dr. Lilith.

The ophthalmologist's performance, in contrast to that of Mrs. Abelson's the previous day, began unemotionally. Matter-of-factly, almost mincingly, he laid out the series of medical deceptions by President Ericson and his personal staff after the examination in the Azores. Then the doctor showed how the lack of knowledge of the previous blindness led to a treatment different from the "right" treatment, which, he said with great certainty, would have been neurosurgery to relieve pressure on the optic nerve. Lilith's presentation, which Fowler knew was being done in front of a blackboard with all appropriate and impressive diagrams, absolved Lilith from blame for the permanence of the Ericson blindness. The doctor made the case—with unjustifiable rectitude, Fowler thought—for the permanent blindness being all Ericson's fault. The psychologist asked himself whether he had become so much a partisan of Ericson, and of blind people, that he allowed his own emotions to influence his medical guesses: Listening to the man Hennessy had cruelly characterized as a "fag," Fowler decided that his emotions had done just that, and he was not unhappy about it.

Dr. Lilith's low-key press conference picked up a nonmedical note when he referred to the President's speech, and its evocation of the biblical Samson. "Anyone who reads that Milton poem today," the eye doctor told the cameras, "cannot help but be struck by this line, spoken of the blind hero: 'How well are come upon him his deserts.' I do not in any way suggest that any human being deserves to be blind, but I do suggest that the President's deliberate lying to his doctors was a primary cause of the permanence of his loss of sight. It need not have been this way; neurosurgery might have made all the difference. President Ericson brought it on himself."

Then the eye doctor cut loose. Fowler winced as he heard Lilith's voice, now beginning to quiver, tell of the "intense pressure directly from the White House" to keep quiet; of threats by the admiral, passing along dire warnings of the ruination of his naval career from "the nondoctor who calls himself doctor," Henry Fowler. The psychologist cringed inwardly, shook his head, and turned back into his office; it was too painful to listen to, directly from the source. Time enough to speedhear it in the summary the next day, or recounted on newscasts, or repeated in the West Wind hallway as part of that series of echoes ricocheting off the White House bunker walls.

Fowler felt dirtied. After the initial wave of unfairness swirled eddies of guilt, his slight variance from the straight and narrow, nothing serious, was being interpreted as terrible pressure. And yet he could see now that at the receiving end, following the admiral's understandable exaggeration, it might well have appeared as terrible pressure. Henry Fowler did not think he was really at fault—it had been the President's idea—but Fowler knew he was at fault, because he was responsible for his own action. Such a little deal, he sighed, to be blown into such a big deal—the television, the editorials, the word-of-mouth denunciations of "more White House deceit." A little slip, an erroneous accommodation of a patient, and he had become associated with—worse, had become additional evidence of—the corrosive Ericson venality, which was taken to be somehow related to his disability.

Or was it? Could a man being attacked as a hateful Machiavelli be removed for being incapable of carrying out the duties of his office? That did not seem consistent to Hank Fowler. He looked along the colors of his internal vista and asked himself how he had helped tie together the unlikely combination of accusations: deviousness and incapacity. He charged himself with failing the President, failing the cause of the handicapped, failing his own long climb from helplessness to respect. Where had he gone wrong? He should have talked it over with Hennessy before he made that call. In this gas-filled room, only experienced men were entitled to carry matches, to be presidential protectors. Ericson was a fundamental force, not a protector; it was not the President's job to guard against the reaction to improper action, but the job of his closest advisers. And they had to be very careful men, not blindly loyal, and not babes in the wood like Dr. Henry Fowler.

He asked himself why he was trying so hard not to blame the President. That analytical question troubled him; he would come back to it when he had time. Meanwhile, the psychologist permitted himself ten minutes to wallow in his misery, and to reflect the fear of a doctor fighting an epidemic, looking at his hands and wondering if he has caught the disease.

The New Chief of Staff / 2

Hennessy surveyed the wreckage of the week laid out before him in the form of pink telephone messages. At the end of a long table, which he had inherited with the job and the office, were a group of messages from congressmen and staffers. Those pink slips were laid out in a fan pattern, like an explosion of complaints about the President's television speech, demands to talk to the chief of staff on matters that now seemed ancient history. Then, arranged in a long row that contrasted with the fan of complaints, there was a batch of Yalta Deceit messages, reaction to the Zophar column, mostly from journalists and those members of Congress who considered themselves "serious"—that is, concerned with foreign affairs. All were determined to pour into the ear of the man who had the President's ear all manner of advice and all kinds of questions. A third grouping, running laterally, like the setup for a game of solitaire—his secretary had done this artistically, Hennessy wearily noted—were from people who had been affected by Herb Abelson's suicide, mainly old friends of the President and his dead doctor. One set in the solitaire group was clipped together before the widow's reaction, a thicker set was dated after Barbara Abelson put on her television spectacular. The post-press-conference messages about the ophthalmologist's outrage were next in the solitaire set, made up of some of the same people who had called earlier in the week, plus a few political types who wanted to sound the alarm about local reaction. Hennessy already had a good measurement of local reaction, in the form of overnight polls, which showed Ericson's popularity eroding in large chunks, from what had been thought to be the "rock bottom" 42 per cent to 30 per cent in a week.

He picked up the intercom and complained to his secretary, "Why are all these phone messages on pink slips? Pink is for girls. Get me message slips for a male executive. Blue maybe. Yes, baby blue. And give all these that are cluttering up my table to somebody else to answer." He picked up the last bundle of messages, the calls he had to return. One from Cartwright, which would tell him how to run this shop, and remind him to stay on top of Duparquet. One from Duparquet, only a half hour old—he would get to that in a minute. One from Hennessy's son, who lived in Boston with Hennessy's wife and daughter, a family he had not visited for more than a month and was just as glad to be away from. Kid probably wanted money, which could wait, or explanations, which could wait longer. One from Smitty: Hell with that, he thought, if it had been important, the press secretary would have come down the hall and barged in. He stopped when he saw the one from "Mr. Goodfriend."

"Mr. Goodfriend" was Marty Quinn, the press agent Hennessy had planted on Bannerman's Committee to Replace the Disabled President. Through Marty, Hennessy had given Bannerman's committee its harsh, direct-attack name, rather than an institutional title that would have been more effective in terms of public opinion. Quinn's message had no return number.

Hennessy started to put in a call to Attorney General Duparquet when his secretary came in, closed the door behind her, and said, "Couple of FBI gumshoes out there, in the waiting room, asking to see you."

"Field checks?" The FBI was always sending a couple of men around on full field investigations of people to be hired or commissioned.

"No. They want to see you about something to do with you. I told them I'd arrange an appointment, but they're persistent—said they'd just hang around till you had a free moment."

Hennessy scowled. Some member of the White House staff had evidently put his foot in it. Irritated, he told his secretary to send the FBI men in right away. This was no day for a middle-level staffer to be caught in some hanky-panky.

The agents were polite, as usual; one had gray in his hair, and did the question-asking; the younger took notes and looked respectful.

"Sorry to bother you, sir, when you have so many return calls to make," the senior agent said, glancing at the display of pink slips.

"I play solitaire with them. What's the problem?"

"How long have you been acquainted with a man named Arthur Leigh?"

"He's not up for a job," Hennessy snapped. "If he is, it's a mistake."

"This is not a recruitment check, sir. Have you known him long?"

"Since the campaign last year." The only thing Hennessy owed Leigh was an apology for mistakenly assuming that the former campaign manager had blabbed to Sam Zophar, when, as it turned out, Leigh had kept his end of their bargain.

"When was the last time you saw him?"

Hennessy's lawyer instincts took over: "What's this about?"

"Not at liberty to say, sir, some preliminary checking. Was he in here recently?" The agent was a skilled interrogator, never leaving a comment alone, always closing with a question. Of course the FBI knew when Leigh had visited Hennessy; every visitor to the White House is logged in by the Secret Service. Hennessy touched the "annoy-me" button under his desk.

"I recall he was in a few weeks ago," Hennessy said, "but I'll be glad to give you the exact date from my records." His secretary knocked and came in, paged by the annoy-me, to say, "They're waiting for you, Mr. Hennessy. They say the meeting can't start without you."

"Marie, these gentlemen want the date and time of the visit Arthur Leigh made a few weeks ago," Hennessy said, looking sorry he had to race off. "Give it to them, and if they like, set up another time to see me tomorrow. Wait, tomorrow's Sunday—Monday, after the staff meeting."

"We can wait till you get back," the older agent said helpfully.

"I don't like to waste taxpayers' money," Hennessy said, "or insult the Bureau by having its best men cooling their heels around here." Gumshoes in the West Wing lobby, attracting press attention, was what he didn't like.

"There's some urgency involved," the agent pressed.

"My duties require me elsewhere at the moment," said the President's chief of staff, still polite, "and I will not give you rushed answers to important questions. I am familiar with Section 1001 of U.S. Code 18." That was a law, sometimes invoked to cause trouble when other laws could not be found for that purpose, that made it a crime to tell a lie to any federal officer. No oath needed—a bad law. Hennessy wanted the agents to know he was not about to be trapped into damaging testimony in an agents' report. He knew why the senior agent had the other man along, and the lawyer was not going into any interview without a witness of his own.

Hennessy left his office, walked down the hall briskly, and disappeared into the Roosevelt Room. He looked at the paintings for a minute—he liked the Remington of Teddy Roosevelt and his men charging up San Juan Hill—and when assured that the FBI men had left, returned to his office and called the Attorney General.

"What the hell is up, Emmett? A couple of your boys are over here snooping around—" Hennessy checked his anger, because the President needed Duparquet as never before. "Did I park illegally outside a massage parlor?"

"I called you a little while ago," Duparquet's voice was formal, which Hennessy took to mean that another person was in his office, "to say that the director of the FBI had assigned some men to an investigation involving Arthur Leigh, and that he and I hoped you would co-operate if you were asked for an interview."

"What's it all about?"

"An allegation of corruption."

"Whose?"

"I can't say." That slammed into Hennessy like a torpedo. It meant he was probably the target of an FBI investigation. Someone must have gotten wind of the deal Hennessy had made to take care of Arthur Leigh's highway problem.

"Mr. Attorney General, let me ask a question that is entirely proper: Am I the target of an investigation?"

"At this stage," Duparquet said evenly, "no individual is a target. If the matter is considered by the United States Attorney in this district to be worthy of grand jury consideration, whoever is the target would be informed, as he has a right to be. As of now, you are not a target. As a federal officer yourself, you are expected to co-operate with any investigation the FBI might undertake." The local United States Attorney was probably sitting at his side, Hennessy thought. His first reaction was how to insulate the President from any corruption charges against his chief of staff.

"As you know, General, I wear two hats over here: chief of staff, and legal counsel to the President. Do you think this might be a good time for the President to appoint someone else to fill the counsel's job?"

Duparquet paused a moment, then said firmly, "Yes. I say that with no prejudice to you, but as a precautionary measure. To avoid any potential conflict of interest."

"I understand." Now came a point it was important to have on the record. "General, please discuss that with the President yourself. It is my intention to co-operate with the FBI, to answer all proper questions, and not to discuss this matter in any way with the President."

"Good," said Duparquet, again after a momentary delay. "I think that's quite proper. The sooner you talk to the agents, the better." Hennessy had the impression he was not talking to one man, but to a Department of Justice; the slight pauses were probably exchanged looks, nods, or head-shakings in the A.G.'s office.

He hung up, made room among the pink slips and put a spoon, a glass, and his bottle of white antacid on the table. His stomach was churning and his heart had begun to pound now that the call was done.

When Leigh had asked for that highway commissioner appointment, Hennessy had passed the word through the patronage man at the White House to the political contact in the Tennessee governor's office. The appointment had been made as he had promised Leigh. Now, Hennessy asked himself, where was the vulnerability? It was probably too soon for the highway commissioner to have made a ruling of financial benefit to Leigh. The patronage man or the governor's man might have blown the whistle, but what crime had been committed? None. Hennessy told himself to relax. He took a spoonful of the antacid, made a face, then took another. He envisioned the walls of his stomach being coated as in a television commercial, and he took comfort from that.

They could possibly charge that he had given the order to appoint the highway commissioner in exchange for Leigh's silence on the previous blindness, which was the truth, but who could substantiate that? Only Leigh, and Leigh had already proven himself to be more trustworthy than Hennessy had suspected. So what was the FBI left with? Just the charge that the White House had acceded to the wishes of an old political supporter in the appointment of a friend of his, which had been done since time immemorial. Without the *quid pro quo,* no venality.

Unless, of course, that bastard Leigh was the source of the allegation. Hennessy started to put that out of his mind, having been burned not trusting Leigh before, but it came back: What could Leigh gain by getting Hennessy and himself in trouble?

"He could gain a whole lot of money," he said aloud to the bottle of antacid. If Leigh had chosen to sell out to Bannerman, he could bring Hennessy down fairly easily—provided Leigh was willing to take a fall as well. Leigh could charge that Hennessy had tried to bribe him, and Hennessy would countercharge extortion—except that the record would show he did the favor for Leigh. Hennessy would have to go down the line claiming there had been no *quid pro quo,* and nobody would believe him. Bannerman did not even need a Hennessy conviction at a trial later—just an indictment now of a White House aide, with maybe a smidgen touching the President.

What would he tell the FBI agents? Hennessy would say, with a witness of his own present, that Leigh had recommended a man for a job, and he had complied —after all, the man had a political IOU. Nothing had been mentioned at any time of keeping quiet about the campaign train blindness. If Hennessy's story conflicted with Leigh's, so be it. No reasonable U. S. Attorney would seek an indictment on the substantiated charge of one man against another. Or would he? Hennessy felt the need for a criminal lawyer.

On the intercom, his secretary told him that "Mr. Goodfriend" was calling again. "We've got a big thing going with the medical associations," Marty Quinn told him from a phone booth. "Bannerman thinks the previous blindness revelation is a lot more important than the Yalta Deceit. He's got control of that eye doctor, offered him a deal outside the Navy, I think. You were right about Bannerman, Hennessy—a son of a bitch of the first water."

Hennessy wasn't so much interested in that: "What's with Arthur Leigh?"

"He was at a meeting with Bannerman and Nichols day before yesterday," Quinn reported. "Just as the Barbara Abelson press conference was taking place.

Bannerman took Leigh outside, I don't know what they cooked up."

"What they cooked up was me," Hennessy murmured. "Look, just in case I have to take off, or I get sick or something, I want you to have another contact here," Harry Bok was the first to come to mind, but the burly man in the wheel chair had been given a rough time in the papers this week, and might shy from the tawdry necessities of staying in power. Hennessy knew that Marty Quinn, who was taking his chances this way, would trust no second-level insider; that left Melinda. Hennessy gave him her private number and put the phone down slowly.

He thought about Melinda. He often thought about Melinda, biting down on his toothache, but now Hennessy thought of her as one of the last human supports left to the President. A lonely woman, everybody said, but everybody could be wrong: A lot of lives intersected with hers. Hennessy took pleasure in getting under her skin, and occasionally let himself think of getting in her pants, but their relationship, he understood, was doomed to banter and byplay and forced trusting. He could not quite figure out the Ericson-McPhee connection, which could not be merely the office-wife, mother-hen relationship that appeared on the surface. How did she feel about the way the President felt about her affair with Duparquet—and how did he really feel about it?

Melinda had turned out to be less tough and more strong than Hennessy had originally thought, and she was getting stronger all the time. He let himself picture her as Beau Geste at Fort Zinderneuf, gallantly propping up dead bodies in the parapets to make attackers think the fort was still defended. Hennessy admitted to himself he was envious of Ericson for possessing her loyalty and jealous of Duparquet for possessing her affection, but it was a good thing she was in both situations: The President needed her now as never before, and her hold on the Attorney General, if it were as serious as Hennessy half-hoped, would help keep Duparquet enlisted in Ericson's cause. Melinda had her priorities in line; she was not the sort who would let infatuation get in the way of loyalty.

She appeared in his doorway—as always, fine figure, dancer's legs, a shade too hawklike—to say, "I just heard. The Boss says they're after you." The Attorney General had made the call, and had undoubtedly advised Ericson not to discuss the matter with Hennessy at all, or to become involved with him in any way.

"The Man wants to see you." He wondered if she was telling the truth.

"I don't think he should. Not about this. Warn him."

"Emmett already told him to cut you off," she said, "but he wants to see you."

"Did The Man ask for your advice, Melinda? What'd you tell him?"

"I told him if he so much as thought twice about not seeing you, I'd break his goddamn long white cane."

"Weakness," Hennessy said scornfully, concealing his relief. "I fucked up. Again. What happens to fuck-ups?"

For the first time, she did not respond to his standard shocker. "They all come to Washington and go to work for Sven Ericson," she said softly. "We all make mistakes. Oh, Hennessy—"

He cut her off. "First I'll talk to my mout'piece. Then I'll see the FBI agents, with my secretary taking notes. Then, if I think it's wise, I'll talk it over with the President. Remember, and I really mean it—remember for later—we can protect the Boss, but he can't protect us. Never forget that, and for Chrissake, buy yourself a low-cut blouse." Again, she did not rise to the bait. That depressed him.

For the next few hours on the telephone, the President's chief of staff went over the matter with a long-time friend who practiced criminal law in New York. Then Hennessy had his interview with the agents. As expected, their questioning went as if based on information supplied by Arthur Leigh. As instructed by his lawyer, Hennessy laid out a simple story and stuck to it: Leigh deserved to have his recommendations considered; the man he recommended was qualified; there was no *quid pro quo;* no talk of "keeping quiet" that Hennessy could recall, and he thought he would remember that. Hennessy never said "he said," only "he indicated," a looser word, and fuzzed it up further with "I don't recall Leigh's words, but his gist, as I understood it, was . . ." Hennessy made himself a difficult defendant to convict, at least on the substance of a "deal." But to indict—that was different.

He was having a belt of bourbon by himself, thinking he might go see the President, when Ericson's cane tapped on the doorjamb and the President appeared behind it. "I should've got you that Seeing Eye dog," Hennessy said, going to the doorway and bringing Ericson in to a chair. "That would have wrung a few tears out of our boys in the bleacher seats."

"You're talking as if you're already on your way out," Ericson said. "What you need is a Hennessy, like I have. He'd put a little steel in your spine."

"You mean, 'shove a ramrod up your ass.' Say what you mean, Sven."

"Presidents don't talk like divorce lawyers." Ericson took a glass of bourbon Hennessy folded into his hand. "Okay," the President sighed, "how do we get our asses out of this one?"

"We keep our eye upon the doughnut, and not upon the hole," Hennessy told him, feeling better enough to use the philosophy he read on the wall of a coffee shop. "You are the doughnut. We give 'em the hole."

"Uh-unh. I need you. There's no need for you to make a martyr out of yourself."

"Here's the thing," Hennessy explained. "They've got a grand jury already empaneled. They've heard Arthur Leigh say I bribed him to keep quiet about the blindness, and I'll bet that bastard Leigh says I told him you knew all about it. The U. S. Attorney's going to run me in there Monday and get me to contradict his story in every way. If I do, they'll have an indictment ready to hand up in a shot."

The President clinked the ice in his glass. "Indict you for what?"

"That's the beauty part. Not for bribing Leigh, with the promise of an appointment that didn't lead to any criminal behavior—that'd be thrown out of court. Nope, they'd indict me for perjury, ten counts, every time I disagree with Leigh. His word against mine— who do you believe? Could go either way at a trial. Neither of us looks very trustworthy."

"But what if you took the Fifth?"

Hennessy shook his head slowly, then remembered and said aloud, "No good. An assistant to the President cannot plead self-incrimination. That would be as much as saying Leigh is telling the truth, and it could be the last straw for you."

"Take the Fifth," said Ericson firmly. "I mean it. I'm not going to let you expose yourself to prosecution. This thing is getting out of hand." Ericson ran his hands through his hair. "I let Herb kill himself, I ruin Harry's chances at a new life, I take a sweet guy like Hank Fowler and get his reputation smeared, and I'm just not going to see you go to jail. Sorry. The job isn't worth it."

"Cut the crap, Sven, we've got to make plans. I couldn't go through life having taken the Fifth on this and you know it. So I'll testify and I'll be terrific. I'll tell the grand jury all about the meeting at Bannerman's house where this was cooked up, with the Vice-President right there. I'll force the prosecutors to call Bannerman and Nichols as witnesses and they'll all have to perjure themselves till they're blue in the face. This grand jury stuff cuts both ways. If we can get some faithless juror to spill our side of the story to a friendly reporter, which we can, we can put those guys on the defensive. I won't go quietly, it's not my style— I'll put up one hell of a scrap. I won't come to trial for six months after the indictment by which time you'll either be in, and the hysteria will be over, or you'll be out, and nobody'll want to be vindictive. It'll be okay."

"Every time you say 'It'll be okay,'" said the President, "I worry. Except for the divorce, and the election. Nothing else turned out okay."

"We win the big ones." They sat silently for a couple of minutes. Hennessy picked up with "Roy Bannerman's no dope. He had this fairly well orchestrated—maybe got to Herb's wife, surely got to the fag eye doctor—did he ever put his hand on your knee? Wonder if they got fag knee doctors. And Bannerman got to Leigh. Could be he had a hand in the Zophar thing. I hear there's some kind of old connection between Bannerman and Zophar. Give the sumbitch credit, he plays hardball without a glove."

"You're paranoid, Hennessy."

"Even a paranoid has some real enemies," he quoted his favorite bit of Freudian wisdom. "Look, if I'm right about that grand jury, I'll be out by the middle of next week. Issue a statement that you're convinced I'm innocent but you agree that I should stand aside until the matter is adjudicated. I'll hit Nichols in a press conference for being in the cook-up session, and you give him the freeze. Who do you have in mind for chief of staff?"

"Smitty, I guess. Circle is getting tight."

"Makes sense, and Marilee gets moved up to press secretary, everybody'll like that. Me going might lance the boil in a lot of ways."

"Great. Who'll I trust?"

"Melinda. She'll have a good contact you don't have to know about in Bannerman's back yard. Don't trust Buffie, by the way. Bang her if you need to but really keep your mouth shut, she's big trouble now. Lucas is solid, still, but Mike Fong is all primed to stab you in the back again—why don't you fire him?"

"Might trigger an impeachment," the President said. "Would show I was scared of my own Cabinet." Hennessy was glad Ericson had given the matter some thought. "What's with you and Melinda, all of a sudden so buddy-buddy? You used to be at each other's throats."

"That's when she didn't know her place," Hennessy

said. "She wears well, doesn't make mistakes. A lot depends on whether she can keep her boy friend in line." For both of us, he thought—Duparquet could decide Ericson's fate in the Cabinet and Hennessy's in the courtroom.

"If you lose your bravado over the weekend," said the President, "and decide to take the Fifth, I'll be pleased. You're right, you'd have to quit here in either case. God, it's like going into an end game and losing your queen."

"Eye doctor's the queen, not me."

"Where was the mistake?" Ericson twisted his white cane in both directions at the same time, one hand clockwise, the other counterclockwise. "What move was wrong, that they could pick you off this way?"

"If you could see, you'd see me shrugging. I had to give Leigh what he wanted, didn't I? You were totally unaware of it, though."

"Totally," Ericson said automatically.

"And the subject never arose when we said good-by."

"Never. I suppose this is good-by, then." That was the purpose of his visit, and it only now seemed to register on Ericson.

"For a while."

"Um." Best thing about working for a blind man, Hennessy thought, was that he couldn't see your eyes. After a few moments, when he trusted his own voice, Hennessy said, "You're in my office, I'm not in yours, remember?"

Ericson rose. "Just point me toward the center of power."

The Personal Secretary / 3

"I don't want to hear the whole News Summary this morning, Melinda," Ericson told her, "just read me the worst." It was past nine, and he was still in bed, as if reluctant to face the day; he had been doing that for the past week, ever since the goddamn speech, and it was a bad habit. She had taken to entering "staff meeting, breakfast room, residence" from 8:30 to 9:30 A.M. on the public calendar.

He was right about the News Summary, though. Tuesday mornings were worst, recapping the news magazine's rehash and interpretation of the previous week, going off like a delayed-action bomb just when you hoped the worst was over. The weekly magazines usually added some extra dirt to stay topical, which was then picked up by the newspapers and television, adding to the impending-disaster momentum. On Tuesdays the News Summary carried all that, plus the developments of Monday that already outdated the news magazines, making the old bad news compete with the new bad news.

"Cover of *Time* is the Yalta Deceit," she skimmed, "montage of Cartwright, Curtice, Harry Bok, and Nikolayev, all in some kind of spider web."

"'Oh, what a tangled web we weave,'" Ericson recited cheerlessly, "'when first we practice to deceive.' That's symbolism. Very subtle. Well, better that than Barbara Abelson."

"She's the cover of *Newsweek*. Or half of it, the other half is Dr. Lilith. Hennessy used to call him the fag eye doctor, and he was right." She swallowed;

482

Hennessy was gone a whole two days, and already it was "Hennessy used to . . ."

"Hennessy's press conference get a good play?"

She put it in the best light: "It got a lot of coverage. The story broke in Zophar's column Monday morning, that he would appear at a grand jury that day, so Hennessy was kind of on the defensive. The headlines were "Ericson Aide Charged with Bribe Try," which ain't good, but there was a clip on television last night showing him zapping Bannerman and Nichols as the 'master manipulators' of the whole thing."

"But that got buried, huh?"

"Well, it's mentioned in some of the editorials this morning. The *Times* says, 'The propriety of the Vice-President's presence at Mr. Bannerman's home while this matter was presumably being discussed is questionable.' "

"What else does it say?"

"Stuff about grand jury secrecy, don't prejudge, and then the needle: 'Whether or not this latest charge turns out to be true, the hard fact is that the American public—after a week-long series of shocks about evidence of White House deceit and duplicity—is ready to believe the worst about President Ericson's ability to control his staff. He has been shown to be a man who—while his own instincts may be good—is in a condition in which he must "go along" with the decisions of the men around him, thereby ratifying a policy of lies. The revelations of the past week, beginning with his own hasty and ill-considered speech, cast serious doubt on the President's ability to govern. His Cabinet, although stacked with his cronies, has a responsibility to invoke the provisions of the Twenty-fifth Amendment. Of course the most rational solution would be for the President to stand aside voluntarily.' "

Ericson slid down in bed and put his hands behind his head on the pillow. "What sort of attention is the Attorney General getting?"

"Emmett's getting a dandy press," Melinda said, irritated. "The U. S. Attorney came to him last week with the Leigh charge, and our boy Duparquet told them to sic the FBI on Hennessy, damn the torpedoes. Everybody likes the way he warned the President to stay the hell out of it—showed his independence."

Ericson gave a rueful chuckle. "When my Cabinet members do something the press doesn't like, I've lost all control—but when Duparquet lets the hounds go baying after my best friend, he's being wonderfully independent."

"I wouldn't kick about the press," Melinda said. "At least they're not writing about how you lie around in bed all morning, with your secretary by your side like some kind of manicurist." She had never become accustomed to that position, still resented it, although, God knew, Ericson had not in recent years taken advantage of it. She enjoyed complaining about it, and he enjoyed hearing the complaint, so it went on.

"Do my nails need cutting?" the President asked, feeling his nails. "You're right, though, I should be in the office, fighting the good fight. Do you have to slosh on all that perfume?"

"Emmett likes it," she said flatly. "I slosh it on for the man in my life, not for you. Also, this place reeks of Lily of the Valley, or Apple Blossom, or whatever cheap stuff—"

"Don't knock my friend's taste," the President smiled.

"Nurses should smell of liniment," she jabbed.

"I don't know why everybody assumes my friend is Nurse Kellgren," Ericson said, cheering up and holding his hand out for a robe, which she gave him. "Harry runs her in and out, and we've never been properly introduced. She's on the quiet side, doesn't complain, good massage—at this moment in my life, exactly what I need."

"You miss Buffie." Melinda could feel his ache.

"Christ, yes. But keep her away, I have enough headaches."

She knew he was teasing her this way for a reason, but she wasn't going to help him. Finally, he broached the subject of the Attorney General: "Melinda, can we depend on Duparquet? Is he a good man?"

"He's a fairly good man," she judged. "I don't know if we can depend on him."

"One of those guys who will defend his integrity, no matter who it hurts, even if it takes him to the White House?"

"Don't be sarcastic, he's done a lot for you." What was she to tell him? That Emmett was a considerate, tender lover? That he was genuinely apologetic about not being available on Sundays and most evenings? That she fixed him dinner at her place last evening, candlelight and wine like a couple of sophomores, and worked him over per Hennessy's careful instructions, with him knowing exactly what she was doing? "He's ambitious, like you. He has principles, like you. But he hasn't been through what you've been through. Nobody's ever really hit him hard."

"I have high hopes for that man," Ericson said slowly. "I want to make it through one term, and then turn it over to somebody I trust. Could be him."

"Never fear," Melinda said dramatically, "I'll never tell him that."

The President, making his way to the barber chair, laughed without bitterness. "If you haven't told him that already, tell him. Every five minutes or so, find a way to bring it up. You see through me with such ease, Melinda—I hope you can see through him. Send in the barber. Do we have a manicurist?"

"You need your fingernails to hang on with," she said, motioning to the man down the hall to gather up his equipment.

"How's your morale, chum?" The President asked her the question lightly, but she knew it was important he be given a serious answer.

"Strange. I feel better now than I did a week ago. I was waiting then, dreading every day, waiting for the other shoe to drop. I knew last week had to come, and it was even worse than I thought, but it's behind us now. As my mother says, that's a blessing."

"Lot more shoes fell than I planned to drop. Sure you're not getting punchy?"

She was not sure at all. "Maybe I'm anesthetized—"

"—as Nurse Kellgren says."

"—or maybe I'm clairvoyant."

"—I knew Claire, the manicurist at the old Roney Plaza."

She was determined to finish. "But I have a hunch we've hit bottom. No other disaster is in the pipeline, that I know of—whatever happens from now on will be a surprise. That's better than knowing something terrible is sure to happen. Know what I mean?"

"Keep thinking that way," Ericson said. "Worst that can happen, we lose our jobs, weaken the presidency, subvert freedom, all that jazz. Darkest before the dawn." An edge of bitterness crept into his tone which she did not like.

"You don't know what I mean?"

"Oh, Melinda, I do, I do, and I wish right now that I could see." He held his hands out as if framing what he could see. "If I could see, I'd be looking at your dark brown, distrusting eyes, and looking out the window at a glorious day, and in a minute looking at the round face of the man who's so proud to be the personal barber to the President of the United States. But all I can see, right this second, is Herb Abelson's face looking at me, accusing me, and Barbara's face looking at me, hating me. It's a good thing I don't know what Hank Fowler's face looks like, because I'd see him looking at me."

"And Shoeless Joe Jackson?" Her reference to Lucas Cartwright's favorite ballplayer made him smile a little.

"Say it ain't so, Melinda."

"Can it," she murmured, "here's the barber." Out in the hall, she spotted Harry Bok being pushed along by Nurse Kellgren. "You better go in with him, Harry, he's a little down." A sudden thought: "Hey, can she give a manicure?"

Harry twisted in his wheel chair. "Can you give a manicure?" Nurse Kellgren smiled and nodded, white hat bobbing. "She can," said Harry. "Probably the best manicure in Washington."

"Stay here." Melinda darted into the upstairs pantry, came out with a soap dish and some soap and a hand towel. She dug in her pocketbook and found an emery board and a cuticle pusher, handing the materials to the capable nurse, who added them to the Lubriderm she always carried in her uniform pocket. "Harry, go in with her, give him a line of patter, and don't let him fool around—get him down to the office in a few minutes. Nurse, why don't you put on some of that lovely perfume of yours, the President likes it, and it helps him know where you are."

Melinda headed downstairs, feeling better. When she spoiled Ericson, it made him feel guilty about his self-pity, and helped him snap out of it. The thought of the blind man's vision of accusing eyes in the dark troubled her, and she shuddered it away; with Hennessy gone, she had a load to carry that day and that night.

The mail, which she supervised, was turning ugly. The mail room had been told not to put together an analysis of pro vs. con, for fear it would leak, but a random sample sent to her had a higher percentage than usual of hate mail. The bomb squad reported fourteen letter-bombs over the weekend, nearly the total of the previous six months in the presidency; those figures were never released for fear of giving the idea to more nuts. What depressed Melinda most were the disappointed-supporter letters, the "Shoeless Joe" mail, and Melinda glanced at one: ". . . trusted you because you were not a politician. But why did you have to lie about the blindness? I would have voted for you anyway. And then, as President, you wouldn't have had any skeleton in your closet." Another: ". . . need to show off your macho. You've given the job all you have, you're obviously not up to it, don't make the country suffer for your handicap. There are plenty of good homes for the blind, and the White House isn't one. . . ."

She dialed a number for the pollster. "Twenty-eight

per cent and falling," he said. "You've just about touched the low point of the Nixon years and you're five points from the Truman low." She did not feel the need to pass that on. Her heart sank briefly as she saw the men from the General Services Administration removing Hennessy's office files, and moving in Smitty's things, but her spirits rose when Marilee showed her how she planned to redo Smitty's press office. Musical chairs to a dirge, but never a dull moment. She plunged into the planning for Law Day the next day in Williamsburg. Emmett Duparquet, who had been so anxious for the President's participation the week before, was no longer sure it was such a good idea. The President had begun to look forward to it, though—no formal speech, just some remarks about the Constitution and the rule of law—and it would be a relief to get away from the bunker atmosphere of the White House. Melinda put herself in charge of the room assignments, and assigned herself to a cottage next to the Attorney General's cottage; they had never spent an entire night together before.

Smitty, the new chief of staff, came into her office, elaborately casual, looking over some of the letters. He probably did not know what to do about Ericson's calendar, she figured, and needed her advice, but he didn't want to give up any of his new authority. She was tempted to let him stew awhile, but decided to be helpful: "Forgot to tell you, Smitty, the President said he hoped you and Lucas Cartwright would spend some time together soon. He was thinking you might run the office the way Lucas did, and not Hennessy."

"That's what I was thinking, too," Smitty said, "more open. Hennessy operated much too close to the chest." That was not quite it, Melinda thought to herself: The President never quite trusted Cartwright, and he doesn't quite trust you. Hennessy, he had trusted. On the other hand, Melinda conceded, Lucas did run a happier shop, and if the President had trusted Lucas Cartwright more and told him about the blindness, much grief might have been averted. "I have the Council of Economic Advisers wanting to see the Boss," Smitty said neutrally.

"He's free this afternoon at five, or tomorrow morning at nine," she replied. "You need a date for Curtice and a foreign-policy briefing, too?"

"If it's not too—"

"That's what they pay him for, being President." She was determined to fill up Ericson's calendar, making it harder for him to mope around. "If you want, you could book the economists in here this afternoon, and Curtice and the CIA tomorrow just before he takes off for Williamsburg."

"That's not too much for him?"

Sure it is, dumb bunny, she thought, and he'll be furious with you, and he'll tell me to tell you to ease up, but she said, "I think he's looking forward to it. And it'll be something for Marilee to tell the reporters, too. You'll be sure to remind the Chairman of the Council to get him a one-page situationer before the meeting, though, that's standard."

"Of course." Of course. Melinda realized that she was suddenly running the government of the United States, or at least running that small part of it in control of the President. Not running it, really, but in the absence of a strong staff chief and with a morose President, it was up to her to force people together. If people, including Cabinet members, thought the President did not want to see them, they did not ask to see him. Everyone was afraid of being rejected. Ericson, in his present state, was passive; available if they wanted to see him, but he would not call them in, or demand a report. It was suddenly up to her to see to it that the President and his Administration thought each was on top of the other. "You got to give him credit," the former press secretary was saying, "the Boss is really hanging in there. I noticed he kind of turned it all around about two weeks ago—started to come back strong—but I thought the shocks of the past week might have gotten to him."

"Nope," Melinda answered, "he hit bottom back when he had that nasty cold, when he couldn't hear or smell too well, and since then he's been getting stronger all the time." If that were only true. Half true, though —Ericson had been taking charge as never before until the goddamn speech episode and all that followed. Smitty was not in close, however, and if he were convinced Ericson had not been set back by the buffeting, that good word would get out far and wide. Especially since he was no longer press secretary: Now he was not a propagandist, but a participant. Reporters would credit him with real inside information. She would have to remind the President about that.

About an hour later, Marilee put her head in: "Hey, Melinda, are you interested in my continued success?" The President's secretary, on the phone to Williamsburg, smiled and nodded that she could listen. Marilee, looking as radiant and aristocratic as Melinda had always wished she could, slouched in a chair and said, "Smitty is acting as if he knew which end is up around here and he doesn't. I have a dinner tonight with three of the bell cows, and I'd like to give them something fresh. Insightful. You know anything insightful?"

Melinda covered the phone. "The Boss was feeling a little shaky over the weekend. Kind of a personal crisis. Then Duparquet came through for him, lot of integrity, the Boss liked that."

"He wasn't sore at the A.G. for sic-ing the FBI on Hennessy? That's what most people think."

"What most people think isn't what goes on here, you know that."

"Keep going," Marilee said, "they'll lap this up."

"The President was glad the A.G. told him not to see Hennessy any more. President cut him right off, even though I happen to know that Hennessy tried to see the Boss to get him to get Duparquet to call off the hounds."

"Hey, this is hot stuff. Does Smitty know?"

"Marilee, ol' buddy, I trust you, but I don't know Smitty all that well. Let's you and me look out for each other, okay?"

"Deal. Smitty will be a super chief of staff, really

he will, but honestly, he was a horse's ass of a press secretary. What else should I know?"

Melinda pretended to look thoughtful, then took some information over the phone, and hung up. "The second reason why Ericson's feeling a lot stronger today. He's glad Hennessy is out of there, and glad Smitty is in."

"Better make notes," Marilee said, borrowing a pencil and paper. "Why's that?"

"Hennessy was trying to take advantage of the President's blindness, grabbing too much power. Ericson doesn't like that, he's his own boss. And he doesn't want his Cabinet dominated by any White House staffer, either."

"Got it. With Hennessy out, you're in a lot better shape, too, Melinda, isn't that so? You and Hennessy —well, lots of tension."

"I don't want to toot my own horn, but I spotted Hennessy for an evil force around here from the start. We're better off without him, and damn lucky to have Smitty in that office instead." She watched Marilee scribbling down all the points. "All of which underlines the main theme of what you want to tell those guys— the Boss is stronger than ever now, and that's why he's acting that way, and why you'll see him taking on a much bigger load of activity."

"I know, I know," Marilee said, shifting her glasses to the top of her head, "Smitty just showed me the new calendar, said the President wants more to do."

Melinda picked up her mail and started riffling wearily through it. She chucked a postcard at Marilee, with a "We get a lot of these." The card read: "Hang in there, Mr. P!"

"Let me have this, I'll leave it on my desk where everybody tries to read upside down."

Melinda made as though to get back to her work. "You pass along whatever you want, I'm no judge of the press."

"This kind of makes Hennessy the fall guy," Marilee said neutrally, "and I know how you feel, but I kind of liked him, in a kooky way. One other thing—do you think I'll be seeing much more of the President now?"

"No," said Melinda, and meant it; Marilee did not press the matter, but thanked her ally and left. The President's secretary got up, closed the door, came back to her desk, and got out her notebook. She flipped through the pages of shorthand, the instructions Hennessy had given her to plant in Marilee's mind for passing along to the press. She had covered them all, even his "evil force" idea that she felt was excessive.

Melinda did not feel bad. She and Hennessy had argued about this, and he had convinced her that since he was leaving, he might as well take some of the hatred out of the White House with him. So she had followed his script. But it would be a long time before Ericson would find another staffer who would put the President's interest first, at whatever cost to his own reputation. Then again, Melinda remembered, Hennessy liked being hated.

The Secretary of Human Resources

Angelo Frangipani did not like squeezing himself into the back seat of a compact car. When mayor of New York City, "the Big Flower" rated a long limousine, equipped with siren, to which he rode to fires in the flamboyant tradition of his predecessor, Fiorello "the Little Flower" La Guardia. But now that he was a Washington big shot, he grumbled frequently, he had to ride around in a dinky little Pinto that had trouble moving when it got stuck on a piece of chewing gum. That was a concession he had made, one grand day, to an antipollution lobby, and he liked to say it was the worst mistake of his sojourn in Washington.

"I'm the only Cabinet member in fifty years without a driver," he told everybody, "because I need the room in my car." In fact, the drive-it-yourself small-car routine was a successful gimmick, adding to his unassailable good-guy image. "The secret to my good-guy image," he would say to his four sons, none of whom would leave home, "is that I really am a good guy."

He parked in the space reserved in the Capitol Hill lot for the Speaker of the House and walked up the stairs to the office of Mortimer Frelingheusen. Twenty years ago, as a freshman congressman from Brooklyn, Frangipani had worked on a committee whose chairman was the man from Wyoming who later became Speaker. Mort was a yellow-dog Republican, Andy a brass-collar Democrat, which meant that they were inclined to like each other, and the Secretary of Human Resources was satisfied that if he had a political friend he could trust in this town, it was the frankly partisan Speaker, who supported the Ericson Administration on foreign policy, opposed it on domestic affairs, and always provided a note of restraint when the "twenty-fivers" were baying.

Andy dropped his white straw fedora on the receptionist's desk, announced himself, and strolled around the ornate old waiting room, taking an interest in the pictures on the walls, thinking about what he wanted to say.

The Administration of which he was a proud part was on the ropes. Although the bureaucracy functioned, and the checks went out, the prevailing mood at Human Resources, his agency—which was inclined to like Ericson—was that the President was a political zombie. In Washington, he knew, moods took on lives of their own, echoing back in the press, reinforced by people who dealt with the press. The town was like the old Coney Island roller coaster, only you never knew if the car was likely to pull out of the dive.

In such a time, a good politician should count the numbers. Andy knew the numbers in the Cabinet; the Speaker would know the numbers in the House, and have a good idea about the Senate. If the numbers to throw Ericson out were not there, the time had come for some sensible pol to pass along this happy news to the President and the savvy press. If the numbers were there, then Angelo Frangipani should think about them and decide what to do.

To the Speaker, a wiry cadaver of a man, Andy came out quickly with what was in his heart: "I don't like what's happening in the country. Nobody sent me to you, Mort, and what we say here is graveyard, but it can't go on this way. It's got to be resolved."

"Is the President unable to carry out his duties?" Good ol' Mort, he got to the point in a hurry.

"He could, if they let him," Andy said, "but they're not letting him, which means that he can't. If everybody thinks you're not able to govern, then you're not. It's a self-sustaining prophecy."

"Fulfilling."

Andy gave his friend a disgusted look. "I know what a self-fulfilling prophecy is. I say 'self-sustaining,' and it's a colorful malapropism. If you understood that, Mort, you'd get ahead in politics."

The Speaker nodded, pulled a bottle and a couple of shot glasses out of a desk drawer, and poured them each a belt of bourbon. They sipped seriously a moment. The Speaker asked, "What is it like with Ericson—personally, I mean. He can't see, he can't tell where the next blow is coming from, he must be suffering. Is he withdrawn? Drinking? Punchy? Nervous? What?"

"They say he screws a lot," Andy replied, "which is a healthy sign. He's not drinking. He sleeps too much, maybe, which I do when I don't want to face the day. On the whole, though, he's been reacting better in the last couple of weeks than most people, under those circumstances. He's a scrapper, Mort—never sell him short. He likes that job."

"Are you getting the decisions you need out of him?"

Andy waved that aside. "Human Resources runs itself. It's by far the biggest department now, and the only dent a President can make in it is to say—'only grow by ten per cent this fiscal year.' He can decide that, whether it's five, ten, or fifteen, in a couple of months when he has to put the budget together. The rest is housekeeping. I can handle that."

"Does he feel guilty about the Yalta Deceit?" the Speaker asked.

"No."

"That's good." Mort surprised him with that reaction. "You can't walk around feeling guilty, and be a chief executive. He was wrong about the previous blindness. He should have said so, and gotten on with it."

"That's what he tried," Andy said, "then the shit hit the fan."

The Speaker shook his head. "He tried to slip past the blindness, and he got trapped in that other thing, the Yalta business. He didn't do the right thing in the campaign, but what's worse, he's handled it badly since."

"Granted," said Andy. "Is that a reason to replace him with Nichols?"

"Now we're down to the nut-cutting." The Speaker studied the amber fluid in his shot glass. "If it were up to me, I'd say to give the man a chance. On the lack of full disclosure on the previous blindness, he must admit he was wrong, frankly, fully. On the Yalta business, he can say his staff did what they thought was best for the country in a tight spot, and he'll back 'em up. He doesn't have to apologize for everything."

Andy put the question squarely: "If the Cabinet doesn't declare him disabled, will the House impeach him?"

"There are enough votes right now to impeach, a bare majority. But the process takes months, and you never know what the mood will be at voting time. Meanwhile, the country would be pretty much paralyzed. That's why I've scotched the impeachment crowd—the House is waiting to see what the Cabinet will do."

The ball was back in Andy's court. "If the Cabinet

votes him out, and he challenges it in the Congress, will the House sustain the Cabinet?"

"You only need a majority of the House to impeach," the Speaker said unhesitatingly, "but you need two thirds of the House to sustain a Cabinet removal. I've given this a lot of thought, and made some soundings, and here's my judgment: If this goes the impeachment route, the House will have its majority to impeach him, and the Senate will probably convict by the necessary two thirds. But if it goes the Cabinet route, using the Twenty-fifth Amendment, then the House will *not* have the two thirds it would need to uphold the Cabinet and keep Ericson out of office."

Frangipani whistled. "Then the situation won't be resolved. You're telling me there's no way of getting there from here."

"I'm telling you that Ericson has a forty per cent rock-solid support in the House. Most of the Democrats, and a few of my Republicans who know what sort of man Bannerman is, and some legal eagles who think a 'high crime' has to be treason. That's enough to deny the Congress a two-thirds vote. Count on it."

"If the Cabinet acts to remove him," said Andy slowly, "then the move to depose the President will fail in the House, you think. If the Cabinet does not act, then you think the House will impeach and the Senate convict him. Do I have it right?"

"You've always been able to count, Andy. You would have had a great future in the Congress. What's your count in the Cabinet?"

"Fong is for removal, of course. Today is Wednesday, the President is down in Williamsburg on that Law Day shindig, with Emmett Duparquet—and the reason Ericson went is to shore up the A.G., who is kind of shaky. Emmett didn't like the Hennessy business one bit, and he considers it a point of personal honor that the President misled him about the previous blindness."

"Cartwright at Defense will stick with the President," the Speaker judged. "He's that sort."

"Of course. Curtice at State will probably—I could

be wrong—vote for removal. At Treasury, Ericson put in Zack Parker, who hates Bannerman so much he'd stick up for the President if rigor mortis set in. So that's two sure for the President, one sure for removal, and two kind of leaning toward removal."

"And the Secretary of Human Resources?"

Frangipani spread his hands. "I dunno. All these years, whenever anybody told me he was 'undecided,' I used to say, 'The son of a bitch, he doesn't trust me.' The fact is, I'm undecided. That's really why I came, Mort. Got some advice?"

"No." The Speaker finished his drink in a gulp. "You have your constitutional responsibility, I have mine. Your move first."

Andy got up to go—more accurately, he got up to talk in the final minutes before going. "Ericson can't govern, because they all say he can't govern. The alternative is Nichols, who's a cat's paw for Bannerman. He's what my Jewish friends in Brooklyn describe as a 'momser'—a wrongo, and a dangerous one."

"I don't envy you the choice, Andy. Lesser of evils."

"Thing I'd like to do," said Andy, he hoped not too craftily, "is come up with an alternative. We're in politics, for God sakes, there's got to be another way out."

"Tell the President I feel for him, and I wish him well," the Speaker said. "I'm worried about this 'ability to govern' argument—that stretches the Twenty-fifth Amendment too far. If the President is physically or mentally disabled, that's one thing. But if he is unpopular, or weak, or has next to no support—we should be stuck with him for four years, because that's the term we elected him for. And I'm not the only one who thinks that way."

"Forty per cent rock-solid, huh?" Andy was hoping he could edge Frelingheusen's prediction over to a commitment, and was surprised not to be disappointed:

"If it should dip under that," said the Speaker, "I have some IOUs to call that would bring it back. I'd sit 'em in the front row, just like Sam Rayburn used to, and if I didn't need 'em, I'd let 'em vote their consciences or their districts. But if I did need 'em, they'd be there."

Andy did not want to press his luck, or give the Speaker time to qualify his remark. He had come as a seeker of advice and some support, and was leaving as a conveyor of the Speaker's voluntary guarantee. Frelingheusen spelled it out for him again in the doorway: "Ericson has a majority against him here in the House, enough to impeach. But there won't be the two thirds here to ratify any usurpation. Act accordingly. If you want to pass that on to the President's ears only, Andy, I'd have no objection, but I'd have to deny it if I read it anywhere."

The Secretary of Human Resources hurried down the hall, down the steps to his little car in the Speaker's space. There was a parking ticket on it. He started to go back up to have it fixed but changed his mind, the hell with it, he'd pay the ten dollars. Frelingheusen had done enough for the executive branch that day.

The Attorney General / 2

Emmett Duparquet stepped to the lectern, nodded cordially to his introducer, and took the welcoming applause during that exhilarating moment before delivering what he was certain was an excellent speech. The auditorium in Colonial Williamsburg was the Hall of Burgesses, redolent with Virginia history, one of the oldest speaking-places in America; the audience, crammed in, was made up of eminent attorneys and jurists, including, as he let his eye contact the group, many he knew. The White House press corps was there, too, spilling along the sides of the long, narrow room, having complained bitterly about bad position, and having been turned down by the Law Day functionaries.

The Attorney General was ambivalent about President Ericson's presence on the platform. On one hand, Ericson's decision to make his first post-ambush foray outside the White House underscored the importance of the occasion; the press corps trailing the President turned what would have been an elite, uncovered function into a nationwide media event. An excellent Duparquet speech, which would otherwise have gone unnoticed, would be excerpted for television that night and seen by 80 million Americans. On the other hand, the Attorney General would have been happier to be dissociated from the President during a week in which the Justice Department was in the process of indicting his chief aide. Duparquet was angry at the President, he admitted to himself: He had been Ericson's advocate in the Cabinet at a time of great crisis, and the client had held back vital information. Duparquet had been had, and he made it a rule never to be had twice.

But the President was right there, in person, his sightless eyes—he was not wearing dark glasses anymore—in full view of the audience. Duparquet was a member of his Cabinet, and his host at the Law Day ceremonies, and any show of coolness would be inflated out of all proportion—actually, into the proportion it deserved. If you help create a situation, the Attorney General told himself, you must do what the situation requires.

"In the Air Force during the war in Vietnam," he began—that reference to his heroism as a pilot was not out of place in this context—"and later in political life, I have been privileged to meet many brave men. It is an honor to share the platform today with a man whose personal bravery is an inspiration to all Americans—President Sven Ericson." Big applause; a salute to Ericson's bravery was unassailable, even to those who disputed his ability to govern, or were disgusted with his tolerance of corrupt or deceitful associates.

"The President will make a few informal remarks later in the afternoon," he said, "which makes me feel like Edward Everett, the man who was the main speaker at Gettysburg." Perhaps that was laying it on a bit thick, but the line was well received by an audience that was disposed to say we-like-you-but-who's-your-friend? Duparquet put on his glasses and launched into his address on the rule of law, which he knew would be interpreted in the light of the investigation of Hennessy and the duplicity of some of his fellow Cabinet members. His most effective passage—the one his press aide had marked for the television cameramen—concluded with a reference to John Adams and the concept of "a government of laws, not of men."

The handsome, tanned Floridian sat down to the right applause, neither polite nor thunderous, a judicious application of admiration from his legal peers. Duparquet was a man in a difficult situation, and the audience knew he knew they knew it.

The chairman, a retired justice of the Supreme Court, thanked him and conscious of propriety, introduced the President with the prescribed nine words. Duparquet and every person in the Hall of Burgesses watched Ericson rise, make a half-left, take five deliberate steps, make a half-right, reach out confidently, and touch the lectern. That was a relief. Then, before the President could say a word into the applause, the visual demonstration began.

Duparquet blanched. At four places in the hall, well-dressed demonstrators, who had blended in with the lawyers in the audience, rose and made their presence known with signs that had been stored under the seats. One sign read "Resign"; another "Deceit"; another "Take the 25th"; and another "Full Disclosure." The audience gasped and the applause died.

Since the demonstrators were silent, Duparquet was in a quandary: Should he go up to the President—

now standing alone at the lectern—and tell him about the signs? Should he let him speak, not knowing they were there? If he went up, that would make the demonstrators' point—that the President was near-helpless without staff aid; if he did not, the agonizing tension would drag on and on. There was no move by the Secret Service to remove the demonstrators or their signs.

"Everybody relax," the President said. "I can tell by the sound of the intake of breath, which is considerable, that the demonstration has begun."

The silent demonstrators looked puzzled; the cameras that had been focused on the signs swung to the speaker.

"For those of you that don't have a good angle," the President said quietly, "the signs read 'Resign' and 'Take the 25th' and similar sentiments. The purpose of a visual demonstration, silent, without the usual shouting, is to show how helpless and dependent I am.

"The truth is, I *am* dependent on others for the faculty of sight. This morning, the Secret Service agents told me that several signs were being smuggled into the Hall of Burgesses, and were being stashed away under the chairs.

"I told the agents to let the plan for the demonstration go forward, because it would be a way for me to demonstrate, too.

"We are met today in an ancient hall, the scene of some of the first stirrings of American liberty. Especially in such a setting, and on a day that celebrates the rule of law, it would have been wrong for me to do anything that would infringe on anyone's right to free speech."

The audience was still too shocked to react; Duparquet's sense of the occasion suggested to him that the President had some well-prepared few words to say that would capitalize on that shock, giving the audience a release from tension, and that would reflect well on him. The Attorney General could not help but root for the man on the podium, as would millions watching later on television film.

"I don't have a speech today," Ericson continued. "Couldn't read it if I had. This is a time for soberly reflecting on all the fine and wise things our Attorney General had to say, about our adherence to the rule of law." Total silence. The audience was mesmerized, the demonstrators frozen.

"One episode in history comes to mind, however. Perhaps it's only a legend, but they say that Lord Nelson, in a naval battle, was told by a frightened lieutenant that they were being attacked by a huge armada. The mate pointed to the fleet of ships coming at them and urged that Nelson order his ship out of harm's way."

The President paused. "Nelson, you will recall, had one blind eye, wore a patch over it. He said to his lieutenant, 'Give me your telescope.' He took the telescope, and in a way that all his men could observe, he held it up to his blind eye. He pretended to scan the horizon, and then he said, 'I see no armada. Sail on.' And they sailed into the Battle of Trafalgar, and won the fight that turned the tide of history."

He paused again, for effect. "As I look around this room today, I see no signs to frighten me. I am going to sail on, and this Administration is going to persevere."

The President turned around, waited for an agent to take his arm, and proceeded off the stage. The place exploded into cheers, with ordinarily reserved jurists shouting encouragement; even lawyers most convinced of the need for Ericson's resignation were clapping vigorously. The demonstrators put down their signs and made no move to reclaim them when the cameramen picked them up for close-ups. Duparquet stood, along with everyone, applauding until the President was well out of earshot.

"Damn good show," the Attorney General said hours later, in the cottage assigned to Melinda. "Fast thinking this morning. Was it Ericson's idea?"

She nodded. "He only got the word a half hour before the chopper was to leave. He called Jonathan Trumbull and they worked out the Nelson thing."

"And the writer just happened to have the Battle of Trafalgar anecdote at his fingertips?"

The President's secretary smiled broadly. "He's been collecting every blind episode that ever happened, from Samson on. This is one Hank Fowler used one day. It's probably not true, that's why the Boss said it may have been a legend, so the history buffs won't come at him."

The phone rang. He frowned as she moved to answer it. "Why don't you tell them you're off duty tonight?"

"I will," she promised. Fair was fair; if he was going to take the chance of not being reachable tonight, the least she could do would be to cut off the calls. "No, Harry, I wasn't going to take the chopper back," he heard her say. "It's an hour's flight and that's too long in one of those things, I have a nervous stomach as is. Is he pleased with himself? Good. No, I'm staying over here, back late in the morning." She bit her lip, uncertain about something. "Hennessy said to block her out. Who? Absolutely not. Never Marilee, you hear? Let it be Buffie then, better the devil we know. All right, but warn him. And tell the switchboard I'm going to sleep now, not to call unless the missiles are on the way. Good night, Harry, it was a good day. You'd have been proud."

"What's all that about?" Duparquet had no right to ask, and was startled when she gave him a direct answer: "The President's girl friend is on Bannerman's payroll. It makes things difficult."

"Roy Bannerman would do that?" Duparquet was genuinely shocked; that was dirty pool, the sort of hardball one associated with Arthur Leigh or Mark Hennessy. On the other hand, he thought, Leigh was evidently associated with Bannerman, and the deceit could be running in both directions.

"I just told you because you asked me," Melinda said. "If you don't want to know something, be careful what you ask. I trust you."

"Why do you look so good to me tonight?"

"Happy my boss did well today, I guess." Then she gave him what he wanted: "And the idea of being with you, and you not having to run off." She poured him a brandy, ignored the couch, and sat down across from him. "Emmett, I'm just not much of a quickie."

"We've got to stop meeting like this," he mocked.

She stretched—he liked to watch her arch her back—and came over to him. Long kiss, just mouth-to-mouth for a long time, no clutching because he had plenty of time tonight. She loosened and took off his tie, slipped her hand inside, and massaged the knot of muscles behind his neck. He cupped her breasts, gently supported their weight as she rubbed, and they nibbled at each other familiarly until she drew back.

"You don't wear lipstick."

"Little chapstick, but nothing anybody'll see on your collar. And why do you suppose you find plain Ivory soap in the bathroom at my place?"

"Because you don't want me to go off smelling like a girl's soap." He hadn't thought about that thoughtfulness before.

"I'm no home wrecker," she said lightly, pulling one of her long black hairs off his jacket. "And I don't want to lose you."

"There's a time to build, and a time to wreck," he told her, not so lightly. He wanted to find a time to plant the seed of an idea that his intentions, as they used to say, were not wholly dishonorable. He did not want to make any commitments, but he wanted her to become closer to him. He was fifty-four, she was thirty-eight; he had long ago lost interest in his wife, and his children were already away at school; he could see himself building a new life with this woman, who didn't need to be briefed on the background of everything. He could talk with her, man to man, make love to her, man to woman, and just be together, friend to friend. He had never found that combination before. He wondered if he had any competition. The affection between Melinda and Ericson seemed to him avuncular; the President would undoubtedly bless the match, if he ever got over his surprise. As far as Duparquet knew, there were no other men that Melinda saw; in the past two months, since Yalta, she had always been available to him, if she wasn't working late.

The phone broke in again. "I thought you turned that off."

She picked it up angrily. "Yeah?" She softened a little. "Put Mr. Trumbull on. Hey, look, Jonathan, I'm taking the night off. Why don't you call the President? He likes to hear good news." She motioned for him to pick up the extension.

"Uh-uh," the writer was saying, "Buffie's with him, and I'll be damned if I'll read the reactions to him with my girl listening in on the other line, bare-assed naked—"

Melinda interrupted quickly, looking at Duparquet listening in on the extension, and the look of mock-horror he put on his face. "The hell with the President, then, Jonathan. Let him suffer. Let him go to sleep thinking his big day got botched up. That'll be your revenge, for the way he's trying to hold on to the girl you're stealing from him."

"Okay." The voice was grudging, but still excited —it was, Duparquet realized, the young man's historical allusion to Lord Nelson that would be remembered in history, and his pride in that took precedence over all other emotions. "And while I'm at it, I'll tell him all the pictures his goddamn official photographer took showed him looking awkward. See how she likes that. Melinda, you're all right—I wish I were old enough to rate you."

"You'll never be that old, Jonathan. Glad you called, don't call back." She put down the phone and walked out on the porch of the reconstructed cottage. Duparquet followed her out into the starless summer night, and sat with her on the anachronistic rocking settee.

"Why did we do away with verandas?" she wondered.

"Bugs," the Floridian answered. "In olden times,

people got bitten all the time, spent half their waking hours scratching. So then we had screened-in porches, which were teats on a bull in the winter. So then we made them glassed-in patios. No more verandas, but no more bugs."

"I'll scratch your back if you'll scratch mine." Duparquet caught that quick bridge back to politics. He took her hand and they swung silently in the sofa for a while. She tucked her legs under her and he pushed.

"You mustn't get euphoric about one good effort by the President," he cautioned her, "or by one part of one newspaper column." Why was he talking politics? Wrong foot. He decided to forget Ericson that evening, but she picked it up.

"Why can't I enjoy some good news, or a decent reaction? This place hasn't been a barrel of laughs over the past week."

"I don't want you to be hurt, Melinda. Don't get your hopes up." He knew of too much bad news in the pipeline, most of which he would have a hand in delivering.

"You mean Hennessy?"

He couldn't not tell her. "Hennessy will be indicted on Friday for lying to the grand jury."

"That's pretty quick."

"You're right," he said, and was uncomfortable about the speed of the process, "but this is an affair of state. When the chief aide of the President of the United States lies to a grand jury, that rates a faster reaction than in ordinary cases."

All she said was "Does it?" which irritated him, because the principle of all men standing equal before the law was, to some degree, undercut in this manner. The U. S. Attorney, who technically reported to the Attorney General, was an ambitious young man who smelled blood and headlines in the Hennessy case, and had acted in undue haste; he was also a little too sure about the timing of his indictment, which meant he had a rubber-stamp grand jury. Duparquet was also disturbed because the U. S. Attorney was generally known to be a "Bannerman appointment," in one of the spoils cuts at the nominating convention last year, and could have an additional interest in embarrassing the White House this week. The Attorney General did not want to betray these doubts to the President's secretary, however; he understood that she personally disliked Hennessy, and blamed him for most of the President's dilemma, but still—an indictment this soon could seem to her to be politically inspired, and he did not want to add fuel to that fire.

"It would have caused quite a hullabaloo," he answered instead, "if I had overruled the U. S. Attorney, and the head of the Criminal Division at Justice, to slow down this case."

"Might have made it look like you were part of a cover-up," she said, in a quiet voice that troubled him. Duparquet felt that she was leading him into a trap.

"That's so," he said warily.

"Would have taken a real jerk to stand up against the threat of a hullabaloo," she said evenly, swinging back and forth slowly in the darkness, "upholding an individual defendant's rights. Sort of a spoilsport who tries to argue with a lynch mob." That stung him. He had repressed his conscience on that score, and did not appreciate the matter brought up by someone he wanted so much to respect him. "Sometimes you have to do something that makes it look like you're not a man of integrity," she continued, "and doing it makes you the only one to know that you really are a man of integrity."

The Attorney General finished the thought for her. "And sometimes you do something that makes you appear to the public to be a person of integrity, which really shows you up to yourself as selfish and venal."

"I suppose that follows," she agreed.

"For God's sake, Melinda, the man offered Leigh a bribe, a position that would have paid money into his pocket, with the authority of the President of the United States. That kind of corruption has to be rooted out immediately, even if a few corners are cut, because the public must maintain its faith in government." That put matters back in perspective, he thought; we weren't dealing here with auto theft.

"That's a very important end," she said in a voice so small he had to strain forward. "Justifies the means, I guess."

"Jesus H. Christ!" He lunged out of the creaking settee and went inside for his brandy. He came back in a moment and sat on the veranda railing, looking at her form in the dark. "Okay. On hard principle, I should have slowed the speed of that prosecution. I should have asked the U. S. Attorney what crime he was investigating in the first place, and why he had to go the perjury route—there's no doubt that Hennessy could have beaten any charge of outright bribery. And in so doing, I would have been tarred with the brush that's ruining everybody near Ericson—not only was I his advocate in the Cabinet, I was blocking the indictment of his chief aide. Obstructing justice, it would have been called. My career would have ended at that point, and I would have had the satisfaction of knowing that you—and I—knew I had done the principled thing."

"I'd have scrubbed floors for us," mocked the form in the dark.

"Be serious. There are a multitude of facets in every prosecutor's decision. When a cop commits a crime, he gets the book thrown at him, and he can't complain about 'equal justice'—he betrayed a public trust, and that's what Hennessy did."

"Why do you suppose he did it? Make a buck for himself?"

She should have been a lawyer, he decided. "I suppose he felt that the end of keeping the President's secret justified the means," Duparquet replied. "And the truth is—sometimes it does and sometimes it doesn't. In the decision facing Hennessy, the end did not justify the means. In the decision facing me, it did."

"That's a sensible answer," she said. "Come sit on the settee, it stopped rocking." He could not; she had him riled up now, and the porch was a good place to pace.

"We might as well have the fundamental issue out," he told her. "One of these days, the ways things are going, the Cabinet will come together again under the Twenty-fifth. The last time, I was the President's lawyer, because I believed in the case. Not because I liked Ericson, which I do, or because it was the smart thing to do politically, which it was. I convinced others, and I convinced myself, on the basis of a set of facts that turned out to be false."

"And now you're going to get even with him."

"Not at all." She did have a way of infuriating him by identifying his self-doubts. "I made a big point out of this: that the American public made its judgment on Election Day in possession of all the facts about Ericson's eyesight. I said that nothing was withheld. That was a lie—I didn't lie, I thought I was telling the truth—but the fact was not a fact, it was a false-hood. The Cabinet decision was made—partially at least—on the basis of an outright lie. Now, when a prosecutor discovers evidence that clears a defend-ant, he must make it available to the defense. In the same way, when the President's defender has used a lie to defeat his opponents, he must find a way to make it up."

"Come on, Emmett, you just don't want to go down with the Ericson ship."

He stopped pacing. "I won't deny that. But there's much more to it. My client lied to me—"

"He did that to protect you. You're innocent. If he had told you, you'd have had to go along, just over-looking the point you made about full disclosure. Aren't you glad now, in your heart of hearts, that he didn't tell you?"

"Absolutely not!" He went back to sit on the rail. "Wait a second now, here come the late returns from the heart of hearts—the answer is yes. I'm clean. But Ericson didn't do it to protect me, did he? From the heart of hearts?"

"He didn't tell you because he thought you had no

need to know," she admitted. "Mistake. If he had told you, you wouldn't have made such a big deal out of full disclosure. But you don't mean you'll double-cross him because he didn't tell you everything—"

"Double-cross is a loaded word," he said, having none of that. If she was going to argue with him, she would go by some rules of evidence. "I'm going to refuse to defend him as a law officer making a constitutional decision."

"You really think he's in a coma, or crazy?"

"That's your definition, and those columnists'. That's not my definition of an inability to carry out his duties."

"He's just too unpopular, you mean?"

"His blindness is a part of it. His psychological reaction to the pressure is part of it. And the nation's reaction to his physical and psychological condition is part of it. It's a vicious circle, getting worse all the time, and the totality of it is such as to cause, in effect, disability."

"You just said you weren't going to defend him. You sound like you're going to vote against him."

"I may." Duparquet went ahead and made the decision: "Yes, I am." He had been kidding himself about keeping an open mind.

The phone rang again. He glowered at her. "I don't mind when it interrupts my love-making, but now it's interrupting my train of thought."

"This may be a good time for a break," she said, and went in to take it. That was bad, he thought, she should have let it ring. If she had let it ring, she would have been telling him something about her priorities.

He made no effort to listen, but heard her talking to a "Mr. Goodfriend." In a moment, she was back, but did not sit down.

"You have it neatly set up," she said coldly. "Fong is going to call the Cabinet together for Friday afternoon. That's just a few hours after Hennessy's indictment is handed down."

"Indictments are handed up," he corrected automatically. "I didn't know the timing, Melinda. It does seem kind of orchestrated."

"And you have your instrument to play. What has Bannerman promised you?"

"That's a cheap shot."

"It was," she said dully, "I'm sorry." He put his hands on her shoulders and she twisted away. "I'm disappointed in you, Emmett."

"We disagree about the President," he said. "We disagree about Hennessy. I may be right on some things, you may be right on others. When this is all over—"

"—it's over. You've had everything Ericson had to offer, and you've had everything I have to offer. Now you move on down life's one-way street."

He would not accept that. She was upset, over-wrought—okay, this was a bad evening. But people did not make decisions about their personal lives and futures on the basis of political disagreements. On the other hand, he recognized, she had nothing from him to suggest that he was serious about her. "When this is over," he continued, "we'll see each other again. And I'm not just talking about love in the afternoon, or playing around. I'm serious about you. I love you. I want—" he stopped before going too far. "I want to discuss long-range ideas with you, about a life to-gether."

"The moment is right here, now," she said in a rush, "on this stupid reconstructed veranda, with no screens to keep out the bugs. You're cutting Hennessy's throat, railroading a man to prison against all your own principles, doing wrong because it looks right. You're conniving to run the President out of office, turning the country over to the worst kind of people, because —mainly, because your nose is out of joint at not be-ing told everything, and partly because you know which way the wind is blowing. You're a politician, Emmett, but you're not a political man."

"And Sven Ericson is?"

"He's becoming one. God, it's a pity you guys have to put us all through such hell to get there."

He stood at the brink of a fierce answer, and controlled himself, because he wanted her more than he wanted to win a point. He sought to narrow the difference between them: "I can't believe that all we have is to be sacrificed because of a political disagreement—"

"You know it's more than that. The kind of man you are is the kind of man Sven Ericson was a few months ago. You think you'll luck your way through, and get everything, no cost, no pain. You'll get it, maybe, but with somebody else. I've already paid my dues."

"I want to stay with you tonight."

"I'll sleep alone. I know how."

"Melinda, have I made myself—I mean, do you know everything you're turning down?"

She nodded. "I had it all figured out. I was not only going to be the second Mrs. Duparquet of Boca Raton, Florida. I was going to be the First Lady after next."

"There is still that possibility." She would make him a damn fine First Lady.

"A lot depends on what you do in the next couple of days."

She obviously meant what she said; disappointed, frustrated, but not confused, he left the cottage and spent the night awake by himself.

The Soviet Leader / 2

At the sound of the bolt sliding back, Vasily Nikolayev looked away from his television set toward the cell door. Since the Lubyanka warden could not decide whether its occupant was to be a traitor, a show-trial star, or a General Secretary, the cell was fairly well appointed, and the prisoner was one of the few in custody permitted to wear a belt. Nikolayev had been watching the Eurovision report, carried to Moscow on a cable restricted to Soviet officials, which showed highlights of the American President's dramatic dealings with demonstrators in Williamsburg. He was pleased for Ericson, linking the President's political fate with his own.

Slovenski, the professional survivor, entered the cell. Nikolayev knew that the neutral bureaucrat, who had made a career out of not offending factions within the Politburo, was usually chosen to bring prisoners good news.

"I have good news," he began, and took a chair next to Nikolayev's in front of the television.

"I know," said Nikolayev, motioning him to be quiet until the newscast was over, as if he had been certain the investigation would clear him. After a few moments, which was all he needed to make his point and all he could stand, the prisoner rose, turned off the set, and looked toward Slovenski. "The investigation revealed the truth?"

"Yes," said Slovenski cheerfully. "You conspired with the Air Force leaders to kill Kolkov and Ericson, and to blame it on the Chinese."

Nikolayev did not let any fear show. "You call that good news."

"No," said Slovenski, "I call that truth, which is what you asked for. The good news is that you have been named Premier by the Presidium. At the next party congress, if all goes well, you will be elected General Secretary."

"Tell me the rest in the car," Nikolayev said. He was free, and although the cell was the best in Lubyanka, he wanted to get out of there more than he had been willing to admit to himself. They walked down the corridor, past the cells where he knew his Air Force coconspirators had been kept. "What happened to them?"

"They died in a plane crash," Slovenski said.

FULL DISCLOSURE

In the Zis limousine, driving through Dzerzhinski Square toward the Kremlin, the neutral bureaucrat explained the seeming contradictions. "After it was determined that you planned the ambush, the question that split the Politburo was whether you did the right thing in getting rid of old Kolkov. Split was deeper than ever, and the matter got out of hand, into the Presidium."

"First time," Nikolayev remarked. He pulled back the drape and looked at the streets, still in daylight. First time, too, that a move of a political prisoner had taken place at a reasonable hour.

"Last, I hope. Took forever. The decision was that Kolkov was planning a pre-emptive strike against the Far Eastern powers, that this was beyond his authority, and that you acted in the interests of the party in eliminating him."

Nikolayev nodded. "And the official results of the investigation will say—"

"Something else. Just as you said, the Chinese tried to kill both leaders to drive the two superpowers apart. It is felt that such a finding is in our best interest, and it follows from that you are to be the Premier."

"And my Air Force friends?" Nikolayev thought briefly of the brave men who had conspired with him to prevent a war.

"Kolkov had many friends. Killing a General Secretary cannot go unpunished. But they are not in disgrace, they died in an accident."

Nikolayev nodded, in resignation or approval, then thought of the three men on the Politburo who had been pallbearers with him at the Kolkov funeral. They would have to be ousted promptly. He asked Slovenski about their whereabouts and was told they were all in Moscow.

"Power stations," Nikolayev said decisively. "One becomes the director of the power station in Irkutsk, the other in Samarkand, the other in Novosibirsk. They are never to contact each other."

When his fellow passenger said nothing, Nikolayev added, "There is a fourth power station. Hard job, cold winter. That is the one that you will direct if those three men are not out of Moscow by eight o'clock tomorrow morning."

Slovenski shook his head. "Perhaps someday, when you are General Secretary. Not yet. Everybody stays in place." Nikolayev sagged inwardly. He was not in power; he was a figurehead. As the car swept through Red Square and swung into the narrow entrance in the Kremlin Wall, Slovenski continued, "Another reason why it was decided you will be declared innocent and falsely accused is that we believe it is in our interest for President Ericson to remain in power."

Nikolayev said nothing, knowing the explanation would be forthcoming. Slovenski went on: "First, the alternative to him is the banker Bannerman, acting through Nichols. Bannerman, as you know, is intractable, and his inclination is to deal separately with the Far Eastern powers. Most of the men in his foundations and on his staff are Chinese and Japanese experts, and he would probably cause a division in the U.S.S.R.-U.S. alliance. Ericson, on the other hand—"

"—is blind. Is weak. Would be grateful for my help." Nikolayev could not believe his fellow members of the Politburo would stand for such nonsense.

"You have a subtler mind than that, comrade." Slovenski grinned. "We have already let it be known, through Gregor, that you and President Ericson's men plotted to make up a story of Kolkov being a hero, saving Ericson's life at Yalta. It is being called the Yalta Deceit. You and Ericson are in it together. That obligates him to you."

Nikolayev waited. That was not enough.

"Second, we have the option of letting the real truth be known at any time, that you ordered Ericson killed. This would put public pressure on Ericson not to react strongly to certain initiatives of ours, for seeming to respond to a personal grudge. He would have to prove he was acting as a careful President, not as a man out to get even."

Nikolayev shook his head impatiently. "Be serious.

This decision to give me a second chance was made in the past few days. Why?"

"Ericson invited you to visit Washington," Slovenski said gruffly, "without checking with us first. Now we could make him look like a fool, which will help drive him from power, or we could make him look very smart, which will help him stay in power. To that extent, his future is in our hands. It is felt, though not unanimously, that we can use you to make him beholden to us."

Now it was beginning to make sense to Nikolayev. His initial instinct—that his own fate was tied to Ericson's—had been right. Just as the Americans had thought that helping Nikolayev through the Kolkov story would obligate the Soviet leader, so the Politburo thought that using him to shore up Ericson would obligate the American leader. Turnabout, fair play. But wouldn't the real truth get out one day soon, since the KBG and CIA were exchanging information? Not officially; Ericson would know that Nikolayev first tried to kill him, then tried to save him. Trying to put himself in Ericson's shoes, Nikolayev found only conflicting emotions.

"He will think I am insincere," Nikolayev observed, and Slovenski grunted a laugh. On balance, the move was sound: Ericson in power thanks to Soviet influence would be better than Bannerman in power contrary to Soviet influence. The trick would be to get Ericson to ask for Nikolayev's help to establish a *quid pro quo* for the future.

They lurched forward as the car stopped in front of Nikolayev's apartment in the Kremlin. The Soviet leader walked upstairs alone and was embraced amidst tears by his wife and three children, who had not known if they would ever see him again. He could not share their sense of joyous relief; he was safe only as long as he was useful.

That night, in the darkened living room of his apartment, he sat alone and worked out his position. If Ericson could serve out his term, Nikolayev would have three years to consolidate his power. The Premier's post was almost meaningless; but if he had the title of General Secretary as well, he could slowly wrest control of the key party posts from the old Kolkov men.

Step one was to get word to Ericson that the Soviet Premier was ready to help if asked. Ericson had to personally make the request, that was essential to lay the basis for the future obligation. Step two was to do whatever was necessary to keep Ericson in office.

How to get in touch with Ericson? The hot line went through two bureaucracies. Possibly he could deal through Curtice, but he could not be sure if Curtice was an Ericson man or a Bannerman ally, in the Byzantine world of Washington politics. There was always Gregor, the official out-of-channels man in the gray world of publishing and diplomacy; he would doubtless inform Nikolayev's enemies in the Kremlin what approaches the new Premier was making, but since Nikolayev was supposed to be getting Ericson obligated, that would do no harm.

Gregor would be the channel, he decided. The next day, he would send a probe through Gregor to ask Ericson when an announcement of the Soviet acceptance of the American invitation would be most propitious. That simultaneous announcement would prove for Ericson's sake that the two leaders were in close touch, that the American President knew what was going on in the Soviet Union, and that he was not only not a blunderer, but a man in masterful control of world events.

The Russian tried to imagine himself in Ericson's position: out of sight, out of popularity, nearly out of power, struggling to hold on. Nikolayev's position was somewhat different: out of power, still in place, with a chance of changing the shadow back into substance. During his visit to Moscow and on the way to Yalta, the American had been a confident, almost cocksure man, the child of fortune. Surely the loss of his eyesight had plunged him into a depression; but the man Nikolayev had seen on the hot-line screen not long ago seemed confident enough. Perhaps that seeming confidence was real, drawn from some hidden well-spring of faith; on the other hand, perhaps the confidence was evidence of Ericson's lack of contact with reality. If they both managed to win back their power, Nikolayev wondered, would he be able to manipulate such an unpredictable person? Would the blindness turn out to be some kind of subtle advantage at a summit?

He yawned, enjoyed a long stretch far from the chilling confines of Lubyanka, rose and strode for the bedroom door, immediately crashing his shinbone against a coffee table that had been moved in his absence. He fell heavily over the table, laden with dishes and a samovar, shouting a curse as the china shattered all around. His wife came running in her nightgown and helped him limp to the bathroom, soaked with tea, laughing at the release from tension and from prison. Nikolayev had, in a sense, put himself in Ericson's shoes, and it taught him a lesson: A blind man has a perverse advantage in knowing he does not know what obstacles lie ahead.

The Official Photographer / 4

"You son of a bitch hack writer, you never wrote a decent speech in your life!" Buffie slammed down the extension's receiver, drew the white terry cloth robe tightly around her, and felt tears stinging in her eyes.

"That was my official photographer," the President said calmly into his extension. "She must have picked up the phone and listened in. Sorry about the eavesdropping, Jonathan, but I have a hunch you suspected as much. She rose to your bait."

She shook her head, mopping her eyes angrily with

the toweling. That wasn't the bait she had risen to. When Jonathan finished reading the President the one decent column about him, and then began going on about how lousy Buffie's photographs were, she knew the writer didn't mean it about the photographs. The man she loved was saying he knew she was there, and worse, listening in to him talking to the man she was in bed with, and Jonathan was baiting her to feel guilty about it. The infuriating part was that she did, first time in her life. So she told him off, and if it embarrassed Ericson, the hell with that. It didn't embarrass him, of course, now that she thought of it; he was putting down the young man by seeing through the whole situation, and probably enjoying it.

When the President put down the phone, she said, "I got a confession to make, Potus." She was curled in the chair, watching his long frame stretched out on the bed, diagonally as usual, probably feeling all pleased after having made good love after a good day and getting good news. Ericson had found his stroke again, moving into her with that steady, self-satisfying rhythm he had long ago in the campaign, not the grabby, needing groping-about of the past couple of months. She liked the old way better, herself, because she went for men who were cool and independent and let her be the same, but Jonathan complicated the picture. She knew that Potus needed her less now, but that—surprisingly—did not draw her back to him. Why did he need her less? Probably because Silent Sam with the big tits was servicing him better than ever. How could a working photographer, with rough hands from working in the lab soup compete with a registered nurse trained in Swedish massage? Buffie's thoughts swerved back to customary shrewdness: That wasn't it. Potus is feelin' better, and he's movin' on. Good thing for both of us. Now she had to get away from Bannerman.

"Don't lay your guilt on me, Buffie, I've got all I can handle."

She went on. "You know I been playin' footsie with Bannerman, and those guys. The baddies."

"I know."

"Nothing serious, I never let on about the campaign train, just little stuff, comings and goings. I figured it would help me later, all his money and publishing contacts, make me an editor and who knows what." Ericson said nothing. "I wasn't being disloyal to you. You know?"

Ericson put his hands behind his head and stretched. He was a good-looking man, for late forties, if you liked a lot of angles and flat planes and knobby joints. "Sure you were being disloyal, Buffie. But you were also there when I needed you, and they canceled each other out. So relax."

"I can't relax. I'm scared shitless."

"I won't fire you. Hell, I can't tell whether your pictures come out or not."

He didn't understand. "Lookit, Potus, it's not you that scares me. You're a good guy. Deep down no heart, maybe, but a friend. But Bannerman scares me plenty, I mean really, no foolin'. I thought I could kind of play both ends against the middle, but I'm over my head. This is no game, this White House life —people play for keeps. They're mean."

"What's he threatening you with?"

"Everything." She started breathing heavily, but she did not want to cave in, so she grabbed hold of herself. "He got my old boy friend fired from his job, just for a sample. All he had to do was snap his fingers and the guy was finished. He can ruin my Dad's business, which isn't hard to do, and make life hard for my sister, and God knows what he can do to black-list me forever in magazines—"

"Those are just threats, Buffie."

"Potus, believe me, this guy likes to hurt. He slammed me pretty good and I could tell he got a kick out of it—"

"He hit you?"

She didn't want Ericson to center on the insignificant part. "I was getting a little hysterical, and he slapped me to shape up, but the part that scared me—"

"He *hit* you?" Ericson sat up in bed and looked toward her, amazed.

"That wasn't the big deal, Potus. It's the way he *could* hit me that's makin' my life miserable. Bannerman's powerful, got friends everywhere, people who have to do what he says."

"He hit you. Where?"

"In the head, where it doesn't show. Forget it."

"Buffie, was it a sexual thing? You been putting out for him?"

She shook her head.

"Answer me, Buffie."

"I'm sorry. No, he's a very moral person. Only straight I ever met who doesn't play around."

"Then he hit you to snap you out of hysterics he drove you into, and then made sure the fear sunk in. Oh, that prick. Okay." The President sat on the edge of the bed, facing her, businesslike. "What does he want you to do?"

"First he wanted me to give you a message, and fast, which is why I told Harry Bok if he wouldn't let me in tonight I'd climb in the window or do something drastic. I would've, too, Silent Sam or not."

"Who?"

"Silent Sam, with the big tits, fast smooth hands, the can of oil in her pocket—"

"What was his message? I hope you wrote it down."

"I made notes," she said, grabbing her photographer's case and pulling out the caption pad. She looked at the notes. "The best thing for the country, he thinks, is for you to resign." She guessed the President knew that already, so she hurried on. "He says you have to think about financial security, being blind and all, and he can guarantee a five-million-dollar package for your memoirs."

"They're worth about three," Ericson commented. "Go on."

"More important, he figures, is 'an ongoing activity worthy of your talents.' Do I have that right? He says the Institute of International Economic Studies would be the vehicle. It's funded with three million now, headquarters in Washington. He says it could be funded with thirty million, and located wherever you like."

"Under his control?"

"Wait a minute, I have something here about that, too. You would have the right to name the new board of directors, and it would be self—uh, self—"

"Perpetuating."

"Bingo."

"Anything else? After all, it's the presidency."

"He said you could name anything you wanted for me. That's not important." She felt awkward about mentioning it. Bannerman thought she had an emotional hold on the President, and did not understand that she and Potus had begun to drift into a kind of friendship.

"No, that's the only important part. Okay, those are the carrots—what's the stick?"

"You mean did he ask me to pass on a threat?" She wished Ericson would not squeeze her for all the information she had.

"Uh-huh."

"I don't think he did. He may have, and I forgot it. No, it was me he was threatening, not you." Bannerman knew better than to threaten Ericson, she reasoned.

"Now Buffie, I want you to get this straight. You got a pencil? Tomorrow morning, that's Thursday morning, you tell him that I consider his message to be an offer of a bribe. Write down these words—'an arrogant attempt to purchase the presidency.'" He said them slowly and she got them down. "Now add this: 'Any action against you or yours would be prima facie'—p-r-i-m-a, f-a-c-i-e—'evidence of coercion of me.' You understand, Buffie? That would be an overt act, evidence of the offer of a bribe."

"Jesus, Potus, was what I said really a bribe?"

"Bannerman would say no. He'd say it was an honorable offer to persuade me to do my duty, and to assure me that I would not become destitute if I resigned. I'd get on my high horse and say it was a dirty, low-down bribe."

"What would I say?"

"What you would say would be very important. You would say the truth, exactly, not a word added. You got those notes you took down of what he told you? Give them to me." She handed them over, wishing her handwriting had been more neat, all the editors complained about her illegible captions. The phone buzzed on the President's bedside table.

"I'll go out," she offered.

"No, stay, I won't say anything that could be beaten out of you." He took up the receiver surely, not groping, and said, "Yes. All right, I'll take her. Yes, Melinda, I'm here with Buffie. Friday? That's fast. Hennessy—the bastards. How come you're there alone? Oh." She must have said something that affected him. "Sorry about that. See you in the morning —I won't need the News Summary, Jonathan read me the good part. Get in on time, I'll be in the office at eight." He put the phone into its cradle slowly, without thinking, and shook his head when he said, "I don't bring people luck any more."

"Luck changes, Potus."

"Come here, give me your hands." She knelt next to him at the bedside, putting her hands in his. "My hands are my worst part," she explained. "My hands and my feet—unattractive. The rest of my body is milk-white, with a delicious dusting of freckles as befits a woman with coppery blond hair and blazing green eyes."

"Who wrote that?"

"Jonathan. He may not write you good speeches, but man, he writes me sizzlin' love letters."

That pleased Ericson, who had a good laugh, pleasing her in turn. She had the foreknowledge that this was to be their last time together, with nobody making a big decision about it. She was sad about that, but relieved in a way; mistressing for a President was high-pressure stuff, and no fun if you felt guilty.

"You kids going to move in together? Cohabit?"

"Hell, no, Potus." He really did not understand younger people, she realized. "That's old-fashioned, seventies stuff. That's for Marilee and her network guy, thinking that hanging loose in life is off the wall. Or for Melinda and the A.G., running away from a decision—there's a screwed-up pair of tight-asses for you. No, thanks. Jonathan and me, we're going to do it like upfront people, the modern way—marriage contracts and babies and mortgages and a-deal's-a-deal. Unless Bannerman messes everything up."

"All right, Buffie, out with it." He held her hands firmly, his own hands swallowing them up. "I can't look in your eyes to see if you're telling the truth, but I have a secret blind man's way of telling through your fingers." Her heart sunk. He knew she was superstitious and would believe that, and she did. "Now, how else is Bannerman planning to use you? What else has he got cooked up for me?"

"You were getting laid on the train when you hit your head," she blurted. "I'm supposed to spill that story to a reporter tomorrow, in time for a big clobber-Ericson day on Friday. I didn't tell him about it, Potus —that bastard Leigh must have. But they figure it shows how immoral you are, a dirty old man who can't wait between campaign stops. Bannerman thinks that'll be a big deal."

"Gives me a venal motive for covering up the accident," Ericson thought aloud. "Hennessy would call that a good, dirty shot." He squeezed her hands. "Here's what to do: Read Bannerman what I told you about the bribe. Tell him you added in the stuff about being with me when the accident happened, because you thought it would scare me. And I said that further substantiates the extortion. Get the pencil, e-x-t-o-r-t-i-o-n. Then you crack up. Go into hysterics, act like a nut. It's all been too much for you. Got it?"

"That shouldn't be hard."

"He'll back off, you'll see. You won't have to go through with the reporter bit, because you're uncontrollable, and he'll know it. He may even get worried about my bribe accusation, and you're central so he'll want you calmed down. That's for the short term."

He leaned back on the pillow and motioned for her to join him in bed. Still in the robe, she lay next to him. "What's with the towel?" She slipped it off reluctantly. He held her body easily, rubbing her arm, thinking. "Buffie, your best insurance policy would be a book."

"Blackmail? That's been done to death."

"No, a book to be published. Your life in the White House, with me. The involvement with Bannerman. Beautiful girl in the middle—"

"—milk-white skin."

"—no, seriously, I mean it. Include the threats to your family. Let Bannerman threaten to sue you, he'd never go through with it, he wouldn't want to give a sworn deposition on this."

"I'm no writer."

"But you're in love with a writer, and the poor sap is out of his head in love with you. Write it together." He was squeezing her arm now, excitedly. She would have a bruise to hide from Jonathan in the morning.

"Be a hell of a first. And a damn good book about me, too. Tell it all—how I really loved you, and gave you up in the end to a younger man." First time Potus ever admitted that. "I've spent some time with Jonathan, figuring he'd write a book one day, and telling him all about my dream for the country. Very uplifting. But if he did a normal White House insider book, pro-Ericson, it wouldn't sell worth a damn. The love story would sell like mad."

"Do they ever have pictures in a book like that?" Potus never quite grasped the idea that she was a professional photographer.

"Oh, sure, pictures and text." He thought a moment. She was thinking the same thing. "Say, you know that roll of film you shot of us that time in Camp David, the weekend before the Inaugural, with the doohickey that you set and got the two of us together? That was pretty intimate stuff, but I wouldn't mind . . ."

"I'd mind," she said. "Jonathan would go up the flue."

"You're kidding." Then he realized she was kidding. "He could handle the whole thing tastefully. No vulgarity, ever. Sincere emotions, the way they really were."

Were. Then why, she wondered, if Potus had become her new uncle, were they lying naked in bed together? He read her question.

"There has to be a last time," he said gently. "A fond farewell. Tomorrow, we'll be friends."

"I was hoping you could handle it," she said, moving in as close as she could, her forehead and nose along the curve of his jaw, as he liked.

"So was I," he said, "this and something else."

"Whoever wakes up first," she told him, "don't wake the other." But she knew he was not ready to go to sleep.

The Secretary of Natural Resources

Mike Fong, seated in the West Wing hallway outside the Cabinet Room on the day that had already been dubbed "Black Friday" by an expectant press, was not so sure that this Cabinet meeting had been a good idea. He had expressed his reservations to Roy Bannerman: The twenty-fivers did not have the votes securely in hand.

The positive decisions of four out of six Cabinet members were needed to remove the President. Fong's vote was one. Curtice's vote, to expiate his growing sense of guilt for the Yalta Deceit, was a second. A possibility for the third was Emmett Duparquet, the advocate for the President on the last go-around who had been taken for a fool by his client; remembering the mistake of putting pressure on Preston Reed before the last meeting, Fong had prevailed on Bannerman to leave Attorney General Duparquet strictly alone.

But where was the fourth? Not Lucas Cartwright, now in Reed's place as Secretary of Defense. Not Zack Parker, a forthright Bannerman-hater from square one. And Andy Frangipani at Human Resources, voting his constituency of the handicapped and the compassionate, was an Ericson stalwart.

"Where's the sense in it?" Fong had asked Bannerman. "If we go in and lose again, Ericson will fire me for sure, along with anybody else who goes against him. Then what hope do we have?" Fong was not looking forward to losing his government job, Bannerman's private guarantees notwithstanding.

"Impeachment, for one," Bannerman had replied. "That's what they impeached Andrew Johnson for, firing a Cabinet officer. We'll need every precedent we can find, if it goes impeachment. Firing you after an abortive Twenty-fifth Amendment move would be a fatal mistake for Ericson. We have to force him to make mistakes."

When Fong had muttered something about not liking to lose in the Cabinet every couple of weeks, Bannerman had let him know who was calling the shots: "Mike, you have to keep crashing into that door of the Oval Office. If it doesn't break down, you go crashing at it again. The pressure on Ericson in these moments has to be enormous. No man can stand it for long."

Orders were orders, and Mike Fong went along. Certainly Bannerman had a point about the pressure: For ten days, the Ericson Administration had been under a bombardment in the press, in the Congress, and now in the courts, with this morning's indictment of presidential aide Mark Hennessy. Suicide, scandal, cover-up, international blundering, deceit, deceit, deceit—the polls showed the American people were fed up with Ericson and his mess. They were no longer sorry for him—after all, hadn't he brought on his own blindness? Mike Fong was convinced any normal man, under those pressures and with an ounce of patriotism left, would resign. But Ericson hung in there, politically paralyzed, and stubbornly paralyzing the country. Nichols was no bargain, Fong thought, as the Vice-President appeared in the hallway for the 4 P.M. meeting, but at least the country could operate. Ericson in office was like having no President at all.

"Shall we have another go at it?" the Vice-President said, leading the others into the room. Nichols took his place at the table, opposite the empty chair of the President's; as the other chairs were filled, Fong was startled to see a strange face sitting in Treasury's chair. Not Zack Parker, the replacement for Bannerman, but a tall, pasty-faced man he had not met.

"Meeting will come to order," said the Vice-President.

Lucas Cartwright immediately said, "The meeting is out of order until the Secretary of the Treasury arrives."

"I'm informed that Secretary Parker has been taken ill," said the Vice-President. "Severe attack of gastroenteritis, which he has suffered from for some time. Since there is no deputy secretary as yet, sitting in his place is the Undersecretary for Monetary Affairs, Albert Hay."

Cartwright angrily argued that no urgency existed that required the meeting be held that day, and proposed it be laid over until the following Monday. The Vice-President said no, the meeting was called in accordance with the Twenty-fifth Amendment, and could not be postponed without the consent of the calling member, which Fong said he would not give.

"I suspect foul play," Cartwright said dramatically. "There is going to be at least a suspicion in the public mind that Secretary Parker's food was tampered with. That will cast a shadow over whatever decision is taken here, especially since it is being railroaded through with such unseemly haste."

"It wouldn't kill us to wait till Monday," said Frangipani, "out of respect to Zack Parker. After all, Zack has never even been to a Cabinet meeting."

"I move the question," said Fong. Why hadn't Bannerman told him about the new man, Hay? Was this why Bannerman was so ready to call the meeting, knowing that Parker would be sick? Was Cartwright right about foul play? Fong was just as glad he didn't know.

"Would the Attorney General give us a legal opinion?" Cartwright looked for help.

Duparquet shrugged it off. "If Mike doesn't want to accept a delay, that's it."

"I don't," said Fong, "because there is an urgency. Just this morning, to cap off an incredible series of revelations, the President's chief of staff has been indicted on six counts of perjury. The government is in paralysis. The President is not in a condition to act. Frankly, Lucas, I think your suggestion of the possibility of foul play is one hell of a terrible thing to say, and I think you ought to withdraw it. I haven't gone around poisoning people's coffee to keep them away from meetings. I was just as surprised as you to see—"

"Hay," said the man in the Treasury chair.

"—Hay here this afternoon."

"I withdraw nothing," said Cartwright. "This is a very fast shuffle and it looks suspicious to me. If you're aiming to strike down a President, for the first time in the history of this nation, you ought to damn well have a full Cabinet on hand." He did not sound like courtly, cool Lucas Cartwright; he was an angry man. Fong took that to mean Cartwright was plenty worried.

"The Attorney General presented the case for the President last time," said the Vice-President.

"I object to your assuming the Chair," said Cartwright.

"Overruled," Nicholas said. "There is a precedent."

"Who's making notes?" Cartwright tried.

"Good point," Nichols allowed. "Andy, would you take the minutes again?"

"We ought to have a verbatim account of this power play," said Cartwright, "available to the public. I move we bring in a stenographer."

"Let's vote on that," said Nichols. Fong knew which way that vote would go; in the last removal meeting, with Cartwright not present, that had been thrashed out. Fong was pleased to win the first vote, five to one. Cartwright was not as adept an advocate as Duparquet had been.

"Will you speak for the President, Emmett?" the Vice-President said.

"I'll defer to Secretary Cartwright," said the Attorney General. "He was chief of staff and knows the President's condition better than any of us."

"What are the charges?" Cartwright demanded.

Fong, feeling more confident each moment, said, "There is only one 'charge,' as you put it. That is, the President of the United States is disabled—unable to fulfill the functions and duties of his office." He took out his wallet, selected the card he had carried since the last meeting, and once again read: "I move that the principal officers of the executive departments, acting under the authority vested in them by the Twenty-fifth Amendment to the Constitution of the United States, do declare the present occupant of the office of President of the United States to be unable to discharge the duties and powers of said office, and that the powers"—here Fong could feel the awful significance of what he was doing, and his voice slowed in solemnity—"and duties of the office of President do devolve upon the Vice-President as Acting President."

"Discussion," said the Vice-President. Nobody seemed to have anything to say. As before, the words Fong had read lay heavy in the room, and the fear that Mike Fong felt, but never expressed, must have been on all of them. What would history say? That they had courageously done their duty? Or that they had been the first American usurpers?

"I would like to hear from the Attorney General," said Cartwright. "No evidence has been presented to show the medical incapacity of President Ericson. The burden of proof is surely on the one who makes such a motion."

"Actually, not," said Duparquet painfully. "This is not an adversary proceeding. The amendment does not say anything about a 'reasonable doubt.' It's a matter of the judgment of the men here assembled."

"You mean they could take a normal, healthy President, and with no evidence, declare him disabled and replace him with the Vice-President?"

"They would surely not, nor was that the intent of the legislation," the Attorney General said. "But theoretically, they could. If the President objected, he has a remedy in law—he could ask for a reinstatement by the Congress."

"We've been through this before," said George Curtice. "We all know the arguments and the law. Let's do our duty."

Fong looked at Cartwright, pale, shaking, as that good man looked across the table at Duparquet. "Does the Attorney General wish to repudiate all he said at the previous meeting of this Cabinet?"

"My evidence repudiated me," said Duparquet. In a resigned tone, he ticked off the reasons why he was deserting Ericson: "I told the Cabinet last time that no voter could anticipate an act of God, and there was nothing in Ericson's record that would have led the voters to believe he was more prone to blindness than anybody. I thought that was the truth, but it was false. Perhaps someone voted not to remove the President on the basis of that lie. I feel the need to correct that now."

"Surely the medical evidence must be newly taken," argued Cartwright—rightly, Fong admitted to himself—"to conform with the legislative intent of the framers of the Twenty-fifth Amendment, which I have right here—"

"We considered the medical evidence from Dr. Abelson, the president's physician, last time," said the Vice-President. "It was such a pack of lies that he killed himself over it. His suicide note contains his opinion that President Ericson is disabled."

"It ill behooves you to let your mouth water," Cartwright snapped at the Vice-President, "at the prospect of seizing President Ericson's rightful powers."

The room tensed. Cartwright had touched a nerve; the Vice-President, Fong thought, was overreaching in taking such an active role in this meeting. "The Vice-President has the power to veto a decision by this Cabinet," Fong said soothingly, "and so I think it would be a good idea if he rescued himself from further comment."

"Butt out," Frangipani told the chagrined Vice-President. "You're not in the Cabinet. We'll handle this."

"I move the question," said Fong.

"Wait." Cartwright looked desperate, nearly ill. "Would everyone just wait one moment, to consider the enormity of the deed we are discussing? History does not deal kindly with regicide. You are striking down a President—a President, gentlemen. For the first time in more than two centuries, a small group of men is taking the most awesome powers on this earth from the elected leader of our people and deliberately handing it to another man."

"If we are wrong," said Curtice, "the President has recourse in the Congress. If we are right, and do not act, the people have no recourse."

"I have worked in this house, on and off, for thirty years," Cartwright said, a loser's look on his face. "You just do not reverse the decision of the people this way. It weakens the very foundations of the White House. . . ."

Fong did not have to move the question again. He looked at the Vice-President, who said, "To the vote to remove the President. The Secretary of State."

George Curtice, seated to the right of the empty presidential chair, said, "I vote yes."

"The Secretary of Defense."

Cartwright said wearily but in a strong voice: "I vote no."

"The Treasury Secretary."

Albert Hay, sitting for the ill Zack Parker, said, "I did not think this was a decision I should make myself, so I reached Secretary Parker in the hospital before the meeting. Treasury votes no."

Fong couldn't believe it. The last-minute substitution for Parker, the Bannerman-hater, was not a Bannerman ploy. The Treasury Secretary must have just been taken ill, that's all there was to it, and nobody in Bannerman's camp had a chance to work this undersecretary over.

"I withdraw my charge of foul play," Lucas Cartwright said mildly.

"The Attorney General," the Vice-President continued.

"Yes," said Duparquet firmly. Thank God we didn't try to pressure him, Fong thought; this is one of those guys who respond badly to pressure. Two to two. We're dead. We need four, and that would leave it to Frangipani.

"The Secretary of Natural Resources."

"Yes," said Fong to his own motion. That's twice he voted on this, and the first time to strike the President down. He cast his vote with the certainty that it would cost him his job.

"The Secretary of Human Resources."

"Yes," said Andy Frangipani.

Silence.

"A vote of 'yes' is a vote to remove the President," said Lucas Cartwright, as if perhaps Frangipani did not understand.

"I know," said the Big Flower, with no expression. "The Vice-President is now the Acting President."

Nobody knew what to do next. Finally, Duparquet said to Nichols, "Mr. Acting President, you have the power to veto the action taken this day by this Cabinet. Do you choose to exercise your veto?"

"No," said Nichols.

"Then I would advise you to declare this meeting—"

"Wait," said Cartwright again. "In the light of the

vote, I would like to propose that we give President Ericson the opportunity to step aside voluntarily, under the provisions of the Twenty-fifth Amendment. Perhaps that would be more seemly."

They all looked at Fong. He knew that Bannerman would expect him to stick the sword in the loser, to make certain that the world knew Ericson was ejected from office against his will. "I think that's a compassionate suggestion, Lucas. I have no objection. Why don't you go see if that's what President Ericson wants, and he can put it in the form of a handwritten note to the Secretary of State."

Cartwright left the Cabinet Room by the door that led toward the Oval Office. The rest of them sat there, saying nothing, for three minutes. Cartwright returned, a note in his hand, looking oddly cheered:

"President Ericson has given me this message: 'Earlier today, I turned down an offer to purchase the presidency. Now I am turning down your offer to let me resign the presidency. The deed you have done this day—to usurp my constitutional power—will link your names with Benedict Arnold. I will fight your action in the Congress until the powers of the President are once again in the hands of the person the people elected to that post.'"

After a moment, Nichols said, "He isn't disputing our right to take this action, is he?"

"No," said Cartwright. "But he has ordered a mattress to be brought to the Oval Office. If you want the President off the premises, Mr. Acting President, you're going to have to throw him out."

V

The President

The President / 1

Ericson ran his fingertips along the edge of the desk used by Herbert Hoover some fifty years before. He sat forward in his chair and laid his forehead gently on the slightly pocked desk top, feeling the cool pressure, rolling his head back and forth. He listened to the almost inaudible quick-ticking of the clock on the left corner of his desk, then to the deep, slow tick of the grandfather's clock near the door to the hallway on his left. To his right, his usual jay was making noise in the Rose Garden. Ahead, slightly to the right, about two o'clock on his mental position clock, was the noise from Melinda's office, a faint phone ringing, a typewriter clicking, muffled voices.

He lifted his head and leaned back, spinning his chair to face the bay window. Maybe he was kidding himself, but the President thought he could make out more shades of gray in what had been only black-and-white images. Yesterday morning, when Buffie thought she was slipping silently out of his bed, she had been silhouetted against a window with the light streaming in behind her, and he could more easily—or so he let himself think—make out her form as she wiggled into her dress. He would have to try that again with Silent Sam.

The buzzer sounded and he reached for the receiver. He called his telephone his "equalizer," the way short hoodlums referred to their guns in the mysteries he had been speedhearing lately. Melinda was on the phone again.

"I don't want to be pushy, but we're all here, ready when you are. Lucas, and Smitty, and Harry and Hank and me. And the constitutional lawyer you wanted, that Lucas picked out. Shall we all march in?"

"Not right now. Talk to each other in the Roosevelt Room, I want to think a little."

He stood up, trailed his finger around the northwest corner of his desk, and then left that familiar island in his office to take the six steps to the door next to the hallway door. He pressed it, and stepped into the narrow passage—a tiny lavatory on his right, the "telephone booth" on his left. He lay down on the small couch that took up one wall. Ericson had asked the White House curator what the room had been used for since Harding's day. The curator had delicately said "naps," and added that the original use—as a telephone booth—was restored when President Kennedy had put in a private telephone extension to bypass the switchboard.

Ericson rested his head on the leather pillow, which his wife so long ago had insisted on calling a "throw cushion." That was one of the few mementos he had of his wife, a loner like him. Never wanted children. He could have used a couple of kids not to come home to in the past ten years, but the White House life would have been rough for children. And it was just as well not to have to explain what had happened in this past week to somebody who wanted to trust you totally. He shuddered her day-of-divorce suicide out of his mind; maybe that's where Herb Abelson got the idea.

Here he was, neither fish nor fowl, neither President nor not President. He had enjoyed zinging that note into the Cabinet Room an hour ago—the Benedict Arnold reference was excessive, now that he thought of it, which was what restraining aides were for. He did not really feel so fiercely defiant. He was leaving Bataan and carrying on the fight at Corregidor, but ultimately that had been a losing position too. He could try to put a good face on things, but he could never win by losing—what on earth, he wondered, possessed Andy Frangipani? The Curtice defection he could understand, a mea culpa to the liberal press. Duparquet had been sulking for a week, and had shown signs of going over; Melinda had tried with Duparquet, gave it all she had, Ericson knew, and at considerable personal cost, but the Attorney General was one to keep his eye on the main chance, and his main chance now was to put daylight between himself and the President. More accurately, the semi-President. Curiously, Ericson harbored little resentment for Fong. Mike was a willing tool of Bannerman's, but sincere in his belief of Ericson's disability. It troubled the President to be the target of a straight-shooter like Mike Fong, who, if he won, would probably be double-crossed by Bannerman. But Andy Frangipani's vote was a shocker; he had counted on his support and paid no attention to him. Maybe that was why—never let anyone feel taken for granted. Something more, there, though: Bannerman might have gotten to Andy, or somebody put the heat on him in another way. Or some arcane New York City political rationale might have been behind his action.

Ericson did not relish going into this fight without Hennessy. Lucas Cartwright was a fine man, and had turned out to be more of a stand-up loyalist than Ericson had ever judged him to be, but he did not have the zest for a no-quarter battle. In this situation, there was nobody Ericson could restrain, calm down, hold back from doing the hotheaded thing; without Hennessy, the semi-President would have to be the source of impetus to do battle, and others would then have to restrain him. Not a customary role for a President, nor one Ericson felt comfortable with.

So much to do, if he could hold on. So much that would be postponed for decades, maybe a generation, if Ericson acquiesced, following the mainstream out the door into honored retirement. He was the first professional economist to be elected President, the first who understood profoundly the forces that underlay the system that moved the country to prosperity or to hard times. Only Ericson, he told himself, the conservative-sounding Democrat with the first Republican Senate in any adult's memory—only Ericson could effect radical reform in the name of the free economy. His first appointment had been significant: a young Friedmanite monetarist to head the Federal Reserve Board, a fellow student of Ericson's. As college roommates, they had dreamed what they could do together if they held the levers of economic power. They shared a vision of America—Ericson smiled ruefully at how often he had used that cliché on the stump —to put through a negative income tax that would reform the welfare system, guaranteeing an end to hunger in the United States as Herbert Hoover, and later Lyndon Johnson, had vowed.

What if we are right, Ericson asked himself—what if the old Keynesian way, the direct government intervention in the economy that has failed so often to flatten the business cycle, is wrong? What if we could guide the economy more creatively, more indirectly, making our central achievement the increase of worker productivity, the only way to a steadily rising standard of living? God knows, economic freedom had been thrown away in so many other countries, pursuing the will-o'-the-wisp of perfect security—couldn't an Ericson Administration show the world what a free economy could deliver to its citizens?

What if we were right, and I caved in, and Bannerman and Nichols took us down the path of more tinkering, more blundering, more recessions, never understanding the opportunity—wouldn't history condemn me for being the worst kind of coward? These economic ideas were not the sort of advice that would be passed on with the keys to the office; such advice had to be married to power, in one person, in the Oval Office, to gain a sustained trial.

The President shifted his position on the couch in the tiny room. The couch was three inches too short for him, but he could not get a larger couch in there. Why couldn't they move the wall for the President of the United States? If he decided to stay on, he would have the wall moved so he could stretch out.

He thought about that, placing his shoe up against the wall. Was his "so-much-to-do" stuff all a rationalization, the necessary back-stopping to his desire to live a full life even though blind, or his inborn obstinacy that always pushed back when pushed, or his love of being Número Uno? At a word, he could have a wall moved, or a mountain. The most powerful leader in the free world. As the power had been snatched away, Ericson could snatch it back.

Power was the wrong word. All the analysts kept talking about "presidential power," as if it were generated by some machine in the basement of the White House, connected to the Grand Coulee Dam, which could be "passed" from one hand to another by constitutional amendment. In reality, his power was checked on all sides—not so much by the Congress or the courts, but by inertia, criticism, boredom, confusion, the forbidding presence of history, and most important, by his own lack of certitude. Even where Ericson felt most purposeful, he had to admit the possibility—"in the bowels of Christ" as Oliver Cromwell put it to the Rump Parliament—that he could be wrong. So, for "power," read "degree of impotence," a level that each President finds for himself, usually by the end of his first year in office.

And yet, and yet; even so; still. So much could be done, or so many mistakes avoided, by one man, especially a man who does not want to merely be President, but wants to act as President. Lying there, one foot on the wall, Ericson came to the conclusion that his own motives in fighting for his office were good, that he did not need the power, or degree of impotence, for the sake of his own psyche. Maybe a while back, not now. At this stage, he knew he wanted to hold on to the reins for what he could do. The real question facing him was whether he could do what he wanted to do, blind and unpopular and under siege. He thought of Arthur Leigh's four jockeys, a labored metaphor Hank Fowler had excitedly passed along to him. The first jockey was the man who needed power and could not handle it—that was never Ericson. The second was the man who needed power and could handle it—that used to be Ericson. The third was the

man who did not need power and could not handle it
—that was Ericson now, and Vice-President Nichols,
too. And the fourth was the man who did not need
power but who could handle it—David Reisman's
"autonomous other-directed man"—could Ericson become that? And if so, soon enough to save his presidency?

To avert apocalypse, Ericson amended Leigh's four
horsemen, placing "the political life" in place of
"power." He did not want power, he wanted to be a
central part of the action. That sounded better; the
President took his shoe off the wall. If he stayed, he
would leave the wall unmoved, as his private symbol
of the limitation of power. Politics, Ericson posited to
himself, was the science of the way out—that is, the
discovery of solutions to dilemmas that created new
problems not as troubling as the original dilemma. In
his own dilemma, he needed a way out. Would he
know one when he saw it? He hoped so.

The President rolled off the short couch and into the
little lavatory, positioned himself carefully, urinated
accurately. He zipped up his pants and his thoughts,
slowly washed his face with soap, put a wet towel behind his neck for a moment, and readied himself for
his sighted aides. He hoped Lucas had found a good
constitutional lawyer, somebody not only sharp on
theory but with some grasp of the human element
in this situation. Ericson chucked the towel to where
the bin should be, and did not hear the satisfying
plunk. He shrugged; it was the bin's fault, not his, if
it was not where it should be. He counted his six steps
back to the Hoover desk and pressed the button for
Melinda. She opened the door.

"Let's get to work," he told her. "Are we still being
paid?"

The others trooped in behind her. "Say hello to
Senator Apple," said Cartwright's voice, "your new
lawyer." Ericson extended his hand. A gnarled old
hand grasped his own and squeezed hard. Lucas'
choice was a pleasant surprise: Apple was in his mid-
seventies, had retired from the Senate a decade ago to

make a pile of money at the head of a Washington law firm. The President hoped the old man's mind was still sharp.

Ericson moved to one of the easy chairs in front of the fireplace, indicating the chair next to him for Senator Apple. That was to show the lawyer he was important, not having to deal with the Chief Executive across a desk, like a staffer. The others took places around them; Ericson could hear Harry Bok's wheel chair, sense Hank Fowler's presence, and smell Melinda's Ma Griffe. Smitty hurried in last and closed the door.

"Mr. President," said the piping, wheezy voice of Senator Apple, "it's my judgment that you're getting a raw deal."

"Raw, maybe. But is it constitutional?"

The senator didn't hem and haw. "It's all been legally done, but I think the Legislative History will show that this despicable action today was not the intent of the framers of the Twenty-fifth Amendment."

"How can you be sure?" Ericson liked his certainty.

"I can be damn sure," the senator wheezed. "I was one of the framers. I was the chairman of the Subcommittee on Constitutional Amendments when the Twenty-fifth Amendment was passed, and I know what I intended."

That's why Lucas had chosen Senator Apple. Ericson was beginning to enjoy this. "You just called me 'Mr. President,' " he said. "Am I?"

"You're called 'Mr. President' till the day you die," Apple replied, "like I'm called 'Senator,' and it means nothing. Your question is, I take it, are you still in fact President of the United States?"

"I find that of interest," Ericson said, taking instruction.

"Yes, you are still President. You occupy the office of President. However, as soon as a written message is received by the President pro tem of the Senate and the Speaker of the House that the Cabinet has declared you unable to carry out your duties and functions— which should be about now—your powers and duties devolve upon the Vice-President as Acting President."

"President without power."

"Right," Apple said matter-of-factly. "You cannot give an order. On the other hand, you are not responsible for the duty of giving an order."

"Can I hire a lawyer?"

"Good question. As an individual, of course, you can. But can you, as President, appoint counsel to be paid by the public? An argument could be made that you do not have that power."

Ericson nodded; that was not a fight he would want to take on. "Then you'll be my personal lawyer. I like that, carries the lawyer-client privilege and all."

"No," said Senator Apple. "Don't give the bastards an inch. You appoint me, and I'll send the government a bill for my services, and as you know, my fees are exorbitant. I'll want to use some of the young fellows in my firm on this, too. My thinking is this: Once you start acting like you have no rights to defend yourself, or to regain your powers, then a certain residual power would disappear."

"What residual power?"

"Look around you," the old man said. "The place, the people. You still have some control over—well, call it influence with—your press secretary, your chief of staff. Remain in the office, go on acting like a President, which you are—let Nichols try to strip you of your powers one by one. It'll make him look like the usurper he is."

Ericson was mulling over something Apple had said a moment ago. "When you say I cannot give an order, what does that mean?"

"Your personal secretary here, Miss—"

"McPhee," Melinda said.

"Miss McPhee. She works for the White House Office. She can, if she wishes, carry out your instructions to make a call, or type a letter, but she cannot pass along an executive demand. As special counsel, I may ask for help from the rest of the White House staff—but I cannot insist upon it."

"How does he get his powers back?" said Lucas Cartwright. "That's what you're here for, Senator."

"Step One," said the lawyer, "is to transmit letters to the President pro tem and the Speaker saying, simply: 'Sir: Pursuant to Section 4, Paragraph 2 of the Twenty-fifth Amendment to the Constitution, this is to advise you that no inability exists, Very truly yours.' I would suggest you write it in your own hand, dated today, and the time, 5:15 P.M."

Ericson did not hesitate. He went to his desk, reached in the drawer for the green-tinted writing paper of the President, picked up the pen, and wrote the two letters, pausing only to say, "Shouldn't it be 'President pro tempore'?"

"President pro tem would do," said Apple, "but go ahead if you want to show off."

Ericson held out the two letters, and Smitty, as chief of staff, took them. "I'll see that these are delivered right after Nichols' letters are delivered."

"What's Step Two?" Ericson was glad something was being moved along.

"The usurpers have four days to challenge your assertion that no inability exists. If they do, and I imagine they will, the words of the amendment read: 'thereupon Congress shall decide the issue.' Since the Congress is now in session, it would have to be decided within twenty-one days from the moment the issue is joined."

Ericson came back from the desk and sat again in the easy chair. He felt detached, as if this were an academic discussion in a political science classroom about how to hand the presidency back and forth. That detachment was never much help to him when it came to the need for what his writers liked to call "bold initiatives," but it was a useful mode for analysis. He asked the Senator, and included Cartwright, what they expected to be the next move from Bannerman & Co.

"If I were them," Senator Apple piped, "the minute I delivered the inability letter and put my name in as

Acting President, my first act would be to seal your files."

"They could do that, personal files as well?" Lucas asked.

"Not only could but should. They don't want you walking off with anything that would help the Acting President run the country. Or would help them prove you were indeed disabled."

"There's my phone," Melinda said quietly and left. Ericson tuned his ears to her office; no phone was ringing. She was—he hoped—going to get his dictabelts out of the safe next to her desk. He felt a flicker of fear at the prospect of his personal diaries coming under somebody else's control. The belts included not only private assessments of men in the Administration and the Congress, but his accounts of the Nikolayev affair—and worst of all, the dictation during those moments of his deep, personal depression, back when he had that bad cold. Hank Fowler had told him that such dictation would be good therapy, and Ericson had said anything that was on his mind—including all the self-doubt. Such a dictabelt could be used to prove his inability, right from his own lips. A man's diary was his most intimate property, Ericson believed—it ought not to be used against him, whatever the case. He trusted that Melinda shared his concern.

As his attention turned back into the conversation, Hank Fowler was chatting about some irrelevancy: A Seeing Eye dog just obtained for the President, which had just been moved into the kennels behind the swimming pool on the south lawn.

The President interrupted: "I don't have the time," he told Hank, "to start training with a dog today."

"Hold on," said Smitty, "it might make a good picture. President, fighting to regain the powers seized from him, takes his first walk with his new Seeing Eye dog. Shows you're not panicking. Hank—a mutt, like we said?"

Ericson said nothing, wondering why the discussion was flying off on this tangent. He knew Fowler must have a purpose in interjecting this at a crucial moment.

"Very smart, but just a mutt," said Fowler. "That's what the President ordered. No pedigree. Kind of a cross between a German shepherd and a—I dunno, maybe a collie. I walked him yesterday, and it made me feel better. I should check him now."

Fowler left. Ericson, still puzzled, was glad the psychologist had snapped out of the feeling of guilt and depression after the eye doctor's press conference. If the dog helped Hank then it would be good to have a dog around. Maybe it could help a semi-President, too.

"After your note is delivered to the Congress," Smitty said briskly, "I'll set up a walk with you and Hank, followed by the press. Be nice, the first training session. I want photocopies of those letters that say 'no inability exists.' That's historic, and the papers will be looking for pictorial stuff."

Lucas Cartwright cut in: "I should describe the look on your face, Senator Apple, to the President. You look like you are thinking—'here we are in the midst of a constitutional crisis, in the very center of power known as the Oval Office, talking about walking the dog.'"

"Oh, not a bit," said the senator. "In the Senate, at some very crucial moments, we used to piss the time away. Relieves the tension."

"They're cheering something." Ericson could hear a commotion in the distance. He went to the french doors and opened them, and they could all hear the sounds of hollering and popping noises, like strings of firecrackers. Smitty went out into the hallway to check the tickers, and returned right away to say "the letters from the Cabinet were delivered. Now I'll send these." Ericson shut out the sound and let some bitterness come out: "The power has passed. You'll hear no orders from me any more. Only requests."

"This is a sad time," said Lucas.

"A historic moment," said the senator, undaunted. "Let us reflect more on it when the power flows back again, redressing the wrong done this day."

"I have a chore to do," said Cartwright, walking out briskly. Ericson, feeling at once drained and angry,

knew what it was; as Secretary of Defense, Lucas had
to make arrangements for the man with the black bag
to switch over to the Acting President. Let Nichols
live with the responsibility of ordering a nuclear strike
if the missiles come in, the President thought, it's not
one of a President's happier tasks. Cartwright's chore
was simple enough: to tell the colonel and the sergeant, now down in the Situation Room, to cross the
street and take up their position in the Vice-President's
suite in the old Executive Office Building. That was
where Nichols would exercise the power from, until
Ericson could be lawfully compelled to vacate the
White House.

The President-in-name went over the language of
the amendment with the senator for ten minutes, learning what his prerogatives were, when he heard a mild
rap on the door from the suite ordinarily guarded by
Melinda and Hank, momentarily unoccupied. "Here's
Director Hewitt," Harry Bok said, announcing the
head of the Secret Service. "Come in, Boss."

Ericson had only met Hewitt once, at some early
briefing; all his Secret Service dealings were through
the chief of detail, first Bok, now Furmark. He recalled a mild-mannered fellow, quiet and respectful,
who had joined the force back in Roosevelt days.

"I thought it would show a measure of respect, sir,"
the director began formally but sincerely, "as well as
the affection all of us have for you, if I came over on
this difficult assignment myself."

Ericson felt an appreciation for the foresight of Senator Apple. "I expect you to do your duty, Director
Hewitt." He wished he could remember the man's first
name.

"The duty is to seal the files," the gentle voice said.
"The Acting President has directed us to slap a seal
on every filing cabinet, safe, desk drawer, and other
storage facility here in the White House. When the
Congress decides the issue, sir"—evidently he had already heard of Ericson's response—"you'll find everything exactly where you left it." That is, Ericson added
to himself, if the semi-President wins; if Bannerman

and Nichols win, these files will be ransacked to find evidence to justify every charge of deceit or inability.

Ericson heard the Secret Service man go to the Herbert Hoover desk. "Here comes the part you might consider offensive, Mr. President. I'm going to have to put this sealer plastic on the drawers of your desk, too. I, uh—"

"Not so fast!" Ericson raised a finger, went behind the desk, and opened the double drawer. "You can put in your report that the President made an attempt to cover up his secret vice." He took out a large plastic bag filled with salt-water taffy sent to him from well-wishers in Atlantic City, New Jersey, and plunked it on the desk. "You can bite into one yourself, for test purposes, but watch your teeth."

"This is a terrible thing to have to do, Mr. President. I hope you know how I feel." The director was genuinely embarrassed. More poignant, to Ericson's mind, was the way the man was upset about what this turmoil was doing to the institution he served.

"I quite understand. Just remember what you promised Harry Bok a couple of months ago."

"I won't forget, nor would my successor." The director passed Harry's wheel chair and murmured something to him about counterfeiting. Harry Bok said, "Thanks, Rufus."

"Oh, and Rufus"—at last Ericson had a first name to deal with—"rest easy about this. It does cut both ways, and I'm glad to know nobody will be poking around in my Administration's files for the next three weeks."

As the Secret Service director left, Ericson could hear his agents already moving about in the offices adjacent to his own. He thought about Melinda, who was off the premises with the suitcase or whatever, containing the dictation belts; he hoped she had not taken them to her apartment, which might also be sealed. He put that out of his mind; she was reliable. "Senator, whatever your exorbitant fee was for today's advice," Ericson told the old man with fervor, "it was worth it."

Senator Apple chortled and launched into a reminiscence of his days drawing up the amendment that was causing so much mischief. As the old man rambled on in a way that Ericson found conducive to quiet thought, an insight suddenly flooded the President's mind. He almost snapped his fingers; "Eureka!" was what one usually shouted when an apparent mystery becomes immediately clear.

Hank Fowler and the dog. The reason the psychologist had brought up the subject of the Seeing Eye dog was not in the least irrelevant. When the senator had mentioned the words "seal the files," and Melinda left the room like a shot, Hank must have thought to himself about his own files. Ericson knew Fowler made copious notes of their conversations, in his capacity as an alienist; he could imagine the same "klong," as Hennessy used to call it, that hit the psychologist at the thought of those cassettes being taken from him. Those were very like a psychiatrist's notes, intensely personal, private, and intimate. Ericson put himself in Fowler's shoes—where could he hide them? Hank couldn't take them home, because he was living on the second floor of the White House. So he had started talking about the new dog, and went to his office, and headed out to the kennels, where—if Ericson was right, and he knew he was—he hid the cassettes in a doghouse. The President could visualize the little psychologist warning the gardener who was in charge of the kennel not to get near the President's Seeing Eye dog, and then crawling in with his package of tapes and stashing it away.

What a resourceful, loyal, and delightful person Hank Fowler was, the President thought. The example did something for him; if a blind psychologist could respond so imaginatively and bravely to crisis, so could a blind President.

Lucas came back, tut-tutting about the way the White House was being battened down—"As Hennessy used to say, I thought I heard a presidential seal bark." Ericson quickly asked him: "Who's our nose-counter in the House? I had been relying on Andy Frangipani for that, but now he's out."

"I shall make discreet inquiries about a floor leader, Mr. President," Cartwright said. "By the way, although I confess to being furious with Brother Frangipani for his despicable vote today, I should tell you he gave me a message in the hallway right afterward. He said to tell you not to hate him, he was a better friend than you thought, and not to do anything drastic."

"You'll be seeing him soon, Lucas?"

"If I decide to remain in the Cabinet," the Defense Secretary answered, "or if I'm not thrown out, I imagine Andy and I will be meeting from time to time."

Ericson was decisive: "Stay in. Dig in your heels. Nichols can't fire you, nobody can fire anybody in this situation." He had a thought, more a suspicion: "And keep a channel open to Frangipani. He carries some weight in the House, and he's a pal of the Speaker's. Could be he's not the bastard we think he is."

2

"Breakfast in this place is a treat," said Jonathan Trumbull, crunching into a toasted, buttered English muffin. Ericson remembered the way the table looked: the flatware gleamed, the linen place mats contrasted with the dark walnut of Grant's Cabinet table, while white-gloved waiters hovered over the Sunday brunchers in the family dining room of the White House, next door to the much larger State Dining Room.

Ericson wanted his close aides, his inner circle, to have the full Sunday-at-the-White-House treatment, both as reward for loyalty and as incentive to future exertions. Melinda seemed a bit grouchy, but Marilee, the first woman presidential press secretary, was especially perky. Maybe that was why Melinda was grouchy. Lucas Cartwright seemed happier as a visiting Cabinet member than as a staff aide; now he was an "in" outsider rather than an "out" insider. Smitty was quieter now that he had the chief of staff's job, which Ericson judged he didn't know how to do, but most of his governmental responsibility had been taken over by the Acting President's chief of staff at the EOB. Harry Bok and Hank Fowler seemed glad their savaging in the press turned out to be short-lived: All the press attention now was split between the President himself and the new Acting President, Arnold Nichols. Senator Apple was absent; the newest member of the "ability advocates," as one friendly newsman called them with some nudging from Marilee, was in his office getting ready for a noon appearance on "Meet the Media."

"We have to get off the defensive," Ericson said. "I'm tired of getting hit with something new every morning. Can't we turn a few of these shots around?"

"Senator Apple has the notes in Buffie's handwriting," said Jonathan, "which he is going to wave on television today. He'll demand an investigation of what he has promised to call 'the most arrogant display of moneyed wealth seeking to purchase high office in the history of this nation.' "

"The senator will be good at that," said Cartwright. "He has the kind of mouth that lends itself to mouth-filling phrases."

"That's good," Ericson conceded, "but it's a one-day wonder. It wasn't a real bribe by Bannerman and it just won't fly. We can use it to muddy up the charges against Hennessy, though." The mention of Hennessy was a depressant, and Ericson hurried on: "We need a villain, and Nichols doesn't make a good enough villain. We have to change the direction of the issue. It's not a whole President versus a disabled President, it should be a legal President against Bannerman and his surrogates."

" 'Stooges' is the word," Smitty put in.

"Bannermanism," Jonathan tried, "the new word for

illegal usurpation." Ericson liked that; at least the kid was trying. "Melinda, maybe your friend can come up with some other meetings that Nichols attended. The plotters, that kind of thing. Some congressman can charge an impropriety." He underscored "your friend." The others, Ericson knew, would think he was referring to the Attorney General. Ericson meant "Mr. Goodfriend," the agent in Bannerman's camp. He felt no need to inform the others of his existence.

"I don't like the way the usurpers have control of the next step," Ericson continued, using "usurpers" to make it a natural part of conversation. "They have four days to respond to my declaration of no inability. Deadline is Monday late afternoon, and I think they'll wait till the last minute. What have we got, Smitty, to counter that? How can we steal the story away from them Monday night on all the TV news shows? Something pictorial, and not walking the dog."

"Great mutt," Fowler said, giving Smitty a chance to think, "everybody loves him."

"You could suddenly appear in the press briefing room on Monday afternoon," Marilee put in, suggesting the obvious. "Say something to get people to write their congressmen, that this is the most crucial twenty-one days ever."

"Twenty-one Days that Shook the Presidency," said Jonathan, overreaching, Ericson thought. But trying.

"That's what I can do," said Ericson, "and I will. Set it up for five o'clock, and we'll dominate the evening news and the next morning's papers. Now is there something anybody else can do?"

Silence. Typical, thought the President; it was always easy to think of ways of generating news by using the President himself. The trick was to use others.

"All this is most important," said Lucas, "but the name of the game is One Third Plus One. Smitty, you are undoubtedly already working on ways to parade individual House members in here to meet with the President and see with their own eyes how un-disabled he is."

"That's two dozen a day," said Hank, good at numbers. "Twenty-four men times twenty-one days equals around 435, the membership of the House."

"Jonathan, work me up a good ten-minute pitch," Ericson ordered. "Check it out with the senator. Smitty, start herding them through here every single morning at eight o'clock."

"Give them one of these breakfasts," Jonathan said, his mouth full.

"And invite their wives," added Melinda.

"Good idea," said Lucas. "I'll tell Mrs. Cartwright to get some congressional-wives-against-Bannermanism going."

"Forget the Senate," said Ericson, his mind skipping ahead. "We'll probably lose there, and I don't want to waste our resources. Concentrate on the House, and for God's sake, nobody knock Senator Frelingheusen, no matter what he does." He rose. "Everybody watch Senator Apple at noon, and call him afterward to tell him how great he was. Smitty, bring his law partners in for a reception tonight if you like. Use this place to a fare-thee-well."

He strode out, using the long cane casually in familiar surroundings. It pleased him to hear Harry Bok say to the others, "The Boss has got the old bug up his ass again."

Ericson was excited because he was about to take a chance. Two days before, Marilee had told him that her network boy friend had come to her with a strange probe. A professional Russian source, Gregor something, was anxious to get a message through to the President, and he wanted somebody to talk to him. Marilee had brushed it off, just mentioning it in passing to the President. Ericson had quickly picked it up and told her to arrange for the Russian to take a White House tour on Sunday morning, with the rest of the sightseers. Melinda was to be in the ground floor China Room, at the display of plates used in the administration of Rutherford B. Hayes—Ericson liked that touch, using a President who stole an election—and would bring Gregor to see somebody unnamed, but "close to the President."

After a day's reflection, Ericson decided that the somebody should be him. If word got out that Lucas Cartwright, Secretary of Defense, was making contact with a KGB man, especially in light of the Yalta Deceit—even he was using that phrase now, the President thought—it could cost Lucas his job. Smitty was likely to prefer not to do it at all, and then to tell the President nobody else should, either, and that could lead to resignations, memoirs, etc. Nobody else around was a heavyweight—not Hank or Harry or Marilee or Jonathan—and the senator did not fit the conspiratorial mold. Melinda could do it, but the Russians probably thought she was only the President's secretary. That's where a Hennessy would have come in handy.

Ericson knew that seeing Gregor himself was daring and possibly foolish, but an alternative did not readily present itself. If the man had a back-channel message from the Soviet Premier, the President of the United States should have it. Ericson told himself it was neither the thrill of secret, highest-level communications, nor the identification he felt between Nikolayev's fate and his own that caused him to deal directly with the agent in this matter. The Soviet leader's position was a blank in the current U.S. intelligence estimates, and Ericson—even without the powers—still felt the weight of some of the duties of the office of President.

On the second floor of the White House, in the Lincoln Sitting Room, the President received the Soviet agent. Furmark frisked him—Ericson could hear the quick, expert patting—and Melinda showed him in. The room was small for the three of them, but Ericson wanted Melinda there to make notes, and to be able to follow up with the agent in a future meeting, if necessary.

"I did not expect to deal on so high a level," the nervous Russian said. "Miss McPhee said only that I would talk to someone close to the President."

"This is not a regular part of the White House tour," Ericson said cheerfully. "As a matter of fact, there is no Sunday morning tour, ordinarily. We had to round up a hundred or so tourists to get you in here confidentially."

The Russian came to the point. "I bear a private message from Premier Nikolayev."

"How is Vasily?" Ericson used the Rooseveltian, old-Joe technique to see if the agent was bona fide.

"I have never met the man," said Gregor. "The message came to me through an intermediary who arrived from Moscow two days ago. I do not know how the Premier looks or sounds. You are understandably interested in some evidence to support the authenticity of the message. I have none."

"Um," Ericson said, showing a frown.

"I can only say something about myself that your intelligence agencies have already informed you of, undoubtedly—that I am the source of the information that was printed in Mr. Zophar's column last week."

Ericson nodded as if that were not news to him. The man was certainly KGB, in the way he overestimated the CIA and FBI; all those fellows were convinced the other side knew more than it did. Gregor probably thought he was being followed around most of the time. If only he let himself look over his shoulder, the Russian would discover nobody was there, but that would only make him suspect he was the victim of more sophisticated surveillance techniques. Ericson put the obvious question to him: "Then what faction are you working for?"

"I am an instrument, Mr. President, used by whatever group, or faction as you put it, is in control."

Ericson said nothing, which he found to be a useful device in dealing with Russians, who did not like silences.

"I have no loyalties," Gregor explained, "just contacts. It is felt that such a person is useful to whichever group becomes dominant, which is why I have done what I do for so long."

"What is the exact message," Ericson said slowly, a signal to Melinda to take everything down verbatim, "which you purport to bring unofficially from the Soviet leadership?"

"First, and I do not quite understand the meaning of this, Premier Nikolayev cautions you not to convey the contents of this message to the marines."

Ericson nodded, not permitting himself to smile; the agent had unwittingly presented his credentials.

"Next, he wants you to know he has returned to his apartment in the Kremlin after a three-week visit to his Uncle Felix." Ericson got the reference: Nikolayev had told him about Lubyanka Prison being on Dzerzhinski Square, named after "Iron Felix" Dzerzhinski of the Soviet secret police.

"Um."

"He says that he is unable to get certain persons, whom the Premier calls 'my Bannermans,' to accept assignments outside Moscow, at power stations."

Ericson thought of Bannerman in charge of the Tennessee Valley Authority. Why did the Soviets choose to send their disgraced top men to run power stations? Was it a Dostoevskian irony, giving the management of natural power to men incapable of handling political power? Gregor was not the man to discuss this with. Nikolayev's point was that the Premier's title was not important—he was not yet in control.

"Premier Nikolayev is prepared to accept your invitation to visit the United States," Gregor went on. "If you feel such a visit would be personally helpful." Ericson could hear Vasily's voice saying, "And then you will owe me one, my friend." To Ericson, the mental picture was of a couple of exhausted heavyweight fighters in the fifteenth round, clinging to each other in a clinch that kept both from collapsing.

"And that's the end of the message." The Russian agent sounded relieved.

"When was it sent? Try to be precise."

"Man arrived here Friday night, must have left Moscow on Aeroflot's SST early Friday morning. Probably was given the message by the Premier Thursday night, which would be late Thursday afternoon here in Washington."

Before the Cabinet meeting of Friday that declared Ericson disabled. If Vasily had used the hot line, at least Curtice's vote might have been turned around. Maybe, maybe not, Ericson thought, refusing to dwell on the game of "if onlys." The question now became: Was the message still valid? Should Ericson respond, or should it be answered in a way that returned the matter to official channels, where it would go to the Acting President?

"Take this gentleman into the Treaty Room for some coffee," he said to Melinda. "I want to consider sending a message back."

When they left, he puzzled it out. The too obvious answer was that the Russians thought it was in their interest to help Ericson stay in power, presumably because he would then be a weak President, grateful to Nikolayev for the assistance. But Ericson knew that was a misreading of himself, and that Vasily Nikolayev knew better—which meant that Nikolayev was playing along with the dominant faction in the Kremlin that thought it would use the weak Nikolayev to help the weak Ericson. Ericson's analysis clicked along: That means that Nikolayev is letting himself be used by a clique he does not control, and he needs me— with my apparent exploitable weakness—to stay in place. So he is offering to help me, figuring if I can stagger through three years of a term, that would give him time to consolidate his own power.

Ericson stopped to ask himself if he was dealing with reality or some movie scriptwriter's idea of international intrigue. Did this cross-fertilization of plots— the internal Kremlin struggle affecting the White House struggle, and vice versa—relate to real-life dealings between nations? The inexperienced President could not know. He expected it did, recalling the "Trollope ploy" practiced by the Kennedys on Khrushchev in the Cuban missile crisis, ignoring a truculent message and answering an earlier one instead. Certainly the assassination of Kolkov was reality, as was his own blindness. These actual events overlaid complex motives of power-seeking. Ericson was pleased that he could analyze them so dispassionately: Curiously, almost inhumanly, he felt no personal hatred against the Far Eastern powers for ordering the ambush, if they did, or against Nikolayev, the man who was personally responsible for his blindness, if the minority view in the intelligence community were right. He explored deeper:

Question: Since the Soviet Union perceived it to be in the Soviet interest to keep Ericson in power, was it against the American interest? Ericson, in a Machiavellian framework, had no trouble with that: The obvious Soviet premise—that Ericson would be a weak President, thankful to Nikolayev—was 100 per cent wrong, and Nikolayev knew it. But Nikolayev would be dependent for his own power on the continued false impression within the controlling Kremlin faction that Ericson was dependent upon him—which false impression Ericson could exploit. This game of three-dimensional chess enabled Ericson to come to the happy conclusion that it was in America's interest for him to regain presidential power. At least as far as dealing with the Soviets was concerned.

Next question: Since circumstances had changed in the White House since Nikolayev's back-channel message was sent through Gregor, and Ericson was out of power, would it be helpful to Ericson if Nikolayev now formally accepted Ericson's old invitation? Or would such an acceptance bolster Nichols, making it seem as if the Soviets had waited to respond until a new Acting President was in place? Exasperated, Ericson shook his head; this was the kind of problem chiefs of state confronted back in the days of sailing ships, when it took months to receive news of a declaration of war or an outbreak of peace. He wished he could write down the time sequences and options on a long sheet of paper.

When he stopped pressing for an answer in his mind, it came to him. The heart of the matter was to convince the House of Representatives that the flap about Ericson's supposed blunder—of hastily inviting a deposed Soviet Premier, not knowing he was deposed—was no blunder at all. The way to prove that was to insist that the leaks about Nikolayev being ousted were totally untrue. Zophar would claim, and the truth might be, that Nikolayev was ousted and is now temporarily back in; but both Ericson and Nikolayev could pump out the word that the story was baloney from the start. No Nikolayev ouster, no Ericson blunder.

Ericson's strategy, then, was akin to Kennedy's Trollope ploy: to have Nikolayev respond to Ericson's invitation of last week as if nothing had happened to either of them. It would seem that Nikolayev got an invitation, considered it for a week or so, and in the course of diplomatic business accepted. All the brouhaha of speculating columnists and leaking Russian agents in the interim could be dismissed as a lot of dust in the eyes. Ericson would appear to have made no mistake; the Cabinet that threw him out would appear to have made its decision in the poisoned atmosphere of false foreign-relations hysteria.

In the Lincoln Sitting Room, Ericson nodded his approval of his thought process; absently, he picked up the life cast of Lincoln's right hand which rested on the corner of the desk. The hand, gripping a sawed-off broom handle, was about the size of his own. Ericson hefted the piece, weighing a new problem that no President had ever had: Since he no longer had the powers of President, he could do nothing—even unofficially—with a foreign power. He would rightly be accused of breaking the Logan Act, which forbids United States citizens from dealing with other nations as if authorized by the United States Government.

Seeing this Soviet agent, now seated in the Treaty Room with Melinda, was a very ticklish thing. If it ever leaked that Ericson had exchanged messages with the Soviet Premier during the twenty-one-day period that Congress was "deciding the issue," the final vote would surely go against him. Ericson had to reject the Soviet overture in a way that still encouraged Nikolayev to assert his willingness to respond to Ericson's—not Nichols'—invitation.

He sent for Melinda and Gregor. "I hope both of

you have pencils," he began. "First point: I am not responding to any private or public message until I am in a constitutional position to do so." He then proceeded to respond: "Second, I consider it reprehensible for anyone, possibly representing a foreign power, to deliberately mislead—change that to 'deceive'—to deliberately deceive an American journalist. Your callous manipulation of Samuel Zophar in this matter is repugnant." That should give Nikolayev the signal to hold to the never-happened line, and to show that the American President had invited a Soviet leader who was in power and not in jail, contrary to reports. This ploy would seriously damage Zophar's reputation, but he had it coming; it would also destroy Gregor, the agent, who did not have it coming, but such were the risks he ran in his chosen line of work.

"Finally," said Ericson, "I intend to report this approach to the Acting President and the Secretary of State in writing, for them to take any action they are empowered to take." Ericson rose and extended his hand to the poor fellow: "Thank you, and good day."

Furmark escorted Gregor out, and Ericson dictated a brief memo to Melinda for Nichols and Curtice—for the record, to protect him from any charge of using presidential powers that were no longer his to use. Sticking tightly to the record, he used the exact words he had spoken to Gregor, "as recorded in shorthand by my secretary, Melinda McPhee, who was present throughout the brief meeting."

"I'll get this to their homes immediately," Melinda said, when his dictation stopped.

"No rush," Ericson said. "Stick it in the interoffice mail. Put one of those little red tags on it, to show it's top priority, which should get it there in a few days. Would the regular mail be slower?"

"Nothing is slower than the interoffice mail marked 'top priority,'" Melinda said, in a heartfelt way.

He picked up the telephone and asked for Smitty, who was still in the breakfast room downstairs with Jonathan and Marilee. "I have just been approached," Ericson said, "by a sleazy character who claims to be a friend of Nikolayev's, claiming to have a message from him. I rejected the approach, and am sending a memo on it to the Acting President and the Secretary of State, to show that I'm not poking my nose into forbidden areas. I'm not sending anybody but you a copy of that memo, Smitty, because you're my chief of staff and I have no secrets from you. Also, this agent says he was the source of the Zophar column. That column turns out to be a crock—Nikolayev is in the saddle, just as he has been since the ambush."

Ericson listened to Smitty make the appropriate noises and then went to the point of the call: "Also, since this memo reflects badly on Zophar's gullibility, you may want to sit down and discuss it with him, as old friends. His first instinct will be to protect himself with some story of the Kremlin flip-flopping power twice in the past couple of weeks, but that's silly. Besides, everybody will be able to get to his secret source now. The source—a Russian named Gregor somebody—will admit he lied to Zophar."

"You're right to want to help Sam on this, Mr. President," Smitty gruffed. "Shows you're not vindictive. Also, he'll owe you a big one, and if he can be turned around—"

"You and he figure out a face-saver for him," Ericson said magnanimously, and could not resist adding, "but nothing where we have to lie."

"Well, we might have to shade the facts just a tad," Smitty cautioned, "but it's in a damn good cause."

Ericson put down the phone and said, "Man was born for troubles, as the sparks fly upward."

"Hallelujah, or whatever you're supposed to say," said Melinda. Ericson was glad Melinda had been there throughout the Gregor ploy; not only was she reliable, but she had the sense to appreciate some creative conniving at the highest level. "You're a lot sharper now than you ever were," she said, "when you were the real President."

He nodded agreement. "I can see the play of power more clearly now. A lot of people think that power is the manipulation of people and the shaping of events.

562

Not so. People and events, and time and chance, all come into confluence to manipulate and limit a man supposedly in power. The trick is to deflect the blows so that they don't hit you, but crash into whatever you see as your obstacle."

"You want me to write that down, or what?"

Ericson laughed easily—he was surprised how easy it was to laugh again—and said, "Nah, it sounds profound, but it always looks lousy in print. I'll talk it over with Jonathan one of these days, and he'll dress it up for his book. Now let's get the telegrams out to the congressmen for breakfast tomorrow morning," he reminded her. "That was the best idea at the brunch, and Smitty'll forget, or not know where to find the list." He had another thought: "If I could see, what I'd like to see most is the expression on Sam Zophar's face when he gets the news that his source is turning on him."

"This is a rough business," Melinda said.

"You're suited for it, like me," he replied. "By the way, on the off-chance that you should abandon ship, where's the suitcase?"

"In a locker at National Airport. I mailed the key to my aunt in Providence, she saves all my souvenirs of the White House."

Ericson thought of his innermost self-doubts, his confessions and admitted duplicity, neatly packed in dictabelt boxes and packed in a suitcase and stored for fifty cents a week in a public facility. "You won't forget to put another half a buck in when the time expires?"

"I never forget a thing," she said coldly. "I'm a walking computer."

She took big chances for his sake. How could he tell her he appreciated her without putting her down? "When you're really tee'd off at me, Melinda, remind yourself how much I need you."

"I always do."

He had not handled that well, he told himself. One day, when all this was past, he would have to figure a way to handle Melinda McPhee.

3

Ericson spent his fifth straight morning giving an inspirational, never-say-die pitch to congressmen, and
fielding their questions: Why did you lie about the
previous blindness? Why didn't you reveal your condition to the people before the election? Why did you
go along with the Yalta Deceit? Why did you fail to
tell the doctors of your history of blindness after
the ambush? None of the congressmen asked about
Hennessy's "bribe" because most of them understood
political job pay-offs all too well. Ericson felt he had
the pitch fairly well mastered at this point, and was
especially effective getting through to the wives.

He went on his training walk with the dog and Hank
Fowler around the Ellipse after the congressional
breakfast. The training session was a daily event he
had come to look forward to, after it dawned on
Ericson that the dog was really training him. After the
walk, the President took a dip in the Ford pool, and
had a good laugh when the mutt jumped in the pool
after him. It was Friday, one week after he had been
"stripped of his powers," as he liked to say, eliciting
a certain sympathy, and Ericson encouraged himself
to think that the tide of opinion might have begun to
turn.

At the edge of the pool, he made the hand-squeezing
motion that signaled the Secret Service that he wanted
a phone, took the receiver, and with his feet dangling
in the water asked for the pollster. No good news: The
level of Ericson support had sunk to 25 per cent, between the worst of Truman and Nixon, but, the pollster
said, reaching for straws, "it's held there, stable, for
three days."

The dog was having some difficulty getting out of the pool, and the Secret Service men had to go in and push him out from behind. In gratitude, the mutt—Ericson would have to give him a name, but didn't want to be rushed—shook himself thoroughly, splattering the two agents who had remained poolside.

Ericson had never been much of a dog fancier but this animal seemed to have a sense of humor. He said, "Lie down by me, mutt" and to his amazement, the wet dog did just that. Ericson heard the whirr of a camera's automatic advance mechanism across the water, and assumed that Buffie was getting pictures. Good; every bit of positive publicity helped. In extremis, he had conquered his distaste for cornball heart-wringing; if he could get away with a shawl and stovepipe hat to bolster his "Lincolnesque image," he would have done it.

He told the telephone operator to play him the News Summary.

Topic A, led all four nets, was Nikolayev's personal response to Ericson, accepting his invitation to visit the United States early this fall. Story stressed Soviet background briefing in Moscow about the way the response was couched. First, directed to President Ericson, not Acting President Nichols, because it was Ericson who made the invitation. Second, Nikolayev said he would be happy to meet with whomever the American government designated, and thus stayed carefully neutral in American internal affairs. Third, Moscow briefers again poured cold water on U.S. press speculation that Nikolayev had ever been deposed or in prison.

This story tied closely to domestic leads (the speeded-up reading of Melinda hurried on), the historic constitutional confrontation being fought out in the Congress. The Nikolayev response is being used as evidence that Ericson did not blunder in making the invitation. However, this was countered by publication of the Gallup poll today, which shows Ericson going through the "Truman Bottom" of 23 per cent approval, which is being used by Nichols supporters as evidence that Ericson has lost the ability to govern.

Other developments: A group that calls itself the Committee to Protect the Presidency—made up of young public-interest lawyers opposed to the Committee to Replace the Disabled President—charged today that the eye doctor who resigned from the Navy yesterday, Dr. Perry Lilith, has been paid off for attacking the President with the offer of a lucrative job at New York Hospital, where the Board of Trustees is headed by Roy Bannerman. Lilith denies this.

Ericson's eyebrows rose. Sounded like a group Hennessy might have formed, but he was out of it, so far as Ericson knew. That was unexpected help.

In the Hennessy corruption case, bad news for Ericson: The man appointed as highway commissioner in Tennessee at White House insistence turns out to have been convicted, under another name, for fraud ten years ago—

"Push the fast forward for about a minute," Ericson told the operator. That should put him in the opinion roundup.

—says that if Ericson does not get at least a 51 per cent vote of confidence in both houses, he should take that as a congressional rejection of his presidency. Although the President would be able to regain his presidency with one-third support in either house, that is a poor technical ground on which to reclaim the powers and duties.

"Balls," said the President aloud. He felt the dog lick his arm in response. "That's not your name," he said. Interesting name for a dog, though.

Columnist Samuel Zophar admits to being ambivalent about the great controversy, backing off his previously militant anti-Ericson stand. Quote, on the one hand, the nation would certainly be better off with a new man at the helm, and Arnold Nichols has the experience and capacity to do the job. However, an Acting President is not a real President when the man elected to the job is constantly hammering at the door. End quote.

In a signed editorial, the editor of *Time* calls for President Ericson to abandon his quest for reinstatement, "not because an inability exists in him, but an inability exists in the nation to cope with two Presidents. Even if Ericson's challenge is defeated—and our latest nose count shows that it might well be— the Twenty-fifth Amendment leaves the door open to repeated challenges and a whole series of twenty-one-day paralyses. "There are none so blind as those who will not see," and Sven Ericson will not see that his duty is first to relieve the nation of this terrible schism of power. . . .

"I didn't start it," Ericson said idly into the telephone.

The Associated Press head count in the Senate stands at twenty-nine for reinstating Ericson, sixty-one opposed, with ten uncommitted. Most observers say that the uncommitteds will break eight to two against Ericson, denying him the one third of the Senate he needs to reassume the powers of the presidency. Over in the House, it could be a different story. A majority opposes reinstating President Ericson, but it is unclear if that majority can reach two thirds, and some congressmen are expressing anger at being nose-counted before the arguments are all presented. . . .

The *Wall Street Journal* chides the "nominal President," as it calls Ericson, for characterizing as a bribe offer a perfectly legitimate and humane suggestion by former Treasury Secretary Bannerman to pave the way for a productive career after his resignation. To return to a somewhat lugubrious quotation of Franklin Roosevelt's, "Never speak of rope in the house of a man who has been hanged." Bribery, after the Hennessy indictment, should be the last word heard from the Ericson White House . . .

They were right about that, Ericson commented to himself, splashing with his feet. A cheap shot, but not an ineffective piece of demagoguery, and it had purchased some surcease from pressure on Buffie. He noted that Bannerman had dropped the campaign train sex angle; the bribe charge had backed him off.

Here he was, Ericson thought, criticized for making some fairly tawdry charges to avoid even tawdrier charges, wrestling for media advantage while the greatest government of free people in the world lay, in Wilson's words, "helpless and contemptible." Was it worth it? Was he really fighting to regain his powers to defend against the weakening of the presidency, or was that a rationalization? Put more accurately, how much of that was a rationalization? He stroked the wet fur of the dog. "This is one of my occasional moments of self-doubt," he told the animal, who would not publish memoirs. "Haven't had many lately." Nor was it severe. Ericson knew that if he lost in the House, if they turned down his challenge to recover his powers, he would not come back to fight again and again. That was something to threaten, not to do. If he lost, he would resign permanently and let the Acting President become President.

Ericson rose and counted his steps around the pool to the changing room. In a few moments, wearing slacks and a sports shirt, he worked his way back to the Oval Office, but did not go inside. With the dog close to him, the President sat on the steps facing the Rose Garden outside his office, conscious of how his simple movement from pool to cabana to Rose Garden had been monitored by the White House police and Secret Service. At least a dozen people had been concerned about the movement, and an electronic box was flashing his whereabouts on the grounds to control centers somewhere underground. A log would be written up afterward filling out spaces on a form: time, moved from where to where, accompanied by whom, protected by whom from what vantage points. At the start of his term, the omnipresence of other eyes had made him feel awkward; after the blindness, comforted; now he felt like a Gulliver trailing hundreds of Lilliputian strings. He took a deep breath of the afternoon's sultry garden air.

"Looks like he's got some collie in him, from the nose."

Ericson tentatively placed the Yankee-twang, nasal voice—the White House gardener, who sometimes said hello, puttering around the Rose Garden—but the President could not remember the man's name or call up his face from past meetings.

"Some collie, mainly Alsatian, I think," Ericson replied, with a tug of guilt: "He been digging up your flowers?"

"No, no, he goes his way, I go mine. Never fouls the footpaths, glad to say. Dr. Fowler takes care of the kennel, too."

Ericson smiled at the picture of Hank Fowler guarding his tape cassettes in the doghouse. He pointed over to the flower bed where he remembered a mass of red-and-yellow tulips had been. "What kind of tulips are those?"

After a pause, the gardener said, "I dig out the tulips in late May. Those were the Queen of Shebas you remember, that were next to the white Triumphators. Long gone."

Ericson realized the spring garden he remembered was not the garden in midsummer. "What's there now?"

"Zinnias coming in good. Delphinium, they're blue ones over there, and the purple heliotrope."

"There were pansies," Ericson recalled, "dark blue and yellow, somewhere over there near the magnolia trees—"

"Marigolds now," said the gardener sharply, as if he were ashamed of that year's pansies. "Rusty red.

And yellow marigolds—President Kennedy wanted them in for Senator Dirksen. He had quite a thing about making the marigold the national flower."

Ericson tried to remember the roses in the Rose Garden, and drew a blank. "Where are the roses?"

"In the four corners, not many. Dunno why they call this the Rose Garden, the roses are the least."

"Red ones," Ericson prompted.

"Hell, no. The Queen Elizabeth is pink and the King's Ransom is yellow. You put red roses in, gives a garden a heavy feeling, makes it sad. You don't really want red roses put in, do you?"

"No, no," Ericson said quickly, conscious that a presidential whim can become a festering tradition. "Any white roses?"

"Right over there," the gardener said proudly, probably pointing somewhere, "set off by the anemones. The shrub rose Nevada, and I raise 'em better than anybody. Get a lot of comment on those."

The President tried to recall what an anemone looked like, and shook his head. He thought of a large shellfish but that was an abalone. So many sights he had paid no attention to that would have served him well today. "Soon it will all be different again," he suggested.

"Mums to go in, few weeks from now. Where the tulips were, that you remember."

The freezing of springtime in his mind's eye was oppressive. The President shot a question at the gardener that he had never asked anyone before: "If you were me, would you quit and go home?" He felt he could safely forecast the answer: Hang in there, Mr. President. The White House permanent staff always personally supported any man who moved into the Oval Office, and Ericson imagined he was not the first President who sought to counter the public-opinion-poll blues with an opinion from a man in the street who never got out in the street.

"If I had a work-connected disability," said the gardener, "and everybody was bitchin' at me, and the people I put in stuck a knife in my back, I'd damn well chuck it."

Ericson decided that was the last time he would be Henry V slipping out among the troops at night. "You don't think I should hang in there?"

"You're hanging in there by the neck, if you don't mind my sayin' so, Mr. President. You better get out while the gettin's good."

"What else can they do to me?" Ericson knew he was not getting the kind of answers he could use in the next inspirational congressional breakfast.

"They can wear you down, make you feel it's all your fault. They can take away your self-respect, so you go home finally with nuthin'. Give yourself a break, Mr. President—chuck it. I'm tellin' you this because you asked me, and I think you're a good man." Ericson did not feel up to replying. "You're wrong to make a pet out of that dog," the gardener said, moving off, "he's a working dog, don't forget."

A few moments later, Ericson said to the dog, "You know what your name is? 'Hang in there.' You hear?" He abbreviated it. "Hangin'ere." Every few moments, he said again, so the dog would get to know his name, "Hangin'ere!"

4

On the twentieth day, the day before the vote in the Congress "to decide the issue," as the Twenty-fifth Amendment read, and after his twentieth breakfast meeting with congressmen, most of whose names began with W, Y, and a couple of Z's, Ericson received a call from Lucas Cartwright.

"I have been approached by Andy Frangipani,"

said Cartwright, "who was approached by Mike Fong, to say that T. Roy Bannerman seeks an audience with you."

"Send him in." Ericson was heartened by the approach. It might mean that Bannerman did not believe he had the tickets in the House. Nobody could be sure, and Ericson's own count—cross-checked with an independent canvass by Frangipani—showed 140 votes to support the President's challenge of the Acting President. He needed one third plus one—146—of the 435 House members. Of nine uncommitteds, seven were likely to go against him. By his own count, Ericson was four votes short. But in any battle, he knew, you knew your own weaknesses, and not the other side's weaknesses. They knew theirs, not yours. Ericson was glad that Bannerman had made the first move, since it could be an indication that he was worried about his count.

"He thinks it would be psychologically debilitating for him to make the pilgrimage to you," Lucas said. "He wants to see you on neutral territory, and no leaks before or after." Ericson could understand the neutral-ground wish. The "or after" on leaks was meaningless.

"What's your judgment, Lucas?"

"Fortunately for the Republic, Mrs. Cartwright has the President's box at the Kennedy Center concert hall tonight. You could be our guest, showing your serenity on the night before the historic vote. Presumably we could wangle tickets for the Bannermans in some other box. During the clanging and banging of the 1812 Overture, you could have a private discussion in the little room with the red walls behind the box."

"I'll be there. You be my second."

"He requests that it only be the two of you."

"Fair enough. What about Duparquet, is he helping us or hurting us in the Florida delegation?"

"Neither. Bannerman leaned on him from one direction, and your amanuensis, Ms. McPhee, from the other. The Attorney General is now so neutral he may never again get into gear."

"Where we going to find those four votes, Lucas? It would be a bitch to miss by so little."

"Andy and I are doing all we can, sir."

Ericson shook his head. "I can't figure Andy. First he cuts my throat, and now he's helping with the bandages. What's he after?" The President had a hunch, but he wanted Cartwright's reading.

"He won't say, Mr. President. He learned his Democratic politics in New York City, and thus could teach the art of contracts in Byzantium. I accept help and ask no questions."

Ericson decided to go to the concert in black tie. It was an opening, he would make a distinguished appearance, and his picture will be in all the morning papers on the day of the vote. He should have thought of going out confidently, Bannerman or not.

Ericson sat in the back row of the President's box, his mind ticking as others were listening to the music, until he was informed that Bannerman was in the room behind. He felt his own way back and extended his hand. Bannerman shook it and led him to a chair.

"There's a split of champagne in the little fridge over there," Ericson said, hoping to show confidence, "let's have a civilized drink."

That left Bannerman no alternative but to go over to the refrigerator, twist open the champagne, and serve it in two awkward plastic glasses. Ericson felt it being placed in his hand and he said, "To the presidency."

"To the presidency," Bannerman repeated solemnly. "That's an apt toast. I have come to see you about a way to strengthen the presidency."

"I'm listening."

"You and I have our counts in the House," Bannerman began. "Mine shows that you will fall a few votes short. Yours undoubtedly shows that you have just enough."

"I'll win," said Ericson.

"If you do," said his opponent, "it will be by the skin of your teeth." Ericson smiled at Bannerman's unconscious use of a phrase out of the Book of Job. "If you do not, it will also be close. My point is that, win or lose, you will have squeaked through by the barest of minorities. You could not conceivably govern in such a circumstance."

"We have a Constitution. I'll govern."

"Your courage does you credit, Mr. President." Ericson shook his head in the semidarkness; Bannerman was a heavy-handed suitor. "But it occurs to me that the presidency would be better off with a real victory—a majority. I have come to suggest that you be given that victory tomorrow."

"And the price?" the President asked.

"Your resignation." A straight deal. Ericson knew what Bannerman was getting at, and he nodded his understanding as the big man explained: "You want to show that no President, not even a man deprived of his eyesight, can be removed against his will. You believe it is necessary to defend that principle for the sake of the presidency itself. I grant that, and assume it is your primary patriotic motive. Therefore, I suggest that the House make your point tomorrow, uphold your right to serve. Having proven your point, in an impressive and unforgettable way, you would then step down voluntarily. The presidency would be as strong as ever, and the nation can move on without putting itself through this unspeakable pressure."

Bannerman, Ericson decided at that instant, was really not sure he had the tickets. Too close to call, so he came up with a fairly sensible deal. Ordinarily the offer would be tempting, but the human element was missing: Ericson would no more voluntarily turn the key to the White House over to Bannerman than he would hand it to Nikolayev.

"If you care about the presidency," Bannerman said, "you'll accept this offer."

"I care about the country, too," Ericson told him. "I'll win this fair and square, and serve my term." On second thought, Ericson thought it would be good to leave the door open a crack. "I'm not an unreasonable man, Roy. This was not an insulting offer, and I'm not rejecting it thoughtlessly. Maybe there's some way we can work together to shore up the presidency after tomorrow's vote."

"Don't decide so quickly," Bannerman urged. "Sleep on it."

Ericson shook his head. He heard the door to the outer hall open and shut as Bannerman strode out. He sat there as the music in the hall rose to crescendo. That was not such a bad offer Bannerman had made. Ericson had not hesitated in turning it down, but he wondered if he had done the right thing.

5

On the twenty-first day, Ericson invited his official family up to the yellow Oval Sitting Room of the residence to watch the vote in the House. He felt light-headed, relieved, fatalistic, as on election day the year before. He had done everything he could think of doing to persuade, wheedle, threaten, and cajole every vote that belonged to him. He felt good that he felt so tired.

Melinda was seated next to him on one of the couches, Smitty and Marilee on the couch facing them. Buffie was moving around, working, walking out on the Truman balcony to shoot through the windows. Jonathan, seated on the floor in front of the TV, was fiddling with the set. "Can't you get that picture better?" the President said and drew an unembarrassed laugh. Harry Bok thrust himself out of his wheel chair into an easy chair. Hank Fowler ordered Hangin'ere to lie down.

To be in the candidate's room when the results came in, Ericson ruminated, was the elixir of the political life: Surrounded by your fellow sufferers, the power flowing in or ebbing out, bound together by Lincoln's "mystic chords of memory," knowing that in a few moments it would be all or nothing. He wished Nurse Kellgren were there, because she was surely on the team, too, but he did not want to make a point of it. Lucas Cartwright and the rest of the Cabinet were in the House of Representatives, along with Senator Apple, who had made a constitutional stem-winder a few hours before, evoking one television commentator's comparison of Daniel Webster's "reply to Hayne." Ericson, observing himself, was curiously content; he was ready to win or to lose.

He picked up the phone and said, "Get me Hennessy." The room fell silent and Jonathan turned down the TV sound. When the operator reached the former chief of staff in New York, the President said, "You watching?"

Hennessy said, "Watching what? I never watch television in the daytime."

"There's a soap opera you want to catch today. We're all here watching, and we don't know how it'll come out."

"Don't worry, the good guys always win," Hennessy said.

"Who are they?" Ericson wished he were kidding.

"That's not determined until somebody wins," Hennessy explained. "So there you sit, surrounded by sycophants, and you decided you missed me."

"No," the President said, "I wouldn't have thought of it till Melinda started blubbering 'Where's Hennessy? He's responsible for this whole mess. Let's call him.' So we called you. I'd put Melinda on, but she's too choked up." Ericson heard an intake of breath and guessed that she was, at that.

"Is Buffie there? With her clothes on? Tell her to send me a picture of this call, it'll dress up the cell."

"I am going to win today," Ericson said, "and you are going to win at your trial." He was unsure about both. If Ericson won, there would then be the pardon problem. If he lost, no problem, except for Hennessy's. "Today, I'm thinking mainly of myself."

"Which is why you called. Okay, ol' buddy, I'll tune in and root for you. Tell Melinda I miss her, it'll crack her up."

Ericson said into the room, so Hennessy could hear, "Hennessy says you're all doing a great job, far better than if he were here."

"Tell Melinda what I miss most is sitting on her desk and looking down her dress."

"He remembers with fondness our evenings around the campfire," Ericson translated to the group. "Take care, chum."

"You were good to call, Sven."

Ericson clicked the phone cradle, asked the operator for Cartwright on the House floor. When he came on, the President asked, "How's your count?"

"One thirty-nine plus two."

"Do your best." Five short. He hung up without announcing the discouraging count to the people in the room. The television sound was broadcasting the clump of the speaker's gavel, and Speaker Frelingheusen's call for the report of the Select Committee on the Disability of the President. Senator Apple had objected to the name of that committee, but the Bannerman forces had rammed it through. The committee chairman, a Republican who had run a fairly sobersided and thorough series of hearings, rose to say, "Each member, Mr. Speaker, has been provided the full report of this committee, a timely transcript of our hearings, and several memoranda of law concerning Paragraph 2, Section 4 of the Twenty-fifth Amendment, along with the brief submitted by the President's counsel and the Acting President's counsel. The committee report, voted unanimously, reads as follows." Ericson had told Apple to work out some innocuous compromise language in the committee report, to let the fight take place on the floor of the House. Every member of the House had then availed himself of his five minutes in the media sun.

"The President of the United States was removed from office by a duly constituted and properly called meeting of the President's Cabinet," the chairman read to a silent House, "and the powers and duties of said office devolved upon the Vice-President as Acting President in accordance with the provisions of Section 4, Paragraph 2 of the Twenty-fifth Amendment. The President, pursuant to the same paragraph, subsequently declared that no inability exists, and the Cabinet, consisting as required by law of the principal officers of the various departments, has informed both houses of the Congress of its disagreement with the President's judgment. The amendment requires that the Congress decide the issue within twenty-one days.

"This committee finds that the decision of the Cabinet was arrived at in proper order and in good faith, reflecting the intent of the framers of the amendment as expressed in the Legislative History. The committee also finds that the challenge of the President, and his personal judgment that no inability exists, is also lawfully arrived at. Thus the decision whether inability does or does not exist rests, as the amendment intends, with the individual judgment of the members of the House and Senate."

Ericson, listening, nodded; the Constitution left it up to human beings to decide on subjective grounds. In a "government of laws, not of men," sometimes the laws had to leave a great deal of discretion in the hands of men.

Frelingheusen's voice was flat. "The clerk will call the roll." The television eye, Ericson knew, was on the electronic tote board, keeping a running score, but he could hear the individual congressmen saying "aye" or "nay," some "yes" or "no," and an occasional "present" to the question. A "yes" vote was to support Ericson's demand for reinstatement of presidential powers; 146—one third—was what the commentators called his "magic number."

The roll call droned ominously on, with the television commentator occasionally interpolating "That was unexpected," or "That nay vote was a congressman the Ericson forces had been counting on." Funny how the small band that stuck with him were characterized as "forces," Ericson thought. His tension did not mount, as he might have expected at the long tolling of this bell; a tightening in his chest remained constant. Two thirds of the way down the roll—in the S's —Lucas Cartwright called with a glum report: "we're not picking up any new strength, Mr. President. Looks like we've got about 140, 142."

"Frangipani agree?"

"Andy thinks we'll make it somehow, but he can't point to the votes."

"How about some of the men who are passing?" Ericson knew that some congressmen would vote their consciences only if they had to, and would prefer to vote their districts. If it were clear that Ericson was going to lose, they would want to be on record as being against him. House rules made it possible to wait until the direction of the wind was clear.

"Of the nine who voted 'present,' wait now, there's another—of the ten, passing, we have them all down on our list as against you."

"Any chance of reaching them?" Ericson's outlook was bleak, but he told himself it was not over until it was all over.

"We have men prowling the cloakroom, doing their best. These men voting 'present' aren't leaving their seats, however. Most of them, now that I look at it, are in the front rows."

"Why's that?"

"Don't know."

"Andy know?"

"Hold on." Lucas came back in a moment. "Andy gives one of his expressive shrugs, spreads his hands, and looks at the ceiling. He may be saying something in Italian."

Curiously, Ericson was more relaxed as the roll call neared its end. He knew he was ready for defeat, which he had never been in his life, and he was also ready for victory, because he was used to it.

"Zwyorkin," the clerk said the last name.

"No!" shouted Zwyorkin.

The television announcer said, "That's 430 congressmen present and voting, only five absent. Ericson needs one third of those voting, or 144. He has 140, he's four votes short. There are eleven representatives who voted 'present,' in effect passing until the end. Most if not all are known to be anti-Ericson. Now here is the clerk's poll of those who have not yet voted."

The clerk called the names. The first voted yes, the next two voted no. Then two yeses. Ericson needed one yes vote out of the remaining six.

The next man voted yes. A shout went up from Ericson supporters in the House, and a moan sounded in the gallery. Then, to put the seal on the vote, the next five congressmen also voted yes. Excitedly, the television announcer said, "There's no doubt about it now, Ericson's got it, he had the votes in reserve!"

Ericson felt his hand being squeezed by Melinda on his left. Harry Bok's wheel chair squeaked over and he felt the firm hand on his arm. At the set, Jonathan was clapping. Buffie's clicking came closer and he felt her lips brush his cheek. He remembered he had to say something for Jonathan's book.

"Forty-one Presidents of the United States salute you," the President said to the Congress on the television screen. To Melinda, he murmured, "There must have been a setup. Frangipani brought it off."

The gavel was banging, and the New Jersey voice of Speaker Frelingheusen affirmed, "Two thirds of the Congress has not supported the Acting President and the Cabinet in their opinion that an inability exists. Therefore, in accordance with Section 4 of the Twenty-fifth Amendment to the Constitution, the Congress has decided the issue." They waited for the words of the decision. "The Vice-President now ceases to be Acting President, and I hereby declare that the powers and duties of the office of the President devolve upon the President."

A few seconds later, Lucas Cartwright called, and in a restrained voice, said, "As Secretary of Defense, it is my duty to inform you, Mr. President, that the colonel and the sergeant who are in touch with our retaliatory forces have now returned to the basement of the White House, from their temporary post in the EOB."

"And only a few moments ago," Ericson replied, "I couldn't even start a small war."

"I can't say I know how it worked out this way," said Cartwright "but it's a good thing for the country it did."

"Lucas, you've been one hundred per cent true blue." Ericson meant that, and felt a surge of admiration for the older man. "Most of my mistakes have been in not trusting you enough."

"I had a need to know that," Cartwright kidded him. Ericson chuckled into the telephone, so Lucas would know he got the point, and said, "Lucas, are the other Cabinet members there, milling around?"

"That would be a fair characterization of their activity, sir."

"Do me a favor." There was menace in Ericson's tone.

Cartwright cautioned: "Remember Churchill's words —'in defeat, defiance; in victory, magnanimity. . . .' "

Ericson had been magnanimous once before, which nearly brought about his downfall. "Tell Mike Fong I want his resignation on my desk before the close of business today. Tell Emmett Duparquet not to bother with a resignation, he's fired."

"Have you forgotten George Curtice?" Cartwright was a mild man, but not forgetful.

"In victory, magnanimity. Tell Andy Frangipani I'd like to see him in the Oval Office as soon as he can make it." Ericson put the phone down, and for the first time, felt the pleasure and the pain of being back in power.

6

"Angelo Frangipani," the President said, behind the desk in the Oval Office, rolling the name around in his mouth, "it was your vote in the Cabinet meeting that plunged the dagger into my back and precipitated the first usurpation of power in American history."

"Rutherford B. Hayes pulled a fast one on Samuel Tilden," the Big Flower opined, and Ericson could visualize him looking at the ceiling, cigar in hand, comparing usurpations. "But I think I topped him."

"And yet," the President went on, "when the chips were down in the Congress, you not only helped me with the New York delegation, but you were a great source of confidence and strength."

"You never said a truer word."

"One theory for your apparent change of heart," Ericson said, "the one that several of your columnist friends have been touting, is that you were struck by a kind of postcoital remorse after the Cabinet vote. You then reversed field and sought to undo the mischief your vote had caused."

"You got a better theory, President Ericson?"

"No," said the President. "I like that theory. It has the virtue of simplicity. I hate to consider the possibilities of intrigue, with you as Warwick the kingmaker." He was telling Frangipani that he did not want to hear about any arrangements made with Speaker Frelingheusen, who had obviously delivered those last reluctant votes, as Andy had seemed confident he would. Ericson could not be so certain of Andy's primary motive, though he had an inkling of the long-range plan.

"It turned out they had the votes to impeach you," Frangipani said, as if changing the subject. "Majority of the House, which would have indicted you, and two thirds of the Senate for a conviction. You squeaked through on the difference between two thirds of the House and half the House—two thirds required by the Twenty-fifth and half in impeachment."

That was it, then; Frangipani had been convinced that if the Cabinet had not acted, the Congress would have—and the route of the Twenty-fifth Amendment offered a little more protection in the House to a President. "It wasn't exactly a vote of confidence," the President agreed.

"That's the next thing," said the Human Resources Secretary. "They'll all be hollering that you technically won, but you didn't really win—that you didn't get a vote of confidence. If we listen to them, all of a sudden we're England."

"Governing won't be easy, this way," Ericson said, thinking he would open the door for whatever suggestion Andy had in mind.

"Governing is going to be a bitch for three long years, and the Democratic party will be in a shambles for the next election," Frangipani was certain. "But don't get me wrong—it would have been worse with Roy Bannerman running the country, the arrogant slob."

"Then I suppose there's no way out." The President snapped his fingers a couple of times, and his dog came to his side. The animal no longer had to be kept in the kennel at all times, protecting Hank's cassettes. Hank had retrieved his cache an hour ago, convulsing the President with the glum comment "Damn mutt chewed up two of them," and enabling the dog to find a new home in the office. "Hullo, Hangin'ere."

"What kind of name is that for a dog?"

"I'm hanging in there, and he's with me."

The big dog nuzzled his hand, then walked over

to the Human Resources Secretary to sniff his shoes. "What would happen," Frangipani wondered to the dog, "if your master and Nichols were both to quit?"

Ericson knew the answer, of course, but hesitated before giving it. "The third in line would become the President."

"Who's that, anyway?" Frangipani rubbed the dog's ear. "The Secretary of State?"

Frangipani's plan, which had flickered in the back of Ericson's mind from time to time, came clear. The third in line to the presidency, as they both well knew, was the Speaker of the House.

"Used to be the Secretary of State," the President said noncommittally, "but they changed it a couple of decades ago."

Frangipani got up to leave. "One of these days, let's go for a ride on that fancy yacht of yours. You and me, Bannerman and Fong. Not Nichols."

"How would the people feel," said the President, addressing the problem inherent in Andy's plan, "about the presidency changing from one party to another during a President's term?"

"Not good," said Andy. "Be a bitch. But a lot would depend on whether you were talking about men who were middle-of-the-roaders, or rootin'-tootin' fire-eaters. You could maybe shift Democrat to Republican, as long as you didn't shift from a liberal to a conservative, or vice versa."

"I suppose there'd have to be some tacit understanding not to rock the boat during the remainder of the term," Ericson fished.

"You couldn't get anything in writing. Have to be a trustworthy sumbitch."

"That it would." Ericson did not want to take the thought any further at that time. He stood up, extended his hand: "Andy, your blessings come in great disguises."

Frangipani held the President's hand in the two of his own. "Invite me about your fancy yacht someday. I'll bring some friends, we'll talk."

"I wouldn't want to be party to anything that looked like a deal," Ericson said.

"That's what Lincoln—the guy you try to look like —used to say," Frangipani told him. "He sent a wire to his campaign manager at the 1860 convention, 'Make no deals in my name.' And David Davis, the manager, said, 'Hell—we're here and he's not.' Lincoln honored the deals."

"And Davis got on the Supreme Court," Ericson added. "You really want to be a judge?"

"Senator from New York," Andy corrected him. "Which I couldn't do next year if you were dragging the country and the party down. Sue me, I'm selfish."

"I wouldn't sue," said the President softly.

7

For two days, Ericson did nothing but practice walking with Hangin'ere, swim, take the sun, and cut himself off from the News Summary, which he knew was filled with apoplectic demands for his resignation after a "vote of no confidence." He gave Camp David to Lucas Cartwright for the weekend, to invite his friends and the key vote-getters in the House fight.

Sitting on the steps leading down to the Rose Garden at dusk, the President said to Hank Fowler, "The jay's gone."

After ten seconds of listening, the psychologist said, "Haven't heard him for a couple of days. You suppose he didn't hear about the House vote?"

Ericson smiled, and wondered at himself for missing the chattery bird. He was a source of sound, a helper; Ericson did not like his basics to change.

585

Maybe the bird didn't like the presence of the dog. You get some help, you lose some help.

"You're acting funny after your big victory," said Fowler.

Ericson leaned back and took a deep breath of the sultry air. Hank was doing his thing, which was fine with the President. "You're now a famous if somewhat controversial psychologist," he said. "You ought to be able to describe my mental attitude with something better than 'acting funny.' " Ericson remembered going through this routine with Herb Abelson long ago, and it depressed him.

"You've suddenly introverted," said Hank clinically. "After a period of daring action, you're withdrawing in fear. In a sense, you're letting the repressed fears of the past week catch up with you."

"And I'm getting all this free," said Ericson. *"Air Force One,* too. You wonder why I want to hang on to the presidency?"

"I wonder if you want to any more," said Fowler. When he did not follow up, the President was curious, but did not want to ask. He waited, and the psychologist went on, "Now that you've risen to the occasion, and defended the office, you'd just as soon chuck it." Ericson thought of the gardener, his use of "chuck it." He made a noncommittal grunt, and Hank kept going. "But you know yourself now, and you recognize the danger of letdown, and you don't want to do anything at a time when you're tired and scared."

The President nodded, did not say "um." Instead he said to Fowler, "You know what you're thinking? You're thinking you've just come through your first brush with scandal, your first career fear since you overcame your blindness. You want a little time in the White House now, to get sanitized, to let everything settle down before moving on."

"Hennessy would say that's practicing without a license," Fowler said, and Ericson could hear the grin in his voice.

Ericson put his hand on his chest. "I always thought the expression 'my heart sunk' was just an expression.

But whenever I think of Hennessy, that part of me, behind bars, my heart feels like it drops in my chest. I'm not suitably detached about Hennessy yet. Let's train the dog." They got up, took a turn around the darkening garden, down the colonnade into the basement of the residence, in and out of the library and across the hall to the Gold Room and the China Room, without a mistake, except for bumping into a Secret Service man near the Oval Office who had been ordered not to make a sound or to get out of the way.

Hank went his way, and Ericson sat behind the desk in the Oval Office in the dark, the dog panting gently at his feet. He could hear Melinda still in her office, and the guard at the hallway door reporting to the switchboard on the President's whereabouts. Ericson had no plans for dinner. He thought about Marilee, then decided he would tell Harry Bok to set up Silent Sam for later that night. The buzzer sounded, and Melinda said that the Secretary of State was there, just happened by after a meeting upstairs, and wondered if he could see the President.

"George, why don't you have dinner with me?" Ericson could sense the surprise and delight as Curtice stammered his acceptance.

"You sure you don't have other plans?" Ericson liked this game. People always had other plans, which they immediately broke at the President's invitation. "If you do, just say so, I'll quite understand—" As usual, his invitee expostulated his protests, anxious to dine with the President, but Ericson kept at it: "You do a lot of work at those dinners in Georgetown, George, I appreciate that—"

"Mr. President, you know I understand something about protocol," Curtice finally broke in, "and the first rule of Washington protocol is that a White House invitation takes precedence over all others. It cannot be turned down on the excuse of a previous engagement. Now, you know I have dinner plans, and you know that the best thing that could happen is for me to send word I can't come because I'm having dinner alone with the President."

Ericson laughed and said, "Follow me, then, the mutt and I will take you there." In Ericson's estimation, Curtice was a useful executive.

At dinner, Curtice put the question Ericson knew was on his mind: "Why haven't you asked for my resignation, Mr. President?"

Ericson's mind framed the honest answer: He didn't have to. In firing Fong and Duparquet, he had removed the possibility of losing another Cabinet vote, so he could keep Curtice on with no danger to himself. Besides, he didn't want to meet new people. And firing Curtice would alienate blacks and some liberals, while ostentatiously keeping him bought Ericson some support in that area. Aloud, he said, "George, I quite understood your vote last month, and if I were you, and had to do something to make good on the Yalta decision"—he would never use the word "deceit" in that context—"I would probably have voted as you did. More important, what you did in Yalta will be remembered kindly by history, no matter what they say now. And most important, I need you. Figure on sticking around a long time."

The man was obviously moved; Ericson was glad he had not been honest. "Mr. President, you have just created yourself the most profoundly loyal Secretary of State any President ever had, from here on in." After a swallowing, the deep voice picked up: "Next topic: How long is 'from here on in'?"

"Figure at least one whole term, maybe two," said Ericson. Curtice, who leaked judiciously in Georgetown, would get that assurance around in no time, and far more effectively than any statement by Smitty or Marilee.

"That's good news," the Secretary said. "Now let's move on Nikolayev. You proved you didn't need him, but he still needs you. Let's get him over here and prop him up."

"I concur," said Ericson. "Concur" was a better word than "agree" when talking statecraft. "You take charge of the whole thing, George, timing, arrangements, everything. Send Nikolayev a personal message from me, and use the phrase 'Felix has iron in his spine.' Got that? It's a cryptic reference to Lubyanka Prison, where he was never held prisoner, no matter what poor Sam Zophar was led to believe. Here's Melinda now." Ericson could smell Ma Griffe at the door, where Melinda was standing; he had buzzed for her a moment before. "Melinda, the Secretary is going to move forward with the Soviet Union in setting up a Nikolayev visit. He's to have charge of my calendar, priority over everything else. George, you work with her, no red tape." Ericson did not want Smitty, his chief of staff, bollixing up the arrangements; Melinda was to be the channel. He would get Smitty busy on something else.

Curtice and Melinda left together. Ericson put his request in with Harry Bok for later that night, asked the butler for a large glass of brandy, and said to his dog, "C'mon, Hangin'ere, I'll show you around this place." The President felt the need to get the feel of the whole White House again.

He strapped the walking handle on the dog, felt the animal become an extension of his arm, and they set out together. From the small dining room into the State Dining Room, around the long table, to the mantelpiece. He felt the inscription cut in the marble, and read it to the dog: " 'May none but Honest and Wise men rule under This Roof.' John Adams. His wife used to hang the washing in here, or maybe it was the East Room." They walked along the corridor through the Red Room, the Blue Room, the Green Room, to the East Room. He felt the dog tense, sensed the Secret Service man directly ahead, said hello, and walked around him. Ericson was really delighted with the way the dog worked, and he hardly knew how to work with him at all. He now had a friend he did not owe anything to; the dog was rewarded by the success of his service. Throughout the House, Ericson soberly told Hangin'ere about the Presidents whose portraits hung on the walls, remembering where each one was; on the stairway upstairs, he pointed to an Alaskan landscape, "where the Huskies come from." It occurred to Ericson that the staff and guards, tracking him from station to station, thought him eccentric, talking to the dog about the pictures, and that pleased him. Everybody needed something for his memoirs, maids and butlers included.

He stopped halfway up the stairs and sat on the landing. Good house, he thought; not a palace, not a museum, and not, as some Presidents called it, "a big white jail." Ericson was sitting in its approximate center, with two floors above and below him, the East and West wings stretching out on either side. Most of the other trappings of office were ego-satisfying—the motorcades, the plane, Camp David, the Marine Band, the cocoon of aides and guards—but the House had what none of those had: the ability to give its occupant a historic sense of place. The House was not too big or imposing; the new Governor's Mansion he had lived in last was almost the same size. The White House was in proportion and tasteful, neither too niggardly nor too lavish, a center for a democracy to be proud of and not for antiroyalists to be guilty about. It was permanent and continuing, with every President adding something or fixing something, only a few diminishing it in any way.

Ericson tried to let the House help him decide whether or not he belonged there, in his current state. Up the stairs and down the hall, the presence of Lincoln made itself felt in the bedroom and sitting room, not as a shrine requiring reverence, but as the place where a man had lived and worked and left a residue of himself, or so Ericson sensed. A shrewd and manipulative man, Lincoln, when you cut through the hero-worship: Ericson always admired the clever way his Emancipation Proclamation during the Civil War freed only those slaves in the states in rebellion, and not in the loyal border states.

Would he weaken the place more by staying or by going? Ericson had shown them all he was a President, a real one, the forty-first in the long line, some of whom must have sat here after a ball or after a crisis wondering how he would look measured against all the others. Sven Ericson had proven he could not be pushed out; the Twenty-fifth Amendment, with all its potential for mischief, would always be narrowed by his precedent. But now Andy Frangipani had most skillfully removed Ericson's second strongest reason for staying—the certainty that the successor would be worse. If Nichols could be removed, if Mort Frelingheusen were the successor, the nation would be well served. The sudden loss of that defense, which had seen him through the grimmest moments, left Ericson feeling that he was standing on a trap door with the spring, like a remote-control switch for the television, in his hand. All he was left with, to keep himself in place, was the "only Ericson" theme —only he had the vision of the good economy that could open the way to the good society. And all by itself, that defense struck Ericson as somewhat egotistical, since it was possible that his economic ideas could be all wrong.

Observing himself going through this process, as Ericson always liked to do, he noted with pride that he was thinking like a patriot: no longer his personal need to hang in, nor the dread of what else he would do, nor the sense that the job now owed him a second sight. He was putting the needs of the country first, weighing what was best without a trace of selfishness or pettiness.

"Really most impressive," he said to the dog, still in harness. "If I'm this good, why don't I stay?"

One answer to that, Ericson knew, was the misleadability of a blind man. Of late, as he signed a bill that had been read to him, or listened to an oral briefing based on a long memorandum that he would have read when he could see, he experienced a nagging worry about how dependent on other people— and on other, imprecise senses—he really was. He had helped crank out the propaganda about how the President had learned to cope, and had come to believe much of it himself, but there was that uncertainty about some moment, sometime—at a crucial moment, perhaps—when he might be taken advantage of. Ericson took a quick think at the thought and suppressed it, because it undermined his confidence.

He followed Hangin'ere up the stairs to the residence, feeling pretty good about himself, aware that he was going through the much-written-about Decision-Making Process. A part of the apparatus was missing, he knew, which had been missing most of his life: a partner, someone to brag to and lean on. A loner's life had its advantages—God, the responsibilities and time-wasting it avoided—but sometimes the blessed privacy wore thin.

The dog took its accustomed place at the door to the President's bedroom, next to the Secret Service man, and Ericson went in, closing the door softly behind him. The welcome smell of his favorite cheap perfume was there; the woman moved in bed and he could hear the covers being slid back for him. He took off his clothes in the familiar darkness and sat on the edge of the bed, wondering whether to make love to Silent Sam first and get a relaxing massage afterward, or to get a stimulating massage first and relax in making love to her afterward. He turned the alternatives over slowly in his mind, savoring each. She touched him, dragging her hair along his leg, and he decided the massage would come later.

He filled his hand with a generous breast, firmer than usual, reflecting the time of the month, he presumed, and kissed her neck, burying his face in the source of that Apple Blossom, or Lily of the Valley, or whatever it was that Silent Sam wore. He had a clear picture of her in his mind, a nude in an Ingmar Bergman movie of the sixties—long, rangy, striking body, a ruddy glow to her skin—and he let himself romanticize her face, it cost him nothing and pleased him to make her more of a perfect beauty in his imagination. She played to his sense of touch, as she always did, working her fingers in his back, and he slid into a gentle, easy rhythm until he broke through to a new level of passion in her, following that pleasurably through to her stormy orgasm and then, less fiercely, his own. She was getting better all the time, he thought, and he was visualizing Buffie less and less during the love-making. He rolled off her after a few moments and lay on his stomach, arms spread, forehead on his hands, awaiting the massage.

Which was not forthcoming. That annoyed him a little, since he had grown accustomed to the finishing touch, but he did not want to ask; it had to be part of an act of love, not a routine in a massage parlor. After a while, Ericson propped himself on an elbow and trailed his fingers along her body, still trembling, moist with perspiration. He touched the long blond hair, typical of Scandinavian women he had known, and after a moment touched it again.

"You got a haircut?"

"Um," she murmured, still far away.

He put his hand on her belly, located the navel, and moved his hand to touch her appendicitis scar. No scar. He touched her nipple again, which was buttonlike on Nurse Kellgren. This nipple was pointed —nice, but not the same. It dawned on Ericson that Harry Bok had slipped a ringer in on him.

His first reaction was annoyance—he never liked to be tricked—but that soon passed to concern whether she was discreet. That passed in a second, too, since Harry Bok would surely have been careful; and was replaced by a wry amusement. He went over several appropriate lines: "Dr. Livingstone, I presume?" came to mind, followed by a direct and polite "Have we met? I'm the President, I live here." He considered a stern accusation: "You are not Lieutenant Kellgren, you are an imposter." Or a mock-scary "You ready now for the whips and chains?"

He was grinning broadly at his range of options when he felt her slide into a sitting position, take a deep breath, and say in a small but very familiar voice, "It's me, Melinda."

That threw him. Ericson had not expected that at all, and he did not respond, except to stop grinning. After a long pause, he managed to get out, "Long time no see."

"That's the sort of thing Hennessy would say," she whispered.

The double meaning of his own line registered on him. "I used to write all of Hennessy's black humor," he said, sitting up next to her. "To annoy you."

"Are you mad at me?"

"Hell, no. A little surprised, that's all. You bring the News Summary?"

"Oh, c'mon!"

He reached over and touched her familiar face, then brought her forward for a serious kiss on the mouth. "You're a lovely woman," he said afterward, "and your timing is right."

"Now I feel awkward," she said. "And I didn't before."

"You weren't and you needn't be. Pour us a brandy, it's in the night table."

She put the glass in his hand and said, "Eight years."

"You've improved."

"You, too."

Ericson allowed to himself that he was really very pleased. "Okay now, what's all this about?" he kidded her. "You want me to give Duparquet his job back? You didn't have to go this far."

"What especially killed me was when you found out about that, it didn't bother you a bit."

In fact, it had, Ericson recalled, but he had seen the importance of their affair to his chances. "Course not," he said. "I never thought of you like this, naked, excited. Hennessy thought about it all the time, though. He had the hots for you, Melinda."

"It hurts just to think about him."

He sipped his brandy and fell into thought. She showered and came back to say, "I suppose I should go now."

"No, sleep with me from now on," he said casually. "You know, I've been thinking, it's pretty scary."

"What is?"

"How completely fooled I was. I expected Silent Sam to be here. When I came in, I smelled her perfume, so I was certain it was her. And I touched her breast, and it wasn't exactly the same, so I adjusted for it, forcing a fact into my preconception. I only saw what I expected to see, not the woman who was there. And I acted on that belief. When you think about it, that's a little scary."

"Look, it was the only way I—"

"I know, I know, and it's for the best. But it sure makes the point about how blind a blind man really is." He thought about that some more, as she slipped into bed beside him. "I am really quite dependent on the impressions I receive from others. It's not all that hard to fool a blind man, and even easier for a blind man to fool himself."

"Never again, I swear."

"You don't understand. And you're an intelligent woman, and you should understand. So I'll explain it at some length. Sit up and pour another drink. What time is it?"

"Only about eleven."

"Get me Frangipani."

"Back to work," she mumbled, picking up the telephone and placing the call. She handed him the receiver when the Secretary came on the line.

"Be at the dock tomorrow night at eight," Ericson said without preliminaries, "for a ride on the fancy yacht. Bring your friends. Good. This is not a commitment, Andy, I'm just checking around to see what my options are. Right." He handed her back the phone. "Tell the Navy I want the *Sequoia* tomorrow night for dinner, four people, sailing about eight-fifteen." She made the arrangements in a quick call.

"Now pay attention," he said. "I want to work this out in my head, thinking aloud. When you see an inconsistency, holler. Don't let me get away with anything, and do not let your own prejudices get in our way. Okay? May take a couple of hours, I've got a lot to say, I think." He felt good that she was there, and not Silent Sam, or even Buffie. "And afterward," he added, thinking of them, "I'm going to take you apart."

8

The President, by prearrangement, was the last to board. Hangin'ere did not seem enthusiastic about leading his master onto the ship, but when Ericson started up the gangway, the dog led the way. The four men sat together aft, in the open air, making conversation about the dog, until Bannerman abruptly said, "Congratulations on your victory, Mr. President, if you can call a vote of no confidence a victory. I think it was a disaster for the nation."

"Good ol' Roy," said Frangipani heartily, "a master of indirection. Stop beating around the bush, Bannerman—tell us how you really feel."

Fong cut in. "You won fair and square, Mr. President. I bear you no resentment." He tinkled the ice in his glass. "Here's mud in your eye."

There was an awkward silence at the foot-in-mouth toast, which Ericson enjoyed; Frangipani relaxed the tension with "Hey, I'm the one who specializes in malaprops, Mike," and Ericson could hear them all laugh except Bannerman.

The *Sequoia* slid down the Potomac toward Mount Vernon as Frangipani launched into a story about the looks on the faces of certain congressmen when the last crop of yes votes squeaked Ericson through. The President, who thought a better way to relax Bannerman would be to flatter his interest in foreign affairs, reported confidentially that George Curtice had arranged with Nikolayev to visit the United States in two weeks.

Bannerman was not having any. "Let's get down to

business. Mike said he and Andy were cooking up a scheme. Let's put it on the table."

"Andy," Ericson said with a trace of disapproval in his tone, "you didn't tell me you had a scheme in mind. You said this would be a smoking of the peace-pipe."

"I lied," said Frangipani. "Mike and I have a bomb to drop on both of you."

"It's Andy's idea," said Fong.

"Here's the problem," said Andy. "Roy here thinks the country is going to hell under a disabled President. He's at least partly right. The President here will be damned if he'll be pushed out of office, and now that Arnold Nichols has grabbed his power for three weeks, the President will be damned if he'll ever re-sign if it means that Arnold becomes President. Right?"

Ericson nodded. That was a good way to play it— not to say that Ericson would refuse to turn power over to Bannerman and his cat's-paw, but to suggest that the President was piqued at Nichols. In that way, Frangipani offered some hope to Bannerman. "If you nod or shake your head," the President said to Ban-nerman, "please make some positive or negative noise for my benefit."

"I didn't bat an eye," said Bannerman.

"Here's the solution," Andy continued. "Banner-man gets what he wants, the President avoids what worries him, and the country gets a President who's one hundred per cent."

"How?" said the President, for Bannerman's bene-fit.

"You resign, Mr. President," Frangipani began.

"The hell with that," said Ericson promptly.

"—you resign upon receiving the resignation of the Vice-President. The Speaker of the House would then become President."

"Ridiculous," said Bannerman.

"The difficulty," Fong said carefully, "which we recognize, is that it would transfer power in the exec-utive branch from the Democrats to the Republicans." Fong, who evidently had worked this out with Frangipani, was acting as if this party-to-party matter would be uppermost in Bannerman's mind. Ericson knew that Bannerman would attach little if any significance to the party switch, but saw that it was a good idea for Mike Fong to argue a non-existent objection first.

"No doubt that's a drawback," said Andy. "That's why the President and Vice-President run as a team, to ensure party continuity. But look at it this way: The country's in a bind. Ericson ain't ever gonna quit unless Nichols quits, too. And there isn't that much ideological difference between Ericson and Mort Frelingheusen. Not like jumping from a radical to a reactionary."

"And perhaps something could be worked out," added Fong, "in a gentleman's agreement, to see to it that a certain percentage of Schedule C appointees stayed on. Half, maybe."

Bannerman did not react further, at least audibly, so Ericson shook his head no. "I don't like it," he said. "It's a constructive thought—I'd certainly not resign otherwise—but it would smack too much of a deal. People wouldn't stand for it."

"People would stand for a lot," Bannerman finally said heavily, "to get you out of the White House."

"I have to feed my dog," said the President. "After I do that, we can all have dinner." He went below, to give Fong and Frangipani a chance to work Bannerman over, and to give the double-resignation idea a final review in his own mind.

The bowl of dry dog meal was on the left of the sink in the galley, easy to hand; Ericson turned the faucet on, let half a cupful run into the bowl, mixed the mess with his finger, stooped and put the bowl in front of Hangin'ere. Hank had told him it was important the master feed the dog himself, with his own hands, and not to delegate the chore to anyone. The President liked doing it; few other ordinary tasks were left to him.

He did not have to make a decision until Bannerman went for the deal. No pressure to decide yet. Ericson could still indulge in the pleasure of "what-if," in a kind of ideas purgatory, without feeling the lash of decision's deadline. If Bannerman said okay, and pulled out Nichols, what would Ericson do then? Go along? Back off, embarrassing Frangipani, who undoubtedly was assuring Bannerman he could deliver the President's agreement?

The dog was making no eating sounds. Ericson could not blame him, the cereal was so unappetizing, but Hank had cautioned not to spoil the animal with meat. The President said firmly, "Eat." He could hear the dog sniff the bowl and back away.

Ericson squatted down, rested a knee on the galley floor, took a handful of the meal and held it out to Hangin'ere, who licked it out of his hand. "There are these four jockeys, see? One of them needs power and can handle it fine, that used to be me." He fed him a second handful. "The second jockey needs power but can't handle it at all, that's been me since the ambush." He fed the dog a third handful. "This is political wisdom, Hangin'ere, Hank got it straight from that bastard Leigh. I hope he got it straight. The third jockey does not have that awful need for power—here, eat from the bowl—but he can't handle power all that well. That's me, today—none of the drawbacks of a power-nut any more, but none of the advantages, either." The dog began to eat less tentatively and Ericson stood up.

"You are wondering about the fourth jockey," he said, leaning against the narrow doorjamb, talking to the dog, "the one that doesn't need the power but who can handle it with ease. Let me tell you, ol' buddy, those kind are hard to find, and I'm sure as hell not there yet." Ericson felt around for the other, smaller bowl on the countertop, found it, filled it with water, and put it down next to the eating bowl. The dog gratefully switched over and slurped it up, returning to the cereal with zest, his license tag rhythmically clopping against the dish as he ate. "Maybe someday, though. Could happen."

The President stretched, smiled, and thought again

about that wondrous, amorphous, always-capitalized mystery called The Decision-Making Process. When had he decided to give up his presidency? Just now, as he was feeding the dog? Or in bed with Melinda, as the realization of the ease at a blind man's tricking himself had sunk in? Or before that, as Andy Frangipani began his maneuvering with Ericson's tacit approval?

The truth about big decisions, Ericson mused, was that they never marched through logical processes, staff systems, option papers, and yellow pads to a conclusion. No dramatic bottom lines, no Thurberian captains with their voices like thin ice breaking, announcing, "We're going through!" The big ones were a matter of mental sets, predispositions, tendencies—taking a lifetime to determine—followed by the battering of circumstance, the search for a feeling of what was right—never concluded at some finite moment of conclusion, but in the recollection of having "known" what the decision would be some indeterminate time before. For weeks now, Ericson knew he had known he was ready to do what he had to do, if only Andy or somebody could be induced to come up with a solution that the President could then put through his Decision-Making Process. That made his decision a willingness not to obstruct, rather than a decision to go ahead, much like Truman's unwillingness to stop the train of events that led to the dropping of the A-bomb—not on the same level of magnitude, but the same type of reluctant going-along.

"I haven't decided yet," he cautioned the dog, who was moving the bowl around with his tongue but no longer making crunching sounds. "A decision is not a decision until it has to be made." Relieved, slightly euphoric, feeling admirably patriotic, Ericson moved to the main cabin to join the others for dinner. He put on a frown and said nothing. After the four had wolfed down their microwaved steaks, Bannerman offered a thought that cast his first light of encouragement on the idea. "If you ever did something like this—and I'm sure Arnold Nichols would never stand for it—the successor would have to have a coalition government."

"Like FDR had in the war," said Andy. "Half Democrats, half Republicans, a government of national unity for a few years. There's a precedent."

"No," Bannerman said, "I mean at the highest level."

They all chewed on that. Fong finally put it forward: "There would have to be some assurance that the new President would appoint a Vice-President from the same party as the resigning President."

"So Democrat Ericson resigns," said Andy, the soul of reason, "along with Nichols, Republican Frelinghuesen takes over, and appoints a Democrat as Vice-President. What could be more natural?"

"I agree with Roy's first reaction," Ericson said, rising from the table, "the whole thing is ridiculous. Nobody will ever get Arnold Nichols to resign, and nobody—and I mean nobody—can commit the next President to do anything. It would be plain wrong to ascend to the presidency on the basis of some kind of promise. Immoral. Forget it. Let me show you the fo'c'sle, Andy."

The two went up front. "He's nibbling," said Ericson, in mild wonderment.

"You shoulda been a goddamn Broadway star," Frangipani said. "You're an actor. I dunno if I trust you any more. What do you suppose he'll take?"

"You're sure he can deliver Nichols' resignation?" asked Ericson.

"I'm sure."

"Bannerman wants the vice-presidency for himself, Andy. That's what he can taste."

"That's kind of a steep price."

"Look. I cannot even consider it. If you think I am considering it, you're mistaken." Then the President added, with care: "But you've been mistaken before. Go talk to him." It was a pleasure dealing with Andy. Ericson would swear he never offered—or permitted to be offered—any assurances to Bannerman that he would be Vice-President, or even to ask the next President for any such consideration.

Frangipani could swear the same thing, right along with Ericson, but he could also say to Bannerman he thought the President might consider it—and what would be the harm in trying?

"You can't be present on that pitch," Andy said. "Come back in ten minutes. You're blind, you got a great poker face, stick with it."

"Make no deals in my name," quoted the President, smiling.

Ericson waited while Frangipani dangled the vice-presidency in front of Bannerman, which the President could deny on a stack of Bibles he had ever authorized. Ericson left it to Andy to get Fong and Bannerman to agree not to ask a President in advance for such an improper guarantee.

When he came back to the open deck aft, the yacht had arrived at the point in the Potomac opposite George Washington's home in Mount Vernon. The crew lined up for the formal salute, the tinny tape played "The Star-Spangled Banner," and the four men joined the crew in the short ceremony. Ericson, saluting, asked his predecessor's forgiveness for what he had to do to protect the office the first President had established. Nobody ever feels toward George Washington quite like the man who holds his job currently, Ericson silently observed. He wondered how he would feel about the Founding Father afterward. "Founding Father" was a great phrase—but who remembered that its coiner was Warren Harding?

"Andy has made clear," said Bannerman, after the salute ended, "that nobody can commit the next President to anything. He has given me his promise of 'best efforts,' that does not require you to say anything."

"I have promised nobody anything," said the President firmly, hoping Bannerman would not believe him, "and I have authorized nobody to promise anything." Trying to sound like he was lying did not come easy—that was a specialty of that bastard Leigh's.

"Of course," Bannerman said impatiently. "I will undertake to get Arnold Nichols into your office tomorrow with his resignation in hand. If I do that, do I have your word of honor that your resignation will be delivered to the Secretary of State within the hour?"

Ericson looked downcast. Finally, solemnly, he said, "You have my word. And do I have your word that nobody discusses this with anybody, especially Speaker Frelingheusen? If anybody approaches him, no matter what the subterfuge, all bets are off."

"Agreed," said Bannerman.

They sat in silence under the stars, as the ship circled and headed back up the Potomac. "It's pretty corny, this setting," said Frangipani, "for a historic moment. We can hope ol' George would approve."

Ericson thought Mike Fong made the appropriate comment, paraphrasing the first President. "More than that—we can hope that the next President will raise 'a standard to which the wise and honest can repair.'"

9

"It's Bannerman," Melinda said. "Can I listen?"

"Might as well," said the President. "And take notes." It had been a long morning.

"Arnold Nichols is here with me," said Bannerman briskly. "He wishes to speak with you."

"Mr. President?" the voice was strained.

"Hello, Arnold."

"I have written my letter of resignation," the Vice-President said, "and I am available to come to your office and sign it at your convenience."

"You're acting in the best interests of the country," Ericson said with sincerity.

"I am doing so," Nichols said, as if reading from a

card, "on the understanding that you will submit your own resignation within one hour after the effective moment of mine."

"Your understanding is correct," Ericson told him. "Say nothing to anybody. Come to the Cabinet Room at four o'clock. The Secretary of State will be there, and he will not know what he will be there for. He's the one authorized to receive our resignations. A few minutes after you do, I will." He reached for something else to say. "After that, we'll both be a couple of has-beens, Arnold." A couple of gunfighters who had polished each other off, leaving the front room of the jail for a new sheriff.

"I'm convinced it's the best thing for the country." The Vice-President, using Ericson's earlier phrase, did not sound convinced; Bannerman must have worked him over severely.

"Be here at four. George Curtice will be here, and you tell him what it's about." The President put down the phone.

Melinda came in. "I better arrange to have the Secretary of State over here, don't you think? We don't want him flying off somewhere."

"Good thought," said Ericson. That would have been embarrassing, forgetting to get Curtice.

"And you might want to write out your resignation, in your own hand," she said quietly. "There's a precedent: It's only one line."

He shook his head, pulling a piece of writing paper out of his drawer. "I'll do it in two lines." He had already given the matter some thought. An inch in from the paper's edge he began: "To the Secretary of State:" On a line below, he wrote, "I am sworn to preserve, protect, and defend the Constitution of the United States of America." He started a new paragraph: "To make certain that my responsibility is carried out, I hereby resign the office of President." He decided not to write "Very truly yours" and simply signed his name, writing the date underneath. He pushed it across the desk. "How's it look?"

Melinda did not respond right away. Ericson remembered seeing her in silent tears once, years ago, when her father died. After a moment, she choked out, "It looks cockeyed. Write it out again." He tried a couple more times, until she was satisfied.

He asked the operator for the Chief Justice, and asked him to come to the Oval Office at four-thirty on a matter of some urgency, and to bring his robes. The jurist agreed, asking no questions, saying only, "Find out for me about 'so help me God,' if it's that." Ericson said he would. He called the Speaker of the House.

"Mort, I wonder if you'd be available to come by the office here about four-thirty today."

"Matter of fact, Mr. President, we have a caucus then. How about six or so?"

"Mort, it's kind of important you be here."

"It's kind of important I be here, too. What's up?"

"I need you here, Mort. I need your wife here, too." Short pause. "We'll be there. Four-thirty?"

"Four-thirty sharp," said Ericson. After he put down the phone, he looked toward Melinda. "What else?"

"We ought to get the press ready for something at four-thirty."

He nodded. "Send in Marilee. I want to have lunch with her." When Marilee came in, he said seriously, "Tell the press to be ready for a, what do you call it, a photo opportunity at four-thirty," he told her. "Be sure the regulars are here, and tell the nets they'll want a live pickup."

"What if they have to know what it's about? They don't like this business of doing anything the President says."

"Don't beg for anything," he told her. "So some network will miss it. They'll think twice the next time."

"Will you be available for questions?"

"No. And don't beat the drums on this, or get everybody excited. Low key."

"I'll get on it."

Ericson felt bad about not trusting her, but if he told her, and she did not pull out all the stops in alerting everybody, she would be blamed later. And he did not want the story out before the event, in case something went awry. She would just have to look uninformed before and after, which is a price press secretaries have to pay to retain their credibility.

"The guy you're going with," he said. "From the network. You serious about him?"

She said nothing for a moment, probably startled at the President's first expression of interest in her love life. "We're close," she said.

"Then be sure he's here." That was all he could do for her. "Send Melinda back in." When the press secretary had left and his personal secretary reappeared, Ericson said impatiently, "What are we forgetting? Got a Bible? I don't want any last-minute rushing around."

"I went ahead and spoke to Mrs. Frelingheusen," Melinda said, "and asked her to bring her family Bible, to lend you for something. Also to bring her two children, who are teen-agers and in town. It's taking a chance on a leak, but you can't leave his family out of this."

He nodded approval, and snapped his fingers. "The oath. It's not the usual federal oath, and the Chief Justice doesn't always know—"

"I have the right one here, right out of the Constitution, typed on a card for him."

"What would I do without you?" Then the meaning of that question struck him. "You're coming back with me, of course. They give me a hundred grand a year for staff, and the memoirs, and the mail—"

"Let me think about it."

"No." He shook his head. A fear clutched at him of what private life would be like without her. "Don't think about it. I need you, you know that. Don't waltz me around."

"This is no time to go into that," she said crisply. "The whole government is about to change—"

"It can all wait," he said, digging in his heels. Uncertainty about what would come after was not anything he wanted. "You coming with me, or not?"

"As what?"

That stopped him. "As everything," he said, surprised. "You know. Little of this, little of that—"

"We'll talk about it later."

"Talk now. What do you want?"

"Christ, you're romantic."

Did she want to be married? He did not want that. On the other hand, what if another Duparquet came along? If she were only a mistress-nurse-secretary, she could be tempted away. Marriage would lock it up.

"I want you to come with me," he said quickly but seriously, "and be my wife."

"I'd like that," she said, "but that wasn't what was worrying me. We'd live together, wife or not."

Ericson, for the life of him, could not understand what she was getting at. What else was there? His expression must have transmitted itself, because Melinda said, "I want to be personal secretary, too."

"Well, of course you'll be that—"

"—starting at my present salary, with cost-of-living escalations."

His jaw set. That would eat up half of his mandated staff allowance. "We'll talk later," he said.

"That's what I thought you'd say."

"You want a hell of a package."

"You're not all that much of a bargain," she replied coolly.

"Taking advantage of a national crisis," he grumbled.

"Where did I learn that from?"

Time was pressing. "No marriage," he said. "Live together. Same salary, with the escalator predicated on the staff allowance escalator."

"A deal," she agreed. She had not been bluffing.

"I'm changing the deal," he said. "We get married in a week."

"A month," she countered. "If we're going to do it, we'll do it right."

"Deal," he said. They shook hands, and he pulled her to him.

"We're in the Oval Office," she said, after a moment.

"You've got no idea what I've done in the Oval Office," he said.

"I have a very explicit idea. Hennessy used to tell

me about it in detail, because it drove me up the wall."

"Okay," he said, his mind moving to the next problem. "What are we forgetting? Get me whatsisname of the Secret Service, the director."

"Rufus Hewitt," she said, going to the phone.

Melinda reached Director Hewitt quickly, and Ericson said, "I want you to know that there will be a need to cover the Speaker of the House and his family after five o'clock today. No, I can't, and I don't want it noised around. Say, Rufus, remember that commitment of yours on Harry Bok? I'd like you to make the appointment to the counterfeiting division close of business today." He listened to the director apologize for the last time they met, and cheerfully said, "Oh, that turned out to be a good idea, most of the files are still sealed and they're better off that way. I still only use one drawer of Hoover's desk, the one for the taffy." He laughed, adding, "You won't forget about Harry."

The President then propped his elbows on his desk and dug his fists in his eyes. He knew Melinda was thinking what he was thinking. "No," he said. "I can't pardon Hennessy. It would be bad for him and bad for me, in the long run."

"Mainly bad for you," she said.

He sighed. "You're thinking that I'm a bit of a shit." She did not contradict him. "It wouldn't be right for me to do. Maybe . . ." he let his voice trail off. Then: "What else?"

"You want to let Nikolayev know ahead of time?"

Ericson had already thought that through. "Tell the hot-line boys to put in a call for four-fifteen sharp. Not from me, from George Curtice. The brownie points can accrue to him, for whatever they're worth. Vasily won't last long." He pulled out a letterhead. "To the Senate of the United States," he wrote. "I hereby nominate Michael Fong, of Arizona, to be Federal District judge to fill the vacancy in the Sixth Judicial District." He signed and dated it, and held it out: "Legible?"

"That's a good thing to do," said Melinda, after reading it. "Takes him out of Bannerman's clutches for the rest of his life."

"I had Mike wrong. I used to think he was only a stooge. He thought he was doing the right thing, kind of a Starbuck. He was a lot of trouble, but Fong was no stooge."

"Any other last-minute acts?"

"I'd like to fire the goddamn gardener," Ericson mused. He turned to the dog at the side of the desk. "You know what I'm going to call you from now on? 'Chuckit.' Here, Chuckit."

"Don't confuse the animal," Melinda said. Ericson reached in the taffy drawer, took out a dog biscuit, and gave it to him, apologizing. That morning, he had reached in absent-mindedly for a salt-water taffy and had wound up nibbling one of the dog's tasteless milk bones. The President didn't tell anybody about that.

"Okay." He leaned back, swiveling his chair and looking out at the brightness, feeling relieved, excited, melancholy, authoritative. Oddly, the thought occurred that all this meant he would have to stop for traffic lights again. Ericson could not remember the last time he was in a car that stopped for a traffic light. He would even have to carry money, if he could figure out a method to tell a finn from a sawbuck. "God bless Captain Vere," he said to nobody, rocking back in the big chair behind the Hoover desk, knowing that—for a change—this was one of those instances when he had started a chain of events that would march to the conclusion he had intended.

10

At five minutes past four, the President entered the Cabinet Room. The shaken voice of Secretary of State George Curtice informed him, "As you know, sir, the Vice-President here has just submitted his resignation."

"How do you know I know?" The President was curious.

"I'll read you his letter. 'Anticipating the resignation of the President immediately following my action, I tender herewith my resignation as Vice-President of the United States.' "

The President smiled. Bannerman didn't trust him at all, even to the point of engraving into the history books that mistrust of some last-minute Ericson deceit. He reached into his pocket and said, "We won't have to wait an hour. I brought along my letter, too."

"No," said Curtice. "Wait. You hold on to that, Mr. President. I'm not sure the Vice-President's letter is legal and proper. It seems, to me at least, to predicate the fact of his resignation on another event. He can't do that. Either he resigns, flatly, or not."

"Perhaps I should consult counsel," Arnold Nichols wavered.

"Look, Arnold," the President said, with events stacking up behind him, like aircraft at a befogged airport, "you see I'm about to hand in my resignation. I'm not pulling any fast ones. Now, why don't you just write 'I resign the vice-presidency effective'—what's the time, George?"

"Four-oh-seven."

"Effective four-oh-seven and the date, and then sign your name."

"In your opinion, Mr. Secretary," Nichols asked formally, "would that be proper?"

"Entirely, Mr. Vice-President."

Ericson heard the felt-tip pen rubbing on the paper, ending with the flourish that was Nichols' ostentatious signature. "Let's let a minute go by," the President said. "George, I took the liberty of placing a hot-line call for you to Premier Nikolayev, so you can inform him first of this action, and of the swearing-in of President Frelingheusen." That was the first time those two words had been used together, he noted. "Arnold, I think it would be good if you and I stood flanking him at that ceremony, don't you? It'll be at four-thirty in the briefing room. You stand next to the Chief Justice, I'll stand alongside Mort. His wife will be in the middle with the Bible. George, don't dawdle on that call from the Sit Room, you'll miss the fun. Tell Vasily time is money." Ericson felt himself beginning to chatter too much. He shut up to match the nature of the occasion.

He unfolded his letter, put it on the table, took out a pen that he intended to keep, and said, "What time is it?"

"Four-oh-nine."

"By that Naval Observatory clock." He pointed at the ticking sound.

"Four-oh-nine," Curtice repeated.

The President wrote the time on the letter of resignation, tapped it against his finger for a moment, held it out, and felt Curtice take it from his fingers. Sven Ericson was no longer President of the United States. He felt no different yet. "George, you go to the Sit Room. Arnold, please come with me." They went through Melinda's office to the Oval Office, and in a few moments, Melinda ushered in the Speaker of the House.

Ericson, in the center of the room, extended his hand. When Speaker Frelingheusen took it, Ericson said, "Good luck, Mr. President."

"I wish you could see the expression on Mort's face," said Nichols, swallowing. "He looks like he thinks you've got the people in the room mixed up."

"A few moments ago," Ericson said, still holding Frelingheusen's hand, "the Vice-President resigned, and then I resigned. Under the Presidential Succession Act, the office—and the powers and the duties—of the President devolve upon you. The Chief Justice is prepared to swear you in, your wife and children are with him now. Your wife brought a Bible. You will be sworn in, before the cameras, in the press briefing room, in a couple of minutes." Ericson thought to add, "If those arrangements are acceptable to you, Mr. President."

"They are," said the President, adding, "Mr. President."

Ericson remembered a couple of items the Chief Justice would need. "You want to 'swear' or 'affirm'? Constitution says you have a choice."

"I, uh—swear."

"And George Washington added 'So help me God' to the end of the oath. It's not in the Constitution, it's up to you."

Frelingheusen blinked.

Ericson helped him out: "Every President except Hoover has added it. He was Quaker, he thought it was excessive. If you want to, I have to tell the Chief Justice, because you repeat after him."

"Yes. Yes, of course."

Ericson smiled. There were certain details not even Melinda thought of, known but to Chief Justices and Presidents. He could not think of any others.

11

"I was dumbfounded," said the President. "For five minutes, it just wouldn't sink in. Did you ever have an experience like that?"

"Never," said Ericson. They were in the wing chairs next to the fireplace in the Oval Office, away from the desk, to avoid the awkwardness of one or the other sitting behind the desk. It was ten in the morning, and Ericson was to leave by helicopter from the White House lawn at noon. President Frelingheusen would move in, wife, kids, and sizable collection of tropical fish later that day. Ericson knew his successor had already been briefed on the black bag; as Speaker, with an interest in foreign affairs, Frelingheusen was current on intelligence estimates. "But there was no way of telling you in advance. I didn't have Nichols' resignation in hand."

"I hope it didn't show," President Frelingheusen said, "the daze I was in. I appreciate the way you made the arrangements, and especially thinking to have my children there. Really, that shows what kind of man you are, and I won't forget."

Ericson wished he had been the one to think of that, or even to be the sort of person who would put family considerations that high on the "must" list. He waved Melinda's thoughtfulness aside, and asked how he could help in the transition.

"Nikolayev," the President said, with an eastern "ev" rather than the "uv" that Ericson used. "You've got him coming here in a couple of weeks. I'll keep the appointment."

"Keep George Curtice on at least through the visit," Ericson advised, "and squeeze Nikolayev hard on lowering the throw-weight. Vasily's the front for the hard-liners in the Kremlin, who thought I needed him to stay in office. Now they're stuck with him for a while, so squeeze—we might not get a chance like this for years. And it might help us hold down the nuclear development of the Arab-Israeli bloc. I've left a long memo for you on that, in the middle drawer of the desk. No copies—use it or tear it up, I'm not telling you how to run things."

His last night in the White House, Ericson had spent dictating that memo, passing along to his successor all he thought could be useful in his relationship with the Soviet leader. He thought it was possible, nearly probable, that Nikolayev would be killed in a plane crash soon, now that his usefulness in dealing with Ericson was ended. But if he made it through the next three months, Nikolayev might last a long time, and the next man in the Oval Office deserved as much information as he could get in judging an adversary-ally.

Ericson had not intended to spend his last night working. On a whim, he had ordered dinner, alone, in the State Dining Room. Forty feet of table and one place mat. He dined on meat loaf, which he liked but had never ordered before—only squares order meat loaf—and a bottle of the 1969 Romanée-Conti. Sitting there, Ericson thought he could make out the blurred light from the sconces and chandeliers, and pictured some of the dinners at which he had presided. High times. He finished the wine with some Stilton cheese on a sliced McIntosh apple—he was going to miss the White House cuisine, no denying that—and had melded his arm to the dog for a final walk around the premises, projecting his mental pictures against the walls. Bidding a sentimental farewell to a place he had not really come to know, he was pleased to note that he was not awash with self-pity. In the Oval Office, sitting behind the desk for the last time, he had the idea for the Nikolayev memo for Frelingheusen, and spent his last hours there productively.

"That could not have been easy for you, under the circumstances," the new President said. He was a sensitive man, if taciturn; Ericson hoped that his admiration for Mort, and his good feelings about the rightness of the passage of power, would repress the natural jealously he felt toward his successor. This lucky man would have the chance to do so much that Ericson had hoped to do, and had expected to be credited by history with doing. "I'm grateful for the advice, and will continue to be." Frelingheusen shifted in the chair. "Yesterday being such a hectic day, did you forget to attend to any last-minute matters that I can be helpful with? I saw you appointed Mike Fong, and I'll push the confirmation, but anything else?"

"The reason we didn't have this talk yesterday," Ericson said clearly, "before you became President, is that I wanted to be absolutely sure that you took office with no commitments, to me or anybody. Especially to me."

"I'm aware of that," Frelingheusen replied. "Keenly. I can't read your mind, though—what would you do in my shoes?"

The President was graciously offering some patronage, but Ericson did not want to snap at it. "First, avoid being assassinated. No, I'm not kidding—let your movements be a surprise. Just pop in places, that's the only security you can ever have. You were a foot soldier in Vietnam, you don't have to prove to anybody how brave you are."

"Got it. What else?"

"Keep a diary. Not the big events you can reconstruct from the clips, but the little things. This meeting, here, now. You'll be amazed how your perceptions change in a short time, and it pays to remember what you were thinking when you did something. But hide the diary, for God's sake." He thought of Fowler and his head in the kennel, and the dog chewing up the cassettes. "Keep a photographic record, too—the official photographer, a girl, is very good. Schedule C, but not really a political appointment."

"I'll want to keep her, then."

"You'll like her work. Chef's good, too—ask for the meat loaf."

"What about the talk in all the papers this morning about a coalition government?"

Ericson leaned forward: "By 'all the papers,' you mean two papers. That's not all the papers. Don't get stampeded by the way they play the news, or what their editorials say, or what their columnists say. They have two big megaphones placed right up against our ears, but it's only two megaphones. Plenty other voices out there. That's what I like about the Presidential News Summary, it has fifty papers, and the opinions of all the media."

"But what about the idea of the coalition government," he persisted, "that a few people seem to be talking about?" Ericson liked that: The new man would not let his train of thought be derailed.

"I don't want to give you my opinion on that," Ericson said finally. "You and I have no understanding on it, unspoken or otherwise. Let it be a mystery."

"Some men, of your party," Frelingheusen went on, "have done important work, and made considerable sacrifices, in the cause of national unity."

"Arnold Nichols is a worn-out hack, and the biggest mistake I ever made was settling for him at the convention. In the name of party unity. If you want to make him ambassador to Lichtenstein, fine—unless you have friends in Lichtenstein."

No sound from the President. "I can't tell if you're nodding or shaking your head," said Ericson.

"I'm trying to wipe the smirk off my face that says, 'What a great judge of character.' "

"I suppose I have to warn you about one man in my party," said Ericson, as if it were painful. "Roy Bannerman. He's a bad man."

"He opposed you rather strongly," said Frelingheusen.

"That would be no reason to say he's a bad man.

Fong opposed me, too, and I made him a judge in my final act, because he's a good man." Ericson had appointed Fong, despite his personal pique, for the single purpose of making this point to the man who would follow him into the Oval Office. "Good men and bad men wanted me out, Mort"—using the first name was not a slip, Presidents could first-name each other—"but Bannerman is a man of great power and cunning, and of bad personal character." Ericson knew Frelingheusen set great store by personal character.

"Any funny business in the Treasury?"

"Not that I'm aware of, although it might be an idea to look into the relationship between the Treasury, the Ex-Im Bank, and the private banks in London. Could be some corruption there that would embarrass you, if it grows." He paused, as if debating whether to go on.

"Bad personal character, you said?"

"He's the sort of man who gets his kicks in slapping around women," Ericson blurted. "It makes my skin crawl, and I can't bear to be in the same room with him."

"You know that for a fact?"

"An absolute fact, from a woman he abused."

"The son of a bitch."

"I've told nobody else, but I suppose you should know." Ericson shook his head slowly, adding, "My one fear in leaving office, frankly, was that the man who followed me might not understand how urgent it is to keep that type of person away from any kind of power."

"Set that fear at rest, Sven. I'll not only not appoint him, I'll watch him."

"Don't be surprised if he comes to you saying he was promised the vice-presidency, and that's why he pulled Nichols out." Ericson wanted to put the last nail in Bannerman's coffin. "Absolutely untrue. I don't know why the hell he did it—Andy talked him into it—but that woman-beater Bannerman got no promise from me on anything."

"Forget about him, he's finished. What's your assessment of the Big Flower?"

"Good man. Going to run for the Senate next year in New York, should win, now that he doesn't have to worry about the Ericson drag." He debated whether to go further. "Be a good senator. Ready for even more, maybe."

"Um." From the nothing that Frelingheusen said, and from the direction of the questioning, Ericson got the feeling that Angelo Frangipani, Democrat, had a good chance of becoming the Vice-President in Republican Mortimer Frelingheusen's Administration. First time in nearly two centuries. It also made Ericson wonder if—in all his manipulating—he had been manipulated.

"What about Curtice?" the President said, as if to cover his intentions by adding another name.

"Personally, I don't like the man. Tricky on tactics, knows how to play the press, always covers his ass. But under pressure, shows a lot of character—I dumped a ton of bricks on him once, and he never budged off a position he thought was right."

"A devious man of character?"

"Good prescription for a Secretary of State."

"Duparquet?"

"Good field, no hit." Ericson did not want to see him climb to the top over the back of the President he double-crossed at the end. "The appearance of integrity is extremely important to him, even when it means not doing the right thing." Ericson also thought of the Attorney General's yearning for Melinda, and he relented a bit: "But good taste, good mind. Reminds me of me before I grew up."

"Speaking as a civil libertarian," said the President, "I thought his prosecution of Mark Hennessy was a disgrace."

Ericson had been hoping for a way to bring up the Hennessy matter. "You thought so, too?"

"I even said so publicly at the time, but nobody printed it," said the President. "It wasn't what anybody wanted to hear. Four days from grand jury appearance to perjury indictment, that's not justice, that's entrapment. Unpardonable."

Ericson shut his eyelids. Not all that subtly, his successor had worked the syllables "pardon" into the conversation, in another context. Frelingheusen was saying he would do the right thing by Hennessy, if Ericson's aide were convicted. Ericson said nothing for a moment, by way of saying thanks, then looked toward the french doors.

"The jay's back," he announced.

"Who?"

"Blue jay, hangs around the Rose Garden, chatters a lot. Part of the background noise, which you miss when it isn't there."

"Your staff is in the East Room," said the President, "waiting to say good-by. I like the way you have it set up."

"Russian style," said Ericson. Instead of a reception line, the staff was gathered in a large circle around the room, and the past and present Presidents would walk around the circle, shaking hands, saying good-by, saying hello. Ericson had taken the idea from a reception the Soviets once held for him in Moscow's St. Vladimir Hall.

The two men left the Oval Office together, went down the colonnade to the residence and up the elevator to the grand reception hall. The Marine Band played "Ruffles and Flourishes" to announce their arrival, then struck up "Hail to the Chief."

Ericson said, correctly, "They're playing that for you, the first time. You're the only one they can play it for."

"No, the next time will be for me," the President said.

Ericson took his time, not making a speech, but working his way around the circle in the East Room, saying farewell individually to everyone from Smitty, the last of the three Ericson staff chiefs, who was choked up, to the White House gardener, who was not.

FULL DISCLOSURE

When Ericson took Lucas Cartwright's hand, he said to the new President, "You're the fifth President this man has served, and he's getting better all the time. There is nobody I trust more." For reasons of his own, Frelinghausen had not asked about Lucas, but Ericson thought it would not hurt to put in a plug this way.

The smell of Femme suggested who was next, though he was no longer willing to trust a perfume for identification. Marilee Pinckney gave him a firm handshake, but the fingers were trembling, and when he reached to touch her face with his fingertips—in a sudden explosion of camera-clicking—he felt the tears streaming down the face of a person that Ericson wished he could have come to know better. Not enough time; he never got around to the back burner.

At Harry Bok's wheel chair, he heard the man who had saved his life say, "You didn't forget—Rufus Hewitt called me last night. I start in the counterfeiting division in a couple of weeks." Ericson squeezed his arm, then reached back to take the hand near the smell of Apple Blossom, or Lily of the Valley.

"Good-by, sir," said Silent Sam, the Air Force nurse who had built his bridge and had eased his transition from Buffie. Ericson touched her face, too, which was dry, then moved to her collar, looking for the insignia of rank. The captain's bars were there, a farewell present, which Lucas had quickly arranged last night. "I want to thank you from the bottom of my heart," Ericson said, meaning it, "for all you have done." Since reporters were near, he added "in helping Harry," but she knew what he meant.

When Jonathan Trumbull said his own name aloud, to identify himself, Ericson replied, "That will be a good by-line on a book. And you alone are escaped to tell them, Brother Jonathan." The writer did not know what to say; Ericson could actually hear the young man swallowing. "Where's your girl?" Ericson asked.

"She's been following you around the room, taking pictures," Jonathan croaked out. "She's taking this right now."

Ericson felt a hand on his arm and a kiss brush his cheek. "S'long, Potus." He closed his eyelids for a moment and took a deep breath.

"Is there a place I can stand?" Ericson asked the agent behind him.

"There is a speaking capability in the corner, sir."

"I was born with a speaking capability," Ericson said. "I just want a place to stand, no mike, a riser about a foot or two high." They took him to a podium in the corner of the East Room, near the piano, and the staff pressed in around him. The standing microphone was taken away.

"There's a lot of sniffling and snuffling out there," Ericson said in a strong voice. "Let's cut it all out. This is not going to be a tear jerker. We've all maintained our cool very well to date, and there's no need to blow it now." He gave them a moment to blow their noses, and for a few of them to get their pocket tape recorders going. He did not want this broadcast, at least not live, but it was important that an accurate record be made.

"The first thing is to stop feeling sorry for ourselves," he began in a flat voice. "A lot of you are thinking you knocked yourselves out putting a man in the White House, and now he's going, and where does that leave you? It leaves you high and dry, that's where. I have no deal or understanding with my successor to keep anybody on. If you're good, you stay; if he has somebody better, you go." There was quickly less snuffling, Ericson observed. "That's the breaks. Your misfortune is somebody else's good luck. Life may be unfair on an individual basis, but when you look around, it all evens up. So take all this philosophically." He had slapped them in the face by facing the reality that many of them were indeed thinking of their personal loss. That laid the basis for unsentimentality on his next point.

"Don't feel sorry for me, because I don't. Oh, I'm sorry to miss all the excitement of being at the center. And I'm sorry I didn't have the chance to do my thing on inflation and unemployment. But I'm not carrying around a crying towel. Because I'm not dead yet, that's why I'm not." That was an applause line but he stepped on it before the reaction could get going. "And the reason why not is that I'm a practical man.

"I'm not about to go riding off into the wilderness and disappear. I'm forty-eight years old and I have a whole generation of active life ahead of me"—the room did explode with applause at that, but he stepped on it again—"please, this is not a stump speech. What I want to say is this: Okay, I'm blind. Not totally blind any more, and I can see a little better every week, so there's some real hope. But blind or not, I'm going to learn to get around, and to communicate, and to use the skills anybody can learn to lead a full life. No pity, thanks, no tut-tutting-isn't-he-brave. After a while, I'll be able to cope with certain jobs as well as anybody.

"That includes political jobs, too. We already had a blind United States senator, who got himself killed crossing the street. Well, I can learn to be careful as hell crossing the street. So I may get active politically in a year or so. Or maybe I'll become the goddamnedest economist you ever saw, or the best damn teacher in the country. One way or another, you'll hear from me."

At that point, Ericson felt there was not a moist eye in the house, which was the unsentimental way he wanted it to be. "As for my personal life," he went on, "I'll get married again one day. I have the woman in mind, but I've made enough news this week." Affectionate applause and murmured guesses. "Let me close on a personal note to a damn good group of people whom I like and respect. With a few exceptions," he added astringently, "but I'll let President Frelingheusen find out who they are.

"This blindness thing. It changes a man. Disables him, scares the hell out of him at first. Sometimes it leaves him in a bog of self-pity and ruins him. Other times it dredges up some compensating strengths.

"Any sudden handicap teaches you something about yourself and forces you to look at other people differently. I was a pretty cool cookie all my life. I haven't turned into any kind of sentimental slob, but I can tell you I'm not as detached as I used to be. Life is not the pure amalgam of thought and action I used to think it was. The cliché word is 'compassion,' which I would use if it had not become a cliché.

"Look." He was silent a moment, seeming to grope for words. "I've never been a religious man—no more than average. But I recall, in church as a kid, an old hymn." Ericson was going to use something now that only Buffie, of all those in the room, would know was stretching a point a little. "The words are familiar to most people—

> " 'Amazing grace,
> How sweet the sound,
> That saved a wretch like me.
> I once was lost,
> But now am found,
> Was blind, but now I see.'

Darkness has a way of concentrating the mind, and can help you to see what's right."

Ericson stopped. He had to stop because the force of his own rhetoric unexpectedly affected him. The hymn he had learned in bed with Buffie, which he had memorized and saved for dramatic use at such an occasion as this, gripped him as he heard himself using it. Maybe he was a born politician after all. He felt he might well be back in this House once again, as an economic adviser, perhaps, or a Senate leader, or even more, but not as a "former" or a long-forgotten visitor. Ericson felt good about that, if slightly troubled by the too-emotional effect the use of the words of the old hymn had on some of his audience, and on him.

Accompanied by the new President, he walked slowly down the stairs, out the diplomatic entrance, to the South Lawn, where the sound told him a fair-sized crowd was gathered. He could hear the clanking and shuffling of the Marine Band double-timing behind him to get in position, and could visualize the long red carpet leading to the helicopter steps.

Standing with President Frelingheusen at the beginning of the carpet out on the grass, Ericson took the honor guard's salute. This ceremony was televised, he knew, and was being watched around the world with the awe, reverence, cynicism, and disbelief that accompany an orderly transition of American presidential power. It struck Ericson, after the moments inside, as anticlimatic. When the band struck up "Hail to the Chief," he came to attention, and despite the knowledge that a telephoto lens might show it on television, said to Frelingheusen out of the side of his mouth, "They're playing our song."

At its conclusion, Ericson gravely shook the President's hand, embraced the First Lady, took his dog's halter in hand, and began to walk alone out to the chopper, where Hank Fowler and Melinda McPhee were already aboard. Ericson did not walk quickly, to show how confident he could be with his Seeing Eye dog; he walked solemnly, in dignity, as befitted the occasion, never wavering from the center of the red carpet.

Halfway out, he heard somebody start to sing "Amazing Grace." The crowd picked it up—young and old, they all knew it—though the people joining in from the crowd did not know the significance given the song by the White House staffers and the new President. Ericson could hear Buffie's reedy voice singing it to him not long ago—certainly, not a hymn in church when he was a kid, as he had said, but that was poetic license—and then he felt the impact, on the singing crowd as on himself, of the last line. Damn, he told himself, hold on, that was more gripping than I planned. He was glad he had not asked beforehand for the sheet music to the hymn to be handed out to the Marine Band, which would have made it all seem contrived.

The dog signaled to him through the halter that he had three more steps to go. He took them, shook hands with the Army pilot at the steps of the helicopter, and turned to the crowd and the camera and the White House. The impact of everyone singing that music with such genuine affection slammed into him; the former President allowed as how some of these rhetorical-ceremonial devices sometimes got out of hand.

Ericson took off his tinted glasses, wiped his eyes, waved once to one side, once to the other, turned, and followed his dog up the steps.